Outback
MAN

MARGARET WAY

T0363707

MILLS & BOON

CONTENTS

Margaret Way takes great pleasure in her work, and works hard at her pleasure. She enjoys tearing off to the beach with her family on weekends, loves haunting galleries and auctions and is completely given over to French champagne "for every possible joyous occasion." She was born and educated in the river city of Brisbane, Australia, and now lives within sight and sound of beautiful Moreton Bay.

The Horseman

Dear Reader,

The Horseman completes my four-book series entitled
MEN OF THE OUTBACK. I do hope you've kept with
me so far, as the stories are linked not only in their setting,
the Northern Territory, the remotest and wildest part of the
continent, but also by the lives of the interlinked families
who call this fascinating place home. If you're one of my
longtime readers you'll know "family" is a recurring theme
in my books. (And if you're not, a big welcome to you!)

I like to portray family with the petals and the thorns.
Families anywhere in the world don't differ all that widely.
They have secrets, running feuds and personal histories
that often contain more than a grain of fiction. As I have
frequently written, the sort of family you grow up in affects
you throughout your life, sometimes to the very end. The
strong and resilient will break free; others are doomed to carry
the conflict forward into succeeding generations. I'm sure
many of you can name a family—perhaps even from your own
street—that runs the risk of being called dysfunctional. But I
like to bring balance to such families by writing of hopes and
dreams, and to introduce heroes and heroines who focus their
energies on making a bright future for themselves and those
they love.

My warmest wishes to you all. Happy reading!

Margaret Way

CHAPTER ONE

The Moreland Mansion
Darwin
Northern Territory
Australia

CECILE MORELAND SAT in front of her dressing table making final adjustments to her bridesmaid's headdress, a garland of silk flowers and foliage scattered with sparkling crystals. Excitement, like a swarm of butterflies, fluttered in her stomach. She wondered how much more excited Sandra was for this was Sandra's day of days, the day she and Daniel were to be married.

The weather was perfect. No bride could have asked for more. Cobalt skies of perfect clarity, a light cooling breeze off the harbor, the mansion's extensive gardens coaxed to perfection, ablaze with flower beds that dripped gorgeous blossoms. Brilliantly colored parrots, chittering and chattering as if they, too, were caught up in the excitement, flashed through the great shade trees that formed a canopy over the long drive, from the massive wrought-iron gates at the entrance up to the house. Everywhere smelled of flowers and cut grass. It was absolutely intoxicating.

Cecile swallowed a rush of emotion she couldn't afford to

indulge; she was all made up and just about ready to join Sandra and the other bridesmaids, but she was still experiencing an overwhelming sense of gratitude and amazement. Daniel, who had grown to manhood with his origins uncertain, had been discovered to be a Moreland; in fact, her first cousin. It was especially hard to believe, because it was less than a year since she had become aware of his existence, let alone that he was part of her family.

They shared a grandfather, Joel Moreland, known throughout the Territory as the Man with the Midas Touch. Daniel, it turned out, was the son of her uncle Jared, who had been killed as a young man in a freak accident at the Alice Springs annual rodeo when Daniel was still in his mother's womb. Whether Jared had been aware of the pregnancy no one would ever know, but the consensus of opinion was, Jared would never have let the mother of his child disappear from his life; it was alien to his nature. Now, Daniel and Sandra's meeting was a wonderful example of synchronicity, the connections that govern human life. Cecile felt moved by that thought. If ever two people deserved to be happy, it was those two.

Softly humming Mendelssohn's "Wedding March" beneath her breath, Cecile rose from the small gilded chair, satisfied with the positioning of her headdress. She smoothed the lovely floor-length skirt of her strapless silk and satin gown, happy in the knowledge it suited her beautifully. The lustrous material was the color of a silver-gray South Sea pearl that under lights, appeared to be shot through with rays of color from her headdress, a mix of pinks, yellows, lilacs and amethyst with accents of palest green. The maid of honor, Melinda, Sandra's friend from her university days, would be wearing an intense shade of pink, the other two bridesmaids, Eva and Denise, sunshine-yellow and a complementary deep lilac respectively. Sandra had taken her inspiration from the exquisite pastel plumage of one of her favorite birds of the Red Centre. This was the elusive Princess Alexandra parrot, named in honor of the Danish princess Alexandra who later became consort to Edward VII of England. Sandra, herself, had been christened Alexandra Mary after her Scottish great-great-grandmother, so it was easy to see the connection. The garlands they all wore on their heads took their theme from the infinite varieties of wildflowers that cloaked Sandra's desert home after the rains. The five of them had settled on their outfits over one very happy get-acquainted weekend on Moondai, the historic station Sandra had inherited from her late grandfather, Rigby Kingston. All four bridesmaids were brunettes, which made a striking contrast with the butter-cup blondness of the bride, Cecile thought. She felt honored that Sandra had chosen her to be part of the bridal party. After all, she was a newcomer to Sandra's life, but their rapport, estab-lished before the big engagement party on Moondai, had been instant, which is about as gratifying as it gets.

Cecile drifted onto the balcony to look over the extensive gar-dens, ten acres in all. Huge white marquees with pink pelmets and tassels had been erected in the grounds: one for the banquet; another to house drinks of all kinds, from French champagne to Coca-Cola; the third for the lavish selection of desserts and coffee. Hundreds of circular white tables and chairs, their backs adorned with huge ivory satin bows, had been set out on the lush green lawn, which swept down to a delightful spring-fed lake that glittered under the tropical sun. Ever since she could remember the lake had been home to a pair of black swans called Apollo and Daphne. Though she recalled how Daphne, initially trying to escape Apollo's attentions, had turned her-self into a tree, the two had mated for life.

The surrounds of the small lake were densely planted with continuously flowering white arum lilies and gorgeous Japanese iris, the water and the boggy conditions ideal for both plants. The actual ceremony would take place not far from the lake in a sheltered glade where countless heads of blue hydrangea were in big showy bloom. The glade had been a favorite haunt of hers as a child, mainly because of the large pentagonal-shaped summer house with its exotic pagoda-like roof. Under that magical roof Daniel and Sandra would be married.

When she was younger—Cecile was now twenty-six and the despair of her mother, who thought twenty-six high time she was married off and carrying her first child—she had thought the glade was where she would like to be married. Stuart, her fiancé, didn't care for that idea at all. He wanted a big cathedral wedding with lots of pomp in their hometown of Melbourne. Stuart was big on pomp and the symbols of success: the grand house; stable of luxury cars; beautiful wife; two perfect kids, boy first, then girl; rich in-laws highly respected in society. A lot to ask for and obviously not yet attained, but she had said yes to his proposal almost a year before. Why, then, was she having difficulty naming a wedding date? Both Stuart and her mother had been pressing her of late to do so—she didn't blame them—but still she couldn't bring herself to commit. She was beginning to realize there was something profoundly significant in that, though she continued to berate herself for her intransigence as though intransigence were a dirty word. She was *certain* Stuart loved her. She loved him. She *did,* didn't she? Why this awful doubt? Why *now*? Their architect-designed house in Melbourne was already undergoing construction. The exclusive site was a gift from her parents. She and Stuart had known one another for years and years. Their families approved, especially her mother, who continued to try very hard to dictate her only child's every move.

Thinking of her mother, Cecile gave an involuntary sigh. Her mother wasn't a happy woman. She was a *good* woman who had tried all her married life to be the perfect wife. She fussed over her husband who was, in fact, a distant Moreland kinsman, so she'd never had to change her name. She was a tireless worker for charity. She kept a beautiful house and a legendary garden. For decades she had devoted herself to endless dinner parties run like military maneuvers to further her husband's business and social status. Cecile's father was now CEO of

Moreland Minerals, a position he held for more than fifteen years. It was confidently expected he would one day take over from her grandfather as chairman. Her mother *should* have been happy, achieving so much. Instead she was a rather driven woman, taking pride but no joy in her accomplishments. Cecile knew for a sad fact that her father had sought physical and mental balm in the occasional discreet affair. For years she had been terrified her mother would find out, but eventually she realized her mother would never question her father until the day she died. Instead, she had made an art form of blocking out any unpleasantness. Her mother's headstone might well read: *Here lies a woman who never delved too deeply.*

Cecile caught back another sigh as the old troubles and tensions of her childhood and adolescence began to creep over her. It was essential she throw off these unhappy thoughts, indeed obligatory, on this happy day, but they kept invading her mind. It saddened her deeply that there was no crucial spark of love between her parents, no special looks they gave one another as Stuart's parents did. There were no intimate, loving glances indicative of a happy shared life, certainly no private let alone public displays of affection. They were more like colleagues who rubbed along comfortably together. There must have been a spark at the beginning surely? Or had her father—as her razor-tongued great-aunt Bea had occasionally suggested—considered that there were more important considerations in marriage than romantic love? Her father was brilliant at business transactions. Were she and Bea too cynical? On such a day as today it was difficult not to contrast what Daniel and Sandra had with what love was in her parents' marriage. Maybe that *blaze* of love happened only rarely. Maybe her mother wasn't destined ever to know it. Maybe, for all her so-called beauty, she wasn't even the kind of woman who inspired passion. Physical beauty certainly didn't reflect all the manifestations of the psyche. There were far more important traits that allowed one to take that enormous step forward.

It was Daniel and Sandra who had been so blessed. In less than an hour they would exchange their marriage vows. It was truly a love match. A fairy story that offered the promise of living happily ever after. Cecile hoped and prayed that promise would come true. Although Sandra was about to become Mrs. Daniel Moreland, the press was still calling Sandra the Kingston Heiress. Probably that label would stick to her all her life. The couple who had wanted a quiet wedding with only family and close friends had a big society wedding on their hands. It couldn't be otherwise with the bridegroom having Joel Moreland for a grandfather. The top journalist from the nation's leading women's magazine was numbered among the guests. The hefty fee for sole coverage of the wedding would go to the charity closest to Sandra's heart, a foundation doing research into childhood leukemia. Sandra had once had a little friend called Nicole, who had lost her life to that cruel disease.

At his death over a year before, Rigby Kingston, Sandra's grandfather, one of the Territory's most prominent and influential cattlemen, had shocked the entire Outback by doing what had never been done before. He had bypassed his son and his grandson to leave Moondai and the bulk of his estate to his estranged granddaughter, daughter of his deceased firstborn son and acknowledged heir, Trevor, who had been killed when the station Cessna plowed into the purple ranges that lay at Moondai's back door. That tragedy had marked the family forever. When Trevor's daughter inherited, many believed it was Kingston's effort to "make things right." Moondai would have gone to Trevor had he lived. That his daughter inherited was seen as reparation for Kingston's having banished her and her social-butterfly mother shortly after the tragedy. At that time Sandra had been ten going on eleven—not the best time to be banished. Sandra had suffered because of it, but it was apparent to everyone who knew her that she hadn't broken. Rather, she had grown strong in adversity, a sign of her strength of character. Cecile greatly admired her for it.

What happened after Sandra arrived on Moondai to take up her inheritance was the stuff of romantic fiction. Destinies converged when she met Daniel. He had been Rigby Kingston's overseer at the time of his death, and Kingston's right-hand man. With the future of Moondai at stake, Kingston had left Daniel a substantial legacy to ensure he would remain in place until such time as his granddaughter, Alexandra, could find a suitable replacement to help her run the historic station should Daniel wish to leave. Her uncle and cousin would be no help to her. Something Kingston had clearly taken into account. Neither by their own admission were cattlemen. They had no taste for the job, let alone the talent. Daniel, however, was highly regarded by everyone in the industry. Some thought having the brains and the sheer *authority* to run a vast cattle station had to be in the blood.

And so it had proved. Daniel had grown up in humble circumstances not knowing the identity of his father. His mother, physically and emotionally fragile, had been badly affected. She had gone to her grave never revealing his name. Daniel, not surprisingly, grew to manhood despising the man who had abandoned his vulnerable mother in her time of need. His mother's fate had always rankled him far more than his own rejection at his father's hands. Daniel was tough. But blood, like the truth, will out eventually no matter how long it takes. Daniel in maturity carried the stamp of a Moreland—the looks, the voice, the manner—and the double helix, the DNA that binds blood. A deathbed confession had led to an investigation that in the end established Daniel's identity. Daniel, born posthumously, was the son of Jared Moreland.

It was their grandfather Joel who had acted on that staggering deathbed confession made by his own wife, Frances. Now Daniel had taken his rightful place within the Moreland family. It had come as a further shock to Cecile to discover she and Daniel shared the "family face." Indeed anyone seeing them together could easily mistake them for twins. Both were happy to settle for first cousins, and she had the honor now of being in his bridal party.

Weddings, she reflected, had a miraculous way of bringing everyone together. She rejoiced in the mantle of happiness that had fallen over the Moreland household. Their grandfather Joel was in splendid form. All those long years without his beloved son, Jared! Now the wheel of fortune had turned full circle. It had restored to him his grandson. All the Morelands were gathered here today, happy to share in this joyous occasion. Three hundred guests from around the country and overseas had already arrived. A great many were roaming all over the grounds like butterflies that flew around the great banks of lantana, pink, white and gold.

It had been decided in a family conference that the logistics of holding the wedding at isolated Moondai in the Red Centre were much more difficult than holding the wedding at "Morelands" in Darwin. Sandra had had no objection; the guests could attend and find accommodation. She wanted nothing more than to marry her Daniel. But then, too, Sandra had grown close to Joel Moreland. She knew intuitively that a wedding held at Morelands would have very special meaning for him. Cecile couldn't have been more pleased. Her grandfather was as good and kind and brave a man as one could ever wish to meet. That Daniel shared many of their grandfather's characteristics had made her warm to him at once.

Graceful as a swan in her bridesmaid's regalia, Cecile glided over to the white wrought-iron balustrade, dazzled by the scene in front of her. Everyone looked resplendent in their wedding finery—many a dashing morning suit among the well-dressed men, glamorous gowns, gorgeous hats, the glitter of expensive jewelry. The children, too, were decked out in formal dress, the little girls adorable in silks and taffetas and organzas, with shining hair drifting down their backs, though no one could stop them from darting all over the grounds, calling to one another, ignoring the pleas of their parents as they hid behind billowing bushes of hibiscus, frangipani and oleander. She could remember doing exactly the same thing with her friends at the innumerable functions her grandparents had held in the grounds.

It was a few moments before that special sense of hers told her she was under surveillance. There were no words to explain where that sense came from; it was just *there*. She stayed perfectly still, though she was aware her breath was coming unevenly. Then, not making a business of it, she shifted her gaze slowly...slowly...following the magnetic beam.

To the left of her, a man was standing alone in a little pocket of quiet. He was staring at her with single-minded concentration. It wasn't simple curiosity in his gaze, and the *quality* of it, indeed his whole body language, locked her in place. For a weird moment she thought she was falling...falling...plunging over the balustrade right into his arms.

Wedding hysteria? The delusion of falling lasted no more than a second or two, yet she remained in a state of confusion, steadying herself with one hand on the wrought-iron banister. She was positive he had been staring at her for some time. Indeed he inclined his head in what she interpreted as a sardonic bow to which she found herself giving him the smallest nod in response. It was a graceful but essentially aloof acknowledgment that wouldn't have been amiss in royalty.

Heat burned in her cheeks. Even now his eyes didn't let go. In fact, the connection, which defied interpretation, grew stronger. They might have been illicit lovers or sworn enemies, so strong was the focus each had on the other.

He was impressively tall. As tall as Daniel, which meant well over six feet, with a similar athletic build. He was dressed in a beautifully tailored camel-colored suit, a deep blue shirt with a white collar beneath, and a wide blue silk tie with broad white stripes banded in either black or navy; she couldn't at this distance tell which. A shaft of dappled sunlight was shining directly on his thick, springy hair, picking out blond strands in the dark caramel. She couldn't see the color of his eyes. She thought dark. What she knew for certain was that they were holding her in place while he took his fill of her.

She registered the strong bone structure, the high cheek-bones, fine straight nose, beautifully sculpted jawline. It was a face not easily forgotten. His skin had the dark tan of a man who spent long hours in a hot sun. He looked to be around thirty, thirty-two, no more. She had never seen him before in her life, but she thought she could pick him out of thousands. He exuded power and vitality as though at any moment he could morph into a man of action, striding across the desert or tackling the world's highest mountains.

A shiver passed through her; it was as though no man had ever looked at her before. She wanted to pull away from the balustrade, but the hypnotic quality of his gaze blocked her every attempt to move. It seemed like an age but it could only have been moments. She couldn't believe this was happening. It *shouldn't* be happening, yet she stood there as if she wanted to do nothing other. What was his expression? It wasn't re-laxed. It wasn't smiling or even pleasant. For an odd moment she thought his gaze was judgmental. Was he sizing her up and finding her wanting? Why should that be? They were perfect strangers. She felt a little dizzy as though not enough oxygen was getting to her brain. It was clear she had to do something to break the deadlock.

She closed her eyes tightly in an act of defiance, wishing Stu-art was by her side. Did she think herself in need of protection?

When she opened them again, the man had moved into the cool green shadows of a feathery poinciana, where he was joined by a trio of attractive young women with their arms interlaced with one another. She could hear their laughing voices as they introduced themselves. One took hold of his sleeve, gazing up into his face, while the others talked excitedly. But then, a man who looked like that would have a steady stream of women beating a path to his side.

At last she felt free to move away from the balustrade. She

was shocked by the impact a total stranger had had on her, especially when neither had spoken a word. As she moved back into her bedroom, a ripple of something approaching antagonism passed through her. She made a real effort to control it. Who *was* he? She didn't know him and had no desire to. Her well-honed intuition told her he would be dangerous to know. Perversely she speculated on who he might be. He had to be a guest of Sandra's or someone from Daniel's past. She knew just about everyone on the Moreland side. She couldn't remember a time any man had so caught her attention. Whoever he was, he was a force in his own right.

Sandra's huge bedroom was abuzz with excited young women in beautiful gowns, but none more beautiful than the bride, who was executing a dreamy little waltz around the room, her arms raised as if to her groom. Sandra was wearing traditional white, an exquisite high-necked Edwardian style lace-and-silk bodice, with dozens of seed pearls hand-applied, the full-length sleeves a continuation of the bodice lace, pegged down the arm. The tightly fitted sashed waist emphasized the billow of the silk skirt. The style suited her petite frame and the blue and gold of her looks. On her head she wore, set straight on her forehead, a garland similar to her bridesmaids', only her flowers were in shades of ivory and cream with the addition of a short shimmering white tulle veil.

The excitement in the room was palpable. Cecile thought she could reach out and grab a handful out of the perfumed air that had as its top notes a floral bouquet of rose, gardenia and lily of the valley.

Sandra flashed a radiant smile. "Ceci, you look wonderful!"

Cecile hurried to her, hugging her with real affection. "I couldn't possibly rival you. You're as lovely as a tea rose." Cecile could feel tears rise to her eyes.

"Don't you dare cry!" Sandra warned, not very far away from bursting into emotional tears herself.

Cecile bit her lip, calling to the other bridesmaids in warm tones, "You look great, too!"

"It's the wedding of the year, my dear," Denise answered, with a flourish of her skirt.

"Ladies, please!" The hairstylist who had been employed to do their hair clapped his hands to get their attention, but that proved impossible. For Sandra's mother, Pamela, looking as glamorous as a film star in a short-skirted Chanel suit and a sexy fascinator on her blond head, chose that moment to walk into the room carrying the beautifully wrapped gifts from Sandra to her bridesmaids. She presented one to each young woman in turn while they exclaimed in delight.

Melinda lost the least time pulling off the elegant wrapping. What she saw made her suck in her breath. "Oooooh!" Slowly she withdrew from the jeweler's box a rope of freshwater pearls fashioned into a choker with a large central clasp of deep pink tourmaline. "Sandy, is this for me?" Her voice wobbled in a mix of awe and delight.

"No one else!" Sandra smiled. "As you can see—" she looked at each of her bridesmaids in turn "—each clasp was chosen to coordinate with your gowns. Pink tourmaline for Melinda, topaz for Eva, amethyst for Denise, pave diamonds for Cecile."

"How absolutely gorgeous, and so generous!" Denise rushed to the long pier mirror to put on her choker. Once fastened, she stared at herself wide-eyed as the big central amethyst caught the light.

"I'm going to treasure this all my life!" Eva was poring over her gift, her fingers caressing the lustrous rope of pearls.

"Here, let me help you put it on," the hairstylist offered, thrilled he had been chosen for what was a big society wedding, one that would get national coverage.

Denise moved away from the mirror to allow Cecile her turn. Beautiful before, the choker with its sunburst of pave diamonds complemented Cecile's gown dramatically and drew attention to the silver shimmer of her eyes.

"Perfect!" Sandra murmured in satisfaction, smiling at Cecile's shoulder.

"Heavens, don't blind us, Cecile!" Denise joked, wishing she could look like Cecile Moreland if only for one day. "Hey, Sandy," she addressed the bride, "you've got to have something old now, something borrowed, something new..."

"And something *blue,*" Melinda chimed in.

Sandra waved her magnificent sapphire-and-diamond engagement ring in the air. "Here's the blue. Mama—" she pointed to her youthful-looking mother "—supplied the something old, but that's a closely guarded secret."

"A very fancy garter, I bet," Denise giggled.

"*Nooo,* Denise," Pamela dragged out the word humorously, "not a garter. So are we all ready?" Pamela picked up her daughter's exquisite trailing bouquet and passed it to her. "You look beautiful, darling. I'm so proud of you." Pamela hugged her daughter one last time. "We're going to get through this splendidly. That means no tears to ruin your makeup. All right, girls, the bridegroom, his attendants and hundreds of guests await!"

Laughing happily, they moved in succession out of Sandra's bedroom, excitement alone lending them all a special loveliness. Weddings spread their own magic, Cecile thought. This was a day when nothing could go wrong. Or nothing would *dare* go wrong. So why did she feel something already had?

CHAPTER TWO

THE CEREMONY WAS one of high emotion. Family and guests were infused with the bliss that surrounded the bride and her groom. As the couple came together for the ceremonial kiss, many of the women guests yielded to an emotional tear, remembering their own wedding day or perhaps the wedding of a beloved son or daughter. Taking her new husband's arm, Sandra led the way to the wedding banquet, which turned out to be brilliant. The food and drink were superb. There were speeches, short and entertaining, that had people laughing; others were deeply touching, such as Joel Moreland's welcoming the bride into the family, an event he said couldn't have taken place had his grandson, Daniel, not have been restored to him.

Afterward there was a great deal of catching up to do as relatives who hadn't seen one another in ages came together and friends from either side of the bridal party were introduced to one another. Professional photographers were on hand to record the happy occasion. The press photographer, with a large video camera in hand, worked his way through the throng while guests took photographs destined for private albums. The bride found herself surrounded by old friends all wanting to embrace her; the groom found he had even more cousins than he had ever dreamt of. There were people everywhere: inside the flower-decked house, with all the French doors standing open to the garden; in the main reception rooms, the huge living room, dining room, library, garden room at the rear of the house. Young people sat all over the steps of the grand staircase, eager to make new friends and, who knows? meet the love of their life. Or dancing to the excellent band had already begun on the broad stone terrace that wrapped the rear of the mansion. Many more guests, champagne flutes in hand, were wandering about the beautiful grounds, admiring the flowers and the antique statuary. Some of the children had stripped off their wedding finery to dive near naked and shrieking into the lake, with inevitably a few adults who'd had too much to drink falling in to join them.

Cecile roamed freely with Stuart, the two stopping frequently to converse with family and guests. Invariably someone, most often a woman, told them archly, "You two will be next!" At such times Stuart always drew Cecile close, dropping a kiss on her temple beneath the lovely garland of silk flowers. "Can't come soon enough for me!" was his most favored response.

It was an answer that should have made Cecile glow. Instead something twisted inside her and on this day of days she found herself badly unsettled. Was it being witness to the love between Daniel and Sandra that had crystallized her long-growing uncertainties? Or was it having that man look at her as he did? She wasn't a temperamental woman—she rather prided herself on her composure—but that look had shaken her. To think that out of the wild blue yonder she had been plunged into what amounted to panic! Such things didn't happen to her. It didn't seem possible that a mere look could turn her world upside down. The answer presented itself. Because it was so primitive, so much man-woman, so irrevocably *physical*. She might as well have been standing on the balcony with her gown transparent. She had to force herself to stop quivering

For a fraught moment Cecile felt like slumping onto one of the stone garden benches, head in hands. There would be a terrible backlash from Stuart and his family if she ever thought to break her engagement. They, who were all so much *for* her, would overnight turn against her. Bitterness and anger would take hold, never to let go. She would be made to feel their public humiliation. In her heart she knew part of her appeal for Stuart and his family was her being Joel Moreland's granddaughter. She had grown up knowing that being the *only* granddaughter of one of the country's richest men affected her relationship with others. Some actively pursued friendship, others, motivated by envy became detractors behind her back. She was never one hundred percent sure who actually liked her for herself except for a trusted few, whose friendship *she* cherished. Even Stuart, by his own admission, was a man on a mission. He wanted to be a real player. He was already on his way. A very bright associate in a leading law firm, Stuart Carlson was looking at being made a full partner within a year or two. He had political aspirations, as well, perhaps borne of his longing to be in the spotlight. She had often teased him about his ambitions. Now she thought they were too overriding. Even in the past year Stuart had become increasingly bent on cultivating the *right* people and discarding those he judged as not really going anywhere. It seemed to her sadly false, though she realized Stuart wasn't alone in setting his goals on climbing the social ladder to the top rung. Marrying a Moreland greatly increased his chances.

And what of her mother? Cecile had spent her life trying to appease and placate her nerve-ridden mother, so she knew Justine would be devastated by any change of plan. For reasons she had never really been able to fathom, Stuart and her mother were huge allies. Of course, Stuart had always gone out of his way to charm her—very attentive, bringing wine and flowers, the special handmade chocolates her mother loved—but even that didn't explain it. She knew her mother saw Stuart as someone on side with *her*; a young man who would make a good son-in-law, who with her guidance could develop into a pillar of society; steady and reliable, a one-woman man who could be depended upon to honor his marriage vows. A judgment Justine knew in her heart of hearts didn't fit her husband.

All the while they were roaming, Cecile was very much aware of Stuart's arm clamped possessively around her waist. She couldn't bring herself to hurt him by breaking free, but it struck her that she wanted to walk alone, not linked to the man she had chosen to marry.

It will make it so much easier for you to find the stranger, said a harsh little voice inside her head. It was excruciating to have to acknowledge it, but it was true. She was actively searching for his tall striking figure among the milling crowd.

You idiot! the harsh little voice whispered on. *He's trouble. You know that. He's someone who can upset your whole life.*

She couldn't claim she had no portent of this. Every nerve in her body was shrieking a warning. Wasn't it extremely foolish then to ignore that warning when she should be listening? It was out of character for her to behave this way, but she found she couldn't stop.

Stuart told her repeatedly how beautiful she looked. "There's not a woman here to touch you!" Pride transformed his smooth, self-assured face, his *lawyer's face* as she thought of it. They were standing in the dappled shadows of a shade tree, he playing with her fingers. Slowly, almost reverently, he lifted the hand that bore his splendid diamond engagement ring to his mouth.

"Ceci?" He looked longingly into her eyes. "You have to marry me very soon. I'm *crazy* about you, don't you know?"

"I do, Stuart, I do!" Her heart felt as though it could break. How could she possibly betray him and his love? How could she even think about it? She had given her solemn promise to marry him. She'd had any number of admirers to choose from since the age of sixteen, but none she'd been able to take as seriously as Stuart. She wanted to marry. She wanted children. She loved children. She would be a good mother, shielding any child of hers from all the pressures that had attended her own childhood. There wasn't going to be any grand passion for her. No use waiting around for it. The knowledge was a factor in her decision to marry Stuart, who had many attractive qualities and, she believed, genuinely loved her. Everyone knew lightning strikes were dangerous, anyway.

There was absolutely no way out.

Stuart threw back his dark head and laughed triumphantly. "That's the very thing I'm desperate for you to say—'I do.' A June wedding would be perfect, wouldn't it, darling? We need to be together, man and wife. I know you love the idea of Morelands for the wedding, but surely you'd want to be married from your own home? You couldn't possibly disappoint Justine. Or my mother, for that matter, though she's neutral. She thinks the world of your grandfather. Morelands is an incredible venue, no denying that, but Justine and I have our hearts set on Melbourne. Tell me that's what you want, too, Ceci. I've known you for a dozen years and more, but sometimes I think I don't know you at all."

She had the eerie feeling that was true. She couldn't tell him that many changes were taking place inside her. In retrospect she realized she rarely confided in him. Stuart was a little like her mother in that he had a tendency to close his ears on what he didn't wish to hear. "Let's just enjoy today, Stuart," she begged gently. "I can't always do what you and my mother want. Oh, look—" she shifted her gaze gratefully "—there's Sasha Donnelly calling to us."

"I say, she's looking very glamorous." Stuart was distracted by the shortness of Sasha's skirt and the sassiness of the gala confection she had on her head.

"She is, and she's still carrying a torch for you," Cecile pointed out lightly.

Just when she thought the stranger must have left early, she saw him standing with a knot of older guests. Profound disappointment, even despondency, was transformed into soaring spirits. They rose alarmingly, threatening to make her airborne.

You fool! You're not even putting up a struggle.

She ignored the little voice. At the center of the group was her grandfather. Her mother and father flanked him, both of them looking extremely stylish; they were handsome people. With them were close friends of the family, Bruce and Fiona Gordon and the Ardens. Bruce Gordon and George Arden were among her grandfather's oldest friends and business partners. All of them were smiling warmly.

"Ceci, darling! Stuart!" Joel Moreland caught sight of them, gesturing them over. When they were close enough, he put out his arm to gather his much-loved granddaughter to his side. "I don't think either of you have yet met Señor Montalvan, who is visiting us from Argentina. When Fiona told me she and Bruce had a houseguest, I insisted he come along with them today." Joel turned his aristocratic silver head to smile at the well-to-do couple.

"Cecile, my darling—" he beamed down at her as he began the introductions "—may I present Señor Raul Montalvan from..."

She didn't hear another word for the roaring in her ears. Every dormant cell in her body fired into life.

Damn it, damn it! This isn't like you. Get a grip!

She might have been standing at a distance, looking at her double. The tide of feeling she was experiencing was not untainted with remorse, even shame. There was Stuart, her fiancé, proud and smiling by her side. She wore his ring. She should only be thinking of Stuart, while all the while she was racked by her attraction to another man.

He was even more stunning close up. Indeed he could have stepped out of a bravura painting. The bronze of his skin was in striking contrast to the dark caramel of his hair with its glinting golden strands. How dark his eyes were! Not black, but a brilliant dark brown with gold flecks. Their expression was very intense. She didn't think she had seen such intensity in a man's eyes before. They made her feel more conscious of herself as a *woman* than at any moment of Stuart's most passionate love-making. It was as though that dark seductive gaze pierced right through her breast to her heart.

"Miss Moreland, I've heard so much about you." He spoke with exquisite gentleness. "The whole of it glowing!"

This drew a smile from her grandfather, who Cecile guessed correctly had been singing her praises.

There was an intriguing hint of an accent. No more. It was a cosmopolitan voice, coming from deep in his chest, the timbre dark, beguiling, with a faint cutting edge.

Good manners demanded she extend her hand. "My grandfather has a very natural bias, señor. I'm very pleased to welcome you to our country." Her skin seemed to sizzle at his touch. She thought she flushed. He didn't shake her hand as she expected, but bowed over it in a way that showed his heritage. It was an entirely natural and elegant ritual courtesy that didn't demand his lips touch her skin. She didn't think she could have borne that given what the mere touch of his hand could do. His hands were as elegant as the rest of him, but she could feel calluses on the pads of his fingers and the palm. Was that the cause of that extraordinary surge of electricity?

Then it was Stuart's turn. He gave a hearty, "Happy to meet you, Mr. Montalvan." To Cecile's ears that didn't quite ring true. Stuart hadn't taken to the newcomer, she could tell, but he was shaking the other man's hand vigorously. "What brings you to the Territory?" he asked.

Montalvan gave a very European shrug. "Pleasure, business. I have always wanted to come to Australia." He spoke in a relaxed fashion, but the *gentleness*, it seemed, had been reserved for Cecile. "Your Top End is not so very different to my home in Argentina. Very beautiful, very isolated, hot and humid, plenty of rain when it comes, glorious vegetation, vast open spaces."

Joel Moreland nodded his agreement. "This is still largely frontier country, Señor Montalvan."

"Please, do call me Raul!" Montalvan turned to his host with a charming half smile.

"Raul it is," Joel Moreland responded, his expression revealing that unlike Stuart, he had taken a fancy to this young man. "Raul is in the ranching business," he informed Cecile and Stuart, "so we have a lot in common. His family have been in ranching for many generations. Ranching and mining, isn't that so? He's also a very fine polo player, I've been told."

"Not surprising, when he hails from a country that has won the World Cup every year since 1949," Cecile's father, Howard, contributed with an admiring laugh.

"True." Montalvan gave another elegant shrug of his shoulder. "But you have some wonderful players here," he added appreciatively. "I'm hoping I'll be invited to participate in a few matches during my stay. Australia is nearly as polo mad as Argentina, I believe."

"It's the great sport of the Outback," Moreland confirmed, "but we can't challenge your world supremacy. Don't worry, Raul, I'm sure we'll be able to arrange something. I used to be a pretty good player myself in the old days."

"I'm certain that's an understatement, sir." Montalvan gave a respectful inclination of his head.

"My father was absolutely splendid!" Justine, who adored her father, spoke proudly. "We have two polo fields on Malagari."

"That's my flagship cattle station toward the Red Centre," Moreland explained before turning to his daughter with a teasing smile. "The polo fields, my dear, are still there. You should come and visit sometime."

"I will, I will, I promise." Justine flushed slightly. "When I get time. Father breeds some of the finest polo ponies in the country," she added.

"So I believe." The Argentinian's expression lit up with interest. "My family breeds fine ponies, too, but nothing like Señor

Moreland's operation, which we do know about in Argentina. I believe, sir, you sold ponies to our famous Da Silver brothers?"

"So I did," Joel Moreland said with great satisfaction. "A heroic pair! I've seen them play. Their team won the World Cup no less than four times, the last time—that was in the mid-90s—riding Lagunda ponies. That's my horse stud in the Gold Coast hinterland of Queensland where the climate, the terrain and environment are ideal."

"I'd love to visit it sometime," Montalvan replied. "It would be a great honor."

"And I'd be delighted to show you, Raul. Both Malagari, which is in the Territory and very dear to my heart, and Lagunda, way across the border. The flame for the game still burns very bright, but inevitably time has sidelined me. I still ride, of course. Now my son, Jared, was far more talented. He had effortless style, the physical strength and power to excel at the game. He had a physique like yours." Moreland had been speaking with spontaneous enthusiasm but he stopped abruptly.

"Very sadly, Uncle Jared died young," Cecile told their guest softly. She knew the comment had simply slipped out, borne of her grandfather's obvious liking for their visitor. Her grandfather rarely spoke his dead son's name. Nearly thirty years later, the pain was too great.

"I am so sorry," Montalvan answered quietly, briefly raising his hand to touch Joel Moreland's shoulder.

"Thank you." Moreland bowed his silver head.

"So where are you staying, Señor Montalvan?" Cecile asked with a return to her normal fluent poise.

"Why, with us, Ceci dear," Fiona Gordon, who had been Justine's chief bridesmaid and was in fact one of Cecile's godmothers, smiled fondly.

"Bruce and Fiona have been very kind to me." Montalvan flashed the couple a smile that was simply marvelous, Cecile thought. It had much to do with his fine white teeth against his deep tan, but it went further, lighting up his whole face.

Yet another powerful tool in his seductive armory, she thought, listening to him say he couldn't impose on Bruce and Fiona much longer.

"I'm thinking of leasing, perhaps buying an apartment overlooking the harbor," he told them. "As I've come this far, I intend to make my stay fairly lengthy."

"You have no one at home demanding your presence?" Stuart asked with the faintest lick of challenge. "Not married, I take it?"

No wife in her right mind would allow this man to roam at will, Cecile thought, acutely aware she was hanging on his answer.

"I'm still waiting for the *coup de foudre*, as the French say." Oddly, Montalvan echoed Cecile's earlier thoughts. "May I congratulate you on your engagement." He returned Stuart's gaze directly.

"You may," Stuart answered, blue eyes very bright. "Getting Cecile to say yes wasn't all that easy, but she's made me the happiest man in the world. Or at least as happy as Daniel on this day of days. It's been the perfect wedding."

"Indeed it has!" Justine gave a voluptuous sigh of satisfaction. "I can't wait until Cecile and Stuart tie the knot. You've no idea, Mr. Montalvan, how long I've been planning it in my head."

Cecile, glancing across at her father, caught the rueful expression in his eyes. Planning was Justine's forte. What she planned had to come off.

The celebrations went on long after the bride and groom had left for Darwin airport on the first leg of their honeymoon trip, which would take them to Hong Kong for a few days, then on to the great capitals of Europe. Sandra had thrown her beautiful bouquet from the upstairs balcony into a sea of smiling, upturned faces and waving, raised arms. There was a great deal of laughing and scuffling, especially on the part of the chief bridesmaid, Melinda, who had her eye on a certain someone in the bridal party, but despite the fact Cecile had just stood there smiling, the bouquet flew to her as though carried on guided wings. Because she made no move to catch it, it came to land on someone directly behind her who, with a swift movement of the hand, sent it back over Cecile's bare shoulder and into the arms she hastily raised. Sandra's bridal bouquet was much too precious to allow to fall to the ground.

"Oh, good for you, Ceci!" Melinda, disappointed, declared.

"Isn't that sweet? You'll be next, Ceci darling!" An elderly Moreland relative flashed her an arch smile.

There were shouts of delight, exaggerated groans of disappointment. Stuart, who had been cheering the loudest threw his arms around her and kissed her mouth. "That settles it, Ceci. We *are* next!"

Cecile kept her eyes fixed steadily on the beautiful waving bride on the balcony.

She knew *exactly* who was behind her, it wasn't her mind that told her. It was her body. She could *feel* him, feel his aura the warmth off his skin, the unique male scent of him that she inhaled into her nostrils. Jubilant at her side, Stuart got into a long, laughing exchange with another guest about where the bouquet had actually landed before being catapulted over Cecile's shoulder. "All's well that ends well!" he cried, and swooped to kiss Cecile again, reveling in the knowledge he was a much-envied man.

She ought to turn around. She *had* to turn around. She managed to do so, her eyes locking on his. The graceful little remark she made sounded quite natural and perfectly composed. It was important she did not let him see how much he affected her. Of course he *did* know.

She could weep for her own susceptibility. Especially now when she had given up thinking any man could evoke such a response. How could such things happen so fast? Nothing seemed real. Nothing was as it had been before. It was as simple and as momentous as that.

* * *

With the bride and groom gone, the party kicked up several more notches. Moet flowed like the water from a great fountain. Inside the house, the older guests settled into comfortable arm-chairs and sofas, relishing the opportunity for a good long chat away from the boisterous young ones. Youth was so wearing. Outside the music from the band was so compulsively toe tapping it had couples everywhere up and dancing: on the brightly lit terrace and in the grounds where the trees had been decked with thousands and thousands of fairy lights, around the huge pool area where they risked getting splashed. There was a lot of hilarity, a lot of flirting, abandoned kisses in the scented darkness, holding hands. Everyone clung to the magic of the day, the marvelous haze of pleasure. No one wanted it to end.

CHAPTER THREE

CECILE KNEW THE moment he would come to her, though her head was turned away. She had, she realized, been waiting for him, as though she waited for him every night of her life. She had even deliberately engineered the moment she would be alone, by sending Stuart off for a cold drink she didn't want. She could see Stuart in the distance being detained by a group of their friends, which included a slightly tipsy Sasha who was holding on to his arm as if she didn't intend to let him get away. Her grandfather, who was enjoying himself enormously, was a good distance away from her, as well, his handsome silver head thrown back as he laughed at something one of his cronies said.

So *finally,* they were alone.

She hoped he couldn't see she was trembling. She moved back into the protective shadows, realizing every defense she had consciously or unconsciously raised over the years to protect herself lay demolished.

"A pretty spectacle?" He indicated the nighttime scene with a turn of his hand. It was a dazzling kaleidoscope of brightly colored dresses, many of them full-length and sweeping the grass. The illuminated gardens were extravagant in their beauty, their intoxicating fragrance unleashed by the warm air. The great shade trees stood like beacons of light, covered all over with tiny white bulbs that pulsed like stars.

"Yes, it's beautiful," she agreed quietly, thinking the man beside her added his own element of splendor. "Everything has gone so well. Granddad waved his magic wand and it all happened."

"The Man with the Midas Touch!"

Something in the way he said it, a barely perceptible nuance, wasn't quite right. She turned her head toward him. "So you've heard that already?"

He gave her a slight smile. "I couldn't tell you how many times."

"I'm very proud of my grandfather," she said, startled he had thrown her onto the defensive when, really, he had said nothing out of place.

"And he adores you." Was there the barest trace of mockery in that fascinating voice? She had the idea there was.

"That's fine by me. *I* adore him."

"I saw that very plainly. Would you care to dance?" he asked, not taking his eyes off her face. "I would have asked you earlier, but your fiancé has never left your side."

Until you sent him away!

She recognized that uncompromising little voice, resisted the accusation though her stomach gave a lurch. How could she say to him she was afraid to dance with him? It was a very strange sensation having a man's aura wrap her like a flowing cloak.

"I'm a little out of breath from the last dance," she said in a low voice, mortified there was a throb in it.

His eyes dropped for a mere moment to the rise and fall of her breasts. "Come, Ms. Moreland. I regard that as an excuse."

"It *is* an excuse." What was the point of saying otherwise? The silent communication between them was as keen as a blade's edge.

"You ought not refuse me," he told her ever so gently. "I'm a visitor to your shores. I think I can say I have your grandfather's approval. But most especially because I was the one who caused the bridal bouquet to fall right into your arms."

"I realize that, Señor Montalvan." She couldn't laugh or smile.

"Please… Raul, I insist. Señor Montalvan is much too formal. I freely admit I maneuvered the bouquet because I was intrigued you weren't making the slightest effort to catch it. Why is that?" He held out his hand. "Come, you can't plead fatigue. You look like you could dance right through the night."

She was so acutely conscious of him she almost wished she were wearing gloves. Once again skin on skin proved so electric it was as though one or the other had thrown a switch. She had never experienced anything like it in her life. There had to be some scientific explanation. Did *he* feel it? She was certain he did. She felt once again the rough calluses. Why wouldn't he have them, a cattleman and an experienced polo player? They moved out of the shadows and he pulled her near, very quiet about it, yet she had the strangest sensation her body was unfurling like a flower. Where was Stuart now? Stuart, her safety net?

She had to say something, anything. This entire sizzling scenario couldn't be happening to her, but it was. "The party doesn't appear to be winding down." She was grateful her voice wasn't shaking like her hands. Dancing was a source of innocent pleasure and relaxation. It could also be a potent form of lovemaking with a certain person.

"Even the children are still running around." There was a note of amusement in his tone. "I wouldn't dare guide you anywhere near the pool. It's fun watching them splash, but I couldn't bear to see your lovely gown marked. Not many could wear a gown the color of crystal rain unless they were beautiful and had eyes like the diamonds you wear at your throat."

Her heart skipped many dangerous beats. "A charming compliment, but the color of my eyes is genetic. Both Daniel and I inherited our gray eyes from our grandfather."

"Gray doesn't say it," he said, studying her face so intently he might have been trying to discover her whole history.

She had half hoped closer contact might lessen some of his mystique, anything so she could regain her balance, but the excitement was fierce.

They were moving in a dream, their steps melding and matching as though their bodies were no surprise to the other. Indeed she fit so perfectly into his arms she wondered if those strong arms would leave an imprint on her. It was so wonderful, so exciting, so *scary,* she grasped as she had never done before how attraction could overpower. And with such violent attraction came the potential to destroy lives and ruin reputations.

The band segued into a haunting romantic ballad that struck a chord deep inside her. The blood coursing through her body was full of sparkles, hot sparkles from all the electricity that raced up and down her spine. She felt a dull heavy ache in the pit of her stomach as though she was about to start her period, which she wasn't. She knew what it was: powerful sexual desire that acted like an erotic charge. It brought on a physical change in her, like deep contractions in the womb. She, who had been brought up to be a fluent conversationalist as befitting a cultured young woman, could say nothing. Excitement was growing inside her at a tremendous rate. She couldn't shut it off. She was in thrall, so much less of herself, much, much, more of him.

Once his cheek touched her temple as he whirled her away from another couple, also intent on each other. She felt the faint rasp of his beard on her soft skin. He was a beautiful dancer. She might have known that from the way he moved. Did they have golden pumas in Argentina? she wondered. She was taken by the image. He was beautiful as a man can be beautiful, with an undeniably exotic air, but she couldn't see his *Spanish* heritage. His eyes were more a velvety brown than black. His hair so thick, and well-groomed, was a warm caramel softened by those sun-kissed streaks. If she hadn't known he was Argentinian and heard for herself that fascinating hint of accent, she wouldn't have known exactly *where* to place him. If Daniel had introduced an adventurous friend back from wandering the world, she would have accepted it readily. Suddenly there were many questions she wanted to ask him.

Not a good idea, Cecile! Her warning voice struggled to get through again. *He'll only be here for a short time. Then he goes back to where he belongs. Much wiser to keep your distance.*

Too late to tell her that now. She had moved into a new, potentially dangerous dimension.

Her grandfather had taken a strong liking to him—she knew her grandfather well—which meant lots of invitations would be issued to the visitor. Her own time in Darwin was short. When her vacation with her grandfather was over, she would have to return home to Melbourne to her work. For the past four years she had achieved her ambition, practicing as a child psychologist in a large private hospital that had excellent accreditation. It was work that was important to her, a career choice perhaps influenced by her own struggle in childhood. At any rate she had another life.

But how to shut him out?

Look on it as a brief encounter, the voice in her head instructed.

One could live a lifetime in an hour.

"So quiet?" he murmured. She had removed her lovely headdress, revealing a waterfall of raven hair that flowed straight and glossy down her back to her shoulder blades. From a central parting, the sides were secured behind her ears by two glittering leaf-shaped diamond clasps. It was a classic style that greatly appealed to him.

"I'm not usually." She allowed herself one roving glance across his face. His mouth was beautifully cut, firm but sensual. She wanted to reach out and touch it very gently with her finger, trace its outline. "You understand," she murmured, "weddings are very moving occasions."

"This one in particular," he agreed, drawing her, unprotesting, closer.

Thousands of twinkling lights from the trees poured over them. There was a cry from a night bird somewhere close by. Two perfectly pitched notes, in a descending cadence.

It was repeated.

God! She could hardly bear it! Her heart was thudding so hard it had to be moving the bodice of her gown.

The ache in her stomach wasn't fading—it was growing. It tormented her she could feel this hungry for sex. It was no romantic longing and so relatively harmless. She wished for sex with a perfect stranger. The very thought threatened her ordered life and disassociated her from her engagement. She could have been one of her own patients: an adolescent whose hormones raged out of control.

"One doesn't always see such a true love match," he remarked after a long pause. "It's commonplace in Argentina and many parts of the world for material considerations to be put first. Fiona explained to me how your cousin came to be restored to his family. It's an extraordinary story, though many families have dark secrets and tragic histories. Still…incredible to think it took all this time before his identity came to light. Your cousin deserves his great happiness."

"He does. Blood is very binding," she agreed in a low voice.

"No matter the separation." Again there was a certain nuance that caused her to look up at him.

"You sound as though you know all about the trials of separation."

"What gave you that idea?" He stared down into her eyes.

"You *do* know though, don't you?"

He was silent a moment. "You're obviously a woman of admirable perception. Separations happen all the time. Some perhaps in a way that others do not. Some separations bring misery and trauma, others make us, as they say, fonder. You and your cousin are very much alike. Anyone seeing the two of you together would assume you were sister and brother. You don't have a brother of your own?"

She shook her head with deep regret. "I'm an only child. I would have liked a brother, preferably brothers and sisters, but my mother had difficulty having me, so no more family! It was wonderful when Daniel came into our lives, and now Sandra. We've become good friends. And you, señor, you have siblings?"

"Didn't I beg you to call me Raul?" His tone dropped low into his chest. It was almost a deep purr. "After all, I intend to call you Cecile."

He pronounced it in the French fashion. It sounded…lovely. Like being stroked. Featherlike strokes all over her face and up and down her body. He was using his voice like the finest of instruments. One could fall in love with such a voice, she thought shakily, even if the owner were plain.

That night bird called again. Was it serenading them? The scent of gardenias was heavy in the air, their waxy white flowers dazzling in the dark. "I don't think we'll be seeing much of each other, however."

"You say it like it cannot be," he challenged. "Your distinguished grandfather has already invited me to a dinner party he's giving Wednesday of this coming week. Perhaps you are wrong. I might be often on your doorstep. I understand you are staying with your grandfather for a month? There is much you could show me if you would only be so kind to a stranger to your country."

Kind? Kindness wasn't what he wanted from her, of that she was sure. Though he mesmerized her with his charm, the idea that he might have an agenda of his own wouldn't have shocked her. He could even be exploiting her. Such attempts had been made before, but she had easily staved them off. "I'm sure there are many others who would be delighted to play that role," she said with a slight air of irony.

He didn't appear to notice.

"But you'll have some time on your hands, Cecile. I could at least be some company, as your fiancé has to return to Melbourne."

She stopped dancing, aware of her burning cheeks. "My grandfather told you that?"

"He did when he issued his invitation."

A curious thing—he kept hold of her hand. "He also told me your fiancé is a lawyer with a prestigious Melbourne firm."

"He is," she said, defeated and unnerved by the thought that Stuart didn't mean as much to her as he should. How, if she loved Stuart, could she put herself into Raul Montalvan's hands? "He should make full partner in a year or so."

"You see yourself as the perfect wife to a man of law?"

"What's behind that question, Raul?" She withdrew her trembling hand and walked on.

"Ah. So I've made you a little angry." He caught her up easily, bending his head as if to search her expression.

"You would *know* if I were angry."

He only smiled. "Fire and ice. However, I don't think your eyes could sparkle any more dangerously than they do now. I apologize if I've somehow given offense. I never meant to. You asked if I had siblings. I have. A younger brother, Francisco, and a sister, Ramona, who is so beautiful she turns heads. But then you would know all about that." The resonance of his voice deepened. "So tell me, do you feel rewarded working with children who are in much mental pain? Your grandfather told me you were a child psychologist. I'd very much like to hear why you chose such a profession. It seems to me to reveal a deeply maternal streak, does it not?"

In her high heels she stumbled slightly over an exposed tree root and he swiftly steadied her. "Thank you," she murmured, fathoms deep in awareness.

"So?" he prompted with what sounded like real interest.

She made an effort. "I do love children. I want children of my own. My guiding star is to help ease the pain. It's greatly rewarding to be able to steer badly hurting young people through very real and sometimes just perceived crises in their lives."

He nodded agreement. "There are so many areas of conflict to contend with, especially during adolescence."

"Children are far less secure these days than ever before. Marriages break up, and the fallout can be very damaging. Some children tend to blame a particular parent for the breakup of the marriage. Usually the mothers. Daddy's gone and Mummy drove him away. This can lead to profound upset for the parent who has to bear the blame. Then again, I find a lot of the time that problems originate with the parents' behavior. They have one another and kept the children at arm's length. That can make change very difficult. Other parents persist in keeping up a front. They disguise, disown or actively lie about the part they play in these conflicts. Children are so helpless. They suffer loneliness, excessive stress and acute depression just as we do. I have a little ten-year-old patient at the moment, a girl called Ellie. I'm trying very hard to help. In fact, she's been constantly on my mind while I'm here on holiday. Ellie has a good many behavioral problems that are getting her deeper and deeper into trouble both at home and school. In some ways she's a contradiction. I'm prepared to back my initial impression she's highly intelligent, yet she's earned the reputation for not being very bright, even with her parents."

"Good people?" he questioned, frowning slightly.

"Good, *caring* people at their wits' end," Cecile confirmed. "So far I haven't been able to make a breakthrough, either, though it's early days."

"Then I wish you every success with young Ellie," he said, sounding earnest. "Perhaps she's grieving about something she can't or won't talk about? The innocent grieve. It is so very interesting, your choice of a profession. Surely you wouldn't have known suffering or conflict in your privileged life? A princess, Joel Moreland's granddaughter?"

She felt a moment of unease. "Is that your *exact* interest in me, Señor Montalvan? I'm Joel Moreland's granddaughter? I have to tell you I'm long used to it, consequently forewarned. I saw how you were secretly studying me while I was standing on the balcony."

"Perhaps I was only thinking how beautiful you were," he answered, smoothly turning her into his arms again. "As serene as the swans that glide across your lake."

She had little option but to continue dancing. "Somehow I don't think that was it. The look wasn't at all an admiring glance or even friendly."

"What was it, then?" he asked, his wide shoulders blocking the light.

She wished she could see his expression more clearly. "Extremely disconcerting."

"Perhaps that was only an illusion. I was simply admiring a woman exquisite in her beauty and outward appearance of serenity."

She couldn't fail to pick up on the *outward*. "You think something entirely different goes on inside me?"

"Would it be so strange if I did? I, too, am a student of psychology. No one could say it's a simple life any more than we are simple beings. The inner person and the outer person can be significantly different."

"Of course. It's no easy thing to become a well-integrated adult. We all continue to harbor the fears and anxieties we had as children, but we've had to learn how to master them or seek help. I see young patients in terrible self-destructive rages because they've had to live through years of conflict and unhappiness. I see a great deal worse, physical and sexual abuse sometimes where one least suspects."

"That must be extremely upsetting?"

"It is." She drew a deep breath. "I've seen children sent back to the care of the very people who've abused them and I've been helpless! Some of it I'll never get out of my mind. It's ghastly stuff. That's one of the reasons I needed this holiday with Granddad. It's not easy what I do and I can't always stand aloof. In childhood we all assemble the building blocks that go into making the adult."

"So when the building blocks are in extremely short supply and the conflicts never resolve themselves, one is left scarred and without an inner haven to shelter."

"Exactly." It was obvious he was following her words closely. "The violent pattern most frequently repeats itself."

He sighed, his breath warm and sweet. "It's difficult to disassociate oneself from intense traumas in childhood. Didn't William Faulkner once say something about the past not being over or even past?"

"I'm not going to disagree with the great man."

"Me, neither. So you see we do have much to talk about, Cecile, if only our mutual interest in the development or the destruction of the human psyche. The great human values of love and honor coexist with hate and evil. Now, I must surrender you to your fiancé. He's heading very purposefully in this direction. I don't know that *I* would care to see my beautiful fiancée in another man's arms, either."

CHAPTER FOUR

STUART TOOK HIS leave at noon the following day. Exactly one minute after Cecile drove her grandfather's Bentley through the front gates of Morelands, the argument broke out just as she knew it would, when there was no one around to overhear.

"Damn it all, I wish you were coming back with me!" Stuart exclaimed, his handsome face marred by an angry expression.

"You don't begrudge me my vacation, surely?" She winced. Even with her sunglasses on the sunlight was much too bright.

"I simply want you with me."

"I know." Stuart had been simmering ever since he'd joined her and Raul Montalvan the previous night, leaving her with the sensation she was caught in the eye of a storm. Even when they met up at breakfast, she'd sensed the continuation of his mood, but as a guest in her grandfather's house he could scarcely vent feelings of outrage or jealousy. She was very much aware he'd had to make a huge effort in the final hours of the party. The celebrations had continued unabated until after two in the morning. When they'd left the mansion, the grounds were thronged with the staff of the firm that supplied the huge marquees and the tables and chairs, among other things.

Cecile tried to remain calm. Inside she knew she was approaching her own crisis point in life. It was a real struggle to hide it; harder yet to fight back.

"I just hate the idea of your being away from me," Stuart said tersely, equally off balance.

"Goodness, it's only a month!" She tried a soothing, sideways glance. "We'll be speaking to each other every day."

"Count on it." He stared moodily out the window. "That bloody Raul made a hit with your grandfather."

"That's not very nice, is it, *bloody* Raul."

"I know it isn't, but I can't help it. He's too suave, too charming by half."

"That's his Latin blood," she offered by way of explanation. "You're not going to blame him for being charming?"

Stuart had the grace to look embarrassed. "I just wish he hadn't turned up. He's the sort of guy that stirs everything up."

God help her, hadn't Stuart put his finger right on it? "You are in an odd mood, Stuart. No sleep?"

"Not when you wouldn't join me," he said, sounding painfully rebuffed.

"Not with a house full of relatives, Stuart. I told you that wasn't likely to happen."

He gave an angry snort. "Sometimes I think you don't give a damn if you sleep with me or not."

Her heart was beating painfully fast. She hadn't asked for any of this. It had just happened. Anyone could become madly infatuated. It was what one did about it that counted. "That's not true, Stuart." Even to her own ears her response didn't sound terribly convincing, yet she enjoyed their lovemaking. Stuart was a considerate lover, able to give satisfaction and not lacking finesse. "Do we really have to ruin a beautiful day with all this? I promised to marry you, didn't I?"

"But, Ceci—" Stuart twisted in the passenger seat to stare at her "—you won't set the date. You've no idea how insecure that makes me feel. Hell, it's like Justine says. We should be married and expecting our first child by now. You told me you loved children. I'm no longer sure."

Normally slow to temper, she felt intensely irritated. "What an alliance you and my mother have formed! Both of you pushing me into marriage and motherhood like I was the wrong side of forty. I do love children, Stuart. I think my choice of a profession proves that. If you and my mother continue to hound me—" She broke off, breathing a sharp sigh of frustration.

"It's not like that." Stuart reached out to stroke her arm. "Darling, it's not like that," he said softly.

Nothing. She felt nothing. She was greatly shocked.

"We would never be guilty of that." Stuart faced front again as though he thought it crucial he, too, mind the road. "Justine just wants the best for you, Cecile. You can be very difficult sometimes."

That was grossly unfair. She shook her head weakly. "I thought I rarely gave trouble. In fact, I was the model child. Ask anyone. I always did *exactly* what was expected of me. I had to be top in everything, grades, sports, ballet, piano. I worked so hard to keep my mother proud of me. I was never under that kind of pressure from my father, thank God. I was always obedient and respectful. I've never played around. I've never touched drugs. My mother wants *her* idea of the best for me, Stuart. I'm not my mother. I love her, but I'm not like her. She means well, but she spends every day of her life making plans for me. She had to give up on Dad. I want her to stop. I'm twenty-six, but she continues to act as though one day I'll screw up. Maybe she's right. Now there's a thought! My mother has always been too focused on me as her only child. I wish to God I'd had brothers and sisters. Anyone to take the heat off me. It won't stop even after we're married. Not with you encouraging her. Or is *that* going to stop when you've finally won the prize?"

Stuart's whole face turned stony, an expression she rarely saw and decided she didn't like. "I don't deserve that, Ceci," he said coldly. "Of course you're a prize, but I'm genuinely fond of your mother. She's a marvelous woman."

"It's a pity you didn't meet someone like her," Cecile shot back. "You have so much in common."

Censure was in his voice. "You sound pretty darn resentful, do you know that? As a psychologist, you ought to know it. Justine and I do have a lot in common. We both love *you.* Look, I don't want to argue, Ceci. I'm like a bear with a sore head today. I had way too much to drink last night and I'm no drinker, as you know. It's just that I'm worried about leaving you here, especially with that bloody Argentinian hanging around. They fancy themselves as great lovers, you know."

Cecile took a deep breath, trying to rein in her anger. "Well, he certainly gives the impression he might be. You don't trust me, is that it? You were furious I was dancing with him. Your coldness to him made it pretty apparent. You didn't get the opportunity to take it out on me, not with a party going on. You're acting as though I can't conduct myself in an appropriate manner if you're not around, just like you're bloody well braking now with your foot while *I'm* driving the car. Do you think I'm going to fling myself at a complete stranger like in some fruity melodrama?"

"You want the straight answer? *Yes,*" he said in a goaded voice. "There's so much about you, Ceci, that's beneath the surface. You act so cool and composed, but that could be your training. There was *something* between you, Ceci. You're trying hard to deny it, but I'm not a complete fool. I'm your fiancé, the man you're going to marry. Need I jog your memory? I have the *right* to question you."

"Really? I might have to start questioning if you're the right man for me. I hate people who go on about their rights, Stuart, unless it's the right to life, liberty and freedom. So to hell with your right to interfere with *my* freedom."

Stuart scowled. "You're being childish, Ceci. It's not like

you to rebel. Maybe you *were* on too tight a leash as a child. My aim is to protect you. I've always trusted you in the past."

"How sad, then, I've committed a very serious breach."

"Ceci, you of all people appeared to be encouraging him." He turned to her, his expression deadly serious.

She groaned. "You just can't leave well enough alone, can you?"

"You think I *want* to speak like this?" His voice was a rasp. "I feel I have an obligation to point certain things out. I do respect your high moral standards, my darling. It's Montalvan I don't trust. You don't have much vanity, but you're a very beautiful woman. Who could blame him if he was attracted to you?"

"How the heck do you know he was?" she demanded, her anger fueled by feelings of guilt.

"Oh, he's attracted all right!" Stuart declared with great conviction. "You could have been alone on an island. Forget there were three hundred bloody guests all around you."

"You have to stop this, Stuart," she said. "My head is starting to pound. Jealousy is a terrible thing. Lots of relationships can't survive jealousy. So we were enjoying the dance. No big deal. I reserve the right to choose the men I wish to speak to or dance with without consulting you, fiancé or not!"

Observing the hectic flush in her cheeks, Stuart backed down. "Of course you can, Ceci. It was the way the guy was holding you, looking at you, that put me in a rage. He knows bloody well you're *my* woman."

She felt like stopping the car and jumping out. It would be so much easier than trying to push him out. "Don't you love to get your tongue around the word *my,*" she fumed. "You've got a whole list starting with *my* career, *my* ambitions, *my* political aspirations, *my* new house, *my* new Beemer, *my* fiancée. I'm right down the list." She realized in her agitation she was over the speed limit and quickly slowed. "Raul Montalvan is a beautiful, natural dancer. Why not? Argentina is the home of the tango after all."

"Ahhh, Ceci," he groaned, "You're making quite an effort to put me off the scent, but there was a little more to it than that. Even Sasha noticed."

"Sasha?" Cecile gave an incredulous laugh. "The two of you were spying on me?"

"Of course not." Stuart spoke in an aggrieved tone. "It was only by chance she spotted you."

"I bet!" She swung her head toward him. "Sasha always was a troublemaker."

"Actually she's very fond of you. She wouldn't want to see you put a foot wrong any more than I would. Women are very sharp. You catch on to things we men don't. But the way the two of you moved together it would have crossed anyone's mind, even trusting ol' me. There was just some aura for all to see."

"Could it have been an alcoholic haze?" she asked with some sarcasm. She was rebelling against the accusations, even as she knew she was in denial. "Sasha was sloshed. I could equally well point out you had no objection to Sasha's clinging on to your arm."

Stuart grimaced. "She doesn't mean a thing to me and you know it. I bet you weren't a bit jealous of Sasha even though she's a damned sexy girl. Doesn't that tell you something about *our* relationship?"

"I've learned to trust you, perhaps?" Cecile maneuvered the big car into the busy right lane so she could take the freeway turnoff.

"You *can* trust me. I don't want anyone else but you, Ceci. And I have some ethics, if that bloody Argentinian doesn't. Who is he, anyway? He appears out of nowhere and makes a beeline for you."

She felt like she wanted to sleep for hours. Shut it all out. "One dance!" she said sharply. "You call that making a beeline?"

Stuart sat straighter, rubbing his trousered knees. "Steady on."

Cecile gritted her teeth. "Do you want to miss your plane?

I've had a license since I was seventeen, Stuart. I've never had an accident, which is more than I can say for you."

"Don't be so touchy!" He raised his brows. "I know you're a good driver, very controlled and decisive about what you do, but this is a big powerful car. Women shouldn't really drive big powerful cars in my view, and you do have a worrying tendency to be impetuous, especially if you're running late. As for my *one* accident, how was I to know a bus was going to pull out in front of the car ahead of me?"

"By studying the road well ahead," she said tartly. "Look, let's stop this, shall we?"

"Certainly. I'm sorry, darling. I apologize. I was jealous. I freely admit it, but I can only say what I fear. To get to know this Montalvan would be to court danger. Knowing your grandfather, the guy's bound to be offered plenty of entertainment while he's here. He's not a suitable companion, that's all. I'm five years older than you. I work in an area where I see a lot more suspect characters than you."

"To hell with that!" she said hotly. "Do you see children and adolescents who've been sexually, physically and mentally abused? Do you see suffering on the grand scale? Little people who've been beaten, burned, tied up with rope or whatever is to hand, had their bones broken, their bodies violated and infected, been threatened with weapons? The most you see, Stuart—you're so bloody pompous at times—is white-collar crime. The socially prominent scoundrels you help beat the charges."

"Well, really, that's a bit extreme, isn't it?" Stuart's voice was taut with shock. "And there's no need to swear. It scarcely suits you. I've never heard you call me pompous before."

"Clearly, sometimes you are!"

"This is too much, Ceci," he complained. "Personally I don't believe attack is the best form of defense. All I was saying is I don't think business-pleasure is all there is to it with this Montalvan guy."

"Why don't you have him investigated?" she suggested, suddenly very aware of Stuart's tendency to patronize her. "That should solve the problem."

Stuart, the lawyer, took the suggestion seriously. "It could be done," he said, nibbling hard on his lip. "All that charm, the expensive clothes, the handmade shoes, the solid gold watch, the meticulous grooming—it could all be window dressing. He could be an experienced con man, for all we know. There's nothing would suit a con man more than to latch on to a beautiful heiress. Seduce her if he could. He certainly latched on to you and your grandfather."

So he did, said that harsh little voice in her head. *He made a huge attempt to reach you and succeeded.* As a man, Raul Montalvan was very, *very* seductive. It was one way to cut across all borders.

"You can't deny it's a possibility." Stuart frowned as he searched her tense profile.

"Fascinating if you were writing a novel, Stuart, but I haven't the slightest doubt Señor Montalvan is who he says he is. I think you'll find he comes from a wealthy well-respected family. Bruce and Fiona must know all about him. I'm sure you could find the Montalvan estancia on the Internet, as they breed polo ponies."

"Maybe he's using someone else's identity," Stuart suggested, still frowning hard. "It's been done before today. Australia is a long way from Argentina."

She clicked her tongue angrily. "Nowhere is a long way from anywhere these days. Granddad would soon discover if Raul knew little about ranching, and polo isn't the sport for a man without means. Besides he has all the graces expected in the son of a cultured family. He's bilingual. I wouldn't be a bit surprised if he didn't speak other languages, as well. Italian, French, who knows?"

"I'm getting the strong impression you admire him," Stuart said angrily.

"I'd say a lot of people admire him," she said dryly. "Actually, Stuart, I'm on side with you. For all his charm, there's something mysterious about Raul Montalvan. Something steely, possibly dangerous? He's an enigma."

Stuart reeled back at some note—perhaps betrayal—in her voice. "Aw, bugger that!" he said with a burst of violent jealousy. "All I know is, such men are best left alone."

Such a pity, then, you've already burnt your fingers!

CHAPTER FIVE

CECILE GAZED DOWN the beautifully appointed dinner table, her eyes on her grandfather, who was swirling a deep ruby wine around his crystal goblet before drinking it and nodding to Robson, the major domo responsible for running the domestic affairs of the mansion smoothly. Her grandfather had always kept an excellent cellar, the best wines from home and around the world. The conversation at a table for fourteen guests eddied around her, her grandfather at one end, Great-aunt Bea at the other. The guest of honor for the evening was a well-known political figure, Senator Brendan Ryan. He sat to her grandfather's right, her mother to his left. She herself sat a few chairs away with Raul Montalvan sitting opposite her across the gleaming table, set with the finest bone china, sparkling crystal and solid silver flatware. A set of six beautiful caryatid candlesticks, her favorites, supporting tall white tapers were set at intervals down the table. Her late maternal grandmother, Frances, had acquired them in London when she and her grandfather were on their honeymoon. Grecian goddesses rose from domed circular bases to support the wax pans and sconces above their heads. Her grandmother had always promised them to her. Frances had doted on her, whereas Justine claimed she had spent a lifetime trying to gain her mother's love and attention. Sadly, from all accounts it was true. It was her uncle Jared, her mother's late brother, who had been the apple of Frances's eye. She had adored him to the exclusion of her daughter, a deprivation that had badly affected Justine and perhaps explained her unswerving, single-minded focus on her only child.

The scent of the wines mingled with the scent of the flowers in the low, very beautiful central arrangement of white lilies and orchids. Montalvan wasn't looking at her. He was talking to her friend Tara Sinclair, his tone too low for her to hear, but it was easy enough to read Tara's expression. She looked enthralled.

There, what did I tell you? It's not difficult for any woman to become infatuated with an exciting man. Possibly he doesn't even realize his hypnotic powers. Then again he most assuredly does.

Tara threw back her blond head and laughed. She was wearing a red silk dress cut low to show the upward swell of her breasts. She had lovely creamy skin, not a conventional beauty but attractive and vivacious. She and Raul appeared to be drawn together in an intimate joke. A peculiar feeling akin, not to jealousy, but to rejection rose in her. She had made a fool of herself the other night. She had quarreled with Stuart, sending him back home to Melbourne with no harmony between them. Of course he had since rung any number of times from his apartment and from work, but during these intervening days she had agonized over, not whether, but *when* to call off the engagement. She knew her mother's reproaches would go on forever, Stuart being her mother's idea of an excellent match.

I can't believe what you're thinking, girl!

She was beginning to tire of her inner voice. She hadn't really done anything stupid, thank God. She took a sip of her wine, no more, quickly turning to one of her old beaus, an architect, newly married, as he asked for her impressions of a recent showing of aboriginal art they had both attended. She was happy to tell him. It took her mind off Raul and Tara.

After dinner her grandfather asked her to play for them, as

she'd known he would. She was a gifted pianist. Glad, in the end, her mother had forced many long hours of practice on her, so that she had collected a clutch of diplomas, all high distinctions, even before she left school. Ordinarily she was happy to perform for dinner guests, but tonight *his* presence made her incredibly nervous when nervousness had been bearing down on her all day.

Everyone took their seats in the living room, all in wonderfully mellow spirits, induced by good conversation and a truly memorable dinner. It had been definitely on the sensual side, with superb oysters topped by caviar, succulent garden-fresh asparagus to accompany the melt-in-your-mouth beef and small pots of velvety smooth, ever-so-seductive chocolate mousse to finish. Certainly Raul Montalvan appeared to have enjoyed it. She had the idea that in nineteenth-century France a bridegroom was encouraged to eat several helpings of asparagus before joining his bride in the connubial bed, just as Montezuma consumed copious amounts of hot chocolate before visiting his harem. Just looking across the table had been enough for her to be devoured by her senses.

Her grandfather went to the big Steinway grand, lifting the lid. It was a small task he loved. Her mother played, or rather, *had* played until her daughter's abilities had overtaken hers. After that, Justine never touched the piano again, which was an awful shame, because Justine desperately needed the relaxation. The magnificent Steinway her grandfather had bought Cecile some ten years back replaced the fine old Bechstein her mother had learned on.

Cecile settled herself on the ebony piano seat already adjusted to her height and particular requirements. Knowing she would be asked to play, she had spent an hour or so of the preceding days practicing. Her hands were slender, long-fingered, deceptively strong. Her technique had never let her down. Tonight, unfortunately, her emotions were all over the place. Should she not play well, her mother would be deeply disappointed in her and make a point of telling her so afterward.

Cecile bowed her head over the keys, her long graceful neck revealed by her hairstyle for the evening, an updated chignon. Normally she was very comfortable in this setting, surrounded by family and friends, none of them, outside of her mother, critical. For a moment her nervousness threatened to overwhelm her. She glanced up at the ceiling; the ceiling stared back. God, she was nothing without her confidence. No performer was. Someone was laughing, a soft little giggle. Sounded like Tara. Etiquette demanded an audience be quiet, but it was hard to quiet Tara, who wasn't a music lover, anyway.

What was happening to her? Stage fright? Panic attacks could happen right out of the blue. She had seen them with sad regularity in the course of her work, but she had never actually experienced one until she'd laid eyes on Raul Montalvan.

Play something easy. Start with a couple of Chopin waltzes. Everyone just wants to enjoy themselves.

She glanced down at her hands, wondering if she had simply lost it.

Then suddenly *he* was approaching the piano, asking her very charmingly if the Spanish composer Albeniz was included in her repertoire. He pronounced the composer's name in the Spanish fashion. She had never heard it sound so good. She had intended to start with a Brahms rhapsody, but Spanish music had always captivated her. She had kept up the repertoire. Why, given he was South American, had she not thought of it herself?

"As long as you don't expect me to measure up to the great Alicia De Larrocha," she said, finding she was able to breathe again.

"You're an artist, I'm sure." He looked deeply into her eyes. Then he moved back to his position on the sofa between Tara and Great-Aunt Bea, who claimed to have been in her youth— she was now seventy-eight—a regular love goddess. Bea certainly liked good-looking men, never depriving herself of their company.

The lights turned on again in her brain. Normally she would never have started with the very difficult "Malaga," one of the most passionate pieces of Albeniz's great work for piano, *Iberia*, but the fact he had come to her aid—his eyes told her that—fired her blood. She turned with a smile to announce to the room what she intended to play. She saw her grandfather clap with delight, turning his head to say a few words to his Argentinian guest. Bea gave her such an animated wave of her heavily bejewelled hands, Cecile thought for a moment she might get up and dance; her mother sat with a slight frown as though doubting whether, without practice, she could pull it off.

Thank you, Mother, for the vote of confidence.

She knew well how difficult it was to treat children whose parents, especially the mothers, were overly demanding. Her old professor at the Conservatorium had always refused to let her mother sit in on any lesson, even rehearsals for exams. *Helicopter mothers, Cecile, forever hovering over their children. I cannot abide them!*

She sat quietly for a moment before the keyboard, bringing all her concentration to bear. Then when she was ready she launched into the piece that in essence represented the wonderful dance rhythms of the *malaguena*.

Never for a moment had he allowed his purpose for coming here to fade from his mind. What he wanted was revenge. It was a kind of mania, really. Sometimes more than others—when he was riding alone far out on the *pampas*—he saw himself as a grown man bound by the vows of his youth. A boy lost, his face hot and flushed with tears for all the misfortune coming his beloved grandfather's way. It was obvious even to him forces were at work to drive them off their land. Land that one day would be his. Land was everything. It spoke to him with a passion. There was an explanation for what was happening.

The Morelands.

"They're determined to ruin us!" He wasn't sure how he was going to achieve revenge—strip a powerful man of at least some of his prestige—but he was hoping ways and means would present themselves as he was drawn deeper and deeper into their world. He had achieved his prime objective of working his way in with little difficulty. It had turned out to be so easy he could scarcely believe it. He had the motivation, now he needed the necessary guile. There would be opportunities. This family, like all families, had secrets. Dark, damning secrets that needed to be exposed to the light of day and public censure. Since he'd been a boy he had dreamed of striking a blow at the family responsible for his own family's long years of suffering and exile: the Morelands, with their powerful army of sympathizers and supporters.

His mother had found peace in her second marriage, giving birth to Francisco, his stepfather Ramon's heir, then two years later, little Ramona. His own father, who had been enticed to Argentina to play polo and was later employed by Ramon to help breed his polo ponies, was long dead, dying in hospital a few days after taking a bad fall at a home match. He would have survived the fall, only it was his blighted destiny to be trampled by his agitated pony. Polo, the way the *gauchos* played it, was dangerously fast in what was the fastest game in the world. What had happened to his father should have put him off playing polo for life, but he, too, thrived on the element of danger. Horsemanship was in his blood. He had inherited his father's speed and finesse and his near-complete range of strokes. Unlike his father when he played it was with *one* objective in mind: to win. He knew Joel Moreland had been a fine, enthusiastic player. He knew his son Jared rode as hard and fearlessly as the best. He knew a great deal about Jared Moreland, the predator, canonized in death.

What he hadn't anticipated was meeting this beautiful creature, Jared Moreland's niece. She couldn't be allowed to get in his way. Then again, he knew he had her at his mercy. If he could only bring himself to be so ruthless, she could play a big part in showing the all-powerful Morelands what it was like to suffer. He relived the moment he'd looked up to see her standing above him on the central balcony of the mansion. She had appeared in her wedding finery like some splendid apparition or a beautiful illustration out of one of Ramona's golden books of fairy tales. Her gown was a lustrous silver. She wore a crown of flowers on her head. That first sight of her might well haunt him the rest of his life, he thought bleakly. Just the sight of her had made him think for the first time he should be building his own life, not forever seeking revenge for a past that was gone. Were the vows he had made eternally binding? Why had she made him feel they no longer meant anything?

For long moments he'd been a stranger to himself. She hadn't been aware of him, so he continued to stare with this queer hunger, as a man might stare at the unattainable. She *shone* in her bridesmaid's gown. Her skin gave off a lovely, luminous glow. Her effect on him was unprecedented in his experience, when his family's adopted Argentina was full of beautiful women, his for the asking. He had not dreamed of *this*, when it was essential he remain true to himself.

She had turned her head; stared down at him, her beautiful face unsmiling. Impossible to smile at that moment. He remembered he'd saluted her in some way. She had acknowledged him, regal as a princess. He'd wanted to climb up to her, using the thick, flowering trumpet vine that wreathed the white pillars as purchase for his eager feet. He was a passionate slave to beauty in all its forms, but for no woman had he been aflame with a terrible desire. It was *unimaginable* she should be a Moreland.

He had known that at once. She was Cecile Moreland, very much her grandfather's princess and heiress. She was far more beautiful in the flesh than in her photos in newspapers and the social pages of magazines, arresting as they were. He'd made it his business to find out everything there was to be learned about the Morelands. He already knew much, since he had lived with that hated name since his childhood. He had started his updated research with the Man with the Midas Touch, Joel Moreland. He now knew where every member of the entire clan lived, what they did for a living, the circles they moved in, their particular friends, their habits. He might have been commissioned to write an unauthorized book on the family, entitled *A Study of the Morelands*. Joel Moreland, the patriarch, father of the dead Jared, was way up there with the richest men in the country. His interests were vast. He doted on the young woman who now sat at the piano, her raven head bent over the keys.

She could complicate things drastically if he allowed it. Or she could become the all-powerful pawn. He had no stomach for causing grief to a woman—certainly not one who had so easily ensnared him—but he couldn't forget how much the women of his family had suffered. His grandmother, his mother, his aunts. The entire family had been forced off the land as his grandfather went deeper and deeper into debt. Land that one day his grandfather had promised would be his. Land was everything. Only, his grandfather had gone bankrupt. His creditors had moved in and they had moved out. Exile was like an amputation. There was an explanation for it all, the never-ending problems and misfortune. The way the family was ostracized.

Moreland wrath.

"They're determined to ruin us, boy!" his grandfather had said, shaking an impotent fist at the clear blue sky. The memory would always remain with him: the boy and the old man. The boy's face hot and flushed with tears, his heart as heavy as his grandfather's. What was to be his was no more. His inheritance, his future hopes had been swept away on a wind straight from hell.

Even in the middle of his tortured thoughts, Raul had sensed Cecile was under some strain, as intensely nervous as he was intensely on edge. He'd been observing her closely all through dinner even with her charming but frivolous friend's voice buzzing like a bee in his ear. He rose when Tara began to giggle softly, walked to the piano knowing intuitively he could restore her nervous energy. It was all part of their subterranean communication.

The instant Cecile's hands touched the keys, the magic of the wonderful opening bars put his somber thoughts to rest. He sat back simply to listen, to absorb the music and the spectacle of her beauty as she sat at the grand piano in her lovely chiffon dress. The color put him in mind of the jacarandas, native to the high deserts of adjoining Brazil. They grew everywhere in Argentina and in flower lit up the Montalvan estancia. He knew they flourished, too, in many parts of temperate and subtropical Australia.

She played beautifully, powerfully. More important, she had mastered to perfection the particular rhythms of Spanish music. His stepsister, Ramona, was an accomplished pianist, but nothing like this. He knew the piece she was playing. He knew practically every piano piece the composer had written, the *Iberia* suite well, although Ramona always said the "Malaga" was too hard for her. Ramona had played the "Suite Espanola" so often over the years he could have whistled every note. In fact, he did whistle the catchy melodies as he rode the *pampas*. Ramon had been the kindest and most generous of stepfathers, adopting him and lending him his name. But Ramon had his heir, Francisco, who would soon turn twenty-one. Stepbrothers, they had never grown close. There was the big difference in age. He was nearly eleven years older, and Francisco was burdened by an intensely jealous nature that came much between them. With him out of the way, perhaps Francisco could find himself and become a better man.

As it was a weekday, all the guests were ready to take their leave not long after midnight. The senator as he was leaving complimented Cecile on "a wonderful performance." The other guests, too, as they moved out the front door expressed their enjoyment. Tara, who had come with her parents, grasped Cecile's arm rather painfully, drawing her swiftly aside.

"He's not married, is he?" she asked excitedly, color in her creamy cheeks.

"You mean Raul?"

"What's wrong with you all of a sudden? Of course I mean Raul. He's *devastating!"* Tara rolled her eyes.

"Don't get your hopes up, girl. I understand he has six children. Argentinians marry early."

Tara elbowed her in the ribs. "You're joking! He's not married at all. *Is* he?"

"He says not. Do you think we can believe him?"

"Well, *I* intend to." Tara readjusted the bodice of her dress to better show off her cleavage. "Listen, Ceci, I need to see more of him. Can you arrange it? Don't tell me now," she whispered hurriedly. "Here he comes. I don't want him to know we're talking about him. Have coffee with me tomorrow, okay? I'll ring you."

"Fine. I look forward to it."

Tara directed a brilliant smile and a little flutter of her hand at Raul Montalvan, calling sweetly, "Hope to see you again, Raul!"

"Is someone giving you a lift?" Cecile inquired of him politely. Fiona and Bruce had had a previous engagement, so they weren't able to attend the dinner party.

"I don't need a lift." He looked down at her gravely. "Your grandfather has already asked. I intend to walk back to the house. It's a beautiful night, and only a couple of miles to the residence. I'm used to very long treks, so a couple of miles could scarcely bother me. That said," his handsome mouth twitched, "perhaps you can walk me to your front gate? I've been wanting to tell you for close on two hours how much excitement I heard in your playing. It gave me enormous pleasure."

"Thank you." She inclined her head. "And thank you for helping me through a nervous moment. Somehow I *froze* when I'm used to playing for company."

"Perhaps I inspired the nerves, so it was necessary for me to take them away."

"You're very sure of yourself, aren't you?" There was a spirited flash in her silver-sheened eyes.

"I could scarcely answer, sure of *you!*"

"Is that a challenge?"

"Only if you'll respond." He smiled. "Come…" He didn't wait for her to agree to accompany him, but gently took her arm.

"Where are you off to, Ceci?" her mother called brightly from the bottom of the grand staircase.

"Ah, the mother ever ready to watch over her chick," he sighed softly, bending his head to Cecile's ear.

"Only to the front gate, Mother," she replied just as blithely.

"Some mothers never really see their daughters as grown-up," he said.

"Please don't tell anyone, okay?" she said coolly when she felt a fever coming on.

The last of the guests' cars were in line to pull out of the open front gates, their rear lights glowing a hot red. In silence they walked down the short flight of stone steps that led away from the huge three-story, colonial-style mansion with its towering vine-wreathed white pillars and second-floor central balcony. Cecile's heart was racing ninety to the dozen, as adrenaline poured into her blood. Now she knew what being on a "high" was. She didn't need any drugs; she was sizzling with the fever of sexual attraction. She felt she was doing something tantalizingly illicit, yet at the same time she couldn't and wouldn't stop herself from going with him. There was simply no *chance* of stopping. It wasn't that she was so much afraid of *him.* She was afraid of herself. And why not? She didn't know herself anymore. The outwardly serene Cecile people were used to had been replaced by someone quite different. She was now a woman who was ready to take dangerous chances.

The night sky was glorious, crowded with stars that hung

over the harbor. The sea breeze stirred the leaves of the trees and shook out the perfume of a million tropical flowers. They had moved beyond the wide semicircle of exterior lights from the house, but the huge lantern lights set into the massive stone pillars that supported the wrought-iron gates showed the path clearly.

"You grandfather has very kindly asked me to his flagship station, as he called it, Malagari."

"When will this be?" She lifted her head in surprise. She didn't know how to take it—things were moving so fast.

"Would you believe toward the end of next week?" he said smoothly. "He had to consult his diary. He told me he had promised you a trip also, that Malagari is one of your favorite places."

"*The* favorite," she said.

"I expect he will want you to come along as well." His voice dropped deep into his chest. "Perhaps we could enjoy some marvelous Outback adventure together?"

The very thought sent cascading ripples down her spine. "There's absolutely no way I can do that, Raul. You know I can't!"

"But you *can!*"

The way he said it thrilled her. This was the moment she should pull back, but he had the speed and grace of a big cat. With one arm around her he whirled her off the driveway into the dense shadow of the trees.

"Wait! *Wait*, Raul! What are you doing?" Her voice shook; her body trembled violently. She might have been stripped naked.

He ran a finger down her satin cheek. "Cecile, my behavior is wholly known to you."

It was a waste of time denying it. "That doesn't mean it's not wrong." She felt herself flush deeply.

"I know that, too—" his answer was clipped "—but I can't seem to help myself."

"Raul, I'm *engaged*!" She despised herself for using it as a shield.

"I remember," he said quietly.

"Then you must realize this shouldn't happen."

"Astonishingly it has!" He pulled her close. "And engaged isn't married. I don't much like your fiancé. I feel strongly he isn't the man for you."

Her agitation intensified. "I don't know what I'm expected to say to that. He's my fiancé. I love him. You don't know anything about Stuart. He's—"

He stopped her mouth with his own.

Delirium!

Moondust fell from the skies, settling like a golden net around them.

His kiss was so deep and so passionate all thought of withstanding it evaporated like the dawn mist. It was a total assault on the senses, too devastating in its power for a mere kiss. Sensation upon sensation rushed through her body, hot, sweet, incredibly fierce. If he had drawn her down to the thick grass where they stood, she wouldn't have resisted. Resistance was impossible, even though she knew she was flouting her own code of honorable behavior.

In moments it was over. She stood there panting, trying to regain some semblance of control. He was still holding her in his arms, but she couldn't get her balance back. It was moments more before she could pull away.

"Dear Lord!" She gave a soft moan, lamenting how much of herself she had delivered up.

"Look at me." His tone was quiet but commanding.

"No way!" She had to lean against a tree for support even though the rough bark caught at the fine fabric of her dress.

"*Please* look at me." He moved nearer. "You are the loveliest thing I've ever seen."

"Raul, go. Just go."

"You feel guilty?"

"Of course I feel guilty," she said angrily. "I'm engaged to be married. I'm kissing you. What sort of a person does that make me?"

His laugh was faintly discordant. "Maybe you're just setting yourself free? Maybe you've wanted to be free all along?"

"And maybe for your own reasons you would like to seduce me?" She threw out the challenge. Certainly it had happened to her before. "I actually knew someone who proposed to do that just to settle a bet. It isn't unusual for a certain kind of man to have that idea."

"Of course this certain man didn't succeed?"

She spoke in a contemptuous tone. "In the end he wished he'd never thought of it. He or his friend."

"So where are we now? Only a fool would mess with the Morelands. Is that it?"

"I wouldn't care to mess with you," she retorted. "Was that kiss a blatant example of what I might expect if I were fool enough to join you on Malagari?"

"I know you want to," he said with stunning self-confidence. "It should happen. It will happen, Cecile. You're the beautiful princess locked away in the ivory tower. It's time for you to break out." His hand rose to lift her chin, then slowly, voluptuously, he pressed another kiss onto her warm pulsing mouth. "Must you marry this fiancé of yours? He seems to me to be what they call a stuffed shirt. He isn't your soul mate."

"And you are?" Her voice betrayed high emotion, but she'd gone beyond caring.

"I can make you tremble," he pointed out gently. "I can make you open your mouth to me."

"The next step my thighs? I think not," she said sharply, a blue vein beating in her temple. "I must go back to the house," she said, albeit much too late. "If you're looking for a holiday affair—"

He caught her wrist, his sensuous voice abruptly harsh.

"Don't talk such nonsense. I am as much compromised by whatever it is that exists between us as you are."

"Nothing exists between us," she declared with no truth whatsoever. "I'm to be married very soon to the man I love."

He gave a short laugh. "Forgive me, but isn't this a bad time to drag that up? It's humiliating, I know, to lose control, especially for someone who represses emotion. Both of us appear to have been blindsided. Fate works in strange ways, Cecile."

She shook her head, feeling like she wanted to cry. What had happened to her self-control? It was sliding away from her. "I must go back." She started to move toward the path and the beam of light. Her high heels were sinking into the grass, and again he took her arm.

"Ah yes, Mamma will be waiting," he said in a sardonic voice. "I picture her now, on the central balcony, a pair of binoculars in hand. She's an impressive woman, your mother, but very controlling. You must try to get past that, Cecile."

She surprised herself by a confession. "Sometimes I think I never will. I'm caught, you see, by love and…compassion."

"Useful tools when one needs to apply emotional blackmail," he said. "How did your engagement happen?"

She gave an angry little laugh. "Maybe I was bored. Maybe I felt pressured into it. Maybe I felt my youth ticking by. I want children." She shrugged a little. "Surely you have no right to question me. Let's say, I fell in love. Stuart loves me."

"*That* part I believe," he said, sounding grim.

"Do you always talk this way to strangers?" She was angry that she felt incompetent to deal with him. "I have to tell you, student of psychology that you are, you know nothing about my mother, my family, my fiancé, nothing about me, except I play the piano rather well—"

"And you forget everything and everyone in my arms." He turned her toward him.

"You don't need to remind me." She drew away as if he were

the devil himself. "I think I should make a vow right now *never* to go back into your arms again."

"Will the moon never come out again at night?" He gave a brief, sardonic laugh.

She had trouble even thinking of an answer. Instead, panic rose in her like a flock of startled birds. "Raul, you must stay away from me."

He touched her cheek "That, too, seems to be out of our control. Your grandfather appears bent on throwing us together."

"He's simply being kind." Even as she said it she was tormented by the notion he was right.

"Perhaps he doesn't think your fiancé worthy of you, either?" Raul suggested. "You deserve better. Already I know a side of you he will *never* see. I'm sure he tells you your playing is very *nice*?"

"Well, he would, as he's tone deaf. You should never have kissed me, Raul," she told him bleakly.

"You should never have kissed me back." His answer was calm.

"I'm ashamed."

"I'm quite certain I'm not," he clipped off. "He wants to *own* you, Cecile."

There was too much truth in what he said, however unpalatable, for her to deny it.

"It can't be a fate your grandfather would want for you. You are your own woman."

"Yes I am, though I won't be if we continue like this." She turned her face sharply toward the house. "I can deal with my problems by myself, you know."

He shrugged. "Forgive me if I thought you could use some help. It seems to me from what your grandfather has told me, much has been expected of you."

"Hasn't much been expected of you?" she countered. "Who *are* you, anyway?" She couldn't conceal her unease.

"Perhaps someone you need?" While she sounded angry, he sounded calm, almost fatalistic.

Her eyes, more accustomed to the low level of lighting, registered the expression on his face. "You don't appear to me as a *friend!* I confess a concern you might have some private agenda."

"But of course I have!" He made a little foreign gesture with his hands. "I can promise you that."

"I don't care for the sound of that."

"But you don't want to *stop* seeing me."

She had no idea how to cope with him. *None!* Not when he had come at her like some blazing meteor from out of space. How could a mere mortal reach her in unreachable places? It didn't seem possible otherwise. She turned on her heel, throwing her words over her shoulder. "Don't draw me into your plans, Raul Montalvan, whatever they are. I'll say good-night."

He raised a mocking hand. *"Buenas noches*, Cecile. Until we meet again!"

CHAPTER SIX

SHE WAS UNDRESSED, ready to climb into bed, when her mother tapped on her door.

"May I come in for a moment, Cecile?" Justine, in one of her collection of luxurious satin nightgowns and matching robes, swept in before Cecile got a chance to say yea or nay.

"It must be important if it can't wait." Cecile, long used to these late-night encounters with her mother, slumped onto the bed, her head already pounding and in a whirl. "It's well after one."

Justine spun around, a handsome, dominant woman whose frequent aggressive actions masked deep insecurities. "Be that as it may, I have something very serious to say to you, Cecile. I don't believe it *can* wait. I'll be off in the morning, as you know. Your father and I have a big function to attend Friday evening."

"Fire away then," Cecile answered, unable to keep the weariness out of her voice.

Justine pursed her mouth at her daughter's response. "*Don't*— I beg of you—don't when you've finally got your life together, allow anything to threaten it."

Realistically speaking, wasn't it a possibility? "Words to live by, Mother," Cecile said. "Anything in particular bring this on?"

Justine moved to one side and took a seat in a brocade-covered armchair. "Don't take that tone with me, Cecile. Your manners have slipped. You used to be very respectful. I'd like you to remain that way. It's the least you can do when I've devoted my life to you. You've been reared in the lap of luxury with every advantage. You've had much love, not to say adulation. I certainly never had that. My mother scarcely acknowledged my existence. We, however, have been very close. I'm very proud of that. You've always heeded my advice and acted on it. Maybe I didn't want you to pursue your career, which must be very ugly and distressing, but I didn't put up any real objection."

Cecile stifled a snort. "How can you say that, Mother, given your numerous objections? It was Dad and Granddad who supported my desire to become a child psychologist. You might challenge Dad and you did, but you've never challenged Granddad."

Justine's outraged expression showed she didn't like that fact pointed out. "I *adore* Daddy. You know I do." At fifty Justine didn't find it at all incongruous she should continue to call her father "Daddy."

"But you've never forgiven him, either," Cecile pointed out quietly. What made her say that, however true? How many times in one day could she shock herself, Cecile thought.

"Cecile, what are you saying?" Justine sat straight, holding her shoulders rigidly.

"Something I've known for a very long time. I'm not trying to upset you, Mother, but I think I should tell you, *you* upset me a lot of the time. You're too ready to interfere in my life, always advising, exhorting. There's always something, if not wrong, not quite right with what I'm doing, no matter what it is. Sometimes I think I'm not the daughter you wanted at all, though God knows I've tried to be. I saw your face tonight when I announced I was going to play the 'Malaga.' Anyone would have thought I was about to disgrace you."

"Nonsense!" Justine rejected that firmly. "I merely thought

you wouldn't do yourself justice. I'm sure you haven't practiced that piece in ages and it's technically very demanding."

"But I did play it well?"

For the first time Justine's taut expression relaxed. "You were wonderful, Cecile. I've always been very proud of you. Haven't I told you often enough?"

"Forgive me, Mother, you have. What are we talking about here, anyway?"

Justine pursed her lips again. "I understood you to say I've never forgiven Daddy. Whatever prompted that?"

"The truth, Mother," Cecile sighed. "You grew up believing Granddad didn't do enough for you." She held up her hand as her mother went to interrupt. "I scarcely mean in the material sense. You didn't think Granddad supported you enough against Nan. He gave you love, support, comfort, solace when you didn't get those things from your mother, but—"

"Believe me, I *didn't!*" Justine said harshly, stony-faced.

"Grandma cared more about Granddad and Uncle Jared than she cared about you?" Cecile asked gently.

"Some women are like that," Justine said bitterly. "Husbands and sons are the only ones who matter. Daddy was away so much of the time. It was always business, business, business. I had no one but servants to look out for me. In many ways I was a lost child. I know my mother loved *you*, extraordinarily enough, but she skipped a generation. She never bonded with me. Ask anyone. Ask wicked old Bea. There's another one who loves you and not me."

"You won't let yourself be loved, Mother," Cecile said. "I think it must have taken Granddad—a very busy man as you say—a long time before he realized what was going on with you and Nan, the lack of warmth and affection. But it wasn't Granddad's fault any more than what happened to Daniel and his poor little mother. It was necessary for Granddad to be away on his many business trips. We've all benefited from his great success. His family and any number of friends and charities.

It seems incredible to me now that Nan was so cruel to Daniel's mother."

"Ah, Johanna! She was just the maid, a no one!" Justine sighed. "Let me tell you your grandmother did have a cruel streak. No way was Johanna, however pretty, going to be allowed to get her hooks into Mother's beloved Jared. My mother solved the problem by driving Daniel's mother away. Now Daniel's back."

"You don't want him back, though, do you, Mother?" Cecile brought it out into the open.

Justine's fine, regular features sharpened. "How dare you say such a thing!"

"Aw, Mother, admit it. You think you know me. I know *you*. I already love Daniel. You've tried very hard to do the right thing. You've acted perfectly, but it is *acting*. You're Daniel's aunt, his own flesh and blood, but you have no feeling for him. Is it because you fear Granddad's love for Daniel will lessen his love for you? It won't. You should feel secure in Granddad's love."

Justine sighed deeply. "Well, I never have. I know Daddy loves me, but he would have gotten over *my* death a whole lot sooner than he's survived Jared's. You can't know what it's like, Cecile, to forever walk in someone else's shadow. When Jared died I wanted to be dead myself. I know my mother would have sacrificed me in an instant to save Jared. She *knew,* I'm convinced of it, that Daniel's mother was pregnant when she sent her away. That meant she sent away her own grandchild, but she didn't care. She had Jared. Thank God Daniel is more like Daddy than Jared ever was. Otherwise I couldn't abide the sight of him. You're right, I can't take to poor Daniel, I'm sorry."

"You will in time, Mother. Give yourself a chance. You know the source of your bitterness and resentment. Daniel had no part to play in that. Daniel was an innocent victim. He's *good,* like Granddad is good. You'll come to see that."

Justine looked unconvinced. "Cecile, I'm hoping I'll have little to do with him, though I do like Alexandra. She's a lovely girl. It's *you* I'm worried about. I want to prevent something bad happening here. You're attracted to this Raul Montalvan, aren't you?"

"Definitely." Cecile saw no point in not admitting it. She had given herself away. "Tara found him extremely attractive, too."

"Then leave him to Tara," Justine said in a clipped voice. "Let Tara entertain him. She'll *love* that. I can see his very obvious attractions, but I don't trust him. Daddy is so generous with his time and money I'm sure he'll be wanting to entertain this young man while he's here. My advice to you, and it's good advice, stay clear of him. He's most definitely trouble. I know Stuart was very concerned."

Cecile flared up. "You don't mean to tell me Stuart discussed the subject with you."

"He didn't have to," Justine answered irritably. "Stuart and I are on the same wavelength. Besides it was *appallingly* obvious our visitor was attracted to you. I don't have to remind you being a Moreland gives you added brilliance. He could be on the lookout for a rich wife for all we know."

"So you think he's a fortune hunter?" Cecile's hackles were well and truly up.

Justine smiled bitterly. "I was an heiress myself, Cecile."

"What's that supposed to mean?"

"It means that made a difference to your *father*," Justine said dryly, shocking her daughter. "I know you think I blind myself to the truth. Most of the time I do, but I have my moments when the shutters come down. Your father and I have a good stable marriage. Each of us got what we wanted. He will never leave me. I'm absolutely certain of that. If he ever tried it, I'd ruin him."

"Oh, Mother!" Cecile sighed deeply, thinking Justine had more of her own mother, Frances, in her than she ever imagined.

Justine stood up, putting a hand to her thick, deeply waving hair, one of her best assets. "Promise me you won't see any more of this Raul Montalvan, Cecile. I can't trust Daddy not to throw you both together. I don't think he truly appreciates what a good husband Stuart will be for you. You have a lot going on inside you, Cecile, that needs curbing. Don't think I'm not aware of it. You seem to be searching for some new way of defining yourself when you're on the threshold of marriage, your life settled. Your job is to be a good wife to Stuart and raise beautiful children."

"You don't think *my* future development is important, Mother?"

"Of course it is," Justine said irritably. "You have the rest of your life for self-development. Look at me. I've been a great asset to your father as you will be to Stuart with some help from me. I love you, Cecile. You've always made me proud. Don't let me down now, I beg of you. Raul Montalvan, no matter how fascinating, is nothing but trouble. Such men always are."

Cecile saw her mother off at the airport, her mother reluctant to let go of her dire warnings until the very last minute, then drove back into the city to have coffee with Tara.

"Tell me first—" Tara put a hand across their al fresco table to grab Cecile's "—did he say anything about me?"

Cecile made a play of looking back at her friend blankly. "Who?"

"For God's sake, tell me." Tara shook Cecile's hand.

"Can we order first?" Cecile asked mildly. "Terrible to say it, but with my mother gone I feel like a kid let off school. When was this anyway?"

Tara looked at her friend with dismay. "When you were walking with him down the bloody drive," she responded tartly. "I *saw* you, but I promise I won't tell the pain in the ass."

The pain in the ass was Tara's private name for Stuart. "Shouldn't you avoid those precise words when you're talking about my fiancé?" Cecile suggested, withdrawing her hand from Tara's surprisingly strong grip. A petite five foot two, Tara was a featherweight due to a strict dieting regime, which veered by the week from one method to another, none of them particularly healthy.

"Why? He's just so bloody pompous," Tara responded, thinking she couldn't bear the idea of her beautiful Cecile marrying Stuart Carlson. "Okay he's good-looking, he's clever, he's the man destined to marry the beautiful Cecile Moreland and go right to the top of the tree, but he's too much the go-getter and he's got bugger-all sex appeal."

"You're not sleeping with him, are you?" Cecile asked.

"If I thought it would stop you marrying him, I would do it in a split second," Tara said with some force.

"Ah, Tara!" Cecile shook her head. In the space of a few hours, her oldest, closest friend was saying one thing, her mother the very opposite. She picked up the menu, ashamed of the fact she had to make a real effort to dredge up a few words in Stuart's defense. "It's as well I'm used to your straight shooting, sweetie. In fact, I love you for it—most of the time—but let me assure you, Stuart's libido is in good working order. I can see why Mother has always considered you an unsuitable companion for me."

"Ah, yes, Mother," Tara replied gleefully. "Gee, you know, if she were only twenty years younger *she* could marry Stuart. They always seem to have such a lot in common."

"They do." Cecile's tone was dry.

"He's not the man for you, Ceci," Tara mourned, shaking her lovely blond helmet of hair. "You're angelic on top, but you're hot and spicy underneath. You can't fool me. We've been friends since we fell into Joel's pond."

"You pushed me in, you mean," Cecile said, recalling the hot afternoon when the two of them had first met at one of her grandmother's garden parties. Six going on seven, complete opposites.

"I was jealous of your party dress," Tara admitted, a nostalgic smile on her pert face. "And *you*. You looked like a little princess and you spoke oh so prim and proper, but you turned out to be a lot of fun. You never told on me, either. But to get back to the delicious Señor Montalvan. I bet he'd be a *wonderful* lover! Did he say anything about me?"

Cecile took her time to answer, not knowing what to say or in what direction she should steer her friend. "Actually he didn't," she said after a while, "which doesn't mean he didn't find you a very attractive dinner companion."

"Oh I hope, I hope!" Tara clasped her hands together in an attitude of prayer. "He's *gorgeous*!" she raved, "and the bloody *voice*! Mel Gibson with a bit of Antonio Banderas thrown in. He doesn't actually look South American, though, does he? Not like South Americans look South American, if you know what I mean. You know, the raven hair and the flashing dark eyes. He could be a very sophisticated Englishman, Australian, American, only for the fascinating trace of accent and I suppose, the manner. Now *that's* South American. What's he here for, anyway? I tried to question him very discreetly."

"You, discreet?" Cecile cocked an eyebrow.

"You don't think I can be discreet?"

"Frankly, no!" Cecile shook her head.

Tara didn't take offense. Her mother told her that all the time, and her young brother, Harry, called her *motormouth.* "Anyway, he was charming but very astute at not answering my questions. Joel's taken quite a fancy to him."

"Yes, he has," Cecile agreed, lifting a hand to a waiter. Tara was one of the few people, certainly of her age group, who called her grandfather Joel. But then, Tara was a great flirt and it amused her grandfather, who had always found Tara as engaging as her mother found her "vulgar." Not true and rather cruel. Impetuous, impulsive maybe, but very loyal.

"I overheard Joel inviting him to Malagari," Tara went on excitedly.

"Puh-leeze, you were *listening,*" Cecile chided her.

"So I was!" Tara gave her infectious gurgle of laughter. "I

might as well confess it, you know me so well. Are *you* going? I got the feeling it was quite soon."

"I don't know." She would need serious counseling herself if she did.

"Come off it!" Tara scoffed. "No woman in her right mind would turn down the opportunity of spending a little time with Señor Montalvan."

"There is the fact I'm an engaged woman," Cecile suggested. "The accent is on the second-last syllable, by the way. Mon-*tal*-van. I think there are a few Spanish marks thrown in the spelling, like the French acutes and graves and cedillas and what not."

"What's a cedilla?" Tara asked with interest.

"Didn't you take French?"

Tara put a finger to her cheek, turning her large blue eyes upward. "Let me think. *Henri Quatre est sur la Pont Neuf.* I know, it's the little comma thing."

"Right. It's under *c* to show it's sibilant."

"Okay, do you have to keep reminding me you've more brains than I have? So it's Mon*tal*van? I *see*. I call him Raul. What does Raul mean, smarty-pants?"

Cecile laughed. "I imagine it's the Spanish form of Ralph." She broke off as the waiter came to take their order.

"So like Raul, you haven't answered my question. Will you go, too?" Tara asked.

Cecile sighed. "Tara, I can't go running off with devilishly handsome Argentinians."

"Force yourself. Or look on it as a kind of escape from Stuart. You've got nothing in common with him. It's all that pressure your mother puts on you! God, does she ever stop? I know mothers nag, but your mother takes the cake. I've worried about it for years. Why does she think Stuart is so great, anyway?"

Cecile rested her chin on the upturned palm of her hand. "God knows."

"There you go!" Tara crowed. "That wasn't the response of

a woman in love. Wake up to yourself, girl. There must be at least two or three billion men left in the world for you to choose from. Me, I'd just like to take a shot at Señor Montalvan. I've never ever seen anything quite like him. He's got wonderful shoulders, don't you think? A wide back too. He looks great in his clothes. I'm just stopping myself from contemplating him without them. The thing is, if *you* go, Ceci, you can ask me. Well? Why are you staring at me like that?"

"Don't you have a job to go to?" Cecile asked, giving herself time to mull over Tara's proposal.

"Sure, only I work for my dad," Tara gloated, "which means I can easily persuade him to give me some time off. Especially if I'm going with you. Unlike your mother with me, *my* mother holds you in very high regard. You're my friend. I would never wish to steal your fiancé, but I sure would like to steal Señor Mon*tal*van away."

"Be my guest," Cecile offered in a wry voice.

Tara took her literally. "Bloody hell, you *mean* it?" Zesty as always, Tara jumped up from her chair to give Cecile a big hug. "I can come?"

"Don't get too excited," Cecile said gently. "I can *ask,* Tara, but it's up to Granddad."

Tara resumed her chair, waving a nonchalant hand. "Then we don't have a worry in the world. Whatever you ask, Joel gives. Anyway, Joel's got a soft spot for me."

"Because you give him heaps of blarney." Cecile smiled.

"Would you *mind!* I love him. Joel is a beautiful man, everyone's image of a distinguished gentleman. Anyway, I've been asked to Malagari plenty of times before. Raul is going to love it!" Tara's blue eyes grew dreamy. "I can see myself sitting across the campfire from him. Dingoes are howling in the hills. I shiver. Immediately he gets up to comfort me. The night is full of stars!" She exhaled blissfully. "Romance with a capital *R,* wouldn't you say?"

"Now that you mention it, yes."

"Next day we go exploring our great desert monuments, Uluru and Kata Tjuta. We pick wildflowers in the canyons. We go horse riding—not far, I'm not much good on horses as you know. Swim in a billabong—who needs suits? Make love on the warm sand. It turns into an orgy. Hey, all I need is a chance!"

CHAPTER SEVEN

THE LANDSCAPE BELOW them put Raul in mind of the pictures coming back to Earth from Mars. It was also the fantastic fiery-red landscape he inhabited in his dreams. Now he was regarding it afresh. His mother had escaped the country of her birth, in truth still too heartsick to ever wish to return. He had never escaped, no matter how far away they had settled. From the moment his mother had arrived in Argentina all those years ago, she had made herself fit in by sheer force of will. She had escaped them all: the people who had thrown the maiming sticks and stones, blaming her simply because of who she was. He and his dad, who had never given a tuppenny damn for what anyone said, had never made a successful transition, not that his dad was given much time to fit in anywhere.

Later on, after that terrible grief had been sprung on his mother and him, Ramon with his money and his beautiful estancia had made himself their deliverer. The fact that his mother was meltingly lovely and courageous had a lot to do with it. Still, Ramon had been good to him even when he'd been a hurting, hotheaded, wildly rebellious boy—practically a savage without the controlling hand of his father—but he had never learned to think of Argentina as his home or his future. He had always been determined that one day he would go back. One day he would make the Morelands pay. He would chase down all the people who had hurt his family. He would solve the puzzle and fulfill his ambition to once more walk his desert home.

Now Moreland's granddaughter and heiress with her silver-rain eyes and her beautiful face had literally fallen into his arms. That rocked him to the core even as an ungentle voice inside his head, cried out triumphantly, *Yes! Yes!* He didn't have to work on any other plan beyond her. He could, however, with his inside influence and knowledge, throw a considerable spoke in Joel Moreland's plans for doing business with Argentinian polo pony breeders and front-line players. A word here, a word there, and it was done. He was as trusted within the Argentinian industry as was his stepfather, Ramon.

Raul continued to look earthward, averting his head to conceal his expression from watching eyes. Had he known it, it was darkly brooding with a turbulent edginess. Yet he had to be careful not to alarm anyone. No one was to see he was plotting anything, but the urge for revenge had become almost meat and drink. Now it was laced with a perverse sense of misgiving. A woman, almost a stranger to him, was at the center of his changing heart. Old scores had to be settled surely? He had to keep remembering that. The slur on *his* family's name had to be lifted.

Beneath them the great inland desert captivated him. It was an endless world of fiery colors: bloodred, bright rust, strong yellow, burnt umber, dusty pink and glaring white. Land always had filled him with a fierce exhilaration. He worshiped the land like some early pagan, the roar of the winds, the fantastic electric storms that rolled back and forth without delivering life-giving rain; canyons that in severe drought opened up unexpectedly right at one's feet. Floods that concealed these undulating red dunes and the isolated mesas, set down as they were in the great emptiness. It was unlike any other part of the world. He realized he had never experienced quite this level of nature worship riding the gorse-covered *pampas* that stretched out to the majestic snow-capped Andes, though their isolated splendor and the wonderful horses had consoled him greatly. He would be forever grateful to Ramon and Ramon's beloved Argentina, but his heart, his *wild* heart, belonged to only one place.

It was the Timeless Land that truly called to his heart.

To the south the endless plains, parched by the blazing sun, met up with eroded ranges that in the distance glowed an extraordinary purplish-blue like the heart of a black opal. Infinite stretches of the living desert lay to either side. It took monsoonal rain from the tropical north or winter rains from the south to carry here to transform the barren Inland into a world of flowers of immense numbers and incomparable perfume. He still remembered as a small boy waking up to a wonderland, jumping out of bed and without bothering to dress, racing out into the horse paddocks to be one of the first to witness the desert flora burst into ecstatic life.

The exhilaration he felt was not unmixed with a deep melancholia that had begun the moment they flew out of the tropical Top End with its crocodiles and magnificent lily-covered lagoons and into the arid Red Heart with its all-pervading atmosphere of deep time. The Northern Territory was bigger than France, Italy and Spain put together, but within its borders lay two vastly different climatic zones: rain forest and desert.

On no account could he allow his melancholia to grow to the point it would swamp him. There would be plenty of ghosts down there on Malagari. Ghosts on the other side of the purple ranges where lay hidden the small operation his family had worked for five generations. Through thick and thin, through drought and a terrible bush fire that had claimed the life of his great-uncle Harry, they had held on to it. He wondered what had happened to it after his grandfather had been forced off. His granddad, a man of tremendous strength and energy, had died of a massive heart attack exactly six months later. That terrible event had drained all the life out of his grandmother. She had survived, eventually falling back on the loving kindness of her married sister who lived far away in the South Island of New Zealand.

So much that had gone catastrophically wrong, and all in a lamentably short time. What had his grandmother called the family suffering? *All the afflictions of Job.* His uncle Benjie had been only fifteen going on sixteen when his life had changed within the space of a few minutes. Benjie was more a big brother than an uncle. He had been killed in a bar fight at the age of twenty-two. What had been his assailant's intention? Murder? Of course the man had denied it strenuously, but he had been charged with manslaughter and given a ten-year jail sentence with parole after six. He'd be long out by now. Probably had his old job back on Malagari. Joel Moreland wasn't just a very rich man. He was an Outback icon. So many people, through his vast interests, relied on him for their livelihood. He had then, as he had now, a veritable army of henchmen to do his bidding.

Yet how could a man who looked and acted as straight as a die in deed and word be so cruel? How could a seemingly delightful man like Joel Moreland, so kind and distinguished, go to such remorseless lengths to punish a boy who had been unfortunate enough to be in the wrong place at the wrong time? Not only the boy, his entire family, as though they had all connived to cause Jared Moreland's death. It hadn't been Benjie who had triggered Jared Moreland's violent end. Jared Moreland, who had been the instrument of Johanna Muir's catastrophic fall from grace, had by his callous behavior contributed to his own death. Innocent high-spirited Benjie had been used as a pawn in a murderous game.

Beware those of you who are left. The exile is back!

Moreland's pilot banked into a right turn lining up the private jet for Malagari's runway. At the far end he could see the roof of a massive hangar far bigger than the one on the Montalvan estancia. The silver roof glittered in the hot sun, the surface giving off shimmering waves of heat. On the roof was emblazoned the name of the station, Malagari, in royal blue, the edges picked out in red. On the ground to the right of the hangar was a towering flagpole from which the red, white and blue of the Australian flag fluttered. Beneath it flew a pennant carrying the colors of the station with the addition of a white circle of stars. He knew that was a Moreland logo.

The tires thumped and bounced hard on contact with the first-grade all-weather strip, sending a cloud of red dust over the wings. He could have managed the landing better, though it was okay. He could see from the flags there was a brisk cross wind. The brakes made their usual high-pitched squeal, then the pilot cut the engines back to idle, taxiing toward the hangar.

They had arrived.

He looked across at Cecile, who was looking out the porthole. Her friend, Tara, was chattering ninety to the dozen in her ear. Cecile's wondrous femininity that put him in mind of a white lily was strangely enhanced by the almost masculine severity of today's outfit, tailored black linen slacks, a silk camisole showing beneath a deeper cream linen safari-style jacket. A wide embossed leather belt with an ornate silver buckle was slung around her narrow waist. Her friend, on the other hand, wore a short, bright blue dress that exactly matched her pretty eyes. While Cecile had greeted him at Moreland's private airstrip with deliberate formality, her friend had stood on tiptoe to kiss him on the cheek. No chance of a kiss or embrace from the woman who barely a week before had swooned in his arms.

There were intense moments in life, Raul mused. Some were more intense than others, but he had never for all his traumas experienced anything approaching the power and complexity of the feelings he was trying to master now. A few feet away from him she sat, a gold clasp gathering back her long hair, totally unaware of what was in his heart. She had that inviolable self-assurance that came with being a beautiful woman of class and money. It would be so easy to hurt her. He would hate to hurt her for a thousand and one reasons. He wasn't a cruel man by nature. But he had been shown a way, perhaps the most symbolic way, to avenge Benjie and his family. Benjie might have turned out the great loser, but Raul reminded himself Benjie was a better man than the scoundrel who had been Moreland's only son.

Pain twisted in his stomach. The bitter irony was he'd had no way of knowing the powerful effect a woman of a hated family would have on him. This was a woman who inspired love, not hate.

On the ground the heat was like a dry oven. He reveled in it; felt it soak into his skin, already darkly tanned. Off in the distance the mirage was playing its remembered tricks, creating inviting vistas of phantom lakes. Chains of them shimmered in the distance, their shores surrounded by tall waving desert palms.

"My man will be here shortly to drive us to the homestead, Raul," Moreland told him, gripped by his own pleasure at being back on Malagari. "Ah, here he is now."

Raul turned slightly. A dusty Land Rover was roaring cross-country, eventually driving up onto the huge concrete platform that surrounded the hangar on all sides and met up with the runway. The engine cut and a big bearded man in his early fifties stood out of the vehicle waving a hand.

"Afternoon, all! Good flight I hope, sir?"

"Couldn't have been smoother, Jack," Moreland said cheerfully, turning to his guest, while Cecile and Tara stood smilingly to one side. "Raul, I'd like you to meet Jack Doyle, my chief steward on Malagari. Jack has worked for me in one capacity or the other for close on thirty years. His wife, Alison, is our resident chef and housekeeper. Ally's in charge of the domestic staff all of them our own aboriginal girls, born on the station. It's a large house. Needs a lot of maintenance. I'm lucky to have such loyal employees."

"Glad to meet you, Mr. Doyle," Raul responded, shaking the other man's hand. *Jack Doyle*. He knew the name. Doyle had moved up in the world. One did when one delivered big on *loyalty*.

"Likewise," Doyle said with a friendly grin. "And it's Jack. No one calls me Mr. Doyle. Welcome to Malagari, Raul. Ah... Miss Cecile—" Doyle turned to smile at her with open affection "—it's great to have you back. We've been missing you. You too, Miss Tara. What practical jokes have you lined up for us this time?"

"Got to be a surprise, Jack," Tara told him breezily.

"Best get us up to the house, Jack," Moreland intervened. "It's pretty darn hot on the runway."

"Right, sir. I'll just load on the luggage."

"I'll give you a hand." Raul was already moving to do so.

"Gee, thanks, mate!" Jack gave their visitor a quick smile. Miss Cecile's fiancé had never on any occasion made such a suggestion. There were servants to do things like that. Delusions of grandeur, Jack always thought.

Ahead of them, set in a desert garden of greens and ochres and flourishing orange-and-scarlet bouganvillea blossom, was the Malagari homestead, an oasis in the wilderness. He had seen pictures of it in pastoral magazines and large coffee table books of historic homesteads, but nothing had prepared him for the heroic scale of the place nor the raw majesty of its setting. In a way, it was rather like the first glimpse of Uluru's great dome, rising out of the infinite plains. Malagari appealed to his heart, his senses and his mind when he had wanted most deeply to loathe the place. The surrounding gardens, huge by any standard, would depend on bore water from the Great Artesian Basin for survival. He knew that. The homestead, he thought, depended on its great overhanging hipped roof to anchor it to the bloodred earth and take care of those who sheltered beneath it. The main single-story structure had wings that formed a squared-off U. Only a man of Moreland's immense wealth, cattle king and business magnate as he was, could afford it.

Raul knew the station, all 10,000 square kilometers of it,

carried a Santa Gertrudis herd of over a quarter of a million. It formed one of the largest operations in the country and certainly the world. Malagari was the Moreland flagship of the arid zone. The Moreland flagship of the Top End, the tropical zone, was Kumbal Downs. Kumbal, he had discovered, ran around 100,000 Brahman. There were other stations in the chain, vast Opal Creek in Queensland's Channel Country for one, Lagunda in Queensland another, but Malagari remained the backbone of the operation just as it had in Raul's grandfather's day.

"This is it!" Joel Moreland announced proudly, waving an arm toward the historic homestead.

"It's splendid!" Raul was able to respond without difficulty, which was as well since Moreland's keen regard was leveled on him. "A desert paradise." Raul turned to admire the courtyard's central marble fountain. It was playing in the blazing fire of noon, creating an aura of coolness. The great bowl, one in a tier of three, was supported by four magnificently carved rearing horses. It would have to be horses for a man who had lived his life in the saddle.

"Italian," Moreland said, following Raul's gaze. "Cost a fortune, plus another fortune to get it here. I bought it in Rome, one of my favorite places in all the world, not long after my beautiful Ceci was born. Right, girls, we'll go inside. Must protect those beautiful complexions." He put an arm around his granddaughter and Tara, turning them toward the house. "Come, Raul. We'll get settled, then we'll have lunch. Jack can attend to everything. I can't wait to hear what you think of the interior. Ceci has been my most recent decorator. She knows exactly what I like. I have to say my late wife and I didn't always see eye-to-eye in that department. Frances had more of a city eye, if you know what I mean. I'm an Outback man through and through. It was Frances who chose to live in Darwin, which I enjoy—it has its own fascination—but in latter years she rarely visited Malagari. In that sense Justine is like her mother. She's a city girl at heart. My Ceci isn't." He dropped a quick kiss on his granddaughter's gleaming head.

So why then did you choose a man who means to keep you pregnant in the suburbs? Raul thought.

Cecile sensed it as if he had spoken his thought aloud. His expressive glance subtly mocked her, catching her up in the now familiar black magic. For a moment she had the strong impression he was going to address her directly. To make it worse, although her grandfather had never interfered in her choice of Stuart or openly criticized any aspect of his behavior, she knew he had never taken to Stuart the way he had so obviously taken to Raul Montalvan.

Damn him!

Raul saw the light flush color her high cheekbones, felt her little wave of hostility. She tilted her chin. It only served to enhance the lovely line of her throat. He was becoming very aware of the fact that she wasn't slow to pick up on his wavelength, read his thoughts. He would have to be careful there. Her friend, Tara, turned her head over her shoulder to smile at him. He couldn't help knowing Tara was attracted to him, but like a madness, he had his heart and his mind set on Cecile.

Raul followed them through the deeply recessed double doors, which appeared to have been carved from Indian teak, and into the world of the very rich. The floor of the grand entrance hall was covered in a wonderful mosaic tile that brought him up short. It had all the glowing colors of a Persian carpet.

"Again an Italian artisan." Joel Moreland smiled at his guest's look of appreciation. "It's beautiful, isn't it?"

"Indeed it is." Raul glanced around him. It was a very handsome house, but as they continued on their way he saw the decoration had been handled in a manner that welcomed.

Inside all was serene, cool and quiet. The main rooms he was able to glimpse through tall pedimented archways of dark gleaming timbers. The furnishings, the pictures, all the valuable objects around the place—one such resting on a console in the entrance hall looked like a Tang Dynasty horse and probably was—created an aura of richness, but the overall effect was one of a comfortable, inviting, large country house. There was a graceful *balance,* Raul thought, like Cecile Moreland herself. The spaces between the beautiful paintings were exactly right. Some of the large canvases depicted the very best of aboriginal art which he knew was attracting a world following. He found himself seduced. Cecile, he noticed with some irony, walked with easy familiarity past all these treasures. Outback royalty, he thought, staring after her.

The color scheme was pale: ivories and creams and dusky golds. It made a cool contrast to the dark timbers, as did the light and airy drapes that billowed gently at the series of broad French doors. The floors weren't carpeted in the desert heat. They were polished to the color of golden honey, the hardwood scattered here and there with magnificent rugs. There were intimate womanly touches to counteract the sheer richness, books, flowers, a very pleasing juxtaposition of objects. He caught a glimpse of an ebony concert grand in the living room. She had a most indulgent grandfather, this Cecile. Life would have been idyllic for her as she was growing up, loved and indulged at every turn. Unlike his, her life had not been vandalized.

Alison Doyle, the housekeeper, came rushing out to greet them, a little flustered, excusing her late appearance as having to get something out of the oven. Introductions began again. Doyle's wife was a slim attractive woman in her late forties, auburn hair, lightly freckled skin with bright blue eyes and a sunny smile.

"I've got everything ready for you, Mr. Moreland," she said. "Lunch in a half hour if that suits?"

"Fine, Ally, fine!" Moreland said, in his easy charming voice. "I know I can always rely on you. I've brought a couple of CDs for you to add to your collection. Ella Fitzgerald and Peggy Lee."

The housekeeper's face lit up. "That's great. Really great!"

"Ally has discovered the great female jazz singers," Joel

Moreland turned to Raul with a word of explanation. "I don't think anyone has topped Ella."

"I know I'm going to love them," Ally said. "Now if you'll excuse me I'll get on with preparing lunch." She gave another smile that encompassed them all, then moved off.

"If you'd like to come with me now, Raul, I'll show you to your room," Cecile said.

"Thank you." Raul turned his eyes away from her to smile at his host. "You have a very beautiful home, sir." He was able to say it with perfect sincerity.

"Look here, you've got to make it Joel." Moreland didn't hold back on extending the friendship. "You can't keep calling me sir."

Raul flashed his illuminating smile. "I'd be delighted to call you Joel if that's your wish." He gave a slight inclination of his head. "I'm looking forward to hearing from Cecile which parts of the homestead have benefited from her elegant hand."

"Why, nearly the lot!" Tara told him blithely. She was relishing the fact that she was here with him. "Ceci is multitalented. You know, good at everything!"

Cecile laughed. "Easy to see Tara are I are old friends. She likes to praise me. My attentions most notably, Raul, have been directed to the living room, the formal dining room and the library. It's a big house. I'm working my way through it gradually." She turned her head to her friend. "You're in the Blue Room, Tara. I know how much you like it."

"I love it!" Tara responded, the excitement she was feeling evident to all.

In the elegant guest suite that had been allotted him, the French doors stood open to the garden and the warm desert breeze. Cecile walked briskly toward them, wondering how on earth she was going to handle this inflammatory situation, though she felt fortified by having Tara's company. Raul followed more slowly, moving out onto the broad veranda that ran the length of the entire building at the rear.

"The casuarinas are what I call monumental," he remarked after a while, his tanned, long-fingered hands spread out on the balustrade as he gazed at the magnificent desert specimens, four in all, that graced that section of the garden. Around their base to a considerable depth were planted the extremely hardy sunbursts of the blue flowering agapanthus.

Cecile glanced at him in surprise. She had now joined him at the balustrade, but keeping a distance away. "You have casuarinas in Argentina?"

That was a slip. "Well, I know what they are." He shrugged.

"You're very knowledgeable about our native desert plants. Yet you can't have been here very long."

"I'm sure there's one in Fiona's garden."

"No, there isn't," she said. "They don't grow in the torrid zone."

"All right, I've seen a picture." He moved his hand along the railing so it covered hers where it lay.

"*Don't,* Raul," she said, low voiced. "Nothing can come of this." Yet he had only to touch her hand for *something* to happen.

"I can't stop this thing between us any more than you can," he answered, the golden sparkles in his eyes catching the light. He didn't remove his hand.

She had to do something. Anything. Only, she was overtaken by the incredible languor he was able to induce in her body while her mind remained on high alert.

"Come here to me."

Four simple words to make up a sentence, yet the effect on her was electrifying. She should have been shocked at his audacity but wasn't. Instead she tried to imagine herself physically putting up barriers...

He straightened and pulled her toward him, fluidity in his every movement. He kept one arm around her waist. "I understand you're perturbed at having me here."

"Why wouldn't I be?" She arched back slightly, looking up into his face. "You're increasing my fears, Raul. You're not doing anything to dispel them."

His velvet brown eyes smoldered. He was trying hard to crush his own feelings of vulnerability without much success. She was not what he had been expecting at all. "I want to kiss you," he said, abruptly abandoning control. "I want to bury my face in your neck, between your breasts. I want to pull your beautiful hair out of that clasp. I want to stroke it with my hands. Feel how soft and silky it is. Do you mind?"

Before she could answer, if she could even find her voice, he lifted his free hand and removed the gold clasp that held back her long hair. Immediately it slid forward, rippling around her shoulders.

"Does your fiancé ever sit with you and brush it?" he asked, smoothing a sensuous hand down a long glossy coil. He had seen Ramon brush his mother's long, thick blond hair many many times. Probably a prelude to their lovemaking.

"No," Cecile answered shakily, fighting an overpowering urge to move right into his arms. Finish this thing they had started.

"You sleep with him?" His hand slowed as he studied her face closely.

"Is that so strange?" she countered self-consciously. "He's my fiancé. I'm going to marry him."

"You're wrong," he said, his voice curt. "You're not going to marry him. I think you already know that. My sister now, Ramona, will go to her bridegroom a virgin. I find I hate the idea of that man touching you."

She could see it in his face. Hear it in his voice. "You have no right to hate," she said. "No right at all."

"Haven't I?" he answered, still in that oddly curt voice. *Careful,* Raul thought. *Careful.* He lifted a hand to encircle her nape. Her beautiful hair cascaded over his hand and wrist. He allowed his callused thumb to massage her skin. How cool her skin was! Smooth as satin.

Cecile could have moaned aloud from the pleasure he was giving her. Perhaps she did. "Things must be different in Argentina," she breathed, realizing how wonderfully well he knew how to touch. Stuart had never stirred her like this even in the wildest throes of their lovemaking. All those sharp little contractions she associated with being touched by this man were starting up again, stabbing deep into her vagina. She touched the tip of her tongue to suddenly parched lips.

"You are *so* beautiful," he said, lowering his head. His mouth was very close. "Lift your face to me, Cecile." He spoke very quietly, but the effect was infinitely powerful.

"Where are we going with this, Raul? The consequences could be disastrous." She was terrified, too, someone would come and catch them in this compromising tableau.

"Need you ask?" He bent his head then, kissing her so softly but so passionately, his mouth savoring the texture of hers, the kiss might have lasted through eternity. "What bright spirit impelled toward delight was ever known to finger out the cost?" His arm remained locked around her as though he knew without being told that the sexual languor that had overtaken her could cause her to sway.

Her heart was beating so high up it was almost in her throat. Her mouth was open to his. His to hers. Their tongues mated. There could be no one else like him in the world.

So this was how a woman fell from grace? If he had picked her up and carried her back inside to the bed? Impossible to do anything now, but if the opportunity arose? God, she hadn't just gone out on a limb, she had already made her decision. The only honorable thing left to her was to break her engagement. That thought, the sudden flare of resolution, gave her the strength to pull free.

There was no look of triumph on his face at overcoming her every scruple. Rather, his expression was deeply brooding. "I

wonder which one of us will surrender first?" he said in a perfectly hard, considering, way.

His words burned into her. "I ought to have you thrown out,"
she muttered, realizing she was wound up as tight as a spring. If
there had ever been a moment to reject him, it had long passsed.

"I daresay you would have in the old days." There was a
flash of sexual antagonism in his own eyes. "You look like a
princess. You even act like one. So ready to turn imperious."

"Because you frighten me, Raul. You really do." Frantic in
case they were interrupted, she tried to draw back her long hair,
but skeins of it escaped. "Please, my clasp, give it back to me."

"When I thought to souvenir it." He loosened a long silky
strand of hair that had twined itself around her throat, then removed the clasp from his pocket and put it into her trembling
hand.

"Thank you," she said raggedly.

Somewhere along the corridor a door shut firmly.

"That's Tara," she said with a touch of panic. She looked at
him with a plea in her eyes. "How do I look?"

"Exquisite," he said, openly mocking. "You have the most
astonishing eyes. Silver. You know the name Argentina come
from the Latin word *argentums*, which means silver?"

"Yes," she said, breathlessly. "Do you prefer dark eyes or
light? You must have had many affairs. Women and girls with
hair as dark as my own but flashing black eyes?"

That smile touched his handsome mouth, lighting up the
tiny space between them. "I forget that part now I've met you."

"You're trying to seduce me, aren't you?"

"Aren't you doing the same with me?"

All the magnetism in the world was in his eyes.

When Tara finally came to the open doorway, Cecile was pointing out three splendid Chinese bronzes that sat atop a yellow
rosewood cabinet. "Tang Dynasty," she said, amazed her voice
sounded quite normal. This particular guest room had been fur-

nished with a male guest in mind. The color scheme was neutral, the furnishings Oriental.

"So what do you think of your room, Raul? Pretty classy, eh?" Tara all but danced into the room, her hair a light nimbus around her pert, glowing face. She was feeling so happy it was all she could do not to pinch herself to prove it was really happening. Her attention, so deeply focused on Raul, allowed the highly nervous Cecile to beat a swift retreat to the door, speaking over her shoulder as she went. "Bring Raul to the garden room when you're ready, Tara," she said, worried there might be some lingering touch of agitation in her voice. "That's where we'll be having lunch."

"Will do!" Tara called, so busy smiling at Raul she wouldn't even have noticed if there were. Tara was longing to question this fascinating guy about what he would like to do that afternoon. He would probably want to go horseback riding. She wasn't much of a rider unfortunately. Mounted so far from the ground always made her nervous, that and the long neck that stretched away in front of her. She'd had to work hard in the early days to overcome her fear of horses, but Cecile had coached her to the stage she could tell which end of the horse was which and if given a quiet work horse she could not only stay on but manage to look quite fetching in the saddle. She'd brought a brand-new outfit with her, bum-hugging sexy moleskins, glossy new riding boots. Raul seemed the sort of guy that noticed those things. Tara shook out her blond hair and began to ask him if Buenos Aires was as exciting a capital city as everyone said. This was one Argentinian who knew how to take a woman's breath away!

CHAPTER EIGHT

As was her routine when she visited Malagari, Cecile rose at dawn to take an early-morning gallop before the heat of the sun became too fierce. She had always loved these early-morning rides, moving about the stables complex, talking to the stable boys, who were always up and about, fluttering and fussing around their charges, feeding, cleaning, grooming, exercising. No point in trying to wake Tara to accompany her. Tara wasn't an early riser; neither did she take much pleasure in riding. Let her sleep.

By the time she reached the cobbled yard, the sun was rising in its fiery glory, dispelling the layers of pinks, indigos and pale yellow on the horizon. Blue light was starting to pour from the sky, the legions of birds were shrieking and whistling as they called to each other, and the desert wind was busy lifting the tantalizing mauve river of mist that hovered over the garden, blowing it away.

As chance would have it, there was no one around, though it was clear work had already begun. The place was lit, and fresh, sweet-smelling hay covered the floors. She walked about, speaking affectionately to the horses, Arabs and Thoroughbreds, all groomed to a silken shine. The horses nodded and whinnied back before she turned her attention to her favorite mount, the beautiful palomino, Zuleika, a separate breed from the others. Horses were just like people, Cecile thought. They had different, sometimes highly individual, personalities. Zuleika was the perfect match for her—or that part of her personality that was mostly hidden. The palomino with her golden coat and light blond mane and tail was sweet-tempered but high-spirited, with a sense of adventure and a certain unpredictability that often kept Cecile on her mettle.

Humming beneath her breath, Cecile pulled the girth tight and adjusted the buckles automatically while Zuleika tried a playful nip or two with her teeth and stamped her lively feet in a show of pent-up energy. The palomino was as eager for a gallop as she was. In fact, Cecile had to hold her back until they were well clear of the home compound. Then she let loose.

The blood sang in Cecile's veins. It was glorious! Such a thrill to have a spirited horse beneath her, a horse that was galloping strongly, pulling at the bit, its hooves thudding into the ground. Moments like this she lived for. They were just what she needed to clear the mad jumble of thoughts out of her head.

A mile from the Pink Lady Lagoon she relaxed the pace. Way across the flats she could see a large mob of cattle being moved toward a water course, which at this time of year would be full of shallow, yellowish water from the clay bed. The omnipresent flights of budgies, a symbol of the Outback, swirled above her in long ribbons of emerald and gold before finally flying off toward the lagoon where she herself was heading. She wondered what her grandfather would have lined up for today to entertain their guest. He had been talking about flying to Lagunda, deep across the border, sometime soon. Lagunda was a working station and one of the country's premier polo farms, producing outstanding polo ponies shipped anywhere in the world where playing polo was a passion. She'd overheard Raul telling her grandfather he'd played in his first tournament when he was fourteen. His team had won. He was now on seven goals, so he had to be pretty darn good. No surprise!

Yesterday her grandfather had set a cracking pace. She was particularly proud of his stamina and fitness. He had always taken pleasure in having young people around him. In the afternoon, after a leisurely lunch, they had traveled in the Land Rover around the station, so Raul could get a good idea of the operation. The two men, despite the huge age difference, had quickly developed an excellent rapport. Indeed one might have thought Joel Moreland had long been Raul's mentor. Her grandfather drove; Raul joined him up front, both of them keeping up a near nonstop conversation with the emphasis on station operations. She and Tara sat in the back throwing in a comment from time to time. Hers, informed, as it should be, Tara's so frivolous it had made them all laugh.

As the afternoon wore on, it struck Cecile, that the Argentinian was perfectly at home on a big Australian cattle station. He was deeply familiar with a station's workings, was able to communicate easily with the station staff, in particular Brad Caldwell, the station manager who had risen through the ranks. Raul loved and knew horses right down to the yarded brumbies awaiting "schooling" from Brad. Most significantly Raul gave every impression of being at one with their desert environment, which, after all, in character was unique in the world. She'd had an idea she intended to check out: that the vast plains of the Argentinian *pampa* were black soil and wonderfully fertile like Queensland's Darling Downs. That would make a stunning contrast to the aridity of the Red Heart, with its fiery, shifting sands, yet Raul Montalvan seemed as much at home in Australia's Red Centre as was her grandfather and for that matter, herself. It struck her as somewhat unusual. Of course he had been reared in vast open spaces, but a lot of visitors to Malagari found the isolation and the sheer starkness of the wild landscape with its infinite horizons quite intimidating. Not so Raul. Cecile had caught many of his passing comments as they had traveled around the station. The man was fathoms deep.

Approaching the Pink Lady Lagoon, so called because of its

thick mantle of exquisite water lilies, Cecile noticed off to her left, parallel to the line of river gums, a swirl of red dust that resolved into a horse and rider traveling at speed. She knew the horse, the magnificent, black-as-coal stallion, Sulaiman. He was being given his head. Out in the open she recognized the rider, Raul Montalvan. Instantly she felt a mad rush of blood to her head. She should have noticed the stallion wasn't in his stall. Their powerful rhythm over the ground flooded her with a breath-catching emotion.

He rode splendidly. She had been prepared for that. He was Argentinian raised on an estancia, but he had obviously adapted in the blink of an eye to the Australian saddle. She was stunned. So, he had set off before her! No time to make her escape either—horse and rider were coming right for her. No way she and Zuleika could outrun them. Zuleika, in fact, was becoming jumpy and excited so by the time Raul had slowed to join her she'd just got the palomino under control.

"Buenos dias!" He swept off his wide-brimmed hat with an engaging little flourish that showed his background. "Pretty horse." He studied the palomino with a smile. "You must learn how to handle her."

"I beg your pardon?" Cecile's chin came up before she saw the teasing look in his eyes. "You're joking of course."

"Do you mind I joke?" he asked, his eyes moving over her face and lovely supple body with an admiration he didn't bother to hide. "I thought I might see you out on an early-morning ride."

She breathed in deeply. It was exciting just to look at him. In fact, he was so damned handsome it nearly brought tears to her eyes. "No doubt Granddad told you?" she said, sounding a little vexed.

"Saved my having to ask," he mocked. "Do you wish to ride down to the lagoon? The horses would appreciate a breather. This Sulaiman is magnificent." He leaned over the stallion's neck, stroking it with his hand.

"He is. How did you get used to our type of saddle so quickly?"

A smile flickered across his dynamic features. "Cecile, I've learned more about riding than you can ever imagine. Do we go down to the lagoon or not?"

"If you give me your promise to—" She broke off, not quite knowing how to continue.

"Not to play games?" he asked with a wicked glint in his dark eyes.

"Exactly."

"But it's no game I'm playing," he assured her. "I should tell you I can't help admiring *your* riding style."

"But you haven't had time to judge it."

"On the contrary, I took time out to watch you put the palomino to the gallop. A remarkable display. I was tempted to run out and applaud." He inclined his head in the direction of a copse of trees. "I hid back there, sorry I didn't have a camera with me. I've seen a lot of women riders where I come from, but you're as good as the best."

"Praise indeed." She sounded cool, but her nerves were running riot.

"The simple truth," he said.

Sunlight filtered a greenish-gold through the avenue of feathery acacias and bauhinias that lined the banks of the lagoon on one side. On the other was a stand of coolabahs, and at their arrival, a flock of gorgeous parrots exploded out of it and rose high above the canopy. She saw Raul lift his head, an expression of pleasure passing across his face. He truly did understand the bush.

Cecile dismounted quickly, tying the reins to a low branch before making her way across the expanse of golden sand to the water. The beautiful pink water lilies were profuse, holding their heads above the silver-sheened dark green water. She had removed her akubra, and now she bent to the crystal-clear stream to splash her face with water, throwing back her head afterward to let her skin dry in the warm breeze.

Cooled and refreshed, she began to take deep, calming breaths. One thing she was really afraid of was this new lack of control in herself. She had never believed in love at first sight. She still didn't. But she had since been converted to *desire* at first sight. Its suddenness, its power, though it was far more than sexual attraction that was between her and Raul Montalvan. Whatever it was, it had real meaning to it. She was *dying* for him to touch her. When had she ever been dying for Stuart to touch her? It was like she was a different woman. This sensuality, this awareness of her body, had come over her all at once. If ever a man had power over her, it was Raul Montalvan.

He came behind her as though he easily read her thoughts, pulling her hair free of its thick plait so it uncoiled across her back. Then he turned her to him, speaking in his dark, faintly accented voice. "You were with me last night," he said, staring deep into her eyes. "Was it a sin to dream it, Cecile? You were with me when I awoke at dawn. I think you are beginning to possess me. What more could you wish to know?"

"If it's *real*?" she answered very seriously.

His nod was solemn. "You think we need more time?"

She turned her face away. "I don't know what to *think,* Raul. Since I first laid eyes on you I haven't been doing much thinking."

"It upsets you to *feel*?"

"No problem if one can handle it," she said wryly.

"Isn't being able to *feel* a miracle?" he asked. "Some people can go through life not even knowing what the word means." His finger stroked her flawless white skin. She wore a touch of lipstick, nothing more. "You look ravishing first thing in the morning," he said. She was a truly beautiful woman, his for the asking; but the enormous *want* he felt for her could so easily turn to love and thus wipe out any thought of reprisals. It was turning into a big dilemma with the joke on him.

Little currents of electricity activated the muscles of his hands. He cupped the perfect oval of her face, conscious his fingertips were rough against that magnolia skin, then he lowered his head and pressed his lips to hers as if her mouth was luscious fruit and he was ravenous.

"Raul!" It was a noble exercise in restraint for Cecile to voice a protest. Only, he ignored her, continuing to nibble on her lips and then the tip of her seeking tongue.

"Don't worry," he whispered into her open mouth. "I'm only kissing you. I promise I will only kiss you until you break your engagement."

"And what happens then?" She was shocked by the heartbroken sound of her voice. "We run away together? We create a scandal? What is this, anyway, Raul? A want, a need, a simple desire?"

"Simple?" He drew back, contemptuous of the word. "Simple desire is not an agony. There's such affinity between our bodies." He set his hand to doing what he desperately wanted. He palmed her breast, his long fingers shaping it, taking the tender weight. It was delicate, yet full. He wanted to tease the nipple with his tongue. Instead, he thumbed the bud, feeling it come erect.

Instantly passion seized her. Cecile arched her neck while a soft moan gushed from her throat. Her shirt clung damply from all the splashing at the stream. Beads of water glistened on her skin at the V neckline of her shirt. Her nipples were now ripe little berries that strained against the thin fabric. She had this violent need to be against him, her breasts crushed to his chest. Why had Stuart never had this effect on her? She had wanted Stuart, but never with such intensity. She should feel guilt, but the strength of her feelings brushed the guilt off.

"Look at the contrast of my brown hand against your white skin," Raul said in an hypnotic voice. He had slipped open a button on her shirt so he could splay his fingers against the upward swell of her breast. "I've never felt such desire for a woman in my life!"

It was so strange the way he said it that she opened her eyes, fixing them on his face. His expression seemed to say his desire for her made him both defensive and angry. "You sound as though you don't want it at all."

He breathed in deeply. "There's this thing called losing control, Cecile. Losing oneself in a woman could mean losing one's own identity."

"Has it never happened to you?" She tilted her head to one side.

He laughed. Not a happy sound. "A couple of weeks ago I wouldn't have thought it possible. You are something utterly new to me, Cecile."

"And it upsets you, though you're trying to cover it."

"As you are trying to cover your beautiful breasts." He shifted her hand away. "Why don't you take the shirt off altogether? It would make it so much easier for me to caress you."

Like him, she exhaled hard. Arousal and anger were naked on her face. "I daresay it would, but I think we should call a stop."

"*This* time," he said, narrow-eyed.

"You're assuming there will be a next time?" Her voice had sharpened.

"Tell me you don't want it."

She bit down on her bottom lip. "Tell *me,* Raul. Am I part of some plan? Watching you makes me think so. What goes on inside your head?"

Her beautiful eyes begged him to tell her. For a moment he even *wanted* to but it was all so complicated and she wouldn't want to ever see him again. "Maybe someday I'll share it with you." His shrug lifted his shoulder. "For now I can tell you it was no plan of mine for the two of us to become enmeshed. It just…happened."

"Maybe the novelty will wear off as quickly as it started," she said, a certain bleakness in her words. She wanted him to keep on doing what he was doing to her; she also wanted him to stop.

His smile turned cynical. "Perhaps we shouldn't miss the opportunity to find out."

Cecile drew away. She was a woman who had once had self-control. "I think not. I'd better obey my inner voice. Do you have one?"

"Yes," he acknowledged. "But no matter what it tells me, fate holds the cards."

She had no answer to that. "I know so little about you, Raul. Even our being here together is completely crazy. Forget Fate. We're ignoring all the *rules!*"

"Which astonishes you?"

She looked away. "I don't want to be astonished at myself."

"I wouldn't have thought you a coward." He watched the shadows play across her face.

"Pretty close," she said, thinking what would be in store for her once she broke off her engagement.

He read her mind. "You can't be frightened of this fiancé, surely?"

"I'd be a darn sight more frightened if I tried to break off any engagement to *you!*"

"It wouldn't happen."

She shrugged and raked her long hair from her face. "The few things I do know about you, Raul, I don't understand."

"No matter!" He couldn't stop himself from kissing her again. It was brief, but so much harder than before. The need just got worse and worse. He slipped the button of her fine cotton shirt back into its hole. "Anyway," he said smoothly, "we have a whole week and more to fill in the gaps."

"While you content yourself with your dreams."

"Of course! Remember what I told you?" He caught her left hand, lifted it to the sunlight so the diamonds blazed. "We don't sleep together until you get rid of this ring. Why are you wearing it? I don't remember your wearing it last night at dinner."

She hadn't, but she had put it on this morning in a rush of guilt. Was she really willing to break Stuart's heart, or she stopped short thinking, badly damage his pride? "This has nothing to do with Stuart, has it?" she asked very quietly. "I've sensed that all along."

His smile was crooked. "Which clearly shows you have very sensitive antennae. It has absolutely *nothing* to do with your fiancé," he confirmed.

Cecile knew she should say something to Stuart. God knows he rang every evening…but she should say it to his face. In the whirlwind days that followed she couldn't seem to summon up her courage to even give a hint. Night after night in bed she composed opening sentences in her head:

Stuart, the last thing in the world I want to do is hurt you….
Stuart, I'm so sorry. I never meant it to happen this way….
Come right out with it, girl! *Stuart, I don't love you. I don't think I ever loved you….* No, too cruel. *Stuart, I've been thinking a great deal about this and I've come to the sad conclusion we're not really meant for each other.*

And then there was the house under construction. *God, oh God, please come to my aid.*

God, no more than her mother would understand what she was doing now. Guilt racked her. Why had she taken so long to discover she didn't love Stuart? She was twenty-six not sixteen. She was a professional woman, earning the respect of people she admired. She thought she knew her own mind. In all probability if she hadn't met Raul, she would have gone ahead and married Stuart. Made her mother very happy. Or would she? Maybe a wedding wouldn't have gone ahead at all. She wasn't lying to herself. Her doubts had set in well before she laid eyes on Raul Montalvan. But now having done so, the question of whether she would marry Stuart was settled.

She went over and over the burning issue so much sometimes she wanted to scream, and once she started to cry in the shower from sheer frustration, unable to figure out what was happening in her life. Yet for the most part she was being carried so high on a wave of euphoria she wouldn't have swapped places with anyone on the planet. So the days passed in a blaze of excitement. Raul was a sorcerer, placing a spell on her.

Her grandfather couldn't bear to sit still, either. It was almost as though he had decided to fill up every moment of the rest of the life that was left to him. It would have worried her greatly, only he was looking wonderfully well. Eating well. Full of energy.

"What do you think?" he announced one morning at breakfast. "I've finally been able to line up a couple of matches for Saturday afternoon. I've been waiting on Chad Bourne, but he's back and rarin' to go. The Farrington brothers are available. I thought Raul could team up well with them. They're all fine horsemen, Chad much more experienced—he plays the sort of game I imagine Raul does—but you have to even the teams up. As for the other team, Vince Siganto will captain it with Chris Arnold and the Dashwood twins, Mart and Matt. I thought we could have a party to follow. People will travel for miles to attend. We have to give them a good show, turn on our stuff. What do you say?"

"Sounds like a great weekend coming up." Raul smiled at the other man's enthusiasm. "What do I do for a polo pony? We've only got four days. I have to get to know the animal. One's horse has a direct effect on the play, as you know. I generally play to win."

"I'm sure you do." Joel Moreland beamed his pleasure. "Don't worry, I'm having one of my very best polo ponies trucked in. It will be here by midday, a Thoroughbred gelding. Called it Churchill, plenty of guts and needless to say he's well trained. I don't think you'll have any problems." He turned his silver head to smile at Cecile. "You girls can take care of the party, can't you? Whatever you want, have it flown in."

"Who's to come to the party, Granddad?" Cecile asked.

"Everyone who turns up." He laughed. "Best make it a big barbecue out of doors."

And to heck with the numbers! Cecile thought. She should

have some idea how many would make the trip to the station most likely from Alice Springs by Thursday if she started to ring around now. In the Outback, where horses were a passion, people loved the game. Once word got around a game was on with high-calibre players, they could count on having quite an influx of spectators. Then there were the two teams with their womenfolk and personal entourages. Just as well she'd had plenty of experience handling her Granddad's impromptu parties. Tara would be a big help; her family did a lot of entertaining. She was pleased Tara was having such a good time even if she knew her friend was disappointed she wasn't getting enough of Raul's attention.

"He probably would like to spend some time alone with me," she lamented to Cecile in a quiet moment, "only that never seems to happen. Joel is a dynamo. He's over seventy, but he's getting around like a teenager. Do you think Raul likes me?"

"Come on, everyone likes you," Cecile said. "Don't feel bad. There's nothing wrong with you. He's probably got a girlfriend back home in Argentina. A dazzling *señorita* called Brunhilde."

"You're joking. Even I know Brunhilde is German."

"All right, Carmelita, then."

"I think maybe he has." Tara gave it her consideration. "He's a pretty dark horse. I'm starting to think there's *someone.*"

"I'd be amazed if there weren't," Cecile said dryly.

"I guess." Tara drew a deep sigh. "It's not every guy who can make your knees buckle."

"Anyway, you really want to live in Argentina?" Cecile smiled. "It's a long way away and you're a real Daddy's girl. I always thought you were interested in Chris Arnold. He'll be here at the weekend."

"So he will!" Tara said, brightening somewhat.

Cecile lowered herself into a planter's chair on the veranda, feeling a little tired. Getting this party organized had taken time and effort, but at last she had everything under control. Tara, usually a bundle of energy, was pretty looped. She had gone off for a lie-down. It was now Thursday; Saturday morning everyone would start arriving: players, their entourages, friends and spectators. They were flying in, coming by charter bus, driving overland in convoys of dusty 4WDs. Generally speaking, everyone had a wonderful time at polo matches, and when the matches were on Malagari where the hospitality was legendary, they could expect the crowd she had catered for. Any food left over could easily be distributed among the station staff and the nomadic aboriginals who traversed the station on walkabout.

One such was Loora, a pure-blood aboriginal woman who had to be, on her grandfather's reckoning, a good twenty years older than he was, which put her well into her nineties. Nineties or not, Loora looked and acted like a sprightly seventy-year-old, an eater and collector of a great variety of native seeds, nuts, bean-sprouting plants and edible fruits that grew wild across the desert plains. No one knew more about the botany of the desert than Loora. For tens of thousands of years the aboriginal people had been like scientists, probing the secrets of the wild bush around them. The early settlers, including her own family, had relied on the aboriginal people to reveal many of the secrets they had unlocked. Which plants were poisonous, which fruits were edible, which contained medicinal compounds, which had therapeutic qualities, which were hallucinogenic. Aboriginals in remote communities of Western Australian were already harvesting and selling their fragrant sandalwood to leading French perfumeries, the sawn sandalwood sent to a distilling plant from whence the aromatic oil was airfreighted to France's top perfume houses.

For decades Loora had been harvesting various barks off the desert trees for her paintings, a collection of which was hung on one wall of her grandfather's study. Loora also collected a bonanza of wild fruits that included wild plums, wild rosella, desert limes, wild pears and many types of berries, which were probably packed with antioxidants. These she presented in an attractive basket she had woven herself at Malagari's kitchen door whenever she was on walkabout. Her grandfather had gone to the trouble of having the plums tested, seizing on the idea they might be a wonderful source of Vitamin C. Loora had known they were, decades before a Darwin laboratory came back with a glowing report.

Yesterday when Cecile and Raul were returning from a practice session at the polo field, they had encountered Loora on her way to the homestead, basket in arm. Raul had stopped the vehicle, astonished to hear from Cecile the old lady was considered to be well into her nineties. Loora, who had spent her entire life traversing the desert, had been moving along in a quite vigorous fashion, her full head of snow-white hair unprotected from the rays of the sun, which were still very strong even though it was coming on to sunset. Cecile's mind went back to the strange encounter, which had been very much on her mind…

"If you are what you eat we'd better find out what it is she's eating," Raul said, half joking, half serious as he stopped the Jeep.

"One hundred percent organic bush tucker," Cecile replied. "The aboriginal traditional diet, plus the fact Loora's always on the move. God knows how many miles she walks every day. She lives her life in the open air without all the stress that goes into *our* lives. I suppose the utter simplicity of life helps and she's doing what she loves to do."

"So let's say hello." Raul was already climbing out. "I don't like her carrying that basket. It looks heavy."

Cecile called a greeting. Loora answered with a big smile that displayed fine teeth, a startling white against her black skin. Even her skin was in the sort of condition a woman half her age might envy.

It was when Cecile turned to introduce Raul that Cecile was caught entirely by surprise.

Loora laid her basket down, then went right up to Raul as though she recognized him. "I know yah, don't I?" Very softly she touched his arm as though eager for him to answer. "Yeah, I know yah," she repeated.

Cecile looked on, puzzled. Raul, however, stood perfectly still, seemingly unperplexed by Loora's behavior. "How can you tell?" He spoke slowly, his accent to Cecile's ears far more pronounced than usual.

Loora lifted a bony arm to tap several times on her right temple. "I got the gift!" she murmured. "I got it when I was just a little one."

"I can see you're clever, Loora," Raul said, "but I come from far away. A country called Argentina. It's in South America."

"I know South America." Loora tapped her temple again with a clawlike hand. "Longa go part of Gondwanna Land, but it break away. You not one of dose people, are yah." It was a statement not a question. Loora flexed her tight facial muscles into a smile. "You come from different direction. Beyond the ranges." She pointed off in the distance to where the sun was slipping down in a splendor of crimson, gold and purple behind the glowing ridges. Ridges that in prehistory were once sand on the shores of the inland sea. "I walk over dere many, many times collectin' stuff in me dilly bag. You belong *dere*. Nasty times. I see it!"

Raul continued to stare at her. "You know all that just from looking at me?"

"Was given to me," Loora explained. "The gift—the double power—it goes right back to the Dreamtime. Besides, I've seen your face before." She lifted her head and stared at him keenly.

"No," Raul replied, shaking his head. "*No,* Loora."

Loora stepped closer, saying the word *no* over as though testing its meaning, then giving it some deep thinking. "So Loora got it wrong," she said eventually. "I *don't* know yah."

"Not possible," Raul said quietly, "but it's a pleasure to meet *you,* Loora. Let me take that basket for you. It must be heavy."

"Used to havin' me hands full," Loora said, but let him pick it up, something she didn't always allow.

"You'll come up to the house, Loora?" Cecile invited. "Say hello? Everyone will be pleased to see you. My grandfather is at home."

"You always kind to me, missy," Loora said. "I say thank you. You ready to learn plenty about woman-business. You fall in love with this fella?" She cocked her head to one side, chuckling as embarrassment whipped color into Cecile's cheeks. "Got no man now. He die longa longa time ago. Up there in the sky with the old people now. This one got a restless spirit!" She gazed up at Raul for a moment. "Bold fella! Spirit wrestling goin' on inside, though."

"I've sensed that, Loora," Cecile said, her eyes seeking Raul's. What did she really know of him except that he had become very important to her?

"Never mind." Loora leaned in to Cecile, her voice dropping to a mere whisper. "He got powerful magic, as well. Magic important. I know." She brought up a hand, spoke from behind it. "He brings a child."

Cecile gasped. The whites of the old woman's eyes grew large. "I'm sorry, Loora," Cecile said, shaking her head to indicate she didn't understand.

Loora spoke again, even more quietly, though her words seemed to *roar* in Cecile's ears. "He bring a child," she repeated, her gaze more intense than ever.

Later on from the veranda outside her bedroom, Cecile caught sight of Raul walking away with Loora across the home gardens into the mauve mist of twilight. Raul had his sun-streaked head—it was so much blonder now—bent to the old aboriginal woman's. They were obviously deep in conversation.

What about? With no contact with the aboriginal people, how had he so easily made a connection? She couldn't pretend to know. So much about Raul Montalvan was a mystery. In some ways she could lock in to his thoughts; in others she had no key.

Then there was the thing that had most shocked her, which

even now made her swallow. *He brings a child.* Did that pronouncement carry a warning? Or could Loora have possibly meant the tranquil little desert wind that aboriginal artists sometimes depicted as a child? There were human figures to represent east winds, west winds, soft winds, harsh winds, winds that brought great dust storms, others that brought thunder and lightning flashing across the desert skies. How could she remain calm when a tribal woman of acknowledged powers had made such a profound pronouncement?

Raul and the station manager, Brad Caldwell, had been meeting up late afternoons to acquaint each other with their playing styles and to trial maneuvers. It was when they were taking a break that Brad brought up Jared Moreland. It could never be said then that he had initiated the conversation, Raul thought, settling in to listen while endeavoring to keep the intensity out of his expression.

"He was a damned fine player," Brad said, wiping sweat from his eyes as he sprawled his long limbs on the grass. "Played his shots like you. Sorta graceful, if you know what I mean. Some players are as rough as guts. That's what brought Jared to mind. We were pretty much of an age. He was a few years older and Joel's son and heir of course. In other words, one hell of a broad canyon between us, but he was a good guy. No side to him like his old man."

"He died in a freak accident, I understand." Raul contrived to sound sympathetic. "The family don't speak about it and naturally I don't ask."

"Well, you know there was a bit of controversy about that." Brad chewed thoughtfully on a blade of grass. "Not at first. In fact, not for a few years. It was supposed to have been just a kid who was involved, but the rumors got started the kid hadn't acted alone."

"What?" Raul heard his voice snap, but he was unable to prevent himself.

Brad gave him an odd look. "Actually I get nervous just talking about it."

"That bad?" Raul swiftly modified his tone. "Sorry if I over-reacted. You really shocked me."

Brad shrugged his big shoulders. "Kinda shocked us all. Talk was there was some bad blood between Jared and one of the stockmen. A guy called Frank Grover. He was pretty friendly with Jack—Jack Doyle up at the house."

"Ah, yes, Jack." Raul leaned back, trying to take in a vital piece of information totally new to him. "Did you have any idea what it was about?" How had it happened Frank Grover's name had never been mentioned within his family? "Surely Joel knew everything there was to know concerning his son's death?"

Brad offered up a deep sigh. "I tell you, mate, Joel in those days wasn't in the frame. Losing his son almost destroyed him, though he managed to soldier on. Too many people depending on him in one form or another. It was the missus, Mrs. More-land, Joel's wife—a powerful lady—that stirred up a hornet's nest of trouble for the kid's family. Ben Lockhart, that was his name. Nice-lookin' kid. Looked like butter wouldn't melt in his mouth. Good people, the Lockharts, so they said. It was a crime they met with such bitter enmity from the missus. Lockhart went broke—starved out I reckon, so much bad feeling whipped up by you know who—and the creditors moved in. The whole lot of 'em moved away. I remember the sister, Lori, Lorianne or something. Boy, was she a looker! Had this glorious head of thick wavy hair. A bit like yours, only lighter, a dark blond. A real shame!" Brad shook his head from side to side.

For a moment Raul felt he really was a stranger in a strange land. There was a terrible tension right through his body. How did Moreland's wife get into this? "So what caused the bad blood between Jared and Grover? Do you know?"

Brad's lean face wore the laconic expression of a man for whom life held no surprises. "No big mystery! A woman, what else? Frank was real sweet on Johanna Muir, a maid at the homestead. Very pretty she was, too, but not a patch on that Lori. Turns out Jared was pretty keen on her, too. Can you beat that! With all the girls he coulda had, he falls for the housemaid. Got her pregnant, anyway. Turns out that baby was Daniel, you know, Daniel...?"

Raul nodded. Daniel Moreland wasn't one of his faceless figures. In fact, he had liked him. "I was at the wedding. Daniel is Jared and Johanna's son."

Another wry smile from Brad. "Nothin' would have come of it if Jared hadn't been killed. People reckon he would have married her. I say *no,* not with *that* mother! Not to speak ill of the dead, but she was a regular monster mum. Odd because Mr. Moreland is one of nature's gentlemen. The missus drove that girl away. One day she was there, the next she wasn't, and she would have needed help. You don't just walk off into the desert. Somehow she was spirited out. Then on top of it, Jared was killed. I'd have believed it if someone told me the missus had had Johanna killed off. I tell you, Mrs. Moreland was ruthless when it came to her family. She thought the sun rose and set in her son's eyes. Me, I'd have run a million miles from her. Maybe Jared would have, only he was destined for disaster."

A kind of numbness was spreading through Raul's body. Why hadn't his family ever pointed a finger at Mrs. Moreland? Joel Moreland had been the sole aggressor, according to his mother. Now Brad Caldwell, who would be in a position to know, said it was the *woman* who had been filled with visceral hatreds. He needed time to think about this. This wasn't the story he'd always been told. The past was unraveling and it wasn't in sync with his mother's version of the sad tale. "So Frank Grover hated Jared Moreland. Is that what you're saying?"

"Sure! Frank started to hate him when he found out about the affair. I reckon Johanna might have told Frank she was pregnant. Got him all fired up. He was one for the booze when he hit town. I know he got tanked up the minute we hit the Alice.

Not that he couldn't hold it. He was one of those guys who liked to hang tough."

"And that's how Jared Moreland got himself killed?" Raul realized he was giving off too much intensity, but thankfully Brad wasn't looking at him.

"You know what they say, crimes of passion!" Brad gave a heavy-hearted sigh.

"So how did the boy come into it?" Raul asked, aware all the certainties he'd carried in his head had fled him. "What did he have to gain but a long prison term?"

A strange smile distorted Brad's mouth. "Maybe the kid had nothin' to do with it, after all," he said in his lazy drawl. "Maybe he was *pushed* off that fence. Coulda happened, a quick shove. All the crowd was interested in was the bulls and the broncos. No one woulda noticed. But one way or the other both Jared and the boy finished up in the path of one mad, stampeding bullock. Jared was kinda known for his reckless courage. He had a real cavalier way about him. I remember he moved without hesitation to protect the boy. In doing so, o'course, he got himself killed. There were minutes of utter silence, like we'd all turned deaf and dumb, then all hell broke loose. It was like there'd been an assassination. The crowd came together in swift judgment. Including me, I'm sorry to say. Always regretted it. But at the time, it was a big thumbs-down for the boy who had done something monumentally stupid. In the crowd's eyes Ben Lockhart was guilty of murder, not just criminal recklessness. He had to pay for it somehow. A man was dead. Joel Moreland is revered in the Outback. Everyone knew how much he adored his only son. Hell, Jared was hardly more than a boy himself. Just twenty-three years old. I'm gettin' a clear image of him now. That bullock did a job on him, I can tell you that." Brad shuddered, fighting off the vision. "Somethin' terrible!"

Raul, who had seen plenty of blood spilled on sand, couldn't talk about it, either. "Where's this Frank Grover now?" He had to find him, speak to him.

Brad snorted. "God knows! You'll have to ask Jack. He might know. Last I heard of him he was workin' on a croc farm in North Queensland. That was years ago. He wasn't wanted here after Jared's death. I figured the missus told him to pack up and go. She would have known he was sweet on Johanna. She probably told Frank where Johanna was. That's if she knew. The woman knew *everything!*" Brad shook his head gravely. "Suppose we'd better try another few shots? You're a great player. It's a privilege to be on the same team."

Raul came to his feet, feeling so profoundly disturbed he barely heard the compliment. He had hated the name Moreland for so long. In particular, Joel Moreland, the Man with the Midas Touch. Now it seemed, if Caldwell could be believed, his family had found the wrong Moreland guilty. A deep sense of frustration was building inside of him. What he desperately needed was hard evidence to prove it was so. Either way, the Morelands had acted like feudal barons.

CHAPTER NINE

THE BREEZE WAS UP. All around the playing field plastic multi-colored pennants flapped, sounding for all the world like ocean waves breaking on the shore. The crowd of spectators had been building all day. Now they sat on three sides of the field in high good spirits waiting for the match of the day to begin. Chris Arnold, an exuberant pilot and captain of one team, had actually landed his Bell helicopter on the middle of the field and taken off again before Jack Doyle, who was in charge of proceedings, rode over to tell him to get the hell off. The crowd had loudly applauded Chris, who was well-known on the circuit, except for those who got the worst of the flying red dust.

Marquees had been set up to serve tea and coffee, soft drinks and light refreshments, sandwiches, pasties, sausage rolls and so on. There was a bar for a cold beer or two, but that was it. No one wanted any drunken behavior or a fight to break out, though Cecile was sure a few of the spectators—not the regulars of whom some had been coming for years—had managed to sneak in a couple of cartons. Everyone mixed well at these occasions, entering into the spirit of things, the rich station owners, stockmen, station workers, town folk from the Alice, a smattering of tourists, all dressed pretty much the same in cool casual gear, their heads covered by the ubiquitous wide-brimmed akubras, both sides rolled up, which somewhat defeated the purpose.

For Cecile, however, the excitement of the day was marred by the fact that Stuart and her mother had thrown a few things into an overnight bag, chartered a flight and turned up on Malagari at ten-thirty that morning. Great-aunt Bea had hitched a ride, as well, which was fine with Cecile. She was very fond of Bea—they'd always been close—but when her autocratic mother teamed up with Stuart, the nerves of Cecile's stomach all twisted in knots. Neither her mother nor Stuart had ever shown the slightest interest in the game of polo, but it became obvious both of them were truly concerned about Raul Montalvan's continuing presence on Malagari.

Then there was the matter of setting the wedding date! One couldn't go on and on with an engagement. One had to tie the knot. Her mother, Cecile realized, wouldn't stop her campaign until Stuart was her lawful wedded husband.

"How much do you love Stuart?" Justine asked the moment they were inside her bedroom door. She didn't wait for an answer. "You've done enough sleeping on the matter, Cecile. My advice is set the date and do it *now.* This very weekend. I don't think I need tell you people are talking about this Argentinian."

"Talking? *What* people?" Cecile looked as amazed as she felt. "We're here in the middle of nowhere, Mother, not back in Melbourne with all the gossips looking on."

"Word gets around nevertheless," Justine said, her voice taut with concern. "Doesn't he have somewhere else to go? And why is Daddy making such a fuss of him?"

Cecile laughed without amusement. "I should think that's obvious, Mother. He really likes him. Raul is very much at home on Malagari, and he's mad about polo, just like Granddad."

"Well, I'm sorry to say I don't like him." Justine passed judgment, tight-lipped.

"But then, who *do* you like?" Cecile asked. "Apart from Stuart, that is. Look, Mother, we can't go into this now. I'm busy and I'm a little tired. We had to fast-track this event. You know what Granddad's like when he's caught up by an enthusiasm."

"The whole thing is a waste of money," Justine said, dismissing the event as a triviality. "All those people! Freeloaders, I call them."

"They're *Granddad's* guests," Cecile pointed out. "It's costing *you* a big fat nothing."

Justine's eyes flashed. "No need to speak to me like that, Cecile. You say you're tired. You don't look it. In fact, I've never seen you look better." Justine sounded quite irked. Cecile was wearing a lacy white halter-necked top that plunged a little too much for Justine's liking, with an eye-catching skirt printed with huge cobalt, yellow and white flowers. She wore yellow wedge-heeled sandals on her feet. Her long hair was pulled back from her face, but flowed freely down her back. Even mothers could feel stabs of jealousy from time to time, Justine thought. It was hell to grow old.

"Malagari has always agreed with me, Mother—I love it," Cecile was saying, aware her control freak of a mother was as mad as a wet hen.

"Which has always struck me as really weird. I was never happy here." Justine turned away, removing an emerald kaftan richly embroidered around the neckline and sleeves from her suitcase and putting it on a padded hanger. "I'm highly tempted to say you've got a crush on this foreigner. He's certainly got an interest in you."

"You really should refrain from using the word *foreigner,* Mother," Cecile chided her mother mildly.

"How else can I put it?" Justine demanded to know. "This whole thing has gone far enough."

"So you've come to save me from myself, is that it?"

"Of course I have, you poor girl!" Justine drooped onto the bed, holding her hand to her head. "If only you'd listen to me. The very last thing I want is an argument, but there's a little *situation* going on here. You can't deny it. Well, not to a woman like me. I know men. Raul Montalvan will go back to Argentina where I'm sure he has a string of women panting on his return. This little flutter or whatever it is will be over. That's life. I just don't want you left crying. I don't want you to jeopardize your future, all our plans. And I beg of you not to humiliate Stuart with this. You may not believe me, but tongues are already wagging."

That was the last straw for Cecile. "Don't you mean *your* tongue, Mother? I bet Stuart rings you every night for a pow-wow right after he's spoken to me."

Justine's finely cut nostrils flared. "Don't speak to me that way, Cecile," she said, looking mega-offended. "I'm not stupid. I'm your mother. I know you backward. As soon as I laid eyes on Raul Montalvan, I sensed trouble. There's something about that young man. He's dangerous. Too hard to handle, let alone tame. Stuart on the other hand is perfect for you."

Cecile started walking toward the door. "He's perfect for *you*, Mother," she corrected, "but unfortunately you're taken. Now, I really must fly."

"Very well, Cecile," Justine said in a wounded voice. "Run away. Ignore my advice. What a thankless job it is being a mother."

Cecile was moving head down along the corridor when she almost collided with Bea coming in the opposite direction.

"What's up with you?" Bea put two hands to her head to straighten her zebra-patterned turban, which sat high above spectacular dangly earrings and platinum kiss curls. "You were coming like an express train."

"Oh, I'm sorry, Bea!" Cecile said, looking at Bea with a feeling of gratitude and affection. Why was Bea always so cheerful when her mother never was? Why was Bea's voice always filled with such friendliness and warmth when her mother invariably sounded so bloody hoity-toity, as befitting her position of prestige and privilege? Bea loved a laugh. Her mother acted as though a laugh was frivolous. Oh hell!

"Having a few words with Mother, were we?" Bea rolled sympathetic eyes. "When is she going to stop trying to boss you around?"

"It's way too late for that, Bea." Cecile shook her head. "She *can't* stop. She doesn't know how."

"There must be a medical term for it," Bea pondered. "Something that ends with *itis*. Of course there *is* the menopause thing. It knocks some women about, but I took a good dose of hormones. You're not out of love with Stuart, are you, dear girl?"

Bea, who had grown considerably shorter over the past few years, tilted her turbaned head to look at the much taller Cecile, sounding hopeful. "Could be," Cecile lamented. "Why do you think Stuart and Mother are here?"

"Checking up on you, my darling. Need you ask? So, you're out of love with Stuart and in love with another man? Have I got that right?"

Cecile bit her lower lip. "Oh, Bea, I'm acting so unlike myself."

Bea, whose outfit for the day was a kind of haute-couture tribal, patted Cecile's arm, setting her dozen or so bracelets a-jangle. "Well, I have to say he's pretty damned *hot!* I won't mention any names of course."

"You'd better not." Cecile sighed. "I have to do the honorable thing, Bea. I have to tell Stuart I can't marry him."

"Well, he was only on probation, wasn't he?" Bea asked, very reasonably.

It was a very Bea-like answer. "It's all very well for you, Bea. You've always been a bad, bad girl."

"So I have!" said Bea, with complete satisfaction. "You on the other hand had the misfortune to be saddled with Justine for a mother. You're worried how she's going to take it?"

"Of course! But shouldn't I be more worried about hurting Stuart?"

"Look, he'll survive, lovey. He really will. You can't get yourself arrested just for breaking an engagement. It happens all the time. Look on the positive side. It would be far worse if you went ahead and got married. The thing that really amazes me is how you got engaged to him in the first place. You don't even speak the same language and he's so bloody *smug!*"

"I thought I loved him, Bea," Cecile said with some sorrow.

"Who could fall in love with a lawyer?" Bea argued. "The way they talk to you! You'd swear you were in a courtroom. My advice to you, my darling, is get it over with. Your mother has to stop trying to run your life. You'll meet someone else *if you haven't met him already*?"

Cecile shook her head as Bea underscored her words. "Not *Raul,* Bea. If that's what you're thinking."

"Can *I* have him, then?" Bea joked. "Charmed the pants off you, has he?"

"Not as yet, Bea." Cecile frowned severely. "And you are a bad, bad girl." Tears glittered for a moment in her eyes. "It's frightening what I feel, Bea," she confessed. "I don't understand what's happening to me."

Bea swooped on her and kissed her. "Well, they do say falling in love is a madness," she pointed out very gently. "But nothing can beat it, believe me."

"It seems not!" Cecile's voice shook with emotion. "I used to be so...so..."

"You don't have to explain it to me, love," Bea said. "I wasn't always this goddamned old and dyeing my hair." She pulled at a platinum kiss curl.

"You? You'll never be old! Look at you today! Not many people could carry off an outfit like that! You're enormously chic!"

"Thank you, darling." Bea's smile was complacent. "When I was your age I was a household name for glamour. Nowadays I'm just a wealthy pampered old bat. You don't think it's a wee bit over the top?" Bea lifted her arms in an exaggerated model's pose.

"Well, it *has* to be because you're so *amazing*," Cecile said, putting her arms around her frail great-aunt and hugging her. "Why wasn't I one of a dozen kids, Bea? Then Mother would have had a lot of us to get around, not just me. Why did it have to happen she could only have *one* child?"

Bea stared at the floor directly in front of her, apparently mulling that over, then she lifted her head, earrings swinging. "I think it's high time I told you all that 'only one child stuff' is a disgusting case of guff. I'm not saying Justine didn't have a tough time having you, but you were her first. Lots of women have a tough time with the first baby. The thing is, Justine had no intention of ever trying again. She had better things to do with her time."

For a moment it wasn't easy to take that in. Cecile opened her mouth to speak, but no sound emerged. "What are you saying, Bea?" she asked finally. Her voice held no anger but a lot of sadness.

"What I should have said long ago, dearest girl. Justine hated childbirth so much she was never going to try it again. There was no physical reason why she couldn't have more children. I know your father wanted more, but he couldn't have *everything* now, could he? Justine was the wife he wanted and she's been a good wife in many ways. I believe they look on it as a successful business partnership. There's something else, too. Justine was able to avenge herself for his other women by not giving him more kids. There was just poor little you for Mother to take care of and run your life. Hell, for all I know you could have been Justine's one-night stand."

"Bea!" Cecile protested even though she was about ready to believe anything.

"Sorry, love! That was in bad taste. I apologize. I'm sure they have a sex life. But next time your mother gives you the baloney about how she suffered so much having you she was advised not to have any more, tell her that ain't so. You can tell her wicked old Bea clued you in. I don't mind. I should have done it long ago. Of course it's not all Justine's fault." Bea shook her head slowly. "My dear sister-in-law Frances was a woeful mama. She ignored Justine for most of the time and got down on a prayer mat to worship her son. There's lots of stuff you don't know about this family, Cecile. Most of your mother's problems stem from the past. You can't afford to worry about what she thinks. If you don't love Stuart, you must tell him so. Let it go on any longer and things will only get worse." Bea pulled her great-niece to her and kissed her.

"I know that, Bea," Cecile murmured. "I'm glad you're here with me. I'll tell him this weekend before he leaves. I can't confront him now. Not with this match on and the party. I think he already suspects bad times are coming."

"And this is one of those times," said Bea prophetically.

The crowds that had gathered around the marquees were back in their seats or sitting on rugs on the grass to watch the main match. A lead-up game had been played earlier with teams of modest handicaps from various stations, but now a great chorus of cheers broke out as the players for the big event of the afternoon took the field. There were four players to a team, two to ride offensively, the third and fourth to play back in the defensive position. In the Outback, polo, a difficult game to learn, let alone the most dangerous, wasn't just a game. It was much much more, like the jousts of old. Chris Arnold's team wore sapphire-blue-and-yellow jerseys; Vince Siganto's team, which included Raul and Brad Caldwell, wore red-and-white with their numbers on a wide white band on the short red sleeve. Brad, at forty-six, was the oldest player, but he was wonderfully fit and played regularly. Even so, he knew his playing days were coming to an end. Earlier Cecile had overheard Raul talking to Vince in the area where the polo ponies were being held. Both of them looked magnificent in their gear, white breeches, color-ful jerseys, high polished boots, which emphasized their lean, long-legged muscular bodies. They weren't at the time wearing their helmets. Second-generation Italian, Vince, who was distinguishing himself internationally as a polo player, had thick raven hair that glistened in the blazing sunlight. In strong contrast, Raul's hair, bleached by the desert sun to coppery blond, burned like fire. Their body language spoke of easy camaraderie, but where she had been expecting them to be speaking English as a matter of course, she found their conversation was being conducted in mellifluous Italian.

Why be surprised?

For all of the play Stuart sat beside her in a collapsible chair battling manfully to look and sound enthusiastic. Her mother and Bea, along with the usual socialite friends, were part of the group sitting behind them under the shade of the trees. Tara, always popular, sat on Cecile's other side looking very fresh and pretty in her favorite blue. A short distance away under striped umbrellas a young group from the Alice had congregated. They were fervent followers of the game and well-known to Cecile; one of them kept up a running commentary that Cecile found both well-informed and funny.

It was evident right from the start that both teams were pretty evenly matched, which was the charm of the game. The best players—and it immediately became obvious who they were, going by their individual handicaps—were Vince, Chris and Raul, so the rest of the players were allotted to one team or the other to ensure neither team was hopelessly outclassed.

Raul, charging at full tilt, scored the first goal.

"Oh, well played!" Tara called excitedly, clapping her hands.

"That was a bit reckless, wasn't it?" Stuart whispered into Cecile's ear. "Frankly this game is so dangerous I think it should be condemned."

"Lighten up, Stuart!" she said. "Far from being reckless that shot was played with great finesse. Just look at Granddad down there." She turned her head to where her grandfather was sitting amid a group of pastoral men, all friends, all former polo players with a vast affection for the game. "He's loving it. So are the rest of them. Try to appreciate the horsemanship and the courage and skill of the ponies."

"I'm just worried some reckless fool is going to gallop right into us." Stuart shuddered, his eyes on Montalvan as the man made another full free swing. Montalvan's teammate Brad Caldwell was very wisely giving him plenty of room. Stuart could just see that mallet connecting with Brad's head, helmet or not. *Show-off,* Stuart thought, upset by the burst of cheering at Montalvan's dashing display of skill. A few minutes later the crowd leapt to their feet as Vince took a forward pass from Raul, shooting for goal. The larrikin in the crowd beside them let out an ear-piercing whistle that Stuart thought should have startled the horses. But then again, could you startle a horse that was used to having a club swung near its head?

"What the heck is this all about?" Stuart was driven into asking. He couldn't follow the game at all, mainly because he didn't want to. Though he had never dared tell anyone he didn't actually enjoy the Melbourne Cup—the nation's and the horse racing world's big event—all that much, either, except for the socializing and having his beautiful heiress fiancée on his arm.

"It's a battle of wits, Stuart," Cecile explained patiently, knowing Stuart was bored by the game. "See what Raul is doing? He's endeavoring to eliminate his opposite number. Some do it by blocking, hooking, barging, all sorts of tactics designed to slow the other man down. The crowd's getting so excited because he's doing it with speed and intelligence. No roughhousing. They appreciate that. Try to think of it as a very fast game of hockey on horseback. The rules are much the same."

"I prefer hockey," Stuart muttered.

"God, you're a spoilsport, Stuart!" Tara groaned. "They ought to put it on your epitaph."

"Not behind the door when it comes to airing your opinion, are we, Tara?" Stuart merely lifted supercilious brows. "Lord knows how Ceci has continued so long with your friendship."

"Ditto!" said Tara.

* * *

Eight chukkas were played with four-minute breaks for the players to change ponies. At halftime the score was 6-4 for the Red team. Three of the Red team's goals had been scored by Raul, the other three by Vince. Chris had scored three of the four goals for his own team. The rest of the match promised to be the cliff-hanger the crowd wanted.

And to everyone's pleasure and excitement it was. The Red team finally won by the narrowest of margins and Cecile presented the impressive trophy to Vince Siganto amid much cheering. It had been a great match and everyone was in the best of spirits. It was now sunset. The barbecue was due to start at 6:30 p.m. In the meantime the crowd was free to roam the station and use the facilities at the staff quarters. The evening's entertainment would include line dancing, which usually proved to be a lot of fun for all age groups. The only exceptions to the universal good behavior were a couple of youths dressed in flashy cowboy outfits who had obviously been consuming alcohol from their own source.

Cecile saw Jack Doyle lead one away, probably to give him a good talking-to, the other, less boisterous and sedate enough until Jack was out of sight, then took it into his head to dart in and out of the milling crowd like an exuberant ten-year-old. Had he continued what he was doing he would have eventually been stopped and by someone, only soon he changed tack and made off quietly toward the enclosure where the polo ponies were being held. Once there, he slipped under the rope, whooping softly. The ponies began to bunch up, tails swishing, not happy to have him there.

"Hey, fellas! Take it easy!" The youth tried to cajole the restless animals. It would really cap a great day if he could get on one's back. "Only havin' a bit of fun!" he explained, looking around him in case a horse minder turned up. Horses thrilled him, not that he could afford one of his own. Maybe he could catch himself a brumby and train him. That Argentinian guy was the quickest and most daring rider he'd ever seen. He'd give anything to be able to ride like that.

Cecile walked down the path to check on the animals.

God, what the hell is that kid doing here? She wondered. *The silly fool is going to spook the horses.*

Cecile picked up her pace, her level of alarm rocketing as she saw the youth raise his arms to shoulder height before spreading them out like wings. Who was he supposed to be, Batman? Next he lifted himself up onto the toes of his boots, and before she knew what he was about, kicked out vigorously as though at an imaginary ball.

"Get out of there!" she yelled, breaking into a run.

He didn't even appear to hear her. Instead, to her acute anxiety, he gave vent to a great raucous squawk like a bird. Perhaps he was supposed to be an eagle? The string of ponies reacted just as she knew they would—with fright. Didn't he know horses could inflict a lot of damage on a person? The horse closest to him reared in a display of raw animal power. Too small to be trained as a racehorse, it was nonetheless a threat.

Too late the cowboy saw how very precarious his position was. He gave one long drawn-out wail, which only served to further spook the horses. The most troubled horse reared again, its front legs beating the air, before it broke free of its restraint and plunged past the youth, who miraculously was able to throw himself out of the way.

"Yikes!" he screamed, tears gushing spontaneously into his eyes with the agony of a struck elbow.

Oh my God!

Cecile stopped running and stood her ground as the horse bolted out onto the rough path. Those that had wandered into the vicinity frantically fell back, looking for cover. No one was prepared to intervene or stop the horse's mad flight for the very real fear they would get kicked or trampled.

Cecile, herself, felt an instant of paralysis, but she stalwartly spread out her arms, calling "Whoa!" in a voice not all that much above normal level but with enough command in it for the horse to get the message and skid to attention. It was all about communication. She rarely encountered the horse that wouldn't do what she wanted. She hoped to deflect the runaway to the side opposite the packed crowd.

The horse read her signals and faltered in its tracks. This was a horse well used to commands. But Cecile's hopes were short-lived. There was a loud whooping yell from behind the trees and the animal was spooked again, breaking into a gallop...

Farther off, Raul had been waylaid by an elderly polo aficionado who was bent on congratulating him for his fine play, but even so he noticed the crowd had changed shape. Always alert, especially when crowds and horses were in close proximity, he held up a staying hand to his companion, concentrating all his attention on what was happening around him.

"Something's wrong," he said to his admirer, then without looking back, took off down the path toward the pony enclosure.

"What's happened?" he called to a middle-aged couple who were beating a hasty retreat through the trees.

"Bloody horse loose, mate!" the man answered, still running. "Some stupid bugger spooked it."

He *knew,* and afterward he marveled that he did know, *she* was in danger.

Raul had never run so fast in his life. It was as though he had been given a shot of a powerful speed-enhancing drug. He saw station men coming from all directions. He was by far the closest. Cecile was standing perfectly still in the horse's path. He heard her call "Whoa!" in much the same sort of voice he himself would have used in the same circumstances. The animal obeyed, nearly skidding to a stop. All might have been well, only from near a stand of trees someone let out a great whoop. The horse was off again.

He could wait no longer. Any thought of revenge on the Morelands evaporated like smoke. This was *Cecile.* Raul arced like an arrow out of the crowd and shot toward his target then gathered her to him. Strangely it wasn't fear he felt but a crazy kind of exultation born of his iron determination to free them of danger. "Here he comes!" he told her, locking his arms around her like a vise.

Cecile's heart seemed to cease beating. She thought he would crack her ribs such was the steel of his grip. They would go down together. Another dreadful accident for the Morelands. Perhaps fatal.

Time crystallized. So this is how it happened, she thought. Her uncle Jared's face sprang to mind. Did he know terror with a rampaging bullock coming right at him? Or like her did he feel the numbed acceptance of someone facing a firing squad?

To the crowd who witnessed what happened—and would talk about it for many a long day—it was an extraordinary act of bravery. It didn't seem like mortal man could react so swiftly. It was more a blur of movement that brought to mind the spring and pounce of a lion. Transfixed with horror, people looked on in sick fascination as two entwined bodies blasted as if out of a cannon across the rough track before crashing to the ground on the other side. It was mere seconds before the horse exploded past the very spot where Cecile had been standing and continued on its mad flight. The man had turned his body at the last minute so the woman was almost completely cushioned from the worst of the fall.

"God almighty!" A brother of one of the players gasped in high relief and admiration. "That's the gutsiest thing I've ever seen."

There was a ragged chorus of agreement.

A distance off, Chris Arnold and Brad Caldwell, working together, had managed to get the trembling polo pony under control. The pseudo cowboy, formerly full of mischief and now condemned as a "brainless young fool," was moaning and groaning, his arms pinned behind his back by a big burly spectator. "Arrest me. Go on, arrest me. I didn't mean no harm. How did I know the bloody horse was going to bolt?"

Ashen-faced and panting, Justine Moreland ran awkwardly, to her daughter who could so easily have been run down and pummeled into the dirt. "Cecile!" she cried, her mouth working with emotion. "You bloody idiot!" She turned her head to vent her rage on the youth with a passion she rarely showed. Her brother Jared's death inevitably came to mind. "I'm going to press charges! You wait and see!"

Joel Moreland, who had moved off some time before, now arrived back on the scene, his tall frame crumpling at the sight of Cecile and Raul lying prone on the ground. For a moment he had to be supported by his friends. "Tell me they're all right?" he begged as Jack Doyle ran to him. "Go to them, Jack."

Cecile was the first to sit up, though it was obviously a struggle for her.

"Thank God! Oh, thank God!" Justine's face was ghastly with shock.

Cecile couldn't speak. She was winded and hurting, but she reached out a hand to her mother, looking dazedly into Justine's tortured face. For all the difficulties between them it couldn't have been plainer her mother loved her. Behind her mother were Bea and Tara, their faces similarly pale and stricken. There was no sign of Stuart, but Cecile wasn't looking for him. He had probably run for his life.

Cecile twisted her aching torso to look down at Raul. He was lying with his eyes shut, apparently unconscious, but her fevered inspection revealed no external signs of injury, apart from a rapidly swelling lump on his head. Blood trickled from where the skin had been broken. There was blood on her white halter top. *His* blood.

"Oh, Raul!" She found her voice, bending over him with breathless concern. Her tone of voice and the expression in her eyes reflected her powerful feelings for all to see, but she was oblivious to everyone but him.

"He's coming round," Justine said with relief, putting aside for the moment the fact that starkly revealing expression on her daughter's face was deeply perturbing. "Look—he's opening his eyes."

"Let me take a look there, lovey." Jack Doyle was with them, dropping to his haunches beside Cecile. Swiftly he took in the disposition of Raul's limbs. Everything looked normal. "Praise the Lord, that's all I can say!" Jack breathed. "I reckon he's okay." Jack looked into Raul's dark eyes. "How yah goin' there, fella?" he asked gently, taking note of the bump on Raul's head where his hair was matted with blood. "How many fingers, mate?" He held up three fingers of his right hand.

"Three," Raul answered instantly, putting a hand to his bleeding head. "What did I hit?"

"The tree." Jack chuckled. "You must have a pretty hard head there, mate. Like to squeeze my hand? Right. Let it go."

"Let's get them both up to the house, Jack," Justine said, some color returning to her face. "That head wound needs a sterile dressing. Ahh, here's Daddy. He looks terrible. Oh, poor Daddy! This shouldn't have happened. Sometimes I hate bloody horses," she raged. "They're so unpredictable, the brutes! Daddy's got George Nelson with him." George Nelson was Joel's friend and personal physician.

"There's the Jeep coming," Jack said. "Let's have Dr. Nelson take a look at you both before we do anything else."

"I'm all right," Raul protested, pushing himself up into a sitting position, though he was very pale beneath his dark tan. "I've had plenty of spills before today. How are *you,* Cecile? Did I hurt you? I'm so sorry."

"Hold on, mate!" Jack gave Raul several comforting pats on the shoulder. "You're a bloody hero!"

"No! No way!" Raul shook his head, then winced.

Cecile, whose eyes were blazing out of her face, reached out to lay a tender hand along his cheek. "We're both safe, Raul."

Dear Heaven! thought Justine, all her worst fears confirmed. When had she ever seen such a frank expression of love on a woman's face? When had she ever seen her daughter look at Stuart that way? The answer was *never.* Where the hell was he, anyway? Wherever he was, it was too late.

"Chris and Brad have the horse under control," Jack Doyle was saying. "That kid and his mate will never be allowed on Malagari again."

"Don't be too hard on him," Raul said, Benjie's fate never far from his mind.

"Don't you go worrying about a thing, Raul dear," Bea exhorted him. "You saved our darling Ceci's life. I'm going to include you in my nightly prayers for the rest of my life," she declared fervently.

"*You,* Bea?" Justine whipped her head around to challenge her aunt. "When did you start praying?"

"About five minutes ago, Justine," said Bea. "Aren't you glad they were answered?"

CHAPTER TEN

THE BARBECUE WENT AHEAD. Everything was in readiness, the crowd had to be fed, so as they said in the theater the show must go on. Cecile couldn't claim she remembered much of it afterward. Shaken and bruised—the discolorations were already coming out—she was fussed over all night. Good-hearted efficient women cheerfully banded together to take the running of the party off her hands. They were all very experienced at these outdoor events and had no difficulty feeding the large crowd and keeping them happy.

For once her grandfather had retired early, reassuring them he was feeling fine, only a little shaken by the events of the afternoon. George Nelson had checked four patients over: Cecile and Raul, and also Joel and Bea, the latter of whom had had a sudden attack of tachycardia. All four had been given the all-clear, though Dr. Nelson had recommended they have an early night. Even so he had checked on Raul, Joel and Bea at frequent intervals during the evening. In Raul's case, though he was a splendidly fit young man, any injury to the head was potentially serious. Raul admitted under questioning to "a bit of a headache," but he showed no other worrying symptoms.

Both men, however, took the doctor's advice and made a reasonably early night of it.

"I'll never forget what you did today, Raul," Joel Moreland told him as they said good-night. He squeezed Raul's hand in gratitude. "If there's any way I can help you—with anything— you have only to say."

"You've already been kindness itself to me." Raul could speak with sincerity. "There are a few questions I might ask you one day."

"Ask them now!" Joel Moreland stared into the young man's eyes, frowning a little in perplexity.

"I don't think so," Raul said. "A bad shock can't be under-estimated. You need your rest."

"I am a bit shaky," Joel admitted. "It was so eerie this after-noon. Time stood still. I've never got over the death of my son. I never will. Had anything happened to Cecile, indeed *you*, I seriously doubt I could have gone on."

"I understand that," Raul said quietly. "One day perhaps you can talk to me about Jared's death." *Starting with the truth,* Raul looked into Joel Moreland's remarkable eyes. "It might help."

Joel gave a sad, twisted smile and placed his hand on the young man's shoulder. "My gut feeling is you'll understand. Good night now, Raul. You sure you're feeling okay?"

"I'd do it again without hesitation," Raul answered.

For a long moment Joel Moreland's eyes remained on the dynamic young man who stood before him. "Anything to pro-tect Cecile, eh?"

Raul's strained-looking face broke into a smile. "Whatever it takes."

An hour or so later, having said her thank-yous and good-nights, Cecile made her way into the house, her head aching and her nerves frayed. Dr. Nelson had given her something to take be-fore bed, but the reality was she and Raul could have been very badly injured or killed today. For that matter, her beloved grandfather could have suffered a heart attack, his color had been so bad. Not that there was anything wrong with his heart to date, but one never knew. The incident had cast a pall on the evening. And then there was Stuart. And her mother. So many times over the past few hours she had seen them with their heads together. Would it ever stop? Stuart had belatedly arrived on the scene, claiming he had been making his way back to the house for something. He then proceeded to make a big display of loving relief and gratitude to Raul. He had been very solicitous ever since. He had even given her her own space for most of the evening, even though he'd stayed close.

She hadn't, however, reckoned on his following her back to the house.

"Ceci!"

She came to a halt in the entrance hall, waiting for him to reach her. She didn't feel up to talking about anything now.

"Could I talk to you for a minute?"

"Can it wait until morning, Stuart?" she asked quietly.

Her plea and the paleness of her face did no good. "I promise it won't take long."

"All right. Let's go into the library," she said, leading the way. There, she switched on the light, taking comfort from the familiar surroundings. It was a world of columns and dark gleaming timbers; bookcases filled with hundreds and hundreds of leather-bound books, a mahogany ladder to reach the top shelves; rich upholstery and rugs, several large canvases of hunting scenes, two Georgian library tables, piled with books, a desk and chair in one corner, two large globes, terrestrial and celestial on stands. She loved this room. It calmed her. It might calm Stuart.

"Sit down, Stuart," she invited, herself sinking into a wing-backed chair. "What is it that can't keep?"

Stuart pulled up his burgundy leather armchair so their knees were almost touching. "Us, Ceci," he said. "I wasn't really sure what was going on before I arrived, but I do now. You're besotted with Montalvan."

Cecile dropped her head in her hands. "Oh, Stuart!" she

breathed, thinking it was finally time to get this thing over with no matter how she felt.

"Be honest with me now," he said. "And don't hang your head. Look at me, Ceci, if you don't mind. What are you afraid of?"

She pulled herself together at his faintly hectoring tone. "There *are* things in life to be afraid of, Stuart. However, I'm not afraid of you. I deeply regret that I must hurt you, but you have to know the truth. I have fallen in love with Raul Montalvan, Stuart. I never meant it to happen."

"You mean you *let* it happen," he shot back accusingly. "Your mother's been right all along. You're not really what you appear to be."

Should she scream in frustration or burst into tears? She did neither. "Perhaps I'm not," she agreed. "I suppose we don't really know ourselves until someone who has the power to do so holds a mirror up to our real selves. I thought I loved you. But what I called love then and what I call love now are two very different things. I'm sorry, Stuart."

"You mean love's ugly twin, don't you?" Stuart's voice had a contemptuous edge. "It's all *sex* with this guy, isn't it?" Stuart's eyes brimmed with hatred.

"I haven't had sex with him, Stuart."

"Liar!" he said bitterly. "Your mother told me you had."

That shook her, but only momentarily. "Now that *is* a lie, Stuart. I'm certain my mother said no such thing."

"Indeed she didn't," Justine thundered from the open doorway. She sailed into the room in her glamorous kaftan and closed the door firmly behind her. "What I did say in the past was I didn't *trust* Raul Montalvan. But after what he did today, putting his own life on the line for Cecile, has left me and our family indebted to him forever. So she's in love with him, Stuart. Who could blame her? He's certainly an extraordinary young man. Maybe it will work out, maybe it won't. Either way—I'm very sorry, Stuart, I realize you're hurt—my daughter is no longer in love with you." Justine smiled tightly. "There it is! We had plans, but that young man knocked them all down with one look from those dark eyes."

A strangled groan from Stuart. "So you're turning against me too, Justine?" he cried. "You've been right behind me up until now."

"I know. I know." Justine put a heavily be-ringed hand to her head. "Stuart, you can't make me feel worse than I do already. I think you're a fine young man. I can't help it if Cecile has fallen out of love with you."

"How do you know she truly has?" Stuart demanded quite savagely.

"Because I *said* so, Stuart," Cecile answered. "The way you and Mother rattle on together as though I'm not in the room is quite extraordinary. I'll say it again, Stuart. I'm very sorry it has come to this, but I can't marry you. I'll return your ring in the morning. I've told you how I feel about Raul. I should point out, I'm not at all sure what Raul feels about me. Certainly he's as attracted to me as I am to him, but right at this moment I don't know where any of it is going. There's so much we don't know about one another."

"You can say that again." Stuart's handsome face darkened. "So he's a glamorous sort of character and he can play polo. He's here on a *visit!*"

"It's not about Raul," Cecile said. "It's about *us,* Stuart. There *is* no us. You're quite right. I'm not the woman you thought I was. Almost certainly I wouldn't make you happy. Our engagement was shaky for some time before Raul came into my life."

"Don't you think you're just trying to justify what you've done?" Stuart asked, his characteristic composure shattering like glass. "We were very happy. Everyone said so. Justine told me pretty well on a daily basis how happy she was about us."

"I had no right to do that, Stuart," Justine suddenly confessed, her supreme confidence in herself shaken. "Call me a very interfering woman. I am. Cecile is far better able to choose the right man than I am."

Stuart totally lost it. He sprang to his feet. "This is an appalling situation. You've made a fool of me, Cecile. I'll never forget that. Neither will my family. Do you know or even care I was going over *our* house with the architect only a few days ago? What about that?"

"My husband and I will take care of the house, Stuart," Justine said in an effort to placate him. "You won't suffer any financial pain."

"I should bloody well think not!" Stuart swore, his breathing fast and shallow.

"I think that's enough now, Stuart." Justine held up her hand. "You and my daughter aren't the first young couple to call off an engagement and you won't be the last. There's no stigma attached to it, nor should there be. The hurt is regrettable."

"The hurt and the *humiliation,*" Stuart answered, the muscles in his lean jaw working. "I'm telling you both now, I'm not taking this lying down. I'm going to dredge up every bit of information I can on Raul Montalvan. Okay, he is who he says he is, I've already checked that out, but you can bet your life a guy like that with his eye for women, and their eye for him—" he gave a hard cackling laugh "—will have a few secrets tucked away he doesn't want anyone to know about."

Cecile looked up at him, smiling sadly. "Stuart, if Raul has love children all over Argentina, it wouldn't help *you*. Our engagement is done. Please try to forgive me for the hurt I've caused you. I should have done this a long time ago. We really aren't suited, are we?"

Stuart gave that odd cackling laugh again. "Skip the self-delusion, Cecile. Raul Montalvan wrecked our engagement. I swear I'll get the dirt on that guy, and when I do you'll be the first to know."

Next morning when Raul walked onto the veranda outside his room, he saw Jack Doyle at the side of the house, giving instructions to a couple of groundsmen. He took in a lungful of pure desert air, trying to rid himself of the lingering miasma of his dreams, nightmares really, intensely vivid, that were connected to the deaths of both Jared Moreland and his uncle Benjamin. Not used to any kind of medication, he put a lot of the feverish brain activity down to the sedative, or whatever, Dr. Nelson had given him for the painful lump on his head. It was still aching and not all that much diminished in size.

He wondered how Cecile was this blue cloudless morning, heavy with the aromatic scents of the bush. The birds were darting through the trees showing flashes of incredibly brilliant color as they called to one another. Beautiful butterflies were drawn in large numbers to the profusely flowering lantana. He watched them fluttering, wondering how he had kept himself from going down to Cecile in the still of last night. Even the thought made his blood stir. The need to reassure himself she was all right had been overwhelming, but so was the need to be with her, to hold her lovely supple body in his arms. More than anything, to make love to her. Once he had seen them on opposing sides, but that feeling had passed. She was in his blood. It was as simple and as hopelessly complicated as that!

Since speaking to Brad Caldwell, the station manager, he had awaited his moment to strike up a conversation with Doyle. With any luck at all, it might lead to his finding out where Frank Grover, Jared Moreland's alleged rival, might be. Whether the man was in or out of the country, Raul silently vowed he would find him. There were a whole lot of questions that needed answers. No way would the Benjie he so lovingly remembered have been involved in any plan to hurt a living soul, let alone Joel Moreland's only son. The most likely scenario could prove Brad right. Someone with a pressing motive had pushed Benjie into the arena, certain that Moreland would be the first to go to his aid.

Chiseled features taut, Raul walked down into the garden and rounded the east wing of the house.

"Well, now, how's it goin'?" Jack Doyle called out a friendly greeting the moment he spotted him. "Bet you've got a sore head."

"It's not too bad, thanks, Jack." Raul smiled at the older man, digging his fingers into his thick hair.

"That's a relief. No ride this morning?"

"I think I'll leave it until this afternoon," Raul said wryly. "It was a great pity Mr. Moreland had to be there yesterday. He was badly shaken."

"Sure was!" Jack agreed. "He's never got over what happened to Jared, even if he never lost the Midas Touch in other ways. I suppose it was trying to block out the grief that drove him to concentrate so fiercely on his business affairs."

There was irony in that, Raul thought. Even cut down, Joel Moreland had remained a workaholic and an increasingly formidable business mogul. In his seventies he was still very much in charge. Raul stared off across the garden to where a large flock of sulfur-crested cockatoos were making a commotion. "So what were the circumstances of Jared's death? Do you mind my asking, Jack? I only hear snatches here and there. I've never had the full story. Brad told me a little about that terrible day. About the young fellow that was held responsible for the tragedy."

"Just a kid—I remember him well," Jack said. "What he did—or what he was thought to have done at the time—was incredibly stupid and wild, but according to those who knew him, which I didn't, he wasn't wild at all. He did, however, have a passion for rodeo, which we all know is a pretty foolhardy recreation. What's the pleasure in courtin' broken bones, countless bruises and mashed insides? I've seen guys who've had their thumbs ripped off calf ropin'. Jared had a passion for the arena as well. It was real dangerous and his mother was very much against it. Even Joel, who used to have a lot of fun with the ride-'em-cowboy routine when he was young, begged him to wrap it up. Got 'im all the same. That was one mean, murderous beast that killed him."

"He must have been very brave, as well as tough." Raul found he was having to revise just about everything he had been told about the Morelands as a boy growing up.

"Brave like *you*," Jack said simply. "Nuthin' fake about it. Real guts."

"He would have known he was taking a terrible risk."

"Nearly pulled it off," Jack lamented, "only he tripped on something and went sprawling flat on his back in the dust. It was bloody horrible, I can tell you. I had nightmares about it for years."

"You said something Brad implied, Jack." Raul was anxious to keep the conversation going without alerting the other man to his deep-seated fixation. "There was some speculation the boy could have been pushed, wasn't there? Brad spoke about bad blood between Jared and a friend of yours, Frank Grover— I think I've got the name right."

"Name's right, but Brad gave you a bum steer about the *friend*." Jack slapped at a biting insect on his arm. "Grover was no friend of mine. How the hell did Brad figure that? We worked together. Rode together. We weren't mates. Hell, I didn't even like the guy. He had real pale, pale blue eyes, kinda empty. He was mad about Johanna, the little housemaid up at the home-stead. I guess you know that story?"

Raul nodded and changed the subject. "What I saw of Dan-iel I liked. He and Cecile could be twins."

"Ain't no one as beautiful as Miss Cecile," Jack said, eyes twinkling.

"You won't get any argument from me," Raul said dryly. "So where is this Grover now? I gather he no longer works on the station?"

"Crikey, you wouldn't wanna know," Jack leaned toward him, near whispering. "He was taken by a croc up in North Queensland about four years ago."

No! That Grover, the bastard, was dead was the one thing

Raul hadn't counted on. He was so busy trying to rein in his crushing frustration he barely heard the rest of Jack's story.

"It was in the papers," Jack was saying in a matter-of-fact voice. "Silly bugger was sitting on a jetty fishing, legs dangling apparently, and a bloody croc reared up out of the water and bit him near in two. They shot the croc when it was just doing what crocs do. Grover was the fool. Any mug would have known better. To make it worse he'd worked on a croc farm for a few years. Got a mite too complacent."

Raul could have smashed his fist into the trunk of the tree they were standing under. "Is it possible Grover pushed the boy, or is that theory just plain crazy?"

Jack took a deep breath and slowly let it out. "Actually not," he said. "No one considered it at the time, but I think Grover let a few things slip one time when he was drunk. He hated Jared for stealing his girl."

"And was she his girl?" Raul tried to moderate the intensity of his tone.

Jack shrugged a broad shoulder. "Lordy, I wasn't close enough to any of them to know. Grover was a good-looking bloke even if he was a bit strange. Johanna couldn't have thought to look as high as Jared. Hell, he was the boss's son. His mother had big plans for him, which didn't include no little housemaid. Maybe Frank *was* her boyfriend, at least for a while. I don't know. All I do know is Johanna was pregnant by Jared."

"Could it have been a deliberate ploy to get Jared to marry her?" Raul was compelled to ask.

"God knows, mate," Jack shook his head. "Who knows what goes on in anyone's head when sex is involved? Fact is, Daniel is the result and Daniel is Joel Moreland's heir. It wouldn't pay to start talkin' about Frank Grover, or the boy. Some things it's better not to discuss. Especially around here. Jared's memory is stained with blood. Lockhart was the boy's name. He was killed, too, believe it or not. It was like a bloody jinx was on all of them. All of them gone."

Raul fought down the racking cry that tore at his chest. "It's a very strange and disturbing story," he said. "You must have some opinion, Jack. You were there that day."

Jack's blue eyes went hazy with memory. "I thought the same as everyone else. It was an act of sheer bloody criminal stupidity had caused Jared's death. Everyone was so shocked and angry they wanted to tear the kid to pieces, poor little bugger...though he wasn't little at all. He was a big strappin' fella. Neither Joel nor Mrs. Moreland were there on the day, but Mrs. Moreland—now there was one terrifyin' lady—she was determined the boy and his family would be punished. She had the power to make it happen. The Morelands were even then huge Territory benefactors. It only took a word in someone's ear to make it pretty difficult for the boy's grandfather to run his property and get help when he needed it. Hired hands, mechanics, truckers, fencers, contract choppers, suppliers of all kinds, even vets had pressing reasons to be somewhere else. The word had gone out, you see. Most stuck with the strength, for fear of reprisals. I reckon Mrs. Moreland would have turned on them. The old boy couldn't get any additional credit from the bank to tide them over the bad patch everyone was experiencing. They came down mighty hard on him when they were lenient with others. It finally finished up with the bank foreclosin' on their station. No one in their right mind would have crossed Mrs. Moreland or, God forbid, been the cause of the death of her son. It wasn't until some years later that the rumors starting goin' the rounds. All of us quick to condemn had to sit down and reexamine the whole event and the people who could have been involved in some way. To this day nobody actually *knows*. Nor will we ever know if it was a horrific accident or bloody murder. I feel real bad about the whole thing. So do most of us, I reckon. Ben Lockhart might have been an entirely innocent young man."

Nevertheless he was condemned and is now dead.

* * *

The strain between herself and Stuart was of such magnitude Cecile judged it would be easier for everyone if she didn't accompany her mother, Bea and Stuart to the airstrip where the charter plane waited. She would bid her farewells at the homestead.

Now she stood on the veranda with Justine and Bea. "God knows what your father is going to say, Ceci," Justine said with that familiar note of censure in her voice.

"No, no, *no!*" Bea protested, waving her arms in the air. "Don't start that again, Justine."

Jaw set grimly, Justine ignored her. "There's going to be a scandal," she said. "Judy Carlson is a truly dreadful woman."

"Ho, ho, we all thought you liked her!" Bea winked laconically at Cecile.

"Keep out of this, Bea, would you?" Justine's nostrils flared, then deflated.

"Lighten up, can't you, Justine?" Bea groaned. "It'll be a nine-day wonder and Howard won't lose any sleep over it. He wants his daughter to be happy. Stuart was a terrible choice for Ceci, anyway. Where the hell is he, by the way?" Bea looked behind her into the interior of the house. "Uh-oh, take cover. Here he comes."

Stuart strode out onto the veranda with a very aloof expression. "Sorry to keep you waiting," he said icily. "I just wanted to have a word with Montalvan."

"Did you find him?" Bea asked with the greatest interest.

"I think you know very well I haven't. He's probably gone into hiding."

"Don't be so ridiculous!" Bea burst out laughing. "Hide from *you*, Stuart?"

Raul chose that precise moment to appear in the entrance hall, then catching sight of them walked out onto the veranda. "Everyone set?" he asked pleasantly.

"Not until you give me another kiss," said Bea cheekily.

"It will be my pleasure." He smiled at her. "You wanted to talk to me, Stuart?"

Stuart drew himself up to his full six-foot height. "You don't have a shred of guilt, do you?"

Raul looked puzzled. "I'm not sure what for."

"No shame! No remorse, either," Stuart continued. "Cecile was *my* fiancée."

"Stuart, *please,*" Cecile begged.

Raul appeared to think about it. "I really can't be held responsible for your inadequacies as a fiancé, Stuart," he said finally. "However, would it be out of line for me to say I understand your pain?"

"I don't want your bloody sympathy, damn it!" Stuart burst out.

"Right, I'll withdraw it."

"I think that's our cue for departure, kids," Bea suggested dryly. "Kiss me, Raul, before I go."

"He heard you the first time, Bea." Justine frowned, obviously thinking her aunt was just too embarrassing.

"Just because you've lost your charm doesn't mean *I* have, thank you very much, Justine," Bea came back with a snap, moving toward Raul. "You know I always thought Lord Nelson said, '*Kismet,* Hardy.' Not that silly, 'Kiss me.' It wouldn't have set a good example for his men, would it?"

Stuart took no notice of her and pointed a finger at Raul. "You're nothing but a con man," he said contemptuously.

"Really?" Raul's response was outwardly mild, but inwardly he sought to put a rein on his temper. "I'll kiss our beautiful Beatrice—I'm quite sure Nelson said *kismet,* too, Beatrice, then I'll walk with you, Stuart, to the Land Rover."

Stuart declined the offer. "I don't like being threatened," he said, his voice tight. "I don't have the stomach for this sordid mess, either. Goodbye, Cecile," he threw at her harshly, almost running down the steps as though he couldn't bear to look at her a moment longer. "You'll be hearing from me, don't worry."

* * *

"What was that all about?" Raul asked after the Land Rover, driven by Jack Doyle, disappeared from sight. "It sounded very much like a threat."

Cecile sighed. "I think Stuart intends to contact the FBI to see if you're on their Most Wanted files."

Raul's mouth compressed. "He thinks I'm an international criminal?"

"He thinks you're a mystery man," Cecile said quietly. "So do I."

"So what is it you want to know?" Raul went to her, linking his hands around her waist and drawing her to him.

She stared up into his burnished eyes. "It's more what *you* want to know, Raul. You've been asking a lot of questions."

"Such as?" He wasn't surprised she'd realized that. He hadn't been all that subtle.

"The circumstances surrounding my uncle Jared's death."

"Wouldn't anyone want to know?" He gave one of those very European shrugs he had picked up along the way. "It's a tragic story. I'm close to you, aren't I? *Aren't* I, Cecile? Tell me, who thought it necessary to report back to you?"

She felt the hot color rise to her cheeks. "No one reported, Raul. It only came out in conversation."

"Yes?" he prompted, unaware his features had gone tight.

"It was Brad, after the match. He mentioned that your playing style, which very much impressed him along with everyone else, reminded him of Uncle Jared's. Then he added you'd shown a good deal of interest in how the whole tragedy occurred."

Raul forced a laugh he didn't feel. "Forgive me if I don't find that the least bit unusual. Perhaps being a Moreland makes you overly suspicious of people, Cecile, is that it?"

She was still staring at him, overwhelmingly conscious of his sexual attraction for her and because of it, her utter vulnerability. "You may be right."

"Don't you love me a little for saving your life?" he asked gently, bending his head so he could murmur in her ear.

It would have been impossible to suppress the excitement that ran through her...except a shocked voice called from the open doorway.

"Excuse me, am I interrupting anything?"

It was Tara. The poleaxed expression on her face made Cecile feel not only embarrassment but a real prickle of alarm. "Not at all, Tara," she said as Raul with no haste withdrew his arms. "Seeing Stuart off wasn't terribly pleasant."

"Well, it looks like you have Raul to comfort you!" There was more than a thread of outrage in Tara's voice. She looked from one to the other, having realized in a split second what she should have picked up on long before if she hadn't been so stupidly blind. Cecile and Raul Montalvan were sexually involved. No question about it. Tara had never felt so upset and so horrendously jealous. She wanted to pack her bags on the instant and leave. Didn't Cecile have enough? She was beautiful. She was gifted. She was filthy rich. Tara would have given anything to attract Raul Montalvan to her side, but she couldn't compete with Ceci. She'd never been able to. She should never have tried.

Tara gave a little agonized cry at the pity she saw in Raul's eyes. Burning with humiliation, she turned on her heel and rushed back into the house.

Cecile stared after her, heart torn. "Oh, Lord, I have to go to her!" She realized, too late, she hadn't taken her friend's interest in Raul half seriously enough. But then, Tara always had been good at covering her deepest emotions with frivolity and amusing banter. She couldn't bear to see Tara hurt. It was far worse than having had to hurt Stuart, and now she'd done both at the same time!

She found Tara facedown on her bed.

"Oh, Tara, I'm so sorry!" Cecile approached hesitantly, feeling weighted by sympathy and something like guilt.

"I've made a bloody fool of myself, haven't I?" Tara railed, thrashing her slender legs on the mattress.

"Of course you haven't." Cecile went to sit on the side of the bed.

"Is *he* why you broke your engagement?" Tara swung her unhappy face to Cecile accusingly.

"No!" Cecile stroked a damp blond strand from Tara's face. "No, Tara. I would have broken my engagement to Stuart if I'd never even laid eyes on Raul. You said yourself that Stuart and I weren't soul mates."

"And you and Raul are?" Tara lashed out with such dislike and contempt that Cecile drew back. She felt for the very first time that their long friendship was in peril.

"I don't know what you thought you saw, Tara—"

"Oh, come off it," Tara retorted furiously. "Have you been to bed with him? What's he like? Bloody marvelous, I bet."

Cecile stared at her friend's puffy, tear-streaked face in utmost dismay. "I haven't been to bed with him, Tara. And really, it's none of your business, is it? You're my dearest friend. I don't want to hurt you. But be reasonable. I didn't come between you and Raul. I couldn't have stopped him falling in love with you if he wanted to." Cecile tried to put an arm around her friend, but Tara threw it off.

"Who's going to fall in love with me with *you* around?" Tara asked with great bitterness and resentment. "It was the same for years and years until you got yourself engaged to Stuart. You turn your bloody charm on them and I don't stand a chance."

"I had no idea you felt this way." Cecile shrank from Tara's contorted face. "Who did I take from you exactly?" she asked in bewilderment, searching her memory.

Tara punched the pillow violently. "Oh, you didn't do it deliberately. I know that. But the combination of beauty and big bucks is too much for most guys. It could be the same with Raul. Canny old Stuart—he is a top lawyer, after all—could well be right. Our devastatingly handsome and charming Raul could be a fortune hunter."

Cecile tried to maintain some dignity and control. "Do you honestly believe that, Tara?"

"Ohhh! I don't know what I believe!" Tara made a terrible keening sound. "I'm outta here. I can't stay, Ceci. I know I'm going to be terribly ashamed of myself later, but I think it advisable if I go home now. You won't suffer in my absence, anyway. You've got Raul."

Cecile stood up from the bed, unable to believe this was Tara, her friend, who was mad with jealousy and rage. How long had Tara been harboring such thoughts? She had always treasured Tara's loyalty. Now it appeared she'd been deceiving herself. Tara, like many others, had only been using her. That was the downside of being Cecile Moreland. Envy inspired deep resentment. Even hate.

In the heat of the day Cecile felt chilled to the bone.

CHAPTER ELEVEN

HE WAS A man at war with himself.

To be free, even momentarily, of all the myriad agonies going round and round in his head! They were causing him many nights of lost sleep. Raul put down the phone after a brief call from Cecile saying she was coming to see him. She didn't say about what and he didn't ask. Just to see her was enough. But it did leave him to speculate on the nature of this unscheduled visit. They were to have dinner that evening. He had always been aware a man like Joel Moreland had the wherewithal to have him thoroughly checked out. Any good private investigator would be able to establish without too much trouble his mother's background: her maiden name, her marriage to his father, her first husband, then to Ramon Montalvan, her second, who had legally adopted him at age twelve. Further investigation would reveal the young man held responsible for the death of Jared Moreland, one Benjamin Lockhart, deceased, had been his mother's younger brother and thus, his uncle.

Was that it? Was he about to be unmasked as the impostor in their midst? So be it! It would almost come as a relief especially as the results of his own investigation had diluted Moreland responsibility for the terrible downturn in his family's lives. But justice must prevail.

Raul walked out onto the terrace of the spacious Darwin apartment he had recently moved into. The vast Darwin harbor sparkled a deep turquoise in the late-afternoon sunlight. Moreland Enterprises owned the exclusive apartment complex, which featured every amenity, including a fifty-meter swimming pool and a superbly equipped gym, so securing a very cozy place indeed to live had been an easy matter.

What deeply troubled him now was the shift in his position. A gradual letting go. He hadn't foreseen it. He hadn't foreseen Cecile. He couldn't help but see the shift as a betrayal to his family. He had returned to Australia with vengeance on his mind. Revenge on the Morelands had twined itself around his life like a great python twined itself around a tree. He seemed as though he had never been free of its coils. Only, what he had long believed as being the truth wasn't revealing itself to be so. There were baffling aspects to the whole thing. A bigger cast of characters than he or his mother had ever imagined. He was certain his mother hadn't lied to him; they were very close. The truth now appeared to have been buried beneath a mountain of grievances, hearsay and outright misinformation. The more he came to know Joel Moreland the more he liked and respected him. No one could have been kinder or more helpful to him than Joel. He was a grandfather figure with a wonderful combination of wisdom, charm and command, as well as a personal history that was the stuff of Outback legend. Add to that the fact that Joel Moreland had a very tolerant way of looking at the world. He believed now, as he had never done before, that Joel had *not* been the deliberate instrument of his family's ruin. It had clearly been Joel's wife, Frances, but the woman had died, only a handful of years back, thus escaping having to admit to him and then the world what she had done. His family name would never be cleared. He had taken a great gamble coming here. The gamble had not paid off.

They were all dead, Raul thought wretchedly. All the main characters in that tragic tale. Even Frank Grover had met with a horrific end. If Frances Moreland had been prepared to turn her back on a pregnant young woman carrying her grandson, she was capable of anything. He had talked about that with Beatrice, who hadn't held back on what she thought of her late sister-in-law.

"Wicked! What she did was wicked!" Beatrice had said, her tiny face pinched in remembrance. "The sad thing was, Frances was totally fixated on her son. She adored him. She had little time for poor Justine. None of us, most of all Joel, had any idea she was going to change so drastically after only a few short years of marriage. Joel was away a lot—it was always business, business, business. He thought Frances had accepted that's what he did. He'd talked seriously to her about it before they married—so for that matter did I—and she seemed to understand. She was madly in love with him. She clearly enjoyed being his wife and all that went with it. Frances was a beautiful woman, but obsessive, as is sad to say Justine. It's in the genes. As the years went on, Jared, not Joel became Frances's obsession. He became her whole life. Whatever persuaded Daniel's mother to set her sights on Jared, heaven only knows. It was madness! Frances was more than capable of ruining the life of anyone who got in her way. Having a lot of money encourages megalomania sad to say."

A sickening perception but in many cases true. He had longed to question Beatrice about the circumstances surrounding Jared's death, but he knew Beatrice, as shrewd as they come, might be alerted to the quality of his interest and see it as a suspicious intrusion into Moreland family matters.

As for Cecile? It was hardly the scenario he had planned. Cecile had grown into his own personal obsession. She'd woven a web around him, in fact around them both. He knew how much Tara's running off had hurt her. It wasn't hard to realize Tara had, without any encouragement, taken a fancy to him. He couldn't help that. He knew he was attractive to women, but he was no womanizer. Anything but. Once or twice he had divined that beneath the breezy banter, Tara was deeply envious of her friend, of Cecile's stunning natural beauty and very privileged lifestyle. It didn't seem to matter that Tara, from all accounts, had long enjoyed the benefits of having Cecile Moreland for a friend.

In another week Cecile was due to return to Melbourne to her family, to her professional career, to her wide circle of friends. He could understand how being an heiress had complicated her life. Most people would assume, as Joel Moreland's granddaughter, she lived a charmed life. She was certainly free of any worrying financial burdens, but that wasn't the whole story. She'd had to accept she was a target for fortune hunters and supposed friends only too willing to help her spend her money. Tara appeared to have been one such experience. Even if at some later date Tara apologized for her behavior, the damage would have been done. It was sad and disillusioning. But Cecile was strong and she was independent. She could have given herself over to a life of pleasure, yet instead had chosen a serious career working with children in deep distress and dire need like her patient, little Ellie, who appeared to be never far from her mind. Cecile was a deeply caring person. Even Justine, who couldn't quite approve of him, involved herself heavily in charitable work. He had also learned from a number of sources the extent of Joel Moreland's philanthropy. As Moreland's empire had grown, his endowments to hospitals, medical research centers and a whole raft of charities grew apace.

This wasn't a man who destroyed lives.

Cecile arrived about forty minutes later. He let her through the security door at the entrance to the building, then waited for her at the elevator.

His first glance told him the mystery of Raul Montalvan had been unraveled. He couldn't say he hadn't seen it coming. Neither of them spoke but walked in silence to his apartment, of which there were only two to a floor. Once inside she turned to face him, a cool, grave beauty in a lovely white silk dress, belted at the narrow waist in silver-studded turquoise that matched her high heels. "You deceived me utterly, *Rolfe,*" she said. "I suppose I should call you Rolfe from now on...but why?"

"Sit down, Cecile," he responded quietly, but there was a flash in his gold-flecked eyes.

She remained standing as though she intended to have her say as quickly as possible, then leave. "What is your state of mind? Do you hate us so much?"

"What is it you know or think you know?" he countered, steeling himself against hearing her grandfather had had him investigated. Like Cecile, Joel Moreland had gotten under his guard.

"I received this in the mail today." She opened her handbag and withdrew a long, thickly padded envelope. "It's from my ex-fiancé, Stuart Carlson, God bless him. I'm sure it gave him a lot of pleasure seeing it all compiled."

"May I?" He held out his hand.

She gave a slight elegant shrug. "Why not? It's all about you, anyway. Your entire background, I would say."

"Then I am who I claim to be—Raul Montalvan," he returned curtly, stung by her tone. "In Argentina Rolfe somehow became Raul. So you might apologize for having said I deceived you. I just didn't give you the full story."

"But it's all *about* the full story, isn't it, Rolfe? Tell me, is the fascinating accent assumed?"

"Don't be ridiculous!" he said shortly, opening out the pages.

She visibly trembled and he relented. "Are you cold?" It was eighty degrees outside, but the air-conditioning was set at seventy.

"I'm frozen," she said. "With shock."

Her wonderful eyes surveyed him the way he imagined a woman might look on a hero found to be badly flawed. "Sit down," he repeated. "You're not getting out of here before we talk."

"Is that a threat?" she asked quietly.

"Take it any way you like," he clipped off. "But you know you're in no danger." He waited until she sank gracefully into an armchair, then he bent to reading Stuart Carlson's vitriolic covering page. Apparently simple decency in dealing with his ex-fiancée was beyond the man.

"I was always suspicious of you, Rolfe," she murmured, even though she knew he was too engrossed in what he was reading to focus on what she was saying.

"Well, they certainly amassed a great deal of information!" Rolfe observed dryly some moments later. He refolded the pages and put them back into the envelope, laying it down on the coffee table in front of her.

"Was everything just for revenge?" she asked. "Did you have any *real* feeling for me, or was that only an elaborate pretense? Perhaps you despise me. Perhaps your plan was to make me fall in love with you, then publicly reject me. Anything's possible." Only her pride saved her from breaking down.

"I'm not going to deny I thought about it," he said, his expression dark and brooding. "For about two minutes, maybe ten. I've lived with the hated name of Moreland for most of my life, Cecile. Can you understand that?"

"But what did we do?" she cried in bewilderment.

His anger exploded, made all the more potent because he felt he had disgraced himself in her eyes. "You ruined my entire family," he rasped. "My grandparents were forced off their land. Land they had worked for five generations. My grandfather—I was named for him—had a massive heart attack not long after. My grandmother exiled herself to New Zealand just as my mother and father took refuge in Argentina. All of us exiles. Do you know what that means? It's like having an arm cut off. My father died there in a strange land."

"Yes, and I'm so sorry." Tears sprang to her eyes.

"Spare me the tears," he said harshly, even as his heart twisted. "I don't doubt you're sorry, but Moreland sympathy has come too late. It's my uncle Benjie's treatment at Moreland hands I most deeply hold against you. He was hounded to his death."

"But he was killed in a bar fight. Surely that's right." She had read it in the report.

"Provoked into a fight, I'm certain. There was far more to your uncle Jared's death than you've been led to believe, Cecile. I know you grew up thinking it was a tragedy caused by his heroic response to a young fool's reckless stupidity."

"And wasn't it?" She had always looked on her uncle as a hero who had given his life to save another's.

Rolfe's mouth, generous in its lines, tightened. "There's some evidence Ben was pushed off that fence by a man called Grover, Frank Grover. He was a stockman on Malagari."

Cecile was beginning to feel quite ill. "You can't be serious!" she gasped. "I've never heard such a thing. Why would anyone want to harm my uncle, anyway?"

His tone was quiet but it commanded attention. "Crimes of passion happen all the time. Grover was in love with the same young woman, the housemaid Johanna Muir, who was to bear Jared's child. I was told there was bad blood between your uncle and Grover."

Cecile looked as shaken and baffled as she felt. "I know absolutely nothing of this."

"You don't *want* to know anything," he countered, between clenched teeth. "You *fear* the truth."

Cecile jumped up from her chair. "I don't! Stop it, Raul.... *Rolfe!*" she cried, wondering if there was anything straightforward in life. "I can't listen. I'm going."

"That's right, run," he challenged, his expression conveying he thought her response cowardly. "You all ran from the truth. Because of that my entire family suffered. My grandfather was hounded off the family land. All right, it was no Malagari, but it had been in the family for five generations. I lost my inheritance. Nothing to you, I dare say, but everything then to me.

My uncle Benjie, an innocent young man lost all direction and eventually died at an attacker's hands."

Cecile saw the burning anger in his eyes. "You hate us, don't you? You really hate us." Would she ever recover from it?

"I hate your grandmother," he said. "I doubt Daniel thinks very kindly of her, either. She was a cruel, ruthless woman."

"But what has my grandmother got to do with this?" Cecile was so shocked she could scarcely draw breath. "She was kindness itself to me."

"You didn't *threaten* her, Cecile." The word was bitterly emphasized.

"There's no peace anywhere, is there?" Cecile's face was as white as her dress. "It's not safe to trust anyone."

That was the worst of it. She had lost all trust in him. He made an attempt to explain. "I couldn't have shown my hand too early. I had to get to know you."

"You mean you had to infiltrate the family." Cecile struggled to keep her voice steady. "You had to become the spy among us. Learn our secrets."

"Of course," he admitted grimly. "I knew most of them already but I had to be in a position to turn your dire secrets against you."

"So that's all it was, seeking revenge?" She was certain that was so.

"All?" he asked harshly. "My family was publicly condemned. I had to set the record straight. I needed to show you up to yourselves. At the beginning, anyway."

"So what changed?" she asked contemptuously.

"*You.* You turned my head. And my heart."

Abruptly she swung away, the hem of her skirt flaring around her slender legs. "I'm not taken in by what you say," she said bitterly. "From the moment you laid eyes on me you saw how I could be used in your little game."

"No game, I assure you."

Cecile spun back to face him, seeing his brow furrowed with

strain. "How could you dream of making a fool of my grandfather, of all people?" she asked bleakly.

Rolfe shrugged. "I hardly think I did. Or *could.* It wasn't Joel who victimized my family and Daniel's hapless mother, as I believed. It was Joel's wife, Frances, your grandmother. She behaved in a manner I believe your grandfather never could. The female is often deadlier than the male."

Cecile made a huge effort to remain calm, although she was dreadfully upset. "I repeat, I know nothing of this," she protested. "You're a man driven by the demon of revenge, yet you were only a child at the time. It would have been impossible for you to form an adult opinion. Too much was put on your shoulders. You accepted whatever was told to you. Small wonder you've become so embittered. So your family's lives were smashed? Did that mean ours has to be smashed, too? Your accounts settled?"

"There are consequences to our actions, Cecile," he said with the gravity of a judge. "Unfortunately for me most of the people involved in that terrible saga are dead. The truth, the real truth, may never be known. It appears to have gone to the grave with them."

Although she was appalled by his words, she steeled herself against him. "If they did wrong, they don't go free," she said. "Don't you believe in God?"

"Maybe not." He shrugged. "If there *is* a God, He wants none of what's going on down here in this deeply troubled world. Did no one know your grandmother was so deeply implicated in my family's ruin?"

Her hackles rose again. "Where's your evidence?" she challenged him. "Have you got a scrap of this so-called evidence to show me?"

"I've spoken to your own people," he retorted. "People in a position to know some of it. You know that. What I have is a good deal of hearsay, I admit, but I'm certain if I dig deep enough, I can get all the evidence I need. I'm not trying to

prove anything in a court of law, Cecile. I'm not trying to sue
the mighty Morelands for stacks of money. I simply want acknowledgment of a terrible miscarriage of justice. I want to remove the slur from my uncle's name. I believe him to have been
the victim of another man's sinister plot. That was Grover. But
Grover's dead—a crocodile beat me to him. Your grandmother
is no longer alive. What did she die of?"

Cecile was wrenched by painful memories. "Something horrible," she said. "Does that appease you? It was stomach cancer."

"I'm sorry." Hurting Cecile was hardly what he wanted. "You
loved her."

"Yes, I did. I can't believe all this…business you're telling
me," she said vehemently.

"When you already know she turned her back on her own
grandson, Daniel?"

Cecile stumbled into a chair, burying her face in her hands.
"Who told you? I can't believe Granddad spoke of it."

"He didn't, but whoever told me had no love or even liking
for your grandmother. And wasn't that the action of a ruthless,
heartless woman, Cecile?" He kept up the challenge. "Turning
the penniless, pregnant mother of her own grandchild out of
the house with nowhere else to go to."

"She gave her money," Cecile said, deeply distressed. "At
least she did that. She wasn't a bad woman. Bad things happened around her. I know that what my grandmother did to
Daniel and his mother was unforgivable, but I believe she paid
for it. Guilt gnawed away at her health, her strength and her
mind. There was such an air of desolation about her at different
times, especially in those final days. Even *you* would have felt
sorry for her. Now you want to heap *more* sins on her head?"

"It's the role I was handed, Cecile. The badness arose out of
your grandmother's obsessive love of her son. You're the psychologist. You would have read widely on such things. Your
grandmother wasn't getting the love and attention she craved
from her husband, so she moved on to the son. You can relate

to controlling parents. Forgive me, but you must have discovered that in your own mother. Your grandmother carried her obsessive love to extremes. She wanted to be in control at all stages of her son's life. He certainly wasn't going to be allowed to further his relationship with a housemaid. A suitable young woman had already been picked out for him. Doesn't it all sound familiar?"

"Controlling parents are common," she said bleakly. "You haven't been free of parental conflicts. They must have been forced on you from childhood."

"Never *forced,*" he said angrily. "I saw with my own eyes how the women of my family suffered. I had to listen helplessly while my mother cried."

"So you lived with a lot of unhappiness and a lot of rage. You lost your father at a significant stage of your development. Not only that, you lost your mother in a sense when she married another man. There must have been a lot of conflict there."

"My stepfather is a good man," he answered repressively. "It's not my life we're examining."

"Yet it explains this drive for revenge. Great stress was put on you, Rolfe. Stress that no child or adolescent should have to bear. I can't believe you didn't clash with your stepfather in the early days, though I accept your saying he's a good man. I expect your mother talked about the past to you from time to time. The past was never allowed to die."

"Especially as it's true the past never does die."

"So your goal has always been revenge? It must be very painful, then, to have that goal dashed."

"Who says it is?" He gave a harsh laugh.

Cecile found herself wringing her hands. "It couldn't have been as you've said. You didn't know my grandmother."

"From all accounts she ignored her daughter, your mother."

Cecile couldn't return his searing gaze. "You're making it sound worse than it was."

His gaze was unwavering. "You weren't there."

"Neither were *you!*" she shouted, losing all control. She loved this man, yes, *loved* him. Betrayal and all. She would have given herself to him in a minute, offered up her heart and her mind and her body, but every step he had taken was carefully planned to bring her down. He meant to use her, then reject her. Revulsion for her own colossal stupidity, her *weakness,* made her rush to the door where she paused, her back to it. "There's no point in talking about this anymore. I have no intention of letting my grandfather see the letter. I love him too much, though I haven't the slightest doubt Stuart will do as much damage as he can."

"Then shouldn't you tell your grandfather even if it's only to stop Carlson?" Rolfe suggested harshly, moving toward her as though she were a magnet. "I'm sure he could. A word in someone's ear should do it. The senior partner in Carlson's law firm. One would have to be a fool to cross Joel Moreland."

"You're admitting you're exactly that, a fool?" A nonviolent person—violence shocked her—Cecile found herself wanting to push him hard, to pound him, to hurt him as he was hurting her. Naked hostility made her eyes blaze like diamonds. "Worse, you're a—"

She got no further.

Rolfe snapped. He hauled her into his arms, the fire of aggression crackling along his veins. It was impossible to have her so near to him yet so far away. She struggled wildly, but no woman was a match for his strength. She was unable to prevent his mouth coming down crushingly on hers.

Cecile couldn't draw breath. Her blood was seething. It was brutal. It was devastating. It was deranged, because at his first touch, she longed for it. Yes, longed for it. She couldn't get enough of him. Nor he of her. She had the sense of being caught up in a great electrical storm. Energy was sizzling all around them, coming off his body, galvanizing her. The sheer force of the sexual attraction swept her off her feet. She could only follow where he led. He was muttering something into her open mouth—she didn't know what, English, Spanish—but she knew what it meant. He *wanted* her. Whatever his initial scheme had been, he was hoist by his own petard. That gave her a sick satisfaction.

"I hate you," she muttered desperately, as they wrestled and weaved across the room. She was shocked by the sound of her own voice. The weight of passion in it.

"Don't say that." Rolfe tried to subdue her without hurting her. "You have to try to understand."

"Well, I can't!"

"*Won't!* Won't is more like it. You're a coward."

"You should talk!" She was frantic as his hand moved to her breast. He cupped it with his hand, a strangely adoring gesture that further incited her passion.

"You're so beautiful," he groaned, "even when you're fiercely hating me."

They were moving, half stumbling, half staggering toward the master bedroom, the two of them breathing as heavily as though they were involved in a marathon. The tears were spilling down her cheeks. "What are you going to do, Rolfe? Rape me?"

Instantly he backed off, his handsome features drawn so incredibly taut for an instant his face looked like a dark golden mask. "No, no, *never.* Just stay with me a while." He was begging, resting his head against hers in a way that conveyed to her how genuinely desperate he was. No way could she mistake those feelings. They were her own.

She could feel herself melting, her limbs giving way. She could despise herself later, but for now her driving needs were too powerful to subdue. She wanted him with an urgency that could not be denied. If this were the only time she was going to experience sex on the scale of grand opera, she was prepared to do it. She didn't love him any longer, she told herself. She *didn't,* yet he pulled her like the moon pulls the tides.

Her hands were fumbling at the buttons of his shirt. She loved the smell of him, the clean male fragrance of his skin that always lingered in her nostrils. Physically he was perfect to her. She slipped her hand inside his shirt, letting her fingers range over the width of his chest, her nails digging into the golden bronze mat of hair.

"I can't stop now. You know I can't!" His mouth slid across her face, wet with tears.

"All this will stop tomorrow," she warned, doing what she had never done before, or even imagined doing—tearing at a man's clothes. "I'm not worried. It's *safe*. You can't trap me that way."

Now they were inside his bedroom and she was pulling off her beautiful white silk dress, throwing it so wildly it was a wonder it landed over a chair and not on the floor. Her sandals came next. She was straightening to start on her slip, only he stood her back against the wall, lifting her arms high above her head.

"You're as frantic as I am, aren't you? Go on, *say* it," he mocked her, leaning over her, his body pressing into her thighs, drawing the tip of his tongue across her mouth.

"I'm saying nothing," she gritted, though the excited color had risen to her face, making her beauty dazzling.

His tongue was against her teeth, determined to gain entry. "Really?" His voice was a low growl in his chest.

Now he was kissing her without restraint. Fierce and fiery. As though she had given him permission to do with her whatever he wanted. She could hear her half-stifled moans. Her slip came off, her bra, her panties. Sunlight was filtering into the room through the blinds, turning her skin radiant.

"You're exquisite!" he muttered. "And, God, how I want you!" His arms closed around her, then he lifted her without effort and threw her trembling and wildly aroused onto the bed.

"The quilt is turned back!" she said furiously. She kicked at the thick folds at the end of the bed. "Did you have it all planned?"

"I don't think there's a moment that I haven't had it all planned." He turned back to her, stripped naked.

The splendor of his body gave her such enormous illicit pleasure she could do nothing else but reach out to him with hands that were a blend of pleading and intense longing. It was no invitation. Only a painful mime of a woman's ultimate surrender.

"This is *all* there is, remember!" She repeated her warning, acknowledging her own surrender, but determined to salvage something of her pride. "No follow-ups, no tomorrow."

He didn't answer but his expression was eloquent of high scorn. He swooped onto the bed beside her, half poised above her, drinking her in with dark eyes that sparkled with gold chips. Then he began to make love to her with his masterly hands, neglecting no part of her body, until her heart was fluttering in her throat.

She could think of nothing. Her mind went blank as every cell in her body sparked into vibrant life. There was only this mind-blowing sensation. Sensation she never wanted to escape. She felt so ecstatic she was impelled to lift an arm to draw his marvelous mouth down to hers. She was thirsting for it as a woman lost in the desert thirsts for flowing water.

At last!

He might take her for his pleasure. He might use it against her, even blackmail her into going to bed with him again. He might do all of those things, but she could never say she hadn't been party to it. She wanted him, she realized, as much as she wanted life itself.

CHAPTER TWELVE

QUITE UNEXPECTEDLY CECILE had reason for cutting short her holiday with her grandfather and thus putting herself beyond Rolfe's orbit. She was in pain and unsure of her ability to withstand him. Maybe at some time in the future she could confront the issues between them but for now so volatile were her moods she knew she couldn't discuss anything with him without swiftly veering into anger. He had *deceived* her. On the face of it he had *used* her. She badly needed time away from him to work out where she was going with her life. Her mother's phone call gave her the excuse to pack up and go home.

Justine rang that very evening, sounding so unlike herself, so nearly hysterical, for a moment Cecile doubted it *was* Justine on the other end of the line.

"What is it, Mother? Just tell me." She had immediately jumped to the conclusion that Stuart, out of spite, had gone to Justine with his report. Not that it would do anyone any good; nor did she think it could make her mother sound so out of control.

"I need you, that's all!" Justine cried. "I can't go into it now. I want you to come home immediately. You've spent enough time with Daddy. I am your mother, after all."

"Well, of course I'll come!" Cecile felt panicked fearing her mother might have discovered she was ill. The frightening prospect of breast cancer came to mind. Her mother sounded desperate enough. "I'll speak to Granddad now. His pilot will fly me back to Melbourne."

Which was what happened. Her grandfather exacted a promise from Cecile before she left to ring back and let him know what Justine's problem was. "Such a secretive girl, Justine," he said, also worried his daughter may have received bad news regarding her health.

When Cecile did finally arrive at her parents' palatial home, the house where she had grown up, the maid let her in. She found her mother upstairs in the master bedroom frantically pulling her father's expensive suits off the hangers in the dressing room and flinging them all round the place with furious abandon. Justine's tall slim body was encased in a satin robe, though it was midafternoon. Her eyes were wild and her luxuriant mane of hair, always so meticulously groomed, was a tangled mess. She wore no makeup either, and Cecile had rarely seen her mother without it, even first thing in the morning.

"Mum, what in the world is happening?" Cecile was so shocked she dropped the more formal "Mother" Justine had long insisted was preferable to plain Mum.

"Your bloody father is leaving me, that's what!" Justine shouted, her actions growing wilder and wilder by the minute. "Can you believe it? Nearly thirty bloody years together and the bastard is leaving me for another woman."

"Oh, my goodness!" Cecile sank like a stone onto a pile of her father's clothes that were scattered all over the bed, too shocked to shift them. Whatever scenario she had imagined on the flight home, it was never *this!* Her parents' marriage vows—and she supposed the prenuptial agreement—were set in stone.

"Of course he's had his women," Justine said in a voice filled with the greatest contempt and anger. "He's *always* had his women—and don't try to tell me you didn't know about it," she rounded on Cecile as though Cecile had long been her father's coconspirator. "Howard and I had an understanding—as long as he was discreet. I've never been a great one for sex. Why is sex so bloody all-consuming?" she ranted. "I always found it bloody messy!" She shuddered fastidiously. "But it was understood we would always remain married. Now he tells me he truly loves some bitch of a woman who has worked for him for years."

Cecile released a pent-up breath through her nose. Her mother *never* swore, but she was giving "bloody" a serious beating. Her mind immediately began to range over any number of attractive women who worked for Moreland Mining. It could be any one of them. Married or not. Her father was only in his mid-fifties, a handsome vigorous, *wealthy* man. In other words, a prize. Would his job still be secure? She doubted it. He could and would be voted out if her mother had anything to do with it. She had the sick certainty her mother would become extremely vengeful now that she knew herself a wife scorned.

"You're not going to believe this," Justine was saying, her body visibly shaking with rage. She picked up a large pair of scissors and hacked through a dozen or more beautiful silk ties.

"Must you do that, Mum?" Cecile implored, upset at such senseless destruction.

"Yes, I must!" Justine started on some long winter scarves. "I bought the bloody things anyway."

"I'm so sorry, Mum." Cecile was tempted to go to her mother and hug her, but she knew her mother disliked physical contact. "I know this is very very painful for you."

"You bet your bloody life it is!" Justine said, slaughtering the sleeves of a dress shirt. "How can I be expected to cope with public humiliation? I have a position in society. Now there's you and your father and your broken promises. Two of a kind, it seems."

"How very unfair," Cecile lamented, unable to bring herself to a more angry response. "You've been speaking to Stuart?"

"I gave him a hearing," Justine said. "I don't have to justify myself to you or anyone. Stuart mightn't be perfect, but he would have made you a faithful husband."

"You don't know that, Mum." Cecile felt too miserable to argue. "It was a painful decision breaking my engagement. I should have done it a lot sooner. This woman we're talking about—she's young, around my age?" Cecile thought that would be the case. It usually was. Men in a desperate bid to recapture lost youth.

"She's *my* bloody age." Justine gave a gut-churning screech, seemingly more affronted a *mature* woman could steal her husband rather than some blond bimbo. "He says he loves her. Love?" she cried, tugging a pair of trousers across the carpet. "What does that mean?"

"Sorry, I don't know, either," Cecile said forlornly.

"Bugger you! You had a good man and you sent him packing. I thought what I did for your bloody father all these long years was love. I've fussed over him like he was a bloody teenager. I even laid out his bloody clothes. You know that. I keep a marvelous house. I'm a leading hostess in this town. My garden is admired by everyone. I always look impeccable. It didn't mean a thing! I'm Joel Moreland's *daughter,* dammit! That's why he married me. Don't stare at me saucer-eyed. He married me because I was Joel Moreland's daughter. It wasn't any silly bloody love match. It was for the long haul. Compatibility, companionship, moving in the same circles, having the same goals. Forget this idiotic love at first sight business. That's over before it's begun," she snorted, hacking the trousers above the knee.

"Dad wanted a son, Mum. More children," Cecile pointed out just for the record. "You wouldn't give them to him."

Justine's scissors shut with a snap. "What are you talking about?" She stared at Cecile with a stab of near hatred.

"Don't let's have any more deceptions, Mum." Cecile, her own emotions raw, made a stand. "There was no reason why you couldn't have had more children. You just didn't want them. You've been living a myth all these years. I would have loved a sister or a brother, preferably both. Have you ever thought of that?"

Justine strode over to the bed looking like Lady Macbeth about to plunge in the dagger. "Who told you?" she demanded, attempting to drag more clothes onto the floor. "Don't bother to answer. It was Bea, wasn't it? She never could keep her mouth shut, the wicked old bag."

A small part of Cecile knew her mother could be dangerous, but her face stayed composed. "She's kept it shut all these years. What does it matter *who* told me, Mum? You made a very big mistake there. Dad is a virile, handsome man."

"He's bloody well past middle age."

"He doesn't look it or act it."

"Good one, good one!" Justine yelled, attacking with relish a Ralph Lauren polo shirt that had obviously never been worn. The price tag was still attached.

"Think about it, Mum." Cecile had second thoughts about trying to take the tailoring scissors from her mother. "You denied him more children and you denied him a full sex life by your own admission. Didn't you see that was destructive to your marriage? Didn't you see it was the reason he went elsewhere?"

"Reason?" Justine spat out the word, tossing back her thick tangled hair. "Whose bloody side are you on, anyway? Anyone would think I was a terrible person, instead of a splendid wife and mother."

"I'm not on any side, Mum," Cecile said quietly. "I love you both. But I can't help seeing things from Dad's point of view. Is there no possibility of a reconciliation?"

Justine's face went a life-threatening red. "You can't think I want the bastard back, can you?" she asked with incredulous outrage. "He's betrayed me once too often."

You mean he's actually found someone to love, Cecile thought, but didn't have the courage to say. Not with her mother wielding a lethal pair of scissors. "I'm so terribly sorry, Mum.

Sorry for your pain. But you must see you allowed this whole situation to arise."

Justine's face went from a hectic red to chalk-white. "I'll never forgive you for that, Cecile," she breathed hoarsely.

"Oh Mum, *please!*" Cecile took her chances. She jumped up from the bed and crossing to her mother, tried to put her arms around her, but Justine, a strong woman at any time, in a manic phase, tossed her off easily.

"I've given you everything you ever wanted, Cecile. The best of everything! You've never been exposed for a minute to the harsher aspects of life."

"That's not true!" Cecile protested. "In my job I see and hear some of the most reprehensible, most shameful, things in life."

"Well, whose fault is that?" Justine pressed on. "You didn't have to do a bloody thing, as I've told you many a time. You could have helped me with my charity work. The thing is, Cecile, you've been overprotected all your life. I spoilt you terribly."

It simply wasn't true. "No, you didn't, Mother," Cecile said, shaking her head. "I tried as hard as I knew how to please you. I excelled at everything because I knew there was no other way. Yet you continued to bully me mercilessly. When I think about it, you practically hounded me into getting engaged to Stuart, the rattlesnake."

"Stop it!" Justine thundered. "It was *time* you got engaged. You could still finish up an old maid. You're a frail creature under that beautiful face. A natural-born victim. You might be clever, but you've got no common sense at all and no good instincts. Stuart told me all about that bloody impostor you've got yourself in deep with."

"Deep as the *Titanic,*" Cecile admitted sadly.

"No good will come of it, mark my words!" Scowling darkly, Justine shook the scissors. "And I thought like a fool I had your promise to stay away from him. Ah, well! You're going to find out the hard way. Stuart was naturally reluctant to come right out with it, but I can read between the lines. You're no more interested in sex than I am."

Cecile laughed, though there was no humor in it. "Put it this way—sex with *Stuart* wasn't all that interesting," she said dryly, having experienced the greatest sex of her life but not about to tell her mother.

Justine narrowed her eyes. "So it's this Raul, Rolfe, whatever the hell his real name is. I just hope you haven't spread your legs for him."

Cecile flinched. "That's my business, Mother," she said, thinking her mother could be as vulgar as the best of them.

"The only thing that surprises me is he's not married."

"God knows how he missed out!" Cecile gave a wry sigh. She looked at her mother, who she believed, deep in her heart, loved her. "Have you forgotten so quickly how he saved me from certain injury, possibly death?"

Justine's smile was terrible to see. "Oh, he's brave enough, I grant you that. A marvelous-looking man if you want to be seduced, but from what Stuart tells me, he's a con man. It's written all over him. He set the whole thing up. Meeting Daddy, then you. He knew he was bound to get you to fall in love with him. Your head has always been in the clouds. He broke every rule of decency, lying to Daddy—"

"He didn't actually lie, did he?" Cecile found herself defending Rolfe, even though her heart was broken. "He is who he said he was. Maybe Raul is actually Rolfe, but his stepfather legally adopted him."

"That much might be true, but the rest is all deception," Justine said with lofty disdain.

"What about the deception in *this* family?" Cecile countered sharply. "According to Rolfe, his family suffered terribly and the person who made absolutely sure they suffered was Nan. Even now I can't believe it."

Justine looked poleaxed. "What in the world are you talking about?"

Was it possible her mother knew no more than she did? "Didn't Stuart hand over a copy of his report?" Cecile asked. "It doesn't tell the whole story, according to Rolfe, but he claims that Nan used all the Moreland clout to ruin Rolfe's grandfather and drive the family off their land."

"Whatever for? I read no report." Justine frowned ferociously, resuming her destruction of a charcoal-gray cardigan. "I don't want to hear all this. It's ancient history, anyway. Stuart told me Raul Montalvan is really Rolfe Chandler. His father, from all accounts, was a nobody who got himself killed playing polo over in Argentina where he presumably went to get a job and make some money. His mother's brother was the young hoodlum who was responsible for the death of my brother—*your* uncle I might point out. This Rolfe, this con man, came back to Australia for the grand hustle. He's in the polo game, isn't he? He breeds ponies. He thoroughly researched his mark. Can't you see that? Once he met you, he counted on your falling into his arms. You have, haven't you, you little fool! You couldn't possibly handle a man like that."

"Maybe not," Cecile admitted, picking up her handbag. "You haven't had a lot of success, either. I was a *fool* to come here, Mother, a fool to try to support you. You turn people away. This is a beautiful big house—you have done a great deal for me and Dad—for which I thank you. You are a wonderful hostess, a stunning-looking woman, but you're cheerless and so is this house. I don't wonder Dad wants to get out from under. I don't wonder he wants to know some happiness in the years ahead. And it's disgusting what you're doing." She indicated with a thrust of her chin the piles of ruined clothing that lay on the carpet. "There's no dignity to it. I think you should stop."

"Stop!" Justine's voice rose to glass-breaking point. She rushed forward, robe flying like wings, and before Cecile knew it was coming, struck her daughter across the face. "How dare you!"

Cecile staggered, slowly righted herself, her distress tinged with relief her mother had dropped the scissors. She couldn't imagine at this point how they would ever make their way back. "But I *do* dare, Mother," she said quietly. "I am sorry for you. I'm very sorry for you, but it's impossible for me to stay any longer. You're not—what was it?—*frail* like me. You're one tough lady. I've no doubt you'll get through this, then make up another cover story. You're good at that. You don't love Dad, anyway. At the risk of another smack in the face, I suggest you don't know *how* to love, Mother. Now, I don't think there's anything more I can do for you, so I may as well be on my way. I'll see myself out."

"You do that!" Justine shouted after her daughter. "You and your father, both of you traitors. *Ingrates!* You might have Daddy wrapped around your little finger, but from this day forth in my book you're disinherited."

"Probably a good idea," Cecile answered coolly from the doorway. "Use some of the money to see a good psychiatrist, Mother. You've got lots of problems. It's about time you confronted them."

For days after Cecile returned to Melbourne, Rolfe battled his demons. It was an unexpected twist for someone to make *him* feel really bad, but she had succeeded, a *Moreland*. Now he was far too involved with Cecile not to put away all thoughts of revenge. His dark quest had obsessed him for too long. After that afternoon when they had made such sublime love he had discarded all his old hatreds like so much broken furniture held for too long in an attic. History hadn't been kind to his family. It hadn't been kind to the Morelands, either. He had to look to the future.

There *was* no future without Cecile. No future that offered such glorious promise. But what could he offer her? Well, he had worked hard and put away enough. Wealth didn't automatically bring happiness, anyway. More often, it was the reverse.

Finally he made up his mind what he should do. He would

go to Joel Moreland and make a clean breast of everything: his background, his dark intentions, his once all-consuming quest for revenge. He would tell Joel Moreland what he had managed to find out. Joel Moreland, because of his grandson Daniel's sad story, already knew what his late wife, Frances, had been capable of. He had to lay it all on the line. Make a full confession. He had hated deceiving Joel, anyway. He would tell Joel everything save his love for Cecile. That was a secret he intended to hold close to his heart.

She had gone away without a word to him, no parting message. He knew she was shocked at his deception. He knew she no longer trusted him, and trust was very important to her. It would be a long road back to regain her confidence. But what they had shared that tumultuous afternoon, the glory of it, continued to warm him, heart and soul. It gave him the courage to confront the Man with the Midas Touch.

When he arrived at the Moreland mansion, the house manager, a pleasant, competent man in his late fifties, showed him into the garden room at the rear of the house. A large collection of tropical orchids was in spectacular bloom, many he was familiar with from his mother's extensive collection. Great luxuriant ferns suspended in baskets from the huge beams that supported the soaring ceiling drew the eye upward. It was a beautiful room. Joel was sitting at a large circular glass-topped table surrounded by papers, enjoying a cup of tea, but he rose and held out his hand.

"Raul, how nice you've come to keep me company."

The welcoming smile made Rolfe feel even more sick at heart. How long would the smiles last? "How are you, sir?" His nerves on edge, he slipped back into formal address.

"Missing my beautiful Cecile." Joel sighed. "Apart from that, I feel like a million bucks. And you, Raul? You look a little tense. Sit down, sit down. Would you like tea, coffee, a cold drink?"

"Nothing, thank you, sir."

"You're very formal today." The remarkable eyes scanned him. Eyes that took in everything about a person.

"I hold you in the greatest respect," Rolfe answered gravely.

"So what's on your mind?" Joel asked. "You've obviously got a problem. I suspect you're missing Cecile, too?"

Rolfe's face went taut. "I doubt she's missing me."

"Oh? I thought you two were madly in love?"

Rolfe's expression registered his shock. "I beg your pardon, sir?"

"I've got eyes, my boy!" Joel scoffed. "You must remember I'm Cecile's granddad. I know every expression that crosses her face, every little inflection in her voice. She's the closest person in the world to me. Closer than my daughter, who has never forgiven me for neglecting her with my absence. Closer even than my grandson, Daniel, so new to me. But I love all three. So you could say Cecile is an open book to me."

"Then you must have sensed she's finished with me now?" Rolfe asked somewhat grimly.

"Well, I knew something was wrong," Joel acknowledged. "There was the trauma of the broken engagement, but then there has been another major concern. You'll find out soon enough. My daughter, Justine, and her husband are splitting up after thirty years of marriage. I understood that was the reason Cecile hurried off home."

"I never knew," Rolfe confessed, feeling more and more rejected. "I had thought Cecile's parents' marriage was rock solid."

"Well, it might have appeared to be. It was certainly no battlefield, but sadly at the end of the day it has no real meaning. In many ways Justine and Howard led isolated lives. Howard devoted himself to the business. I have nothing but praise for him in that regard. My daughter devoted her life to being the perfect wife, and in many respects she was. But one reaches a stage in life when all the old ambitions take a back seat. People as they age begin to think very seriously about the quality of their emotional life. Making money, keeping it intact is no longer as important as it once was. I would have traded everything in the blink of an eye for the life of my son. That was not to be, but I have Daniel, for which I daily thank God. My daughter Justine is understandably devastated, but I'm confident she'll slam down a few barriers and regroup. She has never suffered from loneliness you see, or introspection."

"So it was Cecile's father who wanted to leave?" Rolfe remembered Howard Moreland as being an uncommonly attractive and charming man.

"Apparently. There's another woman, of course. There always is. But this woman—it's not a case of Howard leaving my daughter for a much younger woman—must be able to make my son-in-law happy. Cecile flew home to be with her mother, but that wasn't overly successful, she tells me. Justine is quite capable of doing Howard a lot of harm. I'll get drawn into it fairly soon. So will you."

Rolfe gazed unseeingly around the beautiful plant-filled room. "Not when you hear what I have to say. There are things about me, Joel, you don't know."

"Why don't you go ahead and tell me," Moreland invited briskly, then held up a staying hand. "I think I will get a fresh pot of tea made and some coffee, maybe a few sandwiches?" he suggested. "You look like you need a bit of bucking up. I'm happy you've come to me with your problems, Raul. I'll help you in any way I can."

Would he be happy afterward? Rolfe thought. Having made his decision, he had no option but to launch the missiles that would shatter Joel Moreland's good opinion of him. He suddenly realized that the man's opinion mattered a great deal.

Rolfe began to speak in a low measured tone. He started from when he first arrived in the Territory. He didn't attempt to tone down his reason for returning to the place of his birth. He had meant to cause the Morelands pain....

He was not interrupted. No matter what the revelation, Joel Moreland never said a word. He waited until Rolfe finished speaking before sitting back in his chair, removing his glasses and rubbing the bridge of his nose.

"Revenge never works, Rolfe, does it?" he said finally, in a quiet musing tone. "Rolfe suits you better than Raul, by the way. Hate is corrosive. It eats away at the soul. I've firsthand experience of that—not so much myself, hate doesn't seem to be part of my nature—but I've seen it become an integral part of the lives of so many others. First of all I must tell you not all of this comes as a surprise."

Rolfe pulled upright in his chair. "I should have known."

"Yes, you should," Joel agreed. "I had no intention whatever of doing any check on you if that's what you're thinking. I liked you, that's all there was to it. I took to you on sight. My instincts have never let me down. I could see Ceci was attracted to you. But I have many contacts in the international world of polo. You must realize that."

"Of course." Rolfe had allowed for the fact Joel Moreland might check on him. He had taken the chance.

"I sell many of my polo ponies overseas, including Argentina," Joel explained. "However, it was sheer chance that drew me into conversation with a South American buyer, a Brazilian actually, who knows your stepfather, and has in the past done business with him. I had accepted you were who you said you were—Raul Montalvan. I mentioned your name in passing. When this man told me something of your story, which he'd had from your stepfather, my heart went out to you. I heard how your father was killed, how your mother was left virtually a penniless young widow in a strange country with a young son to rear. How she later married Ramon Montalvan, an excellent man. I received quite a shock when I further learned your mother was an Australian, as was her late husband and of course, you. I hadn't been expecting that at all. After that, I made my own inquiries. I felt in my bones—some presentiment, some fragment of memory—there was a connection. Possibly it was your father's name. I vaguely remembered him as being a promising polo player. It was easy to fill in the rest."

"Dear God!" Rolfe leaned forward and buried his face in his hands. How long had Joel known? How could he still smile?

"My son's death overwhelmed me," Joel said. "You must understand that. You, too, know all about grief. I was desolate. For a time all the life drained out of me. My success, my position in life, meant nothing, though I was forced to keep going. So many people, towns, depended on me for their livelihood. I know now my wife, Frances, was the cause of great unhappiness, great hurt and great wrong. I should have been more aware of what was going on, so I, too, bear the burden of guilt. I can only plead I was adrift in a nightmare and ask for forgiveness. I had such grand plans for Jared. Plans that differed from my wife's. One of her pet objectives was to marry him off to some young woman suitable in her eyes and one I imagine Frances thought she could control. Instead all my son got was a marble headstone. I have arranged that fresh flowers be laid on his grave every day that I live."

"My uncle Benjie didn't get that," Rolfe pointed out quietly. "When did you first know?" He looked into Joel Moreland's eyes. "You gave no sign. You never told Cecile, obviously."

"I think I'm a good judge of men, Rolfe. I held my tongue, waiting to see what you would do. I've gone further. It's something I felt I should do. I've bought back your grandfather's property. It's very run-down, but it's yours to do whatever you like with. Work it, put a manager on it. I don't imagine you want to sell it."

Rolfe looked back in a daze. "But surely..." He could get no further, spearing his hand into his hair in distraction. Whatever he'd expected of today's traumatic encounter it wasn't this.

"I've made other investigations into my son's death—far too late—though nothing will bring Jared back or your uncle Benjamin. It seems appalling to me to malign my poor Frances—

I know she passed many many unhappy years—but she held to denying her own grandson until she was on her deathbed. She carried the secret of how she had imperiled your family to her grave. I ask you to forgive her. To forgive me. On the level of family, Frances was obsessive to a cautionary degree. She adored Jared. That he fell in love with one of our little housemaids and got her pregnant goaded Frances beyond endurance. Then Jared was killed. I knew my son. I'm absolutely certain he had no idea Johanna was carrying his child. If he had, he would have married her and I would have stood beside them both. Your family had the great misfortune to face a bereaved mother's wrath. It falls on me, Rolfe, all these many years later, to make retribution. I ought to have known. With Johanna and my son, I was too involved with my business affairs to notice a romance going on right under my nose. When Jared was killed I was like a man in a coma. I functioned on one level but not on another. That's not much of a defense, I know."

"I think it is, sir." Rolfe's voice was both gentle and understanding.

"You've suffered greatly, haven't you, Rolfe?" Joel asked, looking into the younger man's dark eyes.

Rolfe shrugged off the many blighted areas of his life. Something so far he had been totally unable to do. "Not in any material sense," he said. "My stepfather, Ramon, is a generous, good-hearted man. He adores my mother and because of her he tried very hard with me. Gradually I settled down, though for a long time I was pretty wild. For the last five years I've been in charge of the breeding program of our polo ponies and their training, as you now know. Horses are my passion. I have a special way with them. Ramon thought so, too."

"Horses are my passion, as well," Joel confirmed. "I understand from my Brazilian friend, you were gaining quite a reputation. I've been told your stepfather is particularly proud of your ability to turn out the finest polo ponies. I've checked the sales for the Montalvan estancia. Top prices."

For the first time Rolfe smiled. "It's a great satisfaction to my family—my Argentinian family—I've been so successful, but it wouldn't have happened without my stepfather. It was Ramon who gave me the opportunity and authority over others much longer in the business. If he hadn't, perhaps I would be dead on the polo field like my father from a fatal kick in the head."

Joel visibly shuddered. "Don't say that, Rolfe!" he implored. "Has what I've said given you any peace at all?"

Rolfe looked away, much moved. "I thought you'd brand me an impostor, a fortune hunter, someone utterly untrustworthy."

"Well, there are such men about," Joel said dryly, "but I was and am still prepared to put my trust in you." He put out his hand.

Rolfe took it. "I can never thank you enough for the kindness and understanding of your response. It means a great deal to me. I know I've lost and deserve to lose Cecile's trust. In her beautiful eyes I'm a badly flawed man."

"Then you'll have to work to persuade her otherwise, won't you?" Joel told him bracingly. "I can say it now, but I wasn't happy about her marrying Stuart Carlson. I didn't think I had the right to interfere. Although before you appeared on the scene, I was getting around to it. My daughter Justine is a very strong-minded woman like her mother before her. She has always tried to deny Cecile complete freedom of action. Stuart was *Justine's* choice."

"Carlson had his own dossier compiled on me." Rolfe brought it out into the open.

"Did he now!" Joel whistled softly. "I think I'll have to persuade him to burn it. Not that there could be anything in it to actually discredit you in any way, which obviously was what he hoped. Cecile knows about this?"

Rolfe nodded. "He sent it to her. She thinks the worst of me."

"He sent it to her, did he?" Joel Moreland's voice filled with contempt. "Tells you what sort of man he is. Give Cecile a little time," he advised. "My granddaughter is not the sort of woman

who likes to think the worst of anyone. She has a compassionate heart. That's why she's so successful with her little patients.
She's compassionate and she's clever. She comes up with breakthrough ideas. She's very highly regarded by her peers. She has
the gift of healing."

"I don't doubt that for a moment," Rolfe said with deep fer-
vor. "She healed me."

It was early afternoon some three weeks later. Cecile was sitting at her desk, looking at Ellie Wheeler's drawings. Cecile,
who thought she was beyond being shocked, was brought to
the edge of actual nausea. Since returning to her practice, she
had made special time for Ellie, fitting her into her very busy
schedule to the extent she was starting earlier and finishing
late with many a lunch break missed. But what did that matter? Ellie was in need of intensive therapy. Ellie's mother had
brought in the girl originally because Ellie's latest school had
insisted on Ellie's getting counseling. There would have been
no counseling otherwise, Cecile knew. But as hard as she tried,
she hadn't been able to make the breakthrough she was seeking, although they were doing a lot better now that Cecile had
confined Mrs. Wheeler to the waiting room. Mrs. Wheeler had
been adamant she be allowed in, but Cecile had quietly said
no. Ellie was a very difficult child, physically abusive to her
mother, to her schoolmates and of recent times to her younger
brother. Both parents—Cecile had met the father once—to all
appearances were good caring people, patient and understanding. But they were almost at the end of their tether, now that
Ellie had begun attacking her brother. Ellie was under a two-
week suspension from school—her previous school had asked
for her to be removed—because she had spat at and kicked the
male sports master when he attempted to help her tie up her
shoelaces. Ellie had been deliberately dawdling, holding up the
class. "A small fury!" was the way the teacher described her
during the attack. "She even punched me!"

Ellie, despite her angelic appearance, beautiful blond hair and big blue eyes, acted as much like a little devil. Cecile had tested her for a number of personality disorders, as well as ADD and autism. Her behavior didn't match any of those. Previously Ellie had been considered of exceptional intelligence—her father was a doctor, her mother a music teacher—but at her new school Ellie had gained the reputation for not only being highly disruptive and aggressive, but downright stupid. Many teachers along the way had tried to help her, baffled and challenged by the child. Because of her looks, other children had tried to befriend her, only to be met with bites, scratches and hostile rejection.

"Is she psychotic?" Dr. Peter Wheeler, Ellie's father, had asked in his pleasant cultivated voice, his gray eyes behind dark-framed glasses deeply concerned.

"She wasn't always like this," Marcie Wheeler added, sounding so close to tears her husband had grabbed for her hand.

Ellie wasn't stupid. Far from it. Cecile had divined that from the moment she had met the child. But Ellie was emotionally disturbed. There had to be good reasons for why the child was acting so badly. Cecile knew there was a lot going on behind the either perfectly blank or wildly mutinous little face. Just those two expressions. With her mother present Ellie was given to extreme temper tantrums that her mother appeared totally unable to control. Now that Cecile was working with the child alone, Ellie's behavior had settled closer to normal, and the way she swiftly solved puzzles showed an exceptional intelligence at work. She was even allowing Cecile to come close and she was directly meeting Cecile's eyes, something she hadn't done until that very week. Cecile knew she had been under close scrutiny by the child, and thankfully she appeared to have passed whatever tests Ellie had set. To gain the trust of a child was great progress. Cecile had been quietly thrilled.

Now *this!*

Of course she had considered this possibility, but rejected it. Dr. Peter Wheeler had been described on all sides as a good caring man and a fine doctor. He had certainly come across that way. Cecile had focused all her analyzing powers on his mannerisms, expressions, body language and his account of his troubled little daughter's history. Here was a devoted father.

But my God! The reality could not have been more different! And the mind-blowing arrogance of the man allowing counseling to go ahead! Of course the school had insisted on it and Ellie was fast running out of schools, but there was so much to *hide,* so much that didn't bear examination. Yet Peter Wheeler obviously thought he had such control over his child, or Ellie was so much in fear of him—she would have been threatened with punishment should she ever speak the unspeakable—that the whole sordid story would never see the light of day. Her father's power over her was central to her life.

Only, Ellie had broken free! Dr. Wheeler hadn't allowed for Ellie's intelligence and courage. She was a remarkable child whose range of behavioral problems had not as yet progressed beyond the problems of other children Cecile had treated who were not the victims of sexual abuse. Ellie was truly a fighter. Cecile took a shuddering breath, thinking that because of her, because she'd been away, this brave little girl had been left longer in hell. Drawing had long been used as therapy when dealing with emotionally disturbed children. Ellie's drawings to date had been a series of wild interlocking circles always in black and charcoal signifying, to Cecile's mind, that Ellie regarded herself as being in a prison. Some days the strokes suggested barbed wire.

Now *this!*

Ellie had sat quietly while she had been drawing what could only be described as a sexually abused child's cries for help. Sexual abuse was routinely considered early in therapy, but Ellie had been positively brilliant in hiding what had been happening to her and was probably still happening. So much for the slowness or the stupidity! Tears sprang to Cecile's eyes as she took the colored drawings in hand. Here was a child with long curly blond hair, big blue eyes and *no mouth*. Tears splashed from her eyes to the floor. Another showed the same child in bed with a tall figure with huge black wings like a bat looming over her. Another showed the child locked in a forest with a woman—her mother?—running away from her to the extreme edge of the trees.

"Do you see?" Ellie came around the desk to whisper, a terrible sadness seeping out of her eyes. "Do you see what's been happening to me?"

Cecile lifted her head to meet the child's eyes. "Yes, I see, Ellie. I want to tell you you're a very brave girl. I'm proud of you."

"Are you?" Ellie's voice showed a tiny burst of pleasure. "I wanted to tell Mummy, but I knew she wouldn't listen. She's afraid to say anything to Daddy. We all have to be very careful around him, even Josh. He loves Josh. He doesn't love me. He tells me he loves me, but he's killing me. He wants to kill me."

Cecile didn't admonish the child. She didn't murmur, "That's a terrible thing to say about your father, Ellie." She remained silent, listening for what else Ellie would say.

There was more. A lot more, utterly conclusive as far as Cecile was concerned. And it had to stop *today!* For a ten-year-old child to so graphically describe tearing, searing physical pain, the things that were done to her body. The landscape of a man's body. The *weight* of her abuser. It was all being taped. Cecile's gentle voice encouraged the child in telling her appalling tale, without ever leading her. This was Ellie's terrible story. Ellie had to be protected.

But first there were procedures to be followed. Children's Services. She was well acquainted with the people there. One woman in particular, a woman of enormous understanding and sensitivity. Cecile picked up the phone, after telling Ellie she needed to talk to her mother.

"Do I have to stay there?"

"No, dear."

Ellie looked relieved, though there was still profound fear in her eyes. "She won't believe me. She'll tell Daddy."

"You want this to stop, don't you, Ellie?" Cecile asked quietly.

"Oh yes! Will you help me? I don't want to go home. I don't ever want to go to bed. It's not my fault."

"Never!" Cecile shook her head, taking the trusting hand the child held out to her. "You must never ever blame yourself."

"Daddy said he'd kill us all if I told."

Such sickness of the soul! It seemed almost inconceivable Dr. Peter Wheeler, who presented so well, was the father from hell. Cecile would never have guessed such a depth of depravity in the man. She was stunned he was a doctor. And alarmed. Other children could be under threat. "That's not going to happen, Ellie," Cecile said, radiating comfort and quiet authority to the child. "You have *me* to help you. *I* have the support of kind people who devote their lives to helping children like you. It will be safe for you to talk to them and I'll be there. You and your mother *and* Josh are going to get help. I promise."

Only it wasn't that easy. Ellie's mother at first called her child "a lying little monster" and refused to believe what Ellie had said. "She's made it all up. She's not stupid. She's cruel and cunning and a shocking little troublemaker. She's trying to come between me and my husband. Peter's a *doctor!* A man who cares! He's a saint!"

"He'll get the opportunity to prove it, Mrs. Wheeler," Cecile said, keeping all trace of revulsion out of her voice. "Children do lie. They make certain things up. They can even fool experts, but I'm prepared to believe a medical examination will prove Ellie is telling the truth. No child I've ever spoken with, living in the suburbs with a saint for a father, could describe so graphically sexual abuse. Ellie has a great deal of courage. I'm wondering if *you* knew about it and kept quiet?" Cecile, though sickened, gave the woman a chance. "You were too frightened to get help? I understand how that can happen."

Understand but never never condone.

Cecile played back the tape of Ellie's story, while her mother cried convulsively, the bitter tears streaming down her face as she listened and stared at the drawings. "Where is she, my little Ellie?" she asked finally, looking beaten into the ground. "Will she ever forgive me? I'm not a mother at all. I'm a gutless coward who has lived at my husband's mercy, but not anymore! Tell me what to do."

Cecile returned to her apartment that evening feeling utterly drained. Damning evidence of sexual abuse had been found during Ellie's medical examination, conducted by a kindly woman doctor Cecile and her colleagues often called in. Josh had been picked up from school by the police. The family had been taken to a safe house, pending charges being laid. "We'll never be safe," Mrs. Wheeler had murmured fearfully to Cecile at the last moment, her shoulders hunched in strain. Her two children stood quietly a little distance away, hand in hand. "There's *no* safe place."

"You'll be safe if he's in jail," Cecile told her, placing a hand on the woman's shoulder, feeling the rigidity there. "Your husband can't get away with this anymore, Mrs. Wheeler. You have to be strong for your family."

"He was such a sweet man," Marcie Wheeler confided in the voice of the lovesick teenager she once had been. "He was hurt badly in a car accident five years ago. Do you think it was that? Something twisted his mind?" she asked hopefully. Eyes as blue as her daughter's appealed to Cecile. Marcie Wheeler was a very pretty woman.

"I can't help with that, Mrs. Wheeler," Cecile said flatly, shaking her head, "but I *can* help you."

* * *

At home Cecile played back her phone messages, which included one from her father confirming their lunch date for the following week. Soon after her disastrous confrontation with her mother, she had conceded to her father's plea to meet the new woman in his life, Patricia Northam. Patricia had a beach house on a beautiful stretch of the Mornington Peninsula, which Cecile discovered was set in native bushland with a wonderful view of the sea. The two of them were waiting to greet her at the front of the cottage, their arms entwined.

Her father looked ten years younger and an altogether different person. She'd rarely seen him out of his tailored business suits and his expensive smart, casual clothes. But here he wore an ordinary pair of cargo pants, a black cotton T-shirt and canvas trainers on his feet. The woman tucked beneath his arm looked as fragile as a china doll. She had very curly red hair that reached past her shoulders, unlined skin warmly sprinkled with freckles and eyes as blue as the sparkling sea. As casually dressed as Cecile's father, she wore espadrilles on her feet; even with the wedge heels, she was tiny. She couldn't have looked more different from Cecile's mother. Her father had always appeared to admire the "glamour girls," tall, confident women as well-groomed as racehorses, always dressed in the height of fashion—like Justine. Patricia, or "Patty" as he called her, was a big surprise. She was fresh and natural, quite without artifice.

Her father had come forward to give her a hug and kiss her cheek, thanking her a little awkwardly for coming before introducing Patricia. This was accompanied by a loving look Cecile had never seen when he looked at her mother. Cecile had expected the meeting wouldn't be all that easy for any of them, but she found herself warming to Patricia despite her loyalty to her mother.

Cecile learned Patty's invalid mother had died several months back. Patty had been devoted to her, never marrying. Her mother had left her the cottage and their Melbourne apartment.

"She's led a life of service," Howard had told Cecile quietly. "Now I want to look after her. Your mother never needed looking after. She never needed me except as the obligatory husband. She actively discouraged me from playing a larger role with you. But that's all over. I want us to be close, Cecile. You're my daughter, my only child. I never wanted to hurt Justine, but I think you'll find it's mostly her pride that's been stung."

Cecile hadn't had the heart to comment on the hatchet job her mother had done on his clothes and he didn't mention it, either. Her father looked and acted a different man, more *real* than she had ever seen him. He had resigned his position as Moreland Minerals' CEO. "Joel never asked for my resignation," he told her. "Your grandfather knows how long and hard I've worked for the company, but we both agreed that my staying on would be nigh on impossible with your mother on the board. So, I'm taking early retirement. I intend to enjoy what's left of my life, Ceci!"

Cecile had found it hard to blame him.

She moved to her bedroom and quickly changed out of her elegant gray suit, hung it in the closet, then deciding to take a quick shower, walked into the ensuite bathroom. She brushed her teeth first in an effort to get the taste of evil out of her mouth. She wasn't surprised to see her hands were shaking. The whole Ellie episode had upset her tremendously, although Ellie was far from being the only sexually abused child she had treated. Ellie, however, had been very much better at keeping her dark secret padlocked.

Beneath the shower she allowed herself to weep for all the abused children of the world. The tears streamed down her face. Jets of water washed them away. This was her private place for crying. No one had to know about it. Sometimes her job made her very emotional. She knew she had to guard against it or go to pieces, but children like Ellie made that very difficult.

Afterward she rubbed a deliciously scented moisturizer over her face and body, as though the aroma and the massage would help her relax. There was no way she could banish her sadness, but she was feeling a little better. She had done as much as she could do. The authorities had to do the rest. Lack of faith in Marcie Wheeler had crept over her slowly. She had confided this lack of faith to her good friend Susan Bryant at Children's Services. Susan, ten years older and very experienced, wasn't particularly surprised. "Usually the mothers know about the abuse," Susan said, "but they're so emotionally battered themselves they can't bring themselves to do a thing about it. For all we know the good Dr. Wheeler could have been abusing *her,* too. I wouldn't be in the least surprised."

The fact Susan had picked up on Marcie Wheeler's vulnerability made Cecile feel easier. It would be dreadful if Ellie had to be taken from the only parent that was left to look after her.

Dressed in a cool ankle-length caftan, she poured herself a glass of white wine from her refrigerator. She felt incredibly lonely. Something she had never really experienced until she banished Rolfe from her life. He'd opened a door onto a rapturous world for her. He had been *everything* to her, so his deception had left her shaken to her core and accusing herself of every kind of weakness, so much so that when she had first arrived back, she doubted her ability to pick up and go on with her stressful job. She'd refused to take his calls, though she'd played his messages over and over just to hear his voice. He'd begged her to allow him to see her, but her underlying fear was he was still using her and would continue to. He had seen himself as an avenger on her family since his childhood. Powerful obsessions didn't disappear overnight.

If ever!

She had spoken to her grandfather many times. On one occasion he confided he bought back the old Lockhart cattle station, which was very run-down, and deeded it over to Rolfe.

Could that have been one of Rolfe's goals? The loss of his own inheritance had plagued him. He'd told her so.

"Not that it could possibly compensate him for what he and

his family suffered," her grandfather had offered as a reason for his generosity.

Quite simply Raul Montalvan or Rolfe Chandler, whatever he in his heart called himself, had won over the Man with the Midas Touch. No mean feat! It had been a coup on Rolfe's part to go to her grandfather with a full confession. Her grandfather was a decent, highly principled man. He had wanted desperately to make amends for the sins of her grandmother.

And as for her, she had fallen madly in love with him, or at the very least been engulfed by powerful emotions, at their first meeting. Whether it was possible to trust him again she was a long way from deciding.

She was drawn to the kitchen to make herself something to eat—a light pasta with ricotta and prosciutto? She had fresh herbs growing on her balcony—chives, basil, coriander, mint, dill and fiery little chillies—but she couldn't be bothered cooking a sauce. The loud buzz of her security monitor startled her. Who could it be at this hour? She wasn't expecting anyone. Her friends always rang before they called. Maybe it was a mistake, a visitor wanting someone else. It happened.

She checked what she was wearing. Perfectly presentable to go to the door if she had to, in fact, very pretty if a bit on the sheer side.

She walked the few steps to the wall-mounted monitor and saw a messenger wearing a cap with a logo on it. She couldn't read what it was. He was holding a bouquet of flowers so big they obscured his face.

Well, well, life was indeed surprising! "Yes?"

"Delivery for Ms. Moreland."

"Thank you. I'll let you in." She pressed the button to release the security door. Was it possible the flowers were from Rolfe? She couldn't help the involuntary rush of hope, then chided herself not only for the feeling, which clearly betrayed her ambivalence, but for being stupid. He didn't even know where she lived. What an exercise in futility it was trying to clear all thoughts of him from her head. It was becoming more and more difficult, not easier, with the passing of the days and weeks. The flowers could be from a longtime admirer of hers, Adam Dahl, who'd begun ringing her since her breakup with Stuart had become common knowledge. The bouquet looked enormous. Adam always had been one for going over the top. She had already accepted one of his invitations to dinner. No reason why she couldn't. She was a free woman.

No, that was far from true. In her present mood and state she felt she would never be free of Rolfe.

A faint sigh on her lips, Cecile opened the door, startled to see the messenger already there. He must have stepped straight into the lift. She felt a momentary pang of anxiety. Wasn't it too late for a delivery? Although it *was* Friday, late night shopping.

She put out her hand to take the bouquet, but before she had time to think what was happening, the messenger shoved her back forcibly into the entrance hall of her apartment, shutting the door behind him. She gave a tiny shriek of alarm.

"Afraid, are you?" Peter Wheeler snarled, pitching the bouquet violently across the living room where it fell in a scatter of tall, bloodred gladioli and silver wrapping paper.

Through her fear, Cecile managed to think hard. "What are you doing here, Dr. Wheeler?" she demanded, succeeding in her effort to keep her voice from sounding too panicked. "I'm expecting a friend to drop by any minute now."

"Dressed like that?" He ran his eyes over the contours of her body, revealed by the sheer fabric. He showed not the slightest interest in her. Oh, no, this was a man who liked *little* girls! He wasn't wearing his glasses. She suspected now they were mostly for effect. His eyes were cold and hard like dull gray pebbles that gave back no light.

"I assure you he *will* be here," Cecile said with a show of confidence. "If you have any sense at all, you'll go."

"Go? Where do I go?" he asked in furious frustration. "Thanks to you, the police are out looking for me."

"Then shouldn't you be giving yourself up," Cecile retorted. "They *will* find you."

"They'll find you, too," he said, with a peculiar sliver of a smile.

Cecile felt a sickening sensation in the pit of her stomach. "You're threatening me, are you?" Her voice was absolutely steady. "It's not a good time for you to do it. My friend is a lawyer."

"Then the one thing you must not do is warn him," Wheeler said, not taking his eyes off her. "I don't want to punish him. Just you. You've ruined my life. I face jail. I face the loss of Ellie. You wouldn't know, you sanctimonious bitch, but I *love* her." His face twisted in genuine anguish.

Cecile felt bile rise to her throat. "Love?" she exploded, thinking she would be forever haunted by what Ellie had told her. "You mean you've been abusing her for a very long time. You're a sick man, *Doctor* Wheeler. But you couldn't help your-self, could you? You will wind up in prison, though. I wouldn't want to spend any time there, a man like you, a pedophile. A man who's preyed on his own little daughter. The other pris-oners will—"

"Shut your mouth!" Wheeler threw a savage punch, but Ce-cile was too quick for him. Adrenaline pumping, she ducked and picked up a vase, then hurled it as hard as she could—not at Wheeler but at the etched-glass partition in the entrance hall. It broke into great shards with a loud shattering sound. The apartments were pretty soundproof, but someone might hear something and come to investigate.

Cecile was thinking rapidly. Where was her mobile phone? Damn it, it was still in her bedroom, though she had taken it out of her bag. Joyce Walden, a widow in her early seventies, lived in the adjoining unit. Joyce was inclined to be nosy, which would help, though her sliding glass doors to the rear terrace would be shut with the television and the air-conditioning going full blast. She wouldn't want Joyce to be drawn into any danger, but she could shout, "Call the police!" should Joyce take it into her head to knock.

She began to yell, "Help!" at the top of her voice, but Wheeler sprang at her, a big strong man bent on shutting her up.

And then what? Cecile thought. Would he kill her? How had he found out where she lived? Why hadn't he already been picked up by the police?

"You stupid bitch!" His fierce open-handed slap connected just enough to send her sprawling backward. She fell onto a sofa, where he leaned threateningly over her. "Don't try that again or I promise you you'll be sorry."

"Who told you where I lived?" She threw up her chin, determined not to show fear. He'd had enough of that from his wife and poor little Ellie.

"Easy," he sneered. "I followed you to this building weeks ago. You were trouble right from the beginning. Ellie liked you. She's never liked anyone else. Her bloody fool mother actually rang me to tell me to run. Can you beat that?"

"Your *wife* tipped you off?" Cecile thought of Marcie Wheeler with disgust and pity.

"She loves me, don't you know?" he crowed with sickening triumph.

"Then she is indeed a bloody fool," Cecile said with the utmost contempt.

His face turned to granite. "I told you to shut up. You can't, can you? You're the psychologist, trained to keep people talking. But this should do the trick." With that weird smirk on his face, Wheeler withdrew a syringe from the inside pocket of his bomber jacket. Cecile saw it contained a colorless liquid.

Her throat went so dry she had difficulty speaking. "What do you think you're going to do with that?"

"Shut you up of course. For good. Only fair, don't you think? You ruin my life. I finish off yours."

"Before you do, what I want to know is this. Indulge me,

can't you? You have the upper hand. If your wife warned you, why didn't you simply run? Make your getaway. You can still do it. Isn't that more important than killing me? Getting away?" If she *could* keep him talking, humor him in some way, maybe she could make a break for it. He hadn't locked the door to the apartment, only closed it, before moving into the living room.

"You want to see Ellie again, don't you?" She hated using the child's name, but that was the only connection she thought might work. "Can't you tell me how this first happened? I want to hear. I'm used to listening. What destructive impulses drove you? Or were you forced into it? Were you so unhappy with your wife—the sex was so inadequate—you turned to the child? How did you keep your secret from your wife, or did she know? Evil is completely foreign to a moral man. Aren't you a moral man, Dr. Wheeler? Were you the victim of sexual abuse? Please—help me to understand."

He paused, his face twisted as though he really sought to pinpoint the time when his pedophilia began to manifest itself. He was as pale as a ghost and there was a small involuntary twitch on the left side of his mouth.

"It's all right, you can trust me," she said in a calm, quiet voice.

"I didn't feel that way about other children, other little girls," he said, a vein pulsing in his temple. "It was only Ellie. She was so affectionate with me, kissing me and sitting on my knee. You know all about what bloody Freud had to say. Fathers, daughters, mothers, sons. I fell in love with her."

"Didn't that scare you out of your mind?" she asked with no vestige of pity.

"Yes. I *hated* myself, but I couldn't stop it."

"You didn't seek treatment, a way of fighting back?"

"God Almighty, who could I tell? You? I have a reputation in this city. Who could I have gone to?"

"You know perfectly well the code of confidentiality. You

could never have been at peace. What you were doing was a crime. It was your God-given duty to keep your child safe."

"Damn it, I didn't *hurt* her," he shouted. "I loved her. I wanted her."

"Pig!" Before Cecile could consider the lack of wisdom she spat out the word.

"Ah, I see." He shook his finger. "You were playing for time." He turned away, holding the syringe up to the light. "I'm a doctor, remember? I should know what you're up to. You were hoping to make a dash for it. It won't happen. You've destroyed me. I have no career anymore. And I'm a *good* doctor," he declared with desperate pride. "My patients love me. When they wake up and read the newspapers they won't believe it. There's been some terrible mistake. Not Dr. Wheeler! It can't possibly be *him*. There's only one way out for men like me," he said in quite a different voice.

"You plan to shoot *yourself* up, as well?" Cecile asked with contempt. "What is it in that syringe?"

He threw back his head and laughed. "A lethal dose. You have to be punished for making this happen. You understand that, don't you? I'm not a natural-born killer."

"You're natural-born scum!" Cecile, who had been pretending the near paralysis of acceptance, was on her feet very fast indeed, screaming, "Police! Police!" Surely to God someone would hear her! Even if they didn't, Wheeler had become very agitated, his bloodless skin blotched now with red.

Please God, let him forget me and run!

He didn't. He came after her. Cecile picked up the stainless-steel coffeepot on the stove, prepared to throw it. He intended to kill her. In her own apartment, of all places, with its excellent security system. How could she have been so careless to open the door to anyone? Assumptions could be very dangerous. His voice had been distorted, the bouquet of flowers had all but covered his face. She wondered how many other women had been taken in by such a ploy. A lone woman should never be so trusting. She would never see her family again. She would never see the one man she had ever loved. Life was beyond her frail understanding.

The extent of the man's breakdown was carved on his face. It resembled a devilish mask. He looked horrible, quite mad, worlds away from the calm, caring professional who had presented himself at her office.

The energy was draining out of her as the demands on her nervous system had to be met. She hurled the pot, realizing she could throw as many things as she could lay her hands on, but in the end he would overpower her and a terrible sequence of events would ensue.

Still, she had to fight. She didn't have to sit down and wait. As a last resort, fearing the use of such a weapon, Cecile reached into a drawer and pulled out a wicked-looking carving knife, knowing he might well end up using the knife on her, instead of the syringe.

"Hey, hey, hey," he chided, skidding on drops of water that had fallen from the coffee percolator and reaching for the counter to steady himself. "Put that down."

"I'll carve you up if you come near me," Cecile gritted, her eyes glittering brilliantly.

"No one is coming to rescue you, my dear." He laughed. "It's just you and me. It will be bloody easy just to end it!"

CHAPTER THIRTEEN

ROLFE CHECKED INTO his Melbourne city hotel around 5:30 p.m. He had been traveling most of the day, so he had a quick shower and changed his clothes. It was coming up to a month since he had seen Cecile. A lifetime, when he missed her so badly. He had given her a breathing space, but the urge to come to Melbourne to confront her had been building so powerfully he had surrendered to its demand. He realized the very fact her grandfather had bought back the old Lockhart cattle holding and presented the deed to him would work against him. She would think of it as a continuing con, though he doubted a true con man could put anything over Joel Moreland. Joel knew a great deal of life. He had learned even more from the revelations following the death of his wife, Frances. The discovery he had a grandson called Daniel had made him more deeply understanding of the way Frances Moreland had turned the cool ruthless eye of an enemy on his own family.

Cecile hadn't even been born at the time all this was happening. She couldn't know. She wasn't ready to face it, anyway. It would seem too incredible to her. And why not? From all accounts, Frances Moreland had been a loving grandmother to her. Cecile's thinking would be that had he taken her into his confidence early, it would have validated any *real* feeling he had for her. Instead, by not doing so, he had grossly deceived her. On top of her broken engagement and her parents' marriage breakup, little wonder she had retreated into her shell. Finding out he'd been born in the Northern Territory and not in Argentina would have come as an additional bolt from the blue. Nearly twenty years spent in that country and he could have fooled anyone. His Spanish was Ramon's, the cultivated upper class.

Joel had advised him not to put pressure on Cecile, but he didn't intend to make any demands. It was more she couldn't be allowed to lock him out. That prospect was too grim. What they had shared had affected her as powerfully as it had him. He would stake his life on that. It was a miracle to find bliss in being with another human being. Having experienced that miraculous connection, he couldn't bear to lose it. He had to convince her he was someone on whom she could depend. Someone who most deeply and truly loved her.

He had no intention of returning to Argentina except to visit. His life was here in the country of his birth. His life was with Cecile, if only they could talk through their problems and reach an understanding. He had hesitated about ringing her. He knew she wouldn't answer, but at least she would hear his voice. Tonight he reasoned it would be better to simply arrive on her doorstep rather than alert her with a phone call. It was almost a pity it wasn't pouring rain, though he had heard on the radio a late storm was forecast. She might feel sorry enough for him to let him in. Perhaps even the shock of having him on her doorstep would gain him access for a little while?

In the end, sick of indecisiveness, Rolfe took a cab to where she lived. Her address wasn't listed in the phone book, but Joel had given it to him. Joel was playing Cupid even as he was trying to play negotiator in his daughter's marital crisis. One way or another Joel was being kept very busy.

Rolfe was paying off the cab driver when he saw a messenger carrying a large bouquet of flowers approach the front entrance of the elegant, up-market building. For some reason, a hunch, he thought they might be for Cecile. Perhaps her ex-fiancé was trying to get back into her good graces. He waited at the curb for a few moments watching the messenger press one of the numbers, then say in a crackling sort of voice that carried on the still air, "Delivery for Ms. Moreland."

For an instant Rolfe considered arriving with the flowers, then rejected that as not a good idea. He waited until the messenger was well inside the building before he made his own approach. He was lucky. Two attractive young women were on their way out. They greeted his arrival with bright faces and bold, assessing "Hi's!" He smiled back, as though he found them equally interesting, then walked with cool confidence inside as though he was either a resident or visiting one. Obviously they hadn't judged him any sort of a security risk.

The lift was sitting at the ground floor. Why hadn't the guy delivering the flowers come down in it? He'd had ample time to hand over the bouquet. Rolfe stepped into the empty lift and pressed the button for Cecile's floor, fully expecting to see the messenger up there waiting to get in. Instead an elderly lady was hovering in the quiet hallway, looking very agitated. When she caught sight of Rolfe, she pressed a finger to her lips indicating she wanted him to be quiet, then beckoned him to an alcove with a tall plate-glass window giving an expansive view over the park opposite.

Rolfe followed, though his reassuring smile had vanished. What was she going to tell him? His face tight, he looked down at her.

"Are you visiting Cecile?" she asked, pointing an arthritic hand at Cecile's door.

"Yes. Is anything the matter?" He wanted her to get to the point.

"I don't know," the woman wavered. "I heard a crash. At least, I thought I heard a crash. My television is on. It's one of my favorite quiz shows, but it's rather noisy. Then I thought I heard Cecile shouting."

Rolfe waited for no more. Fear clamped into him like a steel claw. "Call the police," he instructed. As the old woman scurried back to her apartment to do so, Rolfe considered his options. Knock? Call out her name? Instinct warned him against doing that. He had seen the messenger delivering flowers to her apartment. The messenger had come up. He hadn't gone down. So where was he? Rolfe stood in absolute attention, his ear pressed to the heavy door.

No sound at all from inside. Very cautiously he gripped the doorknob, immensely relieved to feel it turn. What a godsend! He opened the door slowly, his nerves strained against making the slightest noise. One look at the shattered glass partition was enough to make his chest heave. Carefully he sidestepped the shards. Gladioli as red as blood had been tossed all over the floor.

So he *was* here! Kidnapper, rapist, psychopath? Rolfe suppressed a powerful urge to shout out a threat. The police might arrive soon but they would be too late to save anyone who had hurt Cecile from getting pulverized.

There was no one in the living room. He couldn't as yet see into the kitchen. He dropped into a crouch to inch his way silently across the thick carpet to a position behind one of the sofas. Now that he had a clear view, he was able to see there was no one in the galley kitchen, either. Where had he taken her—the bedroom?

Rolfe's blood ran cold. He stood upright, quietly removing the leather loafers he was wearing before moving cautiously down the hallway.

Still no sound, but he was absolutely certain he wasn't alone in the apartment. He paused for long moments, not daring to draw breath, then he heard a man's voice say tauntingly, "I don't think your friend is coming, my dear. I don't think anyone is coming."

Aren't I, you bastard! Rolfe swore in silent fury, his strong features compressed into granite. He had no fear of confronting another man, even a dangerous, violent man with a weapon. He just had to be very very careful and as silent as the mountain lions of Argentina. The one thing he didn't have was the luxury of time. He wasn't even certain Cecile's elderly neighbor had done as he'd instructed. She'd looked almost too frightened to speak coherently over the phone.

"Do you really think you're going to get away with this?"

His heart leapt at the sound of Cecile's voice. *Thank God!* His hope grew. She sounded quiet, controlled, even quite extraordinarily patient. Patient with a madman?

Then came the man's laugh. An ugly unnatural sound. "Well, *you'll* never know, my dear. Don't struggle. It's quite useless." The voice became pleasant, even admiring. "I have to confess I'm rather impressed with you, Ms. Moreland—"

Rolfe waited no longer. His body poised to lunge, he inched his face around the bedroom door. The man's back was to him. His right arm was raised. In his hand was a syringe filled with a clear liquid.

Electrified, Rolfe lunged. He landed heavily on the man's back just as Cecile either fainted or slid deliberately to the floor.

"The police will be here soon." Rolfe let out a loud menacing growl, putting all his strength into the lock on the man's wrist. "But not soon enough for you, pal." The man struggled ferociously. He was strong, but Rolfe was stronger. He was also fueled by fury. The syringe fell harmlessly to the floor. Rolfe twisted the man's arm behind his back, increasing the pressure till the fake messenger cried out in pain.

"You're pulling my arm out of its socket!"

"Is that so?" Rolfe allowed himself a harsh laugh. He wrestled the guy to the floor, straddling the man's body, forcing him to lie still.

Cecile hadn't fainted. She had engineered a way to get clear of the syringe. She was up in a crouch now, her face paper-white.

"We need something to tie him up, Cecile." There was an urgent command in Rolfe's voice. All of his considerable strength was given over to controlling her attacker, whose breath was hissing like a steam train as he struggled to get free of Rolfe's hold. Rolfe banged the man's head hard on the floor, just barely resisting the urge to keep going. That quietened the man a little, but soon he resumed his struggle.

Of all things, Cecile put a child's skipping rope into his hands. She swiftly fell to her knees bending over the man's head with a glass water jug. There was no water in it, so presumably she intended to clobber him with it if he got out of control.

"You know him?" Rolfe grunted, binding the messenger's two hands very tightly behind his back.

"Yes." Cecile's voice was ragged. "He's the father of a patient."

"Is he now?" Rolfe stood up, delivering one sharp kick to the ribs of the would-be murderer, who bleated piteously. "Stand away from him, Cecile. He's not going anywhere."

"You'll answer for this!" Wheeler moaned, turning his head to give Cecile a black, betrayed look. "There was no abuse. Ellie was lying. That's what she is, a little liar."

"*You're* the liar, Dr. Wheeler," Cecile said. "Long term abuse has been confirmed."

That appeared to astound him, though why it did Cecile was at a complete loss to know. Wheeler began to bash his own forehead against the carpet in intense frustration. "She *belongs* to me," he cried as though offering the perfect defense. "She's my own flesh and blood. It's my *right* to do to her whatever I want."

"God Almighty!" Rolfe was filled with revulsion. "Shut up!" He directed another kick at the man's ribs. He turned to stare into Cecile's brilliant eyes. "What *is* this guy?"

Contempt was etched into her expression. "A pedophile. A monster. My little patient, Ellie, is ten years old. His *daughter*!"

"You sick bastard!" Rolfe began to flex his powerful right hand, punching it into his left palm like a boxer. "And what did you intend doing to Ms. Moreland?" he asked with quiet menace.

"He was going to kill me," Cecile's voice was toneless, but her whole body was shaking. "He was going to jab me with that syringe. God knows what it contains, but he told me it would have done the job. I think we can believe him. As a doctor he has access to drugs. The police will be wanting to take the syringe into evidence."

"For God's sweet sake!" Rolfe groaned. He moved toward her, feeling in some ways she was handling the shock better than he was. "I arrived in the nick of time, then."

"Funny you should say that!" She gave him the faintest little smile before crumpling slowly to the floor.

There was a whole lot of noise outside. Rolfe laid Cecile on the bed, welcoming the pounding on the door. It was followed up by the crunch of glass being trampled under heavy boots. There were loud identifying shouts of "Police, Police!"

"In the bedroom," Rolfe yelled back. "The woman's safe."

Their weapons drawn, two police officers responded, inching their way along the hallway, much as Rolfe had done, the first officer's nose rounding the door frame of the bedroom, neither man prepared to trust an anonymous voice.

"Clear!" One notified the other.

What they saw was a young woman lying on the bed, moaning softly, a young man standing beside her, his hands up and turned palm out in the universal gesture of no threat, another man trussed up on the floor. The trussed man was bawling like a baby.

Rolfe watched as the police car carrying Dr. Peter Wheeler drove away. It was well over an hour later. The streetlights were on. A storm was threatening. He and Cecile had given their statements. Wheeler would have attempted murder added to his list of charges.

"That should put him away for a long long time," Rolf observed with intense satisfaction. "Suddenly your little patient has a future free of fear."

"They'll have to keep an eye on the mother," Cecile said, feeling oddly numb. A policewoman had made her a cup of tea with lots of sugar. She had drunk it even if it had been sickeningly sweet. "I wouldn't be in the least surprised if Marcie Wheeler rolled up to prison every month for a visit. Why is it certain women are drawn to evil men like moths to a flame? I would never have guessed at that hidden evil when I met him. He seemed so caring, and he *was* a doctor!"

"Plenty of doctors are murderers," Rolfe commented, "the infamous Dr. Crippen for one. People who knew him described him as a pleasant man who wouldn't hurt a fly." He moved back into the living room, shutting the sliding glass doors. It was hot and humid outside—a thunderstorm was building—but inside the apartment it was pleasantly cool. "How do you feel now?"

She let her head fall back against the sofa. "Shaky, whereas you're a rock."

"Don't you believe it!" He sat down on the white upholstered sofa opposite her, a marble-topped coffee table the barrier between them. "I'm still in a rage. I wanted to beat that guy to pulp."

"I thought you were going to," Cecile murmured dryly, laying her head back again and closing her eyes. "His wife warned him, you know. She told him to run. I can't believe it. I mean I *can* believe it, but I'm shocked out of my mind. I'd be dead by now if you hadn't arrived."

"When you feel better, maybe you can say thank-you," he suggested lightly.

"Maybe." She rubbed her arms.

"You're not cold, are you?" His eyes ranged over her. She was still very pale.

"A little. It's just the shock. There are shawls on one of the shelves in the walk-in wardrobe. Could you pick one out for me?"

"Sure." He stood up at once. "Do you want to lie down?"

"I think I can hang in there for a little while yet."

Rolfe rummaged through the shawls and picked one out—long black and fringed, lavish with amethyst, blue and emerald scrolls. The label said silk, but to him it looked and felt like velvet.

"This do?"

"Perfect." She went to take it from him, but he arranged it around her shoulders. "Thank you." She waited until he'd resumed his seat. "In all the excitement I forgot to ask how you knew my address."

"Does the word *granddad* mean anything to you?"

"Of course!" She gave a little click of her tongue. "What exactly does he think he's playing at?"

"One of the oldest games in the world. Cupid!"

Cecile frowned at the levity of his tone. "Granddad has been very successful at just about everything he's attempted, but he'll come a cropper here. I'm finished with you, Rolfe. I thought I'd made that abundantly clear."

"You'd better not say that," he warned. "You might need me. I seem to get to you faster than anyone else."

Cecile exhaled a long breath. "And I'm grateful, but you've lost all your power over me. I can't trust you. Trust is very important."

"Can't you give me a chance?" He leaned forward, speaking as persuasively as he knew how. "I don't make a living out of lying to people, Cecile. I'm not the hustler you seem to believe I am."

"I'm past caring, Rolfe." She shook back her long hair, but it kept sliding over her shoulder. "You've got a lot to answer for. I let you make love to me."

"You *gave* yourself to me completely," he corrected, his gaze dark and mesmeric.

"And it was wonderful! The only thing missing was the all-important trust I'm talking about."

His eyes stayed on her. So beautiful! The fairest of them all. She was wearing a loose turquoise caftan of some almost sheer material that clearly displayed the contours of her body. The silk shawl twisted around her made an exotic contrast. Her skin shone luminous under the lights. Her eyes sparkled. Yet she looked fragile. And why wouldn't she with a maniac bursting in to kill her?

"Don't let's talk about it now," he said quietly. "You need a chance to recover from your ordeal. So do I, for that matter. The bastard's strength was unbelievable."

"He was the one facedown on the carpet," Cecile pointed out dryly.

"Yes, in the end and blubbering like a baby. Why is it those who inflict the most pain on others have such a low pain threshold themselves?"

"Bullies and cowards," Cecile said, her voice racked with emotion. "That little girl has lost something irretrievable. She's lost—" She broke off, unable to go on.

"You'll help her. You've already helped her." Rolfe offered swift consolation, wanting to go to her, but knowing he had to hold back. He had to wait until she came to him. He had visions of tenderly peeling off her clothing, entering her body, feeling her surge up against him. He wanted her to beg him to make love to her. Would that ever be again?

"Don't tear yourself to pieces," he went on. "I know it can't be easy but you know you have to maintain your emotional balance just to function. How about I make us something to eat?" he said in a brisker tone. "You can't have had anything. Neither have I."

For the first time Cecile gave a real smile. "Seriously, can you cook?"

He gave his elegant shrug. "Not terribly well, now that you mention it. In my stepfather's house there are lots of servants."

"Speaking of which, what name are you going to call yourself from now on?" she asked with cool sarcasm.

"Rolfe Chandler," he confirmed. "When I go back to Argentina to visit my family, I'll be Raul Montalvan. I never lied to you about that."

In the end they shared what Cecile had originally intended to have for dinner, the light pasta with ricotta and prosciutto. She let Rolfe handle the pasta. Lack of experience in the kitchen or not, he was characteristically adept. She prepared a green salad, tossing it in a Thai chilli dressing. Rolfe opened a bottle of very good shiraz, which they continued to drink long after the meal had ended.

"You've got your color back," he said, greatly relieved. "You seem more yourself."

She shook her head. "Don't be misled. I'm still very angry with you, Rolfe. It's just I'm not up to showing it tonight. You did save my life."

"I'm getting used to it." He smiled ruefully. "Would you like coffee?"

"If you can find the percolator. I hurled it at Wheeler."

"It's okay. Our nice policewoman retrieved it and she cleaned up the glass."

"She *was* nice," Cecile reflected. "I'll remember her name. Coffee beans are in the fridge in a canister. Grinder on the bench." She sat back trying to compose herself. A hot prickle of something like shame ran through her. She remembered all the nights of lying awake congratulating herself she'd found the will to finish with him! Oh, frail resolve! Desire crackled in the atmosphere, turning the air inside as electric as outdoors.

At around ten-thirty, the storm that had been threatening for the past few hours finally broke over the city with the usual spectacular display of pyrotechnics.

"You can't stay here," she warned him, beating down her tormented longings.

"I know. But you can't toss me out until it's over," he argued. "You're going to be all right?"

"Of course, but I can't guarantee not having a few nightmares." They were back to sitting on opposite sides of the coffee table. A squat crystal vase was atop it, filled with the beautiful full-blown heads of yellow roses. The perfume was so heady Rolfe could taste it. "I'll never let anyone in like that again," she said with a shudder. "I couldn't see his face. I saw the flowers. That put me off my guard."

"Who would the flowers have been from?" he asked, keeping his eyes on her beautiful face, the beauty she wore so lightly.

"Strangely enough my first thought was they might be from you. Then I realized—I *thought*—you didn't know where I lived. I'll be having a word with Granddad. He doesn't usually interfere. This incident can't fail to get into the papers."

He nodded, already seeing the big black headline: Moreland Heiress Threatened By Crazed Sex Offender. "The press have gathered down on the street. I don't know if the police made any statement there and then. Someone tipped them off."

"Someone always does." Cecile shrugged.

"I suspect a couple of reporters will hang around hoping you'll drive out of the building. Your phone would have been ringing, only you're not listed. Is there any other way out, a back street?"

She shook her head. "You *can't* stay."

"Why not?" His eyes flowed down her throat to her breasts.

"Because we'd only sleep together," she said harshly.

"Is that so bad?"

His voice was so filled with tenderness, it shook her badly. She'd seen his face when it was taut with passion. The expression he wore now was incredibly *sweet*. It reached for her, attempted to gather her close. He had an excess of sexual power and he was bringing it to his service right now. Only, she was committed to fighting temptation.

"*Now,* Rolfe." She leapt to her feet. "Go *now!*" She had to spare herself this dangerous dance of seduction. Remember how he had deliberately deceived her.

"Okay, okay. No need to get agitated." He hunted up his jacket, shouldered into it. "You're so cruel. It's still raining."

"I'll lend you an umbrella." Her voice was brittle.

"No thanks. I expect it's like something a model on a catwalk might carry. Is there a cab rank handy or do I need to call one?"

"I'll call one," she said, then visibly jumped when the sliding doors to the terrace lit up brilliantly from a flash of lightning.

"Oh, sit down again." She waved him back helplessly as a great rolling thunderclap followed. "Why did you come here?"

"Thank God I did."

"And I can't wait for you to leave." She made to retreat to the safety of the sofa. But he caught her arm.

"I want you so badly," he told her passionately. "I want to put my arms around you. Comfort you. May I?"

"*Don't,* Rolfe!" Her voice was pitched high. "When the storm is over, you must go."

"I *long* to hold you."

His voice was the perfect instrument for seduction. "Oh, spare me the razzle-dazzle," she said angrily, throwing back her head and exposing her long elegant neck.

Immediately he released her. "No razzle-dazzle, only truth. What's the number of the cab company? I'd walk back to the hotel if I knew which way I was going."

Cecile put a hand to her temple. "Just a moment. I have to look it up. I rarely take cabs." She was desperate for him to go yet the price of maintaining her self-respect appeared to be desolation.

Her face reflected her tormented feelings. So did the agitation of her movements.

"Come here to me," he said.

How could gentleness be so deeply erotic? Her willpower was fading under the impact, her body thoroughly aroused. She was baffled and beaten by the complexity of her feelings. She had sought respite from him. But she couldn't lock him out. He had only to look at her, smile at her, speak to her with his voice flowing like honey. She couldn't, however, let him touch her. But oh, that *sinking* feeling!

She laughed, a trembling little laugh. "You never give up, do you?"

Her beauty swept over him, her vulnerability. "Not on you," he said. "One kiss, the price of having saved your life. *Then* I'll go."

She saw the little flames leaping in his eyes and caught her breath.

First he buried his face in her neck, then he kissed her. The now familiar languor stole into her limbs. It wasn't a gentle kiss. It was the kiss of a man who had known and possessed every inch of her body. That knowledge alone was an unbreakable bond between them.

Instantly she was drenched in desire. It flowed from him to her. In a way it was a revelation. She had never really known what it meant until he had first made love to her. Now she would never have to wonder again. The composed mask she wore had been stripped from her. All for *him*. Her mouth opened to greet his questing tongue. Her fascination for him was overwhelming. She had no defense against it, however hard she tried.

She couldn't resist him or his touch. There was a kind of fear in it, the fear of loss of self. It was as though she had lost all choice. His hands were moving loverlike across her shoulders and down her back while she fell into a thrilling reverie, letting him do what he liked, moving her this way and that, molding her body to his. She slid her arms beneath his jacket, locked them around his waist, feeling his powerful erection settle against the slight curve of her stomach. What an instrument of pleasure and torture that was!

Briefly he lifted his mouth from hers, staring down at her. "If we start this, I'll *never* leave."

"Well, we *have* started it, haven't we?" she answered with a little twist of bitterness. She wanted to hurt him as he had hurt her. She still wondered if she was part of his plan, but the most primitive sexual excitement had taken hold of her and transformed her into someone else. His for the taking. Was it any wonder she was frightened?

They were lying naked together on the bed, while the storm raged outside the shuttered doors as if trying to get in. She was spread out beneath him, arms and legs, toes and soles of her feet sliding across the smooth surface of the bed linen. His palms sought the creamy undersides of her breasts, lifting first one dark pink nipple then the other to his mouth. The horror of the early part of the night was obliterated by the flames of passion that now enveloped them like a great bushfire.

"Forgive me," he whispered into her ear.

"No." He had exposed her to too much pain, too much self-doubt.

"I'll keep doing this to you."

She had opened herself wide to him. Now she cried out as the pleasure mounted too high to be checked.

"Are you going to thank me for saving your life?" He didn't say it was one of the worst moments of *his* life.

"Thank you," she gasped, while outside the storm howled.

"No, no, you mustn't come yet." He taunted her softly, continuing his ministrations that excited her to the point of tears.

She was shaking all over, her body flushed, but she wasn't going to beg.

Then when she thought she couldn't stand the shattering ecstasy a moment longer, he moved his hand away and began to thrust deeply into her. In and out. Back and forth, his penis growing so big it seemed to fill her right up to her throat. Swiftly she caught his rhythm, reveling in the ease with which they fitted together. Groups of muscles clenched and relaxed. Their movements were as smooth as oiled pistons, moving smoothly together until they fired. He lifted her legs high and her finger-

nails dug into his powerful shoulders. It was excruciating torment and it made her eyelids flutter and her heart pound madly.
How much more did he want of her? What part of her body was
he trying to reach? Her penetrated womb throbbed with heat as
if his penis had put a brand on it. The small of her back strained
to arch up from the bed, fell back as his mouth swooped on hers
again. She had the crazy sensation she was flying…her flailing
arms were wings…the whole world was vibrating…

Rippling sensations began deep in the cave of her body,
slowly at first, then gaining strength and speed. She tried to
control the onward surge, but it was hopeless. Ah, the power of
the flesh! The will was as nothing. It was hopeless to control this
tumult or contain it. She had to go with the tide until the tumult
subsided. Her heart was hammering. Inside she was convuls-
ing. Rolfe loomed over her, his own orgasm powerfully fierce.

A cry gushed from her mouth. His name?

Tears slithered down her cheeks.

Faster and faster they rocked. It was a mating dance designed
by nature to bring forth new life. Pleasure soared to the highest
point she had ever reached.

She was split open.

Then….release! Deep internal shifts began that took long….
long…minutes to shudder into calm. Minutes more for the heart
to settle.

Utterly spent and dangling one arm over the bed and one
across Rolfe's chest, Cecile in her mind's eye had a sudden vision of a perfect little boy with golden blond hair and eyes of
velvety brown. Rolfe as a child? There were wildflowers all
around him. She knew those flowers. They were the yellow and
white paper daisies that carpeted the Red Centre after rain. She
could hear him laughing. Such a merry laugh, full of security
and happiness. What kind of vision was that?

She was dreaming. She was in an abandoned building, a hotel
or a derelict apartment building. She could see numbers on the

doors although it was very murky with deep shadows. Some numbers were hanging upside down. One of them was hers: 24. A crashing sound came from behind her. Something heavy. A fallen beam? She knew the building was condemned. Then the sound of pounding footsteps. Someone was coming after her. She began to run, too, her heart beating violently in her chest, but the faster she ran, the farther away the end of the corridor grew. There was a terrible sense of danger all around her. Those heavy footsteps belonged to a killer. *Her* killer. She called on all her strength, but she could hardly breathe. There was a bad stitch in her side. He was coming after her, deadly in pursuit…

Help me!

"Cecile!"

She awoke with a great start. A bedside lamp was on. Rolfe was holding her shoulders, staring into her face. "It's okay," he was saying. His face and voice were full of concern. "You're quite safe. I'm here with you. Cecile, wake up!" He shook her gently.

She responded more fully, throwing an arm over her eyes. "Oh, God, I was having a nightmare. It was dreadful."

"I know." His hand curled around her bare shoulder.

"I was running through a derelict building. One of the doors had the number of my apartment on it. Aren't dreams strange? Someone was coming after me. I was running fast but never fast enough. It was so *real!*"

"They always are." His arm beneath her, he settled his body alongside hers, savoring their closeness as if at any minute it might be over.

"What time is it?" She was immensely grateful he was there with her. He was so strong and *physical.* A man of action.

Rolfe glanced at the digital clock. "Three-thirty. Breathe deeply." He began to breathe with her as if to show her.

After a while her heartbeat quietened. She was feeling better, though the terror of the nightmare clung to her like a fume.

"Would you like a drink of water?" he asked, stroking her blue-sheened hair back from her face.

"Yes, please." She swallowed on a dry throat.

"Okay. I'll be back in a moment." He slid out of the bed, as gloriously naked as a sculpted work of art.

When he returned to the bedroom, she was propped up against the pillow. "Thank you." She drank thirstily. He had water from the dispenser on the refrigerator door, so it was deliciously cold. "The storm's over?"

"Long over," he said.

"And you're still here."

"It seems so." He walked to the sliding glass doors with superb unselfconsciousness. "The moon is riding high in a cloudless sky," he told her, opening the door wide so she could breathe in the rain-washed air.

"The odd time, I have the feeling I can't do without you, Rolfe," she told him.

"And this is one of those times," he answered dryly, coming back to the bed and stretching himself out alongside her.

She turned on her side to stare into his gold-flecked eyes. There was hunger in them. Hunger renewed. She wanted to hold her tongue, especially at this time, but she found she couldn't. "I can't put aside the fact you deliberately deceived me, Rolfe," she said heavily. "Surely you see it was a deception of some magnitude. You made a fool of me. Made me suffer. I can't forget that."

His response was simple. "You're going to have to."

"Or you'll depart for Argentina?" she asked, a war waging inside.

His handsome face tightened as he stared back at her. "I've come *home,* Cecile. Home where I belong. It was a dream I never abandoned. Thoughts of my return have been with me practically my whole life."

"Along with thoughts of revenge. They never left you, either. Was revenge at the heart of it?"

His eyes glittered with a kind of vehemence. "It was part of it," he admitted grimly. "But far more important, more important than even I realized until I came back, was the love of *my* land. It's not just the aboriginals who have it. The white man can have it, too. The red desert sand is in my bones. When I die they can scatter my ashes to the desert winds. I can think of no better end."

"Please...." Cecile reached out impulsively to stop his mouth. "You have a long life ahead of you. I don't want to hear you talk about dying." She visibly shivered.

"We all die, Cecile," he said, lifting the sheet around her. "The price of having any life at all. You asked if I'd return to Argentina. The answer is certainly. Argentina is my second home. My mother is there. Ramon, my stepbrother and sister. But it will only be for visits."

She lay back. "How would you describe your mother?" she asked, staring up at the plastered ceiling.

He answered instantly. "A beautiful woman inside and out. I love her dearly."

"Did you have problems when she married your stepfather? You were still a boy, not an adult. Even adults have problems when a much-loved parent remarries. You'd lost your own father in terrible circumstances."

"What is this, a therapy session?" He loomed over her so she could see clearly the fine grain of his dark golden skin and the glinting blond streaks in his thick mane of hair.

"Well, you *are* lying down," she pointed out. "In *my* bed. How did you get here?"

"The same way you did," he said crisply. "You wanted me as much as I wanted you. *Want* you," he amended, hunger still spilling out of his dark eyes.

She shielded her face from it with her arm.

"The lamp too strong?" he asked with a measure of sarcasm.

"No, leave it on. Is *want* what holds us together?"

He didn't answer for a minute, settling himself back. "A lot of people would think the way we want one another is more than enough. But no, I don't just want your body, Cecile, though it gives me unbelievable pleasure. I want your heart and your mind. You're more real to me than any other woman I've ever known."

"So why didn't you *talk* to me," she demanded, engulfed by a kind of desolation. "I would have listened. I would have listened to everything you said. Even though you've had much to say about my family that's really bad. Your story wouldn't have fallen on deaf ears. You know that now from my grandfather's reaction. Granddad is a wonderful man."

"I know that now," he said. "I didn't know it before. Your grandmother's role in our downfall was all new to me." And to my mother, he thought bleakly, almost ready to reveal to her the true story.

"Well, Granddad tried to make amends by buying back your old property," Cecile retorted. "It's *yours* now. You have your inheritance back. So one of your objectives has been fulfilled." Even after their sublime lovemaking she was unconvinced he wanted her for herself alone.

It must have been the worst thing she could have said because he suddenly caught her chin with strong fingers and dropped a punishing kiss on her mouth. "Time to go, I think," he said in a clipped voice. "I've got enough scars without your adding to them, Cecile." He slid out of the bed and squared his shoulders.

She raised herself on one elbow, a whole range of emotions running through her so fast she couldn't grab hold of a single one. "But it's the way of things, isn't it? Each of us hurting the other." She stared at him, following each swift decisive movement as he pulled on his clothes.

Rolfe waited until he was fully dressed before he looked back at her. Her black hair was tumbling down her back and brushing her shoulders, accentuating the magnolia texture of her skin. Her eyes were pools of light. Her delicate breasts and her body down to her waist were fully exposed. He couldn't help the leap of desire, but he choked it down. "I deeply regret I've hurt you, Cecile," he said in a voice she thought had no apology in it, "but I'm not going to spend the rest of my days apologizing for what I failed to tell you," he confirmed. "I didn't, however, *lie*. You must have learned other things about me. A few good things, surely?" he questioned with a trace of bitter challenge.

She drew herself up, trying to reach for her kaftan to cover her. "I can't... I don't deny I—"

He cut whatever she was trying to say short, shouldering into his jacket. "Don't get out of bed," he said, already on the move. "I can see myself out."

CHAPTER FOURTEEN

THE PUBLICITY THAT followed the arrest and charging of Dr. Peter Wheeler on two counts, one of attempted murder and the other of incest, combined with the fact it was the Moreland heiress, Cecile Moreland, who had been the victim of the murder attempt in her luxury apartment, caused Cecile to want to take flight until the worst of the media coverage had died down. Her family hated publicity. Now they had plenty of it. Her face and her life all over the newspapers. She wouldn't look at a newspaper for days on end in case it carried yet another photograph of her. So many on file? Why was she always smiling? This was a dreadful business that was being reported. Surely they didn't have to pick photographs where she was smiling, did they? The only plus for her was that she and her mother were talking again. In fact, her mother had rushed to be with her, shocked out of her mind such a thing had happened to her daughter.

"I've told you, I've warned you, Ceci, you're in a dangerous profession." Justine had sobbed. Something she never did. "Thank God for Rolfe! How we owe him! Where *is* he?" She looked around wildly as if he were hiding away in the apartment. "I have to thank him personally. You could never, never, have faced that maniac alone."

A lot of people arrived. The apartment was jammed with

them. Relatives, friends, colleagues. Justine stared at the crowd for a few minutes, counted heads, then organized lavish refreshments from one of her innumerable sources. She didn't appear in the least heartbroken over her marriage breakup, Cecile thought. She looked in her element, taking over. Her daughter needed her. That was all that mattered to Justine.

Her grandfather sent the Learjet for her. Her mother tagged along, saying she couldn't bear to have Cecile out of her sight. They returned to Darwin where the population respected the family's privacy. At the weekend they would go on to Malagari where Cecile felt her happiest. She had advised the police of her whereabouts. Her senior colleague, Susan Bryant, would be taking over Ellie's counseling. Children's Services would be conducting routine checks on Marcie Wheeler and her children, though Mrs. Wheeler had notified everyone concerned of her intention to move permanently to New Zealand where she had relatives. Cecile was pleased to hear it. She and Ellie and Josh would be out of harm's way. Mrs. Wheeler further told Cecile when they spoke she never wanted to lay eyes on her husband again. "What he could have done to you and it was my fault!"

Cecile couldn't bring herself to pat the woman's hand soothingly and deny it. Marcie Wheeler had acted very foolishly indeed. Much as she appeared to hate the thought—and who could blame her?—she would have to sight her husband when the case came before the court. She would have to be strong. So would Ellie.

"He doesn't scare us anymore," Marcie told Cecile earnestly. "He deserves to be behind bars. Ellie is so much better you wouldn't believe. We're going to make a fresh start."

Wherever they went Ellie would need further counseling. Possibly for years. Cecile made sure Marcie Wheeler fully understood that.

It was their first night home in the Moreland mansion. Cecile was preparing for bed when clearly her mother was ready for another heart-to-heart. "What's she like, this Northam woman?" Justine asked, studying her beautifully manicured nails. She was sitting in a Louis armchair, looking very much like she'd used up most of her olive branches. The worst of the scare was over. They were safe with Daddy now. Justine wanted to get down to business. "I know you visited them at her beach shack…" Her quick glance was accusing.

Was there anything her mother *didn't* know? "Actually it's quite spacious. I'd be happy in it."

"You'd be happy anywhere Rolfe was around," Justine scoffed. "Where is he, by the way?"

"The last time I spoke to him he was still in Melbourne," Cecile evaded.

"Don't worry, he'll be back. You're making a huge effort to play it down, but I know you. Now, to get back to your father. Gilly Massingham saw the two of you having lunch. She said he'd put on a lot of weight."

"Nonsense! He looks great, Mum," Cecile said. "Just great!"

"Really!" Justine raised beautifully shaped eyebrows. "He's a great-looking man. She's in it for the money. Not that there'll be anything like what she imagines." Her laugh was full of angry satisfaction.

"She's not in it for the money, Mum." Cecile took a brush to her long hair. "She loves him. I don't want to hurt you, but he appears to genuinely love her."

"Gimme a break!" Justine's voice deepened with sarcasm. "Your father can go to hell, for all I care. If he genuinely loved any of the women he's been involved with over the years—"

"But that's it, isn't it, Mum? Your marriage would have been over long ago. He didn't love any of them, but he loves *her*. They need each another. You never did need Dad. Not really. You had Granddad. He's been the rock in all our lives."

"I realize that, Ceci," Justine snapped. "No need to rub it in. I understand she's quite *plain*. A nondescript little thing?"

Cecile knew she was supposed to say, "And stupid to boot!"

Instead she said, "She's neither, Mum. She doesn't have your striking good looks or presence, but there's something really attractive about her. She's fresh and wholesome, well scrubbed."

"Good God!" Justine was genuinely appalled. "No wonder she couldn't get a man till now. Well scrubbed? Sounds like she had to hang herself out to dry."

Cecile sat down in a matching chair. "Okay, here's the story. She had an invalid mother to look after. She was devoted to her. Her mother died not so long ago."

Justine thought about that and what it implied. "So with Mum out of the way Howard decides to call our marriage quits?"

"It does look that way," Cecile said, not without sadness.

"And what am I supposed to do—roll under a bus?" Justine inquired bitterly.

"The stats on getting run over by a bus are very low, Mum. Start looking for another husband," Cecile suggested.

"Another husband? What, more of the same?" Justine asked incredulously. "Besides, I'm getting old...older."

"Nonsense. You're in your prime. Bob Connaught might fit the bill nicely."

Justine gave that some thought. "Actually he *does,* now you mention it. You wouldn't mind my remarrying?"

"Whatever makes you happy makes me happy, Mother dear."

"I'm so sorry for behaving badly!" Unfamiliar tears filled Justine's eyes. "I'm not sorry for cutting up your father's clothes. It made me feel really good. He won't be needing all those Italian suits, anyway, now he's taken a golden handshake."

"He worked very hard for it, Mother," Cecile reminded her.

Justine was silent for a few moments. "How about you start calling me Justine?" she suggested.

"Fine, Justine!" It was no good protesting.

"By the way, I forgot to tell you Daddy took care of Stuart and his blabbermouth." Justine smiled as she said it. "Remember Stuart, your ex-fiancé?" she asked waspishly.

"Vaguely." Cecile put down her hairbrush and began to rub some cream into her hands.

"Thought he was going to humiliate us, did he?" Justine shook herself in outrage.

"It's not as though he was in perfect ignorance of what you might do."

"Indeed!" Justine performed a tattoo on the wooden part of the chair with her long fingernails. "Whatever did I see in him? There must have been something?" She frowned as she looked into her daughter's eyes.

"You like people who agree with you at every turn—could that have been it?" Cecile suggested mildly.

"I don't think I'm going to get that from Rolfe," Justine said slyly.

"Rolfe and I aren't an item," Cecile said, determined to maintain her privacy. Justine couldn't help interfering, she knew. It was her nature.

"Codswallop!" said Justine rudely.

"What a very odd word. I wonder what its derivation is?"

Justine shrugged. "Who cares! It simply means nonsense. I don't blame you if you're not yet ready to totally forgive him. In fact, I suspect you're relishing keeping Rolfe uncertain about you and the whole situation. It's really weird because you'd die if he looked in another woman's direction."

True.

"But then, that special problem has always existed for us, hasn't it?" Justine said soberly. "Are we loved for ourselves, or has it more to do with being the daughter and the granddaughter of the Man with the Midas Touch? I was fairly paranoid as a girl when it came to trust. I know you are, too. It goes with the territory, my darling."

"You think I should trust Rolfe?"

"You're madly in love with him, aren't you? He's saved you from great harm on two separate occasions. Some might say you owe your life to him. That's a big plus in my book."

Cecile looked away. "He's brave. I know that. I'm not so without self-confidence that I don't know he's attracted to me."

"He's conquered you *and* Daddy in a remarkably short time. That's it, isn't it?"

Cecile couldn't answer. Her mother had too much insight into her particular problems. She had trusted Tara, her friend from childhood, but that episode at Malagari when Tara had turned on her had really hurt.

"You're *not* terrified someone else will get him?" Justine broke into Cecile's ponderings, uncannily on her daughter's wavelength. "What about that little opportunist, Tara?"

"What about Tara?" Cecile asked with false calm, unsurprised her mother had read her mind. Justine did it all the time.

"Don't tell me! You've had a falling out? We are *soooo* sorry," Justine gloated. "She's a devious miss, that one! Warned you, didn't I?"

Cecile shrugged. "She rang me immediately she read about what happened. She sounded genuinely distressed for me."

Justine harrumphed. "Just so long as she doesn't come for a visit. But she'll try. Mark my words. I've always said that girl can get in where the ants can't." She rose majestically to her feet. "I'll say good night, darling. You don't mind if I don't come with you to Malagari, do you?" She didn't wait for an answer, but swept on. "I've never been one for the great outdoors. If I weren't so obviously a Moreland, I'd begin to wonder if I were Daddy's at all."

A sad little smile edged Cecile's mouth. "Are you saying Grandma slept with someone else?" As far as she was concerned, the things that Grandma Frances had gotten up to were mind-blowing.

"Good gracious, Ceci, that's not nice." Justine turned to reprimand her. "Even in fun."

"I apologize. She simply wouldn't have had the time. She seemed to have spent most of it creating great traumas for other people. Daniel and his poor abandoned mother. Rolfe's entire family. No one was spared."

Justine in her gorgeous peach-colored peignoir paused at the door, one elegant hand to her temple. "Please, Ceci, not another word. I can't bear to hear it. Even as a child I knew there was always something going on with my mother. She would have been quite at home with the Borgias. All the secrets, the scandals and the downright lies have come as no surprise to me." Justine opened the door, then turned with a bright conspiratorial smile. "Do you really think Bob Connaught and I are suited?"

However had her parents stayed together long enough to have her? "I think it would work," Cecile said. For all she knew, Bob Connaught, a very nice man, could be abstemious in the sex department, too.

"Perhaps." Justine shrugged. "You know what they say. What's good for the goose is good for the gander."

A couple of days after Justine's return to Melbourne, Joel joined Cecile in the garden room where she was endeavoring to reply to a stack of Thinking of You cards, to tell her he had given Rolfe, who was back in town, permission to take one of the station helicopters across the ranges to the old Lockhart cattle holding.

"I think it would be a good idea if you went with him," Joel said. "In many ways Rolfe has been alone a long time. He had his mother of course, and his new family, but it's obvious he never forgot his own world. Rolfe has the same connection to the land that you and I have."

"He deceived us, Granddad. That's what I can't accept."

Joel sighed. "At the beginning deception was his only cover. I'll stake my life he isn't a man who normally dealt in deception. I think he hated having to lie to you, but that desire for revenge on the Morelands was deeply entrenched."

"You say, *was,* past tense."

"I think his quest for revenge is now over, my darling. You're the trained psychologist. Revenge must have filled up the terrible void in his life. But only love can heal a wounded heart. I believe he loves you. You must see it. You must feel it don't you? In its way it's a wonderful redemptive love. It's within your power to lay the ghosts of Rolfe's painful past finally to rest."

Rolfe put the chopper down on the perfectly flat ground that ran away to the ranges at the front of the old homestead. Red desert forever. A world of color. The marvelous contrast of blazing blue skies, fiery earth, ghost gums with their stark white boles, dusty khaki misshapen trees and bushes, great cylindrical clumps of spinifex scorched to a dull gold and looking for all the world like the biggest wheatfield on earth.

Painters would revel in it, he thought. This was his first visit here in over twenty years, and it was as he had fully expected it to be: emotional. But he had to hold his emotions in check, remembering what his grandmother had said to him as a six-year-old when he'd broken his arm: "Brave boys don't cry, Rolfie!"

He'd cried plenty. But always when he was absolutely alone. Tragedy had haunted his life. It was only since he had met Cecile all the pent-up anger and bitterness inside him had all but crumbled to dust. He had thought to get on with his life. Only it wasn't so easy.

A deception of such magnitude!

That's what she had said with such hurt in her eyes. What could he do to win her trust? She felt herself tricked and betrayed. It had been impressed on him enough that heiresses feared not being liked or loved for themselves. It wasn't difficult to understand. Not when people wore masks. At least today she had consented to come with him, although he knew he probably had to thank Joel for that. Joel was turning into the grandfather he had once known.

As they walked toward the single-story homestead, he felt his profound link with it rise up through his very boots. Gradually he became aware of a general *tidiness* about the place. "There's no doubt about him, is there," he murmured.

"Granddad?" she asked.

He nodded, staring about him. "Someone has been here to clean up. Everything is much too neat and tidy for a deserted old homestead."

"That's Granddad for you!" said Cecile slightly discordantly, pausing to take in the old building. "He probably sent a couple of the men over."

"A couple of dozen is more like it." Rolfe lifted his eyes to the purple-hazed ranges that lay in the exact center of the continent. Known collectively as the Macdonnell Ranges, they stood in stark relief against the cloudless sky, among the oldest geological formations on the planet. Extending east to west some hundred miles across the floor of the sandy desert, they were famous for their extraordinary shapes and colors. There was a spectacular gap in the ranges, he remembered. A great chasm of multicolored scalloped layers, rusts, yellows, pinks and creams that impressed itself upon the eye. That was what was so extraordinary about the Red Centre, its stark primal beauty, the inviolability that told you plainly no one could own it.

Close by a flock of white corellas took flight, and he stared after them appreciatively. His head began to fill with childhood memories: riding through canyons and gorges with his grandfather, the sheer cliffs towering to either side; sparkling water holes and great stretches of *Ginda Ginda* flowers. He remembered the magnificent wedge-tailed eagles that soared on high, the huge flocks of budgerigar that seemed to follow them around. He remembered his father letting him ride pillion on his motorbike as they raced across the iron-red plains. He remembered being allowed to join in the chase for brumbies. Was there ever a time he hadn't loved horses? Most of all he remembered when he was very small, racing out into the open paddocks to be the first one in the family—they let him believe he was, anyway—to sight the miraculous appearance of the zillions of paper daisies that appeared after rains.

Sadly he remembered, too, the man from the bank who traveled all the way to tell his grandfather the bank was repossessing the property. He remembered how he had run away and hid for days after his father and Benjie had carried his grandfather's body home. His grandfather's fatal heart attack had happened when he was driving stray cattle into the holding yards.

He couldn't bear to remember the sound of his grandmother's screaming or his mother's brokenhearted sobbing.

"Everything okay?" Cecile asked, seeing somberness come into his expression.

"Sure. Fine." He recovered immediately.

"Good." Perversely she couldn't bear to see him unhappy. She turned slowly to take it all in, the golden sea of spinifex washing right up against the larkspur ranges. "I like this place." It was tiny by Malagari standards, a mere cottage, but it had definite appeal.

"It's a wonder it hasn't fallen down," Rolfe murmured, thinking at some stage the building and the old sheds would have to be demolished. How had they all fitted in there? he wondered. A comfortable home to him as a boy, now it seemed much too small to have sheltered them all. He couldn't recall a single argument. They were a family. They pulled together. They never fell out. Not a one of them wanted to hurt the other. His grandparents had adored him. His grandfather had always called him "my little mate." There had been a unique warmth and companionship between them that had even exceeded the close bond with his father.

"The ranges look quite different from this side," Cecile was observing, shading her eyes. "Namatjira was such a great artist, so much a part of this desert country. He painted with complete accuracy. I've heard city collectors say the colors are too vivid to be true, but we know differently." She looked about her with obvious pleasure. "It's all the Northern Territory, yet there's a great division between our tropical region north and this so-called arid center. No one who has ever seen our desert gardens could possibly call it arid, could they? Lovely, lovely flowers of every kind and color." She was conscious of his eyes on her. "So very strange and so romantic."

They continued to walk toward the old homestead. It was much too hot standing in the sun. "Didn't the early explorer Ernest Giles want to name Palm Valley after all the beautiful flowers he found there?" Rolfe asked. He'd all but forgotten about that.

Cecile nodded. "In the end the palms were so magnificent he called it Glen of Palms, which later became Palm Valley."

"Nothing has changed at all," he said in deep, reflective tones. "Hard to believe now, but we all lived here. My grandparents. Mum and Dad and me until Dad could get a run of his own. Uncle Benjie. Granddad was the patriarch. I was remembering we never fell out as a family. We were very closely knit. We had to depend on one another. Benjie might have been my uncle, but he was more like a big brother. He was tall, over six feet, with a lopsided grin and eyes as blue as my mother's. She's a very beautiful woman. Blond. I inherited my eyes, the shape and color from my dad, but I look a lot like her. I think that's why Ramon took it so easy on me—because I resembled my mother. It couldn't have been my sunny nature. I turned into a savage after my dad was killed."

Something in his expression brought her close to tears. "How very sad, Rolfe." So much trauma for a young boy to contend with. It was no wonder he lived in such pain. "You never did tell me how you felt when your mother remarried."

He grimaced faintly, drawing her up the short flight of stone steps that led to the wide veranda. The homestead itself was set some four feet off the ground by brick pillars. The veranda wrapped around three sides of the house, protecting the core of the building from the fierce inland heat. "I acted like I couldn't care less, but for a long time I hated the situation," Rolfe said. "I couldn't bear to think of my mother being disloyal to my dad, but I didn't accept Ramon at all. Not as my mother's husband. Not as my stepfather, although he adopted me almost immediately."

"And how do you feel about your stepbrother and sister?"

He shrugged. "It's possible one day my stepbrother and I will be friends. No one could help but love Ramona, though." There was much affection in his voice.

The entrance portico, Cecile saw, was simple but attractive, flanked by double timber columns and a fretted timber gable and spire. The roof was corrugated galvanized iron decorated with rather picturesque roof ventilators to aid the cooling of the homestead. Two pairs of French doors to either side of the front door gave onto the veranda. It was a good example of an early pioneering building, but maintenance had not been a priority of subsequent owners who had all gone broke, her grandfather had told her. Cecile didn't think it would warrant restoration work. Possibly the whole structure would have to be demolished. She wondered how Rolfe would feel about that but didn't like to ask.

"Shall we go in?" She turned to him, her eyes sparkling like cool crystal pools in the heat of the day.

He acted completely on instinct. Effortlessly he swept her high in his arms, staring down into her startled face.

"I didn't realize we'd just been married." She tried to make a joke of it that didn't come off.

"I feel like we belong to each other," he said, his handsome face unsmiling. He pushed the door—it wasn't locked—and carried her into the entrance hall. There he lowered her to the polished timber floor, keeping his arms around her. "Thank you for coming today. I know Joel was behind it."

She laid her hand against the flat of his chest, then turned away.

"Even so I wouldn't have come if I didn't want to. Let's take a look around." She felt she could snap at any moment, yet she spoke calmly enough.

His mouth twisted a little. "The place is called Currawa."

She nodded. "I saw the brass plaque beside the front door."

She paused to look up at the original cypress pine ceilings, easily twelve feet high. "Doesn't *currawa* mean the tree—"

"From which gum was obtained to fasten the heads to native spears," he finished for her. "There are other meanings, such as rocky river. There aren't too many rivers around here, barring the oldest, driest river on earth, the Finke, and the Todd, of course, running through the Alice."

"Did you ever get to see the Henley-on-Todd Regatta?" Cecile asked without thinking. She was referring to the annual bottomless boat race, leg propelled down the dry bed of the river. A day of great fun!

"No," he said, standing quite still watching her, "nor the Alice Springs Rodeo where your uncle Jared was killed and Benjie was held responsible."

She bowed her head. "I'm sorry. I spoke without thinking. Why don't we say a prayer for them?" she said quietly. "The two of us together. Members of two families who suffered."

He came away from the wall, straightened his wide shoulders. "I stopped saying prayers when my dad was killed, Cecile," he said, his voice echoing through the empty house.

Toward midday they sat on the front steps in the shade of the gable and ate their picnic lunch straight from the esky. Nothing fancy. Sandwiches and coffee from the stainless-steel flask, a crisp apple for dessert.

"King's Canyon and Palm Valley aren't far away," Cecile said. "We could do a flyover on the way back. It amazes tourists to find wonderful green oases slap bang in the middle of the desert. Beautiful crystal creeks and gullies."

"Remnants of long, long ago when the Centre was once as lush and green as your tropical North."

"Do you remember the wild bush after rain?" she asked, taking a last bite of her red shiny apple.

"Of course! It's a sight no one could forget. My grandmother used to say to my grandfather—it was for *my* benefit

of course— 'The paper daisies will be out by morning, Dad!'
That was all I needed. I used to get up so early the sun hadn't
even crested the ranges. By the time I reached the first horse
paddock the landscape was flooded with golden light. I think
I was around six or seven at the time."

"You must have been a very sensitive little boy," Cecile said,
unable to keep the tenderness out of her voice. "Sensitive to
beauty." She vividly recalled her extraordinary vision of that
beautiful little boy who looked just like Rolfe amid a glowing
landscape of wildflowers.

"I defy anyone to be insensitive to the sight of the arid red
desert transformed overnight into a vast garden," he replied.
"Miles and miles of everlastings, the one color to one area, yellow, then pink, then white. I never did figure out why that was
so. You'd think the seeds would intermingle. After the showers
of winter rain the sand used to be wreathed with trailing stems
of Stuart's crimson desert pea, the bellflowers, the foxgloves,
the pink parakeelyas. When the scorched spinifex sent up its
tall seed-bearing stems, it looked more like we were growing
giant fields of wheat than raising cattle. All those years ago and
I remember it as vividly as though it were yesterday."

"You want to spend the rest of your life here?" She spoke normally, when she was desperate to know his plans for the future.

"What—here on Currawa?" He reached into the esky and
found to his satisfaction a bar of orange-flavored dark chocolate.

She spread her hands. "Well, if not Currawa, this region?"

"I thought I made that clear. It's a *magical* place, Cecile." He
broke off a square of chocolate and handed it to her.

"Thank you. This has been a feast." She slipped the rich
dark chocolate into her mouth, letting it melt. Chocolate had
been considered an aphrodisiac since the time of the Pharaohs.

"I don't intend to work Currawa, if that's what you're trying
to find out. I don't intend to sell it, either. Joel's handing me the
deed was a symbolic gesture. We both knew that. What I was
thinking was at some time in the future turning the site into a

tourist destination. A small working station taking in selected guests. It's a hop, step, and a jump to the Alice and from there Uluru, Kata Tjuta and the rest of the desert monuments. Just an idea, a fairly long-term project. What do you think?"

"Have you spoken to Granddad about it?" So many things he talked to her grandfather about. Why not her?

"In due time I'll ask his advice," he said, capturing and holding her gaze. "It's *you* I'm telling first. *You* I wanted to be with me when I returned here. That's the big reason I delayed."

"Then I'm honored," she said, her throat tight. "You've become quite a favorite with Granddad."

Gold flashed in his dark eyes. "Joel and I connected easily. It could have been very different."

"But you took the gamble?" Inside a voice said, *leave this alone.*

"I can't deny that, Cecile," he said, suddenly looking grave. "I was a different person then."

"Is that likely, your changing so quickly?" she asked, unable to resist the challenge.

"I think falling headlong in love changes people pretty smartly," he retaliated. "You say you would have gotten around to breaking off your engagement to Carlson without my coming into your life. I have a little trouble believing that. I think your meeting me changed you overnight."

"You're so sure of yourself." Cecile began to busy herself tidying up.

"How can I not be when I have you in my arms?" he countered, his voice deep in his throat. "Stop that. What are you so afraid of?" He reached out to lock his hand gently around her wrist.

"Let me go, Rolfe." She trembled as she said it.

"Why can't you look at me? I feel like holding your head still."

She stopped what she was doing. "All right, are you listening?" She reacted emotionally. "As soon as you touch me I spin out of control. I don't even know how to put a stop to it. You can't fall madly in love with someone you hardly know."

He laughed softly. "You're not the first person to say that nor the last. Can't you accept a great thing has happened to us?"

She looked away from his eyes. "I can accept something cataclysmic has happened to us, certainly to *me,* Rolfe," she said more quietly, "but I have more difficulty accepting your dramatic change from a man hell-bent on exacting whatever revenge he can on my family to a recent convert. It's like men in jail suddenly finding God."

He stood up and looked down at her. "I think you better stop there."

"So do I." Her heart was going madly. She didn't want to fight with him, but it was happening.

"And you'd better start questioning if you're as much in love—or lust—or whatever the hell you call it—as you claim to be. Falling in love *is* a time of transformation. I know it if you don't. You might also consider whether you're not the least bit neurotic. The poor little rich girl always condemned to testing people. Is there *anyone* you can trust? Mightn't that mean you haven't sufficient sense of yourself? I love you. I'll shout it out loud. *I love you!* But today, right now, I don't even like you."

Cecile too came to her feet. "Didn't take you long to admit it," she said angrily. "Maybe you have difficulty distinguishing love from hate? I'll never forget the way you were looking at me when I was standing on the balcony at Daniel's wedding. It was so—" She sought for a word. "So…"

"Desiring?" he suggested curtly.

"I was going to say, calculating. I *saw* that, Rolfe. I didn't dream it up."

"So I'm supposed to feel guilty for the rest of my life? Why can't you just let a man be?"

"I'm sorry we started this conversation," she said.

"You brought it up in the first place."

"That's right, blame me." She rushed back up the step, catching the toe of her shoe in a split timber plank. "Damn!" She pitched forward and he caught her.

"Careful," he said. "You are so trouble prone."

She lifted her head, saw the tormenting little smile in his eyes. "Are you after the job of minder?"

"I'm after the job of *husband,*" he said bluntly, getting his arms around her. "Maybe I should keep you here like this until you say yes. My prisoner." He bent his head and kissed her, not stopping until she was making little moaning sounds of surrender.

"I'd be shattered if you ever wanted to leave me," she told him passionately. "Think about it, Rolfe." She hit a hand to his chest. "You *say* you're not going back to Argentina to live, but you might want to at some stage. It happens."

"And you wouldn't come with me?" He rocked her slightly.

"I could say my life is *here.*"

"If we married *you* would become my life," he said, looking deep into her eyes. "As I would become yours. You mustn't fear I'll return to Argentina. I've already promised you I won't."

"So what happens now?" Cecile asked, feeling near helpless. "Where is this great tide of feeling going to carry us?"

"Toward the future, Cecile," he said with great confidence. "Not the past. Think how terrible it would be if we parted. Do you really want that?"

No! "I'd never get over you," she said, finally accepting whether it was safe or not, it was true.

"Then you have to believe in me."

The answer didn't drop out of the sky. That night Cecile stood at the French doors of her bedroom staring up at the great copper moon of the tropics. This was decision time. She had to make up her mind for good. She wanted Rolfe in her life. Indeed she couldn't bear the thought of life without him. She was a child psychologist. She had studied and treated many kinds of conflicts that arose during the early years of life. As the granddaughter of a very rich man, she had virtually been programmed to look very carefully at the people around her before she offered her trust. Trust had become of paramount importance to her. She had suffered little betrayals over the years any number of times. But being left totally in the dark by the man she had come to love had crushed her. It had precipitated an emotional crisis, but to resolve it she had to get out from under. Rolfe, for his part, had been programmed from a blighted childhood to hate the family who had wreaked such painful trauma on his own. His mother apparently hadn't known the full story, either, but it was certain she, too, hadn't let go of her loathing of the Morelands. Looked at objectively, putting aside her own troublesome fears and anxieties, it was easy to see Rolfe had been made a victim, not once, but many times over. It was characteristic of a man not to want to talk. Men walked away from talk, whereas the need to talk things through, sometimes exhaustively, came naturally to women. She had to take that into consideration. Rolfe had acted on his programming. She had acted on hers.

Their crisis had reached a peak. Resolution had to come from her. Hadn't Rolfe confided with deep emotion that she had offered him redemption? Why doubt him? She understood so much about children and how their experiences formed them. Now she had to turn her clear professional regard on herself and Rolfe. The sins of her grandmother, Frances, could no longer be allowed to visit themselves on her and Rolfe. She was the one who had to take meaningful action.

"You have to believe in me!"

Their happiness together rested on that foundation. She had to start turning herself in another direction. There was no one else like Rolfe for her in the world.

CHAPTER FIFTEEN

THE MONTHS SINCE Daniel and Sandra had left on their honeymoon had flown by on wings. The happy couple were due home in a couple of weeks. Their honeymoon trip—from all accounts glorious—had taken in all the great capital cities of Europe and had been extended when the newlyweds decided they wanted more time to explore the countryside of the various regions.

No sooner had they learned the details of the return flight home than Joel started planning a reunion party.

"Nothing big, around a hundred or so, Ceci. I'm sure Sandra's bridesmaids would like to come. We can organize their tickets. Bea will want to be here. I'll send the jet for her and your mother."

"Don't you think you should give Daniel and Sandra a little time to recover, Granddad?" Cecile asked. "There's such a thing as jet lag." Nevertheless she was as excited as her grandfather Daniel and Sandra were coming home.

Joel looked up from some property development plans he had spread out on the coffee table. "They'll be fine, Ceci. They're young." He dismissed jet lag with a wave of his hand. "Let's see. They'll be home early morning of the Wednesday. We'll plan it for the following Saturday night. What do you think?"

Cecile didn't have the heart to say, "Wait a while!" Her grandfather was living his life as though every day was his last.

"Something else I wanted to talk to you about, my darling. Sit down now. Those flowers are just right." Cecile had been twitching a dried oleander branch around her arrangement of orchids and Asian lilies in a celadon vase.

"I'm sitting." She smiled at him affectionately and began to twiddle her thumbs.

"Serious now." Her grandfather took another sip of his coffee and put it down. "I'm thinking of offering Rolfe much the same job he was doing so wonderfully well for his stepfather. Breeding and schooling fine polo ponies for the international market. That means second in charge to Jock Lindsey at Lagunda. Jock has been with me for donkey years, as you know. He isn't far off retiring. At that time Rolfe would take over. What do you think?"

A faint trembling began in Cecile's hands and spread to her body. "It's a lot to take in, Granddad. Have you discussed it with him?"

Joel shook his head. "Not as yet. I'm sounding you out first."

That made sense. "On the face of it, Granddad, it sounds a perfect solution for both parties," she said quietly, "but I don't really know what Rolfe's plans are."

"Then you'd better find out, my darling," Joel advised her. "Rolfe and I have discussed his idea of turning Currawa into a small working station and tourist destination. He told me he'd already discussed it with you. More and more tourists are visiting the Red Centre. Many like the idea of staying on an Outback station and getting an idea of Outback life. It could work well, handled the right way. But Rolfe's got a wonderful way with horses. He said himself horses are his passion. What could be better than working at Lagunda? His stepfather will be very sorry to lose him, but I'm hoping his loss will be my gain. Of course if you're against it, I know he won't consider it."

"Are you sure of that?"

"Surer than *you* are apparently," he said shrewdly. "Rolfe has been working very hard to restore your trust, my darling."

"I know." She touched her grandfather's hand. "Both of us are working to iron out whatever problems we have left. The process is almost complete, but making that final commitment is a huge decision, Granddad. You weren't happy in your marriage. Neither were my parents. I can't hide the fact I love Rolfe. I don't want to. I want to shout it aloud, but some part of me, down deep, is very sensitive to how marriages, even marriages founded on love, can fail."

"Well, marriage is a big gamble for anyone, Ceci." Joel sighed. "We all pursue happiness but it's very elusive. The thing is, time passes. You can't let your life slip by. You have to take action one way or the other. The failure of your engagement to Carlson was a setback. You're too intelligent to set the stage for another failure. Rolfe is a very different man from Carlson."

Cecile's eyes glittered with the depth of her emotion. "I love him so much, sometimes I'm *afraid* of it." She spoke the simple truth.

Her grandfather leaned back in his chair, deep understanding on his face. "Ah, Ceci," he said. "With love there's always the underlying fear of loss. Fear one party will profoundly change and cease to care. Fear of a third party entering the marriage to rock the boat. Fear of terrible things happening to the loved one. That happened to me with Jared. I started having bad dreams a couple of weeks before he was killed."

"I didn't know that, Granddad." Cecile looked at her grandfather with compassion in her eyes.

"Sometimes I had such a tight feeling in my chest I thought I might have a heart attack, though I was only in my forties, very fit and strong. Still, that's how I felt. Presentiments. Hordes of people have had them. I had an intense passion for Frances at the beginning. God knows why, but it faded fast. I suppose the things that mattered to me didn't matter at all to your grandmother. She only pretended in the early days for my benefit.

She told me that herself. We grew apart. I have to accept blame. There was always the pressure of business on me. It wasn't that I was dedicated to making money. That wasn't it. I had *vision*. I wanted to do good things. For the community, for the Territory, for my country."

"You succeeded, Granddad. Have no fear. You're an Outback icon. We're all very proud of you."

"And I'm proud of you, Ceci," said Joel. "And Daniel, my fine grandson. Your mother, you and Daniel are the three most important people in my life. But I have to tell you I thoroughly approve of Rolfe. We get on like a house on fire. At times we seem like family. I sense he's missed a grandfather figure in his life. I'm happy to be it. I would be absolutely delighted to welcome him into the family—which wasn't exactly the case with Stuart."

"Stuart turned on me very quickly," Cecile said, disenchantment in her voice.

Joel shrugged. "Well, one couldn't blame him for being tremendously upset. But he should have stopped there. Of course he was trying to discredit Rolfe in your eyes, but he can't be allowed to put private business on the public agenda. You'll have no trouble there. But getting back to Rolfe, I know I have to wait until you two make a decision regarding your future, but tell me this—could you consider life at Lagunda?"

The reality was she would consider Mars as long as she was with Rolfe. Yet she couldn't commit herself at that moment. "I have to think about it, Granddad. Malagari is my favorite place, but I love Lagunda, too. It's a different world."

"Subtropical, glorious location, the Pacific ocean at your doorstep. Most people would think they'd died and gone to heaven if they lived there."

"I know. But I'm still sorting out a few aspects of my life."

"Of course. As far as Malagari goes, I need Daniel to take over the running of it. He's a born cattleman. But Malagari will always remain the ancestral home. Half goes to you, half to Daniel. I know how much you love it. Lagunda, as you say, is a very different world, lush and green. Would you want to continue your career? It has its dangerous side. That's been brought home to us."

Cecile looked down at her ringless hands. "I trained hard for it, Granddad. I've been able to help a lot of children. That was my aim."

He looked pointedly at her. "You want children yourself?"

She flushed and looked up. "Of course I do. What a question! I love children."

"Sorry. I know you're very different from your mother. Justine always made the excuse that having more children was dangerous. It wasn't true."

"I know. Bea told me."

He clicked his tongue. "Bea got wise to Justine early. She fooled the rest of us for years. In that sense I feel sorry for your father. This other woman, you like her?"

"Yes, I do." It was no shock he knew they'd met. "I believe and I hope she and Dad will be very happy together. Life is too short to be unhappy."

"Absolutely," Joel said. "I can tell you something that would make me enormously happy." His whole face lit up.

"Tell me, it's yours!" Cecile felt a great wave of love.

"That's a promise?" He leaned across the table and put out his hand.

"Yes, if I can." She shook his hand.

"Then make me a great-grandfather someday soon," he begged. "You *and* Daniel. I can tell you now I can't wait."

Two days later Cecile and Rolfe and Joel flew to Queensland, Joel's pilot landing at the Gold Coast airport. From there they rented a car to drive to Lagunda in the beautiful hinterland. Jock and his wife, Valerie, welcomed them warmly. A delicious lunch was waiting, and afterward Cecile, Rolfe and Joel made an inspection of the property—an entire world especially designed for horses—with Jock at the wheel of the 4WD. It was a delightful trip. This was some of the prettiest country in Australia. The blue ranges formed a background for the lush green pastures, there was abundant wildlife, swans, ducks, even a couple of pelicans on a big spring-fed lake just deep enough for a horse to enjoy a dip. There was the tang of salt in the air as the wind blew in from the ocean.

In the white-fenced paddocks was the sweet familiar sight of horses galloping around the perimeter, full of the joy of life, tails and manes flying. Jock stopped from time to time to point out a special horse. Others, each as beautifully groomed as the next, trotted over to the fence to see what was happening and hopefully be petted. There were mothers standing in the paddocks with their foals, a heart-melting sight. The place was filled with incredibly beautiful horses, around three hundred at any given time. Back at the stables they looked in on the latest addition, a foal that had arrived just the previous night. A little colt, he was all legs with a bobtail that he flicked the minute he caught sight of them. Cecile waited long enough to see him cuddle up to his mother to nurse, his little tummy fast filling with milk. A feed, a satisfied sigh, then a nap.

The reason they had come was for Rolfe to make his own inspection, to see what he thought, and from there make a decision as to whether he wanted to take up Joel's offer. He and Jock had hit it off immediately. If they hadn't, there would have been a problem, but both had a relaxed manner and there was the great common bond of the love and deep knowledge of horses.

After the horses came the lengthy discussion on programs, with breeding charts produced. Cecile found herself a little light-headed from the flight, so she returned to the homestead to enjoy a quiet talk with Val. They were old friends, so the time passed quickly.

"Well, what's the verdict?" Joel asked as they drove away a couple of hours later.

"It's a splendid property, Joel," Rolfe, at the wheel, answered. "Jock is a good man. You must value him highly."

"I do, but I happen to know Jock is just about ready to retire. He's well into his sixties now. He and Val have always spoken about traveling. You wouldn't have long to wait to do your own thing."

"I would *want* to," Rolfe said, making that clear. "Some of my methods are quite different from Jock's. I'm not saying *better,* Jock is obviously doing all the right things, but *different.* You're being incredibly generous to me, Joel. Let me think about this." He caught Cecile's silver eyes in the rear view mirror.

She knew then she held the answer. She had to think no more to give it. Hadn't Rolfe's eyes told her, *"I will always, always love you."*

First light woke her. No point in lying there. She rose quickly, then fell back on the bed again, shocked by the wave of nausea that rolled through her stomach. She lay back, waiting for the sick feeling to subside. Mercifully it did. She tried to tell herself it was a quick drop in blood pressure. Or maybe she'd caught a bug. She'd been feeling vaguely off color and light-headed for days, without her usual energy. It could have been a bug, but she knew better. Regular as clockwork she had missed her period. She had waited a week for it to make its appearance, but she *knew* it wasn't going to.

She was pregnant.

A blood test would confirm it. She had pretty much invited it. She had been so emotional after her estrangement from Rolfe she had stopped taking the pill. Her love life was a disaster, wasn't it? She had subsequently gone back on the pill, but she'd known at the back of her mind she was putting herself at risk the night Rolfe had rescued her from the abominable Dr. Wheeler.

No protection.
Exquisite timing!
Such a night!

Was it any wonder, then, she would wind up pregnant?

Yet wasn't that what everyone wanted? She lay there with her hand over her eyes, waiting for her stomach to settle. Her mother, her grandfather? The two of them would be wild with joy after they got over the initial shock. She realized that, mingled with her dismay and sense of trepidation, she herself was already thinking ahead to when she would hold her own child in her arms.

It's not you, my darling, my beautiful love child who jumped the gun. It's me! She patted her stomach, talking to the embryo she was certain at that very moment was growing in her womb. *I love you already.*

She would have to tell Rolfe. When? After she had her own diagnosis confirmed by a blood test? She could arrange that quickly enough. On her own reckoning—she fully expected to be proved right—conception had taken place three weeks before. She couldn't bear to wait six weeks to tell him.

Would he turn on her, his voice rising in dismayed accusation? No, Rolfe wouldn't turn on her. That wasn't his way. But how *would* he take it? Would he have a sense of being tricked? As though she, being the mother of his child, would have control? It would certainly bring any plans he might have rapidly forward. He claimed he wanted to marry her, said he wouldn't take up the position on Lagunda without her.

Should she subject him to another test? He had brought her little habit of testing people out in the open, after all. That aspect of her character might continue with certain people but not with Rolfe. She no longer swung back and forth like a pendulum. Her trust in him from this day forth was rock solid.

The wave of nausea had subsided. This time she stood up more slowly and walked into the bathroom to take a shower. She pulled her nightgown over her head, then turned to look at her naked body in the mirror. She looked exactly the same. No changes in her breasts. She couldn't have been more slender

without being downright thin. Yet it was momentous to think
a baby was growing inside her. She rubbed a hand over her flat
stomach, circling it gently. How long would it be before anyone saw a difference? Five months, six, maybe into the seventh
month? She was taller than average and it was her first child.

She was feeling a lot better now. In fact, she had never felt
more womanly.

*I'm carrying a baby. Rolfe's baby. I'm the luckiest woman
on earth!*

Midmorning when her grandfather and Rolfe were closeted in
the study, discussing God knows what—they'd been in there
an hour and a half—Cecile took a call from a Detective Superintendent Bormann from the Melbourne police in connection
with the Peter Wheeler case. Cecile listened to what he had to
say in absolute silence, thanked him for ringing, then hung up.

She knocked on the study door, then entered the room at her
grandfather's response.

"Cecile?" Rolfe was very quick to his feet, her grandfather
more slowly, their faces mirror images of concern. "Is everything okay?"

She was aware that Rolfe started toward her. She thought she
said his name. She knew she put out her hand to him, but her
vision was wavering. It was like lying at the bottom of a murky
pool. A dark shape swooped down on her from the surface of
the water, gathering her into its cold embrace.

She came to within moments. She was lying on the burgundy
leather sofa, both legs raised on a cushion.

"One in five people faint at least once in their life," she
quoted medical opinion somewhat woozily.

"That's the second time for you. One time too many." Rolfe
was sitting beside her, eyeing her anxiously.

"I'll get a doctor." Her grandfather, too, was looking agitated.

"No, Granddad!" she protested. She would be seeing a doctor soon enough. "Please. I'm okay."

"It wouldn't hurt to get one here." Rolfe backed Joel.

"I'm telling you there's nothing wrong with me." She put strength into her voice. "I've had a shock. Peter Wheeler is dead. He was killed in the jail laundry by one of the other inmates. That was a Detective Superintendent Bormann on the phone. He rang to tell me before it got into the papers."

"Good God!" Joel sat down heavily in the nearest club chair. "What a terrible business. He's not the first man guilty of such a heinous crime to come to a violent end in jail."

"He'd been making threats against his wife, as well," Cecile added.

"Don't talk for a moment," Rolfe advised. "Just lie quietly."

"I will if you'll stop fussing." She looked into his eyes.

"You're the one who fainted."

"Her color is coming back," Joel said, placing a comforting hand on Rolfe's shoulder.

"I'm still here," Cecile reminded them. "I haven't left the room."

"Behave yourself, Ceci," her grandfather admonished. "It's right for us to worry. You're very precious, you know."

"You might put a trip to the doctor on the agenda," Rolfe suggested. "I know the news was ugly, but a faint?"

"I promise I'll go and have a checkup," she reassured him. "You can come with me, if you like."

"I just might do that," he replied.

"At least Wheeler's death has taken the terror out of his wife's life," Joel mused.

"You're not worried about your part in anything, are you?" Rolfe's dark eyes were still intent on Cecile.

She shook her head. "My job was to save Ellie. Peter Wheeler should have sought help a long long time ago."

"How about if I ring for tea?" Joel suggested the universal fix-it. "I could do with a cup. It's a good thing Rolfe is so quick on his feet. It's a pretty hard floor and you were about to hit it, my girl."

"Rolfe has heaps of assets," she murmured, smiling into his eyes.

"May it be my destiny to be always there to catch you," he said.

It was Joel and his cronies' card night—a thirty-year fixture when Joel was in residence—so Rolfe suggested he and Cecile go out to dinner.

She dressed very carefully in a white crepe jersey dress, sleeveless with a low V neckline and a fluid skirt. She left her hair long and flowing the way he liked it. At the last moment she added the long string of lustrous South Sea pearls that had been her grandfather's twenty-first birthday present to her. They fitted perfectly inside the V neckline and looked beautiful against her skin. The pearls were so big most people would assume she was wearing lovely costume jewelry and not the real thing. There was some safety in that.

She and Rolfe popped into the card room to say hello, and her grandfather introduced Rolfe to his friends, looking extremely pleased with himself and the world. He was especially chuffed to see Cecile wearing his birthday gift to her. "Pearls can't hide away, my darling. They have to be worn and they're absolutely perfect on you."

"How is it possible you get more beautiful every time I see you?" Rolfe asked as they walked to the car.

She could tell by the light in his eyes that the trouble she had gone to was well worth the effort. "I pay attention to all the little things." She smiled.

"Like perfume." He lifted aside her long gleaming hair, breathing her in while he kissed her neck.

By the time they parked and walked into the Darwin restaurant, the place was almost full. The maître d' saw them to their private table for two. It was out of the way of the main room, just as Cecile liked it. The floor-to-ceiling windows reflected all the light and glitter from the large elegant main room, and they could also enjoy the outside harbor lights, which glittered like a fairyland.

"Champagne?" Rolfe asked, his eyes savoring her. She was beautiful at all times, but tonight she seemed to have extra bloom. "Or would you prefer something else?"

She shook her head, already concerned for the well-being of their baby. "Usually I have champagne," she said sweetly, "but tonight I'm on a diet."

"What?" He drew back in his chair. "What would you have to go on a diet for?"

"The party," she invented. "Daniel's and Sandra's party. I have a beautiful strapless dress I want to get into."

He shook his head, letting his eyes assess her. "I don't believe this."

"I've put on a pound or two," she fibbed.

"Have you really?" His mouth turned down in disbelief. "Well, I'll check that out tonight."

"You're assuming I'm coming back to your apartment?" she challenged

"You're assuming right," he said dryly. "No wonder you fainted if you've put yourself on some silly diet."

She reached over and touched his hand. "I promise I'm eating all the right things. It's just that I'm off alcohol. But you go ahead."

She didn't remember much about what they ate, but she would always recall with great vividness the deep joy and excitement of being with him.

Over dessert he asked curiously. "You're hiding something. What is it?"

She was feeling so incandescent she wasn't surprised it

showed. "Why would you say that?" She was going to hold on to her secret a little longer.

"Because I *know* you. There's something you're not telling me."

"Maybe." She smiled at him. "You told me you wouldn't take up Granddad's offer if I didn't want to go to Lagunda. Did you mean it?"

He looked perfectly self-possessed. "I said it, didn't I? You're the only woman who could have that kind of power over me."

"Lucky me!"

He clasped her hand across the table. "Seriously, if you think you wouldn't be happy on Lagunda, we won't go there. I'll find something else. I'm not without resources. I understand perfectly if you don't want to give up your career. You've worked hard for it and you're obviously very good at it. At the same time I am concerned, like Joel, about the dangerous situations people in your line of work can become involved in."

A shiver passed over her. "Don't remind me. I do get satisfaction out of my work. Having said that, I am prepared to put my career on the back burner for a while."

"What's a while?" he asked, watching her closely.

"Oh, a year or two. And I'm not stopping you from taking up the appointment at Lagunda. You're so good at what *you* do. As I can't bear to be parted from you, I'll go along as well."

"So I should accept?" His focus on her was intent.

"Yes."

"You were testing me?"

She snapped her fingers. "My darling Rolfe, I've moved on from that. Do you want to stay here any longer or are we done?"

For answer he put up his hand to signal the waiter.

In the bedroom he began to tenderly undress her, removing her beautiful pearls first and laying them on top of a chest of drawers. "So let's check out these extra couple of pounds, shall we?" His voice was a deep sexy purr.

She was down to her underwear, a white bra with fine silk lace and matching delicate lace briefs.

He stood back to allow his eyes to travel all the way over her. "Beautiful, beautiful, beautiful!" He delivered his verdict, moving back to her again and drawing her against his aroused body. "Have you actually checked yourself out in the mirror lately? You don't have an ounce of excess weight on you. Not that I'd mind if you put on a few pounds." He let his hands run down her back to the curves of her taut rounded bottom.

"Maybe I will!"

"Okay by me." He pinched her bottom lightly. "Then I'll have more of you. You are going to marry me, aren't you?" He bent his head, planting kisses all over her face. "We're not going to Lagunda to live in sin as they still say in Argentina."

She started some caressing of her own. "On the contrary I'm going to put pressure on you to marry me. I don't want to wait."

"What about tomorrow afternoon?" He reached behind her back and unclipped her bra, setting her breasts free.

"Great," she said. "Fine with me!" Her breathing was coming faster. She was trembling with pleasure as his hands took the weight of her breasts.

"I'm serious, Cecile." Now his thumbs were circling the nipples, moving from the outside of the rose-pink areola to the tightly furled buds. He began to massage them very gently, watching her face.

"So am I," she moaned.

"Then it has to be sometime very soon. A good thing I've got an engagement ring."

Her eyelids, weighed down with desire, snapped back. "What?"

"I'll just get you comfortable on the bed, then I'll show it to you." He lifted her so quickly, so smoothly, she was lying on the king-size bed before she knew it.

She sat up, amazed, her hair tumbling around her shoulders. "Have you really got a ring for me?"

His back was to her as he opened a drawer in the small desk that occupied a corner of the bedroom. "You didn't really think we were just having an affair, did you?"

She shook her head dazedly. "You are so full of surprises!"

He came back to her, this wonderful man who loved her, and she felt the tears begin to rise to her eyes.

"Open it," he said. "But before you do, tell me what stone you think it is."

She screwed her eyes tight, clutching the small box to her naked breasts. She began to run her fingertips over the polished lid. "It's...it's *not* a diamond."

"It's not a diamond," he confirmed, sinking onto the bed beside her. "I'm not telling you anything else."

Her eyes were still closed. "So it's a ruby, a sapphire or an emerald. It could be a royal purple amethyst, but I don't think so."

She opened her eyes, staring into his face. "If I had blue eyes I'd say a sapphire. I would *love* a fiery pure red ruby, but that's the rarest stone of all. For that matter, I would love an emerald. But I would love and cherish any ring you gave me."

"Perhaps you ought to open it," he said.

"Oh, this is wonderfully exciting!"

"I think so. I've never been engaged before, so you're one up on me."

"Could you puh-lease not mention that!" she begged, aiming a soft slap at him.

"Never again," he promised, making a pretense of defending himself.

"Aaah, Rolfe!" Delight fell over her like a silken net. Inside the box glowing up at her, sat a glorious oval-shaped ruby surrounded by a blaze of diamonds. "Wherever did you get this?"

"In my spare time I was a jewel thief."

"Darling!" She reached up to kiss him. "I can't marry a jewel thief."

"I've changed a lot." He smiled, watching her return to admiring her engagement ring. "Actually it's a long story and fascinating, to boot. How I came by the central stone I mean. I had the ring made to my own design. A few years back I saved a fellow polo player from a potentially fatal fall. Anyway, as it turned out, he was a relative of the Sultan of Brunei."

"Wow! No wonder you galloped after him," she retorted facetiously, turning the boxed ring this way and that to catch the light.

"I'll tell you the full story later," Rolfe said dryly. "Let's put that ring on, shall we?" He took the box from her and extracted the beautiful piece of jewelry. With it in hand, he slid from the side of the bed, kneeling before her like a supplicant to a naked goddess.

"You are my chosen woman out of all the women in the world," he said, taking her hand and raising it to his mouth. "With this ring, Cecile, I swear my everlasting allegiance. I shall love and treasure you until the day I die."

His words struck her ears like heavenly music, and tears of joy started streaming down her cheeks.

"Don't cry, darling. *Please.*" He was torn between laughter and tenderness.

"Hey, that's what women do."

"Right-o, go ahead. I can lick all those tears up." Keeping his eyes on her, he slid the ring over her knuckle to the base of her finger. It came to rest there as if made for her alone. "It looks wonderful on your beautiful hand."

"It *is* wonderful!" She tried to halt the flow of tears, but they continued to stream from her eyes. Maybe her being pregnant had something to do with it? she thought. Pregnancy, fulfillment, happiness. A good strong man who loved her, the father of her child.

"All right!" Rolfe started stripping off his clothes very purposefully. "I know one way to stop those tears. I'm going to get naked, then I'm going to make hot, impassioned love to you and it's going to go on for a long time."

"Well, that's what I'm here for," she said. "Impassioned love *is* your specialty!" She threw herself languorously onto the pillows, holding up her ring to the light. "Hurry, darling," she said. "I'm calling a wedding officiant first thing in the morning."

They were lying quietly in the aftermath of truly beautiful sex, still marveling at the miracle of their love.

"How do you feel about babies?" she asked as though sounding him out on his views for their future. She was turned on her side, snuggling into him, her ring hand splayed across his chest. The Bruneian ruby, a splendid pure red, was the perfect symbol of their love.

He took a moment to answer, continuing to wind a raven lock of her hair around his hand. Then very seriously, "I love babies," he said.

* * * * *

Outback Man Seeks Wife

Dear Reader,

Welcome to the first story in my OUTBACK MARRIAGES duet. I could never have enough space to tell you how much I love my country, but my loyal readers will know I've been writing about it for the past thirty years. My aim at the beginning of my career was the same as now: to open a window on Australia for the pleasure, interest and expanding knowledge of our global readership. The first custodians of this vast land, the Australian Aborigines, have lived here for some sixty thousand years, and their presence has had an enormous bearing on the incredible mystique of the Outback. While the majority of the Australian population—a scant twenty million people, who live in a vastness of some three million square miles—cling to the lush corridor of coastlines, we're all very much aware of the great beating heart that lies beyond the rugged dividing ranges.

The focus of our national spirit belongs to the Man of the Outback. The Outback represents the real Australia. So much of my inspiration has been the heroic men and women that people the inland. Our cattle kings, our sheep barons and the men who work for them: heroes who, because of the extreme isolation of their workplace and the resulting lack of opportunities to meet partners, have had to devise some pretty bold strategies to find the right women with whom to share their lives and bear their children—young women ready and able to accept all the challenges that living in the Back O' Beyond brings.

My two heroes, Clay and Rory, recognize the indisputable fact that behind every good man stands an even better woman! See how Clay and Rory go about making two feisty heroines their own!

Good reading and warmest best wishes,

Margaret Way

Margaret's anecdotes:

1. Outback people, like all people on the land, work extremely hard. They play hard, too. One only has to attend a gala Bachelor and Spinster Ball, or the legendary Birdsville Race Day—Birdsville is about as remote as it can get—to know that. Everyone enters wholeheartedly into the spirit of fun. Australians are great horse lovers. Not surprisingly, polo is the great game of the Outback and incredibly well attended. Whenever the opportunity arises to have fun and meet up with other Outback people, it's seized with both hands.

2. Outback people know how to have fun. Along with polo, rodeo events are popular, as well. The Alice rodeo in Alice Springs—the town at the very center of Australia—offers big prize money. Then there's the Camel Festival, and the hilarious Henley-on-Todd Regatta, where teams race in bottomless boats, leg-propelled down the dry, sandy bed of the river!

CHAPTER ONE

'YOU CAN'T MISS HIM,' said a languid female voice from behind her. 'He's with the other guys making their way to the starting line. Dark blue shirt, yellow Number 6 on his back.'

Carrie McNevin turned her blond head. 'Your cousin, right?'

'Well *second* cousin!'

Carrie felt rather than saw the look of arrogant dismissal on Natasha Cunningham's face. 'I've barely spoken to him since he arrived.'

'Well you've made contact at least,' Carrie felt very sorry for the young man who had been treated so badly by his family. She couldn't remember Natasha's cousin herself. Or she *thought* she couldn't. There was some tiny spark of memory there. But she'd been little more than a toddler when he and his parents had disappeared from their part of the world like a puff of smoke.

'It was purely by accident I assure you,' Natasha retorted, with familiar derision.

There was a moment's respite from this edgy conversation while both young women followed the progress of the entries in the Jimboorie Cup, the main event in Jimboorie's annual two-day bush picnic races. The amateur jockeys, all fine horsemen, expertly brought their mounts under control. The horses, groomed to perfection, looked wonderful Carrie thought, the familiar excitement surging through her veins. She loved these special days when the closely knit but far flung Outback community came together from distances of hundreds of miles to relax and enjoy themselves. Many winged their way aboard their private planes. Others came overland in trucks, buses or their big dusty 4WD's sporting the ubiquitous bull bars. Outsiders joined in as well. City slickers out for the legendary good time to be had in the bush, inveterate race goers and gamblers who came from all over the country to mostly lose their money and salesmen of all kinds mixing with vast-spread station owners and graziers.

Picnic race days were a gloriously unique part of Outback Australia. The Jimboorie races weren't as famous as the Alice Springs or the Birdsville races with the towering blood-red sandhills of the Simpson Desert sitting just outside of town. Jimboorie lay further to the north-east, more towards the plains country at the centre of the giant state of Queensland with the surrounding stations running sheep, cattle or both.

It was early spring or what passed for spring; September so as to take advantage of the best weather of the year. Today's temperature was 27 degrees C. It was brilliantly fine—no humidity to speak of—but hotter around the bush course, which was located a couple of miles outside the small township of Jimboorie. It boasted *three* pubs—what could be sadder than an Outback town with no pub, worse no beer—all full up with visiting guests; a one man police station; a couple of government buildings; a small bush hospital manned by a doctor and two well qualified nurses; a chemist who sold all sorts of things outside of pharmaceuticals; a single room school; a post office that fitted neatly into a corner of the craft shop; a couple of shoe and clothing stores; a huge barn that sold just about everything like a city hyper-dome; the office of the well respected Jimboorie *Bulletin,* which appeared monthly and had a wide circulation. The branch office of the Commonwealth Bank had long since been closed down to everyone's disgust, but the town continued to boast a remarkably good Chinese restaurant and a bakehouse famous for the quality of its bread and its mouth-watering steak pies.

This afternoon the entire township of less than three thousand—a near boom town in the Outback—was in attendance, including the latest inhabitants, the publicans, Vince and Katie Dougherty's six-month-old identical twins, duly cooed over.

The horses, all with thoroughbred blood, were the pride of the competing stations; proud heads bowed, glossy necks arched, tails swishing in nervous anticipation. This was a special day for them, too. They were giving every indication they were ready to race their hearts out. All in all, though it was hidden beneath lots of laughter, back-slapping and the deeply entrenched mateship of the bush, rivalry was as keen as English mustard.

The Jimboorie Cup had been sponsored in the early days of settlement by the pioneering Cunningham family, a pastoral dynasty whose origins, like most others in colonial Australia, lay in the British Isles. William Cunningham second son of an English upper middle class rural family arrived in Australia in the early 1800s, going on to make his fortune in the southern colonies rearing and selling thousands of 'pure' Merino sheep. It wasn't until the mid-1860s that a branch of the family moved from New South Wales into Queensland, squatting on a few hundred thousand acres of rich black plains country, gradually moving from tin shed to wooden shack then into the Outback castles they eventually began to erect for themselves as befitting their social stature and to remind them of 'Home'.

Carrie's own ancestors—Anglo-Irish—had arrived ten years later in the 1870s with sufficient money to take up a huge run and eventually build a fine house some twenty miles distance from Jimboorie House the reigning queen. In time the Cunninghams and the McNevins and the ones who came after became known as the 'sheep barons' making great fortunes off the backs of the Merinos. That was the boom time. It was wonderful while it lasted and it lasted for well over one hundred years. But as everyone knows for every boom there's a bust. The demand for Australian wool—the best in the world—gradually went into decline as man-made fibres emerged as strong competitors. The smart producers had swiftly switched to sheep meat production to keep afloat while still maintaining the country's fine wool genetics from the dual purpose Merino. So Australia was still riding on the sheep's back establishing itself as the world's premium exporter of lamb.

The once splendid Jimboorie Station with its reputation for producing the finest wool, under the guardianship of the incredibly stubborn and short-sighted Angus Cunningham had continued to focus on a rapidly declining market while his neighbours had the good sense to turn quickly to diversification and sheep meat production thus optimising returns.

Today the Cup was run by a *group* of station owners, working extremely hard but still living the good life. Carrie's father, Bruce McNevin, Clerk of the Course, was one. Natasha Cunningham's father another. Brad Harper, a relative newcomer—twenty years—but a prominent station owner all the same, was the race commentator and had been for a number of years. One of the horses—it was Number 6—Lightning Boy was acting extra frisky, loping in circles, dancing on its black hooves, requiring its rider to keep a good grip on the reins.

'He's an absolute nothing, a nobody,' Natasha Cunningham continued the contemptuous tirade against her cousin. She came alongside Carrie as she moved nearer the white rails. Flemington—home of the Melbourne Cup—had its famous borders of beautiful roses. Jimboorie's rails were hedged by thick banks of indestructible agapanthus waving their sunbursts of blue and white flowers.

'He certainly knows how to handle a horse,' Carrie murmured dryly.

'Why not? That's all he's ever been, a stockman. His father might have been one of us but his mother was just a common little slut. His father died early, probably from sheer boredom.

He and his mother roamed Queensland towns like a couple of
deadbeats, I believe. I doubt he's had much of an education.
Mother's dead, too. Drink, drugs, probably both. The family
never spoke one word to her. No one attended their wedding.
Shotgun, Mother said.'

She *would,* Carrie thought, a clear picture of the acid tongued
Julia Cunningham in her mind. Carrie thoroughly disliked the
pretentious Julia and her even more snobbish daughter. Now she
knew a moment of satisfaction. 'Well, your great uncle, Angus,
remembered your cousin at the end. He left him Jimboorie.'

Natasha burst into bitter laughter. 'And what a prize that is!
The homestead is just about ready to implode.'

'I've always loved it,' Carrie said with more than a touch of
nostalgia. 'When I was little I thought it was a palace.'

'How stupid can you get!' Natasha gave a bark of laughter.
'Though I agree it would have been wonderful in the old days
when the Cunninghams were the leading pioneering family. So
of course we're still important. *My* grandfather would have seen
to Jimboorie's upkeep. He would have switched to feeding the
domestic market like Dad. But that old fool Angus never did a
thing about it. Just left the station and the Cunningham ancestral home fall down around his ears. Went to pieces after his
wife died and his daughter married and moved away. Angus
should never have inherited in the first place. Neither should
James. Or Clay as he calls himself these days. No 'little Jimmy'
anymore. James Claybourne Cunningham. Claybourne, would
you believe, was his mother's maiden name. A bit fancy for the
likes of her.'

'It's a nice tribute to his mother,' Carrie said quietly. 'He
can't have any fond memories of your side of the family.' What
an understatement!

'Nor we for him! But the feud was on long before that. My
grandad and great-uncle Angus hated one another. The whole
Outback knows that.'

'Yes, indeed,' Carrie said, long acquainted with the tortured saga of the Cunninghams. She angled her wide brimmed cream hat so that it came further down over her eyes. The sun was blazing at three o'clock in the afternoon. A shimmering heat haze hovered over the track. 'Look, they're about to start.'

'Oh goody!' Natasha mocked the excitement in Carrie's voice. 'My money's on Scott.' She glanced sideways, her blue eyes filled with overt malice.

'So's mine,' Carrie answered calmly, visibly moving Scott's two carat diamond solitaire around on her finger. Natasha had always had her eye on Scott. It was in the nature of things Natasha Cunningham would always get what she wanted. But Scott had fallen for Carrie, very much upsetting the Cunninghams, and marking Carrie as a target for Natasha's vicious tongue. Something that had to be lived with.

Three races had already been run that afternoon. The crowd was in fine form calling for the day's big event to begin. There was a bit of larrikinism quickly clamped down on by Jimboorie's resident policeman. The huge white marquees acting as 'bars' had been doing a roaring trade. Scott, on the strapping Sassafras, a rich red chestnut with a white blaze and white socks, was the bookies' favourite, as well as the crowd's. He was up against two fine riders, members of his own polo team. No one had had any prior knowledge of the riding skills of the latest arrival to their far flung bush community. Well they knew *now,* Carrie thought. They only had to watch the way he handled his handsome horse. It had an excellent conformation; a generous chest that would have good heart room. The crowd knew who the rider was of course. Everyone knew his sad history. And there was *more!* All the girls for hundreds of miles around were agog with excitement having heard the rumour, which naturally spread like a bushfire, Clay Cunningham, a bachelor, was looking for a wife. That rivetting piece of information had come from Jimboorie's leading publican, the one and only Vince Dougherty. Vince gained it, he claimed, over a cold beer or two. Not that Clay Cunningham was the only bush bachelor looking for a wife. In the harsh and lonely conditions of the Outback—very much a man's world—eligible women were a fairly scarce commodity and thus highly prized. As far as Carrie could see all the pretty girls had swarmed here, some already joking about making the newcomer a good wife. Perhaps Clay Cunningham had been unwise to mention it. There was a good chance he'd get mobbed as proceedings got more boisterous.

He certainly cut a fine figure on horseback though Carrie didn't expect Natasha to concede that. The black gelding looked in tip-top condition. It had drawn almost as many admiring eyes as its rider. A fine rider herself—Carrie had won many ladies' races and cross country events—she loved to see good horsemanship. She hadn't competed in the Ladies' Race run earlier that day, which she most likely would have won. She was to present the Jimboorie Cup to the winning rider. Her mother, Alicia, President of the Ladies Committee and a woman of powerful persuasion, had insisted she look as fresh as a daisy and as glamorous as possible. A journalist and a photographer from a popular women's magazine had been invited to cover the two-day event with a gala dance to be held that night in Jimboorie's splendid new Community Hall of which they were all very proud.

A few minutes before 3:00 p.m. the chattering, laughing crowd abruptly hushed. They were waiting now for the starter, mounted on a distinguished old grey mare everyone knew as Daisy, to drop his white flag... Carrie began to count the seconds....

'They're off!' she shouted in her excitement, making a spontaneous little spring off the ground. A great cheer rose all around her, lofting into the cloudless cobalt sky. The field, ten runners in all, literally leapt from their standing start. The horses as was usual were bunched up at first. Then the riders began battling for good positions, two quickly becoming trapped on the rails. The field sorted itself out and the horses began to pound along, hooves eating up a track that was predictably hard and fast.

When the time came for the riders to negotiate the turn in what was essentially a wild bush track, half of the field started to fall back. In many ways it was more like a Wild West gallop than the kind of sophisticated flat race one would see at a city track. The front runners had begun to fight it out, showing their true grit. Scott, his polo team mates and Jack Butler, who was Carrie's father's overseer on Victory Downs. Clay Cunningham's black gelding was less than a length behind Jack and going well. Carrie watched him lean forward to hiss some instruction into his horse's ear.

'Oh dear!' Carrie watched with a perverse mix of dismay and delight as the gelding stormed up alongside Jack's gutsy chestnut, then overtook him. Jack, who would have been thrilled to be among the frontliners, was battling away for all he was worth. At this rate Clay Cunningham was a sure thing, Carrie considered, unless Scott could get some extra speed from his mount. Scott was savagely competitive but the newcomer was giving every indication he'd be hard to beat. One thing was certain. Clay Cunningham was a crack rider.

Natasha, too, had drawn in her breath sharply. The possibility Scott could be beaten hadn't occurred to either woman. Golden Boy Harper, as he was popularly known, was captain of their winning polo team and thus had a special place in Jimboorie society.

'Your cousin looks like winning,' Carrie warned her, shaking her own head. 'Damn it, *now,* Scott! Make your move.' Carrie wasn't sure Scott was riding the right race. Though she would never say it, she didn't actually consider Scott had the innate ability to get the best out of a horse. He didn't know much about *coaxing* for one thing.

Natasha belted the air furiously with her fist. 'This shouldn't be happening.'

'Well it *is!'* Carrie was preparing herself for the worst.

She saw Scott produce his whip, giving his horse a sharp crack, but Clay Cunningham was using touch and judgment rather than resorting to force. It paid off. The big black gelding had already closed the gap coming at full stride down the track.

'Damn it!' Natasha shrieked, looking ready to burst with disappointment.

Carrie, on the other hand, was feeling almost guilty. She was getting goose bumps just watching Clay Cunningham ride with such authority that Scott's efforts nearly fell into insignificance. That feeling in itself was difficult to come to grips with. The fast paced highly competitive gelding, like its rider, looked like it had plenty left in reserve.

Carrie held her breath, still feeling that upsurge of contrasting emotions. Admiration and apprehension were there aplenty. Sharp disappointment that Scott, her fiancé, wasn't going to win. Elation at how fast the big gelding was travelling—that was the horse lover in her she told herself. That animal had a lot of class. So did its rider. There was a man *determined* to win. After the way Jimboorie had treated him, Carrie couldn't begrudge him the victory. She liked a fighter.

Two minutes more, just as she expected, Lightning Boy flew past the post with almost two full lengths in hand.

What a buzz!

'Oh, well done!' Carrie cried, putting her hands together. For a moment she forgot she was standing beside Natasha, the inveterate informer. 'I wonder if he plays polo?' What an asset he would be!

'Of course he doesn't play polo,' Natasha snapped. 'He's a pauper. Paupers don't get to play polo. Where's your loyalty anyway?' she demanded fiercely. 'Scott's your fiancé and you're applauding an outsider.'

'Insider,' Carrie corrected, looking as cool as a cucumber. 'He's already moved into Jimboorie.'

'For now.' Natasha made no effort to hide her outrage and anger. 'Just see if people deal with him. My father has a great amount of influence.'

Carrie frowned. 'What are you saying? Your family is ready-
ing to make life even more difficult for him?'

'You bet we are!' Natasha's blue eyes were hard. 'He'd be
mad to stay around here. Old Angus only left him Jimboorie
to spite us.'

'Be that as it may, your cousin must intend to stick around
if he's looking for a wife,' Carrie said, really pleased that after
a moment of stunned silence the crowd erupted into loud, appreciative applause and even louder whistles. They were willing to give the newcomer a fair go even if Natasha's vengeful
family weren't. 'Well there you are!' she said brightly. 'No one
rated his chances yet your cousin came out the clear winner.'

'We'll see what Scott has to say,' Natasha snorted with in-
dignation, visibly jangling with nerves. 'For all we know there
could have been interference near the fence.'

'There wasn't.' Carrie dismissed that charge very firmly. 'I
know Scotty doesn't like to lose, but he'll take it well enough.'
Some hope, she thought inwardly. Her fiancé had a considerable antipathy to losing. At anything.

'I'll be sure to tell him how delighted you were with my cousin's performance,' Natasha called quite nastily as she walked
away.

'I bet you will,' Carrie muttered aloud. Since she and Scott
had become engaged, two months previously, Natasha always
gave Carrie the impression she'd like to tear her eyes out.

A tricky situation was now coming up. It was her job, graciously handed over to her by her mother, to present the Cup.
Not to Scott, as just about everyone had confidently expected,
but to the new owner of historic Jimboorie Station. The Cunningham ancestral home was falling down around his ears and
the once premier cattle and sheep station these days was little
more than a ruin said to be laden with debt. In all likelihood
the new owner would at some stage sell up and move on. But
for now, she had to find her way to the mounting yard for the
presentation and lots of photographs. Come to that, she would

have to take some herself. For two years now since she had returned home from university she had worked a couple of days a week for Paddy Kennedy, the founder and long time editor of the *Jimboorie Bulletin*. Once a senior editor with the *Sydney Morning Herald*, chronic life-threatening asthma sent him out to the pure dry air of the Outback where it was thought he had a better chance of controlling his condition.

That was twenty years ago. The monthly *Jimboorie Bulletin* wasn't any old rag featuring local gossip and kitty-up-the-tree stories. It was a professional newspaper, covering issues important to the Outback: the fragile environment, political matters, social matters, health matters, aboriginal matters, national sporting news, leavened by a page reporting on social events from all over the Outback. The rest of the time Carrie was kept busy with her various duties on the family station she loved, as well as running the home office, a job she had taken over from her mother.

Her work for the *Bulletin* stimulated her intellectually and she loved Paddy. He was the wisest, kindest man she knew whereas her father—although he had always been good to her in a material fashion—was not a man a *daughter* could get close to. A son maybe, but her parents had not been blessed with a son. She was an only child, one who was sensitive enough to have long become aware of her father's pain and bitter disappointment he had no male heir. He had already told her, although she would be well provided for, Victory Downs was to go to her cousin, Alex, the son of her father's younger brother. Uncle Andrew wasn't a pastoralist at all, though he had been raised in a pastoral family. He had a thriving law practice in Melbourne and was, in fact, the family solicitor.

Alex was still at university, uncertain what he wanted to be, although he knew Victory Downs would pass to him. Carrie's mother had fought aggressively for her daughter's rights but her father couldn't be moved. For once in her married life her mother had lost the fight.

'You know how men are!' Alicia had railed. 'They think women can't run anything. It's immensely unfair. How can your father think young Alex would be a better manager than you?'

'That's not the only reason, Mum,' Carrie had replied, thinking it terrible to be robbed of one's inheritance. 'Dad doesn't want the station to pass out of the family. Sons have to be the inheritors. Sons carry the family name. Dad doesn't care at all for the idea anyone other than a McNevin should inherit Victory Downs. He seems to be naturally suspicious of women as well. Why is that? Uncle Andy isn't a bit like that.'

'Your father just doesn't know how to relax,' was Alicia's stock explanation, always turning swiftly to another topic.

It had been strange growing up knowing she was seriously undervalued by her father but Carrie was reluctant to criticise him. He was a *good* father in his way. Certainly she and her mother lacked for nothing, though there was no question of squandering money like Julia Cunningham, who spent as much time in the big cities of Sydney and Melbourne as she did in her Outback home.

People in the swirling crowd waved to her happily—she waved back. Most of the young women her age were wearing smart casual dress, while she was decked out as if she were attending a garden party at Government House in Sydney. Alicia's idea. Carrie's hat was lovely really, the wide dipping brim trimmed with silk flowers. She wore a sunshine-yellow printed silk dress sent to her from her mother's favourite Sydney designer. Studded high heeled yellow sandals were on her feet. Her long honey-blond hair was drawn back into a sophisticated knot to accommodate the picture hat her mother had insisted on her wearing.

'I want you to look really, *really* good!' Alicia, a classic beauty in her mid-forties and looking nothing like it, fussed over her. 'Which means you have to wear this hat. It will protect your lovely skin for one thing as well as adding the necessary glamour. Never forget it's doubly essential to look after one's skin in our part of the world. You know how careful I am even though we have an enviable tawny tint.'

Indeed they had. Carrie had inherited her mother's beautiful brown eyes as well. Eyes that presented such a striking contrast to their golden hair. Carrie, christened Caroline Adriana McNevin had *no* look of her father's side of the family. She didn't really mind. Alicia, from a well-to-do Melbourne family and with an Italian Contessa as her maternal grandmother, was a beautiful woman by anyone's standards.

'You're a lucky girl, do you realise that? Scott Harper for a fiancé.' Alicia fondly pinched her daughter's cheek. 'I don't think the Cunninghams will ever get over it. Julia worked so hard to throw Scott and Natasha together.'

As if you didn't do the same thing with Scott and me, Mamma, Carrie thought but didn't have the heart to say. Scott Harper was one of the most eligible bachelors in the country. His father's property ventures were huge. Even Carrie's father had been 'absolutely delighted' when she and Scott had become engaged. Obviously the best thing a daughter could do—her crowning achievement as it were—was to marry a handsome young man from a wealthy family. To prove it her father seemed to have a lot more time for her in the past few months. Could he be thinking of future heirs, not withstanding the fact he had already made a will in favour of Alex? It wouldn't be so bad, would it, to pass Victory Downs on to someone like Scott Harper, rich and ambitious?

Sometimes Carrie felt like a pawn.

Clay was agreeably surprised by the number of people who made it their business to congratulate him. Many of the older generation mentioned they remembered his father and added how much Clay resembled him. One sweet-faced elderly lady actually asked after his mother, her smile crumpling when Clay told her gently that his mother had passed on. He hadn't received any congratulations from the runner-up, the god in their midst,

Scott Harper, and didn't expect any. Leopards didn't change their spots. Aged ten when his parents uprooted him from the place he so loved and which incredibly was now his, Clay still had vivid memories of Scott Harper, the golden-haired bully boy, two years his senior. Harper had treated him like trash when he'd never had trouble from the other station boys. For some reason Harper had baited him mercilessly about his parents' marriage whenever they met up. Once Harper had knocked him down in the main street of the town causing a bad concussion for which he'd been hospitalised. His father, wild as hell, had made the long drive in his battered utility to the Harper station to remonstrate with Scott's father, but he had been turned back at gunpoint by Bradley Harper's men.

Clay's taking the Jimboorie Cup from Scott this afternoon was doubly sweet. Soon the surprisingly impressive silver cup would be presented to him by Harper's fiancé. He had been amazed to hear it was Caroline McNevin, whom he remembered as the prettiest little girl he had ever laid eyes on. How had that exquisite little creature grown up to become engaged to someone like Harper? But then wasn't it a tradition for pastoral families to intermarry? His father—once considered destined for great things—had proved the odd man out, struck down by love at first sight. Love for a penniless little Irish girl now buried by his side.

There was a stir in the crowd. Clay turned about to see a woman coming towards him. He drew himself up straighter, absolutely thrown by how beautiful Caroline had become. Her whole aura suggested springtime, a world of flowers. Her petite figure absorbed all the sunlight around her.

She seemed to *float* rather than walk. For a moment an overwhelming emotion swept over him. To combat it, he stood very, very still. He wondered if it were nostalgia; remembrance of some lovely moment when he was a boy. The hillsides around Jimboorie alight with golden wattle, perhaps?

Now they were face-to-face, less than a metre apart, and

he like a fool stood transfixed. He was conscious his nerves had tensed and his stomach muscles had tightened into a hard knot. She was *tiny* compared to him. Even in her high heels she only came up to his heart. She still had that look of shining innocence, only now it was allied to an adult allure all the more potent since both qualities appeared to exist quite naturally side by side.

He couldn't seem to take his eyes off her while she consolidated her hold over him.

Caroline had beautiful large oval eyes, a deep velvety-brown. They were doubly arresting with her golden hair. Her skin, a tawny olive beneath the big picture hat, was flawlessly beautiful. Her features were delicate, perfectly symmetrical. No more than five-three, she nevertheless had a real presence. At least she was running tight circles around him.

'James Cunningham!' The vision smiled at him. A smile that damn near broke his heart. What the heck was the matter with him? How could he describe what he felt? Perhaps they had meant something to each other in another life? 'Welcome back to Jimboorie. I'm Carrie McNevin.'

Belatedly he came back to control. 'I remember you, Caroline,' he said, his voice steady, unhurried, yet he was so broadsided by her beauty, he forgot to smile.

'You *can't*!' A soft flush rose to her cheeks.

'I do.' He shrugged his shoulder, thinking beautiful women had unbounded power at their pink fingertips. 'I remember you as the happy little girl who used to wave to me when you saw me in town.'

'Really?' She was enchanted by the idea.

'Yes, really.'

Her essential sweetness enfolded him. Her voice was clear and gentle, beautifully enunciated. Caroline McNevin, the little princess. Untouchable. Except now by Harper. That made him hot and angry, inducing feelings that hit him with the force of a breaker.

'Well, it's my great pleasure, James, or do you prefer to be called Clay?' She paused, tipping her golden head to one side.

'Clay will do.' Only his mother had ever called him James. Now he remembered to smile though his expression remained serious even a little sombre. Why wouldn't he when he felt appallingly vulnerable in the face of a beautiful creature who barely came up to his heart?

Carrie was aware of the sombreness in him. It added to the impression he gave of quiet power and it had to be admitted, mystery. 'Then it's going to be my great pleasure to be able to present you, Clay, with the Jimboorie Cup,' Carrie continued. 'We'll just move back over there,' she said, turning to lead the way to a small dais where the race committee was grouped, waiting for her and the winner of the Cup to join them. 'They'll want to take photos,' she told him, herself oddly shaken by their meeting. And the feeling wasn't passing off. Perhaps it was because she'd heard so many stories about the Cunninghams while she was growing up? Or maybe it was because Clay Cunningham had grown into a strikingly attractive man. She felt that attraction brush over her then without her being able to do a thing about it. She felt it sink into her skin. She only hoped she wasn't showing her strong reactions. Everyone was looking at them.

Natasha might well continue to denounce her cousin, Carrie thought, but the family resemblance was strong. The Cunninghams were a handsome lot, raven haired, with bright blue eyes. Natasha would have been beautiful, but her fine features were marred by inner discontent and her eyes were strangely cold. Clay Cunningham had the Cunningham height and rangy build—only his hair wasn't black. It was a rich mahogany with a flame of dark auburn as the sun burnished it. His eyes, the burning blue of an Outback sky, were really beautiful, full of depth and sparkle. He looked like a *real* man. A man women would fall for hook, line and sinker. So why wasn't he married already, or actively looking for a wife? If indeed the rumour were true. Something she was beginning to doubt. He had to be four, maybe five years older than she, which made him around twenty-eight. He was a different kind of man from Scott. She sensed a depth, a sensitivity—whatever it was—in him that Scott lacked.

It had to be an effect of the light but there seemed to be sparkles in the space between them. Carrie never dreamed a near-stranger could have this effect on her. Her main concern was to conceal it. Up until now she had felt *safe*. She was going to marry Scott, the man she was in love with—yet Clay Cunningham's blue gaze had reached forbidden places.

Their hands touched as she handed over the Silver Cup to the accompanying waves of applause. She couldn't move, even *think* for a few seconds. She felt a little jolt of electricity through every pore of her skin. He continued to hold her eyes, his own unfaltering. Had her trembling transferred itself to him like a vibration? She hoped not. She wasn't permitted to feel like this.

Yet sparkles continued to pulsate before her eyes. Perhaps she was mildly sun-struck? She had the unnerving notion that the little frisson of shock—unlike anything she had ever experienced before—was mutual. She even wondered what life might have in store if he decided to remain on Jimboorie? All around her people were laughing and clapping. Some were carrying colourful balloons. The thrill of the race had got to her. That was it! Her course was set. She was a happily engaged woman. She was to marry Scott Harper in December. A Christmas bride.

And there was Scott staring right at her. Too late she became aware of him. She felt the chill behind his smile. She knew him so well she had no difficulty recognising it. It came towards her like an ice-bearing cloud. He was furious and doing a wonderful job of hiding it. A triumphant looking Natasha was by his side, the two of them striking a near identical pose; one full of an overbearing self-confidence. Maybe arrogance was a better word. Scott as Bradley Harper's heir certainly liked to flaunt it. Natasha, as a Cunningham, did too.

Now Scott sauntered towards the dais around which the VIPs of the vast district milled, calling in a taunting voice, 'You'll absolutely have to tell us, *Jimmy,* where you learned how to ride like that? And the name of the guy who loaned you his horse. Or did you steal it?' He held up defensive hands. 'Only joking!'

As a joke it was way off, but Clay Cunningham held his ground, quite unmoved. 'You haven't changed one little bit, have you, Harper?' he said with unruffled calm. 'Lightning Boy was a parting gift from a good friend of mine. A beauty, isn't he? He could run the race over.'

'Like to give it another go?' Scott challenged with an open lick of hostility.

'Any time—when *your* horse is less spent.' Clay Cunningham gently waved the silver cup aloft to another roar of applause.

Bruce McNevin, a concerned observer to all this, fearing a confrontation, moved quickly onto the dais to address the crowd. Even youngsters draped over the railings managed to fall silent. They were used to hearing from Mr. McNevin who was to say a few words then hand over the prize money of $20,000 dollars, well above the reward offered by other bush committees.

Her father was a handsome man, Carrie thought proudly. A man in his prime. He had a full head of dark hair, good regular features, a bony Celtic nose, a strong clean jawline and well defined cheekbones. He was always immaculately if very conservatively dressed. Bruce McNevin was definitely a 'tweedy' man.

While her father spoke Carrie stood not altogether happily within the half circle of Scott's distinctly proprietorial arm. She was acutely aware of the anger and dented pride he was fighting to hold in. Scott wasn't a good loser. Carrie didn't know why but it was apparent he had taken an active dislike to Clay Cunningham.

Now Clay Cunningham, cheque in hand, made a response to

her father that proved such a mix of modesty, confidence and dry humour that time and again his little speech was punctuated by appreciative bursts of laughter and applause. The crowd was still excited and the winner's speech couldn't have been more designed to please. The race goers had come to witness a good race and the Cup winner—a newcomer—had well and truly delivered. Not that anyone could really call him a newcomer. Heavens, he was a Cunningham! Cunningham was a name everyone knew. There was even a chance he might be able to save what was left of that once proud historic station, Jimboorie, though it would take a Herculean effort and a bottomless well of money.

'Who the hell does he think he is?' Scott muttered in Carrie's ear, unable to credit the man 'little Jimmy' Cunningham, the urchin, had become. 'And what's with the posh voice?'

'He *is* a Cunningham, Scott,' Carrie felt obliged to point out. 'It's written all over him. And it may very well be he *did* get a good education.'

Scott snorted like an angry bull. 'His father left here without a dime. Everyone knows that. Angus Cunningham might have sheltered them to spite the rest of his family but he couldn't have paid his nephew anything in the way of wages. Reece Cunningham cut himself off from his own family when he married that little tramp.'

'You know nothing about her, Scott.' Carrie pulled away from him as discreetly as she could. '*My* mother says there was *no* proof whatsoever to any of the cruel stories that were circulated about her by the Cunninghams and the Campbells. Remember Clay's father was expected to marry Elizabeth Campbell or Campbell-Moore as she is today.'

'But the fool of a man didn't,' Scott retorted, staring down at her with a mixture of hurt and displeasure. 'Whose side are you on anyway?'

She turned away from the glare in his eyes. 'The side of fair mindedness, Scott. Now you'll have to excuse me. Mamma wants me for more photographs.'

'Go to her by all means.' Scott bowed slightly. 'I just hope Cunningham doesn't plan on showing up tonight.'

His voice was iron hard.

CHAPTER TWO

WRESTLING WITH HER unsettled feelings, Carrie dressed for the gala dance. Her party dress at least gave her uncomplicated pleasure. It was of white silk chiffon, feminine and floaty. White always married well with the golden tint in her skin, a legacy of that generous dollop of Italian blood. The bodice of her evening dress was perfectly plain, dipping low into the cleft between her breasts and hung from double spaghetti straps. The midcalf swishy skirt was richly embroidered with swirls of tiny seed pearls and silver sequins. She wore her hair hanging loose down her back—the way Scott liked it—but pulled away from her face and secured behind her ears with two beautiful antique hair combs encrusted with dazzling faux jewels. She should have felt on top of the world, instead she felt...*apprehensive* as though something unpleasant was going to happen or she was going to make a single irreversible mistake. So that's what meeting up with Clay Cunningham had done for her!

Her mind kept jumping back to the look in Scott's eyes. The hardness, the jealousy and the defiance. Scott scarcely knew Clay Cunningham. Scott could only have been twelve when Clay's father had finally packed up and moved his family away, but she could have sworn Scott's antagonism to Clay Cunningham, perhaps buried deep within him, had re-surfaced with a vengeance. She already knew about Scott's jealous nature, but usually he kept it under control. Scott actually disliked even his own friends smiling at her let alone attempting a playful flirtation. It was a terrifying thought he might have intuited her spontaneous reaction to the man Clay Cunningham had grown into. She realised, too, with a guilty pang ever since Clay had told her she used to wave to him in the town when she was a little girl, she had been trying very hard to evoke a forgotten memory.

Goodness, what's the matter with me? she asked her reflection. She was usually very level-headed. She even felt an impulse to start praying the evening would go well. Glancing up at the silver framed wall clock she saw it was almost eight. She really should be on her way. Scott was going to meet her in the foyer It was only a short walk from Dougherty's pub where she was staying to the new Community Hall. The band had been underway for at least an hour, the infectious toe tapping music spilling out onto the street. The band was good. Her mother had arranged for the musicians to come from Brisbane. She started to sing along a little, trying to lift her spirits.

A final check in the mirror. Turning her head from side to side, she saw the sparkling light of her hair combs, one of innumerable little presents from her mother. Her parents were staying overnight with friends. She had elected to stay with Vince and Katie at the pub, as they always looked after her. The pub was spotlessly clean, the food not fancy, but good. She stayed there overnight when she was working for Paddy at the *Bulletin*. It was preferable to making the long drive home, then back again the following morning. Victory Downs was over a hundred miles west of the town—no distance in the bush—but she had to multiply that by four when she worked in town as she mostly did, two days in a row.

She had her silver sandalled foot on the second bottom tread of the staircase when Scott, wearing a white dinner jacket, and looking dazzlingly handsome, swung through the front doors.

'Hiyah, beautiful!' His blue eyes travelled over her with pride of possession. 'I *am* impressed!'

The overhead light glinted on his smooth golden hair and the white of his smile. If they had children—she wanted three, four was okay—they were bound to have golden hair, Carrie thought, holding out her hands to him.

'There's not going to be anyone to touch you!' Scott continued to eye her, appreciatively. She looked as good to eat as a bowl of vanilla ice cream. He'd had a lot of girls over the years but Carrie was unique.

'You look great yourself!' she told him, sincerity in her velvety eyes.

'All for you.' He'd had a few drinks: now, he badly wanted pull her into his arms. He wanted to race her back upstairs, strip that pretty white dress off her, throw her down on the bed and make violent love to her. Only he was afraid of what might happen. Carrie, by his reckoning, had to be the last virgin over fifteen left on the planet. If that weren't astonishing enough, she wanted it to remain that way until they were married. Could you beat it! He would *never* have agreed, only he saw her resolve was very strong. Or maybe she was playing it smart, teasing the living daylights out of him. She was his fiancée yet he had to keep his hands off her. Well, within limits. It was excruciatingly frustrating—more torture—when she filled him with such lust as he had ever known. Not that he had taken a corresponding vow of celibacy. He got release when he wanted it. Most girls were his for the asking including that bitch Natasha Cunningham. He'd had an on and off relationship with her for years. She was mad for him—and he knew it.

But it was innocent little Caroline McNevin he had always wanted. He guessed he had started to want her from when she was a yummy little teenager with budding breasts. He'd confidently thought virginity was a relic of the Dark Ages. He'd been stunned when Carrie told him she wanted to remain a virgin until their wedding night. At first he'd been sure it was a damned ploy to keep him interested, on a knife's edge. As a ploy it certainly worked, but then he came to realise she was fair dinkum. It was impossible to believe! But, boy, wouldn't he make up for the long hungry years of deprivation! Their wedding night couldn't come soon enough.

They had scarcely made it into the packed hall with huge silver-blue disco balls suspended from the ceiling like glittering moons, when Scott's grip on her arm tightened. Carrie let out a surprised little whimper. 'Hey, Scott, you're hurting!'

'Sorry.' He shifted his arm to around her waist, hauling her close to him. 'That bastard has had the nerve to show up,' he ground out, his eyes quickly finding Clay Cunningham's rangy figure across the room.

So it wasn't going to be a happy evening! Carrie's heart began to thump. She lifted her eyes to Scott's tight face. 'Scott, please settle down. We're here to enjoy ourselves aren't we? Everybody will be watching. Clay Cunningham has a perfect right to be here. I expect there would be a lot of disappointed girls if he hadn't shown up. Surely you're not looking for trouble?'

'He'd do well to steer clear of me,' Scott gritted, unable to conceal a flare of jealousy so monstrous it startled even him. He tried to calm himself by sheer will power. So far as he was concerned it was Cunningham versus *him!* Across the packed hall Cunningham was standing head and shoulders above a group of silly giggling females. One let out a burst of ecstatic laughter, obviously thrilled there was an eligible bachelor in their midst. A man, moreover, who had expressed his desire to find himself a wife. Hadn't they heard, the little fools, Jimboorie House was falling down? Didn't they know Jimboorie Station would never be what it was again? Or would any man do? Girls fell in and out of love so fast. They were like kids with some wonderful new toy.

All right, Cunningham was handsome. Scott was honest enough to admit that. All the Cunninghams were. Even Natasha. And Cunningham had that look about him, he recognised, of a fine natural athlete. How had that little weed of a kid who he'd loved slapping around turned into this guy? Scott wasn't even sure he could take Cunningham in a fight, even though he was a good amateur boxer, a welterweight champion at university. The fact Cunningham had beaten him for the Cup Scott took as a scalding defeat. And he'd been beaten so *easily!* That was what stunned and humiliated him. He was used to being king pin. To cap it off his fiancée had presented Cunningham with the Cup. He'd watched their eyes, then their hands meet. It had only taken him a second to register the look on Carrie's face. It had filled him with jealousy and unease.

Cunningham had stirred her interest and attention. That wasn't going to be allowed to happen. Carrie was *his*! He owned her. Or near enough. She was wearing his ring.

I mightn't be able to stop you looking, but don't touch, you bastard! Scott swung Carrie into his arms, whisking her onto the dance floor. At least the music was great. It filled up the room.

After each bracket of numbers, the crowd clapped their appreciation. One of the band, a sexy looking guy in tight jeans, a red satin shirt and cowboy boots, took over the microphone to a roar of applause and began to sing, launching into the first romantic ballad of the night; one that was currently top of the charts. His voice was so attractive the dancers gave themselves up to it....

Carrie didn't have the usual succession of dance partners she'd had in the past. Things had changed since she had become engaged to Scott. She realised she was starting to worry that Scott was so possessive. She wasn't *property.* She was a woman, a human being. The last thing she wanted was a stormy married life with a control freak for a husband. But then her thoughts turned to how understanding Scott was about her desire to remain a virgin until their marriage. It pleased her that he was so considerate of her wishes. She had never been one to bow to peer pressure so she hadn't been part of the general sexual experimentation that had attended her university years. She knew some of her fellow students had labelled her a bit of an extremist, but the idea of sex without genuine strong feeling had little appeal for her. It was *her* body that would be invaded after all. Men came from a different place. Most of them she had found, saw sex as satisfying an appetite like food and drink. At the same time they were notoriously quick to pin cruel labels on their willing female partners. Carrie thought there was not only a moral standard, but a health standard that made fastidiousness matter.

Then again she had to take stock of the fact she had no real conflict with remaining a virgin. There was even the odd moment when she had to consider perhaps she hadn't met the man who could overturn all her defences? Or maybe her libido wasn't of the intense sort? Not that Scott hadn't awakened her romantic desires. He had. She knew about sensual pleasure. But still it had been relatively easy to keep to her vow. Or it had been up until now.

She was momentarily alone. Scott was caught up in settling an argument about some polo match when she heard her name—her *full* name—spoken.

'You dance beautifully, Caroline. Will you dance with me?'

He was standing in front of her, looking down at her from his superior height. The corners of his mouth were upturned in a smile. His dark blue eyes held a current of electricity that bathed her in its glow.

She managed to smile back. It felt like taking a risk. A tremble shook her body. The music…the laughter…the voices… oddly started to recede. She knew her lips parted but for the smallest time—maybe a few seconds—no words came out.

'Caroline?'

The oxygen came back to her brain. 'Yes of course I will,' she said, unaware a nerve was pulsing in the hollow of her throat.

His arms came around her. He held her lightly yet his arms

enclosed her. Letting him hold her—she knew—vastly increased the risks.

She couldn't relax. Not there and then. He was, she realised, gifted with sexual radiance and he was using that gift. Consciously or unconsciously? She couldn't tell.

She tried to distract herself by looking at the sea of happy, excited faces around them.

'I know, I'm too tall for you.' Clay's voice was wry. 'And I'm not much of a dancer. Never had time to learn.'

'No, you're fine.' Indeed, it seemed to her he moved with natural ease and rhythm.

'And you're kind.' He pulled her in a little closer and she lifted her hand higher on his shoulder. She could feel the strength in it; the warmth of his skin. He wasn't formally attired like Scott . He wore a beige coloured linen jacket over a black T-shirt and black jeans. A simple outfit, yet on him it looked very sophisticated. He would have absolutely no difficulty finding a wife. In fact, the frenzy had already started. It was her role to watch. Never let it be forgotten she was taken!

She realised she was luxuriating in his clean male scent, redolent of the open air, of fragrant wood smoke. Inhaled, it left her with a feeling akin to a delicious languor. The overhead disco lights dazzled, throwing out blue and silver rays over the swirling crowd, their faces and clothes streaked with light.

For long minutes they danced without speaking, he leading her expertly for all he claimed he couldn't dance. She was beginning to feel a degree of trepidation at the forces set loose by their physical contact. She didn't want it. She certainly didn't need it. She didn't even understand it. Her reaction wasn't *normal*. She couldn't allow herself to think it was akin to being in a state of thrall!

Be careful with this! A warning voice said.

There was a pressure behind Carrie's rib cage. Could he incite emotion as easily as he could incite his high mettled horse to victory? She feared that might be the case. It was even possible he could be looking at *her* as a conquest? Retribution for the way he had been treated? A perverted desire to win over Scott Harper's fiancée? She saw how he had won the Cup. His was a powerful determination and maybe she was next on his list? Only time would prove her right.

Meanwhile he was making her feel decidedly odd. It was as if she were someone else. She couldn't allow that. She had to be herself, yet the feel of his arms around her had deep chords resounding within her. His hand on her back could even be playing her like a master musician. What was he really thinking?

'You look very beautiful,' he said. His voice, which was resonant and deep, had considerable emotional power.

Carrie took a quick breath, thinking she wasn't going to give him any help.

'Harper is a lucky man.'

Now she tilted her head to stare into his eyes. 'What went wrong between you two? It seems strange—you were both so young when you moved away, yet I sense a history between you and Scott. An animosity that still clings.'

The flash in his eyes was as blue as an acetate flame. 'Scott Harper used to like to scare me when I was a kid.'

She felt shame on Scott's behalf. 'It still matters?'

He shrugged. 'You saw how your fiancé was. I'm sure he'll be right with us any moment now. Do you mind that most of the guys here, though they're dying to dance with you, are keeping their distance?'

That hit home. 'I *do* realise,' she said, more severely than she had intended, 'but Scott is my fiancé.'

He nodded. 'A pity'

'A pity he's my fiancé?' Now she was really on the defensive.

'How do you know I don't want you for myself?' He unfolded a slow smile, keeping his tone light.

Hectic colour swept into her cheeks, enhancing her beauty. 'I'm sorry, Clay, but I'm taken.'

'Have you set a date for the wedding?' he asked, with interest.

'Why aren't *you* married?' she countered, aware something potentially dangerous was smouldering between them.

'Because I believe a man has to be able to provide for a wife before he embarks on matrimony.'

She realised she was becoming agitated. She had to rein herself in. 'The rumour around town is you're looking for a wife. Could that possibly be right?'

His smile was self mocking. 'You might very well see me on the doorstep of the *Bulletin* some time soon. I understand you're Pat Kennedy's right hand woman. You can help me run an ad. "Bush Bachelor Seeks A Wife!" You could advise me what to say, maybe help me read through what replies come in.'

'You're joking!' She felt an odd anger.

Clay's blue, blue eyes were alight with what? Devilment? A taunt? He was still holding her lightly but she was starting to feel she couldn't breathe.

'I couldn't be more serious,' he replied. 'I want a wife beside me. I want children. I've been so flat-out working all my life, I've had little time to play the courting game. Besides, eligible young women aren't all that easy to find. I thought an ad might work. It would certainly speed things up.'

He was obviously waiting for her response.

It came out soft but tart. 'Why don't you simply walk up to one of the girls here?' Carrie challenged him, wishing she was older, taller, more experienced. As it was she was a little afraid of him.

He wasn't smiling. 'Forgive me, but it's hard to see past you.'

That transfixed her. She, so light on her feet, a lovely dancer, missed a step, nearly causing him to tread on her toe. 'Must I remind you that I'm taken?' she said as though he had broken a strict rule.

'So you are!' His voice was deeply regretful.

What should she do? Walk away? Abandon him on the dance floor? She didn't *want* to. At the same time she knew she had to.

Run, run away! Far from temptation!

'Give yourself plenty of time to make sure it's going to work.' He steered her away from a whirling couple.

'Is that a warning?' This man was deliberately casting a spell on her. To what end?

'I don't see the two of you together,' he said.

'How can you possibly judge?' Despite herself she began to compare him with Scott. It was something she couldn't control. 'You don't know me and you don't know Scott. We have a fine future ahead of us.'

'Why, then, the fright in your eyes? If he's the love of your life?'

There was such a whirring inside her. It was as though some part of her hitherto not properly in working order, suddenly sprang into life. 'Why are we talking like this, Clay? It's getting very personal and private.' Not to say out of order.

'I told you. I don't have much time. Besides, I feel I could talk to you far into the night.'

'You've just told me why.' She pointed out, not without sarcasm. 'You're lonely.'

'It's possible that's part of it,' he agreed smoothly.

Carrie sucked in her breath; waited a moment. 'I must tell you I wouldn't have agreed to marry Scott if I didn't love him.' Now her voice sounded stilted.

'As I said, Harper is a very lucky man.'

This was too much. Just *too* much. She couldn't play this game if that's what it was. Dancing with him wasn't the same as dancing with Scott. Or any other man for that matter. She could feel the blood beating in her throat, in her breasts, in the pit of her stomach. She had never been so breathtakingly conscious of her own *flesh*.

The same tipsy couple almost careened into them. Clay's arm tightened around her as he swiftly drew her out of harm's way.

She knew it was well past the time to break away, but she made the excuse to herself that would only draw attention to them. So change the subject quickly! 'You're not planning to leave, then?'

'Caroline, I've just arrived,' he replied, mock-plaintively.

'Everyone calls me Carrie.' She spoke as if to correct him when in reality the sound of her name on his lips was like a bell tolling inside her.

'I'm not everyone,' he said quietly. 'Carrie is pretty. Caroline suits you better.'

'What if I say I want you to call me Carrie?'

'All right, Carrie.' He smiled. 'I'll call you Caroline whenever I get the chance.'

It was totally unnerving how dramatically he was getting to her. 'I used to think when I was little that Jimboorie House was a palace.'

'So did I.' Again his glance like blue flame rested on her.

'You have more than a trace of an English accent. Where did that come from?'

He looked over her blond head. 'From my mother I guess. She was Anglo-Irish and well spoken—and lovely. My father's appallingly cruel family had no right to treat her the way they did. They turned all their fury on *her* because my father abandoned them for her. The accent would have been reinforced by long contact with my late mentor who was English. I became very close to him.'

'Was he the one who presented you with Lightning Boy?' She wanted to know all about him.

He nodded. 'Yes, he was. He handed Lightning Boy over a couple of months before he died.'

She read the grief in his glance. 'What did you do? Did you work for him?'

'I was proud to,' he said briefly, his tone a little curt. 'My boss and mentor.'

'Are you going to tell me his name?'

'No, Caroline.' He refused her. At the same time his gaze gathered her up.

'I'm sorry.' She glanced across the dance floor at all the glowing, happy faces. This would go on into the wee hours. 'I won't intrude. I'm just glad you met someone who treated you well.'

'I can't recall many others.' His expression was openly bitter.

'Are you going to make us all pay for wounding you?' she asked, thinking he had been hurt a great deal.

He ignored her question. 'I'd like to take you out to Jimboorie. Would you come?'

Her heart jumped. Agree and there'd be trouble. *Big* trouble.

'Look at me,' he invited quietly. 'Not away. Would you come, Caroline?'

A back-up singer in the band launched into a romantic number. 'How do you see me?' she countered. 'As someone whose freedom is being curtailed?'

'Is it?' He studied her so intently he might have been trying to unmask her.

That put her on her mettle. 'I'd be delighted to come,' she said shortly, consoling herself she had been driven to it.

'Good. I confess I find a woman's views necessary.'

'Is it your intention to put in your ad that Jimboorie House is falling down?' She met his eyes.

'Certainly. It's the right thing to do,' he replied smoothly. 'But it's not in the utter state of decay it appears to be from the outside. The best materials were used in its construction. The finest, stoutest timbers. The cedar came from the vast forests of the Bunya Bunya Mountains. The house itself is built of sandstone. There *is* a tremendous amount of restoration to be done—I can't deny that—but somehow I'll get around it.'

'Perhaps you should say in your ad that you're looking for an heiress?' she suggested, bitter-sweet.

'Now that's a great idea.' His face broke into a mocking smile.

Unnoticed by either of them Scott Harper, who had been further detained by two of his father's friends wanting to know if he thought his team could continue their unbeaten polo season, was quickly canvassing the crowd.

The blood flooded into his face the moment he saw them together. He drew in his breath sharply, catching his bottom lip between strong teeth and drawing blood. How could Carrie possibly do this thing? She knew how he felt about Clay Cunningham. All his childhood antipathy had returned but one hundred times worse. He made his way towards them, threading a path through the dancers, some of them, marking his expression, getting out of his way.

Just look at her, Scott inwardly raged, his jealousy violent and painful. Her beautiful blond head was tipped right back as she stared up into Cunningham's eyes.

This is wrong, all wrong. Let her go!

His progress was stopped when a woman got him in a surprisingly strong arm-lock. 'Scotty, you're not ignoring me are you, darling?'

He swung, catching the hateful expression of malice on Natasha's face. 'You can't let your dewy little fiancée have a bit of fun, can you?' Her voice dropped so low he could barely hear her. 'And she *is* having fun, isn't she?'

'Let go, Natasha,' he rasped. If she'd been a man he would have hit her, so tense was his mood.

'Sure. One dance and we'll call it a night.' She stepped right up to him, a stunning figure in violet banded in silver, putting both hands on his shoulders. 'Don't make a fool of me now, Scotty,' she warned. 'I've kept my mouth shut up to now, but things can change.'

'You're a real bitch! You know that?' he muttered, contempt built into his voice. Nevertheless he retained enough sense to draw her into his arms.

'You don't say that when I'm making you happy.' Natasha, a tall woman, stared with hard challenge into his eyes.

'I should never have started with you,' he said.

A shadow fell across her blue eyes. 'You told me once you were in love with me. I'm still in love with you.'

'Why don't you get over it?' he suggested harshly.

'Easier said than done, Scotty. Don't get mad at me. I'm your friend. I've loved you far too much and far too long. You've made a big mistake getting yourself hitched up to Carrie McNevin. You haven't got a damned thing in common. And how ridiculous is that virgin bit?' Her lips curled in a sneer.

'Shut up,' Scott hissed violently, in the next minute thankful the dance music had changed to something loud and upbeat. Why had he ever told Natasha about Carrie and himself? He was a thousand times sorry.

'Watch it!' she warned, an answering rage in her eyes. 'You don't want people to see how jealous you are my cousin is fascinating your beloved little virgin. I have to admit he scrubs up pretty well. That's the Cunningham in him, of course. Why don't we sit this out for a while? Or we could go outside?'

'Forget it,' he said bluntly.

Her expression was both wounded and affronted. 'What is it she's got? I'm beautiful, too. Is it the hunt? The thrill of the chase? Once you've had her you won't want her anymore.'

'You don't understand *anything*,' Scott said, shaking his head as if to clear it. 'Carrie appeals to the best part of me. When I'm with her I remember I have a soul.'

That affected Natasha more than the cruellest rebuff. 'You fool!' she said.

Scott gave up. In the middle of the dance floor he dropped his arms from around her and walked away, leaving Natasha feeling hollowed out, gutted. Why did she love Scott Harper? It dismayed and humiliated her. She was well aware of his character flaws, which that little innocent Carrie wasn't. Living through this engagement was a long nightmare. She knew Scott had used her up—she had let him, was still letting him—but damn if he was going to throw her away. Maybe it was about time she had a little talk with darling Carrie even if she risked having her own life torn apart.

Carrie danced twice more with Clay Cunningham. It was driving Scott crazy, but he couldn't seem to do a damn thing about it. Cunningham set the pace. Other guys lined up to dance with her. He was drinking too much and he knew it. Alcohol was flowing like water from a bubbling fountain. His mind swirled with crazy thoughts.

Get Carrie on her own.

She had denied him for far too long. They were engaged now. It was his right to have her whether with her consent or not. In his experience girls said *no* all the time when what they really meant was *yes, yes, yes!* He could have any girl he wanted. Natasha Cunningham. Why did he want Carrie so desperately? There was even a strong chance she didn't go for sex. That would be a disaster. Sex was as essential for him as breathing air.

It didn't take him long to come up with an idea. He could tell her he had something for her in the SUV. A little present. Women loved being given presents, though to be honest, Carrie was no gold digger. But couldn't she feel his pain, his desire? No, she was oblivious to everything except remaining a *virgin.* Scott's anger turned ugly, a red mist swirling before his eyes. He remembered the expression on her face as she'd looked up at Cunningham. What *was* it exactly? Curiosity, a deep interest? More than that. A *craving* for something she had never had. Scott only knew she had never turned such a gaze on him. His face darkened.

Finally he had her to himself. They crossed the street with Scott holding her firmly by the arm. 'No, I won't tell you. It's a surprise!' he said in a playful voice he dredged up from somewhere.

She turned to him, puzzled. 'Why did you leave it in the car, Scott? Is it big?' She laughed a little although she was uneasy, concerned Scott had had far too much to drink. Not that he was the only one. The whole hall was filled with tipsy people, singing, dancing, chanting, full of high spirits that would last through until dawn. She couldn't worry about them but she was afraid Scott might make something of a spectacle of himself with his father around. Bradley Harper just wouldn't understand. Usually Scott held his drink well, but tonight was different. He was slurring his words. He never did that.

It was dark under the shadow of the trees that ringed the town park. The gums were smothered in blossom. There was a lovely lemony scent in the air. A little way in the distance she could see couples strolling arm in arm through the park, their bodies spotlighted by the overhead lighting. Others had moved off to cars either to catch a nap or indulge in a spot of canoodling. The big question was, why didn't she want Scott to make love to her? Saying he'd had too much to drink wasn't answer enough. She was going to marry him in three months time. My God, she should be ravenous for his lovemaking. She was so perturbed tears sprang to her eyes.

'Let's sit in the back for a moment,' Scott said, opening up the rear door and all but pushing her in.

'I don't know,' she wavered. 'We shouldn't stay.'

'You're not a bit of fun, are you?' Scott climbed in beside her, turning to her and cupping her face hard with his hand.

'What's the matter with you, Scott?' She shook her head vigorously to free his grip. 'You're in a mood.' It couldn't have been more obvious now.

'Thanks to you,' he said bitterly, abandoning all pretence.

'I've no idea what you mean!' She tried to defend herself. 'Where's the present?' She couldn't have cared less about any present. She just wanted this over.

'What do you know?' he laughed. 'I forgot to bring it with me.'

'Ah, Scott!' She tried hard to fight down her dismay.

'You don't want to be here with me, do you?' he accused her, his hot temper rising.

'Not when you're making me nervous,' she answered truthfully.

'Kiss me.' His voice grated harshly.

She could smell his damp breath, heavy with bourbon. She tried to draw away. 'We have all the time in the world for kisses. Not *here,* Scott. Our parents expect us to set a certain standard.'

'Damn them!' he said violently, getting his arms around her. 'You tell me you're a virgin, but I'm worried you're *not!* You females are full of wiles.'

He sounded terrible, hardly recognisable. A different Scott from the one she knew.

'I refuse to have this discussion now, Scott,' she said quietly, though she was starting to shake inside. 'Let's go back to the hall. Please.'

'Why don't I find out right here and now?' he responded, making his intentions very clear.

She hit him then, a cold spasm of dread causing a real ache in her stomach. It was absolutely spontaneous, her cracking slap to the side of his head. 'I don't lie, understand?' she panted. 'I demand respect from you, Scott!'

He gripped her delicate shoulders, all male force and threat. 'Now isn't that the strangest thing of all! Little Carrie McNevin attacking me.' With a grinding laugh he hauled her to him, hard and tight, crushing her body against him. 'You're *mine,* Carrie. You better believe it. I'm sick to death of holding off. Can't you feel me.' He forced her hand down to his powerful erection. 'I'm mad for you! What is making love anyway, a big mortal sin?'

He cranked up his offensive. He was half on top of her, shoving his tongue deeper and deeper into her mouth. Carrie almost gagged.

'Now we're talking!' he crowed in triumph, his hand buried in the front of her dress, his fingers clamping on to her breast. 'You're the freshest, sweetest girl in the world,' he grunted.

'You made me a promise, Carrie. You accepted my ring. Now accept *me!*'

Quick as a striking snake his other hand was under her skirt, while he rammed her body back into the seat.

'Stop, Scott. *Please.*' She was forced to beg, but she was damned if she was going to scream.

'Relax, you're going to love this.' His hungry hand was at the top of her panties.

'Dammit, I said *stop!*' Carrie cried, cursing her own stupidity. She was frightened of his brute strength. Drunk or not, he was physically in control. Even his weight was relentless. She could never get clear of him.

It was time to think, not give in. The day hadn't arrived when she was going to lie back and take it. Not like *this* anyway. This wasn't love. This was catastrophe. Rape. She let her body go slack, seemingly quiescent, as his hand plunged between her legs. He was moaning now. Moaning with a kind of fierce animal pleasure, primal in its mindlessness.

It was now or never. Carrie gathered herself, fiercely ignoring that his hand was going where it had never gone before. There wasn't much of her but she was fit. And she was an expert horsewoman with strong legs and knees. She waited her moment then when his fingers were about to thrust into her, she rammed one of her knees hard into his sensitive scrotum.

He *howled*! He actually howled! The sound was wild and appalled. Sexual passion turned to a stunned rage. 'God, you bitch!' He lifted a hand to hit her, only the contempt in her voice stopped him in his tracks.

'Don't hit me, Scott. Don't even attempt to go there.'

'You bitch!' he repeated, thinking she needed teaching a lesson. Some part of him was ashamed, the rest was in a whole lot of pain. He let out another moan, rolling across the seat away from her and hunching over, clutching his throbbing parts.

With a dazzling turn of speed Carrie was out of the SUV and on to the grass. Anger burned inside her. She tried desperately to straighten her clothing. What motivated men to behave the way they did? It was a very big question that had never been answered.

A voice called sharply from the other side of the street. 'You all right, Caroline?'

She could have died from humiliation. Clay Cunningham. This was a nightmare. What was she supposed to do, wave? Call out her fine handsome fiancée had just tried to rape her? 'I'm okay. It's nothing,' she answered, her mouth so dry she could barely form the words.

Clay didn't seem too impressed with that. He strode across the street, moving towards the parked vehicle. He watched in disgust as Scott Harper, holding his crotch staggered out of it. 'Mind your own bloody business, Cunningham,' Scott gritted, his voice full of hate and loathing.

'Sorry.' Clay Cunningham had made the transformation from Mr. Nice Guy to one tough looking character, powerfully intimidating. 'I'm not the kind of guy who walks away from a lady in distress. Come over here, Caroline,' he instructed.

'Don't do a damn thing he asks you,' Scott snarled her a warning.

That really bugged her. She responded by running around the front of the vehicle, clearly making her choice. When she was on her own maybe she'd have a good howl herself, but for now she had to get away from Scott. At least until he came to his senses. That she was running to Clay Cunningham was just one of life's great ironies.

'You've torn your dress,' he said, his eyes moving swiftly over her. The light from the street lamp revealed to him the stress on her delicate face. The bodice of her gown had fallen so low it disclosed the rising curves of her lovely high breasts. One of the thin straps that held it was ripped, the other fell off her shoulder. He watched her straightening it.

'I'll get her another one,' Scott lurched towards them, ready and willing to do battle. 'Why don't you get the hell away from here, Cunningham? Do you really think you're capable of steal-ing *my* fiancée?'

'Where do you want to go, Caroline?' Clay asked, ignor-ing Scott.

'I can't go back into the hall,' she said, fighting down her humiliation. She had lost one of her hair combs. She couldn't retrieve it. Not now. It would have to stay in the SUV. 'You can walk me back to the hotel if you would. I'm calling it a night.'

'Don't go, Carrie,' Scott called to her with great urgency. 'Let's start remembering *I'm* your fiancé.'

'I thought that meant I could trust you, Scott,' she retorted, as though he were beneath contempt. 'I don't want to talk about this.'

'If you walk off with *him* our engagement's finished! That's right, finished!' he shouted, as if she were about to make the worst mistake of her life.

'Then let's get it over with!' Carrie didn't go to pieces— though she felt like it. She tugged at the diamond solitaire on her finger, then when it was off, she threw it directly at him. 'You might like to give this to Natasha. She's got a reputation for making out in cars.'

My God! For a shocked moment Scott went cold. Did Car-rie *know* about him and Natasha? 'Hey, come on,' he cajoled, trying to get a grip on himself. 'Natasha means nothing to me.'

When did you find out? he wondered, but didn't dare ask.

Carrie, however, still had no idea of the secret liaison be-tween Scott and Natasha that continued right into their en-gagement.

'Be careful you don't stomp on the ring,' she warned. 'It will do another turn. Good night, Scott.'

'Carrie, don't go!' He reverted to pleading as she and Cun-ningham began to move off. 'I love you. I've had so much to drink.'

Clay Cunningham intervened. 'There's no need for everyone to know, Harper. Keep your voice down.'

'You talkin' to *me*?' Still hurting, Scott made a maddened charge forwards, full of bravado, fists flying, ready to show Cunningham a thing or two. His mind inevitably flew back to the way he had knocked Cunningham down when they were kids. He could take him now. Cunningham was a good three inches taller, but he was heavier and he'd had years of training.

'Oh for God's sake, no!' Carrie was fearful they would soon have an audience ready to cheer a fight on. She couldn't help knowing some people would enjoy seeing Golden Boy Harper get a thrashing.

Only Clay Cunningham didn't want any fight. He threw out a defensive arm to block Scott's vicious punch. At the same time he threw a single punch of his own. It landed squarely on the point of Scott's jaw as he knew it would. Scott staggered back in astonishment, trying desperately to recover from the effects of that blow. Only his legs buckled, then went out from under him as he fell to the grass groaning afresh.

'You've hurt him,' Carrie said, in a sad and sorry voice, but not feeling encouraged to go to her ex-fiancé.

'He'll live,' Clay assured her in a clipped voice. 'The fight's over. Let's get out of here, Caroline, before we draw a crowd.'

This was a turning point for Carrie. Her life could go in one of two directions. With Scott. Or without him.

CHAPTER THREE

'SO WHAT EXACTLY HAPPENED?' It was ten o'clock the next morning. Carrie and her mother were sitting in a quiet corner of the pub having coffee which Katie had served with some freshly baked pastries.

'I don't want to go into it, Mamma,' Carrie said carefully.

'But darling, I need to know.' Alicia leaned forward across the bench table. 'One moment you were there, the belle of the ball. Next time I looked you and Scott were gone. Did you have an argument? I wouldn't be surprised if you did. Scott has a jealous streak and you did appear to be enjoying yourself with Clay Cunningham, who incidentally, is an extraordinarily attractive young man with a strong look of his father. He disappeared as well and he didn't come back.'

'Scott and I did have a few words,' Carrie confided, unwilling to upset her mother.

Alicia frowned slightly. 'Scott's hopelessly in love with you, darling. You *are* putting him under quite a bit of pressure.'

'Are you suggesting I sleep with him, Mamma?'

Alicia glanced away. 'Who would blame you if you had that in mind? You *are* engaged. You're to be married in December.'

'So I should feel free to jump into bed? Or rather Scott should feel free to force me into sex?' Carrie took several hot, angry breaths.

'Gracious, darling, that's not what he tried to do?' Alicia looked extremely dismayed. 'Everything has been going so very well.'

Carrie began to spoon the chocolate off her coffee. 'He was drunk, Mamma. I've never seen him like that before. Losing to Clay Cunningham set him off.'

'That's one of his little failings,' Alicia said, thanking God it wasn't a whole lot worse. 'Scott's a bad loser.'

'I don't know that we should count that as a *little* failing,' Carrie said. 'In many ways Scott has been spoiled rotten. His mother idolises him—'

'Heavens, she couldn't love him more than your father and I love you.' Alicia looked at her daughter dotingly.

'Does Dad love me?' Carrie asked bleakly. *Lord, did I really say that!* 'I'd really like to know. He *wants* to love me, he tries hard to love me but it seems to place too much of a burden on him.'

'Sweetheart, you shock me. Please don't talk like that.' Alicia's beautiful eyes filled with tears. 'Your father is a very reserved man. You know that. He doesn't know how to be demonstrative. You have to take it into account.'

'I assure you I have done. For years.' Carrie couldn't let go of the mountain of pain that was inside. 'Why did you marry him? You're very different people.'

Alicia laughed shakily. 'I suppose we are.' She didn't attempt to deny it. 'But we were very much in love.'

'Well, that's good to hear. Actually Dad loves you to death! He tolerates me, because I look like you.'

Alicia's dark eyes grew wide with shock. She bowed her graceful head. 'Carrie, you're upsetting me, darling.'

'That's certainly not my intention,' Carrie reached out to take her mother's hand. 'There couldn't be many fathers who would bypass their only child—a lowly daughter—for their nephew who's nowhere near as smart as I am, could there? Alex would be the first to admit it. I'm not even sure he *wants* Victory Downs.'

Alicia's voice was heavy with irony. 'He will when he's old enough. I console myself you don't need it darling. You're going to marry Scott. You will be so well looked after. His will be a splendid inheritance.'

'*His* inheritance, not mine, Mamma,' Carrie pointed out. 'Even the Japanese government is driven to pass a law to allow the little princess to become Empress in due course.'

'And so she should!' Alicia said emphatically, when she had to all intents and purposes given up the fight to have Carrie inherit the McNevin station. 'Now regards Scott. Give him time to apologise for his less than acceptable behaviour last night. I know he will. He's mad about you, Carrie.'

'Why exactly?' Carrie asked, staring at her mother, waiting for her answer. 'It's becoming as much a mystery to me as you and Dad. Scott worked very hard to sweep me off my feet. He was determined to and he succeeded. You welcomed him as a prospective son-in-law, so did Dad. At long last I'm in Dad's good books. He's been much more relaxed with me since the engagement, hasn't he? I pleased him, made him proud. It was a good feeling. For a while.'

Alicia's hand on her coffee cup was shaking. 'Don't make any hasty decisions you might come to regret,' she warned. 'A devil gets into the best of men from time to time.'

'You sound like you know what you're talking about. Actually you sound like you led a secret life, Mamma,' Carrie said, surprised to see her mother's cheeks fill with warm colour. It was so unlike her to blush.

'My past is an open book,' Alicia declared, spreading her hands. 'I can't say I came to my marriage a virgin. You could teach me a thing or two about abstinence, my darling, but I only had one lover—before your father. When I finally got out of a

Catholic boarding school there was no stopping me. I was ravishing in those days. All the boys were in love with me.'

'I bet!' The number of men who had fallen in love with her
mother was legendary, but Alicia had never been known to have
affairs. That would have killed the husband who worshipped
her. 'You know you're a dark horse, Mamma,' Carrie said simply. 'Who was he?' It occurred to her, her mother might have a
whole host of secrets hidden away.

Alicia put her hands together as if in prayer. 'Good gracious,
darling, I'm sorry I mentioned it. No one had what your father
had to offer.'

'And what was that exactly? A well-respected name? Money?
A historic sheep station?' Carrie asked. She couldn't say it—
she didn't even want to think it—but her father could be a very
boring man, given to the silent treatment.

'Not to be sneezed at,' Alicia said briskly. 'There are more
important considerations than romantic love in marriage. Love
is a madness anyway. And so short-lived! There's no such thing
as eternal passion I'm afraid, my darling. Any fool can fall in
love. It takes time and hard work to grow a successful marriage.
It is a bit like gardening. Putting down good strong roots. Your
father and I mightn't appear as demonstrative as other couples
but we understand one another. We'll stay together.'

There had to be something about her parents' relationship she
couldn't see. 'Can you imagine life without him?' Carrie asked,
knowing however much she looked like her mother she had an
entirely different temperament and approach to life. Where did
that come from? she wondered, certainly not her father.

'What a question! This coffee is a bit strong and it's going
cold. Look out for Katie. We'll order more. Your father is in
splendid health. So am I.'

But Carrie persisted. 'Did Dad ever make you feel breathless with excitement? Under a spell?' There was something in
her mother's eyes that was troubling her. 'Did he ever make

you feel you could do something utterly rash? Be powerless to stop yourself?'

'Please...please, Carrie.' Alicia clutched the table as if the whole world had started to spin. 'The emotions you're describing can cause a lot of pain. Even ruin lives that were once full of promise. You're in a very unsettled mood aren't you, my darling girl?' she asked, worried Carrie might be thinking of calling the engagement off.

Carrie began to confirm her worst fears. 'I don't think I want to marry Scott and leave you behind,' Carrie said, staring back at her beautifully groomed mother who always looked that way. 'I've had the feeling recently he'd like to chop me off from my family. He wants me all to himself.'

Alicia stifled a deep sigh. 'And who could blame him! But that first hectic flush will pass. Your father and I will be very much in the picture. Count on it. We're looking forwards to becoming doting grandparents.'

Carrie's voice was shaky, her small face tense. 'I feel differently about Scott today,' she said, thinking of his hard, hurting hands on her body.

Concern flew into Alicia's face. 'Oh darling, give yourself a little time. He shocked you with his demands, did he?'

'He did,' Carrie said grimly.

Alicia's honeyed speaking voice turned icy cold. 'Really! Would you like your father to have a word with him?'

'God, no.' Carrie was appalled.

'It wouldn't bother me to speak to him,' Alicia said, itching to do it.

'Please, no, Mamma '

'Men aren't saints, my darling.'

'I never thought for a moment they were!' Carrie answered.

'You're a beautiful *and* sexy young woman, Carrie, even if you don't see it. In many ways you're unawakened. Of course I respect your decision to remain a virgin. Probably a very smart move with someone like Scott.'

'Smart moves had nothing to do with my decision,' Carrie pointed out, with a trace of admonition.

'Of course not. I don't really know why I said that. My advice is, if it wasn't all that bad—my God, I'm sure we're not talking rape—forgive him if you can. If you can't—' Alicia threw up her elegant hands '—your father and I will always back your decision.'

'*You* will,' Carrie said. 'I don't know about Dad. I think he'd be bitterly disappointed if I went to him and said the engagement was over.'

'But you're not going to do that, are you, darling?' More than anything Alicia wanted to see her daughter make a good marriage. Scott Harper mightn't be perfect but he had a lot going for him. 'One can understand his being in serious need of sex,' she pointed out gently.

'Be that as it may, whatever happened I dealt with it,' Carrie said. 'And Clay Cunningham came along at the right moment to back me up.'

Alicia drew in a sharp, whistling breath. 'Clay Cunningham? Now I do feel rather sorry for Scott. So Clay Cunningham rescued you like a true hero?'

Carrie on the other hand sounded suddenly *pleased*. 'He knocked Scott down.'

'Good God! I must say he had to wait a long time to do that,' Alicia laughed shortly. 'It's no secret Scott put Clay in hospital when they were boys.'

'I had no idea Scott was such a bully,' Carrie said. 'Or I didn't know until last night.' Now she sounded bitter and angry.

'You used to wave to Clay whenever you saw him in town,' Alicia suddenly recalled. 'You didn't wave to everybody.'

'He told me I used to wave,' Carrie said. 'I don't remember at all.' She didn't add she'd been trying very hard to.

'He was a handsome boy. Now a striking young man. That red in his hair he got from his mother, though she was pure Titian. I only saw her once or twice. She was so pretty. An English rose. I wanted to befriend her but your father was very much against it. He sided with the Cunninghams. So did most people. Reece was to marry Elizabeth Campbell. It was as good as written in stone.'

'It shouldn't have been,' Carrie said, acutely aware of her own change of heart. 'You might as well know, Mamma, I gave Scott his ring back.' No need to say she had pitched it at him.

'Darling!' For one extraordinary moment there was a gleam of satisfaction in Alicia's eyes. 'He must have received one hell of a shock, being, as he is, God's gift to women. *My* only concern is for *you*. If you don't want to marry Scott Harper, there's just one thing to do. Tell him. But first give him a chance to apologise. To tell you he deeply regrets causing you pain. I'm sure he'll do just that.'

Katie appeared from the direction of the kitchen and Alicia held up her hand. 'Yoo-hoo, Katie, Carrie and I would love two more coffees. The little pastries were delicious.'

'Glad you liked 'em, Mrs. Mac!' Katie called cheerfully.

Just as her mother had predicted Scott, looking pallid beneath his tan and deeply troubled, sought out his ex-fiancée. The diamond solitaire was in his shirt pocket. No way could he let Carrie go out of his life. She was perfect. What girl ever was or would be again?

It was another brilliant day. A big barbecue lunch had been organised in the park to start at 1:00 p.m. Afterwards entertainment had been arranged for the kids, clowns and games, kites and balloons, rides on the darling little Shetland ponies and for the older, more daring kids, rides on two very aristocratic looking desert camels.

Carrie was helping out at the tables when Scott approached her. 'Carrie, could I talk to you, please?'

'It's okay, love, go right ahead. We're fine here,' one of the women on the committee called to her, giving Scott a coy wave.

'Last night was a nightmare,' Scott began wretchedly. He

took Carrie's arm, drawing her along a path beneath a canopy of white flowering bauhinia trees like a bridal walk. 'I can't tell you how sorry I am any of that happened. I've been agonising about it and I reckon someone had to have spiked my drink. I've never been so out of it in my life.'

'The question is will you be out of it again?' Beautiful as the day was, sorry as Scott seemed, Carrie wasn't ready to forgive. She had come very close to being violated. Scott's assault on her had caused revulsion and a sense of inner devastation. She had trusted him. She knew it was a struggle for him no sex before marriage but she sincerely believed it was worthwhile for both of them. Her mood of desolation was further deepened by the knowledge he had been on the point of hitting her and from the look on his face, hitting her very hard. Physical violence horrified her.

'I swear by all that's holy, I'll never force myself on you again,' Scott said, sounding miserably abject. 'It was all the alcohol, Carrie. That and seeing you in Cunningham's arms. It drove me right off the edge.'

'Why exactly?' Carrie asked. 'We were enjoying a dance in front of hundreds of people. You didn't catch us in some compromising position.'

'It was the look on your face,' Scott said. 'It had a closeness about it you never give me.'

'Nonsense,' Carrie said firmly, though she felt herself under scrutiny. 'You're a frighteningly jealous person. Now I think about it, a domineering sort of man.' *Like your father,* hung in the air.

'What is it, Carrie?' Scott groaned. 'You need me to be perfect? Near inhuman? I'm madly in love with you. I'm a man of twenty-nine, nearly thirty, and you don't want me to touch you? Do you know how hard that is?'

'Yes, I do,' she said quietly, her reaction to Clay Cunningham taking over her mind, 'but I was proud of your sense of discipline, your consideration of my wishes.'

'You can't forgive me for *one* mistake?' Scott just stopped himself from turning ugly.

'That one mistake showed me you're not the man I thought you were,' Carrie said, brushing a spent white bauhinia blossom from her shoulder. 'You were even going to hit me. Don't deny it. You were going to slap me very hard. That was *bad,* Scott. Is that what you do when a woman doesn't give consent?'

'Oh God, Carrie!' Scott's voice was a heartfelt lament. 'I wouldn't really have hit you. I think maybe I thought about it for half a second.'

'Wrong. You were about to do it. Somehow I was able to stop you. Perhaps it was the disgust in my voice.'

Quite simply it had been. 'Carrie, I can't really remember last night,' he said. 'I can't be certain I hadn't been given some drug.'

'Did you take something?' She glanced up at him, knowing there was nowhere designer drugs hadn't reached.

'Carrie, stop punishing me,' he said. 'I love you. I'm desperate to marry you. I'll never deliberately cause you pain again. I beg you. Give me one more chance.' His eyes were extraordinarily intense. 'Is that too much to ask of the girl who's supposed to love me? You can't abandon me for one mistake.'

'Two bad mistakes.'

'We're getting married in December,' Scott pressed on. 'I've tried. God, how I've tried!'

This at least was true. Despite herself Carrie found herself moved by his obvious pain and contrition. 'Oh, Scott,' she sighed in a dispirited kind of way. She had a big problem now deciding she had ever loved him. A problem that hadn't really existed before Clay Cunningham came back into their lives.

'Please, darling.' Scott fumbled for the diamond solitaire in his pocket. 'A commitment has been made, Carrie. We can sort this out. Everyone is so happy we're together. My parents, your parents. Your dad and I are good mates. He thoroughly approves me of as a son-in-law.'

Wasn't that the truth! An outsider if asked might have said Scott was Bruce McNevin's offspring rather than his daughter.

'Let me prove to you all over again how much I love you,' Scott said ardently, lifting her hand and pushing his ring home on her finger. 'I'm nothing without you.' He lifted her hand to his mouth and kissed it tenderly. 'Say you forgive me.'

Carrie shook her head. 'That's impossible for me to say today, Scott.' She had never felt so dejected, so unsure of herself to the point of tears.

'It's your father. He's coming towards us,' Scott told her swiftly, seeing Bruce McNevin hurrying towards them across the grass. 'Don't let me down.'

'Ah, there you are, you two!' Bruce McNevin, having witnessed that heart-warming little moment between Carrie and Scott, called to them in a voice that was almost affectionate. A big concession for him. 'I've organised a corner table for all of us near the fountain. Your mother and father, Scott, Alicia and I and you two lovebirds.' He eyed them both with wry amusement. 'Goodness, from the look of you both, you must have been up all night.'

'Darn nearly sir.' Scott flashed his prospective father-in-law a respectful smile. 'Thanks for organising the table. I can tell you we're definitely hungry.'

Clay stayed in town for three reasons: as the winner of the Jimboorie Cup; to get to know people; and to avail himself of the magnificent barbecue lunch free to all. Or so he told himself. Why he *really* stayed was to keep a watchful eye on Caroline. She had well and truly aroused his protective streak which was always near the surface when it came to vulnerable women. Now he wanted to see how she was going to handle an ex-fiancé who was determined to fight his way back into her good books.

The worst of it was, Harper appeared to have succeeded. Though Clay did his best not to look too often in their direction he had noted Caroline was not only wearing her big solitaire again, but Harper was sitting close beside her, in the company of both sets of smiling parents. As to be expected theirs was the best table set under the trees near the playing fountain.

Last night he had escorted Caroline back to Dougherty's pub where she was staying. He had asked if she were okay, then when she said she was, he said a quiet good-night watching her walk up the stairs to the guest bedrooms. He had longed to stay. To offer a few words of comfort—he had even wanted to rush into some good advice—but he could see how upset and vulnerable she was. The torn skirt of her beautiful dress and the ripped shoulder strap made him so angry he felt like going back outside to find Harper and give him the thrashing he deserved.

Caroline wouldn't thank him for that. She wanted the incident kept as quiet as possible. It was quite a miracle they had made it back to the pub without anyone paying them any particular attention. Caroline had tucked the torn shoulder strap into her bodice and her skirt was long and swishy concealing the rent. Such damage spoke for itself.

Harper had attacked her. Attacked the young woman he professed to love—his wife-to-be! Child, and man, Harper was a born bully. And what was it about anyway? Obviously Harper had wanted to make love to her—just as obviously she had said no. Any man in his right mind would have accepted it. Harper, alcohol driven, had nevertheless revealed the inner man. He had forced her only in this case he had underestimated his fiancée's fighting qualities. A woman at bay, even a pocket-sized one, could inflict damage if she were able to overcome her fear and get in a telling kick where it hurt most.

Clay felt proud of her. Like a big brother. Best to think of it like that. After all she'd used to wave to him from when she was a toddler until she was about six. And what a beautiful little girl she had been.

For another two hours he had sat across the street from the pub keeping an eye on the entrance just in case Harper took it into his mind to try to get Caroline alone again. He hadn't showed, though Clay was struck by the fact at one point in the night he had seen Harper in the distance having what looked like a serious disagreement with his cousin, Natasha. Impossible to miss her tall, willowy figure and the light was shining on her violet dress. Natasha might have been his cousin, but she wanted no part of Clay. On the other hand, why had Natasha been engaged in a violent argument with Harper? She couldn't have been acting on Caroline's behalf. Clay had gained the strong impression during the course of the afternoon and evening Caroline and Natasha weren't at all friendly. Yet a strong link existed between Natasha and Harper. How else could both of them have been filled with such anger? Clay had to admit he found that troubling.

Surrounded by 'family' Carrie was feeling hemmed in. She was tormented by her complex emotions. Had she really agreed to give Scott a second chance? She didn't think so, yet why was she seated at this table as if nothing had happened? Her mother had given her a quick, surprised glance after registering the diamond solitaire was back on her finger. Alicia didn't say anything but she patted Carrie's arm gently. Two lovers had had a fight and made up. It was much easier not to rock the boat. Alicia was in excellent spirits as was her father.

Why am I doing this? Carrie wondered. Was she in such desperate need of her father's approval? The deep reserve of his lifelong manner with her, the distancing, the lack of response, had caused her much grief and pain. She was sure that was why her mother had sent her away to boarding school early. Her mother gave her plenty of love and affection, cared for her as a mother should, but it was never enough. Her mother told her pretty much daily, 'I love you.' Her father—and she had racked her memory—had *never* said it. Surely that was wrong, wrong, *wrong!* Instead of disturbing her less, it disturbed her more and more as she grew older. It suddenly occurred to her, before her engagement to Scott Harper her existence hadn't had much significance for her father. Now with blinding clarity she saw that her father's approval rated higher than Scott's love.

That was immensely disturbing.

Across the green parkland she glimpsed Clay Cunningham seated at a table with the very attractive McFadden sisters, Jade and Mia. They were really sweet girls. The whole family was nice. The sisters sat on either side of him looking thrilled to be there. Several other young people she knew, including the girls' younger brother Aidan, made up the number at the table. If Clay Cunningham was desperate to find himself a bride he had arrived in town at the optimum time. It would be another year before the town saw such a gathering. As she expected, given Clay Cunningham was such a stunning man, both sisters were flushed with excitement as was Susie Peterson of the big blue eyes sitting opposite him. Susie leaned across the table to say something to him, which made them all laugh.

Carrie almost laughed herself. No need to help him out with his Bush Bachelor advertisement. He actually had three eligible young women hanging on his every word. If he were serious about finding a bride he'd better make the most of this glorious opportunity. After today they would all go their separate ways; home to pastoral properties all over the vast State. Distance was a big factor in the difficulties confronting those wanting to form meaningful relationships. Distance and back breaking sunup to sundown hard work that left precious little time for play.

After lunch Carrie helped out with the children's races. Even if she said so herself she had a talent with kids. They always welcomed her around. Afterwards she took a turn leading the little ones mounted on Shetland ponies around the sandy oval, the ponies perfectly behaved if not the kids. It was good to be able to make her escape from the 'family.' Though she had tried her hardest she'd found lunchtime oppressive. Once she had caught Scott's mother, Thea, looking at her with an odd expression in her eyes. A kind of what's-going-on-here? Mrs

Harper's enmity would be deadly if she decided to go ahead and call off the engagement.

To her surprise she saw Clay Cunningham take a turn at leading around the older kids in saddlelike rigs aboard the camels. These domesticated camels came from a Far West property. Camels were such intelligent animals, Carrie thought. Not indigenous to the continent, they had been brought to Australia along with their Afghan handlers in the early days of settlement. Camels had been used on the ill-fated Burke and Wills expedition, by other explorers, miners, telegraph line builders, surveyors, station owners, tradesmen of all kinds. Camels had been *the* beasts of burden all over the Outback. Now they numbered around three hundred thousand, the healthiest camels on the planet. To Carrie's mind their heavy, long lashed eyelids gave them a benign look but she knew in the wild they could be dangerous.

There was no danger today. The camels couldn't have been more docile and obliging. They didn't even mind the excited little sidekicks they were getting from the children, predictably the boys, to spur them on. She was reminded how Scott had used his whip on Sassafras when Clay Cunningham had 'talked' his horse home.

She had a breather from Scott. He had gone off with her father to try their hand at flying the big, wonderfully painted and decorated kites too difficult for youngsters to handle. She could see one swooping up and up in the sky. It really had been a flawless day.

Aidan McFadden approached her, giving her a big smile. 'I'll take over from you now, Carrie. You must feel like a rest from this lot?'

'I sure do.' Carrie returned the smile. 'A cold drink will go down well. Thanks, Aidan. It's been a great weekend, hasn't it?'

'As far as I'm concerned the new guy Clay Cunningham put on the best show. Boy can he ride!' Aidan's open expression registered admiration. 'Do you think he'd mind if I took a look at the old homestead sometime? I was going to ask him. He sat at our table for lunch. He's a nice, easygoing guy. Do you really think he will stay? I hope he will. Only old Angus Cunningham left Jimboorie in a woeful state.'

'He had a breakdown after his wife died,' Carrie said. 'Then his daughter left him. He was a sad, sad man. Clay told me he wants to stay, Aidan. Why don't you simply ask him if you can visit sometime? Unless he's disappeared.' She glanced around the area.

'No, he's still around.' Aidan grinned. 'He can't shake Jade and Mia. Is it true he's looking for a wife? Or is that a bit of a joke? We didn't like to ask him but I can tell you the girls want him for themselves.'

'He can only pick one.' Carrie smiled back, but she felt a prick of something very much like misery.

'Then it's Jade!' Aidan called hopefully after her.

Clay Cunningham had won the McFaddens over it seemed.

One of the committee ladies met her with a home-made lemonade in a tall frosted glass decorated with a sprig of mint. 'Thank you so much, Carrie. You're always such a help. The kids love you.'

'I love them,' Carrie answered truthfully, accepting the very welcome drink. 'Where's Mamma?'

'Talking to Thea Harper the last time I saw her. The wedding's not far off now. You'll make the most beautiful bride,' she gushed.

Carrie smiled but could not answer. Was it possible she was having the first of a sequence of panic attacks?

'Hi, Caroline!' a deep attractive male voice called. A voice she now thought she'd know anywhere.

She paused, turning her head. 'Hello there, Clay.'

'How are you today?' He caught up to her, the both of them moving spontaneously towards an empty park bench.

'Very unsettled,' she admitted, sinking gratefully onto the timber seat.

'I couldn't help noticing Harper is forgiven.' He glanced down at her slender, polished fingers. The diamond solitaire was blazing away in a chink of sunlight.

'Everyone is just so happy we're engaged,' she said.

He knit his mahogany brows. 'Everyone but you.'

She risked a direct glance into his face, bewilderment surging into her voice. 'I used to be happy. Or I thought I was. Maybe I was just basking in everyone's approval.'

'What does that mean exactly?' The question was intense, far from light.

'God you know all about approval and the lack of it, Clay,' she said raggedly. 'I can't talk about it. It's disloyal to my family.'

'What about Harper?' he asked in a taut low voice. 'Hell, Caroline, you're not a schoolgirl. You're a woman. What are you afraid of? You weren't afraid last night. You were astonishingly gutsy. What's happened to change that?'

She didn't answer for a moment. She took a long draft of the lemonade, moving her tongue into a curl. It was delicious and refreshingly cold. 'I was very angry with Scott last night. I'm still not happy about him, but he came to me this morning and—'

'Swore he'd never use force on you again?' he interjected. 'You believed him?'

She had the strong impression he was disgusted. 'May I ask why it's any of your business, Clay?'

'You may ask but I might be less inclined to answer.' He gave a humourless laugh. 'Think of it as I'm catching up with a friendship that never had a chance to get started. I was a pretty lonely kid, living on the fringe of things. My father dishonoured by his own people. My mother spoken about as if she were nothing more than a wayward little tramp. In reality she had more class than any of them. But it broke her as time went on. It might seem like a small thing but I saw the way little Princess McNevin always gave me a wave as a bright spot in my blighted childhood.'

'I can't remember.' She stared at him out of sorrowful doe eyes.

'Sounds like you've been trying?' His voice had a tender but challenging note.

'I know I *will* remember,' she said, clinging to the idea. 'It's going to happen all at once.'

'When can you come to Jimboorie?' he asked, with some urgency because Caroline was never on her own for long.

'It's not a good idea.' In fact it could cost her a good deal.

'Caroline, you *promised*,' he reminded her, his eyes a blazing blue against the bronze cast of his skin.

'Scott hates you.'

His handsome face bore an expression of indifference. 'That's okay. I can live with it. I don't exactly admire him. He's a bully. Man and boy. What days do you come into town for Pat Kennedy?'

She could see he wasn't going to let this alone. If the truth be told she badly wanted to accept his invitation. 'Make it next Friday,' she said. 'I'll meet you at the *Bulletin* office at 10:00 a.m. Would that suit?'

'No, but I'll be there.' He gave her a smile that made a lick of fire run right down to her toes.

'Then another day?' she suggested quickly.

He shook his head, his thick mahogany hair, lit by rich red tones. 'Friday's fine. The sooner the better. Are you going to tell your folks?'

She laughed as if it were an insane thing to ask. 'Oh, Clay, they won't even notice I've gone. Well, my father won't.'

He wanted to touch her cheek but he knew he shouldn't. 'What's the problem with your father? There appears to be one.'

'Maybe I'll tell you sometime,' she said. 'Oh, God!' she muttered, under her breath. 'Here he comes now with Scott.'

Clay rose immediately to his impressive height. 'Don't panic, I'll go. You will turn up?'

She trembled and he saw it. 'Yes. 10:00 a.m. at the office,' she repeated.

'What I'd really like to do is stay and meet your father. Ask him why he turned against the man who was once his friend?'

'Now's not the time for it, Clay!' She looked at him with a plea in her eyes.

'Don't walk into the trap,' he warned, touching a forefinger to his temple before striding away.

CHAPTER FOUR

THEY HAD BEEN driving for well over an hour. There hadn't been much conversation between them, rather an intense *awareness* that made any comment deeper than normal, a potential minefield. She had not removed her engagement ring. She offered him no explanation and he didn't ask for one, yet she carried the conviction he would before the day was over.

She'd told her mother where she was going...

'Darling, is that wise?' Alicia had shown a level of concern, bordering on alarm.

'Wise or not I'm going,' Carrie had replied. 'I really want to see the old house. When I was little I thought it was a palace like the Queen lived in.'

'And you want to see Clay Cunningham.' Alicia didn't beat about the bush.

'I like him,' Carrie said. What she failed to say was he had an extraordinary effect on her. It was something she had to keep secret. Even from herself, but Alicia's expression suggested she knew all the same.

There was Jimboorie House rising up before them. Once the cultural hub of a vast region, it stood boldly atop a rise that fell away rather steeply to the long curving billabong of Koona

Creek at its feet. It was to Carrie, far and away the most beautiful homestead ever erected by the sheep barons who became the landed gentry. It was certainly the biggest, built of sandstone that had weathered to a lovely soft honey-pink. It lofted two tall storeys high, the broad terrace beneath the deep overhang of the upper level supported by imposing stone columns, which were all but obscured by a rampant tangle of vines all in flower. The great roof was tiled with harmonising grey slate that had been imported all the way from Wales. The whole effect was of an establishment that would be considered quite impressive in any part of the world, if only one narrowed one's eyes and totally ignored the decay and the grime.

The mansion was approached by a long driveway guarded by sentinel towering gums. This in turn opened out into a circular driveway with a once magnificent fountain, now broken, in the centre. The gardens, alas, were no more but the indestructible bouganvilleas climbed over every standing structure in sight. A short flight of stone steps led to the imposing pedimented Ionic portico.

Clay drove his 4WD into the shade of the flowering gums, the low trailing branches scraping the hood.

'What it once must have been!' Carrie sighed. 'It's still beautiful even if it's falling down.'

'Come see for yourself,' he invited, with a note in his voice that made her doubly curious.

Carrie stepped out onto the gravelled driveway, a petite young woman wearing a white knit tank top over cropped cotton drill olive-green pants, a simple wardrobe she somehow made glamorous. Their arrival disturbed a flock of rainbow lorikeets that had been feeding on the pollen and nectar in the surrounding eucalypts, bauhinias, and cassias all in bloom. The birds displayed all the colours of the spectrum in their plumage, Carrie thought, following their flight. The upper wings were emerald-green, under wings orange washed with yellow, beautiful deep violet heads, scarlet beaks and eyes. They presented a beautiful sight, chattering shrilly to one another as they flew to another feeding site.

A sprightly breeze had blown up, tugging at her hair which she had tied back at the nape with a silk scarf designed by aboriginal women using fascinating traditional motifs. 'What does it feel like to be back?' she asked him, filled for a moment with a real sadness for what might have been.

'Like I've never been away,' Clay answered simply, though his face held myriad emotions. 'This is precisely the place I belong.'

'Is it?' His words touched her deeply. She looked across at his tall, lean figure. He was dressed simply as she was, in everyday working clothes—tight fitting jeans, and a short sleeved open necked bush shirt. Dark, hand tooled boots on his feet gave him added stature. He had a wonderful body, she thought, starting to fear the effect he had on her. At her deepest level she knew a man like this could push over all her defences as easily as one could push over a pack of cards. It was something entirely new in her life. She wondered could she resist *him* as she was so able to resist Scott? At heart, she was beginning to question herself. Was her decision to remain a virgin until marriage brought about by sheer circumstance? It seemed very obvious to her now she didn't love Scott in the way a woman should love the man she chooses to marry. Everyone else saw him as a solid choice. Did that automatically make for a good marriage?

As for Clay Cunningham? She didn't have a clue where their friendship would lead. In short he presented a dilemma. Carrie's nerves stretched taut as her memory was overrun by images of her father and Scott as they joined her yesterday only moments after Clay had moved off. Both handsome faces wore near identical expressions. Anger to the point of outrage. It chilled her to the bone. She wasn't a possession, a chattel. She was a grown woman with the right to befriend anyone she so chose.

Her father didn't think so and made that plain. 'Better you

don't have anything to do with him, Carrie,' he'd clipped off, his grey eyes full of ice.

'Why not?' She had never in her life answered her father quite like that before. A clear challenge that brought hot, angry colour to his cheeks.

'I wouldn't have thought I had to tell you,' he reprimanded her. 'He's bad news. Just like his father before him. You're an engaged woman yet it's quite obvious he has his eye on you.'

She had waited for Scott to intervene but he hadn't. Best not get on the wrong side of Mr McNevin. At least until he and Carrie were safely married.

'That's carrying it a bit far, Dad,' Carrie had said. 'Clay just came across to say hello. I like him.'

Her father looked pained. 'People talk, Carrie. I don't want them to be talking about *you.*'

'You're very quiet today, Scott?' She hadn't bothered to hide the taunt. 'Nothing to add?'

He shook his golden head. 'As far as I'm concerned your father has said it all.'

That earned him Bruce McNevin's nod of approval.

Clay took her arm as they climbed the short flight of steps to the portico and on to the spacious terrace. 'Careful,' he said, indicating the deep gouges between the slate tiles. 'Just stay with me.'

Guilt swept through her. *Why, why, why did she want so much to be with him?* This was all too sudden. She had the mad notion she would have gone with him had he asked her to take a trip to Antarctica.

The double front doors towered a good ten feet. They were very impressive and in reasonably good condition. When she had *really* looked from the outside, she had seen the large numbers of broken or displaced tiles on the roof and the smashed glass in the tall arched windows of the upper level. Some of the shutters, once a Venetian green, were hanging askew. Panels of glass in the French doors of the lower level were broken as well and replaced with cardboard.

The effect was terrible. Some of the damage could have been caused by vandals. The smashed glass in the doors and windows for example. Six months had elapsed since Angus Cunningham's death and the arrival of his great-nephew. It could have happened then although the talk in the town was Jimboorie House was haunted by the late Isabelle Cunningham. No one had the slightest wish to encounter her.

Clay opened one door, then the other, so that long rays of sunlight pierced the grand entrance hall.

As far as Carrie was concerned, the entrance hall said it all about a house. 'Oh!' she gasped, as she stepped across the threshold. She stared about her with something approaching reverence. 'I've always wanted to see inside. It's as noble as I knew it would be.'

Her face held so much fascination it was exquisite! Clay thought. 'I'm glad you're here, and you're not disappointed.'

Something in his tone made Carrie's heart turn a somersault in her breast. She didn't look back at him—she didn't dare—but continued to stare about her. After the mess of broken tiles on the terrace she was thrilled to see the floor of the entrance hall, tessellated with richly coloured tiles was intact. In three sections, the design was beautiful, circular at the centre with equally beautiful borders.

'What a miracle it hasn't been damaged.'

'The house isn't in any where near as bad condition as everyone seems to think,' Clay commented with a considerable amount of satisfaction. 'Which is not to say a great deal of money won't be spent on its restoration.'

She stood in the sunbeams with dust motes of gold. 'It would be wonderful to hear your great-uncle actually left you some money?'

'He had it,' Clay said, surprising her.

'He couldn't have!' Carrie was completely taken aback. 'How

could he have had money and let the homestead fall into ruin let alone allow the station to become so rundown?'

'He no longer cared,' Clay told her, shrugging. 'Simple as that. He cared about no one and nothing. He only loved one person in his entire life. That was his wife. After she died he slowly sank into a deep depression. She's supposed to haunt the place, incidentally. My mother claimed to have seen her many times. Isabelle died early. Thirty-eight. No age at all! I wouldn't like to think I only had another ten years of life. She was carrying Angus's heir who died with his mother. Their daughter, Meredith, the firstborn, spent most of her time at boarding school, or with her maternal aunt in Sydney who, thank the Lord, loved her. Meredith was never close to her father after her mother died. No one was. Uncle Angus locked everyone out.'

'Yet he took you in? You and your parents?'

'It was only to spite the rest of the family, I assure you,' Clay said, the hard glint of remembrance in his eyes. 'My father worked like a slave for little more than board for us all. Angus kept my father at it by telling him he was going to inherit Jimboorie. Meredith didn't want the place. Mercifully she married well. Her aunt saw to that. When Angus finally admitted he fully intended to sell up, my father decided it was high time to move on.'

'What happened to your father?' Carrie asked, positioning herself out of the dazzling beam of light so she could see him clearly.

His face became a tight mask. 'He was helping to put out a bushfire, only he and the station hand working with him became surrounded by the flames.'

'Oh, Clay!' Carrie whispered, absolutely appalled. No one knew this. At least she hadn't heard anything of Reece Cunningham's dreadful fate. 'How horrible! Why should anyone have to die like that?'

The corners of his handsome mouth turned down. 'To save the rest of us I suppose. I had to concentrate on his heroism or go mad. My mother spent the rest of her life having ghastly nightmares. The way my father died left her not only bereft but sunk in a depressive state she couldn't fight out of. That fire destroyed her, too. I know she actually prayed for the day she would die. She truly believed she would see my father again.'

'Do *you*?' she asked with a degree of trepidation.

'No.' Abruptly he shook his burnished head. 'Still I can't help but wonder from time to time.'

'Mystery, mysteries, the *great* mystery,' she said. She lifted her head to the divided staircase. Of polished cedar and splendid workmanship it led to the richly adorned overhanging gallery. The gallery had to have a dome because natural light was pouring in. Either that or there was a huge hole in the roof. The plaster ceilings, that once would have been so beautiful, were badly in need of repair.

'Does the gallery have a dome?' she asked, hoping the answer was yes.

'It does,' he said, 'and it's still intact. The bedrooms are upstairs of course. Twelve in all. The old kitchens and the servants' quarters are the buildings at the rear of the house. We'll get to them. Let's move on. There are forty rooms in the house all up.' He extended his arm to the right.

More tall double doors gave on to the formal dining room on their left, the drawing room to their right. Neither room was furnished. The drawing room was huge and classically proportioned. The once grand drapes of watered Nile-green silk were hanging in tatters.

She was both appalled and moved by the badly neglected state of the historic homestead. 'Where do you plan to start first?' she asked, her clear voice echoing in the huge empty spaces. 'Or are you going to leave that to your wife?'

'I'll have to,' he said, amusement in his voice. 'I'll be too busy getting the station up and running.'

'So what are you going to run?' Her voice lifted with interest.

'A lean commercial operation geared for results,' he an-

swered promptly. 'Jimboorie's glamour days are over. Beef is
back. There's a strong demand. I'm going to run Hereford cattle.
Angus couldn't envisage any other pursuit than running sheep
even when the wool industry was in crisis.'

'Are you going to tell me where you acquired your skills as
a cattleman?'

He nodded. 'I actually got to Agricultural College where I did
rather well. Then I worked on a cattle station rising to overseer.'

'Would I know this station?'

'Oh, come on, Caroline,' he gently taunted her. 'You would
if I told you.'

'So you think if you confide in me I'll tell everyone else?' She
was hurt he didn't trust her but she made a huge effort to hide it.

'I don't think that at all. Not if I told you not to. It's just that
it's difficult to talk about a lot of things right now.'

She turned away from him. 'That's okay. It's not as if we're
friends.'

'It's not easy to make a true friend,' he said sombrely. 'What
are we exactly?'

'We're in the process of becoming friends,' she bravely said.

'So you'd befriend me and rebuff your fiancé? It's back on
again, I take it?' His tone was sardonic, if not openly critical.

'It's just a mess, Clay,' she said, that tone getting to her.

His brilliant blue eyes seemed to *burn* over her, making her
skin flush. 'Well you can't disregard it. It's your life's happiness
that's on the line. Are you so afraid of increasing the discord between yourself and your father?' he asked with considerable perception. 'He's obviously an extremely difficult man to please?'

She glanced away through the French doors at the abandoned garden. The wildflowers, shrubs and flowering vines
that had survived lent it colour as did the hardiest of climbing
cabbage roses, a magnificent deep scarlet, in full bloom over
an old pergola. She had seen many pictures of Jimboorie House
in its prime so she knew there had been a wonderful rose ar-
bour. 'My father is difficult about some things,' she answered

at length. 'He's a good father in others. I don't know why I'm telling you. I feel I know you.'

'You do know me,' he replied. 'You're the little girl who used to deliver the sweetest smile and the wave of a little princess, remember?'

'May I ask you a personal question?' She turned to face him, held fast by the extraordinary intensity of his gaze.

'You can try.' He smiled. 'And what would it be? Have I ever been in love?' His voice held amusement.

It wasn't her question, but she stared back at him, aware she badly wanted to know. 'Have you?'

'Caroline, I told you.'

That smile was *magic*. Few smiles lit up a man's face like that.

'My lifestyle left very little time for romance,' he explained again. 'There was a girl once. She got spooked by my lack of money. All she had to do was give me a little time.'

'Do you still love her?' The muscles in her slender throat tensed. She told herself it would be wonderful to have a man like Clay Cunningham love her. Something she knew she would agonize over later.

'No.'

'Are you sure?'

'Absolutely positive,' he said. He didn't tell her, nor would he, he'd already dated falling in love from the moment he'd laid eyes on her, albeit rashly. He had already discovered she was the fiancée of Scott Harper, the bully boy of his childhood. Still was, for that matter. She wore Harper's ring. Maybe the death of his mother and returning to Jimboorie had put him in a very vulnerable state of mind. That's why he wanted a wife, a wife and children, a family of his own to love. Having a family of his own had somehow developed into a passion. Caroline McNevin could too easily become a passion. A *doomed* passion. Unless she found the strength to break away from Harper.

Carrie moved on. 'I love the fireplace,' she said. The chimney piece was constructed of flawless white Carrara marble. Instead of the usual large gilded mirror to hang above it—any mirror would probably have been shattered—was a very elegant overmantel in the same white marble. Judging from the staining left on the marble, it seemed a painting had once hung there and on other places around the walls.

'It would take a great deal of furniture to fill this room alone,' she marvelled, finding it easy to visualise the drawing room restored. She loved houses; beautiful houses like this. Clay was quite correct in saying the interior wasn't in any where near as bad condition as everyone thought. At least as much as she had seen.

'A lot of the original furnishings, paintings, rugs, objets d'art, you name it, are in storage,' he said, further surprising her.

'Really?' Her dark eyes opened wide. 'On the property, you mean? One of the outbuildings?'

He shook his head. 'Great-Uncle Angus wasn't so steeped in grief he didn't make sure nothing of real value was left here to be stolen. There's a warehouse full of it in Toowoomba.' He named a city one hundred miles west of Brisbane, the state capital, lying on the edge of the Great Dividing Range and famous for its spring carnival of flowers.

'I think you could safely say your great-uncle Angus fooled the world,' she said wryly. 'Have you seen what's in there?'

'Not as yet, but I have the inventory. I'll make the trip to Toowoomba some time fairly soon. Want to come?'

'Aren't you the bush bachelor looking for a wife?' She gave him a look.

'Most definitely,' he retorted. 'We could talk about what I should put in my ad along the way.'

'You have a devil in you, Clay Cunningham.'

He absorbed her slowly with his eyes. 'Most men do, but *you'll* never stumble on mine, I promise. You speak of loving Harper, but I don't think you do.'

She had learned that in stages. 'Off-limits, Clay,' she warned moving into the huge handsome room that was obviously the library. Cedar bookcases were set in arcaded recesses all around the room, but the collection had gone. A book lover, she prayed it had gone into storage.

'Perhaps you're a little too accustomed to doing what you believe will please everyone?' he questioned, his voice resonating with a certain sympathy.

'Is that a good reason to get married?' She felt wounded.

'It happens a lot,' he said. 'I had no difficulty sensing you badly need to please your father. That desire must be far from new.'

She stopped abruptly. 'You sense far too much. What is it you want from me, Clay?' Without meaning for it to happen— her momentary weakness shocked her—tears filled her eyes.

He stared down at her in dismay. 'Caroline, don't do that,' he implored, slowly rubbing a hand across his tanned forehead. 'I've got plenty of self-control, but your tears might prove my undoing.' In reality he saw himself on the very edge of a yawning chasm. If those tears spilled onto her cheeks, he might plunge into that chasm, taking her with him, his arms enclosing her, cradling her, his mouth closing over hers to muffle her cries.

Oh God, Caroline, stop it! When he was with her his every perception was intensified.

'Meaning what?' She tried valiantly to blink the tears away.

'You know perfectly well what I mean.' His handsome face was grim. 'Why do your eyes contain tears anyway? They're no protection against me. The reverse is true. It seems to me you want to cry from sheer necessity. You're unhappy. You feel caught in a trap. You can get out of it if you're strong.'

Was she strong? She'd thought she was. Now she turned her head away from him and the tremendous temptation he presented. 'It's impossible overnight.' Her hands were shaking. She lifted one to clasp the silk scarf at her nape. She pulled it free, suddenly irritated by the knot of material on her neck.

'No, it's not,' he answered roughly, watching her hair uncoil into long golden skeins. It radiated light like a halo around her head. He couldn't help himself. He moved nearer, lifting a hand and curling a long shining lock around his fingers. It felt like silk, sweetly scented. He tugged on the thick lock very gently edging her towards him.

'Don't *do* this, Clay,' she warned, knowing they had both reached a turning point that was far from unexpected.

'Look into my eyes and tell me that,' he said. His hand moved to the mass of her shining hair pulling her head back so he could stare into her face. 'Caroline?'

'I must be mad,' she murmured.

'I know. So am I.'

Now the tears did seep from her eyes. What she saw in his face was sexual ardour of a nature she had hitherto never even glimpsed. It wasn't crude lust. Lust she had come to despise. There was real *yearning* there, as though he believed she might be the one to cure his deep-seated griefs. She, in turn, was spellbound by the concentration of pure desire that burned so brilliantly in his blue eyes.

She didn't so much go along with it. She surrendered herself to it, deferring to a stolen moment in time. 'This may well be a serious mistake!' The streams of passion that stormed through her veins offered proof.

He nodded solemnly, one hand cupping her face with a tenderness that was profoundly moving. 'You're so small!'

'I'm a woman,' she said. 'A woman of nearly twenty-four.'

'A very serious young woman who has to put a few things right.'

'That's how you see it?' she whispered, her eyes on his clean cut mouth.

'Don't *you*?'

Before she had time to react—did she really have the strength?—he lifted her as though she weighed no more than a child and carried her to one of the recessed alcoves, setting her on top of the solid cedar cupboard, which supported the ceiling-high bookshelves.

'Caroline McNevin, you are *so* beautiful!' He trailed one hand down over her cheek, her throat, lightly skimmed the low-necked front of her tank top that gave a tantalizing glimpse of the upward curves of her breasts.

Her body ached. There was pain, she was learning, in desire. 'Why are we doing this, Clay?'

'It's all I've wanted to do since you walked back into my life,' he confessed.

Her eyes were very dark, her expression strange. 'When kissing me is strictly forbidden?'

'By whom?'

'God help me, not *me*!'

Her words chimed in his mind. He lowered his head, while Carrie closed her eyes, dizzy suddenly with the level of sensuality.

His powerful, lean body stood directly in front of her. Without thought—all she wanted was to get as close to him as possible—she brought up her slender legs to wrap him around. It was something she had never done before but her inhibitions were melting like a polar thaw. Her fall from grace—the full rush of it—stunned her. If indeed fall was what it was. But she had promised to marry another man, for all the decision to make a clean break from Scott was fast overtaking her.

She could pay heavily for this moment out of time. They *both* could. But Carrie was powerless to stop what had already started. The sense of having been caught up in something far beyond the power of either of them to control was strong in her. Fate, destiny, something preordained?

Gently, so *gently* at first, he touched his mouth to hers. A communion. Yet the effect was so overwhelming it drowned her in a wave of the most voluptuous heat. She had never experienced such a powerful sexual reaction. It caught at her breath so it emerged as a moan.

'I'm not hurting you?' He drew back a little.

'No!'

The flame and the urgency of their coming together seemed to devour her. No flutter of conscience troubled her then. His kiss was so deep and so passionate there was no question of denying him what he sought to take from her. No question of denying herself such excitement, such a tremendous physical exhilaration.

She had never dreamed a kiss could be like this.

Never!

At that dangerous moment she was his for the taking. She was *pressing* herself against him with absolute abandon. All the world was lost to her. Instead of her habitual ingrained caution she felt only a magnificent generosity. She was offering herself, shamelessly, ultimately inciting him to take as much as he wanted from her. She was acutely aware he was powerfully aroused but she had no thought of withdrawing herself or calling a stop. Desire such as this was a revelation. It was the most potent of all intoxications and she was drinking it from his mouth.

Why would she call a halt to such a storm of wanting? For all she knew it might never happen again.

'Caroline!' He gasped out her name, getting one hand to her hair that was tumbling all around them in golden sheets.

She realised with a shock he was trying to hold her off.

Oh, God!

Absolute bliss turned to blinding mortification.

His dark head was bent over hers as he smoothed the hair away from her flushed face. 'You know where this is going?' His voice was as taut as a bow.

Wasn't she inviting it? God help her, she was practically begging him to make love to her. She took a deep breath, then pushed him away, one hand flat against his chest.

'I'm sorry.'

'Don't be.' He, too, had been unable to diminish the scale of all that he felt for her.

The whole extraordinary episode couldn't have taken more than a few minutes yet she felt she would remember this encounter until the day she died. 'It's all right. I'm all right,' she said. It took a while—she was cautious she wouldn't slip into a faint she was so dazed—but she was able to slide off the cupboard bench, onto the floor. 'I wanted that as much as you,' she said, her voice full of confusion and regret, 'but we have to watch ourselves from now on.'

A week later Carrie was working in a rather desultory fashion on station accounts when her mother rushed into the office, looking violently upset.

Gripped by panic, Carrie sprang to her feet. 'What is it, Mamma?' For a moment she experienced pure dread. Had something happened to her father? Was her mother ill? Had she received some terrible news? Blows had a relentless way of coming right out of the blue.

'It's Scott,' Alicia gasped, sounding quite breathless.

'What's happened? Has he been hurt?' Carrie began to imagine all sorts of horrendous things. Station accidents were all too common. Even fatalities. She had only seen Scott once since the Sunday of the picnic races. A Scott so repentant, so painfully anxious to please her, she'd found it extremely difficult to say what she needed to say; what desperately needed saying.

Scott, I want out of our engagement!

But the way Scott had acted made her feel breaking their engagement would be too terrible for him to bear at that time. Had she been blinded to the true depth of his love for her? Had she not seen how much he cared? Had she blamed him too severely for that terrible night? She couldn't forget the sight of his hand upraised to her. His excuse was that he was drunk. People acted out of character when they were under the influence of alcohol. Pity for him was part of her self-enforced silence. He had treated her so carefully, as though she were utterly *precious,* and in the end she had let him drive away without saying one word of what was going round and round in her head.

The need for decisive action. It was causing her many a sleepless night. She had the awful feeling once she broke her engagement the recent harmony between herself and her father would break down overnight into icy rejection. Once the thought would have terrified her. But she was a woman now. She was well-educated. She would have to live separate from her parents. That meant she would have to leave her beloved home, the *land* she loved and seek a life for herself in the city. There were far worse things.

Now she led her mother to a chair. 'Mamma, sit down. Here have some water.' Swiftly she poured a glass from the cooler and put it into her mother's hand. 'Scott's been injured, hasn't he?'

'They've *both* been injured,' Alicia said bitterly. Alicia set down the glass of cold water so forcibly it was a wonder it didn't break.

'Both?' Carrie stared at her mother vacantly.

'Scott and that sly, underhanded bitch, Natasha Cunningham,' Alicia said and thrust back a long strand of her hair.

Carrie was stupefied. 'Mamma, what are you talking about? What happened? Where? Why were they together?'

Alicia looked at her daughter with pitying eyes. 'Because he's been seeing her on the side, that's why!'

Carrie couldn't seem to take it in, though she was staring at her mother, hard. 'Scott has been seeing Natasha?' she repeated. Given the way Scott had been behaving towards her—the way he always labelled Natasha 'a bitch'—Carrie found it impossible to believe. Only a few days ago Scott had been literally down on his knees telling her how much he loved her, his voice filled with a I-can't-live-without-you fervour. 'How do you know? Who told you?' Carrie demanded, wondering if there were a possibility her mother had got things wrong.

'The way they found them told the story.' Alicia reached for the glass and drained it as if she were parched to the point of severe dehydration.

'What on earth do you mean?' Carrie's even temper started a slow boil. 'Who found them? Where were they? Spit it out. Mamma, for God's sake! I bet it's all over the district already. Were they in his SUV?'

Alicia clapped her hand to her mouth as though she was about to be sick. 'They careened right off the road and plunged into Campbell's Crossing. It was Ian Campbell who found them. They've already been airlifted to hospital.'

'My God!' Carrie's voice was flat with shock. 'How bad were their injuries?'

'No one knows yet,' Alicia said, forcing herself to steady down. 'Scott was in a worse state than Natasha, I believe.'

Carrie released a devastated groan. 'We must ring the hospital to find out.'

'Carrie, love, did you hear what I told you? Did you take it in? They were *together*. Scott has betrayed you. We all know he and Natasha were an item one time, but everyone thought it was over. What fools we've all been. Obviously their affair has never left off.'

'I can't understand this,' Carrie said and she couldn't. 'I've been agonising over finding the best moment to tell Scott our engagement is off. I felt desperate to let him down lightly. Now I learn he's been seeing Natasha behind my back all the while. It doesn't make a bit of sense!'

'Doesn't it?' Alicia laughed grimly. 'She was giving him what *you* wouldn't,' she said, bluntly. 'It was just sex.'

'Just sex!' Carrie's voice soared to the ceiling. 'You seem to know a hell of a lot about sex, Mamma.'

Alicia laughed even more bitterly. 'I'm a married woman.' Suddenly tears surged into her eyes. 'Oh, Carrie, what a terrible mess!'

Carrie looked past her mother towards the door. 'I'll have to find out what condition they're both in,' she said. 'I can't stand here wondering. Does Dad know?'

Alicia raised her golden head, looking utterly drained. 'He's the one who told me. He's shocked out of his mind.'

'He never thought to come to me.' Carrie's feeling of wretchedness increased. 'After all, I am supposed to be Scott's fiancée. But Dad came to you. As always.'

'He's dreadfully upset.' Alicia made excuses for her husband. 'Naturally he would come to me, Carrie, and allow me to break the news to you. He was being thoughtful. He's only just got the news directly from Ian Campbell. Your father thought the world of Scott.'

'*You* didn't, Mamma,' Carrie pointed out, without emotion. 'You wouldn't have been too upset if I broke off the engagement.'

Alicia shielded her face with her hand. 'I'm your mother. I wanted to see you marry well. Scott Harper is a great catch. *Was* a great catch.' Her voice broke.

'I pray to God he still will be,' Carrie said, her expression badly strained. 'But not for *me*. Why didn't I recognise what was behind all those snide remarks Natasha used to make? The outright malice in her eyes? I put it down to jealousy. Understandable, when she must have been in love with Scott at one time. Now it appears she's never given up on him. Maybe they were going to continue their affair right into our marriage? I'm a complete fool and I've only just found out. Surely *someone* realised what was going on?'

Alicia lifted her hand, her expression stony. 'They erected a pretty good smoke screen, the two of them,' she said with utter contempt. 'I daresay some of his mates would have known what was going on. They'd think Scotty was entitled to a bit of fun on the side.'

'*Fun?*' Carrie's voice rose again. 'Fun, for God's sake, *fun*! Well it's not fun now.'

CHAPTER FIVE

HER FATHER WAS remarkably solicitious. He treated her as if she had been in the accident; as if she were breakable when she didn't feel breakable at all. The town treated her the same way. One would have thought Scott and Natasha had been involved in separate accidents so determined were people not to mention their names in the same breath.

But they *had* been together. There again, no one would tell her what it was about the accident that had so compromised them. Had they been found stark-naked? She rather doubted that. Was Natasha in a state of undress? She finally got it from Paddy when she called into the *Bulletin* office to see him in person—they had spoken on the phone—and ask for time off.

'Needless to say out of respect we won't be printing the full story,' Pat Kennedy told her, studying her face closely. He loved this girl. She was as dear to him as the granddaughter he had wished for but never had.

'At last we get to it,' Carrie sighed, her dark eyes full of misery. 'Tell me, Paddy. Get it over. I guess twenty-four isn't too late to find out you're a gullible fool.'

'You're no fool, my girl,' Paddy said, then added with sudden fierceness, 'it's that fiancé of yours who's the fool. I don't understand this whole business actually. I could have sworn

Scott was madly in love with you. No pretence, he couldn't wait to marry you.'

'That's all over, Paddy.'

'He's still in the induced coma?'

Carrie gulped down tears. 'Yes.' Ever one to visualise she had a clear picture of Scott lying in a hospital bed, hooked up to monitors. He had been badly concussed—the great fear being of brain injury—with a broken collarbone, multiple lacerations and two broken ribs. All Carrie wanted was for him to open his eyes again and talk to someone. His mother. She didn't want to be the one but as far as she was concerned all was forgiven. She had no wish for him or Natasha to suffer, though Natasha wasn't the one to worry about right now. Natasha had been lucky. Compared to Scott she had come through relatively un-scathed. No broken bones but severe bruising and multiple lac-erations that nevertheless were not considered serious enough to leave scars. Carrie was glad of that. Natasha Cunningham was a beautiful woman—if not a beautiful person.

Carrie had spoken to Scott's distraught mother the day of the accident. Thea Harper, after all, was to have become her mother-in-law. All Carrie could do was offer comfort in the face of a mother's agony. Thea was nearly out of her mind with worry, as well she might be. Scott was not only her only son, he was her only child. Both of them had chosen to put Natasha's presence in Scott's SUV to one side. There was enough to worry about without following through on that issue. Time enough for that.

'Are you going to give Scott a chance to tell his side of the story?' Paddy asked, his normally twinkling blue eyes troubled. 'That Cunningham girl is trouble. I've long said so.'

'So what's the full story,' Carrie asked wearily.

Paddy, seasoned journalist, close friend and mentor, with all the wisdom of a fulfilled life, at seventy-three, coloured up. 'It seems Natasha wasn't wearing her, er, shirt. Or her bra,' he added with a shake of his silver head.

Carrie was past shock. 'That seems extraordinarily wild, even for Natasha. Or was it night-time?'

'Must have been,' Paddy said briefly. 'You're going to visit him?'

'Regardless of what they were up to, it's high time I did,' Carrie said. 'I'll look in on Natasha while I'm at it. We've never been friends but I've often thought there's something sad and lost about her. That's why she behaves so badly.'

'Dreadful crowd,' Paddy tutted though he was kind about most people. 'Cruel what they did to Reece and his young family. I've met Clay. He used to be 'little Jimmy Cunningham' back then. I would have met him at the picnic races only for my old mate, Bill Hawkins's funeral in Brisbane. Clay came into the office last week to make himself known to me. I must say he appears to have turned out splendidly.'

Carrie kept her eyes downcast. 'He's a wonderful horse-man. It was quite thrilling to see him win the Cup.'

'Scott must have hated that?' Paddy spoke wryly, showing his understanding of Scott's nature.

'He didn't take it too well,' Carrie agreed. 'Was there some feud in their childhood, Clay and Scott? If so it's carried through to now.'

Paddy's face creased up. 'Scott was a bit of a bully in those days, Carrie,' he settled for, deliberately not mentioning the time Scott Harper had fiercely knocked a younger, smaller child to the ground. 'He chose to pick on Jimmy—I mean Clay—every time he saw him in town. People took sides in those days. Even a child would have been affected. Reece was going to marry Elizabeth Campbell after all. Not that they were engaged. It was just taken for granted. Enter one lovely little English-Irish girl— I never knew which—with blazing Titian hair, and that was that! Elizabeth and Thea Harper were friends. Naturally they turned against Reece and more particularly the young woman he fell in love with.' Paddy's well rounded voice was thin with regret.

'Awful the things that were said about that young woman. Not a single rumour that was sustainable. But mud sticks.'

'I'm wondering how long this particular piece of mud is going to stick?' Carrie sighed. 'I pray for Scott's rapid recovery but I can't marry him, Paddy. I had decided not to even before *this*.'

'Look, who would expect you to?' Paddy asked. He had never thought Golden Boy Harper was half good enough for Carrie.

Carrie stared sightlessly at the wall clock. 'When it happened, Dad was shocked out of his mind. He thought the world of Scott.'

'Yes, isn't that odd?' mused Paddy.

'*You* didn't?' Carrie turned her gaze back on her friend and mentor. He had never said a word against Scott.

Paddy looked embarrassed. 'Well, he's a handsome young fella. He's much admired in certain quarters. He's certainly going to be very rich, but I didn't really see you two as compatible, Carrie. Scott doesn't have your depth of character.'

'Oh, Paddy,' Carrie sighed. 'What depth of character? I'm not much of a judge, am I? Do you think it would be okay if I took this week off? I have to make arrangements to travel to the hospital. What I was going to tell you was, Dad seems to be doubling back on himself. An injured Scott is somehow working his way back to being reinstated in Dad's good books. I can *feel* it! Lately I've been wondering if Dad didn't think my getting myself engaged to Scott was the best thing I've ever done.'

Paddy shook his head. He had to bide his time to speak to Carrie in depth. He had never liked Bruce McNevin any more than he had approved of Scott Harper for Carrie. McNevin, a man of considerable reserve and a dreadful snob, was in Paddy's opinion, a controlling person. In some way he controlled his beautiful, outgoing wife. God knows why! He had long sought to control his daughter as though without his guidance her beauty would cause her to run off the rails. It was all very odd! Both parents had acted as though the sooner Carrie was married off to a young man they judged right, the better.

* * *

Carrie stayed to have a bite of lunch with Paddy and afterwards walked down to the local super market—to stock up on a few items for which her mother had given her a list. It was as she was leaving the huge barn, pushing a laden trolley—why was it one always bought so much more than was on the list?—that she ran in to Clay.

'Hi, I'll take that.'

Her heartbeat stumbled, then staggered on. She watched as he took charge of the trolley. She hadn't spoken to him—neither of them had made contact—since that day on Jimboorie when they had gone into each other's arms. Ecstatic, then, afterwards trying to push away.

'How's Harper?' he asked, following her lead to the parking bay.

'Stable when I rang this morning.'

'And Natasha, my wayward cousin?'

'She'll be coming home. I pray to God they'll both be coming home soon.'

'So how do you feel about it?' he asked, starting to load the provisions into her 4WD.

'I'm just thankful they're alive, Clay. Other than that I feel like a complete fool.'

Clay paused in what he was doing to look down at her. There were faint shadows beneath her beautiful eyes as though she'd slept badly. 'You haven't heard yet what he has to say? I take it at this point you're not *unengaged*?'

'It's a difficult moment to announce the wedding's off,' she countered. 'The town has decided to pretend Natasha's presence in Scott's SUV was quite innocent. She was accompanying him on some journey out to Campbell's Creek a well-known beauty spot for lovers. And at *night*!'

'You don't buy the innocent story?'

She looked away from him, a pressure building up behind her rib cage. 'My mother told me not long after it happened it *wasn't.* She's dreadfully upset. So is my father. Both of them were thrilled when I got engaged to Scott.'

'In God's name, *why?*' There was a lick of anger in his brilliant blue eyes. 'It sounds to me like you were almost railroaded into it.'

She raised a delicate shoulder in a shrug. Let it drop. She realized now there was more than a grain of truth in it. 'Not anymore,' she said. 'When Scott is fit enough I'm going to tell him—'

'For the *second* time—'

'Our engagement is over.' She was wearing a wide-brimmed straw hat, protection against the hot rays of the sun but now a strong gust of wind blew it from her head.

Clay caught it, twirling it in his hand. 'Pretty!' he said, feeling both happy and sad. Something about wide-brimmed straw hats and lovely little faces beneath them made him want to laugh and cry if ever a man was allowed to cry. His mother with a redhead's porcelain complexion, had always worn big shady hats in the sun.

'If he wants to be with Natasha he's welcome to her,' Carrie was saying, sensitive to the changing expressions on his face. *What* was he thinking about?

Clay handed her hat back to her. 'Put it back on. You have the most beautiful skin. I'd say Scott will probably take the line Natasha came onto him. I think that's the sort of thing he would do. The point is, whatever arrangement he had with Natasha, he wants *you.*'

'Maybe for a while.' A little bitterness seeped out. 'But that's not going to happen, Clay.'

'I wish I could believe you,' he smiled ironically.

'What's it to you anyway?' The breathless feeling was increasing. She had never stopped thinking about this man even with everything else going on in her life.

'For a highly intelligent young woman that's a very stupid question,' he said tersely.

She had to breathe in deeply as she looked up at him. His strong features were drawn taut.

'Clay, I'm not taking anything away from…from what happened that day on Jimboorie,' she burst out emotionally. 'I fell…'

'*We* fell…' He corrected, shoving his hands deep in the pockets of his jeans lest he reach out and grab her.

'Are you going to keep interrupting me?' she asked a little raggedly.

'Yes.' He nodded. '*We* fell…'

'Fathoms deep in…*fascination*,' she said, her dark eyes enormous in her face. 'It's not love, Clay. It can't be love. We barely know one another. I've known Scott for most of my life.'

'So?' He pulled at the knotted red bandanna around his bronze throat as though he, too, were having difficulty breathing. 'You got engaged. You pleased your parents, his parents. But he certainly didn't make you happy. Are you going to admit it?'

She looked up at the blazing blue sky—the colour of his eyes—as if looking for an answer. 'I can't abandon him until he's out of hospital and safely home. He could have been killed or condemned to live life in a wheelchair. He could still take a turn for the worse.'

'I hope to God he doesn't,' Clay said, with utter soberness. 'This guy seems to be able to project guilt on you. Are you sorry about *our* time together?' He tilted her chin up. 'Tell me. I'm not here to harass you, Caroline. But I'm not going to stand by and watch you get locked into a bad situation. On your own admission your parents are coming around to dismissing the rumours or ignoring them altogether.'

'Who told *you*?' she asked, curious to know.

'Someone who was there,' he said in a clipped voice.

'Surely not one of the Campbells? You know the story. Your father was supposed to marry Elizabeth Campbell.'

His blue eyes were spangled with silver in the glare. 'Sounds like a lot of railroading goes on in this part of the world. My father told me the only woman he ever wanted to marry was my mother. If you'd have seen them together you would have known how much they loved one another.'

'They both died young,' Carrie lamented.

'Young enough,' Clay said. 'My father never used his name, Cunningham. That's just between you and me. Cunningham was too well-known and he wanted no part of his family any-more. We were the Dysons. Dyson was his second name. We kept ourselves to ourselves. After my father was killed, my mother and I were even more quiet.'

'My heart goes out to you, Clay.' Indeed all of her went out to him.

He could see the sympathy and understanding in her lovely face. 'Don't get upset, Caroline. You know what happened the last time. Do you feel like a cup of coffee?' He was desperate to prolong his time with her.

'I have to get going, Clay,' she made her excuse, seeing sta-tion women she knew wheeling out their trolleys and waving to her, eyes curious. She waved back. So did Clay.

'You don't want us to be seen together? Is that it?' His dark-timbred voice turned hard.

'No, I don't mean that.' She shook her head. 'I feel I must visit Scott in hospital. I have to make arrangements. It's a duty I can't avoid.'

He stood there looking down at her, picturing them both back at Jimboorie. 'If you want I can drive you to Toowoomba,' he said. 'Natasha mightn't love me as a cousin should but I've been thinking of calling in to see her. She might need a bit of sup-port. I bet her family are very unhappy with her. Cunninghams *hate* scandals. When would you want to go or did you intend to fly? Are your parents going with you?'

A whole new excitement opened up. Temptation. Danger. 'Not at this stage. We're all caught in a maze of moral dilem-mas, I'm afraid. But I feel I *must* see Scott. I would never forgive myself if anything happened to him. He's been a big part of my life. God, Clay, I was going to marry him in December.'

'Marry *me* instead,' he found himself blurting out when he could well be ruining his chances by speaking out so precipitously. But, hell, wasn't he a better option than Harper?

Carrie's knees nearly gave way from under her. 'You can't be serious?'

His handsome head blocked out the sun. 'I've never been more serious in my life,' he said, flying in the face of caution. 'I wasn't joking when I said I wanted a wife and family. I do. I fully intended to advertise for the right woman. I'd thought it over carefully, came to that decision. Then along came *you*.'

'At what point did you think I might suit?' She feigned a kind of anger.

'Don't get angry,' he said. 'The last thing I intended was offence. Does it matter at what point?' Hadn't he wanted her *instantly*? But to tell her was really to risk frightening her away. 'I think we could make a go of it, Caroline. You'd never feel trapped with me. You love Jimboorie and the old homestead. I've seen that with my own eyes. We could restore it. I'm sure you know all about that side of things.' She was the sort of girl he'd dreamed of but doubted he'd ever find.

Bees were buzzing in a nearby flowering bottle brush or was it a sound in her head? 'Clay, you can't speak to me this way.' She clenched her hands together in agitation.

'Why not?' He lowered his resonant voice lest it float all over the parking area. 'This is a serious proposal. One I'd be honoured if you'd consider. I'm not stone-broke like everyone seems to think. Miracles do happen in life. I've no great fortune, but quite enough to be going on with. I could make a good life for you. I'd dedicate myself to it.'

'You'd marry a woman you didn't love?' She stared up at him, knowing his dedication wouldn't be enough for her. Scales had been lifted from her eyes. She wanted a man who would love her passionately. As passionately as she loved him. Love that would be there to stay.

'You were going to marry a man you didn't love,' he pointed out very quietly.

She felt like she was being swept along in a turbulent stream. 'Clay, I can't possibly consider this. It would take more than I'm prepared to give. Besides, I'm in an impossible place in my life. Haven't you enough admirers already? You could have had your pick of a dozen at the gala dance?'

'What, pretty little teenagers who don't yet know their own minds?'

'There were others!'

'Stop, Caroline,' he said. 'I understand you're in a difficult place. I daresay your parents wouldn't be happy about me, but I know we can make a real go of it. I can't put it better than that. Except to say I'm as strongly attracted to you as you are to me. Okay, it's not love. You say you can't fall in love right away. But what we have is *good.*'

She couldn't deny it. What they had was beautiful. No one could take that kiss away, but exposing her heart with all that had happened to her seemed an ominous thing to do. Her fellow shoppers would probably think she was flirting with Clay when Scott was lying comatose in a hospital bed.

Knowing what sort of person Carrie was, the other women shoppers *weren't* thinking that at all, but Carrie found herself burdened by unwarranted guilt.

'When are you wanting to leave?' Clay asked, oblivious of anyone now but Carrie.

'Tomorrow morning,' she said. 'It would be a three-hour drive even moving!'

'I'll take you,' he said.

'So how would we meet up?' she asked shakily. God, she wanted so much to be with him when she didn't even know if she could handle it. Her whole philosophy of life was coming under bombardment. It was as though a volcano lying dormant within her was showing perilous signs of erupting.

'What the hell, I'll drive out to Victory Downs,' Clay decided. 'I'll get an early start. What have we got to hide anyway? I'm going to see my cousin. You're going to see your ex-fiancé. No need for me to come in and meet the folks,' he said with extreme dryness. 'You can come out to the car.'

Carrie shook her head. She just couldn't face her father's opposition. It would be like a great icy wind from Antarctica. 'I'll meet you in town. I'll park here.'

'What time can you make it?' He didn't like the idea of her making all these long drives.

'Eight o'clock. Is that too late?'

'Eight's fine. Put in a few clothes. You'll be tired. We might as well stay in Toowoomba overnight.' His blue eyes looked directly into hers. 'Trust me, Caroline. We'll be fine.'

Did she trust him?

That wasn't the question at all. The answer was and it came right away. Did she trust *herself*?

When she found Scott's room, his parents were already there, seated at their son's bedside.

'Carrie, dear!' Thea Harper rose at once, coming to hug and kiss her. 'I'm so glad you're here.'

'Carrie!' Even Bradley Harper's severe face broke into a smile. 'Thanks for coming. How did you get here?'

'Drove,' Carrie said, cutting off the conversation by moving quickly towards the bed. 'How is he?' She bent over Scott's prone frame, gently, even tenderly, taking his hand. 'Any change?'

'They've wound down the drugs,' Thea Harper said, in a shaky voice. 'They're waiting for him to come out of it.'

Carrie lowered herself into the chair Bradley Harper drew up for her close to Scott's head. He looked very young and handsome. Sleeping quietly except for the monitors. 'He's going to be all right,' she said.

'Oh, God, he has to be!' Thea Harper suddenly started to sob.

'Thea, stop that,' her husband commanded. 'You're wearing yourself out. Scotty's going to be okay now Carrie's here.'

Please, please, please, don't put this on me, Carrie thought, something like panic crawling across her skin.

How was she supposed to feel when Scott had been continuing an affair with his old flame? Ready to forgive and forget? It seemed so. As far as the Harpers were concerned she and Scott were destined for marriage no matter what! The Harpers adored their only child so much they were prepared to make any sacrifice for him including *her.* If, God forbid, Scott were to be confined to a wheelchair they would still expect her to go through with the marriage. If she loved him, she would. Now she fully understood she didn't love him.

The Harpers, sick and exhausted, had gone off to have coffee leaving Carrie still sitting by Scott's bed. She, too, had shut her eyes as a headache pressed down on her temples, although she was still gently holding his fingers.

'Carrie?'

Her eyes flew open. She hadn't imagined that. Scott had spoken, sounding perfectly lucid. 'You're awake. Oh, thank God!'

'What happened?'

His dilated pupils seemed impossibly large. 'It's okay. You're all right,' she patted him reassuringly. 'You're in hospital. You were in an accident. You were badly concussed. Hang on, I have to get a doctor in here.' She rose from her chair.

'Don't leave me,' Scott called. 'Don't ever leave me.'

Carrie flew out to the nurses' station, her mind swirling with crazy thoughts of flight.

The Harpers were ecstatic. 'It was *you*!' Thea Harper, laughing and crying gave Carrie all the credit. 'He heard your voice. He felt the touch of your hand.'

'He was ready to come out of it, Mrs. Harper,' Carrie said, aware Scott's doctor was studying her with a close but friendly eye.

'No, *you* were the miracle!' Thea maintained, hugging Carrie yet again, her exhaustion lifted. 'You, Carrie McNevin. You're an angel.'

An angel, imagine!

'Look I'll have to shoo you all out for ten minutes or so,' the doctor said. 'You can come back one at a time and say your goodbyes. This sleeping beauty might have awakened, but he's still in need of plenty of rest.'

'We'll go,' Bradley Harper said, putting an arm around his wife. 'Love you, son!' A hard, tough man, he declared it in a strong, emotional voice. That hurt Carrie. She doubted her father could ever say that to *her*. Certainly not in that voice. 'We'll be back later,' Brad Harper said.

'Don't go, Carrie,' Scott appealed to Carrie, his eyes glassy. 'I need you here. Carrie?'

She looked at the doctor unsure what to do. 'She can come back later,' the doctor said. 'Settle back, young man. You want to get out of here as soon as possible, don't you?'

'Can't wait. Everything is going to be okay, Carrie,' Scott said and it seemed to her there was full comprehension in his eyes. 'Kiss me before you go.'

She bent over him, touching her lips to his temple. 'I'll come back later, okay?'

'I love you,' Scott said, as though there were no other woman in the world.

The Harpers were waiting for her down the corridor. Thea reached out to hug her yet again. 'You're really a godsend, Carrie. *You* are the one he needs.'

The pressure was getting scary. 'We should talk about that, Mrs. Harper, but not today,' Carrie said. 'Are you going to look in on Natasha? She hasn't been discharged yet.'

'Of course we're not going to look in on that scheming young woman,' Thea said. 'She's done nothing but throw herself shamelessly at Scott.'

'It appears I was the only one who didn't know that,' Carrie said quietly.

'My son loves only *you,* Carrie,' Brad Harper told her in a voice that defied her to disagree. 'Natasha Cunningham meant nothing to him.'

'Actually she did, Mr. Harper,' Carrie said, inside objecting to his domineering tone. Why did men want so much power over women? 'But let's not spoil the moment. Scott is going to make a full recovery.'

'Thank God!' the Harpers declared in unison. 'Come and have a coffee with us, Carrie,' Thea invited. 'We're drowning in it but we can have tea.'

'Thank you, Mrs. Harper, but I intend to look in on Natasha,' Carrie said, letting them make what they liked of that.

'Good! Give her what for!' Brad Harper advised, his weathered face grim.

Natasha Cunningham was not in bed. She was sitting in an armchair looking out the window, her back to Carrie. No one else was in the room. Clay must have gone, although they had made arrangements to meet up late afternoon.

'Natasha, it's me, Carrie,' she said in as gentle a voice as she could muster.

A moment of stunned silence, then, 'What the hell are *you* doing here?' Natasha responded roughly. She thrust up and turned around as if prepared for confrontation.

'I would have thought that obvious,' Carrie said. 'I came to see how you are. Knowing what your family is like I thought you could do with a friend.'

'Ain't that the truth!' Natasha was half laughing now, but she looked terrible. She was white and drained, her eyes bloodshot and red rimmed as though she had never stopped crying. The right side of her face was black and blue all around the jawline. Lacerations were clearly visible on her lower neck and arms. She wasn't in hospital garb. She was wearing a T-shirt and loose linen trousers that hung on her. Always bone thin, she had lost even more weight.

'Thank God you got out of it as well as you did,' Carrie said. 'Please sit down again. You don't look so good.'

'How's Scotty?' Natasha asked, leaning over as though her stomach ached. 'I dared not go near his room.'

'I was about to tell you. *When* you sit down. Preferably lie down.'

'Okay, okay.' Natasha waved a hand irritably, but she went back to the bed. 'How is he?' She stared Carrie right in the eye.

'You know he's been in a medically induced coma. He's fully conscious now. He recognises everyone. The fractured clavicle will keep him quiet for a couple of months and he can forget polo for a while longer, but he'll heal. His doctor is expecting him to make a full recovery. His youth and fitness will be a big help.'

There was an unbearably intense look or gladness and relief on Natasha's face. Then she burst into violent tears. 'It was all my fault. Everything is my fault.'

Carrie could only feel pity. 'Are you well enough to talk about it or should we let it go?' Her very nature was preventing her from feeling the ill will towards Natasha she thoroughly deserved.

'You must be furious with me. Furious and disgusted.' Natasha dashed her tears away with the back of her head. 'I'm a bitch. A real bad bitch. I've gloried in it.'

'No, you haven't.' Carrie shook her head, suddenly convinced it was true. 'Somehow I think you've been pushed into that role. I'm not furious with you. I don't exactly understand why. By rights, I should be.' Carrie reached inside her handbag for some clean tissues, which she passed to Natasha. 'Did you have an argument? Was that it? Scott lost control of the wheel?' She could well see it happening. Natasha was such a volatile young woman.

'Do you love him, Carrie?' Natasha didn't answer Carrie's questions but asked one of her own. 'He's a real bastard you know.'

'But *you* love him,' Carrie pointed out, doing her own ignoring.

'God knows why! I've always loved him. I've tried, but I could never get myself free of him. He took *my* virginity, you know. I might have held on to it longer if not for him. And he wasn't too gentle about it, either. Scotty only thinks about *himself.*'

'It certainly looks like it,' Carrie agreed. 'And you've been with him all this time?'

Natasha wept afresh, charcoal smudges beneath her eyes. 'He's as mad as he can be for you, but you wouldn't come across. He told me. I could barely stop laughing. I, unlike you, couldn't keep away from him. Not that he ever turned me down. Sex is very high on Scotty's agenda.'

'A little bit *too* high, if you ask me,' Carrie said, crisply.

Natasha nodded as though they were two friends having a serious discussion. 'He even wanted it the night of the dance when he had that fight with Clay.'

'Oh my Lord!' Carrie groaned softly. 'And that's the man I got myself engaged to! How utterly blind I've been.'

'Don't sound so shocked.' Natasha picked up a few white grapes and popped them in her mouth. 'He needed comfort. He knows I can give it to him. None of this little bit of loving stuff like you dish out.'

'Thanks for sharing that with me, Natasha,' Carrie said. 'You're one underhanded pair and it's starting to show.'

Natasha laughed. 'You're a very dull person, Carrie. Face it. I have more than a few tricks.'

'Of course you have,' Carrie said. 'Even then Scott isn't all that interested in you.'

'*You* don't love him,' Natasha cried, mortally stung.

'You'd have been ready to do violence had I truly taken your man.'

'You bet!' Natasha wiped her mouth with the back of her hand. 'I'd have skinned you alive.'

'Only I wouldn't stoop to prostituting myself with another woman's fiancée,' Carrie said flatly. 'Has Clay been to see you?'

She didn't expect to see a smile break across Natasha's face. 'You know my cousin's a really nice guy when you get to know him. One of the *good* guys. I didn't get to know too many of them. Scott got in the way. Clay would never tell a woman to get herself an abortion.'

Carrie felt like an avalanche had hit her. *Abortion!* She could even feel herself turn pale.

'I'm sorry, Carrie,' Natasha burst out. 'I'm really and truly sorry. You're a good guy, too. You've always been nice to me even when I've been a pig.'

Carrie hardly heard her. 'You're pregnant?' she asked, astonished now Natasha hadn't caused it to happen long before this.

Natasha's answer came right away, not without a trace of triumph. 'I am.'

'Even through the accident?' It was a mystery to Carrie.

'Strong little beggar,' Natasha said, fondly.

'How far along are you?'

'Ten weeks,' Natasha said, patting her flat tummy.

'Did you tell Clay?'

'God no!' Natasha looked astounded by the question. 'Of course I didn't. What's it got to do with him? Strewth, he was acting like *you're* the love of his life. What's with you anyway that the guys get so carried away?'

'*You're* the one who got carried away, Natasha,' Carrie said, her expression firming. 'Either that or you decided to resolve the situation. I wouldn't put it past you.'

'It wasn't like that,' Natasha said.

Carrie shook her head. 'You have a gnat's sense of what's

right and wrong, Natasha. And Scott suggested you get an abortion?'

'Not suggested, dear. Scott's not like that. It was a command. It's *you* he wants to marry. I'm beginning to wonder if you little virgins aren't the smartest of us all.'

Carrie ignored the comment; instead she asked, 'What are you going to do about the baby?'

Natasha touched her stomach tenderly again. 'I don't know yet. This will be a great, great scandal unless I pack up and leave home in a hurry.'

'Do your parents know?'

Natasha shook her dark head vehemently. 'Come off it, Carrie. We're talking the world's most sanctimonious people. It's just you, me and Scotty. And the doctor who examined me, of course and he's not talking.'

'You must keep the baby, Natasha,' Carrie said, trying hard to deal with all this. 'It's precious new life you're carrying. This is *your* child. You'll regret it all the days of your life if you allow yourself to be talked into an abortion. Your little one has put up a fight for life so far.'

'That he has. It's a boy, I know. Scotty's son.' Natasha stretched out a leisurely hand for more grapes, her expression showing maternal pride.

Carrie's head was swimming so badly she might have been drunk. There was an ache in her heart. A worse ache in her head. 'So you'd better get Scotty to marry you,' she said, somehow finding the strength to stand up. 'I wouldn't touch him with a barge pole.'

CHAPTER SIX

THEY SAT IN a quiet corner of a little restaurant at the top of the Range, a twinkling world of coloured lights spread out across the city beneath them.

'No appetite?' Clay asked, having watched her toy with the delicious food.

'I should have stuck with the entrée,' Carrie said, putting down her knife and fork. 'The food's great, but life's getting too much for me.' Her dark velvety eyes registered sadness.

'Scott's going to make a full recovery,' he pointed out. 'That must take a lot of the burden off you.' He hoped to God it did. Maybe then she could tell Scott to let go.

'It does,' she admitted.

'Is there something you're not telling me?'

'Yes.' He was just so perceptive, she dipped her head.

'Thought so.' He let his eyes rest on her. She was wearing a bare little black top with a multi-coloured, multi-patterned gauzy skirt that almost reached her ankles. Her beautiful long hair braided away from her face shone pure gold in the candle-light. Her skin had an equally lovely gold tint. He had never seen any woman he thought more beautiful. No woman to touch her.

'Obviously it's very much upset you?' He topped up her glass of white wine.

'Thank you.' She raised her glass and took a long sip. 'This is in complete confidence, because I trust you.'

Warning bells began ringing inside his head. 'Just so long as you're not about to tell me you're going to marry Harper in December?' His eyes sizzled over her.

'I'm *not* going to marry Scott,' she said and shook her head. 'Chances are when he's fit enough—or even before then—he'll be marrying Natasha.'

Clay sat back, astonished, though Carrie had delivered the news quite matter-of-factly. 'Now that's the very *last* thing I expected to hear.'

'She's pregnant,' Carrie explained, still in that quiet even tone. 'I had to tell someone. I couldn't keep it to myself. Natasha is pregnant with my ex-fiancé's child.'

'God!' Clay was genuinely stunned. 'Doesn't she know about contraception?'

Finally Carrie released a long-baffled sigh. 'Being Natasha I'd say she took her chances. She could even have been trying to push her luck. Who knows? The fact is, she's carrying Scott's child.'

'Then he must marry her,' Clay said as though there were no other course open to the man.

'He told her to have an abortion.'

Clay couldn't disguise his contempt. 'Doesn't that say everything you need to know about Scott Harper? His *own* child and he's ready to destroy it? Natasha can't listen to him. Times have changed so much. She'll get through and she'll adore her baby.'

'I hope so,' Carrie said, thinking the essence of the Cunninghams was their coldheartedness. 'There aren't too many families like yours.'

'They're not *my* family,' Clay retorted, his voice peppered with loathing. 'Nor will they ever be in my mind. I gather Natasha doesn't get along too well with her parents. It doesn't make sense to me, these rich people. They have everything and they have nothing. Then again Natasha is getting looked after so well financially she'd never leave home.'

Carrie drank her wine slowly. 'I would say that's because of Scott.' Natasha wasn't far off thirty and on her own admission she hadn't really looked beyond her first lover.

'The bastard!' Clay exploded, then apologised.

'No need, you're spot on. Scott has always been in the picture.'

'Poor Natasha!' Clay said. 'Though she doesn't seem to have much going for her in the way of morals. But she was nice for the time I was with her. Quiet and introspective. Now I know why. In a way it's the same for her as you. Harper caught both of you into a trap.'

Carrie tasted the bitter truth. 'I'm thinking Natasha turned the tables on him.'

'You said it's over?' Clay caught the tips of her fingers across the table.

'It's over,' she said, reacting to the thrill of his hand on hers.

'But you haven't told him?'

She averted her dark eyes. 'When he's settled back at home Scott and I will be having a serious talk.'

'I'm really happy to hear that,' Clay said, not looking happy at all. 'He surely doesn't think Natasha is going to do as he says?'

'He'd have to be forced to marry her,' Carrie gave her opinion. 'I don't think his parents would force him to do anything. Especially after his accident which apparently Natasha caused.'

'I'm sure she didn't plan it. I guess he went ballistic when she told him.'

'I would say his reaction would be fairly strong.'

'Anyway, that's their problem. Natasha's child is the Harper's grandchild. Surely that means everything to them? Their *grandchild*? The Cunninghams aren't nobodies. Natasha's parents would adjust overnight. So would the town if Scott and Natasha were to marry.'

'Nothing would surprise me,' Carrie said, 'but I have the awful feeling some of the scandal will stick to *me*.'

'You're the innocent party,' Clay said.

'That won't stop it. It never does. I don't feel like I'm walking on solid ground any more.'

'I can understand that,' he said quietly. 'You're in shock. You have to give yourself a little time, Caroline.'

'*You* have to give me a little time.' She looked into his eyes, sealing the rest of the world off.

'I'd give you all the time in the world if only we had it,' he replied. 'I know what's in my head already.' He could, and perhaps should, have said what's in 'my head and my *heart*.' It was true enough, but she still wasn't absolutely free of Harper. 'I know it came out all wrong the last time. I startled you. I see now I could hardly fail to do so, but I'm here for you, Caroline, once Harper is out of the way. I seem to have been alone for so much of my life. It wasn't only my father who left me. My mother left me as well after he was killed. Neither of them returned.'

She pressed her hands against the heat in her cheeks. It flamed through her whole body. 'What if you found you couldn't love me? *After* marriage, for all your best intentions it just didn't happen?' It was a legitimate fear.

All Clay wanted to do was rain kisses on her face, her throat, her breasts, down over her whole body to her toes as beautifully formed as were her slender fingers. Fingers that were doubly pretty because she wasn't wearing Harper's ring. When had she taken that off?

'I refuse to believe it couldn't happen,' he said. 'Didn't a fire burn inside you when I kissed you?'

She was almost ready to tell him his kiss had awakened her to full life only she held back. 'This is the wrong time for a courtship, Clay,' she said. 'You know it's funny, but sometimes, I badly want to call you James,' she confessed.

'So you can call me James when we marry.' He gave her the smile that so easily melted her heart.

'I think it's time to take me back to the hotel,' she murmured, just that little bit scared of so much emotion. When she was with Clay she wasn't prim and proper Carrie. She was someone else.

'Do you intend seeing Harper again in the morning before we return?' he asked, somehow sensing what was actually in her mind. He, too, was overwhelmed by the powerful attraction that had overtaken them. He had wished for the right woman. It had happened. But he could see she was so unguarded she could snap.

'I don't want to, but I will.' Carrie spoke more firmly. 'Hospitals aren't the best places to deliver bad news. And it *will* be bad news for Scott and his parents. Scott has lived his life thinking he can have any girl he wants. For whatever his reasons he's hell-bent on marrying me. Perhaps it was because I wasn't giving him what he wanted? I had to be absolutely *his* and marriage was the only way? Who knows? He was only using Natasha when she lay in bed with him. I feel sorry for her. Nevertheless at this point he's too sick to tell him what I think of him. That will have to wait.'

'So we're going around in circles?' Clay realized he had to accept that. He gestured to the waiter for the bill.

'It's a bit like that.' Briefly Carrie met his gaze.

She was standing quietly in the foyer, admiring the exquisite flower arrangement—this after all was the Garden City of Queensland—while Clay settled the bill.

He joined her after a moment and took her arm. They were barely out the door when they were confronted by a well dressed middle-aged couple about to enter the restaurant. It was the Harpers, even though Carrie had been given to understand that Bradley Harper was returning home, leaving his wife staying with a friend who lived on the Range.

Carrie felt so guilty she might have been caught in the execution of a serious crime.

The Harpers, too, looked startled.

'What on earth are you doing here, Carrie? And with *him*?' Shock quickly turned to outright aggression as Bradley Harper addressed her in his deep, gravelly voice. He snapped a furious glance over Clay who stood, a tall, quiet presence by Carrie's side.

'Good evening, Mr and Mrs Harper,' Carrie said in her usual courteous manner. 'You remember Clay, don't you? Clay Cunningham?'

'Yes,' Thea Harper said briefly, incapable of arranging her face into a smile. She was pale with dismay. 'What are you doing here together, Carrie? I don't understand. Scott's still lying in hospital and you've had dinner with this young man? I really can't believe it. Not *you,* Carrie. You always conduct yourself so well.'

'I hope I'm still doing that, Mrs. Harper,' Carrie said. 'Clay is my friend. Nothing more.' That wasn't true but they didn't have to know. 'Many things have changed since before and after Scott's accident. I'm so glad he's going to make a full recovery but Scott knows in his heart our engagement is over. It just wasn't the right time to make that perfectly plain to him at the hospital. I'll delay our talk until he's well enough.'

The Harpers stood staring at her. 'You're not *serious*? You can't be, Carrie,' Thea Harper moved forward to lay a hand on Carrie's arm. 'You're overreacting surely? My son adores you.'

'That's not true, Mrs. Harper,' Carrie said very gently. 'I don't want to distress you. I know how upset you and Mr. Harper have been, but Scott really is involved with Natasha. I'll allow him to tell you about it himself.'

Bradley Harper broke in so violently he must have reached breaking point. 'Involved with Natasha Cunningham, rubbish! There are always women like Natasha Cunningham in life. What *I* want to know is, what's been going on between *you* two?' His expression turned ugly.

Clay spoke for the first time. 'Have a care, Mr. Harper,' he said in a very quiet, controlled sort of voice.

'What was that? Speak up?' Bradley Harper, a powerful man, began to square up, looking at the six-foot-three, superbly fit young man as though he were an insect to be crushed underfoot.

'You heard me perfectly well the first time,' Clay said. 'We're in public, remember? I suggest you back down. And you might apologise to Caroline. She's the injured party here.'

'*Caroline?*' Harper's expression froze. 'She's not *Caroline*. She's Carrie. Don't get smart with me, son!' Bradley Harper warned, his beefy, still handsome face flushed with blood. 'I saw off your father. I'll do the same for you.'

'I wouldn't bank on that.' Clay's alert stance and sombre tone would have convinced anyone. 'As I understand it you didn't see off my father, as you call it. Your men saw him off your station at gunpoint. You didn't appear at all. I'm not like my father anyway. My father was a *gentle* man. I'm not.'

A rush of contemptuous laughter broke from Bradley Harper's mouth. 'Why you arrogant young bastard!' That peculiar smile broadened as he threw a rage packed right hook, which Clay blocked so effectively the older man went staggering back. Like father. Like son.

Both women were utterly dismayed. 'Please. Please stop it!' Carrie begged. This wasn't what they wanted. Other people were coming out of the restaurant, staring at them, whispering.

'You'll be sorry for that!' Bradley Harper snarled at Clay after he righted himself and regained a little control. 'How dare you lay a hand on me? Do you even have a clue how powerful I am?'

'You're not above the law, Mr Harper,' Clay reminded him, in a voice that held a natural authority. 'What you attempted was assault. *I'll* lay charges if you ever attempt anything like that again. Believe me, I only stopped you because of the ladies and the fact I knew you'd come off badly.'

The tears were spilling down Thea Harper's face. 'Brad, please! You're making a spectacle of us.' She'd had the feeling all along it wasn't a good idea for Brad to bring her here. Now *this*!

'*These two* are making the show,' Bradley Harper corrected her with surprising venom.

'I'm sorry, Mrs Harper.' Carrie, who was trembling badly, took Clay's arm to move him away. She could feel the tension right through his body—the desire she supposed, to pummel Bradley Harper as he had pummelled Scott. There were old issues that had to be settled here, though she knew it wouldn't be Clay who would make the first move. He'd simply finish it.

Neither of them said a word all the way back to the hotel where they were staying.

'I feel like a drink,' Clay said softly, when they entered the hotel lobby. 'Care to join me?'

'I'll sit for a while,' she said, too upset to go up to her room. 'I feel very shaky. He's an awful man, Brad Harper.'

'Of course he is.' Clay led her into the well-appointed lounge where a few guests were seated at the small circular tables. 'You can count your lucky stars you won't be getting him for a father-in-law after all.'

'Mrs Harper is okay.' She sank into a plush banquette, resting her back against it. 'She's easy enough to get on with, but she's right under his thumb, poor woman. He's such a domineering man. Even Scott is intimidated by his father.'

'Bag of wind,' Clay said, dismissing the powerful and ruthless Bradley Harper. 'What can I get you?'

'I don't especially want anything.' Yes, she did. She wanted his arms around her.

'What about a brandy and ginger? You want something to settle you down. I'm for a single malt whiskey. Don't move from this spot. I'll be back in a moment.'

Her mother and father would soon get the news, Carrie thought, watching Clay walk over to the bar. When he arrived there, he turned and looked back at her. Even at a distance his eyes *burned* an electric-blue.

She gave him a little wave, conscious women at other tables were looking at him as well. And why not? He was a marvellous looking man. She hadn't planned on falling in love with him. Yet here she was with him. She saw him give the order to the bartender, then he returned to the table, settling his tall, rangy frame into the banquette beside her.

Carrie drew great comfort from his nearness. Comfort and a kind of bliss that flushed her skin and made her look as though she were lit from within.

'What's with the Harpers always throwing punches?' he asked, wryly. 'Wild punches, I might add.'

'They see themselves as men of action,' Carrie said, with a crazy impulse to lay her head on his shoulder.

'Better to think first and act later,' Clay said, looking towards the waiter who was approaching with their drinks.

Carrie took not a sip, but a gulp of her drink. Things were getting right out of hand. The encounter with the Harpers had really thrown her. Her drink was cold and the shot of brandy added depth to the sparkling ginger ale. 'Mrs Harper won't lose any time ringing my parents to let them know they've seen me with you,' she said, one part of her admiring the paintings around the walls. 'They'll do it tonight.'

'It's always best to say exactly what you're doing, Caroline,' he told her quietly. 'You're a grown woman not a child. You could have told your mother I was giving you a lift.'

'I did,' she said.

'Well, that's not so bad then?' He studied her pure profile. 'Would she tell your father?'

Carrie shook her head. 'No. I'm beginning to think there's lots my mother doesn't tell my father. Sometimes I can't figure Mamma out. She does things I know she doesn't want to, to please Dad.'

'Lots of wives would do that.'

'Mamma does it for a *living*,' Carrie said. 'It's all coming to a head, isn't it?'

'It has to, Caroline. You have to get on with your life. Whether I'm in it or not remains to be seen.'

'Sure you don't want to run that advertisement?' she asked, tilting her head to stare into his eyes.

'Only if you write it up for me.'

'Let's see, how would it go?'

'You're the journalist,' he reminded her.

'Photojournalist,' she corrected with a little smile. 'I take photos for the *Bulletin* as well.'

'I'm certain you'll take a good one of me. Now where were we?'

'Bush Bachelor, twenty-eight, never married, very fit, owns his own pastoral property, is looking for a wife aged between—?'

'Twenty-four and twenty-eight,' he filled in, in a helpful tone of voice. 'Under twenty-four too young to really know their own mind, over twenty-eight older than me. Twenty-four for preference. Petite. Must be a golden-blonde with velvety-brown doe eyes. A countrywoman, loves the land, an excellent horsewoman, interested in restoring a historic homestead, eventually having kids, two or three, must be able to guarantee a daughter who looks just like her. Let's see, what else?'

'You don't need me at all,' she said. She took another little swallow. Even tried a smile.

'Oh, yes, I do. Haven't I just described you?'

'Maybe I was the first one your gaze really fell on?' she suggested. 'Maybe knowing I was Scott Harper's fiancée had something to do with it?'

'What is that supposed to mean, Caroline?'

The question was dead serious. 'Didn't Brad Harper fire up when you called me Caroline?' she remarked, ignoring his question. 'You'd think that wasn't allowed.'

'Answer the question, please.' He gently tapped the back of her hand.

'Maybe you felt like taking something of his?'

He kept looking at her until she looked away. 'Actually I'm fine with that, but the thought never crossed my mind. I saw the connection as a huge complication. I definitely wanted to get to know you better, but there you were, engaged.'

The air around them seemed on the point of igniting. 'I'm sorry,' Carrie apologised.

'So you should be. But I'll forgive you. This one time.'

'It could just as easily have been someone else. One of the McFadden sisters,' she persisted. 'Jade or Mia. Both of them are very attractive and good company. They're station people. They're good riders. Jade and I often battle it out for first place in competitions. They certainly gave the impression they were attracted to you.'

'So we've narrowed it down to the McFadden sisters and *you*.'

Inside she was deeply, *deeply,* shaken. 'I can't see clearly about myself, Clay. You've got to heed it. What I do see is a twenty-four-year-old woman who was about to marry a man who continued to sleep with other women—I bet there were others—while we were engaged, then he impregnated one. Finally to cap it off a man who told another woman to get rid of his own child so he could still marry me. What kind of a fool did he think I was? What kind of a fool am I for that matter?'

'What kind of a callous bastard is he, don't you mean?' Clay responded, with frightening calm. 'Countless people have been deceived, Caroline. Men and women. They give their trust only to have it trampled underfoot. One doesn't have to be a fool for that to happen. It happens right across the board.'

'Trust is so very important,' she said quietly. 'It is to me yet it's so easy to lose faith. What happens then? Does one turn into a cynic, never trusting anyone again?'

'You know what they say! Life's a gamble. Love's a gamble. We come through with courage and a dollop of daring.'

'And there's another thing about me,' she said. 'I don't know my own mind. I'd be devastated if I'd truly loved Scott. Obviously I didn't. I just thought I was in love with him.'

'So when did you wake up to the fact you weren't?' he asked dryly. 'Did it just happen one morning?'

She turned her head slightly. 'The fact I could so easily be attracted to you was a tremendous eye opener. What if it had happened *after* I married Scott?'

'No need to worry about it,' he consoled her. 'You're not going to marry Scott. We might leave the rest of that drink.'

'Are you saying I've had too much?' There was a little flash in her dark eyes.

'Perhaps the tiniest little bit. You had very little to eat and that confrontation with the Harpers upset you.'

'Didn't it upset you?'

'I wanted to hit that man,' Clay admitted, his handsome face taut. 'I wanted to hit him so badly, but he's too old to hit. And then there were you women. Women don't like violence.'

'You're right about that!' she wholeheartedly agreed. 'I'm apprehensive about what my father is going to say.'

'He's very tough on you in his way, isn't he? Why *is* that?' He studied her, a beautiful, refined young woman any father would be proud of. He was quite unable to understand it.

Carrie suddenly picked up her glass and clinked it against his in a funny little gesture. 'Our personalities are incompatible?' she suggested, with a brittle little laugh. 'There's something about me he doesn't like? I suppose it can happen.'

'Leave home, Caroline,' he advised. 'It's time you did.'

'Victory Downs isn't going to be mine, anyway,' she sighed. She didn't want the rest of her drink but she had it anyway.

'How's that?' A vertical line appeared between his strongly marked brows. 'You're an only child. Who else can take over?'

'My cousin, Alex, will inherit. He's still a student.'

'Good God!' Clay found himself appalled. 'So what's your little lot?'

'Did you think I was an heiress?' she asked, outright challenge glimmering in her eyes. 'Did you think you just could land an heiress? You didn't put that in the ad.'

'Caroline, I couldn't care less if you were penniless,' he said a little curtly. 'It's *you,* the woman, I'm interested in.'

'That's what they all say.' He was quite right. She was just that tiny bit intoxicated. 'I'll be "well looked after" I've been told. Besides, I was to marry Bradley Harper's heir. That was considered a compelling reason for matrimony.'

'How very mercenary,' he said with contempt.

'Only I'm not marrying anyone,' she said.

They took the lift to Carrie's floor walking down the quiet, empty corridor to her room. There they paused while Carrie hunted up her keycard.

'You seem to be taking an awfully long time,' he said, an attractive wry note in his voice.

'Damn, where is it?' She knew she had it. 'I know!' She sank her hand into the deep hidden pocket in her skirt.

'Here, give it to me.' He took the keycard from her, opening up the door. 'Good night, Caroline,' he said.

'Goodness, you sound as if you have a very pressing engagement elsewhere. Are you that anxious to get rid of me!' She pushed past him and entered the comfortably furnished room, switching on more lights. Am I about to make a fool of myself? she thought. Why not? He already knows I am.

'Come here,' he said gently, standing just inside the door.

She spun about. 'There's nothing going to happen, Clay.'

'What makes you suppose there was?' His blue eyes gave off sparks.

'The way you're looking at me for one thing,' she said, trying to keep her emotional equilibrium and losing the battle. 'I'm a virgin. Did I mention that? It's a joke these days.'

He stayed where he was. He wasn't smiling. 'Why wouldn't a woman keep herself for the man she truly loves?'

'For fear she mightn't find him and life is flying by. I'm sorry, Clay. I'm trying to tell you I'm not a good judge.'

'You're tired,' he said. 'Exhausted.'

'We both are. Do you want to sleep with me in this bed?'

He didn't say anything for a moment. He just wanted to look at her. 'I don't think I'd be doing much sleeping,' he said, finally. 'I told you, Caroline. There's no pressure.'

'That's something else!' she said raggedly, doing a half spin. 'Scott was ready to wait. Next thing he's trying to rape me.'

Clay remembered that night very clearly; the way he had felt. 'Don't remind me! That would never happen to *any* woman with me, Caroline. You know that. Come on now, you're tired and upset. You'll get over all this. It's been pretty full on, one thing after another.'

'And another to face,' she said, leaning wearily against an armchair.

'I'm driving you back to Victory Downs tomorrow,' he told her firmly. 'We can get your 4WD picked up from the town and delivered to the station. I don't want you pushing on home.'

She wasn't looking forward to it, either. 'There'd be fireworks, Clay,' she warned.

He wasn't worried for himself. 'Your father's temper wouldn't bother me any more than Brad Harper's. I didn't think your father gave way to emotion anyway, he looks so darn buttoned up.'

For a moment Carrie looked quite lost. 'I should have said iceworks, not fireworks. Dad freezes you out.'

'I'm driving you home, Carrie,' Clay repeated. 'Right to your door. Now come here.'

Adrenaline shot into her bloodstream. All her senses lifted and began to soar. 'What for?'

'I want to kiss you,' he said simply, not taking his eyes off her. 'I want to take your *kiss* with me to bed.'

What else could she do? Every cell in her body demanded it. She walked towards him as if she couldn't keep away.

His arms were around her, his hand at the back of her neck,

taking the weight off her head. He was so much taller he was lifting her, enveloping her. He bore her weight so easily her feet were clear of the ground.

'Caroline!' he breathed, over her head.

Then his marvellous mouth came down on hers. She was so hungry, *greedy* to keep it there. What had happened to that *absent* part of her? The part Scott had never been able to reach? Did she only come alive through this man? The pleasure he gave her was so sensual, so limb melting, she thought as she collapsed against him. At any rate she relaxed into a posture of utter submission waiting for him to open her up like a flower.

All her defences were tumbling. She gathered nectar from his open mouth, kissing and nibbling at those cleanly defined, upraised edges as she went.

They were breathing as one.

It was an agony and an ecstasy to kiss and be kissed like this. The one counter-balancing the other. Agony. Ecstasy. But she wanted more. Much more. She realised now she was desperately in need of love. She wanted *everything* a man and a woman in love did together. It was impossible to resist longing such as this. Such was the nature of passion…

Next thing she knew she was lying on the bed, her eyelids closed tight. She was listening to the rapid-fire beating of her heart. It seemed to be shaking her entire being. She lifted a hand to contain her wild heart, slowly opening her eyes.

Only to discover Clay was gone.

CHAPTER SEVEN

CLAY'S BIG 4WD hummed along the highway, its shadow racing after them. A heat haze rose off the never ending black ribbon of road, shimmering in the air in front of the bonnet. The Great Dividing Range that stretched five thousand kilometres from the tropical tip of Cape York in Far North Queensland to the magnificent stone ramparts of the Grampian Ranges in Victoria, loomed to their left, a formidable barrier between the lush eastern seaboard and the vast Outback. The dry, *dry,* land that had taken the lives of early explorers and many an adventurer without trace. Today the Range looked spectacular, Clay thought, its rugged slopes hyacinth-blue in the blazing heat. It was another brilliantly fine day and the huge Spinifex plains were beginning to reveal themselves in wild golds and greens with broad domed, stunted trees dotted here and there over the countryside.

They had long since left the beautiful Darling Downs region with its wonderfully fertile agricultural land, travelling through the fruit and wine zones, the golden Granite Belt and the cotton fields with their high yielding quality crop, out past the gas and oil regions into the real Outback and the sheep and cattle stations.

'Okay?' Clay asked, glancing down at the blond head stirring on his shoulder.

'Oh, I'm sorry!' Carrie straightened abruptly. 'I must have dozed off.'

'You did,' he smiled. 'That's okay. I liked it.'

'I didn't get much sleep last night,' she explained, putting a hand to the thick plait at her nape. That was an understatement. Apart from an initial hour or two she hadn't slept at all she was so overwrought.

'You're worrying about what's going to happen when you arrive home?'

Carrie nodded.

'The authoritarian father,' Clay sighed. 'I'll make sure I'm not like that. I hate to ask but doesn't your mother ever take your side?'

'Of course she does,' Carrie protested. 'She's a wonderful mother.'

'She makes up for your father's distant kind of parenting?'

'I've told you too much, Clay,' she said.

'You have to tell someone,' he said. 'Besides, I worked it out for myself.'

'Why did you go off and leave me?' she asked. 'Last night, why did you leave me?'

'Right now, Caroline, you're immensely vulnerable,' he said quietly. 'You have an ex-fiancé who betrayed you— He is *ex*, by the way?' He gave her a sidelong glance.

'I told him this morning,' she said. 'I know I said I wasn't going to until he was out of hospital, but I changed my mind after the events of last night. It was only the briefest visit to convince myself he was physically, at least, on the mend. And he is.'

'What did he say?'

'Nothing. He expected it. Why wouldn't he?' she said without bitterness.

'Just checking,' Clay replied. 'I know what a tender heart you have. I left you, Caroline, because I just can't bear to do anything to hurt you. By the same token it was the *hardest* thing I've ever done.'

'I was beginning to think I was frigid,' she said.

He laughed aloud. 'Well, you got *that* wrong. You're *perfect* to make love to.'

'Maybe I never knew what making love meant,' she said.

Just under an hour later they were driving over a grid beneath the huge sign supported by two massive posts that marked the entrance to the station. Victory Downs.

Carrie shifted uneasily in the passenger seat. She hated confrontations but she knew there was one coming up. As for Clay who drove so calmly and efficiently beside her, it was as he said—he was well able to take care of himself.

They swept along the wide driveway lined by magnificent she-oaks. Flocks of woolly white sheep were off in the distance. Kangaroos hopped leisurely towards the silver line of the creek. An eagle soared overhead. Station horses grazed in the home paddocks.

Home. But for how much longer? She didn't understand why her father was leaving the station to her cousin Alex and she never would. It almost seemed as if he were telling her to get married or get thrown out! Her father's delight in her engagement seemed to perfectly express his feelings.

After about a mile they came on the homestead.

The dominating double storeyed central section, the original house, was Georgian in style but single storey wings had been added on later. The whole effect was of order and serenity. The paint on the decorative shutters gleamed as it did on the white ornamental wrought iron. The homestead and the surrounding lawns and gardens, irrigated by bore water, were beautifully maintained—in sharp contrast to the tremendous neglect the once 'Princess of the Western Plains' Jimboorie House had suffered. Carrie loved her home, but in her eyes it lacked the sheer sweep and romance of Jimboorie.

'Here we go!' Clay said, laconically, bringing his 4WD to a halt in the shade of a spreading bauhinia.

Around the side of the east wing two splendid Scotch collies came flying, their long silky near orange coats streaming in the wind.

'Here, boys!' Carrie called, patting her knees.

Clay's handsome face lit up. 'What beautiful creatures!'

'Prince and Blaze,' Carrie told him proudly. 'You won't get better than them. They're working dogs. They'll be pleased to meet you.'

'I'll be pleased to meet them.'

Excitedly the dogs welcomed Carrie home, then turned to sniffing the newcomer who bent to scratch one then the other behind the ear. 'Shake hands.' Clay gave the order to the older dog, Prince.

'He mightn't do it. He doesn't know you—' Carrie broke off laughing, as Prince obediently presented Clay with a paw.

'Good boy!'

Carrie looked past Clay to see her mother coming down the verandah steps towards them. 'You're home, darling,' she called, her face wearing a welcoming smile. 'Good trip? Clay, how nice to see you again.' Smilingly Alicia put out her hand to this stunning young man who so recently had entered their lives like a comet.

'How are you, Mrs McNevin?' Clay responded, shaking hands and looking down into Alicia's beautiful face, that scarcely bore a trace of ageing. Caroline was destined to look like this in maturity, he thought. He had been introduced to the McNevins briefly after he had won the Cup. Alicia had been gracious to him then, but he hadn't expected the friendly greeting he was getting now.

'I'm well, thank you, Clay,' Alicia said. 'I'm sure you'd like to come in and have something to eat after that long trip.'

Carrie's eyes sought her mother's. 'Where's Dad?' she asked carefully.

Alicia was totally relaxed. 'He and Harry Tennant have flown off to Longreach for a meeting. Your father won't be back until tomorrow afternoon.' In other words, the all clear. 'Come into the house,' she invited. 'It's hot standing in the sun. So how did you find Scott?' she asked Carrie as they walked towards the homestead, the dogs trotting quietly by their side.

'It's all very upsetting, Mamma,' Carrie said. 'Didn't Thea Cunningham get in touch with you?'

Alicia smiled tersely. 'She certainly did. I'm not sure now if I didn't tell her off, poor woman. She idolises that boy. In a way she's ruined him. But enough of that. Come in and freshen up then we can sit and relax.'

Clay stayed on for an hour of conversation that skirted any difficult issues. Afterwards both women saw him off.

Alicia slipped an arm around her daughter's waist as they walked back to the house. 'Do you know, I can't remember when I met such a charming young man. And so well spoken. I like him very, *very* much.'

'You liked Scott, remember?' Carrie pointed out with a touch of irony.

Alicia's beautiful eyes clouded. 'I had no idea he was so full of deceit.'

'You haven't heard the half of it, Mamma,' Carrie said.

'Good God there's not more?' Alicia asked in dismay. 'Thea couldn't wait to recount your meeting outside the restaurant in Toowoomba. She said Clay threatened to knock Bradley down. I must confess that shocked me though sometimes I think Brad Harper needs flattening.'

'I didn't think Mrs Harper told lies,' Carrie said, angrily. 'It was Mr Harper who threw a punch at Clay. He blocked it and told Mr Harper not to try it again. That was it!'

'She seemed to think *you* were to blame. You'd let them all down.'

They had reached the verandah. Now both sank into planter's chairs. Carrie looked straight ahead. 'Natasha is carrying Scott's child,' she said baldly.

Alicia who had eased back into her chair sat bolt upright. 'What are you saying?' She stared at Carrie, a dazed look on her face.

'Natasha's pregnant. Believe it,' Carrie repeated harshly.

A bewildered look passed across Alicia's face. 'What sort of an abject low life is he?' she demanded to know.

Carrie sighed deeply. 'I daresay Natasha contrived it. Needless to say with his help. She's mad about him.'

'Dear God!' Alicia shook her head slowly from side to side. 'I take it his parents don't know?'

'I wouldn't like to be Scott when he tells them.' Carrie bit on her lip hard. 'Mr Harper would be a pretty violent sort of man once he gets going. He loves Scott, but he expects him to toe the line. Scott, by the way, told Natasha to have an abortion.'

'That was his solution, was it?' Alicia asked in utter disgust. 'Get rid of his own child? God, haven't *you* been lucky? And haven't your father and I been colossally stupid? You're well out of it.'

'You think I don't know that?' Carrie said. 'Dad thought Scott was perfect for me. He'll be shocked. Does he know Clay was with me in Toowoomba?'

'No, and we won't tell him,' Alicia said.

'Is that a good idea?'

'It's the best one I can think of at the moment.'

'I should probably tell the truth. Dad runs too much of my life.'

'He means well, Carrie,' her mother said. 'He'll be really upset about the whole sorry business. But it's Scott who's the villain here, not Clay. Your father has to get over his misconceptions.'

Carrie considered. 'He's too rigid in his ways. I don't think he's ever going to approve of Clay. He's set his mind against him.'

'Not so different to how he treated Clay's father,' Alicia said in a tight voice. 'But what the heck! You're a woman now. You can do as you please.'

'Maybe the day will come when *you* can, too, Mamma,' Carrie said meaningfully and closed her fingers around her mother's.

When Carrie returned to the homestead at noon for a bite of lunch—she had teamed up with the vet doing his morning rounds—her father had returned home. She could hear his voice upraised in anger as she mounted the front steps. Her father rarely raised his voice. It simply wasn't necessary. Arguments with his wife were exceedingly rare, but they were having one humdinger of an argument now.

Carrie hesitated, uncertain whether to go back outside or find her way up to her bedroom through a side door.

'How could he *do* this? How could he spoil everything,' Bruce McNevin was asking in a rage. 'Here you are able to wind any man—any man at all—around your little finger and Carrie can't hold onto her own fiancé. I thought she'd be married in December. I thought we'd have our lives to ourselves.'

'What a dreadful thing to say, Bruce,' Carrie heard her mother reply, her voice full of pain.

'All right I'm sorry. I've done my best, Alicia. God knows I've tried. But she's not *mine*. How can you expect me to love her? I've tried all these years to love her but I *can't*. She's not my blood. Why do you think I've left the station to young Alex. He at least, *is*.'

Carrie reached for something to hold on to.

Click, click, click! It all came together. *She's not mine!*

A trembling began right through her body. A profound sadness filled her eyes. Nonetheless, she didn't step backwards, but forwards. She was devastated, but to her wonderment, not demolished. *She's not mine!* Hadn't such a thing been implied by his behaviour all these years?

'Shut up and keep your voice down,' Alicia ordered in a voice akin to the sharp crack of a whip. 'Carrie will be home soon.'

'She's home *now*.' Carrie found herself in the kitchen, where her parents or her mother and the man she thought was her father faced each other across the table like combatants in a deadly battle. 'Would someone like to explain to me what I just overheard?'

Alicia's face went paper-white. 'Carrie, darling!' She rushed to her daughter who stood stricken but resolute in the open doorway.

Carrie held up her hand, warding her mother off. 'Who exactly am I, Mum? Is there anyone in this world who hasn't betrayed me? My father all these long years isn't my father at all. So *who* is? I'm not going anywhere until you tell me.' Her dark eyes bore into her mother's. 'That's if you *know*?'

Bruce McNevin stood watching Carrie with such an odd look on his face. 'Please don't speak to your mother like that,' he said. 'I'm sorry you had to hear that. I'm just so terribly upset.'

'*You're* upset?' Alicia rounded tempestuously on her husband, unleashing one of her stunning tennis backhands. 'You miserable bastard!' she cried. 'You miserable whining cur! You *swore* you'd never tell her.'

Bruce McNevin stood as stiff as a ramrod against the blow, the imprint of Alicia's hand clear on his cheek. 'I didn't tell her. She overheard. This was just supposed to be between you and me, Alicia.'

'God!' Alicia moaned. 'I don't want to live with you anymore, Bruce. You've killed whatever feeling I had for you. Carrie is my daughter. I love her best in the world. Far more than I could ever love you.'

'But you never loved me, did you?' Bruce McNevin's grey eyes glittered strangely. 'I've been the one who's done all the loving.'

Carrie intervened, saying what she had to say as if it were enormously important. 'You don't know the first thing about love. You don't even know about simple compassion. You're a cold man. You think only of yourself. God, it must have been so hard for you fathering a child that wasn't yours. Why didn't you tell Mum to have an abortion?'

A white line ringed Bruce McNevin's tight mouth. 'She *wouldn't* have it, that's why!'

Alicia shook her head, her eyes full of grief. 'Never, never!'

'So who's my father, Mum?' Carrie ignored the tears pouring down her mother's face. 'Or is it as I said. You don't know.'

'She's knows all right,' Bruce McNevin burst out furiously. 'But she couldn't marry him. He was married already. I was the poor fool who took her to the altar.'

'It was all you ever wanted.' Alicia rounded on her husband with utter contempt.

'I loved you then. I love you now,' Bruce McNevin's grey eyes turned imploring.

'Totally amazing!' Alicia gave a broken crow of laughter. 'You actually believe it. This marriage is *over,* Bruce. All these years I've lived with your emotional blackmail. Now it's out in the open.'

His answer was full of fear. 'You don't mean that. You'll never leave me, Alicia. It would be very wrong and dishonourable. I've been good to you, haven't I? I've tried my best with Carrie, but the way she looks at me! It's like she's always *known.*'

'I guess some part of me did,' Carrie said. 'Now I don't give a damn which one of you leaves. All I need to know is the name of my real father, then I'm out of here.'

'Where to? You have nowhere to go.' Alicia made another attempt to take her daughter in her arms, but Carrie would have none of it.

'Oh, yes, I have,' she said.

'I hope you're not talking about Cunningham?' Bruce Mc-Nevin's breath escaped in a long hiss.

'None of your bloody business,' Carrie said, enunciating very clearly. 'Who's my father, Mum. I *must* know.'

'You're crazy!' Bruce McNevin said.

'Shut up, Bruce!' Alicia looked positively dangerous. She turned her head towards her daughter. 'I can't tell you, Carrie. Maybe one day.'

'One day very soon.' Carrie was adamant. 'Understand? Now tell the truth if you can, Mamma. Did my *real* father know about me?'

Alicia's white face flushed deeply. 'I never told him.'

'He had a right to know.'

'Yes, he did,' Alicia admitted, revealing the depth of her old anguish.

'What would he have done, do you think?'

'He'd have bloody well wrecked his marriage,' Bruce Mc-Nevin suddenly shouted. 'A *good* marriage, mind you. Two small children. Two boys. I never had a son,' he cried, his voice full of bitterness.

'Nothing wrong with *me,* Bruce,' Alicia said. 'You never would see a doctor.' She turned her attention back to her daughter. 'I couldn't tell your real father I was pregnant, Carrie. I couldn't do it to him,' she confessed, brokenheartedly.

'No, but you could do it to *me,*' said Carrie. 'That makes you a ruthless person. I should hate you, Mamma. I'm not sure I don't right now. You were supposed to protect me. Not deliver the two of us up to this man.' Her gentle voice was harsh.

Alicia collapsed into a chair, crumpling up over the table. 'Please don't go, darling. Don't leave me,' she sobbed. 'We'll go together.'

Carrie shook her head. 'You have your husband. You've stuck it out with him all this time. I *am* going to find my father. With or without your help.'

'He'll never recognise you as his daughter,' Bruce McNevin told her, the expression on his face half scorn for Carrie, half misery for himself. 'Not even now when his wife is dead. Scandal can't touch a man like that.'

'Oh, yes, he will.' Alicia's tears abruptly turned off. 'I know that much about him.'

'Then perhaps when you're ready you'll give me his name,' Carrie said. 'I don't intend to embarrass him. I just want to see him with my own eyes.'

'You have seen him, you little fool!' Bruce McNevin had totally lost his habitual cool. One side of his face was paper-white, the other flushed with blood. 'All you have to do is watch television.'

'What's he talking about, Mum?' Carrie asked.

'Go ahead. Tell her,' Bruce McNevin dared his wife.

'Is he some television personality?' Carrie asked with something like amazement.

'No, no, nothing like that!' Alicia shook her head. 'He's an important man, Carrie.'

'Oh, listen to her! He's an *important* man. And I'm not?' Bruce McNevin glared at his wife.

'Oh, shut up, Bruce,' she said yet again. 'I wish to God you'd just been *kind*. I'll tell you when I'm ready, Carrie. Please don't ask me now.'

Carrie could see the trembling in her mother's hands. 'Okay,' she sighed, her heart torn. 'Now I hope you don't mind if I throw a few things in a bag. It won't take me long. I'll get the rest of my things picked up.'

'Carrie, no!' Alicia jumped up, her voice full of emotion. 'Please stay. We'll work something out.'

'Not anymore, Mum.'

'Let me handle this, Alicia,' Bruce McNevin said, striding after Carrie as though she were deliberately causing her mother unnecessary pain. 'Where are you going, Carrie? Answer me.'

'Sorry, Mr McNevin.' Carrie turned with great severity on the man she had called father. 'You've given your last performance. You've waited for this a long time. You wanted me out? Be thankful. I'm going!'

When she arrived at Jimboorie, a red sun was sinking towards the jewelled horizon. Carrie stepped out of her 4WD, which one of their employees had brought back from the town only that morning, looking up at the great house. There was the glow of lights inside. She had parked right at the base of the flight of stone stairs, now she leaned into the vehicle keeping her palm pressed flat on the horn.

I'm on the run, she thought. *I'm a fugitive. A profoundly wounded woman.*

At least Clay was at home. She felt in her jeans pocket for the folded note paper she intended to present to him. He would understand what it was. It was her response to the advertisement for a wife he'd never placed. Surely he'd told her she would fit the bill? She had nowhere else to go. And nowhere else she wanted to be.

Clay's tall rangy figure appeared on the verandah. 'Caroline, what's up?'

She gave him a pathetic little wave, feeling pushed to the limit, yet in the space of a nanosecond the vision of herself as a child waving to him while Clay, the handsome little boy, waved back flared like a bright light. For weeks and weeks she had searched the archives of her mind for that cherished memory. Now like some miracle it presented itself, bringing her a moment of happiness.

Clay lost no time covering the distance between them, moving through the portico and taking the steps in a single leap.

'I've just remembered waving to you when I was a little girl. Isn't that strange?'

'Strange and beautiful,' he said, staring down at her 'That

meant a lot to me, Caroline.' He spoke quietly, gently, seeing her disturbed state. 'What's happened?'

She looked up at him a little dazedly. 'I've left home and I'm never going back.'

He absorbed that without comment. 'Come inside the house,' he said, tucking her to his side. 'You're trembling.'

A parched laugh escaped her lips. 'How come nothing shocks me to the core anymore?'

'You're *in* shock, that's why,' he pointed out, already feeling concern he could have been a cause of the family fallout.

From somewhere furniture had appeared in the drawing room; a huge brown leather chesterfield and two deep leather armchairs. A carved Chinese chest acting as a coffee table stood on a beautiful Persian rug all rich rubies and deep blues. She looked at the comfortable arrangement with a little frown on her face. 'Where did these things come from?'

'Out the back,' he said, offhandedly. 'There's more in store in Toowoomba. So are you going to tell me?' He led her to an armchair, waited until she was seated. 'What happened? Did you have an argument with your father?'

'What father?' she said.

Clay's face darkened. 'He surely couldn't have told you to go?'

Carrie shrugged. 'No, I did that all by myself.'

'Look, would you like coffee?' Clay suggested. 'I've got some good coffee beans. Won't take me a moment to grind them and put the percolator on.'

'I'll come with you,' she said, her movements almost trance-like.

Furniture had been moved into the enormous kitchen as well. It hadn't been there on her visit. He really was settling in. A long refectory table adorned the centre of the room with six carved wooden chairs, Scottish baronial, arranged around it, three to each side. The seats were upholstered in luxurious dark green leather. The huge matching carver stood at the head of the table. 'Expecting guests?' she asked, starting to drag out one chair. God, either it was *heavy* or she had lost her strength.

'*You're* here,' Clay pointed out, directing her to the carver instead, with its substantial armrests. A big man, it suited him fine. It nearly swallowed her up.

'This is a marvellous kitchen,' she said, looking around her. 'Or it could be. These chairs really belong in a dining room, you know.' She ran her hands along the oak armrests. 'Were they shipped out from England? They're antique. Early nineteenth century, I'd say.'

'Plenty more where they came from,' he said, busying himself setting out china mugs. 'While you were visiting Harper, I took a look at what was in storage. My favourite things were still there. Things I remember from when I was a child. There'll be more than enough to furnish the ground floor. I don't know about upstairs. Twelve bedrooms takes a bit of furnishing. At least I have a bed.'

'That's good,' she said wryly. 'Somewhere to rest a weary head. You might want to take a look at this.' She stretched her right leg so she could remove the folded notepaper from the pocket of her tight fitting jeans.

'What is it? Hang on a moment, I'll just grind these beans.'

Carrie covered her ears, counting to about twenty.

A few moments later, the percolator on the massive stove, Clay took the seat right of her. 'So what's this?' He unfolded the crumpled paper, looking at it with interest.

'It's not my best effort. I just had enough time to get down the facts,' she explained, very carefully, very precisely.

He turned his head to stare into her large, almond eyes. She was hurting badly but she wasn't going to say. 'Is this what I think it is?'

'Read on,' she invited, with an encouraging little movement of her hand.

He began again. 'This is truly *remarkable,* Caroline,' he said when he had finished. 'On the scale of one to ten, I'd give you an eleven. No, wait, a twelve!' He refolded the letter and thrust it into his breast pocket.

'Isn't it good,' she agreed. 'I mean it's so good you won't need to advertise for anyone else.'

'Well, that will certainly save a lot of time,' he said briskly. 'It's all happening around here. I have a firm lined up to fix the roof and a team of tradesmen to do the repairs. They'll be kept busy for months. There's an expert on the environment—a Professor Langley, my old professor—calling some time soon to advise about drought and flood management on the station. He's brilliant. He's bound to know someone to restore the garden.'

'Good heavens, you have been busy.' For a few moments he had completely taken her mind from her own problems. 'Where's all the money coming from?

'You,' he said.

She caught the gentle mockery in his eyes. 'I don't come with a dowry, Clay,' she said sadly. 'I daresay I'll be cut out of my ex-father's will without delay. I do have a little nest egg from Nona. That's my grandmother, Alicia's mother. I wish Nona were here, but she went to live in Italy after my grandfather died. You're welcome to that.'

'Why how very sweet of you.' Clay lightly encircled her wrist. 'But such a sacrifice isn't necessary. That money is *yours.* Don't feel bad about not coming with a dowry. I told you Great-Uncle Angus was far from broke. In fact he'd have given Scrooge a run for his money.'

'So he left you the money as well.'

'I guess I was the only one he could think of.' Clay's comment was sardonic. 'One way or another we have enough.' He lifted her hand and kissed it.

'How upset that's going to make your relatives!' Carrie, numb for hours, awoke to sensation. 'They were hoping it was all going to fall down around your ears.'

'Instead of which I get to marry the princess and share the

pot of gold,' he said, gazing deeply into her eyes. 'Now tell me what's causing all this suffering? Take your time.'

'Mum had an affair before she was married.' She spoke in a voice utterly devoid of emotion.

Clay's strong hand closed over her trembling fingers. What was coming next just had to be momentous.

'The man I *thought* was my father all these years isn't my father at all.' Carrie gave him a heartbreaking smile. 'Can you beat that?'

'How could they do that to you?' Clay felt the blood drain from his own face.

Carrie shrugged. 'Apparently he was married with two kids, but he wasn't worried about committing adultery. Neither was Mum. He must have been Someone even then. Mum decided she couldn't break up his marriage. She married Bruce Mc-Nevin instead.'

'So that explains it,' Clay said, steel in his voice.

'At least Mum didn't consider a termination.'

'Thank God for that!' he breathed, unable to contemplate a world without Caroline. 'So how did this all come out? I mean what provoked it after all these years?'

She pulled a sad little clown's face. 'You know the old saying. Eavesdroppers never hear well of themselves? I could hear them arguing when I arrived back at the house for lunch. They *never* argue. I heard my *father* say, "She's not mine! How can you expect me to love her? She's not my blood!"'

Muscles flexed hard along Clay's jawline. 'Go on. You have to get this off your chest.' He stood up to pour the perked coffee, setting a mug down before her then moving the sugar bowl close to her hand. 'Do you want milk or cream?'

'Black's fine.' She spooned a teaspoon of sugar into the mug and absently began to stir.

'Have another teaspoon of sugar,' he urged. 'You're awfully pale. Wasn't your mother worried about your driving?'

Carrie nodded. 'She begged me not to go but I couldn't stay

in *his* house another moment. He's only tolerated me because of Mum. He's still madly in love with her. So what the hell's wrong with *me*? Am I so unlovable?'

Clay felt a rush of anger on her behalf. 'That's the last thing you have to worry about,' he said so emphatically she felt immensely relieved.

'You *really* want to marry me now? I could turn into a pure liability. Well?' she pressed, directly holding his eyes. 'Answer me, Clay.'

'You aren't going to *order* me to marry you, are you?' he asked gently.

'Not unless you want an illegitimate bride. Mum wouldn't even tell me who my real father is. *He* knows.'

'Who, McNevin?'

'Yes. Don't worry, I'll find out.'

'Then what will you do?' he asked very seriously.

'I don't mean to embarrass my real father, Clay,' she explained carefully. 'I just want to lay eyes on him. Can you understand that?'

'Caroline, God!' He was debating whether to pick her up and carry her upstairs. If ever a girl needed loving it was this beautiful traumatised young creature. 'Of course I understand. It's hard to feel *whole* when you only know the identity of one parent.'

'My entire childhood and adolescence lacked *wholeness*,' she said, painfully aware that was so. 'I think I'll be content once I know who my real father is. I can watch him without his being aware of it.'

'What if you're not? What if you're impelled to go up to him and tell him he's your father? He'd have to remember your mother so he'd have to know who *you* are. You resemble her greatly.'

'Clearly I resemble her physically, but not in other ways,' Carrie said, carefully. 'I can't believe she's lied to me all these years. Couldn't she have concocted another story? Couldn't she have married someone else but Bruce McNevin? He's a *mean* man at heart. How could anyone disavow a baby, a little girl, a dutiful daughter?'

'It's no excuse, but I suppose he felt tremendously insecure about your mother,' Clay suggested. 'She's obviously never loved him.'

'Then why didn't she divorce him?' Carrie shot back.

'I can't find an acceptable answer, Caroline.' He stared at her, his eyes full of compassion. 'Who knows what goes on inside a marriage anyway? He must have been doing something right.'

'Not by *me*! But he thought he was the perfect husband. I've even heard him say so.' Carrie picked up her coffee mug again. 'This is good.'

'When did you last eat?' he asked, his eyes moving over her inch by inch.

'Breakfast.' She shrugged. 'I was coming in for lunch when my whole life was shattered. Soon as I heard their voices I knew something awful was going to happen. I think he's actually relieved it's all out in the open. He no longer has to pretend.'

'Should I ring your mother and tell her you're with me?'

'No, Clay, *no*!' She laid a restraining hand on his tanned arm.

'Whatever she's done or *had* to do she loves you, Caroline. She'll be frantic.'

'Don't worry, she won't kill herself,' Carrie said, her voice as dry as ash. 'She knows where I am anyway. I mightn't have told her, but she'll guess. Even my dear old ex-father, guessed I was heading here. That's three ex's in my life. Ex-mother, ex-father, ex-fiancé.'

'Your mother's always your mother, Caroline,' he said. 'Nothing's going to change that.'

Carrie released the gold clasp at her nape so her hair fell heavily around her face. 'Do you realise if all this miserable business with Scott hadn't happened I probably would never have found out?'

'It has occurred to me,' Clay said, thinking however desperate she felt she looked absolutely beautiful. The purity and symmetry of her small features transcended mere prettiness.

'We've all been living a lie,' she said in a melancholy voice. 'I could have married Scott in a few weeks' time.'

'I imagine Natasha would have had something to say about that,' he said dryly.

'Lord, you'd think the accident and all the stress would have triggered a miscarriage.'

'You didn't want that to happen?'

'Oh, my God, no. Dear God, no,' Carrie said. 'Natasha's tough and her baby's tough. They'll have to be. Do you mind my burdening you with all this?'

'Mind, how? Haven't you applied for the position of my wife? I have your application—which I will frame—in my pocket.' There was tenderness on his face and a shadow of physical yearning kept under tight control.

'Well, I don't much care for anyone else,' she said. 'So what's the answer? Or do you want to hear from more women?' She didn't realise it but she sounded incredibly anxious.

'Yours was the winning application,' he said.

'The *only* application.'

'I won't hold it against you. Now as soon as we settle you in I'll have to think about feeding you. By a stroke of good fortune I stocked up the last time I was in town.'

She shook her head. 'I'm not hungry, thank you all the same, Clay.'

'Well *I* am.' He stood up. 'I won't feel happy eating alone. And now I think of it, you didn't mention in your application if you could cook?'

'And you didn't ask.' She smiled weakly. 'I can cook. My mother taught me. I'll never be as good as her. You know *he* didn't want a housekeeper. We have Mrs. Finlay from town come in once a week to do the cleaning. He didn't want *any-one* but Mum I can see that now. And Mum acted as though she *owed* him. What for? For his marrying her when she was pregnant? Is that what Natasha will have to settle for?'

'Don't upset yourself,' Clay said. 'Harper and Natasha will have to solve their own problems.'

Carrie's heart stuttered.

She sat straight up in bed, saying shakily, 'Who's there?'

She looked about her in a dazed panic. Where *was* she?

She waited for full consciousness to kick in. Thank God! She was at Jimboorie with Clay. He had given up his bed for her, a brand-new king-sized ensemble, electing to spend the night in the massive four poster—too big to ever be shifted—in the bedroom just across the hall. They had shared a bottle of red wine over a dinner of tender beef fillet, tiny new potatoes and asparagus—all cooked to perfection by him—and the alcohol had soothed her sending her off to sleep.

The effects had evaporated. She didn't know what time it was but something had awoken her. She willed her memory back to an image.

A slow opening door? A shape of a woman? She was sure it was a woman. Jimboorie House was haunted. Clay's mother had seemed to think so.

Calm down, fool that you are.

Hold down panic. Control the mind. It was only a dream.

She lifted a glass of water from the bedside table; sipped at it, panning her eyes around the huge room, listening intently for the slightest sound. Outside in the night, a full moon was riding high in the indigo sky, its rays washing the room with a silvery light. But it was impossibly dark in the far corners. A strangeness seemed to be in her and at that moment a supreme wakefulness. She didn't quite know how to handle it. Or herself. One thing she did know with absolute certainty was, she couldn't lie in the semidarkness anymore. She couldn't bear to be alone, either. She wanted love. Plenty of it.

She rose from the bed in that unquiet night, catching the scent of gardenia that wafted from her nightgown She always used gardenia sachets amid her under garments and nightgowns. Her Thai silk robe bought in Bangkok was at the end of the bed, the white background scattered with bright red poppies, the edges bound with ebony. She slipped it on, tying the sash loosely. Her heart was aching afresh as the events of the day flooded back to her mind.

At long last she knew what her inner being had always suspected—the man whose name she bore wasn't her father. All he was, was her mother's husband. Twenty-three years of lying. Could she ever forgive her mother for that? Slowly she made her way across the room, heart fluttering, keeping to the band of moonlight.

What was her excuse for going to him? What would she say when he woke to find her standing beside his bed, staring down at him?

Love me, Clay. I desperately need to be loved.

Need had overtaken her entirely. She felt no embarrassment. just the driving need for comfort that only he seemed able to give.

His door was open. Carrie could hear his gentle, even breathing. She glided as silently as a shadow across the floor towards that massive bed. His naked back was turned to her, one shoulder raised high. She loved the shape of him, the shape of his broad shoulders, the way his strong arms could enfold her. She loved everything about him. And she wanted to learn more. Fate had carried her here to this moment, to this beautiful man. Her life had slipped out of focus. He had the power to put it back in place.

She held her flowing hair back with her hand. 'Clay!'

She thought he might take moments to stir but he was instantly alert.

'God, Caroline!' Fast breathing now. He sat up, thrusting a hand through his hair. 'I was dreaming about you.'

'Isn't it better I'm here?' She let her voice fall to a whisper.

'Did something frighten you?' he asked, with concern. 'I could have sworn you'd sleep through the night.'

'Isabelle's ghost,' she said and even laughed. 'She must walk around the house at full moon. May I get into bed with you?'

'Caroline.' Instantly he was aroused, every nerve throbbing. He dared not think what would happen if she did. 'You know what that means?' he managed to say. 'I couldn't possibly resist you. I just *couldn't*. I'm not strong enough.'

'But I don't want you to resist me,' she said. 'I want you to touch me. I want to touch you.' She reached out and moved her fingers, gently, slowly, over his broad chest letting them tangle in the fine mat of hair.

Clay felt his blood come to a rolling boil. 'Caroline!' he said, taking hold of her wrists. 'What are you trying to do to me?'

'You want me, don't you?'

I want you to be mine forever! 'It's for your protection,' he said, valiantly holding her off, at the same time desperately trying to exert the full force of his will. 'I would let you stay with me. I want nothing more in the world than have you stay with me, but I'm worried. I'm worried about *you*. What might happen.'

'Stop worrying,' she said, pulling away from him gently, to slide off her robe. Then she clambered onto the high bed. 'Can't you understand, Clay. I *need* loving.'

Why tell him *that* when he was wild for her! The very enormity of having her there in the bed beside him, inhaling her fragrance, all but robbed him of his precious self-control.

'So you're going to allow me to take your virginity?' He was already utterly aroused and unable to do a damn thing about it.

'Isn't that your wish?'

'I want you to give it to me. I don't want to *steal* it from you. I care about you too much.'

'Well, I can't wait,' she said. 'I *thought* I wanted to wait. I could have waited easily with Scott. But not with you. It's not all about sex, Clay,' she said reaching out to stroke his face. 'I want *you*. I need you. It's as simple as that.'

'And it has to be this very night, my little runaway Caroline?' he asked with immense tenderness, staring down at her.

'Only you can save me from the pain.'

The blood rushed to his head. She thought herself safe with him. She *was*. But he had to be so gentle when the adrenaline was roaring through his body. He tried to slow himself down by kissing first the side of her neck, then the exquisite little hollow in her throat, moving back to her eyes, her cheeks, her nose, then her lovely mouth. He kissed her again and again, until they were both light-headed, his hands moving irresistibly to her breasts, creamy like roses, their pink tips flaring at his touch. While she moaned softly he let his hand slide down over the smooth tautness of her stomach, downward yet to her secret sex.

Her mouth formed words. She exhaled them.

'My true love,' she said.

It was an utterance that reached right through to Clay's soul.

And he was gentle with her, his fingers feathering over her, his mouth following...

'Do you like that?' He wasn't going to do a thing that didn't give her pleasure.

'Perfect!' she moaned, her back arching off the bed.

'You are *so* beautiful!' He turned her over, making long strokes over her satiny back, cupping her buttocks so smooth and round, pressing his lips to them...

She was yearning for him to move into her, her body was demanding release, but he continued to work his magic on her, inch by inch.

She kept her eyes closed tight.

When he gently worked her clitoris, she made a wild strange sound, like a bird keening. The sensuality was profound. Wonderful and unbearable at the same time. She was panting and gasping with excitement, reaching for him frantically, guiding him to the entrance of her sex.

'Yes!' she cried, overcome by the extraordinary piercing sensations that were running riot in her body. She couldn't control them. They were controlling her.

Clay drew back, laying his palms flat on the bed to either side of her. 'I'll be as gentle as I can,' he vowed.

'You're a *magician,*' she whispered back.

'Am I?'

'Yes!' She was desperate for him to push into her. To *fill* her.

There was a twinge of pain. No more. Then a spreading rapture like life giving rain spreading over the flood plains.

'You're okay?' he whispered urgently against her cheek, striving to keep his own driving needs reined in.

'I *adore* you!' she cried.

Was there ever an answer that could please a man more? He threw his head back with sheer joy and she arched up to kiss his throat. 'Adore you. Adore you. Adore you!'

He couldn't hold back a moment longer. Not after that. Their bodies radiated heat and an incredible *energy.* The whole room was filled with it. It crackled like live wires.

He plunged into her in an ecstasy of passion and she met that plunge, spreading her silken thighs for him. It thrilled him to the core. She was spreading herself wide-open to him, her soul as naked as her beautiful body. His heart swelled with pride, exultation, and an enormous gratitude. He felt *free.* Unburdened of the griefs that had long plagued him.

Neither of them held back. They gave of each other unstintingly. At long last they had discovered something they had never known before.

Pure Desire. Pure Love.

CHAPTER EIGHT

CLAY AND CARRIE were coming back from a long ramble down to the creek, when they saw Alicia's Land Rover make a sweep around the circular driveway and park, bonnet in, to the shade of the trees. There had been a fantastic, wonderfully welcome downpour of rain around dawn, which had awakened them to more glorious lovemaking, and now the whole world was washed clean.

'It's Mamma,' Carrie said, unnecessarily, holding Clay's hand tight.

'I'm sure she's only come to see if you're all right,' Clay said, calming her. 'Take it easy, Caroline. Your mother must be under a lot of stress.'

Alicia was waiting quietly on the terrace.

'Why have you come, Mamma?' Carrie started in at once, though her heart smote her at the unhappiness in Alicia's face.

'I *had* to come,' Alicia said.

'Please sit down, Mrs McNevin.' Clay held a chair for her. 'How are things at home?'

'Not good, Clay,' Alicia said, releasing a long sigh. 'And please call me Alicia.'

'I'd be happy to,' Clay said quietly. 'Let's all take a seat.' He put his hand gently on Carrie's shoulder, exerting the slightest pressure. 'Would you two like to talk while I make coffee?'

'I'd be grateful for that, Clay,' Alicia said.

'No problem.' He strode away into the house.

'What a very considerate young man!' Alicia said, sighing as though she'd never had the good fortune to meet one in her life. 'I'm leaving Bruce,' she told Carrie.

'Isn't it about time?' Carrie asked. 'You don't love him, Mum. You've never loved him, have you?'

'Look,' said Alicia, 'give him some credit. When I knew I was pregnant with you I was absolutely desperate—'

'You couldn't tell Nona?' Carrie broke in, not understanding *her* nona was another person to her mother.

'I didn't think I could,' Alicia confessed. 'Your grandmother had—still has—very definite ideas about how a well-bred young lady should conduct herself. She would have been shocked and bitterly disappointed in me. The scandal would have been enormous. It wouldn't have been so bad if I'd been able to marry the father of my child, but I couldn't.'

'Then why have an affair with him?' Carrie asked, sounding stern about it.

'You're in love with Clay, aren't you?' Alicia made a plea for understanding. 'You're in love at last?'

Colour flooded Carrie's cheeks. 'Oh please... Clay's not married.'

'I was mad about him,' Alicia said. 'I truly believe he loved me. Neither of us planned it. It wasn't supposed to happen, yet all it took was a smile. We met at a fund-raiser. I knew who he was, of course—'

'Which is a damn sight more than I do,' Carrie interrupted.

'He noticed me from across the room.' All these years later Alicia's beautiful eyes went dreamy.

'He would. Any man would,' Carrie said, still in that critical voice.

'I'd noticed him back. That's how it started.'

'Easy as that, eh?' Carrie's voice was unwillingly sympathetic. 'When did you start sleeping together?'

'When did you start sleeping with Clay?' Alicia retorted.

'Last night,' Carrie admitted freely. 'And at dawn this morning. It was *wonderful*! Clay has restored my faith in humanity.'

'I hope you used protection?' Alicia went from penitent to concerned mother.

'I'm not going into details,' Carrie said. '*Why* have you come, Mamma? Your husband hasn't threatened you in any way?' The very thought frightened her.

'He's beside himself,' Alicia said.

'I'm quite sure he's blaming me for all this?' Carrie said.

Alicia passed on the answer. 'I want you to come with me to Melbourne, darling,' she said as though it were something both of them simply had to do.

'Melbourne? What for?' Carrie started to picture where her mother would go. To friends? To a hotel?

'For one thing you can't stay here with Clay,' Alicia pointed out quietly.

'Why not?' Carrie turned squarely on her mother. 'I'm going to marry him.'

'And he'll be a wonderful husband, I know.' Alicia took the news very calmly. 'But you want to do it right.'

'Unlike *you*!' Carrie was near tears. But her mother did have a point—Clay was now the owner of Jimboorie Station. He intended to work it. He intended to restore the homestead. He *was* a Cunningham. If nothing else she had to uphold *his* reputation. 'What's in Melbourne?' she asked finally.

Alicia looked sightlessly across the grounds. 'Your *father,*' she said.

'You're back!' Bruce McNevin greeted his wife the moment she walked into the homestead. 'I knew you'd come back. You've got nowhere else to go.'

'I'm only here to do a little packing, Bruce,' Alicia said. 'I'm taking Carrie with me to Melbourne.'

He blocked her way as she walked to the stairs. 'Just how long do you think you can stay with friends?'

'I've almost lost touch with them, haven't I, through you? Let me past, Bruce.'

'Not until we have this out. I'm extremely unhappy with your behaviour, Alicia. You *owe* me. As for Carrie, she's just going from bad to worse. I suppose she was with Cunningham?'

'Why don't you ask them?' Alicia said. 'They're waiting for me in the driveway.'

'They're what?' Bruce McNevin hurried to the front door, looking out. 'How dare they!'

'They don't trust *you* to behave yourself, Bruce.'

'Have I ever laid a finger on you?' He strode back to her looking outraged.

'If you had, I'd have found the guts to move on.'

Bruce McNevin shook his head, something like grief in his eyes. 'I *knew* Leyland's child would split us one day. You surely can't be going to him? You have no place in his life.'

'I know that, Bruce,' Alicia said simply, 'but Carrie does. There have been a lot of changes in society since I was a girl. People are more *accepting*. Carrie wants to meet her father. I'm going to arrange it. Neither of us intend to embarrass him though I know he'll be deeply disturbed.'

'And what about his sons? What are they going to think?'

Alicia spread her hands in an inherited gesture. 'There are secret places in everyone's life. Besides, they're married men now. Or one is.'

'Been checking up on them, have you?' McNevin sneered.

'They're a prominent family, Bruce. The media like to report on prominent families.'

'They'll relish *this* scandal then, won't they? The return of the prodigal ex-lover along with their lovechild. And what about your oh so proper mother? What the hell is she going to think?'

'She's a long way from here, Bruce. I can't worry about her anymore. Or about you. I'm not the panic-stricken girl I once was.'

'My God!' McNevin breathed. 'I love you, Alicia. Doesn't that mean anything to you anymore?'

She met his eyes directly. 'It would have meant a lot had you loved my daughter, too!' Alicia went around him and mounted the stairs.

Clay and Carrie sat waiting for Alicia to reappear. 'I think I should go in,' Clay said. It was he who had insisted on accompanying them back to the homestead, concerned Bruce McNevin might react badly when faced with losing the woman he loved.

'It's all right, Mum's coming out onto the verandah.' Carrie breathed a great sigh of relief. 'She's ready for you to collect the luggage.' They watched Alicia give them a signal then walk back into the house.

Clay restarted the engine. 'I'll drive up to the steps. He might come out, Carrie. Be prepared.' For *anything,* Clay thought, glad he was with them. Even the mildest man could turn dangerous given enough provocation.

Clay was out of the Land Rover when Bruce McNevin strode out onto the front verandah, his manner highly confrontational. 'Ah, it's *you,* just as I thought. I want you off my land, Cunningham,' he ordered.

Clay reacted calmly to the blustering authority. 'I certainly don't want to be here, sir. But Mrs McNevin needs a helping hand.'

'Not from the likes of you,' Bruce McNevin said, suddenly producing a whip.

'I wouldn't think of using that,' Clay warned. 'You'll definitely come off second best. I understand you're upset, Mr McNevin, but don't push it. I'll just collect what luggage Mrs McNevin needs then we'll be on our way.'

'*Where,* may I ask?' Bruce McNevin said in his most pretentious voice.

'There's plenty of room at Jimboorie.'

'That crumbling heap!' McNevin scoffed.

'You won't know it in six months' time,' Clay assured him. 'Jimboorie House will in time be restored to its former glory. Take it from me.'

'You!' McNevin asked with great sarcasm. 'What, that wicked old bastard leave you a few bob, did he?'

'Actually he did,' Clay confirmed casually. 'He was far from broke as you seem to think. What he was, was a *miser.* Heard of them?'

Bruce McNevin's face was a study. 'You're not *serious*?'

Clay nodded. 'Yes, I am. Excuse me, sir. I'll just collect those bags.'

Clay entered the house without incident. Bruce McNevin waited a moment then stalked down the steps and over to the Land Rover.

Seeing him coming Carrie opened the passenger door and stepped out onto the gravel to confront him.

McNevin's face was dark with anger. 'I'll never forgive you, Carrie, for what you've done.'

'I haven't done anything,' she said. 'It's more what was *done* to me. I have to live with the fact my own mother lied to me all these years. I suppose she *had* to, to stay under your roof. Your precious reputation is very important to you, isn't it? But she had to pay dearly. I was to be passed off as your child, but right from the beginning you never treated me as family, much less an adopted daughter. You mightn't be able to see my scars. They're not visible to the naked eye, but they're there. Things might have been very different had you been a man of heart.'

Bruce McNevin flushed violently. 'I know I fed you, clothed you, housed you, educated you. Don't let's forget all that, my girl. You never wanted for anything.'

'Maybe so and for that I thank you, but I went wanting for a bit of affection,' Carrie said quietly. 'I know you couldn't make it to love. You couldn't love another man's child.'

'How many men do you think could?' he asked with the greatest impatience. 'All those cuckolded men, when they find out through DNA the child they've long parented isn't theirs at all, doesn't the love switch off? You bet it does. That bastard, that father of yours, raped your mother.'

For the first time in her life, Carrie literally saw red. Clouds of it swirled in front of her eyes, almost obscuring her vision. Even now he couldn't leave well enough alone. He was impelled to cause more damage. Blindly she moved a step closer to the man who had treated her all her life with such contained severity and cried out. 'That is absolutely unforgivable. And a blatant *lie*. Your miserable mean way of getting even? I demand an apology.'

'Why, you arrogant little girl!' Bruce McNevin exclaimed, quite shocked by her anger. 'To think you can *demand* anything of me.'

Carrie's heart was thudding violently in her chest. 'It's normal enough in parent-child interactions but then I'm *not* your child, am I? My poor mother is *still* in love with that man even today. There was no rape as well you know. No need when they were madly in love with each other.'

'What a mess! What a bloody mess!' Bruce McNevin groaned, burying his face in his hands.

'A mess that has to be straightened out.' Carrie swept her thick plait back over her shoulder. 'I doubt if I'll be seeing you again, Mr McNevin. So I'll say my goodbyes. I feel sorry for you in a way. But I shouldn't. I can only remember my life as your daughter as being *loveless*.'

Her mother and Clay were already out of the house and coming towards them. Now they joined her, Alicia standing close beside her daughter.

'If you must do this, do it, Alicia,' Bruce McNevin addressed his wife, ignoring Carrie and Clay. 'No good will come of it, I warn you.'

'Well it wouldn't be *you* if you wished us luck,' Alicia said in an ironic voice.

'I don't want you upset and embarrassed, Alicia,' he said. 'I repeat. I love you. I've stood by you no matter what. I'm not perfect. I didn't have it in me to take to another man's child. I'm not proud of it but it's understandable. The thing is I've always stood by you. Take all the time you want, but come back to me. *Please!* We have a good marriage.'

'And you think we'll have a better one without Carrie?' Alicia asked.

'I'm *sure* of it,' he responded.

'Please, Mamma, let it be,' Carrie intervened, glad of Clay's rock-solid support at her back.

'I suppose you think this puts you in the picture, Cunningham?' Bruce McNevin exploded, as he could see his whole life changing. 'Scott's out of the way, so you move in?'

'I don't see that that's any of your business, Mr McNevin.' Clay's tone was perfectly even. It was evident he had no intention of being goaded. 'I'll say good day to you.'

'And good riddance!' Bruce McNevin shouted as Clay moved off. 'Make sure you never come on to my land again.'

'You should take it easy for a while, sir,' Clay advised, half turning and looking over his shoulder. 'You could have a stroke, heart attack, anything.'

'Mind what he's saying, Bruce,' Alicia warned her husband. 'The blood has mounted into your face.'

'So why should I care?' he cried in a distraught voice. 'You're leaving me, aren't you?'

Alicia's beautiful face looked incredibly sad. 'There's nothing left for us, Bruce. I should have done this a long time ago but I didn't have the courage to start again. Our marriage never had a firm foundation. I take a lot of the blame. I'll see a solicitor in Melbourne.'

'To start divorce proceedings?' He closed his eyes then looked up to heaven.

'Of course.'

His expression entirely changed. 'Then don't think for one moment you'll get your hooks into *my* money. *You're* the guilty party. I'll make sure everyone knows that. Mark my words, Alicia, you start this and I'll fight you every inch of the way.'

'Bruce. Goodbye,' Alicia said.

Senator Leyland Richards was having a busy morning. He had flown in from Canberra, the seat of Federal Government, to Melbourne, his home town, the previous evening and he hadn't had a moment to himself since.

Ah, well, this was the life he had wanted, wasn't it?

Fame and fortune.

He sighed deeply, putting off a phone call he knew wouldn't wait. Though his plans, as yet, weren't in the public domain, it was his intention to quit politics after giving twenty-five years of his life to it. He had discussed the matter privately with the Prime Minister; they had agreed on the best time for the announcement and he had received a strong message he was a definite contender for the top diplomatic posting to Washington.

'You're just the man for the job, Leyland!' The P.M. had assured him.

The thing was, though it was far from apparent to his family, his friends, his parliamentary colleagues *and* the P.M. he had lost the driving ambition that had set him on the high road to success. Son of a wealthy legal family—he had himself worked for a few years as a barrister in the prestigious law firm established by his grandfather—his entry into politics was put on the fast track when he married Annette Darlington, the only daughter of Sir Cecil Darlington, a senator at that time. It was in the way he had handled a tricky matter for the Senator that had really brought him to Darlington's attention. From then on it had been plain sailing. He was given to understand Sir Cecil was very impressed with him and his style. Meetings were arranged to interest him in running for a blue ribbon seat he eventually won. Annette, so very sweet and earnest, fell in love with him. And that was that! It was a union of *old money.* A union of Establishment families. The beginning of a good marriage and highly successful career in politics.

It had been two years now since he had lost Annette to breast cancer, a great blow. Annette had made him a wonderful wife and had been a loving mother to their two sons. She had wanted nothing more than to serve him and the boys. Most men would have found that an enormous bonus but he had secretly wanted *more* from her. More of *herself.* He had always been regarded as the perfect husband and son-in-law. God knows he had always tried to be. Less than a year after the untimely death of Annette, the retired Sir Cecil who had adored his only daughter, had suffered a massive heart attack while they were out on his yacht, *Lady Annette II.* Leyland had had an ambulance waiting as they docked, but his father-in-law had died before they reached hospital. Two great blows in as many years.

He'd done his duty by everyone. Doing one's duty was extremely important. Now he felt, despite the honours that apparently were yet in store for him, he desperately needed time to himself. Time to breathe. To sit in the sun. Take the boat out. He was fifty-three now. Surely it was time for a sea change? As it was he was at everyone's beck and call. Only an hour ago his press secretary had popped her head around the door to remind him of a press interview she had lined up for the following morning.

He made the phone call to the Shadow Minister in the Opposition who he definitely didn't admire, but as a natural diplomat he was able to get his message across to the extent a date was made for a round of golf at the weekend. At least the man was a fine golfer.

He was working diligently at some papers when his secretary buzzed him.

'I know you didn't want to be disturbed, Senator,' she said in a low, confidential tone, 'but there's a lady here—she has no appointment—who thinks you might see her.'

A lady? *What* lady? There were no ladies in his life since he'd lost Annette, but plenty who'd like to replace her. 'What's her name, Susan?' he asked. 'What does she want?' Dammit, he didn't really have the time.

'A Mrs. Alicia McNevin, Senator,' Susan said in hushed tones. 'She claims to be an old friend. She's very beautiful.'

Leyland felt something like an electric shock go through him. *Alicia! My God! Would the memory of her ever fade?*

'Send her in, Susan,' he said.

Carrie was so nervous she was almost ill. And she missed Clay terribly. He had become her rock and her refuge.

'Are you *sure* he wants to see me?' she begged her mother.

'He sent the limousine for us, didn't he?' Alicia gently smiled and took hold of her daughter's trembling hand. 'We're having dinner with him at his home, which he intends to hand over to his elder son and young family. Lee has bought a penthouse apartment with fantastic views of the city, Port Philip Bay and the Dandenongs. I understand it's undergone a brilliant renovation. We'll get to see it.'

'You call him Lee?'

'I always called him Lee,' Alicia said.

'And what am I going to call him?' Carrie swallowed hard.

'Just relax, darling,' Alicia advised. 'It will come. Lee is a most charming man. He will put you at ease.'

'Will he now?' Carrie said. 'That remains to be seen. And he wasn't angry you never told him about me?' Her voice was quite shaky, but she so desperately needed reassurance.

Alicia glanced through the window of the moving Bentley, the uniformed chauffeur separated from them by a glass panel, which went up and down at the touch of a button on the console in front of them. 'Well, you know, darling, it's as I told you. He was extremely shocked and very upset. But he rallied.'

'It's a wonder he didn't throw you out,' Carrie murmured, imagining the scene.

'That wouldn't have been at all like him.' Alicia shook her golden head.

Tonight she looked even more beautiful than usual in a sophisticated champagne coloured silk and lace blouse over a tight black skirt, her still small waist cinched with a wide black belt. She'd had her hair done and she radiated a womanly allure on a level her daughter had never seen before.

'I'm sorry he lost his wife.' Carrie's mind was inevitably drawn to the *wife*. She wondered whether Annette Richards had known about her mother. She hoped not.

'He loved her,' Alicia said simply, though her heart twisted.

'Does he know about *you*?' Carrie asked. 'Does he know you're going to divorce Bruce?'

'He knows *everything*!' Alicia said.

Carrie's mouth was so dry she didn't know if she was going be able to speak. This was her *father* she was about to meet. Her *real* father, her own flesh and blood. Her mother, on the other hand, looked remarkably relaxed. Alicia was obviously looking forward to the evening. She had gone to some lengths to look marvellous. Carrie had never laid eyes on her outfit. What had gone on at that meeting? Carrie wondered for the umpteenth time.

Impressive wrought-iron gates led to the Richards mansion, a Tuscan style residence that had known functions and parties galore. The house was designed over four levels, drawing Carrie's eye upwards. Impressive as it was, it lacked the sheer breadth, the size, the glamour of Jimboorie House, falling down or not. Garden beds lay to either side, clipped in the classical style. The gates were open in welcome and the chauffeur guided the Bentley into the huge garage to the right.

'We're here, darling,' Alicia said, touching a hand to her hair. 'You okay?' She was clearly anxious. Carrie looked lovely but austere, like a little saint facing martyrdom.

'I'm fine.' Carrie tilted her chin, wishing Clay were there so she could hold his hand. 'Lead on.'

They stood outside a magnificent front entrance door for barely a moment. It swung open revealing a stunning reception area with tall marble columns and a double staircase with beautiful black and gold balustrading leading to the mezzanine level. It usually stopped most people in their tracks but Carrie saw none of it. Her eyes were rivetted on the tall charismatic man who stood staring down at her, so deeply, so gravely. She had seen him many times on television and in the newspapers never dreaming there could be any possible connection, now she saw him in the flesh before her.

My father! My God!

The realisation didn't come easily. He looked what he was: a powerful, brilliant person, but how would he react to her? Would he entertain her briefly then send her on her way? He had the sons he wanted. The life he wanted, albeit as a widower. Perhaps not for long. Would he swear her to secrecy? A man in his position would surely be desperate to avoid a scandal? Would this meeting even have been possible had his wife still been alive?

She saw him reach out to take her mother's hand. She saw her mother reach up to kiss his cheek, a *special* kiss. 'Lee, this is your daughter,' Alicia said, tears falling gently from her eyes.

Leyland Richards looked down at that lovely, strained young face with its beautiful, haunted doe eyes, despairing that they could never find their lost time. But there was the future! He lifted his arms wide, not making the slightest attempt to hide the raw emotion in his eyes. Indeed his handsome face was suddenly ravaged by a mixture of joy and anguish. This was his daughter. He knew instantly and without doubt.

'Caroline!' he cried. 'Oh, God!' The very breath seemed to catch in his throat.

An enormous lightness seized her. Nothing could hold her back now. This was really her father. She had waited twenty-four years for this. Carrie went into those outstretched arms, feeling them close strongly around her. 'That's my beautiful girl!' her father said.

CHAPTER NINE

I COULD LOSE HER!

Two weeks went by before Clay started tormenting himself with that frightening prospect. Each day she sounded more and more as though a wonderful new world had been opened up for her. Which of course it had. Her father had done what *he* couldn't. This was what he feared. She was happy living a life apart from him. And it could go on. Perhaps forever! Her biological father hadn't had a moment's hesitation in acknowledging her, she'd told him with enormous gladness in her voice. Clay loved her, so he was able to share in her happiness. But, Lord, he needed her as much as her father. *More.*

Miracles do happen, Clay!

He'd thought one had happened to him. But she was only going to keep him posted. She had been through bad experiences what with Harper, then Natasha and finally the man she had all her life called Father. He'd caught her at a vulnerable moment in time when she was emotionally fragile. That's why she had come to him—actually putting it down on paper—that she would marry him. Maybe now she thought of her promise as just plain *craziness.*

It occurred to Clay in acknowledging her, her father stood to lose much of his unsullied reputation. He would have to know that. His was a household name. Caroline's father was Senator Leyland Richards, leader of the Upper House. Clay, though not overly struck on politicians of any persuasion, had always admired the man. He was a handsome, distinguished, highly intelligent, highly articulate with a magnetic charm that drew people to him. Senator Richards had long had the reputation for being a man the people could trust. He was also a natural diplomat with an engaging wit that worked well for him in his televised interviews. Women loved him. He got their vote. In short he was just the sort of man Caroline should have had as a father right from the beginning.

Caroline had told him in confidence that Senator Richards intended to retire from politics at the end of the year when he would make his announcement. Who was I going to tell anyway? Clay thought. Bruce McNevin, who must be cursing the day he ever opened his mouth? Clay went over their conversations a hundred times in his head. All too often the line was bad. A lot of work was being done around Jimboorie so he could only take calls at night. Caroline had been gone such a short time, yet she had already met her half brother, Adrian and his wife and young family. The younger brother, Todd, who had won a Rhodes Scholarship to Oxford, was overseas. They were well on the way to becoming one happy family.

Alicia, too, had been welcomed with open arms. Of course Alicia was a stunning woman. Clay was human enough to wonder if Caroline and her mother would have been received so magnanimously had both of them been ordinary people and plain to boot.

By the end of the third week Clay found himself going about his business grim-faced. He missed her unbearably. She may have found her *real* father, but she was in *his* blood, too. He prayed she'd remember that. Absence either made the heart grow fonder or the fond memories faded. Not that she didn't always tell him how much she missed him when she called. But when was she coming home? And where *was* home? He was so lonely without her. He had never known such loneliness. He told himself repeatedly he could scarcely begrudge her this precious time with her father. He was just so worried she might want to stay close to him. Hell, was that so unusual?

Clay worked so hard in an effort to take his mind off his anxieties, he fell into bed each night exhausted to the bone.

By the end of the month he decided to take action. He didn't have to watch every dollar anymore. He would take a trip to Melbourne. He would buy a decent suit and go calling, courting, whatever. Caroline and her mother had moved out of their hotel into the Richards's residence. He had the telephone number and the address. He was hurting so badly he just *had* to see her. If she wanted to remain in Melbourne with her new family he had to face the appalling fact there was *nothing* he could do about it. The very thought made him flinch. Without Caroline, all his plans for the future would be smashed.

They were all over him in the department store where he went to buy some smart city clothes. There was no question it would be extremely easy for a bush bachelor to find plenty of female company in the city but getting a one of them to leave the city for the lonely isolated Outback was another story.

In the end he bought much more than he needed, but the staff seemed hell-bent on outfitting him in a way they considered appropriate. He might have been a sporting icon—they made such a fuss.

You have the most wonderful physique, Mr. Cunningham. Those shoulders!

Thank you, ma'am.

A male staff member, scarcely less flattering, gave him the name of a top hairdresser and how to find the salon. Okay, his hair *was* too long and too thick!

He didn't know himself. He stared in the full-length hotel mirror wondering if he hadn't gone too far. What a change an Italian suit made. Was it really worth an arm and a leg? Where would he ever wear it again? But never mind. He had to look right for Caroline. They hadn't cut all that much off his hair. Just trimmed it and somehow shaped it so it followed the line of his skull. All those people trying to take care of him! He was glad he'd been able to frame his sincere thank yous.

In the hotel foyer he had to be aware he was turning women's heads. He could have laughed aloud. He was no sex symbol. He doubted if they would have looked at him in his usual gear of bush shirt, jeans and high boots. He didn't get the truth of it. He was a stunning-looking man, but he never saw himself that way.

His longing for Caroline was like a hand stretched out to guide him. He had decided on surprising her, not sure she would be at home, but willing to take the chance. She'd told him the Senator was always extremely busy sorting out his affairs but he always managed to make it home for dinner. Why not, with two beautiful women waiting for him! Maybe the Senator and Alicia would revive their doomed romance. They must have loved one another at one time though it would have been a sad thing to break up a marriage, especially when small children were involved.

He took a taxi to the Richards's residence, pausing a moment on the street to look up at the Italianate mansion, four storeys high. The lot would have fitted neatly inside Jimboorie House, he thought, with a surge of pride for the old historic homestead. The workmen he had hired had been going at the renovations hell for leather. It was astonishing what they had already achieved though there was a great deal still to be done. It would all take time and money. With Caroline by his side he had looked on it as a glorious challenge.

A sweet faced maid called Loretta answered the door, telling him Miss Carrie was relaxing by the swimming pool at the rear of the house. She stepped back smilingly to allow him to enter the house. He returned the smile, telling her he didn't wish to be announced. It was a surprise visit. He would walk around the side of the house to the pool, coming on Caroline that way. Loretta grinned at him like a coconspirator.

Following her directions he took the paved path on the western side of the house. A lot of the plants growing to either side were unknown to him. The character of the front and side gardens seemed very classical to his eyes. It was all very beautiful, very orderly, but the only splash of colour was white. Even the flowering agapanthus were white. Clay rounded the end of the rear terrace looking towards a spectacular turquoise swimming pool. The smooth surface was flashing a million sequinned lights. The pool was edged by towering royal palm trees and plushly upholstered chaise longues. A short distance back was a large open living area shaded by a terra-cotta roof with a deep overhang supported by substantial columns. The space was luxuriously furnished with circular tables, rattan armchairs and long rattan divans, again upholstered in an expensive looking fabric.

Sitting on one of the divans, their heads close together, were Caroline and a good-looking young guy, dark haired, bronze tan, wearing blue swim shorts. Clay took a deep calming breath. Then another. Caroline was wearing a brief swimsuit as well with a little bit of nothing over it. Her beautiful hair tumbled down her back. Her skin glowed honey-gold. Her lovely limbs looked wonderfully sleek.

His heart began thudding like Lightning Boy's hooves. He stood perfectly still, watching. Why wouldn't she attract eligible young men? God, hadn't he been struck by her allure, quite apart from her beauty, right off. Why wouldn't this guy who was staring into her face with what seemed to Clay tremendous intensity want her? They were, in fact, closely regarding each other.

Clay's stomach tightened into a tight knot. He braced himself as the guy placed a hand on her shoulder. He'd fallen in love

with her. Of course he had. And Caroline was mightily interested in him. He felt lacerated by that.

I'll be damned if I'm going to let him take her away from me!

They were so close to each other. *Too* close. The guy said
something that made Caroline laugh; a silvery, carefree peal
of laughter.

Clay's built up feelings of anticipation evaporated like creek
water in a drought. He was tempted to confront them, find out
who this guy was, but he had the dismal idea he might finish
up throwing the poor man in the pool. He'd rather die than act
the jealous fool.

Clay turned on his heel and walked away. There was no longer any excitement. No longer the sheer magic of seeing her.

Barely ten minutes later Carrie, having had enough sun, was
making her way back into the house when she met Loretta coming out onto the terrace.

'Enjoy your swim?' Loretta asked with a coy smile.

'It was lovely!' Carrie said, shaking back her hair.

Loretta's gaze went past her to the pool. 'The gentleman
didn't stay long,' she said in a disappointed voice. 'I was just
coming down to see if you'd like refreshments.'

'Gentleman? What gentleman?' Carrie frowned.

'Why the young man who came to see you,' Loretta said,
eyes wide. 'He was gorgeous!' she added.

'Did he give a name?' There was puzzlement on Carrie's face.

'Sure!' Loretta nodded. 'Couldn't forget it. A nice name.
Suited him. Clay Cunningham. Didn't want me to announce
him. Said it was a surprise. I directed him—'

Carrie's voice overlapped the maid's. 'What time was this,
Loretta?' she asked, urgency in her manner.

Loretta considered, head to the side. 'Not more than ten
minutes ago. He was walking around the side of the house to
the pool.'

'Well, he never arrived.' He saw *us,* Carrie thought.

She waited not a moment longer. 'Loretta, tell my mother when she comes home I've gone into town,' she called over her shoulder. 'Tell her I'll try to make it back for dinner.'

It took Carrie under twenty minutes to track down the hotel where Clay was staying, shower, dress and call a cab to take her into the city. Lee had made a car available to her but she didn't want to waste precious time trying to find a parking spot. When she arrived at the hotel she was told by reception Mr. Cunningham wasn't in his room. He had been seen going out perhaps an hour or so before. He hadn't returned.

Carrie retreated to a lounge setting in the spacious foyer ordering a cold drink. Where had he gone? What time was he coming back? Whatever time it was, she was prepared to wait. She was so consumed by her thoughts she almost missed Clay's arrival maybe a half hour later. What alerted her was the ribald comment of one of two young women sitting across from her, sipping highly coloured and decorated cocktails.

'Strewth, would you look at the guy who just walked in?' the one in the sequinned top gasped, putting down her glass and sitting bolt upright. 'Wouldn't I love to wrap my legs around him!'

'We have a Ten!' the other squealed, holding up all her digits.

Carrie's heart catapulted into her throat. She followed the focus of their gaze although it would have been difficult indeed to miss him. It was Clay. He looked absolutely stunning in his city clothes, his marvellous hair barbered to perfection. He had meant to surprise her. Instead, apparently, she had shocked him into leaving.

When the girls saw her staring so avidly, the one with the sequinned top called to her. 'Bet your life someone has already high-jacked him. Wanna come over and join us?'

Carrie stood up quickly, grabbing her handbag. 'Love to, but I can't, sorry. I have to catch up to my fiancé.'

'You mean that drop-dead dreamy hunk of a guy is your man?' the one with the scarlet hair asked.

'Sure is,' Carrie confirmed proudly.

'You're one lucky lady,' Scarlet Hair told her with a wicked grin.

Though she pursued him as fast as her high heels would allow, Carrie saw him disappear into a waiting elevator. She took the next available, glad she knew which floor and which room he was in. Even then he beat her inside his door.

He came at the third knock.

'I missed you at the house,' Carrie said brightly, devouring him with her eyes.

He didn't respond, but stood looking down at her.

'Aren't you going to ask me in?' She had to duck under his arm to get into the room. 'What happened? Why did you leave?' She turned to face him.

He shut the door, leaned against it. 'One's the right answer and the other one isn't,' he said crisply.

'Fire away,' she invited, throwing her handbag down onto the bed.

'Right. One, I was running late for an appointment. Two, I thought I'd give that guy you were being so sweet to some swimming lessons.'

'You were *jealous*!' Carrie gave a little crow of disbelief.

He came away from the door abruptly, all six foot three of him, emanating radiant energy. 'What the *hell* did you expect me to be?' Despite himself Clay suddenly exploded. 'But, hey, I probably had no right. I mean it's not as though we're an old married couple or anything.'

'No,' she agreed, though her heart was fluttering. 'Why don't you try kissing me?' She threw it down like a challenge, moving right up to him and staring into his tense face.

'Why don't I?' He hauled her to him with one arm. 'I'm not enough for you, am I, Caroline?' His blue eyes were so full of emotion they *blazed*.

'I can't tell until you kiss me again,' she said.

He stared at her with those burning eyes, a frown between his brows. 'Do I look like a guy you can manipulate?'

'Manipulate?' She pretended to try the word out on her tongue. 'I don't know what that means!' She knew she was deliberately provoking him but excitement was running at the rate of knots. She was just so *thrilled* to see him and he didn't even know it.

'Of course you know what it means,' he countered harshly. 'Every beautiful woman knows *that*. I didn't aim for your love right off, Caroline. I hoped love would come. But I thought I had your promise. That little letter you wrote me. It said you wanted to be my wife.'

'Well, you didn't take it seriously, did you?' she flashed back. 'You haven't seen me for a month yet you can't even get around to kissing me.'

She actually sounded *aggrieved*.

Clay's strong arms trembled. He'd had enough of her mockery, sarcasm, whatever it was. This wasn't *his* Caroline—what had happened to her?—but he still wanted this Caroline. Madly. Badly. He couldn't look at her without wanting her. He couldn't inhale her fragrance. Clay gathered her up, unprotesting, and carried her back to the deep armchair where he settled her in his lap.

'Go on, kiss me,' she urged, her beautiful dark eyes staring into his, her long blond hair spilling over his arm.

His face tightened into a bronze mask. He wanted to pay her back. Yes, he *did*. But he could never hurt her. Instead he let his mouth move over hers, not punishingly, but letting it convey his deep need of her. His hands moulded her to him. He couldn't make sense of anything. He didn't try. It was the same old magic all over again. Magic that had the power to drain him of his bitter disappointment and anger.

When he finally lifted his head, he saw *radiance* on her face, though her eyes remained shut. 'Caroline?' Surely she couldn't kiss him like that and not love him?

'All right, you've kissed me,' she whispered, opening her dark eyes. 'Now tell me you love me.'

He was moved to reveal his heart. 'I love you,' he said, his voice a deep well of emotion. 'I want you to have my children. I'll love you until the day I die.'

Carrie was trying her hardest not to cry. She sat up a little, holding his face between her hands. 'So why didn't you trust me?' she reproached him.

He shook his head with regret. 'I will from now on, I swear! But God, Caroline, it was understandable, don't you think? I came on the woman I love staring into another man's eyes like he had the answer to all life's problems. A young good-looking guy who had his hand on your shoulder. We'll forget the fact both of you weren't wearing a lot of clothes.'

'Since when do you wear a lot of clothes when you go swimming, my darling?' Carrie asked. 'Haven't I rung you every night? Haven't I told you how much I missed you?'

'Not *enough* apparently,' he said, allowing a deep sigh to escape him. 'I took off before I embarrassed myself. And worse, *you.*'

'Let's face it, Clay,' she said gently, 'you made a mistake. Had you waited I could have introduced you to my half brother, Todd. When he heard about me, he decided on the spot he had to come home to meet me. He's only just arrived. I would have told you tonight.'

Clay threw back his head, stunned. 'Your half brother?' If only he'd phoned ahead he would have been told and saved himself a lot of heartache.

Carrie pressed her lips to his throat. 'My half brother,' she confirmed. 'I can't marry him but I can marry you.'

Clay stared at her until his raging emotions cut back to a simmer. 'I apologise,' he said finally. 'A man in love isn't entirely *sane.'*

'And I accept your apology,' she said, feeling giddy with

sheer delight. 'I can't believe you're here with me.' To prove it she hugged him. 'About time, too.'

'And your new family?' Clay questioned, wanting to get things absolutely right. 'You're sure you don't want to stay close to them? We go back to Jimboorie, they'll be a long way away,' he reminded her.

'They're not going out of my life, Clay,' Carrie said. 'That's not going to happen.'

'Of course not,' he agreed, actually looking forward to meeting them. 'But you won't be able to see them on a daily basis or anything like that. There'll just be *me*.'

She took his hand in hers. 'I'm happy with that.' She smiled into his eyes. 'Hey, this reunion has been *perfect,* but my father and my half brothers have their own busy lives. Incidentally they all understand I love *you*. I've told them all about you. You have to meet them.'

'What right *now*?' Clay's voice was a low purr in his throat.

'No, not now.' She pulled down his head and kissed him lingeringly on the mouth. 'But tonight for dinner. I can't wait to show you off. Besides, I haven't quite forgiven you yet. You still have some work to do.'

'Okay,' he said in a smouldering voice, only too willing to prove his love.

'By the way.' Carrie deferred his ardent kisses for only a few seconds. 'We'd better get busy on our wedding plans.'

Clay laughed. 'I say we drink to that!'

'There's a bit more. If we don't, Mamma and Leyland are going to beat us to it, would you believe? Alicia is *still* Alicia, if you know what I mean.'

Clay smiled back at her. 'And Caroline is still Caroline,' he murmured, starting to seriously make love to her.

This was a wonderful outcome to all his hopes and dreams. One lonely bush bachelor had found himself the perfect wife.

EPILOGUE

Jimboorie House
18 Months Later...

THE ARMY OF TRADESMEN—roofers, carpenters, plumbers, plasterers, polishers, painters and wallpaperers, electricians—had all packed up and gone home. At some stage they would return—there was still plenty of work to be done on the many bedrooms of the upper level—but for now restoration work on the mansion had progressed so wonderfully well that Clay and Carrie had thrown it open to the people of the town and the outlying stations. Jimboorie House, once the hub of social life for the vast central plains of Queensland was set to take its place again as the reigning 'Princess' of the vast district's historic homesteads.

This particular gala day, a Saturday, had been set aside as a house warming for the very popular young couple whose splendid home it was and a fun day for all who had been invited. There was scarcely a soul—maybe one or two who had the sense to keep their resentments to themselves—who wasn't thrilled and proud to see 'the old girl' Jimboorie House rise like a phoenix from the ashes. This was *their* heritage after all.

Guests were milling around the house now marvelling at what had been done. So absolutely *right*—Carrie and her mother, Alicia, had received hundreds of compliments and congratulations. They had worked closely with the decorators over the long months, demonstrating their own considerable artistic flair and innate good taste.

To Carrie, who couldn't quite believe in her own level of pure bliss, everything was a miracle. Finding Clay, her wonderful husband and her soul mate, was a miracle. Finding her real father another. The fact her and Clay's wishes for a baby had been granted was yet another glorious miracle. She had recently had her pregnancy confirmed. She and Clay were over the moon. So were Alicia and Leyland who had married quietly only a few months before. The fact Senator Leyland Richards had a beautiful daughter from an old twenty-year-plus liaison— the revelation had received wide media coverage—in the end proved no impediment to his diplomatic posting to Washington. Alicia and Leyland had, in fact, delayed their departure to attend the restoration party, making it clear they would visit at every available opportunity. Try to keep them away! Prospective grandparents, they were overjoyed by Carrie's news; Alicia promised she would return home for the birth.

Another stroke of good luck was that Bruce McNevin had very quickly consoled himself by taking a new wife, a rich socialite widow, still young enough to have a child. They were in fact on their honeymoon in Europe. Given their shared history and the fact they would be living in the same district, Clay and Carrie had decided, as they lived in an adult world, some kind of peace had to be made or at the very least an outward show of civility. Carrie hadn't the slightest doubt Bruce still loved her mother, but destiny had planned for Alicia and Leyland to be reunited at long last.

Carrie stood at the French doors looking out over the beautifully restored garden and the magnificent central fountain now playing, smiling quietly to herself.

'Now what's that little smile about?' Clay came up behind her wrapping his arms around her. Carrie was his *life*. Together they had made *new* life. He lowered his locked hands a fraction to press them lovingly against her tummy. 'Love you,' he murmured, the flame of desire never far from his blue eyes.

'Love you,' she whispered back, then gave a little ripple of laughter. 'See out there? I was hoping and praying Natasha and Scott would make a go of it.'

Clay looked out at the young couple who were the focus of her attention. Blond and raven heads together, they were pushing what had to be the Rolls-Royce of prams.

'Well it didn't happen overnight,' Clay remarked quietly, 'but it *is* happening, thank God. Natasha is certainly a different woman.' Natasha in fact had become a routine visitor to Jimboorie saying she was *family* all along.

'Motherhood suits her,' Carrie who was looking breathtakingly beautiful in her trouble-free early pregnancy observed. 'I was wrong all along about Scott. He wasn't going to turn his back on his child.'

'I don't believe his parents were going to let him.' Clay's retort was dry. 'But he seems determined to be a father. So good for him!'

'Well he has an excellent reason to get his life together,' Carrie said. 'Sean is a beautiful little boy.'

'And he'll have another cousin before long,' Clay said, bending his head to kiss his wife's satin cheek. 'God, how happy you've made me, Carrie!' he breathed. 'Supremely happy! You've even with your compassion turned Natasha into a friend. Not content with that, you've caused the Cunninghams to beg forgiveness for past wrongs.'

'It was *you* who did the forgiving,' she reminded him, enormously proud of her husband.

'How could I lock the old bitterness into my heart when I had such love in my own life?' he said simply.

Carrie's soft sigh was eloquent of her happiness. A special radiance emanated from her, visible for all to see. She pressed back against her husband's lean strong body, her head on his chest. 'And the greatest joy is yet to come,' she promised, placing her hands over his on her very gently rounded tummy.

'I didn't think it was possible for you to be more beautiful,' Clay whispered, 'but you *are!*'

And his voice was hushed with awe.

It wasn't until the gala day was drawing to an end that Clay was approached by a young man, around his own age, who thrust out his hand.

'It *is* Clay, isn't it?' The man smiled. 'Clay Dyson? Used to be overseer on Havilah a couple of years back?'

Clay's face broke into a warm answering smile as he recognised Rory Compton, scion of one of the wealthiest cattle families in the Channel Country deep into the southwest. 'Cunningham now, Rory,' Clay said as they shook hands. 'Cunningham is my real name, by the way. How are you and what are you doing so far from home? Not that it isn't great to see you.'

'Great to see you!' Rory responded with sincerity. He hadn't known Clay Dyson all that well, but what he had seen and heard he had liked. 'So what's the story, Clay? And this homestead!' He gazed towards it. 'It's magnificent!'

'It is,' Clay agreed proudly. 'There is a story, of course. A long one. I'll tell you sometime, but to cut it short it all came about through a bitter family feud. You know about them?'

'I do,' Rory answered with a faint grimace.

'Mercifully the feud has been put to bed,' Clay said with satisfaction. 'My great-uncle Angus left me all this.' He threw out his arm with a flourish. 'Caroline, that's my wife and I, have only recently called a halt to the renovations. They were mighty extensive and mighty expensive. What I inherited was a far cry from what you see now.'

'So I believe.' Rory nodded. 'I'm staying at the Jimboorie pub. The publican told me about the open day out here. I'm glad I came.'

'So am I.' Clay's attractive smile lit up his features. 'Have you met Caroline yet?'

'The very beautiful blonde with the big brown eyes?' Rory gave the other man a sideways grin.

'That's Caroline.' Clay couldn't keep the proud smile off his face.

'I haven't had the pleasure as yet,' Rory said. 'I only arrived about thirty minutes ago, but I'm looking forward to it. You're one lucky guy, Cunningham!'

'*You* should talk!' Clay scoffed, totally unaware of Rory's current situation. 'How's Jay and your dad?' he said pleasantly.

'Jay's fine,' Rory said. 'He's the heir. My dad and I had one helluva bust-up.'

Clay could see the pain behind the level tone. 'That's rough! I'm sorry to hear it.'

'It was a long time coming,' Rory said quietly. 'The upshot being I didn't have much choice but to hit the road. I have some money set aside from my granddad. I guess he thought I might need it sometime. What I'm looking for now is a spread of my own. Nothing like Jimboorie of course. I'm nowhere in your league, but a nice little run I can bring up to scratch and sell off as I move up the chain.'

Clay looked into the middle distance, a thoughtful frown between his brows. 'You know I might be able to help you there,' he said slowly, already turning ideas over in his head. He knew of Rory Compton's reputation as a highly skilled cattleman with more vision than his dad and his elder brother put together. 'Why don't you come back inside. Meet Caroline. Stay to dinner. You're not desperate to get back to town are you?'

'Heck, no!' Rory felt a whole lot better in two minutes flat. 'I'd love to stay if it's okay with your beautiful wife?'

'It'll be fine,' Clay assured him. 'Caroline will be pleased to meet you. And we'll both have time to catch up.'

'Great!'

Destiny has an amazing way of throwing people together.

* * * * *

Cattle Rancher, Convenient Wife

Books by Margaret Way
OUTBACK MAN SEEKS WIFE*
HER OUTBACK PROTECTOR
THE CATTLE BARON'S BRIDE

Outback Marriages

Dear Reader,

Welcome to book two of my duet OUTBACK MARRIAGES. I hope when you've read both stories you'll be able to say with satisfaction, "I really enjoyed them!" Better yet "And I actually learned something I didn't know before!"

A devoted fan recently asked me what inspired me to write so much about the Outback when I wasn't born there. True, I was born in subtropical Brisbane, a city I love, but when I was a girl I went to a prestigious school called All Hallows. All Hallows took in boarders from all over Queensland's vast Outback. These girls had something special about them. When I used to listen to their stories of "home," I was fascinated. They came from places with legendary names like Longreach, Thargominda and Cloncurry, birthplace of QANTAS—Queensland and Northern Territory Aerial Services—and the Royal Flying Doctor Service, which spread its mantle of safety all over the Outback.

I was introduced to billowing red dust storms, drought, flood, the Dreamtime, Aborigines, billabongs, brumbies, camels, dingoes, private planes and governesses when they were small. For the highly imaginative girl I was, the Outback assumed near-mythical proportions in my mind. As a woman I discovered for myself reality not only matched those stories, it exceeded them. I had to see those amazing dry but vivid, burned ocher colors for myself. Our Australian Outback truly does have an incredible mystique. For the majority of you who can't possibly visit, I hope I've succeeded in opening a window on this unique part of the world.

Best wishes to you all, and a very special thank-you to my longtime loyal fans who have given me so much support throughout my long career. If we didn't have readers, we wouldn't have writers! Take a bow!

Margaret Way

CHAPTER ONE

THOUGH HIS MOOD was fairly grim Rory Compton couldn't help but smile. It was the middle of the day, yet a man could fire a cannon down the main street of Jimboorie and not find a target; not even a stray dog. The broad sunlit street was deserted as were the sidewalks, usually ganged on a Saturday. No kids were bobbing, weaving, ducking about, playing some private game, while their mothers, looking harried shouted at them to stop. No one was loading groceries into the family pickup. No dusty four-wheel drive's ran back and forth, the drivers waving casually and calling greetings to friends and acquaintances which meant pretty well everyone in town.

Seated on the upper verandah of Vince Dougherty's pub, Rory had the perfect view of the town centre, its impressive Community Hall and its attractive park. He drained off the cold beer he'd enjoyed with the prepacked lunch Dougherty's wife, Katie, had very kindly left him; a plate of thick roast beef and pickles sandwiches, cling wrapped so well it took him almost five minutes to get into it. He hadn't a hope of working his way through the pile. The stray dog would have come in handy in that regard. With the possible exception of himself, the whole town had taken itself off to the big 'open day' on Jimboorie, an outlying historic sheep station that had given the town its name. Sitting there, his long legs resting on a planter's chair, he debated whether to go. There was a slim chance it could boost his mood.

It was a restoration party he understood from Vince, who being a publican was always ready for a chat that naturally included dramatic revelations. The old homestead, from all accounts, once magnificent, had been allowed to go to rack and ruin under the custodianship of the former owner, Angus Cunningham. 'A miserable old bastard! Didn't think anyone in town was good enough to talk to!'

Of course Rory knew the name Cunningham. The Cunninghams figured among the roll call Outback pioneers. Sheep men. Not cattlemen like his own kind, their stamping ground, the legendary Channel Country, a riverine desert deep into the South-West pocket of their vast State. The new owner, a great nephew, 'one helluva guy!' had spent well over a year and a mountain of money restoring the place. Lucky old him! Vince had invited Rory along to the open day—'Sure and they won't mind!' Vince was as expansive as though he and Cunningham were best mates.

'Maybe,' he'd said. And maybe not. He wasn't in his best spirits since he and his father had had their cataclysmic row a couple of weeks back. Since then he'd been on the road, travelling from one Outback town to another in a sick, angry daze, checking out if there were any pastoral properties on the market he could afford with the help of a hefty bank loan. He couldn't lift his eyes to the multimillion range. All up including the private nest egg his grandad, Trevis Compton, had left him he had close to two million dollars A lot of money to a lot of people. Not near enough when one was talking a halfway decent pastoral property.

'I haven't left your brother, Jay, anything outside the personal things he loves,' Trevis had told him years back. They were sitting on the front steps watching another glorious desert sunset, his grandad's arm around his shoulder. 'Jay's the heir. He gets

Turrawin. It's always been that way. The eldest Compton son inherits to ensure the family heritage is kept intact. There are problems with splitting it a number of ways. Jay's a good boy. I love him dearly. But he's not *you*. You're meant for big things, Rory. A little nest egg might well come in handy after I'm gone.'

Rory could still hear his grandfather's deep gentle voice. How could two men be so different? His grandfather and his dad? To be strictly fair his grandfather had led a charmed life with a devoted wife as his constant companion. His son Bernard, however, had his life blighted fairly early. Bitterness ate into a man's soul. That last row had been one row too many. On both sides. His father had sent him on his way—hell he was going anyway—hurling the most vicious and unjust insults that even Rory, used to his father's ungovernable tirades, was deeply shocked. He had passed his elder brother, Jay, his father's heir in the entrance hall.

'Damn him, damn him! Damn him to hell!' Jay was muttering, white faced and shamed, furious with his father for attacking Rory but unprepared to go to his defence. Their father had turned big strong Jay into a powder puff, Rory thought sadly. Anyway Jay's intervention would have been in vain. He was going or his own pride and integrity would be hopelessly compromised. What did it matter he ran Turrawin these days and largely for the past four years? His father wanted him *out*! Sometimes Rory thought his father couldn't abide to look at him.

They had never been close. Instinctively Rory had known the reason. He strongly resembled his mother who had run off and left her husband and children when Rory was twelve and Jay fourteen. A *really* bad time. It had brought scandal on the family and a very hard life on Laura Compton's two boys who had worshipped her. From that day forward their father had succumbed to the dark places that were in him. His temper, always volatile became so uncontrollable his young sons lived in a constant state of fear and anxiety. Jay was often in floods of tears after a beating with a riding crop; Rory, *never* which only served to inflame their father further. Both boys regarded boarding school as a god-send. By the age of sixteen and eighteen, both six foot plus, taller and stronger than their father, the beatings had stopped. Their father had been forced to turn his attention back to his whiplash tongue.

'As soon as Dad's dead you and I are going to be full partners,' Jay had promised, his voice full of brotherly love and *pride*. Jay made no bones about it. Rory was everything he was not. 'I won't be able to run Turrawin without you. We both know that. The men look to you not me. *You're* the cattleman. The man to save the station. Dad didn't inherit Grandad's skills or his leadership qualities. Neither did I. You're the *real* cattleman, Rory.'

Rory sighed deeply knowing Jay would get into trouble without him. Bernard Compton had bruised his sons badly. But he hasn't beaten *me*, Rory thought determinedly. I've got everything going for me. Youth, health, strength, the necessary skills. He'd start up his own run. Move up in easy stages. He was as ready to found a dynasty as his Compton ancestors had before him. In time—it would have to be pretty soon, he'd turned twenty-eight—he'd find himself a wife. A young woman reared to the Outback. A woman with a deep love of the land who could withstand an isolated existence without caving in to depression or a mad craving for city lights.

Romantic love wasn't all that high on his agenda. Romance had a shelf life. That was the down side. He had to learn from experience. Most people didn't. History wasn't going to repeat itself with him. His best bet was a *partner* who could go the distance. That meant for *life*; a contractual sort of arrangement that the two of them would honour, working strongly together to build a future. As long as the woman was young and reasonably attractive the sex should be okay. He definitely wanted children. He knew he wasn't and never could be a hard, cruel bastard like his old man. He would be a good father to his children, not bring them up in a minefield. The Outback certainly bred hard men, *tough* men. But mercifully not many like his dad.

So what to do now? Rory stood up and stretched his long arms, staring down at the empty street. He had plenty of time on his hands. Why not take a run out to Jimboorie?

He might as well. Vince had given him directions. A beautiful old homestead would be worth seeing at least. It might even offer some comfort. He'd been intrigued to learn the new owner's Christian name was Clay. Clay Cunningham. He'd only ever met one Clay in his life, but that was a Clay Dyson, the overseer on Havilah a couple of years back. A guy around his own age held in great esteem by his employer, old Colonel Forbes, ex-British Army, now deceased, who had inherited Havilah from his Australian cousin and to everyone's astonishment had remained in the country to work it. Colonel Forbes, universally respected, had thought the world of Clay Dyson, Rory recalled. But it wasn't *that* Clay. Couldn't be. The Clay Dyson he had known had no background of money, no family *name*, though the word was old Colonel Forbes had remembered him in his will.

By the time he arrived on Jimboorie, a splendid property and as far out of his reach as planet Pluto, the main compound was still crowded with people but some were starting to leave making for the parking area crammed with vehicles of all makes and price tags. During the long approach to the station he had seen more than one light aircraft airborne, heading home. He made a quick tour of the very extensive gardens marvelling at the great design and the rich variety of trees, flowering plants and shrubs he presumed were drought tolerant and could withstand dust storms.

Beneath a long tunnel of cerise bouganvillea that blossomed heavily over an all but smothered green wrought-iron trellis, he passed two pretty young women from the town who smiled at him shyly in acknowledgement. He smiled back, raising a hand in salute, totally unaware it only took an instant for his smile to light up his entire face and dispel the dark, serious, brooding look he'd worn since his teens.

Jimboorie House impressed him immensely. He'd never expected it to be so *big* or so grand. It was huge! It rivalled if not surpassed any of the historic homesteads he had been invited into over the years. When his mother had been with them—when they were *family*—they had been invited everywhere as a matter or course. His beautiful mother, Laura, had been very popular, herself an excellent hostess presiding over their own handsome homestead on which she had lavished much love and care.

Why then had she abandoned them? Didn't God decree mothers had to remain with their children? For years he and Jay had accepted the reason their father had drummed into them. City bred their mother had only awaited the opportunity when they were old enough to renounce her lonely Outback life. As young men they came to understand what life for their mother might have been like, though their father had been reasonable enough *then*. Well, for most of the time anyway. He had never actually laid a hand on them when their mother was around except for the odd time when she had protested so strongly he had stopped. In any event she had remarried after the divorce. That happened all the time but it was lousy for the kids.

Their father, as was to be expected given his name, his money and influence, gained custody. He had never been prepared to share it with his ex-wife. The failure of their marriage was her fault entirely. It was one of his father's most marked characteristics, he held himself blameless in all things. Their mother alone deserved condemnation. The sharing was a bad idea anyway. Sensitive Jay had always become enormously upset when it was time to leave her. Equally upset, though he never let on, Rory behaved badly. He had to take the pain out on someone. He had chosen to take it out on his mother. After a while the visits became farther and farther in-between, then ceased altogether.

'Didn't I tell you?' their father had crowed, that hard triumphant gleam in his eyes as he started all over again to trash their mother. 'She doesn't want you. She never did! She's a selfish, self-centred heartless bitch! We're well rid of her!'

Neither of them would have won a good parenting award, Rory thought. But well rid of her? People really did die from grief. All three of them, father and sons, hadn't been able to handle her desertion. Their father, a proud and arrogant man, had never been free of his own grief and crazed thoughts of personal humiliation. Rory's memories of his mother were so heartwrenching he rarely allowed them to touch him. He and Jay had believed their mother to be the sweetest, gentlest, funniest, mother in the world. She could always make them laugh. It just didn't seem possible she had been faking it as their father always claimed. Nevertheless she had left, taking no account of the devastation she left behind her.

In choosing a woman of his own, Rory had long since decided he had to make absolutely sure he kept his eyes and ears open and his feet firmly on the ground. He was as susceptible to a woman's beauty as the next man—maybe more so he thought wryly—but there was no way he was going to allow himself to be seduced by it.

Or so he thought.

Vince Dougherty caught sight of him as he was wandering the grandly proportioned rooms of the old homestead letting it work its magic on him. Whoever had been responsible for the interior decoration—probably a top city designer—had done a great job.

'You made it!' Vince, looking delighted—his enthusiasm was hard to resist—made a beeline for him pumping his hand as though he hadn't seen him for weeks instead of around eight-thirty that morning. 'What d'yah think now? Tell me.' He poked Rory's shoulder which was marginally better than a poke in the ribs. 'You look like a guy with good taste.'

'That's very kind of you, Vince.' Rory's answer was laconic. 'It's magnificent!' His admiration was unfeigned. 'Definitely well worth the visit!'

Vince looked as proud as if he were the owner, decorator, landscaper, all rolled into one. The kind of guy who changed lives. 'Told yah, didn't I? You should have come an hour or so earlier. Meet the Cunninghams yet?'

'Not so far.' Rory shook his head. 'I only came to see the house really. I'm only passing through, Vince. Just like I told you.'

'Well, yah never know!' Vince's face creased into another smile. He was hoping this fine-looking young fella would stay in the district. He glanced upwards to the gallery. 'That's Carrie, Mrs Cunningham up there.' Discreetly he pointed out a blond young woman with a lovely innocent face and a radiant smile. She was standing in the midst of a circle of women friends who were laughing at something she was saying, which they obviously found very funny.

Rory could understand Vince's look of undying admiration. 'She's very beautiful,' he said. 'The house suits her perfectly.'

Vince's big amiable face settled into an expression of pride. 'An angel!' he announced. 'Clay reckons he's the luckiest man in the world. Now how about me taking you to find him? I reckon you young blokes would get on.'

Why not? 'Just point me in his direction, Vince,' Rory said. 'I see your wife beckoning to you.'

'My little sweetheart!' Vince exclaimed, a tag Rory had heard at least forty times during his stay. Vince and Katie were apparently right for each other. Katie wasn't *little*, either. 'Have to get back to the pub sooner or later. Try outdoors, near the fountain. Clay was there a few minutes ago. I don't think he's come back into the house.'

'Will do.' Rory tipped a finger to his temple.

It would turn out to be one of the best moves he had ever made.

The marble three-tiered fountain, monumental in size to suit the grand proportions of the house, was playing; an object of fascination for the children who had to be dragged away from the water by their mothers before they fell in or climbed in as one daring six-year-old had already done and been lightly chastised for. At such times he always remembered how his father had used to bawl him out as a child. It seemed like he had always made his father mad. Madder and madder as the years wore on. And later after their grandad died, the blind rages that took longer and longer to blow over.

A tall, handsome young man stood like a monarch at the top of the broad sloping lawn that ran down to a sun spangled creek. White lilies were blooming all around the banks, an exquisite foil for the sparkling stream and the green foliage of the reeds and the myriad water plants. Rory walked toward him, his spirits growing lighter. Surely it was Clay Dyson? Dyson was an arresting looking guy, hard to miss. Rory let his amazement show on his face.

'It *is* Clay, isn't it? Clay Dyson?' he called. 'Used to be overseer on Havilah a couple of years back?'

The other man turned, his face breaking into a smile of surprise as he recognised his visitor. He walked toward Rory, thrusting out a welcoming hand. 'Cunningham now, Rory. Cunningham is my *real* name by the way. How are you and what are you doing so far from home?' he exclaimed. 'Not that it isn't great to see you.'

'Great to see you!' Rory responded in kind, returning the handshake. He hadn't known Clay Dyson—Cunningham whatever—all that well, but what he'd seen and what he'd heard he'd liked. 'So what's the story, Clay? And this homestead!' He turned to gaze towards the front facade. 'It's magnificent.'

'It is,' Clay agreed with serene pride. 'There is a story, of course. A long one. I'll tell you sometime, but to cut it short it all came about through a bitter family feud. You know about them?'

'I do.' Rory made a wry face.

'Mercifully the feud has been put to bed,' Clay said with satisfaction. 'My great-uncle Angus left me all this.' He threw out his arm with a flourish. 'Caroline, my wife, and I have only recently called a halt to renovations. They were mighty extensive and mighty expensive. What I inherited was a far cry from what you see now.'

'So I believe,' Rory said in an admiring voice. 'I'm staying at the Jimboorie pub for a few days. Vince told me about the open day out here. I'm glad I came.'

'So am I.' Clay smiled. 'Have you met Caroline yet?'

'The very beautiful blonde with the big brown eyes?' Rory gave the other man a sideways grin.

'That's Caroline!' Clay couldn't keep the proud smile off his face.

'I haven't had the pleasure,' Rory said. 'You're one lucky guy, Cunningham.'

'You should talk!' Clay scoffed, totally unaware of Rory's changed circumstances. 'How's Jay isn't it, and your dad?'

'Jay's fine. He's the heir. My dad and I had one helluva bust up. That's why I'm on the road.'

Clay was aware of the pain and anger behind the easy conversational tone. 'That's rough! I'm sorry to hear it.' The Comptons had been an eminent Channel Country cattle family for generations. Where did that leave Rory?

'It was a long time coming,' Rory told him calmly. 'I didn't have any choice but to hit the road. I have some money set aside from my grandad. I guess he knew in his bones I might be in need of it sometime. What I'm looking for now is a spread of my own. Nothing like Jimboorie of course. I'm nowhere in your league, but a nice little run I can bring up to scratch and sell off as I move up the chain.'

Clay looked down to the creek, where children were running and shrieking, overexcited. 'No chance your dad will cool off, Rory? Could there be a reconciliation?'

Rory uncovered his head, his thick wavy hair as black and glossy as a magpie's wing. A lock fell forward on his darkly tanned forehead. 'No way! I wouldn't care if he did. That part of my life is over. The only thing I'm sorry about is I'm leaving Jay to it.'

Clay studied Rory with a thoughtful frown. He remembered now the Compton family history. 'You know I might be able to help you,' Clay confided, like someone who already had an idea in his mind, which indeed he did. 'Why don't you come back inside? Meet Caroline. Stay to dinner. A few friends are stopping over. I'd like you to meet them. You're not desperate to get back to town are you?'

'Heck no!' Rory felt a whole lot better in two minutes flat. 'I'd love to stay if it's okay with your beautiful wife?'

'It'll be fine!' Clay assured him, following his gut feeling about Rory Compton. This was a guy he could trust; a guy who could make a good friend. 'Caroline will be happy to meet you. And we'll have time to catch up.'

'Great!' A surge of pleasure at Clay's hospitality ran through him. Rory whipped out his transforming smile.

Destiny has an amazing way of throwing people together.

CHAPTER TWO

RORY FOUND IT all too easy to settle into the spacious, high-ceilinged guest bedroom that had been allotted him. His room at the pub, albeit clean and comfortable was *tiny* for a guy his size.

'Stay the night, Rory,' Clay had insisted. 'We'll be having a few drinks over dinner. Anyway it's too far to drive back into town. Everyone else is staying over until morning. There's any amount of room. Twelve bedrooms in, although we haven't got around to furnishing the lot as yet.'

His bedroom had a beautiful dark hardwood floor, partially covered by a stylish modern rug in cream and brown. Teak furnishings with clean Asian lines gave the room its 'masculine' feel. The colour scheme was elegant and subdued, the bedspread, the drapery fabric and the cushions on the long sofa of a golden beige Thai silk. It was all very classy. Clay had even lent him a shirt to wear to dinner. Something 'dressier' since he'd only been wearing a short-sleeved bush shirt. They were much of a height and build. In fact the shirt fitted perfectly.

Drinks were being served in the refurbished drawing room at seven. It was almost that now. He'd showered and washed his hair using the shampoo in the well-stocked cabinet. Now he gave himself a quick glance in the mirror aware as always of his resemblance to his mother. He had her thick sable hair, her olive skin, though life in the open air had tanned his to bronze. It was *her* eyes looking back at him; the setting, the colour. They flashed silver against his darkened skin. He had her clean bone structure, the high cheekbones, the jawline, stronger and more definite in him. Hell his face was *angular* now he came to take a good look. He'd lost a bit of weight stressing over the current situation and being forever on the road. Who would have ever thought it bad luck to closely resemble his beautiful mother? Although their old man had scarcely liked Jay more, when Jay was almost a double for their father at the same age. Jay could never be brutal. Jay was a lovely human being who really wasn't born to raise cattle. Both straight A students at their 'old money' boarding school Jay had once spoken of a desire to study medicine. It had only brought forth ridicule and high scorn from their father while their mother had gone to Jay laying her smooth cheek against his.

'And you'd be a fine doctor, Jay. Your grandfather Eugene was a highly respected orthopaedic surgeon.'

'Stop it, Laura!' their father had thundered, his handsome face as hard as granite. 'Mollycoddling the boy as usual. Putting ideas into his head. There's no place for nonsense here. Jay is my *heir*! His life is here on Turrawin. Let that be an end to it.'

His expression darkened with remembrance. He missed his brother. Their father would blame Jay for every last little thing that went wrong now. It was dreadful to wish your own father would just ride off into the sunset and never come back, but both of his sons were guilty of wanting that in their minds.

'You *are* a sick bastard, aren't you?' he berated himself, making a huge effort to throw off his mood. He'd already met most of his dinner companions, which was good. No surprises there. They were all nice, friendly people around his age, maybe a year or two older. Two married couples, the Stapletons and the Mastermans and a young woman, called Chloe Sanders with softly curling brown hair and big sky-blue eyes whose face became highly flushed when he spoke to her. Perhaps she was overcome with shyness, though she had to be well into her twenties and maybe past the time for hectic blushes.

It appeared there was a sister, Allegra, who was staying over as well, but so far she hadn't appeared. Caroline had told him in a quiet aside Allegra, recently divorced, was understandably feeling a bit low. She was staying a while with her mother and sister on the family property, Naroom, which *just could* be up for sale. A hint there surely? The girls' father, Llew Sanders had contracted a very bad strain of malaria while on a visit to New Guinea. Complications had set in but by the time he was properly hospitalised it was already too late. That was six months back, around the time Allegra's divorce had been finalised. All three women had been shattered, Caroline told him, her lovely face compassionate. The daughter who had stayed at home with her parents was Chloe. The one with the fancy name, Allegra, had flown the coup to marry a high flying Sydney stockbroker then had turned around and divorced him within a few years. Rory didn't get it. She was too young for a midlife crisis. Why did she marry at all if she hadn't been prepared to make a go of it? Then again to be fair it might have been the husband's fault? If the sisters looked anything alike, and they probably did, the high flyer husband could well have found someone more glamorous and exciting?

Heaven help me, I might like a bit of glamour and excitement myself!

Rory didn't want to know it, but he was a man at war with himself.

They were all assembled in the drawing room, chatting easily together, drinks in hand.

'Ah, there you are, Rory. What's it to be?' Clay asked. 'I've made a pitcher of ice-cold martinis if you're interested?'

'They're very good!' Meryl Stapleton held up her glass. 'Clay told me his secret. Just show the vermouth bottle to the gin.'

Rory laughed. 'I'm not a great one for cocktails, I'm afraid.'

'A beer then?' Clay produced a top brand.

'Fine.' Rory smiled and went to sit beside Chloe who was sending out silent but unmistakable signals. A man could learn a lot from a woman who wanted him to sit beside her. She flushed up prettily and shifted her rounded bottom to make a place for him. Still no sign of the sister. Perhaps she was all damped down with depression? Maybe their hostess would have to go to her and offer a little encouragement?

Greg Stapleton, a slightly avid expression on his face, immediately started into asking him if he was any relation to the Channel Country Comptons. 'You know the cattle dynasty?'

Obviously Clay hadn't filled him in. Rory was grateful for that. He really didn't want to talk about his family. Nevertheless he found himself nodding casually. 'The very same, Greg.'

'Say that's great!' Greg Stapleton gazed back at him with heightened interest. 'But what are you doing in this neck of the woods? You'd be way out of your territory?'

Rory answered pleasantly though he wanted to call, 'That's *it*!'

'Actually, Greg, I'm looking to start up on my own.'

Stapleton look amazed. 'Glory be! When Turrawin is one of our major cattle stations? The biggest and the best in the nation. Surely you'd have more than enough to do there?'

'I have an elder brother, Greg,' Rory said, making it sound like it was no big deal instead of a boot out the door situation. 'Jay's my father's heir. Not me. I've always wanted to do my own thing.'

'And I'm sure you'll be marvellous at it,' Chloe spoke up protectively and gently touched his arm. Chloe it appeared was a very sympathetic young woman. Nothing wrong with that!

'I'm totally against this primogeniture thing!' Greg announced. 'It's all wrong and it's hopelessly archaic.'

'Ah, here's Allegra!' Caroline rose gracefully to her feet, grateful for the intervention her guest's arrival presented. Clay had told her in advance a little of Rory Compton's story so she knew he wouldn't want to talk about it. But there was no stopping Greg once he got started. She welcomed the newcomer to their midst. 'Just in time for a drink before dinner, Allegra!'

'That would be lovely!' A faintly husky, marvellously sexy, voice responded.

My God, what a turn up!

Rory just managed to hold himself back from outright staring. He was absolutely certain *this* femme fatale had left not just a husband but a string of broken hearts in her wake. He had enough presence of mind to rise to his feet along with the other men as Chloe's sister walked into the room to join them. No, not walked. It was more like a red carpet glide. How exactly did unexceptional Chloe feel about having this beautiful exotic creature for a sister? All Rory's sympathies were with Chloe. The sisters couldn't have looked less alike. He hoped Chloe wasn't jealous. Jealousy was a hell of a thing to haul around.

In a split second his dazzlement turned to an intense wariness and even a lick of sexual antagonism that appeared out of nowhere. It wasn't admirable and it stunned him. He wasn't usually *this* judgemental.

She was a redhead. Not Titian. A much deeper shade. More the lustrous red one saw in the heart of a garnet, a stone he recalled had been sacred to ancient civilisations such as the Aztecs and the Mayans. She wore her hair long and flowing. He liked that. Most men would. It curved away from her face and fell over her shoulders like a shining cape. It even lifted most glamorously in the evening breeze that wafted through the French doors. Her eyes were a jewelled topaz-blue, set in a thick fringe of dark lashes. Her skin wasn't the pale porcelain usually seen in redheads. It had an alluring tint of gold. Very very *smooth*. Probably she dyed her hair. That would explain the skin tones. Her hair was an extraordinary colour.

She was much taller than Chloe with a body as slender and pliant as a lily. Her yellow silk dress was perfectly simple, yet to him it oozed style. He might have been staring at some beautiful young woman who modelled high couture clothes for a living or something equally frivolous like spinning the wheel on a quiz show.

'You know everyone except Rory,' Caroline was saying, happy to make the introduction. 'Allegra this is Rory Compton who hails from the Channel Country. Rory, this is Chloe's sister, Allegra Hamilton.'

She was walking towards him, graciously extending a long delicate hand. What was he supposed to do, fall to one knee? Kiss the air above her fingers? Powerful attraction often went along with a rush of contrary emotions, or so he had read. 'How do you do,' she said in that husky voice, as though equally struck by something in him she didn't quite understand, or for that matter *like.*

It might have been a gale force wind instead of a breeze blowing through the open doors. Rory swallowed hard on the roaring in his ears. What the hell! One could shake hands with a vision. Get it over. Life went on. He knew he hadn't imagined the shiver of electricity. It was a wonder they hadn't struck sparks off one another. It happened. But there was bound to be a scientific explanation. He felt more comfortable with that, though he hadn't the slightest doubt she could cause such a response at will.

Well ma'am, I survived it!

She didn't smile at him, coolly summing him up. He didn't smile at her. Instead they studied one another with an absolute thoroughness that seemed to lock out everyone else in the room.

She looked away first.

He didn't know how to interpret that. A win or a loss?

Over dinner, it turned out stunning Allegra was also smart. Pretty soon he'd be lost in admiration. Lighthearted conversation set the tone for most of the meal. They talked about anything and everything. A recent art auction, remarkable for the high prices paid for aboriginal art, music, classical and pop, favourite films, books, celebrities in the news, steering clear of anything confrontational. He liked the way she entered spiritedly into the discussions, revealing not only a broad general knowledge, but a wicked sense of humour. Now why should that surprise him? Rory had to chide himself for being so damned chauvinistic in the face of the twenty-first century. Why shouldn't there be a good brain behind that beautiful exterior? His mother had been a clever woman, well educated, well read. Not much of a mother, however, as it turned out. Not all glorious looking women kept themselves busy luring rich guys into marriage he reminded himself.

What *really* struck him, was the way sweet little Chloe kept heckling her sister just about every time she opened her mouth. Heckling was the only way he could interpret it. It was all done with a cutesy smile, which he thought rather odd, but towards the end he found himself fed up with it. Sisterly ease and friendliness appeared to be a thin veneer.

On the other hand—further surprising him—there appeared to be no limit to Allegra's tolerance. She had such a high mettled look to her and surely a redhead's temper he had expected a free-for-all. If again that gorgeous mane was natural? But never once did she retaliate to her sister's running interference when Rory had thought of a few sharp answers himself. There was no way Chloe could be totally free of jealousy, he reasoned. Poor Chloe. This was one of the ways she handled it.

'And what's your feeling, Rory?' Allegra startled him by addressing him directly. She looked across the gleaming table, her beauty quite electrifying amid the candlelight and flowers.

'I'm sorry, I missed that.' *I was too damned busy wondering about you!*

She smiled as though aware of it. 'We were talking about the mystery resignation.' She named a well-known politician who had stunned everyone including the prime minister by vacating his federal seat literally overnight.

'He's had a breakdown, I'd say,' Rory offered quietly, after a moment of reflection.

'Doesn't look like that to me.' Greg Stapleton's mouth curled into a sardonic grin. 'Could be woman trouble. The man looks great, fit and well. I saw him only recently on a talk show. He's a good-looking bloke, happily married supposedly. One of the top performers in government.'

'A high achiever,' Rory agreed. 'And he *is* happily married, with three children. He is a man who drives himself hard. When depression hits it hits hard. It can hit anyone. I've met the man and really admired him.'

'So you think all the stress that goes along with the job—the lengthy periods away from home—got to him?' Allegra asked, studying Rory very carefully and obviously waiting on his answer.

'That's my opinion,' he said. 'But I'm prepared to bet he is the man to confront it and win out.'

She gave a gratifying nod of approval. 'I'm sure we all wish him well.'

Chloe at this point, not to be outdone, attempted to start a rousing political discussion, which was met not so much with disinterest but a disinclination to spoil the mood. Subdued she turned her attention back to cutting down her sister at the same time keeping her own brain underwraps. Appearances could be very deceptive Rory was fast learning. He'd initially thought sweet Chloe would make some man a good wife. Perhaps she *would*. Just so long as her sister wasn't around.

Irritations aside, dinner went off very well. A roulade of salmon with a crab cream sauce; smoked duck breast as a change from beef, a lime and ginger brulée. Someone took an excellent approach to cooking. He hadn't been eating well on the road. Clay and his beautiful wife were the best of hosts; the formal dining room recently redecorated and refurbished was splendid and the food and wine matched up.

It was well after midnight before they broke up. Rory was one of the last to make his way upstairs to his guest room because he and Clay had a private conversation first.

'If you want I could have a word with Allegra in the morning,' Clay suggested, drawing Rory into the book filled library. 'There's a possibility the Sanders property—it's called Naroom by the way—could come on the market.'

'You think they're serious?' Rory asked, staggered by all the leatherbound tomes. Did anyone read them?

'We won't exactly know until I broach the subject.'

'Why Allegra, why not both sisters?' Rory asked, fairly cautiously.

Clay's response was dry. 'Not to be unkind, you've met both sisters. Allegra is definitely the brains of the outfit.'

'Is that why Chloe's so darned resentful?' Rory's chiselled mouth twisted.

'I've never seen Chloe quite so bad,' Clay confessed. '*You* might have had something to do with that!' A teasing grin split his face.

'Cut it out!' Rory's voice was wry. 'I'm sure Chloe can be a very nice person when she tries, but I have to say I'm not interested.'

'What about Allegra?' Clay continued, tongue-in-cheek. 'She's so much more beautiful—'

'And brainier,' Rory cut in. 'Sorry, I know what a beautiful woman can do to a man. You're one of the lucky ones.'

'About as lucky as a man can get,' Clay admitted with a smile. 'Anyway, who could blame Chloe for being so miffed. Allegra has so much going for her.'

'Really?' Rory raised a brow. 'I thought she'd just come out of an unpleasant divorce?'

'So she has. I think she's been feeling a bit down lately. Who could blame her?'

'That must account for the way she hasn't got around to telling her little sister to back off?'

'It's all about sibling rivalry, my man!' Clay groaned. 'Anyway if you like I'll suss out the situation for you in the morning.

No harm done one way or the other, but I'm pretty sure they'll want to sell. I'll see what Allegra has to say and let you know.'

'That'll be great, Clay. I much appreciate what you're doing for me and thank you again for your splendid hospitality.'

'A pleasure!' Clay's smile was wide and genuine.

Afterwards Rory found himself following the lingerers, Allegra and Chloe up the grand staircase quite unable to prevent himself from admiring Allegra's long slender legs and delicate ankles. Never in his wildest dreams had he anticipated meeting a woman like this. To try to do something about it would be madness. He was a man looking for a suitable woman to make his wife. He'd be a total fool to lift his eyes to a goddess who found mortal men dull in a very short time.

He was so engrossed in his thoughts, half admiration, half remonstration, when he almost barged into her. As surefooted as a gazelle, she suddenly stumbled, throwing out a slender ringless hand he had already observed over dinner, to clutch at the banister.

'Oh heavens!' she gasped, sounding relieved he had broken her fall.

'Okay?' Rory's arm shot out like lightning. With his arm around her, his whole body went electric with tension. He dared not even open his mouth again. Instead he stared into her disturbingly beautiful face, unaware his eyes had gone as brilliant and hard as any diamonds.

'She's sloshed!' Chloe explained, looking at her sister aghast.

Rory found himself jumping to Allegra's defence. 'Nothing like it!' His answer came out a shade too curtly, causing poor Chloe to colour up. Allegra Hamilton had had no more than three glasses of wine over the space of the whole evening. He knew that for a fact. He'd rarely taken his eyes off her, which could only mean he had more need of caution.

As it was, he held her lightly but very carefully, surprised the silk dress she wore wasn't going up in smoke. He was searingly aware of the pliant curves and contours of her body. He could smell her perfume. A man could ruin himself over a woman like this. He fully understood that. He just bet she haunted the ex-husband's dreams, poor devil!

'Do you feel faint?' he asked, studying her pale oval face.

Chloe looked on speechlessly.

For a moment Allegra's dazzling gaze locked on his, then when she couldn't hold his gaze any longer, she shook her head as if in an effort to clear it. 'Just a little. It will pass.'

'She doesn't eat,' Chloe informed him like it was an ill kept secret. Her face and neck were flushed with colour. 'Anorexia, you know. Or near enough. So she can wear all those tight clothes.'

Now that just *could* be right, Rory thought. She had eaten lightly at dinner. She was as willowy as a reed. He should know. He still had his arm around her. It felt incredibly, dangerously *intimate*. Anyone would think he'd never had his arm around a woman in his life. He was no monk. But he was, he realised to his extreme discomfort, consumed by the warmth of this woman's body and the lovely fragrance it gave off. It blurred his objective faculties, casting a subversive spell. Allegra Hamilton was a heartbreaker. He knew all about *those*.

'Lord, Chloe, will you stop making it up as you go along. I'm *not* anorexic,' Allegra sighed. 'Though I confess I haven't had much appetite of late. Or much sleep. Thank you, Rory. I'm fine now.' It was said with the faintest trace of acid as though she was aware of the erotic thoughts that were running through his head. She shook back her hair, squared her shoulders and slowly straightened up. 'It was just a fuzzy moment. Nothing to get alarmed about.'

'How many times have I heard you say that after a dinner party?' Chloe directed a tight conspiratorial smile in Rory's direction.

'The fact is you've *never* heard it, Chloe,' Allegra answered with a kind of weary resignation.

'I have, too,' Chloe suddenly barked. 'Mark was really worried about your drinking.'

Allegra laughed shakily. 'What, Diet Coke?'

'Why don't I just carry you to your room?' Rory suggested, not at all happy with the way she was near dragging herself up the stairs, one hand on the banister. He didn't want to hear about her ex-husband, either. Not tonight anyway. 'You'd be as light as a feather.'

'You're kidding!' She paused to give him a vaguely taunting glance. 'A feather?'

'If I pick you up I can prove it. You look to me like you need carrying to your room.' Before she could say another word or get out a word of protest, he scooped her up in his arms.

'There, what did I tell you?' His voice mocked her, but in reality he was seized by a feeling of intoxication that was enormously distracting. It came at him in mounting waves. For one forbidden moment he went hot with desire, quite without the power to cool it. Never before had a woman stirred such a response. His every other experience paled into insignificance beside this. A man of good sense should fear such things as not all that long ago men feared witches.

She caught her breath, astounded by his action. Then she gave way to laughter. 'A woman has to be careful around you I can see, Rory Compton. I've never been swept off my feet before. Though it does fit your image.'

'What image?' He looked down at her with his brooding, light filled eyes.

'Man of action. It's written all over you.'

'Look I'm really sorry, Rory,' Chloe said, trotting in their wake. 'Allegra is always doing things like this. It's so embarrassing.'

'Give me a break, Chloe!' Allegra broke into a moan before she was overcome again by laughter. Peals of it. It simply took her over. 'I've never met a man like Rhett Butler before,' she gasped.

Though her mood seemed lighthearted, Rory had the odd feeling she was on the verge of tears. A woman's tears could render a man very vulnerable. He knew when she was alone in her room they might flow.

With his arms around her body, her beautiful face so close, excitement was pouring into him way beyond the level of comfort. Wariness had turned to wonder. Wonder to a dark, albeit *involuntary* desire. She might have been naked in his arms so acutely did his senses respond.

Oh ye of little resolve! A taunting voice started up in his head. But then he hadn't seen a woman like Allegra Hamilton coming.

What he needed now was a long, cold bracing shower. She was an incredibly desirable woman yet he was half appalled by his own reactions, the depth and dimension, the sheer physical pleasure he took in holding her. The breasts he couldn't help but look down on, were small but beautifully shaped; her shoulders delicately feminine. Her arched neck had the elegance of a swan's. What would a man feel like carrying a woman such as this to their bridal bed? It came to him with a fierce jolt he deeply resented the fact another man had already done so. How could that same man bring himself to let her go? He didn't really know but he was prepared to bet it was she who had tossed her husband aside. And how many other men had she ensnared before him?

It was more than time to set her down before she totally messed him up.

Chloe ran ahead helpfully and opened the bedroom door. 'Anyone would think she was a baby. She can walk.' She looked up at Rory sympathetically. 'Just put her on the bed.'

My God, didn't he want to!

He was no damned different from all the other poor fools. Whatever his mind said, whatever his will demanded, underneath he was just a man whose fate was to succumb to woman.

'Please, Chloe,' Allegra laughed. 'I'm the wronged party. It's this cowboy who swept me off my feet.'

'Cattleman, ma'am,' he corrected, now so perversely hostile he barely stopped himself from pitching her onto the huge four-poster bed, its timber glowing honey-gold.

'Rory, I didn't mean to offend you,' she apologised, still caught between laughter and tears.

'Forgive me, I think you did.' He couldn't say he badly resented being put under a spell. He wasn't accustomed to such things.

'I confess I find *your* attitude a little worrying, too.' From a lying position—God how erotic—she sat up on the bed, staring at him with her great topaz-blue eyes.

'Hey, what on earth are you two talking about?' Chloe was struggling hard to keep up. It all seemed incomprehensible to her.

'Nothing. Absolutely nothing,' Rory said, further perplexing her. Allegra Hamilton in the space of one evening had got right under his skin. He was aware his muscles had gone rigid with the effort not to yield to the urge to lean forward, close the space between them, grasp those delicate shoulders and kiss her hard. Only desiring a woman like that was an option he simply couldn't afford.

Maybe it was her utter unattainability that made her so desirable to him? He had to find a reason to give him comfort. On his way to the door Rory turned to give her one last glance.

A big mistake!

She couldn't have looked more ravishing or the setting more marvellously appropriate. The quilted bedspread gleamed an opulent gold, embroidered with richly coloured flowers. Her dress had ridden up over her lovely legs, pooling around her in deep yellow. Her hair shone a rich red beneath an antique gilt and crystal chandelier that hung from a central rose in the plastered ceiling. Hanging over the head of the bed was a very beautiful flower painting of yellow roses in a brass bowl, lit from above.

It was enough to steal any man's breath away.

'Good night, Rory,' she said sweetly, which he translated into, 'Goodbye!'

He nodded his dark head curtly, but made no response.

Witch!

She was accustomed to putting men under a spell. But for all he knew she could have a heart of ice.

Coming as he did from the desert where there was a much higher pitch of light and the vast landscape was so brilliantly coloured, Rory found his trip out to Naroom, enjoyable, but relatively uninspiring compared to his own region, the Channel Country. The bones of many dead men lay beneath the fiery iron-oxide red soil of his nearly eight hundred thousand square kilometre desert domain. The explorers Burke and Wills had perished there; the great Charles Sturt, the first explorer to ever enter the Simpson Desert almost came to final grief—the German Ludwig Leichhardt became a victim of the forbidding landscape. Not only had the early explorers been challenged by that wild land, but so too were the pioneering cattlemen like his forebears who had followed. After good rains, the best cattle fattening country in the world, in times of drought they had to exploit the water in the Great Artesian Basin, which lay beneath the Simpson Desert to keep their vast herds alive. And exploitation was the word. It really worried him that one day the flow of water to the several natural springs and the artificial bores might cease. What a calamity!

To Rory, the desert atmosphere of home was so vivid he could smell it and taste it on his tongue. These vast central plains seemed much nearer civilisation. He had lived all his life in a riverine desert, bordered on Turrawin's west by the one hundred thousand square kilometre Simpson Desert of central Australia. His world was a world of infinite horizons and maybe because of it, the desert possessed an extraordinary mystique.

It was certainly a different world from the silvery plains he was driving through. His landscapes were surreal. They seeped into a man's soul. The desert was where he belonged, he thought sadly, though he accepted it was fearsome country compared to those gentler, more tranquil landscapes; the silvers, the browns, the dark sapphires and the sage-greens. He was used to a sun scorched land where the shifting red sands were decorated with bright golden clumps of Spinifex that glowed at dusk. Scenically the Channel Country was not duplicated by any other region on the continent. It was unique.

Unique, too, the way the desert, universally a bold fiery-red, was literally smothered in wildflowers of all colours after the rains. No matter what ailed him such sights had always offered him relief, a safety valve after grim exchanges with his father, even a considerable degree of healing. There were just some places one *belonged*. Fate had made him a second son and given him a father who had shown himself to be without heart. He was the second son who was neither wanted nor needed.

Well let it lie.

Clay as promised had set up this meeting with the Sanders women. Clay would have come along, only he was fathoms deep in work. Rory would have liked his company—they got on extremely well together—but he didn't mind. It was just the two sisters and their mother. An exploratory chat. Just the two sisters? Who was he kidding? He couldn't wait to lay eyes on Allegra Hamilton again. In fact it hadn't been easy putting her out of his mind.

You can handle it, he told himself.

With no conviction whatever.

Clay had assured him Mrs Sanders *was* seriously considering selling, although the property wasn't on the market as yet. Clay, during his conversation with the beauteous Mrs Hamilton, had formed the idea the family would want between $3.5 and $4 million, although she hadn't given much away. Clay got the impression Allegra didn't really want to sell.

Why not? It wasn't as though a woman like that, a hothouse

orchid, could work the place. Nevertheless Rory had already taken the opportunity of having a long, private phone conversation with one of Turrawin's bankers. A man he was used to and who knew him and his capabilities. He had been given the go-ahead on a sizeable loan to match his own equity. Naroom wasn't a big property as properties in his part of the world went—nowhere near the size of Jimboorie for that matter, let alone Turrawin. The property from all accounts had been allowed to run down following the death of Llew Sanders and the unexpected departure of their overseer who it was rumoured had had a falling out with Mrs Sanders. A woman who 'kept herself to herself' and consequently wasn't much liked. Rory wanted to ask where Allegra had got her extraordinary looks from, but thought it unfair to Chloe who seemed a nice little thing if she could just hurdle the sibling rivalry or trade in her present life for a new one.

Rivalry simply hadn't existed between him and Jay. They had always been the best of friends. The strong bond formed in early childhood had only grown closer with the changing circumstances of their lives. In many ways he had taken on the mantle of older brother even though he was two years Jay's junior. He had shielded the quieter, more sensitive Jay through their traumatic adolescence and gone on to take the burden away from Jay in the running of the station. That old hypocrite, his father, had been well aware of it but chose—because it suited him—to keep his mouth and his purse shut.

Valerie Sanders walked into the kitchen in time to see Allegra taking a tray of chocolate chip cookies out of the oven, presumably to offer to their visitor with tea or coffee. Cooking wasn't Valerie's forte so she had left Allegra to it. Besides she had sacked their housekeeper, Beth, who didn't know how to keep a still tongue in her head, even after fourteen years.

'I hope you're not going to be difficult, Allegra,' Valerie, a trim and attractive fifty-two-year-old now said, picking up their discussion from breakfast. 'I want the place sold. So does

Chloe. Why should you care? You don't live here. You have to stop thinking of yourself for a change.'

Allegra transferred the cookies to a wire cooling rack before answering. She had learned long ago to ignore Valerie's perennial sniping. Crossing swords with her only reinforced it. 'That's a bit unfair, Val,' she said mildly. 'All I said was, we can't simply *give* Naroom away. It's worth every penny of $4 million even if it's not the best of times to sell. Dad would turn over in his grave if we sold it for less. It just seemed to me you and Chloe are prepared to accept the first offer.'

Valerie's light blue gaze turned baleful. 'I want *out*, Allegra. I've had more than enough of life on the land and Chloe has had *no* life at all. I know you don't worry about your sister. But she has to find a good man to marry and she isn't getting any younger. You had a good man and you were fool enough to let him get away.'

Allegra refused to fire. 'Do you actually listen to a word I say, Val? Mark was unfaithful to me. Since when are philanderers good men?' She busied herself setting out cups and saucers. 'As for Chloe, I used to invite her to stay with us often enough. Surely you remember?'

'How could she stay when there was always tension between you and Mark?' Valerie retaliated. 'Though it must be said Mark always did his best to pretend nothing was wrong. Chloe and I have come to the conclusion *you* were the source of all the trouble, Allegra, however much you protest. And you've always gone out of your way to put your sister in the shade. You could have been a real help to her, but you live in your own little world.'

Allegra couldn't help a groan escaping her. 'So you've been pointing out to me for years and years. Now we're on the subject of Chloe, she's not much help around the place. I hear her complaining about putting on weight when the surefire answer is exercise. There's plenty to do around the house since you let Beth go.'

'We couldn't afford her,' Valerie said briefly.

'She been with us for years and years,' Allegra said, thankful she had managed to contact Beth who was now living with her sister

'That awful woman!' Beth, her anger up, had raged. 'I only stayed because of your dad. It was all so different when you left home, Ally love. Personally I think your stepmother drove your poor dear father bonkers! He must have spent years of his life wondering why he married her.'

He married her for my sake, Allegra thought sadly. To give me a mother.

'Now when this young man arrives I want you to stay in the background,' Valerie said. ' If such a thing is possible. Your father spoilt you terribly.'

'I suppose he was trying to make up for you, Val,' Allegra offered dryly. 'I've always irritated the living daylights out of you.' In fact Allegra couldn't recall a happy, carefree period of her life; a time when she was not exposed to Valerie's shrouded antagonism, which nevertheless Allegra was made aware of even as a child.

'So you have,' Valerie admitted. 'You must have irritated the living daylights out of Mark as well. You could have held onto him with a little understanding. We all know men are in the habit of having a bit on the side But your ego couldn't tolerate that, could it?'

Allegra considered this, aghast. 'My ego had nothing to do with it. Dad didn't have a bit on the side as you phrase it.'

'No, he was faithful to the memory of your sainted mother!' At long last Valerie gave vent to the helpless anger she'd been forced to stifle for years; anger that had at its heart jealousy of a ghost.

'Now you've come out with it.' Allegra experienced a hard pang. 'I can see from now on it's going to be no-holds-barred. That's the answer to all our woes, isn't it? I'm guilty of resembling my mother who died before she was thirty. Think about that, Val. You're *jealous* of a woman who died so young? Would you have swapped places with her? It's truly sad, but you've never been able to master your deep envy of her place in Dad's life. The fact I look so much like her has only made you fixate on it all these long years. I suppose it was inevitable.'

'Psychoanalyst now are we?' Valerie jeered, her expression bitter. 'Actually I'm fine. Llew is dead. Naroom will soon be sold. It was never really *my* home. More *her* shrine. No need for us to put up a pretence anymore. But don't kid yourself. The conflicts we've had over the years have been caused by your pushing me or your sister to the limit. I wasn't your darling mummy. You were such an assertive child, always demanding your father's attention. You took your demands to the next stage with your husband. Small wonder he left you.'

'Oh go jump, Val!' Allegra had come to the end of her tether. '*I* left Mark. But don't let's upset your mind-set.'

'Mark told me *you* made him feel alienated,' Valerie persisted.

'Since when did you become Mark's champion?' Allegra asked wearily. 'He's ancient history, Val.'

The expression on Valerie's face was one of primitive antagonism. 'Alienation was the cause of much of his unhappiness and his turning to someone else.'

Allegra groaned with frustration. 'You're talking through your hat. It was more than some*one* else, Val.'

'I bet you had your little flings as well,' Valerie quickly countered. 'You demand constant admiration.'

'None of which has ever been handed out by you. Some stepmothers are wonderful. Heaps of them! But your crowning achievement has been picking on me. All your love has been given to your own child. I had to lean heavily on Dad. You set out early to drive a wedge between me and Chloe. You bred your own resentment into her. As for my marriage, I respected my vows.'

Valerie gave a mocking smile. 'The reason I understand exactly what Mark meant when he said you alienated him is because you alienate *me*.'

'Then I'm sorry!' Allegra threw up her hands, thinking her stepmother's problems with her would never be resolved until the family—such as it was—split up. Her father had held them all together. Now he was gone. 'I have to get changed,' she said, moving towards the door. 'Rory Compton should be here soon.'

'Set to fascinate him, are we?' Valerie called after her.

The facade of caring stepmother was rapidly crumbling.

In her bedroom Allegra changed out of the loose dress she'd been wearing since breakfast into a cool top with a gypsy style skirt that created a breeze around her legs. She slung a silver studded belt around her narrow waist and hunted up a pair of turquoise sandals to match her outfit. It was second nature to her to try to look her best no matter how she felt. For one thing her job as Fashion Editor on a glossy magazine demanded it. Besides, looking good gave her the extra confidence she needed. It helped her present her best face to the world.

Inside, these days, she felt totally derailed. Her beloved father gone. The only person in the world who had truly loved her. Val coming out into the open, spitting chips! No husband to be there for her. What does a woman do when she can't keep her husband of three years faithful? So much for beauty! She had thought in her naivete, she and Mark would be together for life—Mark the father of her children—but she and Mark had been marching to a very different tune. Fidelity simply wasn't in his nature, though he had given every outward semblance of it for quite a while. That was until she received in the mail a batch of photographs, stunning evidence of her husband's betrayal. They were sent anonymously of course. Not a single word accompanied them as though the photographs said it all; which indeed they did. They were from someone who didn't so much care about her pain as showing Mark up for what he was. Allegra had always had the idea that person was a woman.

Someone who may have been a former lover of Mark's and now hated him.

Mark's explanation when she had confronted him with them had been quite extraordinary. He had acted calm, as though he couldn't quite grasp her devastating shock.

'It's long over, Ally!' He'd assured her in his smooth, convincing stockbroker's voice. 'It meant absolutely nothing. All it did was relieve a physical ache at the time. Let's face it, my darling, I don't get as much sex from you, as I want, though I have to admit it increases your allure. Why do women make such a big deal about men having extra needs? It's *you* I love. You're my *wife*. No other woman can touch you. I'll never leave you and you'll never leave me. I'd be devastated if you did.'

She was the one who was devastated but, God help her, she had forgiven him. It was too early in their marriage to call it a day. She certainly couldn't go home to Val to seek advice and comfort. She told herself lots of people make mistakes. She made herself believe it had been Mark's only infidelity. In retrospect, of course it hadn't been. Mark was addicted to sex like another man might have been addicted to golf. It was a necessary relaxation, a *fix*. Mark was handsome, charming, successful, generous. Especially with his favours.

In the beginning he had been a tender, sensitive, romantic lover, eager to please her. She realised now what he had been doing was gradually trying to break her in to his little ways she found vaguely demeaning, though she tried to understand where he was coming from. It wasn't as though there was much harm in what he wanted her to do it. It wasn't even overpoweringly sensual. But she couldn't help feeling titillating little games were ridiculous. Certainly they didn't turn her on.

'Sweetheart, you're not a bit of fun!'

Seeing how she felt, he backed off. Overnight he rectified his behaviour, which had never been evident during their courtship, returning to the considerate, caring lover. She'd believed like a fool they had come to an understanding. Nothing further was going to be allowed to disrupt their lives. Only Mark secretly moved back to the kind of women who were up for the kind of sexual kicks he craved. The other women turned out to be married women from their own circle. Why had she been so shocked? Faithless friends made faithless lovers. All of them had been exceedingly careful, not wanting exposure or even to break up their existing marriages. There was no wild partying, no staying out overnight, much less for long weekends. Their marriage might have survived for quite a bit longer only she had returned home from work unexpectedly early one afternoon only to find Mark and a married friend of theirs chasing one another around the bedroom.

Incredibly she hadn't been laid low. She hadn't screamed or cried or yelled at the woman to get dressed and get the hell out of her house. For a moment she had very nearly laughed. They looked so ridiculous staring back at her. Like a pair of startled kangaroos caught in the headlights of a four-wheel drive.

'Goodness, Penny, I scarcely recognised you without your clothes!'

Then she had turned about and walked straight out of the house, booking into a hotel.

So here she was at twenty-seven, a betrayed wife. A betrayed ex-wife. And having a hard time coming to terms with what a fool she had been. She had truly believed Mark was a man of integrity. Yet love or what she thought had been love had flown out the window. Indeed it had all but taken wing when she had first received those compromising photographs with her clever handsome husband caught in the act, his unflattering position preventing her from seeing his partner-in-crime's face. At one stage, as she bent over the photographs, she had the weirdest notion that partner could have been Chloe—something about the slight plumpness of the legs, what she could see of the woman's body?—but quickly rejected the idea, disgusted with herself for even allowing such a notion to cross her mind. Chloe would never do such a thing. Chloe was far too honourable.

Incredibly Mark had tried desperately to save their marriage, saying she was making something out of nothing. Just how did one define *nothing*? A man wasn't intended to remain monogamous, he said. Everyone knew that. Smart women accepted it; turned a blind eye.

He obviously didn't want to consider the innumerable crimes of passion that hit the headlines. He continued to hold to the line he 'adored' her. He knew he had a problem of sorts, but he would seek counselling if that's what she wanted. They would go together.

She had declined without regrets. She had to face the dismal fact Mark was highly unlikely to be cured. Sooner or later he would break out again. He had found it ridiculously easy up to date. Almost ten years her senior and well versed in the less laudable ways of the world, he had run rings around her. Even after their divorce became final he had stalked her, telling her how ashamed he was of his behaviour and how much he desperately needed her. Didn't he deserve another chance?

Tell me. Whatever it is you want me to do, I'll do it. I've already entered into treatment.

She knew it was a lie. The only thing Mark was sorry about was getting *caught*.

Why had she married him in the first place? He hadn't exactly swept her off her feet, though he couldn't have been kinder, sweeter, or more considerate. His intellect had reached out to her. He was a clever, cultured man, highly successful with powerful friends. She went from single woman with no *real* home—home with Valerie and had felt like enemy territory—to married woman with a beautiful home of her own and an extraordinarily generous husband who showered her with gifts. Was that what she had really wanted all along?

A home of her own?

She never told anyone about Mark's little idiosyncrasies. She could well be confiding in someone who already knew. She didn't blacken his name. She knew quite a few in their circle believed she was the one to bring what had appeared to be a marriage made in heaven to an abrupt end. Mark was 'a lovely guy!' Everyone knew he adored her. The age difference might have had something to do with it. Or Allegra had found someone else. In her work she was invited everywhere with or without her husband—there had to be lots of temptations along the way, men and women behaving the way they did.

Allegra knew people had been talking, but there was little she could do about it but take it on the chin.

CHAPTER THREE

RORY COMPTON HAD already arrived by the time she made her way downstairs. She realized with a prickle of something like discomfort and an irrational guilt she had taken a few extra little pains with her appearance. She was aware too of a quickening of excitement that was gathering in strength. She hadn't expected anything like it. Not here, not *now*. Not when she wanted time to re-evaluate her life. She was a woman trying to recover from a recent divorce. Sad things had happened to her, leaving her feeling low, but the advent of Rory Compton into her life had sparked off some sort of revival. Without wanting to, or without planning it, he had somehow brought her back to life. Could it possibly have something to do with the rebound syndrome? She had actually seen it at work with a friend. Women were very vulnerable after the break-up of a relationship. Was she one of them?

Since she had met him she had started to ask herself that very question. She couldn't stop thinking of him though she had willed herself not to. But like all things forbidden he had stuck in her mind. There was just something about the man that had penetrated the miasma of grief she had been battling since the death of her beloved father and the failure of her marriage. She had been certain in her mind she wanted to remain untouchable. At least for a proper period of time. In a sense she was mourning the death of her marriage; the death of a dream.

Rory Compton had changed all that and in a remarkably short space of time. She would do well to see the danger in that. All it had needed was a glance from his remarkable eyes; the peculiar excitement she had felt when he had swept her up into his arms; the way her heart rate had speeded up. He had drawn from her not only a physical, but an emotional response. It wasn't simply his arresting looks. She had really liked the way he had been at the Cunningham's dinner party; his sense of humour, his broad range of interests and the sympathy and sensitivity he had shown towards the politician, a fellow man battling the depression that had fallen on him so unexpectedly.

Rory Compton was formidable, she had concluded. A real presence for a man his age. There was something very purposeful and intent about him and she had to concede a hidden anger, or at the very least brooding. He had actually made her feel like her old self. Correction. More like she was running at full throttle. Was it the adversarial look in those silver frosted eyes? Or the taunting half smile? He was physically very strong. He had lifted her as though she weighed no more than a twelve-year-old. She sensed his physical attraction to her—given that it was quite involuntary—maddened him. Here was a man who liked to be in control.

Holding her in his arms had quite spoilt it for him. The truth was—she couldn't hide it from herself—she had been as aroused as he was. Powerful physical attraction was a daunting thing, especially when it came out of left field. She would do well to be wary of it. Once bitten, twice shy? What did she know of him after all? Her judgement had been way off with Mark. She wasn't about to make a habit of it. She needed to know much more about Rory Compton. It would be better given her background to mistrust rather than trust.

What you're feeling, girl, are hormones. You have to let it pass.

* * *

He was seated on the verandah at the white wicker table. Valerie and Chloe flanked him, both looking surprisingly mellow. Chloe too had gone to some pains, Allegra thought gently. Her apple blossom skin that flushed easily heightened the colour of her eyes and she was wearing a very pretty dress Allegra had brought with her as a present, knowing exactly what would best suit her sister.

Allegra paused for a moment in the open doorway, hoping she had given them enough time alone with their visitor as requested, though requested was too polite a word.

Immediately Rory Compton saw her he sprang to his feet, the man of dark compelling looks she too vividly remembered. A wedge of crow-black hair had fallen forwards on his forehead giving him a very attractive, slightly rakish look. Worn longer than was usual, his glossy, thick textured hair curled up at his nape. It would be great hair to touch. His eyes glittered against his bronze skin. Today his cheekbones looked more pronounced. There wasn't a skerrick of weight on him. His nose was very straight above his beautifully cut mouth. Not generously full lipped like Mark's, but firm and chiselled. He had the sort of face one wouldn't forget in a hurry.

Despite her little pep talks to herself she forgot about betrayal, failure and the tense situation that existed between her and Valerie. She pretended she was considering a particularly sexy man to act as the foil for the beautiful female model in a fashion shoot. No question he would get the job. Two or three inches over six feet, by and large he was moving from lean to nearly thin even in the couple of days since she had last seen him. It startled her to realise it, but something about him caught at her heart. It was a sentiment that in its tenderness took her completely by surprise. This man was eating away at her defences. No wonder she felt a tingle of alarm.

As on the first occasion when they had been introduced, he didn't smile and he had a wonderful smile. She'd seen it directed at Chloe among others. She didn't smile, either, and there was nothing wrong with *her* smile. Instead she inclined her head in acknowledgement of his presence. Both of them matched up in self-protectiveness, she thought. Perversely she wondered as her eyes alighted on his mouth what it would be like to kiss those chiselled lips?

Don't think about it!

She had nothing to hope for with Rory Compton. He was a near stranger It was the wrong time for starting another relationship anyway, though she couldn't help but be aware there was *something* between them.

'Mrs Hamilton!' He inclined his dark head in greeting.

'Please, Allegra.' It came out more coolly than she intended. She planned to drop the Hamilton anyway.

'Well now we'd almost given up on you!' Val announced, as though Allegra was habitually late and consciously rude.

'Why is that, Val?'

Rory held a chair for her. He hadn't been expecting to hear her call her mother by her Christian name, or to mark the swirling undercurrents now they were together. This wasn't one close-knit family, he swiftly intuited. Chloe had no problem with 'Mum.' In fact Chloe was sweetly affectionate towards her mother and her mother clearly doted on her. That wasn't the case, it seemed, with her elder daughter.

'Well you did tell us you had plenty of other things to do,' Chloe started into a deliberate lie. Why did men have to look at Allegra the way they did? It brought out the worst in her.

'Like making coffee or tea?' Allegra looked down on her sister's silky brown head. 'Would you like to come and help me?' *Since when?* When there was a job to be done it had never taken Chloe long to disappear. Born and reared on a working station Chloe had no love of the outdoor life or work of any kind. As a girl she had always wanted to stay at home with Mum who had never encouraged Chloe to pull her weight.

Valerie, as was her practice, jumped in on Chloe's behalf.

'Chloe has opted to take Rory for a drive around the property. But we would like coffee first. Coffee for you, Rory? Or tea if you prefer?' Valerie smiled at this extraordinarily personable young man. Chloe had already told her how strikingly handsome he was. Not to mention those eyes!

Rory, however, turned to Allegra. She was so damned magnetic he decided there and then caution had to determine his every response. 'Coffee's fine,' he said. 'Sure *I* can't help you bring it out?'

Some imp of mischief got into Allegra. 'Thank you so much,' she said gracefully. 'Please come through.' She turned to lead the way, but not before catching the glare in Valerie's eyes.

Under the terms of her father's will his estate had been split three ways, but not in the way any of them had expected. Certainly not Valerie. She and Chloe had each inherited quarter shares; Allegra half, much to Valerie's outrage.

If I want to invite this man into the house I have a perfect right to do so no matter the scowl on Valerie's face, Allegra thought. Her father's will had further alienated her from her family when she had thought their mutual loss would bring them closer together.

Faint hope! She knew Valerie and Chloe believed she had received a handsome divorce settlement from Mark but she had refused to take a penny. How could she do such a thing? The choice to end the marriage had been hers. She wanted nothing of Mark's, even the beautiful jewellery he had given her. She hadn't even opted to take her wedding ring let alone the magnificent solitaire diamond engagement ring. He could save that for her successor.

Rory followed her into the large well equipped kitchen, definitely troubled by the undercurrents. He was surprised Allegra—who looked like she was used to being waited on hand and foot—was the one to organise the morning tea. He really had to stop being so quick with his assumptions Blame it on his unnatural bias.

'Coffee, you said?' She gave him a glance that just stopped short of challenge.

He understood because he felt the same powerful urge to challenge her. He didn't understand exactly why, but he did know everything had changed since he had met her. 'Yes, thank you.' He looked about him. 'You have a very attractive home.'

'It actually needs refurbishing,' she said, setting the percolator on the hot plate. 'Nothing has been touched since my mother redecorated it in the early days of her marriage.'

That meant well over twenty years surely? Chloe had told him that first evening she was twenty-three to Allegra's twenty-seven. She had made twenty-seven sound more like seventy-two. 'She hasn't felt the urge to try her hand again?' he asked. 'I thought women loved rearranging things.'

Allegra sliced into the fruit cake she had made the previous day. 'So we do, but my mother, sadly, is no longer with us. She was killed in a car crash when I was a toddler. I would have been killed, too, only it was one of the rare times I wasn't with her.'

Initially he felt shock, then an explanation for the things that were troubling him. 'I'm very sorry for your loss,' he said with sincerity. 'So Valerie is your stepmother?'

'And Chloe my half sister,' she nodded. 'My father remarried when I was three. A lot of people think Val is my mother because she's always been there.'

He looked at her keenly. 'But she wasn't the mother you wanted?'

She took a few moments to answer. 'You're going to psychoanalyse me?'

'No, just a question.'

'Why would you *say* that?' She wasn't surprised, however, by his perception.

He gave a self-deprecating shrug. 'I'm an authority on mothers that go missing. Mine left home when I was twelve and my brother, Jay, fourteen.'

'And the reason, seeing we're cutting right through the usual preliminaries?'

'She couldn't take it anymore,' he offered bluntly.

'She was having marital problems?' Allegra began to load the trolley.

'You would know about them,' he answered in a low dark voice.

'Indeed I do,' she returned smartly.

'Yes, she was having problems,' he admitted, thinking the very air scintillated around her. 'My father was and remains a very difficult man.'

'You look like you might have a few hang-ups of your own?' She stopped what she was doing and pinned him with her gaze

'Thanks for noticing,' he said suavely.

'Don't feel bad about it. I have them as well. So name one.'

'I don't trust beautiful women.'

Her stomach did a little flip. He could say that yet it was as if he had reached out and kissed her. 'Never in this world?' Somehow she managed a smile.

'No.' Slowly he shook his head, not breaking the eye contact.

'Wow!' The expression on her face was both satirical and amused. 'We're going to have lots to talk about. I don't trust handsome men.'

'I understood your ex-husband adored you?' Now that was definitely a challenge.

'We had different ideas about what being 'adored' meant. I think you actually *did* adore your mother?'

His eyes turned as turbulent as a stormy sea. 'We both did. Jay and I. Seen from our point of view her leaving was an abandonment.'

'But you see her now?' she asked, fully expecting the answer to be yes.

He picked up three lemons and juggled them in his sure

hands. 'Not for many years,' he said and returned the lemons to the bowl. 'Close on fifteen.'

'Good grief!' She didn't hide her surprise. 'So you haven't seen her since you were a boy?' She wondered how that could have been allowed to happen.

He held aloof. 'That's right, Mrs Hamilton.' He focused on watching her move around the kitchen. She was very efficient in her movements. In fact she was perfectly at home in a kitchen when he had been too ready to think she was the quintessential hothouse flower who lay about gracefully while someone else did the work.

'Allegra,' she corrected, speaking sharply because he was unnerving her and he knew it. 'Sorry, I don't care for Mrs Hamilton,' she said more calmly. 'You don't feel motivated to find her?'

He didn't hesitate. 'No. But I know where she is.'

She had to suck air into her lungs. 'You make it sound like the outer reaches of the galaxy.'

'Might as well be.' Rory had to steady himself, too, unwilling for her to see just how much the old trauma still hurt. 'It's a long, hard road back from betrayal, *Allegra*.' He placed mocking emphasis on her name.

She studied his handsome, brooding face for a moment. 'Isn't it strange how we punish the ones we love? You're absolutely sure you know the reason? She must have been desperately unhappy?'

He took so long to answer she thought he was going to ignore her question. 'That's there under the abandonment,' he conceded. 'I guess she was unhappy. For a *while* at least.' He put a mocking hand to his heart, his luminous eyes dangerously bright. 'She remarried a couple of years later.'

'Life goes on.' She shrugged. 'So did my dad, but he never forgot my mother. One of the reasons he remarried so soon was that he needed a wife to look after me.'

And what a beautiful child she must have been! Rory let his

gaze rest on her, aware his fingers were curled tight into his palms as though he might make some involuntary move towards her. A woman like that any man could lose his senses. But to let himself fall in love with her would be one hell of an ill fated idea. She had wonderful skin, wonderful colouring. He allowed his eyes, at least, to barely skim the low neckline of her top. It dipped as she moved, revealing the satin-smooth upper curves of her breasts. The blue of that clingy little top was the same colour as her eyes. Of course she knew that. She wore her mane of garnet hair in a classic knot. And it *was* natural. Abandoning indifference if only for a moment he had asked Chloe. Chloe said the only nice thing she had said about her sister all night. 'Yes, isn't it beautiful! Hair that colour is rare!'

The sheer power of a beautiful woman!. A lover of beauty in all its forms, Rory felt himself drenched in heat. He had to realise he was achingly vulnerable to this particular woman. A woman like that could take a lot off a man without giving a thing back.

Belatedly he picked up the conversation. 'And that woman was Valerie?'

'Yes.' Allegra for her part, didn't fully understand why this man moved her like he did. It was as though she could see through the layers of defences accumulated through the years, to when he was a handsome, daring little boy. A little boy who had the capacity to be badly hurt.

'A lot of expectations were put on her,' he said.

'Absolutely!' Her answer was faintly bitter in response to the irony of his tone.

'It can't be an easy job trying to raise another woman's child?' He looked at her, lifting a black brow.

'No one suggested it was,' she said bluntly.

'Okay, I'll back off.'

'Do.' She was frosty in her tone. 'To get off the subject, I might as well tell you I've read up on Compton Holdings. I'll ask a few questions of my own now, if I may? Why did you leave? Surely with a huge enterprise and a flagship station like Turrawin there was more than enough room and work for two brothers? Or a dozen brothers for that matter.'

His expression hardened. 'For most people there would be, but you haven't met my father. My father is a very controlling sort of man and I'm long past marching to his drumbeat. I needed to strike out on my own.'

'Then you have the money to buy here?' She resorted to a brisk business-like tone.

'Always supposing I'm interested.' His eyes mocked her. 'I haven't seen over the place yet.'

'You wouldn't be here if you thought it a waste of time, but I warn you I'm no push-over, Rory Compton.'

'Excuse me, *you* inherited?' He leaned back nonchalantly against a cabinet and folded his arms.

What a combination of male graces he had, such an elegance of movement. 'I'm the major shareholder,' she informed him coolly, aware of something else. He offered torment as well as poignancy.

'That's unusual?'

'Well *you'd* know all about that.' She came back spiritedly.

'Touché!' Unexpectedly he gave her his rare smile. It was so heartbreaking it was just as well it came and went fairly rarely. 'I think we got off on the wrong foot, Allegra.'

She wanted to remain as cool as a cucumber but the way he said her name tugged at her heart. Perversely it reminded her of the need for caution. How could her interest in a man re-awaken so quickly after her divorce? The answer? This man was too compelling. 'That happens when people are wary of one another, ' she said.

'*Are* we?' he asked , feigning a wondering voice. Neither of them could deny there was a strong current running between them.

'Isn't that the word you would use?' She kept her eyes on him. No struggle at all.

'As I say, it pays to be wary around a beautiful woman.' Impatiently he slicked that troublesome stray lock back. 'Did I mention I find you beautiful?' Well, she knew that for a fact. No harm in getting it out into the open.

'That worries you?' Her blue eyes checked on his expression.

'Terribly.' He smiled.

The really extraordinary thing was she smiled back. 'Whatever looks I have they haven't done me much good,' she said wryly.

'But I understood from Chloe you're a fashion editor on a magazine? If they wanted someone to look the part you had to be it.'

'Why thank you, Rory.'

He smiled. 'If I know anything about women, it's they like to be complimented now and then.'

'True. Okay, my looks were important there,' she conceded. 'But I wanted a happy marriage far more than a successful career. I wanted children. I wanted family. I wanted years and years and years of watching my kids grow up. I wanted grandchildren. I wanted my husband and myself to grow old together, still in love.'

He gave her a searching look. 'A lot of wants, Allegra. You didn't try for a family?' God a man would so want a child with her.

There was pain in her expression. 'You don't know when to quit do you? That's a very personal question.'

'Maybe, but I'm in pursuit of truth here. It so happens, I'm looking for a wife.'

Her heart did a somersault in her breast. 'Is that your next career move?' Somehow she gave the question an edge of sarcasm.

'Sure is. Total commitment,' he confirmed.

'Don't dare look at *me*.' She issued the warning with a little laugh. 'I won't be thinking of marriage for a long, long time.'

'Afraid?'

'You bet!' she answered swiftly. 'I made one mistake. I'm

sure you'll appreciate I'll be very cautious about making another. To be honest, Rory, I didn't see *your* offer coming.' She gave him a sparkling glance.

'I didn't make one, did I? Hell, I'm as cautious as you, Allegra. But I have to tell you, you impress me.' He made a mock study of her as though she were a possible candidate. 'You're a highly desirable woman in any man's language, but there's that wary bit we both share.'

'Maybe you'd be more in tune with Chloe?' she suggested. 'And here I was thinking you were simply looking to buy a property?'

'But I am,' he assured her. 'It was you who introduced the subject telling me you wanted children. I feel the same way I want a wife and family. It's predictable I suppose. I never really had one.'

'So what's wrong with advertising?' she suggested helpfully.

'Nothing whatsoever,' he said. 'We guys live in such isolation it's not easy to find partners.'

'I understand that,' she said, 'having been reared on the land. I have a feeling, though, if you do advertise you'll be inundated with answers.'

'I'm counting on it. In the meantime, there's *you!*' He flickered a silver glance at her.

It was pathetic, but thrills ran down her spine. 'It's like I told you, Rory Compton. Count me out!'

His handsome face was openly mocking. 'I know better than to argue.'

'That's a relief.' She felt a flush over her whole body.

Footsteps echoed in the hallway. In the next minute Chloe bustled in, eyes wide as she tried to gauge the atmosphere. From the look that came over her face she could have suspected amazing sex on the kitchen table. 'What in the world are you doing?' she asked, transferring her glance from one to the other.

'My fault,' Rory said, and flashed Allegra a smile.

Chloe's cheeks smarted. 'I just thought you might need some help?'

'We're fine thanks, Chloe,' Allegra said pleasantly. 'You can play Mother and wheel the trolley out if you like.'

Forty minutes later Rory was sitting in the passenger seat of the station Jeep with Chloe at the wheel. So far he could see work around Naroom had all but come to a stop. Why wouldn't it without an overseer to run it? Whatever had persuaded Mrs Sanders to sack her late husband's right hand man? It didn't make sense unless that was confirmation she had no intention of remaining on the land. Even then it was counter productive to allow the property to decline. He had seen around the homestead and liked it. It was spacious, comfortable, attractive. The outbuildings for the most part were in good condition. Now he asked Chloe to stop while he spoke to one of the stockmen who was driving a small mob of healthy looking beasts towards the creek.

'We'd be mighty pleased if a good man could buy the place,' the stockman confided within minutes of Rory's calling out to him. He was only too ready to talk and hopefully hold on to his job. 'Things have gone from bad to worse since the Boss died and Jack left. Jack Nelson was the overseer here for the past ten years with no complaints from the Boss, but Jack and the Missus couldn't see eye to eye. Or even half an eye come to that. She never wanted to spend any money maintaining the place. It was a real battle trying to get any money out of her for anything, even paying the vet. Jack reckoned she was only waiting for a buyer so she could sell up. The only one who loves the place is Miss Allegra. Miss Chloe now—I can see her back there in the Jeep—you want to strap yourself in—she won't do no rough work. Not much of a rider, either, which is pretty funny when to see Miss Allegra in the saddle does a man's heart good. She can handle most of the jobs on the station, too. Her dad taught her. Chloe, now, always liked to spend her time indoors with her mum. Both of them are bone lazy if you ask me. Hell, don't tell her that. I could lose my job.' He shut up abruptly.

Back in the Jeep Rory would have liked to suggest he take over the driving but didn't want to hurt Chloe's feelings. She didn't so much steer as wrestle with the wheel. One of her little foibles was hitting as many pot holes and partially submerged rocks as she could, sniffing them out like a heat-seeking missile. It was almost as if it were her bounden duty. Then she groaned aloud as the vehicle reacted with a stomach churning kangarooing. Excuses ranged from, 'Whoops, didn't see that!' to 'That wasn't there last time!' Maintenance on the Jeep would run heavily to shock absorbers he reckoned.

'What did Gallagher have to say?' she asked when they resumed their seats after another bout of catapulting.

Rory thought it better not to pass on Gallagher's indiscretions. 'Nothing much. Just saying hello.'

'It's a wonder Mum didn't sack him along with Jack Nelson,' Chloe muttered, incredibly clipping a branch of a tree.

'Why's that?' Rory wondered how Chloe could possibly drive in a city or even a small town without hitting everything in her path. He even began to wonder if she'd had any proper driving lessons or simply got behind the wheel one day without bothering about lessons or a licence. He recalled he and Jay could drive around the station from a very early age.

'Cheeky bugger! Not respectful enough to Mum or me.' Chloe bridled.

'Who, Nelson or Gallagher?' Both that voice in his head said.

'Both,' Chloe confirmed, her pretty mouth tightening. 'It would be wonderful if you really liked the place, Rory. No one ever thought Dad would die so young. Mum and I are lost without him. Running a station needs a man. Dad needed a son. Instead he got Allegra and me,' she said wryly. 'I stayed. I was the loyal one. Allegra cleared off as soon as she could.'

'Oh, yes, when was this?' He tried not to sound too interested when he found himself avid for information.

'She insisted on going to university while I had to stay at home. Mum needed me. It's so lonely out here a girl could go ape. Afterwards Allegra landed a magazine job. We all know why. She's the perfect clothes horse and she *does* have good taste although it took a few years before she got the big promotion.'

'Was this before or after she married?' Rory asked, intrigued Allegra might have kept working when she had married a rich man.

'The promotion?' She took such a lengthy look at him, Rory was forced to put a steadying hand on the wheel.

'Yes.'

Chloe placed her hand gently over his and took a while to take it off. 'She was fashion editor when she met Mark. She could easily have quit her job and devoted herself to being a good wife to Mark, but she didn't. I think a man deserves that, don't you? He's *such* a lovely man, too, and she *dumped* him. I ask you! Dump the love of your life?'

'Obviously he wasn't,' Rory suggested, not trying all that hard to dull the sarcasm.

'Seems not,' Chloe sighed and headed into a clump of brambles. 'Mum and I really took to him. He's so handsome and clever *and* rich and he worshipped her. It's a bit weird isn't it the way men worship beautiful women? I mean beauty's only a tiny fraction of what a real woman is all about. I tell you when she left him Mum and I were gobsmacked. We even thought he might top himself.'

'Surely not!' Rory groaned before he could help himself. 'Your father liked him, too?' He wanted some perspective on the worshipping husband. Not that he exactly blamed him, tiny fraction or not.

Pretty Chloe scowled darkly. 'Oh, as far as Dad was concerned no one was good enough for Allegra!' she said, her voice betraying her intense jealousy. 'You've no idea what it was like for me when we were growing up. Allegra always wanting the attention and getting it from Dad. Allegra could be an absolute *pig*!' She paused a moment to cool down. She didn't want Rory getting the wrong idea about her. 'We're half sisters, you know.'

'Allegra did tell me,.' Rory admitted, surprised they were any relation at all.

'She would. No matter how much Mum and I tried she would never let us love her and Mum's the sweetest woman who ever drew breath.'

Rory fought a wry smile.

'I hesitate to say this,' Chloe continued with some relish, 'in fact it hurts me, but it might help you understand. My beautiful sister is pretty shallow. I don't think there's a man alive who could make her happy.' To reinforce her opinion Chloe hit the steering wheel with her open palm.

Sibling rivalry could be absolutely deadly Rory thought. Potentially so could Chloe's driving. 'That's your opinion, Chloe, is it? And what about you?' Rory kept his eyes glued ahead for more likely obstacles. If he'd only known what going for a drive with Chloe held in store! 'What are your plans if and when the station is sold?'

Chloe swung her head to beam at him. A woman just waiting to be hit by Cupid's arrow. 'I'm going to find myself a man,' she confessed with a dimpled grin. 'I'm going to have a Big White Wedding I'll always remember. And I won't have Allegra for my damned bridesmaid,' she tacked on wrathfully, heading towards a solitary gum tree like it was a designated pit stop. 'You can be sure of that!'.

Rory gently nudged the wheel. 'Obviously a sore point?' The reason wasn't lost on him.

'Well, I won't want her upstaging me on the best day of my life.' Inexplicably she braked hard as if they were coming to a set of traffic lights mysteriously erected in the bush. 'Can you blame me?' Satisfied about whatever it was—he didn't have a clue—she picked up speed again. 'I won't even let her meet my husband until after we're married just to be on the safe side. I won't be like her, either. Sadly she could only stay married five minutes. Marriage is forever, Rory, don't you think?'

He must have lost a layer of skin. Either that or it was the way Chloe was affecting him. 'Absolutely,' he said, 'or I'd want my money back.'

They insisted he stay for a late lunch again prepared and served by Allegra who, as far as Rory could see, could get a job at a top restaurant.

'Great meal, Allegra,' he complimented her. In fact it was the best meal he'd had for quite a while, outside dinner with the Cunninghams.

Chloe blushed fiercely. 'It's only a chicken dish,' she pointed out with a flick of the head, though she had not only overloaded her plate she had scoffed the lot.

'The secret's in the spices,' Allegra told him, ignoring her sister, instead of giving her the thump on the back of the head she deserved. 'I'd be glad to give you the recipe to hand on.'

'Perfect,' he said.

'Hand on ? Who to?' Chloe looked baffled, staring from one to the other in an effort to get them to divulge the secret.

'Rory is compiling a cookbook to hand over to his future wife,' Allegra said.

'Good heavens! Are you really?' Chloe looked fascinated by such a thing. After all she had a glory box.

'I hadn't been thinking of it,' Rory confessed. 'Now I'm convinced I should do it.'

'Anyone special in your life, Rory?' Valerie asked, irritated beyond measure by the constant exchanges between their visitor and Allegra and trying none too successfully not to show it.

He shook his head. 'No, not really, Mrs. Sanders.' He gave her an easy smile.

'What's wrong with all the girls then?' Valerie favoured him with a girlish one of her own. 'I would have thought you'd be fighting them off?'

Chloe, mouth slightly open, looked like she felt exactly the same way.

'A man doesn't get to meet too many where I come from,' Rory explained. 'The desert is about as remote as one can get.'

'Well then I'm sure you'll do better here,' Valerie said with great satisfaction, aiming a fond glance in her daughter's direction.

Rory vowed there and then not to give Chloe the slightest encouragement.

He took his leave of them thirty minutes later saying he'd have to think things over before getting back to them.

'Naturally' Valerie smiled and touched him gently on the arm. 'We have to put our heads together, too.'

'Walk out to the car with me.' Rory managed to get off a quick aside to Allegra as Valerie wheeled about to have a word—never mind what it was—with her daughter.

'Very well.' Allegra led the way down the front steps, fully expecting Chloe to seize the moment and race after them. All right, Chloe didn't normally race, but there was always the first time. She had obviously taken a shine to Rory. Even Valerie had broken out into sunny smiles. One had to be a good looking young man to get one.

Strangely Chloe didn't come after them. There was only one explanation. It was too hot. 'So do you want to tell me your thoughts now?' she asked as Rory fell in alongside her. She really liked the way she had to look up to him. In her high heels she and Mark had been fairly level.

'Your stepmother made a huge tactical error sacking your overseer,' he commented in a crisp voice.

'Tell me something I don't know,' she sighed. 'Jack got on with everybody.' Except Valerie.

'Obviously he found it pretty hard going with your stepmother.'

Not wanting to criticise Valerie, Allegra said nothing.

'Surely you have a big stake in seeing the place is run properly?' Rory prompted, looking down at her flaming head. For some reason—again beyond him—he felt he could talk to her like he'd known her for ever. She was tall for a woman, around five-eight but to him she *felt* small. Indeed he'd had extreme difficulty keeping the *feel* of her out of his dreams. But there was no way he could volunteer that.

'That's why I'm here.' She showed a little flash of temper. 'Losing Dad was a great blow for all of us. Dad was the one who held us all together. With him gone I'm very much afraid I'll be minus what family I have left. Val and I never did get on.'

'Actually I can understand that,' he said laconically.

When Val had been on her best behaviour, Allegra thought. He should come on them unexpectedly. 'The thing is I was fatally blemished in my stepmother's eyes because I resemble my mother. Val suffered from the second wife syndrome. It's a very hurtful and wounding situation.'

Rory nodded. 'Skewed by the dagger of jealousy! Have you all come to some agreement on an asking price?'

'Not as yet,' she said.

'You *are* going to be able to work it out, right?' he asked dryly.

'Don't worry, we will. I take it you feel you can do something with the place?'

'Not feel, *know*,' he said, sounding utterly confident.

'Ah, the arrogance of achievement!' she said. 'Word is *you* ran your family station?'

'Jay and I.' He put her straight. 'I love my brother.'

'But he's not the cattleman in the family?'

'Would you believe he wanted to be a doctor?'

She picked up on the sadness, the regret. 'So, what stopped him? What finer calling could there be?'

'He's my father's heir, Allegra,' he pointed out. 'That says it all.'

'Okay. I understand. And I don't.' For total strangers they had moved quickly to a very real communication, no matter how edgy. 'It seems to me Jay should have fought for his dream, instead of letting it die a slow death.'

'Only life has a way of falling short of our dreams,' he said, ever sensitive to any criticism of his brother. 'So what decided you to scuttle *your* dream?' he questioned, combining a real desire to know with that little flash of sexual hostility.

'Scuttle is entirely the wrong word.' She gave him her own admonishing glance. 'I wanted to *cure* the situation. My dream was to find harmony and fulfilment. I thought I had a fighting chance with Mark but it blew up in my face like Krakatoa.'

'So you took the only course open to you. You bolted?' He was determined to know.

'What does anyone do when they find out they've made a big mistake,' she asked, very soberly. 'Now I've got to get my life back on track. Incidentally I'm stunned I'm talking like this to a near stranger.'

'It *is* a bit eerie,' he agreed. 'I'm not always like this with strange women, either. Then again we can think of it as pouring out a life story to the person sitting next to us on a plane.'

She laughed. 'I assure you I've never done it. There's too much to you, Rory Compton. Darkness, Lightness. Now I think back, I realise I was running away. I love Naroom. I love station life. After all it's what I was bred to. Yet I was impelled to change my life. It wasn't the best reason to marry.'

'You obviously weren't prepared to stick it out for the next forty years.'

It was said in a voice that so infuriated her, she wanted to slap him. 'It strikes me that's none of your business.'

'True. It's just that I'm dying to know. How long was it again?'

'I repeat. None of your business, Compton,' she returned coolly. 'You don't approve of what I did, do you?' She came to a standstill staring up into his dynamic face.

He almost reached out to tuck a stray lock of her hair behind her ear. 'I don't approve of divorce in general, Allegra, being a child of divorce. Not unless there's a very good and pressing reason. Which you may well have. Forgive me for not minding my own business.'

'You know what they say. Curiosity killed the cat.'

'Curiosity isn't the right word. It implies a passing interest. I aspire to seeing more of you, Miss Allegra. For better or worse, we seem to have bonded. I haven't as yet figured out why. There's one thing jumps to mind. Your cooking. A woman's ability to put out a good meal finds high favour with most men. Other things about you, however, could scare me.'

She acknowledged the mocking glitter in his eyes with a tight smile. 'It's hard to believe any woman could scare you. By the way, it amazes me—I'm not a short woman—but just looking up at you makes me feel dizzy.'

Hell, he felt dizzy just looking down at her. 'Would you believe you appear *small* to me?'

'Then I'll definitely stick to high heels,' she said.

He had a sudden vision of her walking up the Cunningham's staircase, with him admiring her legs. 'When you get to know me you'll realise I am scarable,' he said with a grin. 'Is that a word?'

'They let in new words every day.' They walked on. 'I know you worry about your brother. I know you're desperately unhappy beneath the dark Byronic façade.'

'Please.' So self-assured, he looked embarrassed.

She decided being able to embarrass him pleased her. 'Okay,' she scoffed. 'So there's too much romance about Byron for you. Do you know I actually cooked that special lunch for you today because you've lost weight even since we met.'

'Well fancy!' He gasped in mock surprise. 'You mean you've been studying me with those amazing blue eyes?'

'I figure if *you* can look, so can I,' she answered crisply. 'Why did you want me to walk with you? Any particular reason?'

'I'm certain you walk a lot faster than Chloe,' was his flippant response. 'Why? Did you have something better to do? Like spend more time with your stepmother and sister?'

'Your family's not everything it should be.' She struck back.

'Indeed it's not,' he agreed with a rasp in his voice. 'When you think about it, Allegra, the two of us have lived through a lot of stuff. Though I've never had the unfortunate experience of being burned by a bad marriage.'

'What about singed by a love affair that went wrong?' she asked with feigned sweetness.

He only smiled. 'Not yet.'

'Don't lay money on it not happening,' she said. 'Falling in love is a dangerous business.'

'And your love for your ex-husband wasn't unconditional?'

'You're making me angry, Rory,' she said. In fact he was making her heart pound.

'And I don't blame you. I apologise. You raise my blood pressure, too.'

They had reached his Toyota, now Rory opened the driver's door.

'Don't count on getting this place cheap, either,' she warned, conscious her body was throbbing in the oddest way.

'Then I'll blame you for pushing up the price.' He turned to fully face her.

They were so close, on a panicked reflex, Allegra stepped back, her heart almost leaping into her throat. It was her turn for embarrassment to wash over her.

'So long, Allegra,' he said, his eyes holding a wealth of mockery. He sketched a brief salute. 'I'll get back to you in a day or two.'

'You've made up your mind now,' She slammed his door shut, beating him to it.

He studied her through the open window. The sun was turning her glowing head to fire. 'Be sure of it,' he said.

CHAPTER FOUR

Jay paused for a minute to catch his breath. His arms were aching from thrashing through the lignum swamp. His khaki bush shirt was soaked with sweat, his jeans soaked with a green slime and swamp water up to the knees. He and a couple of the men had been hunting up a massive wild boar as big as a calf that kept threatening the herd. They had chased it into the deepest reaches of the swamp where a man on his own would find it very easy to get lost. The swamp was home to countless water birds and pelicans, but was spell-bound to the aborigines who shivering in fear, refused to go into it. Jay didn't altogether blame them. An unearthly yellow glow emanated from the place, seeping into the air. Rory, of course, afraid of nothing always said it was a sulphur spring. Whatever the eerie glow was, it was almost impossible to get into the swamp's deepest recesses without a machete. A good enough reason for the boar to make its home in the dense thickets, out of the path of danger where it could wallow to its heart's content in the mud.

It had made one last stand, its ugly head lowered for a final charge. It glared at them with its little reddened eyes, a ferocious looking animal, its coarse black bristles caked in mud and slime. Two powerful yellowish tusks protruded from its lower jaw, curving upwards in half circles. Sharp tusks that could easily disembowel a man or gore him to death. Spear carrying aborigines on the plain, would have charged the beast and killed it, a manoeuvre so dangerous it made Jay shudder just to think of it, though he knew boar hunting had been considered an exciting sport for hundreds of years. Jay got off a single clean shot to the boar's heart. Its bulk quivered for a moment on its short powerful legs, then it rolled over with a loud squelching sound into the foul smelling mud.

That exploit had taken them far afield and it was a long ride back before Jay reached the home compound.

He had truly believed he fully appreciated just how much hard yakka Rory put in, day in and day out—how much responsibility he assumed without saying a word. Rory had a natural affinity with animals; all sorts of animals from the wildest rogue brumby hell-bent on freedom to the most docile calf. Rory wouldn't have spent the best part of the afternoon tracking down that boar. He could read the signs as clearly as any aboriginal. Rory had only been gone a month and already he was sorely missed by all.

Jay missed him terribly. First as a brother and his best friend: then as a buffer between him and their father and thirdly as the cattleman, the Boss-man, who ran Turrawin. Rory was the Compton every last station employee deferred to and took orders from without complaint. Rory was a natural born leader. Such men didn't come along every day. Their father, Bernard, Jay had long since recognised, had little going for him these days but bluster and a whiplash tongue. With Rory gone there was animosity where there had never been before. Not only that, it was on the rise among the station staff. Not towards *him* personally—he got on well enough with everyone—but the whole situation. Not content with ordering Rory off the station, their father had let it be known Rory wasn't coming back. Further more Rory had been disinherited.

What that had achieved was nigh on catastrophic. It had

bonded everyone against his father. While the men had greatly admired and respected Rory, working happily in the saddle for him from dawn to dusk, they were becoming discontented and occasionally rebellious under him. Okay they liked him—they even felt sorry for him having the father he did—but they didn't look to him as the boss.

He wasn't a cattleman, though God knows he'd struggled to become one. The trouble was his heart wasn't in it and he wasn't half tough enough. He wasn't much good at giving orders, either, or even knowing what best to do in difficult situations when Rory, the man of action, had always come up with a solution right off the top of his head. Jay's only gift was fixing things, especially machinery. Rory had constantly reassured him that was a considerable gift. He could take any piece of faulty station machinery apart and put it together again in fine working order. Just like he had once longed to put the damaged human body back together.

He was thirty years of age, two years Rory's senior, but he still longed for the beautiful woman who had been his mother. She had understood him but she had never been strong enough to withstand their father. She was scared of him the same way Jay had been scared of him. The only one who wasn't scared was Rory. But even Rory had been known to flinch away from their father's vicious tongue.

Now that Rory was gone their father took it out on him.

He returned to the homestead at dusk, cursing the fact, as he did every day, his father was such a severe man who these days possessed not even a chink of lightness of soul. Bernard Compton had become damned impossible. When Jay entered the kitchen through the back door prior to taking a shower in the adjacent mudroom, he found his father slouched over the huge pine table, a whiskey bottle near his hand. Jay never remembered his father drinking so much but these past weeks he'd been getting into it as if alcohol took his mind off his troubles and what was already going wrong on the station. It was his grandfather and the Compton men before him to whom they owed the success of Turrawin. Then Rory. The necessary skills and attributes had skipped a generation. Oddly enough, his father, like him, was excellent with machinery but he took little pride in Jay's inherited ability. In fact he went out of his way to deride it.

'That's all you're bloody good for, son. Tinkering about!'

His tinkering had saved the station a lot of money.

Bernard Compton looked up as Jay entered the room. There was no welcoming smile on his heavy handsome face but a scowl. His once brilliant dark eyes were badly bloodshot. 'There's a couple of postcards from your brother,' he said, taking a gulp of his drink.

'You've read them?' Jay moved towards the table, feeling a rush of pleasure and relief at hearing from Rory again.

'Why not? They're bloody postcards aren't they?'

'They're addressed to me,' Jay pointed out quietly, picking them up. 'You shouldn't have sent Rory away, Dad. We can't do without him.'

'I'm not asking him to come back, if that's what you think.' Bernard Compton's face was set grimly. 'I don't get down on my knees to anyone least of all my own son. No respect, Rory. No respect at all. Looking at me with his mother's eyes.'

'Mum's beautiful eyes,' Jay said, his glance devouring what was written on the two postcards, each from different Outback towns. 'He's at a place called Jimboorie. Or he was.'

'I can read,' Bernard said roughly, staring up at his son. Jay was a handsome big fellow, strong and clever, but for God knows what reason glaringly inadequate when it came to running the station. 'So what do you want me to do about it?'

'Beg Rory to come home, Dad,' Jay answered promptly. 'The men look to Rory, not me.' *Not to you, either,* hung heavily in the air.

'He made his bed now he's got to lie in it,' Bernard Compton said. 'What we need is an overseer given you're so hopeless.'

'You're not much better,' Jay retorted, almost beyond caring what his father thought. 'Why didn't I have the guts to do what I always wanted to do?'

'Become a doctor?' Bernard snorted, and threw back the whiskey.

'I'd have been a good doctor,' Jay said in his quiet way. 'It's in my genes. I should have pushed for it.'

His father hooted. 'You've never pushed for anything in your life.'

Not with a father I hated and feared. 'Maybe there's still time to make plans,' Jay said. 'Rory told me there was.'

'That's because *he* wants Turrawin.' His father told him with a savage laugh. 'There's no end to your gullibility, son. Rory wants Turrawin,' Bernard repeated.

'Well, I don't want it, Dad,' Jay replied, his unhappiness growing more unbearable every day.

'Why, you gutless wonder! I'm ashamed of you, Jay,' Bernard Compton thundered, striking the table with his large fist.

'Do you think I don't know that?' Jay asked in a weary voice. 'You've bludgeoned me over the head with it for years, Dad. But my inadequacies are modest compared to yours. All you're good for is letting loose with the venom.'

'Why you—!' Bernard Compton, his face flushed a dark red, started to rise, but Jay, a powerful young man, shoved him back down on his chair. 'When I was a kid I used to find you very frightening. Mum did, too. But no more. I pity you from the bottom of my heart. You're a hollow man. Rory should have Turrawin. I'm the one who has to give up on this life I was never meant to lead.'

'What are you saying?' Bernard Compton's bloodshot eyes were filled with shock and disbelief.

'You heard me. Rory should have Turrawin otherwise this historic station will go steadily downhill. Only Rory can save it.'

'Over my dead body,' Bernard Compton exploded, glaring at his son.

'Why do you hate him so much?' Jay marvelled. 'He's your son, isn't he? Is there some bloody thing we don't know? Is that why Mum left? What's the goddamn mystery?'

Bernard Compton gave an awful grunt, clutching the whiskey bottle and pouring himself another double shot. 'Of course Rory is my son, you idiot. And I don't hate him. I bloody well admire him like I admired my old man. But there has to be a lot of space between us. I don't want him on my territory.'

'You're afraid of him aren't you? He's everything you wanted to be. Grandad loved him so much. He loved *me*, but I always knew Rory was the favourite.'

'That old bastard!' Bernard swore blearily. 'He certainly didn't love me. He always made me feel a fool.'

'Then I'm sorry, but it was never his intention. Grandad was a really good man. I'll stay with you, Dad, until we get a competent overseer in place. I thought we could bring Ted Warren in from Mariji. He's more competent than I am to handle things. Then I'm going to get a new life. Up until now I've always had the weird feeling I'm on hold with nothing to hope for. That has to change. But first, I'm going to find my brother.'

Allegra stood on the front verandah watching life giving rain pour down over the burdened eaves in silver curtains so heavy it was impossible to see out into the home gardens. It was well over a week now since Rory Compton had made the two-hour journey from Jimboorie township to Narooma with his offer; an offer Valerie and Chloe had near jumped at. She on the other hand had made it abundantly clear it wasn't enough, although she pretty well believed him when he said it was the best he could do. He didn't seem the man to try to beat them down. Clay Cunningham didn't think so, either. She'd already had a conversation with Clay, a man she trusted, who had revealed a little more about Rory Compton's situation. It was true his brother,

Jay was to inherit historic Turrawin. True by all accounts—word in the far flung Outback flew around with astonishing speed—Bernard Compton had disinherited his younger son.

Rory Compton was no longer part of a wealthy family of pioneering cattle barons. Times for Rory had changed. He was out on his own albeit with the wherewithal to purchase a small-ish run. Nothing that could possibly match what he had come from, but a property a man with his talents could build on and make prosper. Allegra was sure of it.

Rory Compton was a man of substance at twenty-eight. No great age. Her father would have judged him square in the mould of builder-expander. A man who exuded all the drive, ambition, know-how and ideas to turn middle of the road Naroom into a financial success. After that, she supposed, he would move on to bigger and better things. His offer had been basically, their reserve $3.5 million. She was sticking out for $4 million knowing despite depreciation and a big drop in stock numbers, Naroom was worth that. Or were her emotions too heavily in-volved? Naroom was her *home*.

The magic of the place! Yet she seemed to be the only one now her dad was gone to feel it. Anyway as far as borrowing went Rory Compton still had his name. A name to be reckoned with. His bank had approved his loan in what seemed to her record time. Her gut feeling was the bank could go $500,000 more.

No surprises a huge family fight had developed. Her on one side: Valerie and Chloe on the other. If she had ever thought and hoped there was some love between her and her half-sister she soon found out when the chips were down, there wasn't. Even thinking about the things Valerie and Chloe had said to her brought the sting of tears to her eyes. At one point she even thought Valerie would come at her in a rush of physical rage. Valerie was not to be thwarted. She wanted out like a wild horse wanted its freedom. And don't for the love of God get in the way. Whatever Valerie wanted, so did Chloe. The gang of two.

It wasn't as though she had been adamant with a no. Their combined clout equalled hers. All she wanted was a better offer. Or the opportunity at least to see if he could come up with a better offer? Surely that was reasonable? She was doing this for her dad, not for herself. His memory. Yet Valerie and Chloe had branded her with every unjust name they could think of.

'I'll tell you straight! I despise you for being so selfish!' Valerie had raged. 'Why did you come back here? We didn't want you.'

It doesn't take a lot of words to tear a heart out. What point in saying she had a perfect right to come back. Naroom was as much her home as theirs. More. But they obviously thought her marriage, however short, and their long tenancy downgraded her rights.

The following morning they left in a great flurry, catching a charter flight to Brisbane.

'I'm going to make it my business to consult with a top lawyer regarding *my* rights,' Valerie announced a half an hour before their departure. 'I was Llew's wife! Surely to God I had the stronger claim? But no, I finished up with a mere quarter of everything.'

'A quarter of the estate amounts to quite a lot, Val.' Allegra tried to get a word in edgeways.

But Valerie wasn't prepared to listen. 'I'm going to see about contesting the will. It's an outrage your share was double mine. Anyone would side with me on that one. The *wife* should be the main beneficiary. I know you worked on your father. You kept at him and at him until he saw things your way.'

A wave of futility crested then crashed on Allegra. For her and Valerie to reconcile was unimaginable. 'That is patently untrue, Valerie. For your information Dad and I never ever discussed his will.'

'And who would believe you?' Valerie countered, her eyes flashing anger and disbelief. 'Anyway I can't stand around arguing with you. We have a plane to catch.'

'Good but before you go I want you to know I have no intention of holding up a sale if that's what you want. All I'm seeking is the best possible price we can get.'

'Just see you stick to that!' Valerie responded, her voice charged with venom.

There was, alas, little hope what was left of family could survive. Her father gone Allegra felt she was well and truly on her own.

By late morning the rain had ceased and the sun came out in all its glory, dispersing the clouds. Allegra took the opportunity of saddling up Cezar, her father's big handsome bay, and riding out to check on the herd. After one torrential downpour the creek that had been low for so long had risen a good metre, the surging brown water frothed with white. It coursed between its green banks, spewing up spray wherever it encountered boulders and rocks. She had already given the order to move the stock in case there were further downpours, which was a strong possibility. It was the monsoon season in the tropical North. Anything was possible; deep troughs, cyclones. The cattle were now grazing all over the flats on either side of the creek. They all knew what flash floods were like. They had all seen dead bloated cattle with terror carved into their faces. It was not a sight one forgot.

When she was satisfied everything was moving according to plan she rode back to the homestead, rejoicing in a world the rain had washed clean. She loved the air after the rain. She loved riding beneath the trees getting showered with water from the dripping branches. Everything about her, body and spirit, rejoiced in the great outdoors. For sure she had made a name for herself working as a fashion editor. She knew she was very good at her job. She had natural flair but she had always known where her heart was. It was the *land* that made her happy.

She was approaching the house when she saw with a flare of excitement as big as a bonfire: Rory Compton's Land Cruiser parked in the driveway. A moment later she saw his tall rangy figure walk down the front steps, making for his vehicle. Finding no one at home he was obviously leaving. That couldn't be allowed to happen. This man was too much on her mind.

Allegra urged the bay into a gallop.

He saw her coming. The bay she was riding was too big and most likely too strong for most women but she was handling it beautifully. She was wearing a cream slouch hat crammed down on her head, but her dark red hair was streaming beneath it like a pennant in the wind. He remembered what a beautiful natural rider his mother had been. How he had loved to watch her. He was painfully aware his love for the woman who had borne him wasn't buried so deep it couldn't resurface at some time. A tribute to motherhood he supposed.

He found he loved watching this woman, too. Allegra Hamilton was luring him like a moth drawn compulsively to a lamp. From out of nowhere she was all over his life. He was even starting to miss her when he didn't see her. He was even starting to imagine her there beside him. Hell, he wanted more of her. More of her company. The good Lord had either answered his prayers or sent him one heck of a problem.

She reined in a foot or two away from him, one hand tipping her hat the brim turned up on both sides, further back on her head. Her posture was proud and elegant. God, what's the matter with me? he thought

The answer came right away. You've fallen fathoms deep in love.

'What brings you here, Rory Compton?' Her eyes sparkled all over him, his face and his body, setting up a chain of spine tingles.

He damn nearly said, *you*. But no way could her feelings be as well developed as his. He made do with business. 'I've come with my final offer,' he explained.

'Ah, so you've got one?' She dismounted in one swift, graceful movement, swinging her long slender leg up and over the horse's back.

'That's some animal,' he said, running his eyes over the handsome beast.

'Cezar.' She patted the bay's neck affectionately. 'Cezar was my father's horse.'

'I should have known. He's too big and too powerful to be a woman's horse.'

'Are you saying I can't handle him?' She had to narrow her eyes against the glare.

He spread his hands. 'Never, my lady. It was a pleasure to watch you. You're a fine horsewoman. My mother was, too.' He hadn't intended to mention his mother at all. It just happened.

Her beautiful face softened into tenderness. 'You miss her terribly, don't you?'

'Here, let me do that,' he said, ignoring her question because he was too moved by it, coming forward so he could remove the saddle from her heated horse.

'It's okay,' she said, turning her head. 'Here comes Wally. He'll take care of it.'

'Fine.' Rory watched as a wiry-looking lad of around sixteen—he vaguely recognised him—jogged towards them, coming from the direction of the stables. He had a big cheerful grin all over his face. 'Thought I saw you comin' back, Miss Allegra.'

'We both wanted that ride, Wally,' she said and handed him the reins. 'Look after him for me, would you? You remember Mr Compton?'

'Sure do!' The boy, part aboriginal, studied Rory with obvious liking. 'Gunna buy the place, boss?'

'Allow us to work that out, Wally, if you don't mind.' Allegra broke in, her tone mild.

'Sure, Miss Allegra.' Wally's grin stayed in place. He hadn't taken the slightest offence. He took the reins to lead Cezar away. 'Nice to see yah, Mr Compton.'

'So long, Wally.' Rory nodded casually. 'Be good now.'

'Come into the house,' Allegra said as she turned to Rory, struck by the dramatic foil his light eyes, tanned skin and black hair presented. He was so handsome it seemed to her he radiated a spell. She just hoped she was keeping her powerful response underwraps. But surely no red-blooded woman could fail to be aroused by such stunning masculinity, or not enjoy his male beauty. Even after the traumas of her broken marriage she couldn't help but wonder what he would be like in bed.

Face it. She'd been spending too much time wondering. At a time when she should be standing back, taking stock of her life, a new relationship had been thrown open. What to do with it? Briskly she made towards the front steps.

'So where are Valerie and Chloe?' Rory asked, as they moved into the empty house. He would have a huge job in front of him keeping up the businesslike aura.

'They won't be back here until next week,' Allegra said, throwing her cream hat unerringly onto a peg.

He saluted her aim with a clap. 'Are they taking a short holiday?' he asked. He wouldn't cry buckets if they weren't coming back.

'You could say that.' She turned to face him, filled with something very like joy. Where was all this leading? She only knew it was going too fast.

'Would it be considered impolite to ask why?' Rory stared back at her, drinking her in. She was wearing a mulberry coloured polo shirt over cream jodhpurs that showed off the slender length of her legs and her very neat butt. She didn't appear to be wearing any makeup at all. Just a touch of lipstick probably to protect her mouth, but her beauty was undiminished.

'You're loads better off not knowing!' Her answer was wry.

'Tell me. One would have to be massively insensitive not to pick up on the fact you women don't have a warm relationship.'

'Okay, we had an argument,' she confessed.

'I would never have guessed! It involved my offer and your decision not to accept it, of course.'

'Clairvoyant as well.' She turned to walk into the living room and he followed.

God, she could lead me anywhere, Rory thought, not altogether proud of the way he had fallen so easily for her. Did he actually *need* a mad passion? Surely he had decided he didn't. Yet he was thrilled and apprehensive at the same time. Their being alone together could only draw them closer. He already knew he was going to go along with it, even though he recognised she had the capacity to hurt him badly. This was a woman who would want to go back to her glamour job in the city. That was something to be feared.

You fool, Rory! This is getting altogether too serious.

He was getting right into the habit of communing with himself. Now he glanced around the comfortable living room. 'Family arguments are no fun.' Boy, didn't he have some experience!

'You can say that again,' she sighed. 'My family doesn't want me here anymore. That's it in a nutshell.'

'Okay let's sit down,' he said gently, seeing how much that hurt her.

'We're going to haggle?' She settled into an armchair indicating he take the one opposite.

'If you like. A cup of coffee would make me feel better.'

She sprang up as if remiss at not offering him one. 'Me, too!' She was becoming addicted to this man and in such a short while. Yet right from the beginning an intimacy had existed she had never shared with anyone else. Explain *that*? 'Come through to the kitchen,' she invited. 'We can haggle in there.'

It was a big kitchen but his presence filled it up. Allegra busied herself hunting out the coffee grinder then taking the beans from the refrigerator.

'I'll do that,' he offered, moving closer.

'Fine.' Even her pulses were doing an Irish reel. 'Count to

twenty, that should do it.' She opened a cupboard and took out coffee cups and saucers, trying to tone herself down.

'The rain was wonderful,' he said when he finished grinding the beans and the kitchen was quiet again. 'I found myself standing out in it.'

'I can understand that.' She smiled. 'I did, too. I was purposely riding under the trees so I could get a shower from the wet branches. Do you think we'll get more? Rain is so very unpredictable.'

'Certain to,' he said.

'How do you know? Don't tell me it's your aching bones?'

'I can *feel* it. I can *smell* it,' he said. 'Besides the rain is coming down in bucket loads in the North. The last report I heard a cyclone was forming in the Coral Sea. That's all it will take. It's either flood or drought. If the cyclone develops and we get torrential rain, the Big Three—that's the Diamantina, the Georgina and the Cooper—will bring the floodwaters right down into our remote South-West corner. The Channel Country is one vast natural irrigation system as I'm sure you know. You've never been there?'

'I regret to say, no. I spent years at boarding school, then university, then I married. But I will get there one day.'

'It would be nice to take you,' he said. 'The whole region can flood without a drop of actual rain. Seen from the air it looks like the whole country is underwater.'

'Of course!' She looked across at him in quick realisation. 'You *would* see it from the air. You have your own plane on Turrawin?'

He nodded. 'A Beech Baron and a couple of Bell helicopters. We use the choppers a lot for mustering. We also use the services of an aerial mustering company from time to time. Choppers have revolutionised the whole business.'

'I can imagine, with those vast areas.' She stopped what she was doing to study him. 'But it can be dangerous? I've heard of many instances of fatal light aircraft and chopper crashes.'

'Very dangerous.' He shrugged the danger off. 'But it's our way of life, Allegra. We have to keep our fears under control.'

'That's pretty amazing,' she said dryly.

'When fatalities happen our vast community shares in the heartbreak. We're all in it together. I've been in ground searches and aerial searches in my time. We've had two major accidents in the last twelve years on Turrawin. One death I regret to say. A really good bloke, one of our regulars who could fly anything and land anywhere so no one worried about him for quite a while. The other was a crash landing, but mercifully the pilot walked away. I've had a close call myself. Once I came down in the middle of a big paperbark swamp. In the Territory I could have been taken by a croc, but we don't have any crocs in the desert. Well not anymore.' He smiled. 'Though you can see them in our aboriginal rock paintings.'

She stared back at him fascinated. 'You have cave paintings on Turrawin?'

'We don't advertise, but yes. Some of them are amazing. One cave in particular is guaranteed to make you believe in the Spirit Guardians. The hairs stand up on my forearms and I consider myself pretty cool.'

'You *are* cool.' She laughed. 'I'd love to see that cave myself.'

'I wish I could take you there.'

'That would be wonderful,' she admitted recklessly. 'We don't have anything like that around here.'

'I know.'

His mouth, quirked as it was now, was framed by the sexiest little brackets. She realised she watched for those moments. That was what falling in love was all about. It seemed that for her this was the classic coup de foudre. Which by no means guaranteed things were going to turn out fine she reminded herself. As for it happening at such a turning point in her life she was beyond thought.

'You're very passionate about your desert domain, aren't

you?' She said, knowing he would be passionate about most things.

'Yes, ma'am.' His crystalline eyes looked right into hers. 'It's like no other place on earth and Jay and I have managed to see quite a few. Australia is the oldest continent on earth. I think that accounts for a lot of the extraordinary mystique. It's the timelessness, the antiquity, the aboriginal feel, the power of the Dreamtime spirits. Then there's the colour of the place… the vivid contrast between the fiery red earth and the cloudless blue sky. Every country offers its great and its quiet wonders.

'I've stayed a few times with friends, another cattle family, who own and run a magnificent ranch in Colorado. They have the Rocky Mountains for a backdrop. It's like *wow*! Then we had a great trip to Argentina a couple of years back. Business and pleasure. A wonderfully colourful and exciting place. We loved it. We managed to get in a few games of polo while we were there. They're the greatest as I'm sure you know. We even got to fly over the Andes. I love flight. I love flying. Being up there in the wild blue yonder all on your lonesome. It's tremendous!'

'Then you're going to miss it, aren't you?' she said, getting a clear picture of him seated at the controls of a plane. 'Naroom doesn't run to light aircraft.'

He shrugged. 'Well you *are* much closer to civilisation. Turrawin on the other hand is right on the edge of the Simpson. The sand dunes there peak at around one hundred feet and they run for a couple of hundred kilometres unbroken the longest parallel sand dunes in the world. It's really eerie the way they bring to mind the inland sea of prehistory. I've stood on top of our most famous dune, Nappanerica—'

'The Big Red?' She smiled, glad she knew the answer.

'The very same. A Simpson traveller, Dennis Bartell named it. It's closer to one hundred fifty feet. The most amazing little wildflowers come out after a shower. Not the gigantic displays we get after flooding. But it's fascinating to study the little fellas up close. There are so many you can't move without crushing them underfoot, but then they release the most wonderful perfume. You think you've died and gone to Heaven.' He purposely didn't say he thought the fragrance akin to the fresh fragrance that came off her body.

'And after flooding?' she asked. 'I've seen marvellous photographic shots in calendars.'

'Allegra,' he said dryly, 'You have to see the real thing.' As he spoke he was imagining her with a diadem of yellow daisies around her head. As young boys he and Jay had fashioned them for their mother. 'After heavy rain, the desert flora has no equal,' he said with unmistakably nostalgia. 'The landscape is completely carpeted by pink, white and yellow paper daisies. It's like some great inland tide. They even sweep up to the stony hill country. Even the hills come alive with thousands of fluffy mulla mulla banners and waving lambs tails. So many varieties of desert peas come out, fuchsias and hibiscus, our exquisite desert rose. Nature's glory confronts you wherever you look.'

'It sounds wonderful,' she said, moved by the controlled emotion in his voice and face. Nostalgia was written all over him 'The central plains must seem pretty tame to you after your desert home?'

He raised both his wide shoulders in a shrug, but he didn't answer.

'Is there no hope of a reconciliation between you and your father?' she dared to ask the question.

His face angled away from her, looked grim. 'I need to get as far away from my father as is humanly possible.'

Good God as bad as that!' she said, pondering the no-holds-barred bitterness and hatreds in family life. 'It seems to me you're a son to be proud of.'

He looked up then to smile at her, the smile that was impossible to resist. 'Why thank you, Miss Allegra.'

'I'm not trying to butter you up,' she said, a shade tartly to counteract that sexual radiance. 'Just a simple statement of fact.'

Belatedly she put the coffee on to perk. He was just so interesting to talk to she had forgotten all about it. 'Take a seat.'

He pulled out a chair, resting his strong tanned arms on the table. He was wearing a red T-shirt with his jeans, the fabric clinging to his wide shoulders and the taut muscular line of his torso. It was hard to look past his physical magnetism. In fact it was making her jumpy. So jumpy she felt if he touched her she would fall to pieces. Wisely she stayed on the opposite side of the table.

'So what have you got to tell me?'

He was as aware as she was of the glittering sexual tension that stretched between them, but he tried to play it cool as befitting a serious man. 'I can go a little higher with my bid.'

She raised an arched brow. 'How high is *a little*?'

He turned up his hands. 'We'll split it between $3.5 and $4 million. My final offer, Mrs Hamilton, is $3.75.'

'That *Mrs* Hamilton might cost you,' she said frostily.

'What did he do to you?' The intense desire to reach for her—the desire he was endeavouring to keep on simmer—damned nearly boiled over.

'What's made you change your mind about me?' she asked. 'When we first met it was like— What did she do to her poor husband?'

'I've had an epiphany,' he said, deciding there was safety in being flippant. 'For one thing, you're a great cook.'

'So the fact I can cook swung it?' The coffee was perking away merrily. She turned away to shift it off the heat.

'I'm joking!' There was amusement in his eyes.

'I know you are, Rory Compton,' she said tartly, betraying her stretched feelings. There was only one answer to all this. The question was when?

'So what *did* he do to you?' Rory repeated, his gaze very direct. He didn't think he could stop until he knew. That in itself was a danger.

She set his coffee down in front of him and pushed a plate of homemade biscuits his way. 'Isn't this too early in our relationship—for want of a better word—to ask a question like that?'

'One doesn't have to go together a long time to have a relationship.' He let his gaze rest on her. 'I thought we'd agreed we've well and truly bypassed the preliminaries?' He stirred three teaspoons of raw sugar into his black coffee.

'That's way too much sugar,' she murmured, unable to deny the truth of what he had just said.

'I take sugar to rally my flagging spirits. Not that I actually need it right now.' The little sexy quirks bracketed his mouth again. 'If you won't answer my question about your husband, answer this. What do you think of my offer?'

Her hand reached up to brush back a fallen thick coil of her hair. 'Well, I have to see what Valerie and Chloe think.'

'Stop being so damned evasive,' he said swiftly. 'Valerie and Chloe were ready to take $3.5 million.'

'Don't you dare look triumphant,' she warned him, seeing the silver glint in his eyes. 'I can't bear it!.' To her horror she felt tears swim into her own.

'Hey!' Rory reached across the table in consternation. He took hold of her satin smooth fingertips, curling his own work toughened hands around them.

Electricity pulsed the entire length of Allegra's body. She felt the shock of it as much as if he had taken hold of her and thrown her down on a bed.

'What's the matter?' Rory asked. 'Have I upset you? I didn't mean to. It's honestly all I can offer, Allegra.'

She blinked furiously. God, what was the matter with her? She was a quivering mass of nerve endings. 'I know that,' she said, looking down at their joined hands. She had never seen such a contrast in skin tones. 'You can let go of me now.'

'Fine.' He did so before he burst into flames. 'You've got skin like silk. It's your home is that it? In losing it to me you'd be cutting the last ties with your dad.'

'You're very perceptive,' she said shakily, convinced of it.

'Why else would you look so sad?'

The deep note of empathy, smote her heart. 'The grieving never ends, does it? It goes away for a little while then it comes back.'

'Old wounds never cease aching,' he agreed with a philosophic shrug. 'Some people are far less able to cope with the pain than others.' He was thinking of Jay now.

'I don't have anyone anymore,' she said as though it had suddenly occurred to her. 'No father, no mother, no husband, no stepmother, no half sister. No *family*. At least you have your brother. Someone you know loves you and you love him back.'

His brooding expression was back in place. 'It's going to be damned difficult to see him if I can't set foot on Turrawin.'

'Your father must be a monster,' she exclaimed, leaning her head in her palm.

'Is that why you left your husband? *He* was a monster?' The fact he couldn't let the subject alone proved he was in over his head.

'He was a clown!' The words burst from Allegra before she could take them back. 'God that sounds awful. Forget I said it.'

He didn't speak for half a minute, he was so surprised. Clown? He hadn't been expecting that! 'So you don't hate him so much as despise him,' he asked, registering an involuntary wave of relief.

'Why are you so interested in my past life?' she asked.

He smiled. Tantalising. Heartbreaking. It seemed to her that smile was coming more frequently.' You know why, even if I am trying to slow myself down. I don't want to frighten you away, but you're the most romantic, the most glamorous woman I've ever met. And you smell like a million crushed wildflowers.'

Her heart faltered, plunged on. 'That's one sweet compliment for a cautious man, Rory Compton.'

'I just can't help myself. There's something so right about you, Allegra. Too much danger, too.'

'In what way?'

He looked past her. 'I'm an Outback cattleman. You're a woman with a glamorous career in Sydney.'

'So I am,' she said, suddenly plummeted into bleakness.

He wanted to pull her into his arms, stroke that melancholy expression away, instead he spoke bracingly, trying to keep both of them on an even keel. 'It was one hell of a trip around the property with Chloe. Her driving isn't so much dangerous as unlawful. What about the two of us riding out? I know you've still got some good horses.'

Instantly she felt a surge of pleasure that blew her troubles away. 'Great minds think alike! I was planning that myself. You can ride Cezar if you like?' She was aware of her desire to see him on horseback. She hadn't the slightest doubt he'd been a superlative rider.

His eyes widened for a second. 'I'd really appreciate that, Allegra,' he said. 'And I'm honoured. Cezar is a splendid animal.'

'You're welcome.'

'Great!' He stood up, cattleman coming to the fore. 'I hope you've had your men shift the cattle off the river flats. If there is more rain the water will rise above the escarpments of the creek. It will run a bumper and then, you'll have trouble on your hands.'

Allegra rolled her eyes heavenwards. 'Do you think I don't know? I'm not stupid, Rory Compton.'

'I'm starting to think you're a paragon,' he said dryly.

Allegra took the final gulp of her coffee.

'Right!' He pushed back his chair. 'Let's get going while the sun's out.'

CHAPTER FIVE

HE WAS ALREADY acting like Naroom was his own, Allegra thought, torn between acceptance and an understandable sense of loss. It was midafternoon, stiflingly hot and humid even though the sun had disappeared under a great pile-up of incandescent clouds. The smell of sulphur was in the air. It was as though one only had to strike a match for the whole world to go up in flames. Even the birds had stopped singing, lapsing into the silence that precedes a storm. Presently a wind sprang up, gaining velocity. Spiralling whirlwinds danced across the darkening landscape sending out their own clouds of dust, leaves and split, sun-scorched grasses.

There was a lot of water stored in those ominous clouds. The rain couldn't have been more welcome but she dreaded the thought of hail. Many times in her life she'd seen it come down on Naroom with hellish fury, hailstones as big as cricket balls, bombarding the herd and sometimes killing the small game scurrying through the pastures.

Allegra roused herself from her thoughts. Rory hadn't been at all happy with the distance north of the homestead Gallagher and his off-sider Mick Evans had moved the cattle so he rode off with steely purpose to let them know. Allegra sat silently on her horse watching. There was always work to be done on a station; always another job.

Rory would get the men moving, she thought with satisfaction. It seemed only a man, a tough cattleman with a superior knowledge and experience of cattle could fill the shoes of Boss Man. Women need not apply. The outer areas of the run would be safe but he wanted *all* the cattle concentrated in the home pastures mustered and moved off the creek flats. One of the major problems with the station hands since her father's death, then the loss of their competent overseer—Valerie's disastrous decision—was that the men were sinking deeper and deeper into lethargy, understandably uncertain of their future when times weren't easy. Even the cook had taken off, but cooks were always guaranteed of a job.

Well, I gave them their orders, Allegra consoled herself. The *right* orders. 'Remember now. High out of the creek's reach!' It was clear they had only half done the job. She had fully intended to check on them. She knew she had to, but Rory's arrival had set her back. She watched him ride back to her, the stirring sight bringing the sting of tears to her eyes. Cezar was more than a touch temperamental but Rory wasn't having the slightest trouble making a near instant communication with her father's horse, essentially a one man horse although Cezar had gradually accepted her.

'You're not happy are you?' she asked, studying his expression as he reined in alongside.

'No, but there's no use worrying about it. We have to get cracking. We need to shift all the cows and calves on the other side across the creek.' There was a dark frown on his face. 'I've told those two layabouts if they're interested in holding on to a job they'd better shake themselves up. Big time. We'll never get the stock across if the creek starts flowing any faster. As it is we'll have to push them with stock whips. They're certain to be nervous, especially with this wind blowing up.' He glanced heavenward at the threatening sky. 'I've sent Gallagher to get the Jeep and bring it down here. Some of those calves are pretty small. They'll hold the rest up. We can pick 'em up and shove them in the back of the Jeep.'

'Right, boss!' She spoke in a voice of exaggerated respect.

'It needs to be done.' He gave her a querying look.

'Of course it does. Just having a little joke. I did tell them, you know.'

'Obviously they weren't paying the right amount of attention,' he said crisply. 'They will now. If you ride back to the stables you can tell young Wally we need a hand. On the double. Doesn't anyone use their own initiative? What about you?' He cast a dubious eye over her slender, ultrafeminine frame. 'I'll understand if you don't want to join in. It'll be hard work and we're pushed for time thanks to those two. We need them otherwise you should sack them on the spot.'

'They need sacking,' she agreed. 'And don't be ridiculous. Of course I'll help. That's what I'm here for.' She wheeled her horse's head about. 'They're all docile beasts on Naroom. We don't have your mighty herds to contend with. No rogues, no wild ones, no clean skins, either.'

'Off you go then,' he urged. 'We've got a lot to do before the weather worsens.'

A big storm broke around dusk but by then they had every last lowing beast up on high ground. Allegra's ears were ringing from the crack of the whips. They kept them sailing well above the backs of the herd while the loud sound drove them on. Darkness was closing in fast, the sun almost swallowed up. The familiar landscape was shrouded in a sodden mist that drenched them in seconds.

'Dig your heels in!' he called to her.

She didn't need to be told twice. The temperature had dropped considerably and she was shivering. When they arrived back at the homestead, the two of them ran quickly from the stables towards the rear entrance of the house. Once she went for a sickening skid, floundered wildly for a moment before he caught hold of her, amazingly surefooted in the quagmire.

At last they reached the back door, pushing it open and making for the mudroom cum first-aid room.

'While you take a shower I'll hunt you up some clothes,' Allegra told him, gasping from exertion 'That's if you don't mind wearing some of the clothes Mark left here? I was going to give them away. But so far I haven't got around to it.'

'Sentimental reasons?' He was busy pulling off his muddy boots.

'No,' she said shortly.

'I couldn't wear them otherwise.' Now he was stripping off his soaked T-shirt with total unselfconsciousness, throwing it in the tub before he turned back to her. His eyes blazed like diamonds in his dynamic face. His hair was like black silk. A beautiful man. 'Sure there's nothing of yours I could wear?' he joked, putting up both hands to skim back that wet hair.

Her heart skipped a beat and her blood coursed to her most sensitive places. She wasn't sure how she liked him best. Dressed or undressed? Hell, she couldn't just stand there admiring him, though she actually felt like taking the grand tour around him. Instead she managed a laugh. 'We're not really of a size. Don't worry, everything's clean. You can't imagine how fastidious Mark is. Most of the stuff is brand-new.'

'Beggars can't be choosers,' he said, running a careless hand over his wet chest, a gesture she found incredibly erotic.

'There are clean towels in the cupboard.' Never in her life had she drunk in the sight of a man's body like this. 'Everything you need is there. Don't get under the shower before I come back.'

'Why not?' He shot her a questioning glance..

'Naked men make me uncomfortable,' she joked.

He laughed aloud, looking wonderfully vital. 'Really? And you an ex-married woman! Surely you saw a naked man on a daily basis? Anyway there is such a thing as a towel. I assure you I'd have one at the ready. The last thing I want to do is throw you into a panic. I'll sit right here.' He turned, present-ing the wide, gleaming fan of his tanned back and pulled up a chair. Then he sat on it, back to front, aiming his wonderful smile at her.

How had this man got so close to her? Why had she let him? *You didn't have a choice.*

Yet he could cast her adrift. Anything was possible in life. But for now, he was making her feel things she had never felt before. She had to will herself to move. 'Won't be long.' She had already taken off her boots and used a towel to mop up the worst of the mud, now she padded towards the doorway lead-ing into the hall. 'Not much chance of your driving back to Jimboorie.' She half turned back. 'Not in this!'

'So what are you saying, I can stay?' His tone was disturb-ingly mocking, even erotic.

She held his gaze as long as she could, shocked by the wrenching physical sensations in her body. She wasn't a school-girl with a crush on the captain of the football team. She was an experienced woman, twenty-seven years old. 'Well you're welcome to bolt if you think it's too risky,' she said tartly.

'Never!'

Rory offered up a silent prayer.

And lead me not into temptation.

'I'll stay,' he said. 'Thank you most kindly, Allegra. It'll give us the opportunity to have a good long chat.'

Rory washed out his gear and threw it in the dryer. Then he turned to examining Mark Hamilton's clothing most carefully. Everything Allegra had selected was brand-new and fine qual-ity. He read the labels. From the dark blue polo shirt to the beige cotton trousers and the classy underpants. He tried to visualise Allegra's ex-husband. Couldn't. Chloe had called him a 'lovely guy' handsome and clever. Was he *all* of those things? Allegra in a driven moment had called him a clown! What did that mean exactly? A man forever playing innocuous but annoying practical jokes? A man not seriously minded enough for her? He had to be impaired in some way. He was a poor lover? He was a violent lover? Clown didn't sound violent. Who knew what went on inside a marriage anyway? Besides he couldn't trust Chloe. Chloe had made an art form out of putting down her exquisite sister.

Hamilton was a heavier build. And some inches shorter. The shirt was okay. He had to hitch up the trousers with his own belt. Rory was much leaner through the waist and hips. The length fell short but okay, who cared? She had even found him a pair of expensive leather loafers that fitted well enough. He took a look in the mirror, thrust back his damp hair and laughed. He had never worn a shirt of such a wondrous electric-blue.

'Gosh you look like someone famous!' Allegra swallowed when she caught sight of him.

'Don't say a rock star.' He grimaced. 'The blue makes me look swarthier than usual.' He glanced down at the shirt.

'Far from it. It's great. You're a good-looking guy, Compton.' She led the way into the kitchen. 'I could find you work tomorrow.'

'You surely can't mean as a male model?'

'You want to check out what they're earning,' she retorted. 'The guys who get to model here and overseas earn a fortune.'

'No, thanks. For better or worse I'm buying Naroom. All we need is the paperwork done.'

'And Valerie's and Chloe's okay,' she tacked on.

'Consider that a fait accompli.' He watched her take salad ingredients out of the crisper in the refrigerator.

'What are we having?'

'Something easy,' she said. 'Steak and salad and maybe some French fries. This afternoon was pretty strenuous.'

'I did warn you.' He let his gaze rest on her, feeling a surge of desire. She had teamed a delicate little lilac top, which looked like silk—he had a mad urge to feel it—with a flowing skirt. Her beautiful hair streamed over her shoulders and down her back, drying in long loose waves. There wouldn't be a man alive who wouldn't get a buzz from simply looking at her, he thought. She was just so effortlessly beautiful. Exclusive looking yet she had worked tirelessly that afternoon. Tirelessly and extremely well. This might be a woman who looked like an orchid but she didn't hesitate to pitch in. He found himself full of admiration for her. She was a woman of surprises.

'Valerie and Chloe were prepared to say yes to $3.5 million,' he reminded her, picking up the conversation. 'Thanks to you they get more.'

She took two prime T-bone steaks from the refrigerator and put them down on the counter before turning to him. Her expression was brushed with worry. 'Valerie said she was going to consult a solicitor with a view to contesting the will.'

'In what way?' He could see that upset her.

'Dad left me a half share of everything,' she said, 'whereas Valerie and Chloe had quarter shares.'

'Tough,' he said, thinking she didn't have a problem. 'I'm no lawyer but I'm willing to bet your father left his will airtight. Don't worry, Allegra. I'd say Valerie was trying to make you suffer. You can bet your life she's already been on to a solicitor who's told her she hasn't a chance in hell of contesting the will. You won't be embroiled in any lawsuit and this deal will go through more smoothly than you think.'

'I don't really want it to go through,' she confessed, leaning against the table.

'Which part of me don't you like?' He stared at her hard.

'This is *home*, Rory.' She met his challenging gaze. 'My father brought my mother here as a bride. I was born here. Even when I was away from it I still *lived* here, if you know what I mean?'

'I surely do.' He thought she put it well.

'To be honest I'd like to die here.'

He stirred restlessly at that. 'Don't for God's sake talk about dying,' he said tersely. 'You've got a long life in front of you. Would you want to stay here and work it?'

'I *could* do it,' she said. 'I'd have to sack guys like Gallagher and Evans and hire some good men. Then I'd see if I could get our old overseer back.'

'Well, well, well,' he said. 'Like I said, you're a *most* surprising woman. But then I don't know a lot about women. I grew up mostly in an all male environment. Even so I'm sure you're very unusual. Do you have the money to buy your stepmother and Chloe out?'

She lowered her head, picked up a shiny red capsicum and set it down again 'No, unfortunately. I didn't take a penny off Mark.'

'You were entitled to.'

'No.' She shook her head. 'I didn't want to do anything like that. He didn't want to break up the marriage. *I* did.'

'So he was the innocent party?'

'No he wasn't, Rory Compton,' she said with sharp censure. '*I* was the innocent party but don't worry about it. I thought maybe I could borrow like you.'

'Really?' He sat back, his hands locked behind his head. 'You could try but maybe you wouldn't be so successful,' he warned her. 'You're a woman and you have no real hands on experience.'

'All right, I know that!' she said, giving in to irritation.

'And what about your big city job? I thought you intended going back to it? Surely you'd miss city life? I mean it couldn't be a more different world?'

'Rory, I love the land,' she told him passionately. 'I know it's a little unusual my making such a success of being a fashion editor, but that's only a little part of me. I doubt I would ever have left home had my mother lived. At the beginning living in the city was like living in a foreign country. After life on the land, I felt so hemmed in by all the tall buildings and so many people rushing about. All our space and freedom was lost to me. You should understand.'

'Of course I do.'

She nodded. 'It's not a nice thing to say, but Val drove me away. Val and Chloe to a certain extent. I was made to feel an outsider in my own home.'

'Have you a photograph of your mother?' he asked, sitting straight in his chair again.

She sighed deeply. 'Sure. Wait here.'

Rory rose and walked to the sink feeling vaguely stunned. The last thing he'd expected when they had first met, was such a glamorous young woman would want to live in isolation. In his experience it was men who did that sort of thing. Solitary men who had pioneered the vast interior before admitting women and children to their lives. He knew plenty of reclusives who could only live in the wilderness. Not that the central plains country was anything like wilderness but Naroom was isolated enough. God knows what she'd make of his desert home! Or what had been his desert home he thought with a stab of pain.

His mind wheeling off in several directions, he began to run some of the salad ingredients—tomatoes, cucumber, a bunch of radishes and some celery—under the tap. He could see the mixed salad greens had been prewashed. He felt like that steak. He hoped she had some good English mustard. He was hungry.

Allegra returned a few moments later, holding a large silver framed photograph to her heart.

He held out his hand. Ah, genetics! he thought, much struck by Allegra's striking resemblance to her mother. There were the purely cut features, the shape and set of the eyes, the chin held at a perfect right angle to the neck. There was the same flowing hair, the deep, loose waves. The photograph was black and white but he was certain the hair was the same shade as Allegra's. Even the expression was near identical. Confident, forward-looking, self-assured. Yet this woman had died so tragically young. What a waste!

'It would have been hard for your stepmother to be confronted every day by the image of the woman her husband truly loved?' he spoke musingly, finding it in his heart to pity Valerie.

'Hey, I was only *three* when Val became my stepmother,' Allegra pointed out.

'But the extraordinary resemblance was there. And each year you grew it became more pronounced. By the time you were in your teens you were a powerful rival. Or an ever present reminder if you like.'

She gave him a wounded look. 'Whose side are you on anyway?'

His expression softened. 'I'm sorry, Allegra. I can imagine what it was like for you. In my family Jay took after my father. Physically, that is. Jay is nothing like my father, thank God. I took after my mother. I have her eyes like you have your mother's eyes. Eyes tend to dominate a face. My father loved my mother. Or as much as he could love anyone. He sure doesn't love me. I was one terrible reminder she left him. I had to pay for my mother's unforgivable crime.'

'So there's a parallel?' she said more quietly.

'Oddly, yes. Both of us are outsiders.'

The wind and rain kicked up another notch during the night. He awoke to near perfect darkness. Amazingly he had slept. He never thought he would with Allegra sleeping down the hallway. They had talked until after midnight about their lives, their childhood, events that had shaped them, without her ever giving away the reason for abandoning her marriage. He really needed to know. It had become a burning question. Simply put, how could he truly understand until he knew? His mother's abandonment had played such a destructive role in his life he had a natural fear of handing over his heart to a woman who one day might cast him aside. God knows it happened.

Afterwards they had walked around the homestead together like an old married couple, checking all the doors and windows.

Only the sexual tension both refused to let get out of bounds, betrayed them. Their hands had only to come into fleeting contact for Rory's hard muscled body to melt like hot wax. He wanted her. He wasn't such a fool he didn't know she wanted him. Sexual magnetism. Each was irresistibly drawn to the other, yet each was determined to keep control. Besides, there were dangers in acting on the most basic, powerful instinct.

Something had caused him to come awake. Some noise in the house. Downstairs. Maybe they should have made the French doors more secure by closing the exterior shutters? The verandah did, however, have a deep protective overhang. He stood up, pulling on his jeans, which he had removed from the dryer earlier in the night. He opened the bedroom door and looked down the corridor. All was quiet. Why wouldn't she be sleeping after such an exhausting afternoon? They had shared a bottle of red wine as well.

It turned out to be what he expected—one of the French doors in the living room. It was rattling loudly as the wind blew against it. He opened one side, latched in back, then stepped out onto the verandah, feeling the invigorating lash of the moisture laden wind. It felt marvellous! Rain to the man on the land was a miracle. The most precious commodity. In the Outback it was either drought or flood. He knew the creek would be in muddy flood by now. Thank God he'd arrived when he had. A woman no matter how willing to chip in wasn't meant to do backbreaking station work.

It took him only moments to secure the shutters, then the interior doors. One of the bolts on the door had worked its way loose, hence the rattle. He padded back into the entrance hall a little disoriented in a strange house. There was less illumination now that he had pulled the shutters. What he had to do was turn on a few lights before he blundered into something and woke Allegra. He didn't think he could cope with seeing her floating towards him on her beautiful high arched feet. He just might grab her, pick her up in his arms, and carry her upstairs…

'God!' He gave a startled oath as a wraithlike figure walked right into instead of through him. He held the apparition by its delicate shoulders.

'Allegra!' He sucked in his breath. Apparitions didn't have warm, satiny flesh.

'Who did you think it was, Chloe back home?' Her voice in the semidarkness came as a soft hiss.

'Out of the question. Chloe's shorter and a lot plumper than you.'

'Don't for God's sake ever call her plump to her face.'

'I wouldn't dream of it. I tried not to wake you.'

'When you were making so much noise?' Her voice rose.

'Pardon me, I was very quiet. Besides, what were trying to do to *me*? For a split second I thought you were a witch.' Very carefully he took his hands off her. Steady. Steady. He could smell her body scent like some powerful aphrodisiac.

'Witches don't flap around in nighties.'

He was seeing her more and more clearly. 'Are you mad? Of course they do. What's the matter anyway? You're as much out of breath as if you've been running.'

'I was trying to exercise caution as it happens,' she admonished him. 'You gave me a fright, too.'

'Then I'm sorry. There's nothing dangerous about me.'

She laughed shakily. What were they doing here, absorbed in a crazy conversation conducted in the near dark? 'I have news for you, Rory Compton.'

'Better not to tell me. It was one of the French doors. I've closed the shutters. I should have done it before.'

A shiver of excitement came into her voice. 'The wind is much stronger now.'

It couldn't be stronger than her magnetic pull. Rory marvelled at his self-control. Maybe honour could explain it? 'Why are you whispering?' he asked.

'I really don't know and I don't want to find out,' she whispered back. 'We should turn on a light.'

'Damn, why didn't I think of that?'

'The creek will have broken its banks.'

'Any chance of your speaking louder?'

'Oh, shut up!' The tension between then was electrifying. 'I'm *so* glad you were here, Rory!'

'*Am* here,' he corrected. 'Now, where the heck *is* the light switch for the stairs?' He knew it was dangerously wrong to keep standing there. Another minute and he'd reach for her. There was only one answer after that.

'I'll get it.' She slipped away like a shadow. Another second and lights bloomed over the stairs and along the upper hallway.

Behind him the tall grandfather clock chimed three.

'Ah, just as I thought!' he exclaimed. 'The witching hour!'

She was standing beneath a glowing wall sconce. It gilded the dark rose of the long hair that framed her face. He saw she was wearing a magical silk robe, a golden-green, with pink and cerise flowers all over it. It had fallen open down the front so he could see her nightgown, the same cerise of the flowers. It gleamed satin. So did the curves of her breasts revealed by the plunging V of the neckline. For a minute his strong legs felt like twigs.

Allegra drew her robe around her, scorchingly aware of his intimate appraisal. She was so aroused she was nearly on fire.

So why aren't you moving?

'We'd better go back to bed,' she said in another furious whisper. 'You go up.'

'Why not leave those two wall sconces on?' he suggested, not wanting and wanting so much to delay her. No words could describe how he felt. There was something magical about her. 'There'll be enough light to see us up the stairs.' He could only wonder at how composed he sounded when his body was flowing with sexual energy.

'The rain seems to be slowing.' She switched off the main

lights, then padded on her slippered feet to the base of the stairs. 'Coming?'

He was awed by the electric jolt to his heart. 'Coming where?' He had a sudden overpowering urge to tell her how much he wanted her.

Only she cut him off. 'You *can't* come with *me!*' Her voice trembled. She didn't confess she was terribly tempted.

'I can't help wishing I could.' He stared back at her, hot with hunger. 'Don't be scared, Allegra. I would never offer you a moment's worry.'

She almost burst into tears she was feeling so frustrated. 'I'm not scared of you,' she said. 'I'm scared of me. Haven't we progressed far enough for one night?'

'Years have passed off in a matter of hours,' he said wryly. 'Even then you haven't answered the burning question.'

There was a breathless pause. 'Ask it quickly. I'm going up to bed.' She fixed her jewelled eyes on him.

'What was so wrong with your marriage you had to abandon it?'

She might have turned to marble. 'Don't go there, Rory,' she said.

'You have to get it out of your system.'

She shook her glowing head. 'Believe me, tonight's not the night. Good night, Rory!'

'What's left of it.' He shrugged. 'See you in the morning, Allegra. I'll be up early to check everything's okay.'

'Thank you.' She was already at the first landing, intent on getting to the safety of her bedroom and shutting temptation out. 'If you knock on my door, I'll join you.'

With that she fled.

CHAPTER SIX

THE RAIN STOPPED in the predawn .The air was so fresh it was like a liqueur to the lungs. The birds were calling ecstatically to one another secure in the knowledge there was plenty of water. In the orange-red flame of sunrise they drove around the property, Rory at the wheel of the Jeep, revelling in the miracles the rain could perform. Overnight the whole landscape had turned a verdant glowing green. Little purple wildflowers appeared out of nowhere, skittering across the top of the grasses. Hundreds of white capped mushrooms had sprung up beneath the trees that were sprouting tight bunches of edible berries.

They checked on the herd together. It had been little affected by the torrential downpour. The stock had come through the night unscathed and without event. The hail Allegra had feared had not eventuated. Cattle were spread out all over the sunlit ridges to the rear of the homestead. It was great to see them so healthy, their liver-red hides washed clean by the downpour.

The creek as expected had burst its banks. They stood at the top of the highest slope looking down at the racing torrent. It was running strongly, and noisily, carrying a lot of debris, fallen branches from the trees and vast clumps of water reeds torn up by the flow. When the water hit the big pearl-grey boulders the height reached by the flying spray was something to see. The area around the big rocks churned with swirling eddies of foaming water.

For a time neither of them spoke, simply enjoying the scene and the freshness and fragrance of the early morning. Both of them knew what this life-giving rain meant; how important it was to the entire region. A flight of galahs undulated overhead in a pink and magenta wave. Exquisite little finches were on the wing, brilliantly plumaged lorikeets chasing them out of their territory with weird squawks. Waterfowl, too, were in flight. They came in to the creek to investigate, fanning out over the stream. Allegra and Rory watched as the birds skimmed a few feet above the racing water, then collectively decided it was way too rough to land. They took off as a squadron, soaring steeply back into the sky again. Water was a magnet to birds. They would be back, from all points of the compass just waiting for the raging of the waters to slow and the creek to turn to a splendid landing field.

'Rain, the divine blessing!' Rory breathed as he watched the torrent downstream leap over a rock. 'No rain our way as yet.'

Our way! His beloved Channel Country. They had listened to the radio for news. The late cyclone that had been developing in the Coral Sea was now threatening the far North. Drought continued to reign in the great South-West.

'When it comes, the creeks, the gullies, the waterholes, the long curving billabongs will all fill up,' he continued in a quiet but compelling voice. 'The billabongs cover over with water lilies. None of your home garden stuff. Huge magnificent blooms. Pink, in one place, the sacred blue lotus in another, lovely creams, a deep pinkish red not unlike the colour of your hair. When the rains come the landscape just doesn't get a drenching, the vast flood plains go under.

'We've been totally isolated on Turrawin before today, surrounded on all sides by a marshy sea. When the storms come they come with a vengeance. It's all on a Wagnerian scale—massive thunderheads back lit by plunging spears of lightning.

Getting struck and killed isn't uncommon. We had a neighbour killed in a violent electrical storm a few years back.'

Allegra turned to him, registering the homesickness on his handsome face. 'How are you going to be able to settle here, Rory, when your heart is clearly somewhere else?'

He adjusted his hat to further shade his eyes from a brilliant chink of sunlight that fell through the green canopy. 'I told you, Allegra, I can't go back. My home is lost to me.'

'You couldn't find a suitable property in your own region?'

He gave a humourless laugh. 'I could find one, maybe, but I couldn't pay for one. No way! We're talking two entirely different levels here. Our cattle stations—kingdoms are what they're called and it's not so fanciful—dwarf the runs in this area. I have to start more or less around the middle and work my way up.'

Her brows were a question mark. 'But are you going to be happy doing it?'

'Okay, I understand you.' He shrugged. 'The Channel Country is the place of *my* dreaming. It speaks to my soul like Naroom speaks to yours. This is beautiful country, don't get me wrong. Maybe it hasn't got the haunting quality of the desert, or its incredible charisma, but I'll settle here. I have to.'

'I don't think I'd count on it,' Allegra said, shrugging wryly. 'Your love for your desert home won't be shaken off any more than my father's love for my dead mother. Some loves go so deep nothing and no one can approach them.'

'Thinking twice about selling then?' he asked, filling his eyes with her. Her lissom body was clad in a navy and white top and close fitting jeans No makeup again, save for a pink gloss on her mouth. Her thick hair was woven into a rope like plait. He'd never seen a woman look better.

'Valerie and Chloe, when they return, will demand Naroom be sold,' she answered. 'I don't think we could ask for anyone better than you to take it on. You're an astute, ambitious man. I haven't the slightest doubt you'll make a big success of Naroom. And then you'll move on.' She spoke with a lowered head and saddened eyes.

'Hey, that's quite a few years down the line!' He tried to re-assure her. 'But isn't that the way of it, Allegra? One expands, not stands still. Which doesn't mean to say Naroom couldn't and wouldn't remain a valuable link in a chain.'

'How good a cattleman is your brother?' she asked abruptly, moving a step nearer the top of the grassy slope to check it was a log that had smashed into one of the creek boulders and not a lost little calf.

'Jay got pushed into it,' he answered. 'He works as hard as any man. Harder, but—'

'He wasn't born to the job,' she cut in gently.

'I told you he wanted to be a doctor. It's a bit late but he could still be. I wouldn't know but he was a straight A student. Jay has a more sensitive side to him than I have.'

She gazed at him out of her black fringed eyes. 'I don't know if that's exactly right. I haven't had the pleasure of meeting Jay, but I would describe you as pretty deep, Rory Compton. You display your sensitivities in many ways.'

'As when?' he asked the question, then broke off abruptly, seized by a mild panic. 'Don't move,' he ordered. 'You could take a tumble.'

Even as he spoke the ground shifted beneath Allegra's feet. 'Oh...hell!' She threw out an arm. He grabbed it strongly, but the soles of her riding boots were slick with grass and mud. She slipped further down the bank with Rory straining to hold her. Allegra almost righted herself, about to thank him for his help, but in the next second a section of rain impacted earth gave way and the two of them began to roll over and over down the wet grassy slope, gathering momentum as they went. Their bodies crushed the multitude of unidentifiable little flowers that grew there in abundance, releasing a sweet musky smell.

Allegra, though powerfully shocked by their tumble, was experiencing a rush of emotions that included exhilaration and a blazing excitement. They were going to go into the stream. She knew that even if she couldn't look. It wouldn't be the first time she'd found herself in deep, fast running water. She was a strong swimmer. He would be, too. She didn't even have to consider it. His powerful arms were around her. What did she care if they had to fight the torrent? They were together. She felt like a woman is supposed to feel when she was with one particular man. A man who walked like he owned the earth.

Rory was taking the brunt of it, trying to protect her body from any hurt along the way. They were to an extent cushioned by the thick grasses that gave up a wonderfully pure, herbal aroma. As they careened towards the rushing creek he crushed her to him. He couldn't risk flinging out an arm. That meant taking one from her, but he was straining to gain purchase with his boots. Finally he hooked into something—a tight web of vines—that slowed their mad descent.

Another four feet and he was able to slam a brake on their rough tumble. They rolled in slow motion to a complete stop, finding they were almost at the bottom with the roar of the creek in their ears and the near overwhelming scent of crushed vegetation in their nostrils.

'Bloody hell, woman!' It was an eternity of seconds before Rory could speak. Then his words came out explosively. He was poised over her, staring down into her beautiful face vivid with exhilaration. 'Just hold it right there!' He held her captive, as if he believed her capable of jumping up and taking a header into the creek just for the hell of it!

She laughed with absolute delight. The sound was crystal clear. Transparent like an excited child's.

'Why did you stop us?' she wailed. 'I wanted to take a swim.'

'More likely bash your head against a rock,' he told her sternly.' The current is too strong.'

'Still I enjoyed it, didn't you?' She stared into his glittering eyes. 'I'll remember it for always.' The great thing was, she meant it. She raised her hand and very slowly caressed his bronze cheek, taking exquisite pleasure in the fine rasp of his beard on her skin. She fancied she saw little rays of light around his head. An energy that held her within his magnetic field?

'So what are you trying to do to me?' Rory stared down at her, equally bedazzled. 'What a repertoire of alluring little spells you have!'

'All called up with you in mind.'

'Then there's only one thing left to do.' The last tight coils of his self-control broke free. He was so hungry for her he didn't know how he was going to assuage it. He lowered his head, intent on capturing her mouth, only to see with a flame of wonder her lovely mouth ready itself to receive his.

What would he do to her if she let him?

He kissed her very slowly and gently at first until he had her whimpering and moving her head from side to side in agitation. Then his kisses strengthened in pressure and intensity as his passion for her surged. What a fool he was thinking he had schooled himself to restraint. The reality was he was so powerfully attracted to her he had lost the capacity for rational thought.

Time stopped. The whole world stopped. Pain and old grief were forgotten. His weight pinioned her body into the thick, verdant grasses.

'Am I hurting you?'

'Don't go way.' She loved the weight of him. Her eyelids fluttered shut and she caught the back of his neck with her hand.

He kissed her until both of them were gasping and out of breath. His hands were sliding slowly, sensuously, over her body as though learning it. Sometimes she led his touch, the delicate contours of her breasts swelling at his caress. Her heart felt like it was going to break out from behind her rib cage. Never before in her life had she felt such sensual excitement. Being with him had increased her every perception one hundredfold.

The breeze shook leaves from the trees. They flew down to them, golden-green, purple backed, landing gently in the glowing garnet coils of her hair. If ever a man could take a woman with his eyes he was guilty of taking her now Rory thought. In a minute she would lay her hand on his cheek again and tell him to stop.

Only she didn't.

For a woman who had lived three years in a bad marriage, Allegra felt unbelievably ecstatic. She wasn't unafraid of anything that was in him, because it was in *her*.

'Allegra, do you trust me?' His lips pressed against her throat. 'Do *you* trust *me*?'

Did he trust her siren song? The monumental shift in his line of defence couldn't have been more apparent. 'Do I trust life itself,' he murmured, continuing to trail passionate kisses across her face and throat. 'You must know I want you badly.' How could she not when she had been moving her hand over him as he moved his over her?

Allegra's breathing came fast and shallow. She *had* to tell him before his body took total control of his mind. 'It's not a safe time for me right now, Rory.' She tried to laugh, but couldn't bring it off.

'Oh my God!' He stopped kissing her, his sigh deep and tortured. 'Oh God, Allegra!' Frustration whirled through him with the force of a tornado. 'I'd better let go of you,' he groaned.

'Maybe you'd better.' Her own burning desire was at war with all ideas of caution and common sense. She was panicked by the thought that desire for him could very well win if they didn't move. 'I didn't know all this was going to happen so soon.'

'Hell, don't apologise,' he said, his body racked by painful little stabs. 'So you could fall pregnant?' He helped her to sit up.

'It's a strong possibility.' She held a hand over her heart, trying to quiet her breathing.

'I wish to God I'd brought some protection.' His handsome face was taut with frustration.

'So do I.' She laughed without humour, her creamy skin covered in a fine dew of heat.

'I'm so desperate to get close to you,' he admitted, teetering on the edge of saying a whole lot more.

'Are you?' She turned to stare into his eyes, conscious of a sudden joy.

'You know I am. Damn, damn, damn,' he groaned. 'So what do we do? Let the flames die?'

'It might be a good idea.' She didn't bother to hide her regret.

'Would you *want* to have my baby?' he asked very quietly.

'Are you speaking seriously?' It wouldn't be the end of the world if she fell pregnant to him. It would be thrilling.

'Yes,' he said.

'What's going on in your mind, Rory?' She was trying to read it from his expression.

'You haven't answered the question.'

'I want children,' she said. 'I've told you that before.'

He took her hand, looking intently into her eyes. 'Do you think we have enough going for us to consider marriage?' He knew he was being carried to extremes, but maybe extremism was his natural bent? Either that or he had finally found his life's focus.

'Rory!' Allegra began to laugh a little wildly. For a minute she felt like she was flying; caught up by a great wind. She who had come through a catastrophic relationship was being asked to consider marriage again. What was even more astounding was she knew right away what her decision would be. Something extraordinary had happened to her. She had to seize the day.

'Well?' He took her chin, sparkles of light in his eyes.

'You don't have to propose to me to get me into bed,' she said, pierced by the look in his eyes. She was long used to men regarding her but this was something entirely different.

'You think I don't know that?' he said gently. 'I know this has come at an odd time, but can't you see the beauty of it? I want a family. So do you. We're much the same age. Neither of us is content to let things go on much longer. If I've shocked you with my audacity, perhaps you can think of it as a contract that could work extremely well for both of us as we both have the same aims. You wouldn't have to leave the home you love. You'd gain a half share as my wife and partner. You'd be able to hold onto your own money. It's important for a woman to feel financially independent.'

The words were business-like, but the warmth of real emotion was in the sound. 'I should say you're crazy!' Allegra was still flying high. To share a dream! Isn't that what she had always wanted?

'You know I'm not.'

'So what are you leading us into?' she asked as calmly as she could.

'Why a marriage of convenience for two people who just so happen to suit one another right down to the ground.'

'We can't have love, too?'

For answer, he turned her face to him and dropped a brief, ravishing kiss on her mouth. 'Wouldn't you say we're more than halfway there?'

So there was one secret between them. She was already there. 'Maybe we should slow down instead of full steam ahead?' she suggested before binding him to her.

'I'm going to leave that up to you, Allegra,' he said. '*I* won't change my mind. You're the woman I want.'

She kept her eyes lowered. 'You can't have forgotten both of us have a lot of old issues to work through?'

'We can work through them together.' His response was swift and sure. 'Have I dared too much too soon?' He searched her eyes for any hint of misgiving. 'I hadn't planned any of it. It took a tumble down the hill to shake it out of me. Love is a big word. Maybe the biggest in the dictionary. I don't think we're going to have a problem getting into bed together, do you?' he asked dryly.

No problem at all but she had to remind him. 'There's a bit more to marriage than sex, Rory.'

He nearly said what was flooding his mind. *I love you.* But the last thing he wanted was to frighten her off. 'Do you think I don't know that? We really *like* each other, though, don't we? Not that I'm about to knock great sex. Marriage would be very sad without it. But we have a lot in common. All the things we talked about last night. Our love of the land. Don't let any bad experience you may have had with your husband warp you.'

She felt a frisson of shock. She had never said a word to him about Mark. What then had he assumed? 'So much depends on our mutual love of the land, doesn't it?' she said, ignoring the reference to Mark.

'I'd be lying if I didn't say it was a crucial factor.' He didn't drop his gaze. 'I couldn't consider marrying a woman—no matter how much I wanted her—if I knew she might go off and leave me when the going got rough. Worse, leave our kids. You were being entirely truthful when you said the land is where you belong?'

'Of course! How could you doubt me?' She shook her head vigorously. 'I have my own dreaming.'

'Well then, it's a brilliant idea,' he said as though that clinched it.

'More like explosive!' Allegra knew she ought to be filled with doubts but incredibly she wasn't. She felt more like a woman who had been blind all her life then finally opened her eyes. In fact, she had never felt so good. 'You've got to give me a little time to think,' she said, paying a moment's homage to caution. Impossible to *think* when he was holding her hand and making love to her with his eyes. 'This is scary. Or it darn well ought to be. I didn't do too brilliantly the last time.'

'And you won't let me hear the problem. He didn't abuse you, did he?' Rory couldn't abide the thought. 'I'd go find him and horse whip him if he did.'

'And wind up inside a jail? I wouldn't like that. Mark isn't a violent man. In many respects he's the perfect gentleman. Everyone thought so anyway. People can act perfectly civilised but one barely has to scratch the surface to discover they're something quite different underneath. My dad didn't take to Mark. I knew that although Dad never put his concerns into words.'

'I'm listening,' he prompted, feeling an iron determination to protect her.

She bent her head, unsure how much to say. 'Mark was into a fantasy life. A *sexual* fantasy life.'

'One that bothered you?' he frowned.

'Once I found out he'd been unfaithful the marriage was as good as over. I hate to talk about it, actually. I forgave him the first time. I thought it was a one-off aberration and I felt badly about calling it quits so early in the marriage. But it wasn't. Mark continued his brief encounters with married women in our own circle. They made an absolute fool out of me. Opportunity is always present if one is looking for it.'

'Good God!' Rory made a deep, growling sound in his throat. 'He sounds like an oversexed adolescent.'

Allegra's shrug was cynical. 'A lot of men of all ages fit that description. Men and woman have affairs. Married or not. I saw a lot of it. One can't help attraction. The possibility is always there. If one is married the right decision is to consciously turn away from temptation. Some don't.'

'You never thought to get even?' he asked. 'Sorry, I withdraw that. I know you didn't.'

'You're dead right. I respected my marriage vows. I respected myself. That's why I had to get out.' She steadied herself to look into his eyes. 'I liked the way you checked the minute I said it wasn't the right time to have sex.'

'Why of course! You surely didn't think I would force the issue?'

'I didn't, but I *was* responding an awful lot. In a way it was a crisis and you dealt with it the way it had to be. Mark messed me up for a while. He's quite a bit older. Nearly ten years. He set out to mould me to *his* ways but he failed. He actually believed his little affairs were harmless. He swore over and over he loved only me. I was his *wife*. That put me on a pedestal instead of exposing me to ridicule. He swore he'd get help.'

'And did he?' Rory was having difficulty understanding a man like Mark Hamilton.

'I didn't wait around to find out,' Allegra replied flatly. 'I believed I did at the time, but I didn't love Mark. He was more a replacement father figure. Had I really loved him I'd have been devastated at the divorce, instead of just plain *mad* at myself. The state of my home life—the way I grew up—pushed me into trying to find someone safe. Mark had every outward appearance of being safe, except he wasn't safe at all. I made one hell of a mistake. I can't possibly make another.' She was too close to tears to say another word.

He drew her within the haven of his arm.' Did you tell your stepmother and Chloe about this?'

She nodded. 'But not all that much. They thought the world of Mark. In their eyes if anyone was to blame for the breakdown of our marriage it was me. Val has been compelled to find fault with me since I was a kid. I couldn't do a thing right. She used to make up stories for Chloe to believe and Chloe did. I used to be devastated. Not anymore. Over the years, Val has brainwashed my sister. Chloe would be a much better person away from her mother. In her heart Chloe knows it. Anyway there's nothing I can do there. It's all too late. There's a lot of deep resentment. Not love.'

'Was there *any* happiness in your marriage?' he asked.

'I can remember some good times,' she said. 'At the beginning.'

'Then let me make up for all you've missed.' His hand slid to her nape, cradling her head. He allowed himself the sheer bliss of kissing her again, only breaking it by force of will. 'You'll have to be really, *really* patient for the rest.' Mockery sparkled in his eyes.

'I guess I have to be okay with that.' Her voice was soft. He had taken her breath. Sunlight was filtering through the trees, warming them in its streams of golden light.

'I suppose we could live together first like couples do these days?' He put forward the idea as a way of giving her an option. 'Does that appeal to you? A trial run? We could take it in stages if that would make you feel easier in your mind. You can have all the time you want to get used to me. The same goes for me.' He gave a sardonic ripple of laughter. 'Although I'll never get used to you if I live a hundred years.' She had stopped him in his tracks when he had first laid eyes on her. She was even more beautiful to him now.

'You'll make some woman a terrific husband, Rory Compton,' she told him, thus stating her clear preference.

'Then that woman better be *you*!'

CHAPTER SEVEN

VALERIE'S FACE WAS a study. She jumped to her feet, moving towards Allegra as though she would like to slap her. 'How long now is it since your divorce and you're planning to *remarry*?' Her voice rang so loudly it bounced off the walls. 'Even knowing you the way I do, I can scarcely believe it.'

Chloe sat trembling, on the verge of tears. 'What did you *do* when we were away?' she demanded to know, her voice sounding thick in a clogged throat.

'Do?' Allegra repeated. She fell back from the kitchen table, as ever feeling outnumbered. 'I hardly think it's got a damned thing to do with you, Chloe. You should be thrilled I managed to get extra for Naroom, instead of questioning me like this. I haven't heard a word about the better offer.'

'Did you sleep with him?' Valerie threw out an arm so precipitously she knocked over a glass on the sink. It smashed on the terracotta tiles but all three women ignored it.

Allegra sat there wondering why after all these years, she was still stunned by their reactions. 'That's absolutely none of your business.'

A dark look crossed Valerie's face and her jaw set hard. 'I bet you did. 'You take no notice of the conventions. Mark was too much the gentleman to say a word against you.'

'Mark was no gentleman,' Allegra said, sick to death of the way they defended him. 'A gentleman is a man of decency.'

'And Mark wasn't?' Chloe's *pretty* mouth twisted bitterly.

Her tone struck Allegra as odd. So odd, she thought suddenly of those old photographs. '*You* didn't by any chance sleep with him?' Allegra's voice was so tight it was devoid of expression.

Chloe flushed a deep scarlet, then swiftly turned her head away, the very picture of guilt, colour flooding her face.

'What a criminal thing to say. Apologise now.' Valerie was breathing hard, her eyes fixed on Allegra and not her daughter. 'You're beautiful to look at, but you're not beautiful inside. That's the paradox with women like you. Apologise to your sister.'

Allegra ignored her, studying her half sister with contemptuous eyes. '*Did* you, Chloe? I always had a sneaking suspicion you did.'.

'Are you quite m-mad!' Valerie stuttered, looking like she thought Allegra beyond the pail.

'You, Val, are a fool.' Allegra spoke without looking at the woman. 'So am I for that matter. You *did* didn't you, Chloe. You did it as much to spite me as surrendering to Mark's charms.'

Valerie, openly incredulous, shook her head, but Chloe, unable to disguise her guilt but without a glimmer of remorse, put her face down into her hands and promptly burst into floods of tears as her only way out.

'Found out at long last!' Allegra said quietly, feeling sick to the stomach. 'What a hypocrite you are, Chloe. Always playing the role of Goody Two-shoes while you betrayed me in my own house.'

Chloe adopted a victim's expression. 'He wanted me. He waited for me.' She lifted her tearstained face to steal a look at her mother.

'The *bastard*!' Valerie erupted predictably. Nevertheless she took Chloe's shoulder in a hard grip. 'Sit up straight. You're al-

ways slouching about. You slept with your sister's *husband*?'
She gave her daughter a look of the utmost reproach.

'Like I wanted to? He was after me. Anyway, what does it
matter?' Chloe moaned. 'I was nothing to him. The only one
who was ever important to Mark was Allegra.'

'And to think I've been defending him!' Shock was written
all over Valerie. 'You've got a hell of a lot of explaining to do,
young lady.' She stared down at her daughter's mock penitent
head. All Chloe was sorry about was she had been exposed.
'What was in your mind to do such a thing?' Valerie demanded
to know.

'I don't really have an excuse. He took advantage of me. I'm
sorry,' Chloe mumbled, managing to sound shattered, which
in a way she was.

'Sorry? Is that the best you can do?' Valerie was suddenly
seeing her daughter very differently.

Allegra just stood there, her head spinning. 'Only Dad saw
through Mark,' she said. 'But Dad unfortunately held back because he thought I loved him.'

'Which you never did.' Valerie reverted to making Allegra
the scapegoat. 'You just needed a stepping stone.'

'You saw that, did you?'

Valerie smiled grimly, but didn't answer.

'Not loving Mark isn't something I'm proud of, Val. I *thought*
I loved him at the time. In retrospect it's pathetically clear I really wanted a home of my own. Someone to love *me*.'

Valerie turned away to sweep up the fragments of the broken
glass. 'What a swine he was! He seduced my Chloe.'

'Don't believe it!' Allegra scoffed. 'Chloe was right there in
the middle of it, ready to take whatever was going. I don't think
I want to talk to you again, Chloe,' she said. 'Not after today.'

'Who would care!' Chloe shouted. 'All you do is *burn* people.
Now it's Rory Compton who has to pay for coming into your
orbit. You seduced *him*. I haven't the slightest doubt of that. You
have seduction down to perfection.'

'My dear, I could take lessons off you,' Allegra said.

'What *did* happen with Rory Compton,' Valerie asked. her tone condemnatory.

Allegra studied her. 'Nothing as if you have any right to know. Rory came with a second offer, just as I told you. He had no idea you were away. He was enormously helpful shifting the stock to high ground. The creek was running a bumper. It's still high if you want to take the time to go down and look. He had to stay the night. It was raining far too heavily for him to drive back to Jimboorie.'

'And you lured him into your bed,' Chloe hit back. 'That's unforgivable, Allegra. You've always done it. As soon as any guy takes a liking to me you *have* to take him off me.'

'Haven't I told you that all along.' Valerie gave Allegra a venomous look. 'What are people going to say? Think of the scandal and so soon after your father's death. Let alone your divorce. But you scarcely care about that. You don't even know this man. You could destroy him.'

Allegra lowered her head in resignation. 'Val, you should have sought help a long time ago. The animosity that's in you is corrosive to the soul. I'll go back to Sydney until Naroom is sold. I can't stay here the situation being what it is. It's a thirty-day unconditional contract. Rory already has bank approval.'

'I want you to leave tomorrow,' Valerie said, slamming her two palms flat on the table.

'To hell with you and what you want. You forget yourself, Valerie. I'll leave when I'm good and ready.' Allegra's voice was so authoritative Valerie backed off. 'I'd be grateful if you could keep a civil tongue in your head until then. I've put up with your viciousness until now, but no more!'

'Viciousness?' Chloe jumped in to champion her mother.

'It's about time you stopped playing the ingénue, Chloe,' Allegra said . 'You're much too old for it. In your heart you know the situation. Your mother hates me.'

'Mum doesn't hate anyone,' Chloe declared, mostly because

she needed her mother on side. 'I know she can be a little sharp tongued from time to time, but she doesn't *hate* you, Allegra. *I* don't hate you. But you've never let me shine. Can you understand what that does to me? I've always been overshadowed. You're the beautiful sister, the clever sister, the one people ask after. They come up to me and say, 'How's your beautiful sister?' I hate it.' Her blue eyes flashed anger. 'That's why I slept with Mark. To get back at you. I hated myself afterwards. I had to pretend it never happened to live. It was only the once anyway.' That at least was the truth. 'I didn't like it. Rory is different. He would have liked me if you hadn't been around.'

'Wishful thinking, my dear,' Allegra said disdainfully, and walked away from them without a qualm.

Allegra shocked a lot of people when she handed in her resignation.

'But you had such a future with us, Allegra,' Juleanne Spencer, the Editor-in-Chief and something of a national icon, told her, staring in dismay across her magnificent antique desk. Their meeting had already lasted forty minutes but Juleanne, who had great persuasive powers, was distressed she wasn't about to sway her clever and, she would have thought, highly ambitious Fashion Editor. Allegra Hamilton had *real* style and an uncanny ability to combine glamour, excitement *and* wearability into the beautiful and imaginative fashion shoots the magazine was famous for.

'How our best laid plans go astray!' Juleanne lamented, taking a moment to think back over at least a hundred cock-ups. 'Really, darling, the sky was the limit! You had mountains to climb. It might seem impossible now but one day I have to retire.'

'When you're so young!' Allegra exclaimed.

'Young at heart, dear. You know I won't see sixty again.' Juleanne when last she looked had her sixty-sixth coming up, but then she didn't do the normal calculations like everyone else.

'We were actually counting the days until you returned. You're valued around here.'

'Emma is well able to take over from me.' She spoke confidently, referring to her Associate Fashion Editor. 'She's doing it already. I've seen this month's magazine.'

'Emma's good, but she's not *brilliant*.' Juleanne wrung her heavily bejewelled hands, nothing under four carats in sight. 'What about if I offered you a hefty raise?' Money always worked. At least on most people.

'You've already offered a hefty raise, Jules.'

'It's a man isn't it?' Juleanne, three times married, moaned, as if all one could expect from a man once married was mental cruelty or physical abuse. 'One of those—are there any others?—who doesn't want you to have a career?'

Allegra sweetened her answer with a smile. 'I've really enjoyed my time with the magazine, Jules. I've loved working under you. You've been my inspiration. I've turned myself inside out for you. You're a living legend. But I find at the end of the day I'm a country girl through and through.'

'But darling, you don't *look* it,' Juleanne said in horrified amazement. 'You always look sensational. Which is really lovely to have around the place. I just can't see you down on the farm mulling around three million cattle, or is it sheep?'

'More like eight thousand cattle these days, Jules. We're understocked. That means more feed in times of drought. The Outback is where I was raised.'

'You can't take an extended leave and get it out of your system?' Juleanne suggested hopefully.

'No.' Allegra shook her head.

'So you're seriously considering life on the land?' Wonderment was all over Juleanne's marvellously preserved, un-Botoxed face. 'It's a man, isn't it?' she repeated her question. 'Of course it is,' she said sadly, accepting defeat. 'My advice is have an affair with him, darling. You have no idea how marriage can disrupt a good relationship. By the way, now you're well shot of him, I never did like Mark. He reminded me of my second. Kept telling me he loved me then tried to drown me in the hot tub.'

The day after settlement day Rory made another long journey to Naroom to say goodbye to Valerie and Chloe who were taking a long overseas trip with the proceeds of the sale. They were now very comfortably off but they stopped well short of being happy. In fact both mother and daughter were acting like there was no justice left in the world. The greatest offence that was offered appeared to be the fact he *and* Allegra were co-owners of Naroom. Then there was their decision to marry. It was greeted as being on a par with a heinous crime.

He knew Chloe had a minor crush on him—he was sure it would soon pass, and he was sensitive to her hurt, but he hadn't given her the slightest encouragement. Somehow she had convinced herself Allegra had deliberately ruined her chances. Both Chloe and her mother were eaten up by jealousy, using it as a justification for attacking Allegra whenever they could. No wonder Allegra had returned to Sydney until the deal was done.

Unmoved by his every argument, she had insisted on paying for her half share of the station. 'This is the way I want it, Rory,' she told him. 'There's no other way. If you want me, you'll agree.'

'It's blackmail,' he'd said.

'Does it matter? This is what I want. Our arrangement will work better if we're equal partners. I don't want you working yourself to exhaustion trying to pay off the loan quickly. Which is exactly what you'd do. This way money is freed up for other things. Buying more stock, for one.'

Well he had said it was an arrangement to suit *both* of them. Allegra got her way. He was missing her so much his escalating emotions had firmed into an iron determination to take a trip to Sydney and bring her home.

Brilliant sunshine outdoors. A chill inside the homestead.

'I just hope you know what you're doing, Rory,' Valerie said, in the chastising voice she thought she had a right to. Valerie was big on rights. 'You haven't had time to get to know Allegra.'

'Oh, I think I know enough, Mrs. Sanders,' Rory replied, keeping a tight rein on his temper. What an awful woman! Not awful exactly. Totally obnoxious. Llew Sanders had made a huge tactical error there. Or maybe Valerie had kept her true nature underwraps.

Now she looked back at him with bitter eyes. 'Aren't you just the least bit apprehensive, considering Allegra couldn't make a go of her marriage?'

'I believe she told you why,' Rory spoke crisply. 'That good man was unfaithful.'

'Perhaps she drove him to it?' Like the leopard Valerie couldn't change her spots.

'I warned you about Allegra, Rory, but you wouldn't listen,' Chloe, the two-faced deceiver added.

'I believe I'm a much better judge of character than you, Chloe,' he said firmly. 'I can appreciate you've suffered believing yourself outshone by Allegra, but that was hardly her fault. Happiness mightn't have eluded you if you hadn't been so jealous of your half sister.' He held up his hand as she opened her mouth to defend herself. 'No, let me finish. I can't sit here and allow either of you to attack Allegra. You do it all the time. It's upsetting. Worse, it's dead boring. I have an older brother, Jay. I love him very much. *He* will inherit Turrawin, when my father dies. Not me. If I'd allowed myself to become bitter about it, it would have ruined a wonderful relationship. There was nothing either of us could do. That was the way of it with you. Allegra could have been your closest friend, Chloe. Instead something bad happened. Between you and your mother, you turned her into an outsider.'

Valerie sat motionless, but the steam of outrage was rising off her. 'How dare you talk to me like that.'

'I do dare, Mrs Sanders.' Rory unfolded himself to his impressive height. 'If there's something I can do for you to help you get away, I'm happy to do it. Otherwise I'll go.'

'I prefer you did,' Valerie said very coldly.

It was futile to remain a moment longer; or point out the irony of being ordered off what was now *his* and Allegra's property. Rory didn't like to tangle with irate, irrational women. He walked down the front steps, making for his vehicle which he'd parked in the shade of a stand of gums. The trees were bearing enormous quantities of yellow blossoms enticing lorikeets in their dozens to feed noisily on the nectar.

He was surprised when Chloe came running after him.

'Rory, please stop,' she called.

It would have been churlish for him not to, but he was fed up. 'What is it, Chloe?' He waited for her to come up to him. A short run yet she was puffing hard. He suddenly saw it through Allegra's eyes. Chloe, the girl, always making excuses to stay at home with her mother. Chloe not getting outdoors and not getting enough exercise.

'I apologise for Mum's talking like that,' she said, darting a swift glance at his stern expression and away again. 'You must understand she's terribly upset.'

'I'm upset, too, Chloe.'

'She was only trying to help you!' Chloe sought to appease him. 'We've been through so much with Allegra.'

His expression was openly condemning. 'You ought to stop telling howlers, Chloe. It's a hard habit to break. Actually what Allegra's been through springs more easily to mind. But you can't help yourself, can you? It's almost become second nature. It seems to me, your mother has used you to bolster her position in the household. Personally I think she must have given Allegra one hell of a time when she was growing up. When you think about it, it's amazing Allegra has come through so wonderfully well. It's called *character.*'

Chloe couldn't have looked more forlorn. 'You're in love with her, aren't you?' she said, mournfully. ' I can see it in your eyes. It's no *arrangement*. No marriage of convenience. You're hiding behind that word. You *love* her.'

'Maybe I do,' he said, his silver eyes distant.

'Then she's going to make you suffer!' Chloe flared up, the brittle, attacking edge back in her voice. 'Just like Mark.'

'Why don't *you* marry him Chloe?' Rory suggested, wondering at her startled, maybe guilty expression? 'So long now. Have a good trip. I hope you learn something along the way. You might even consider striking out on your own when you come home.' He began to move off then half turned back. 'By the way, suffering with Allegra sounds infinitely better than setting up house with any other woman I know.'

The four weeks had been fairly peaceful for Allegra, though she found herself missing Rory with every fibre of her being. They kept in constant touch. For the most part he reported to her daily and she called him frequently at the Jimboorie pub where he was staying until Valerie and Chloe moved out. The last time he had spoken to her he told her he wanted her home.

Home!

She couldn't believe the momentum her life had taken on. Everyone knew of rebound relationships. They happened all the time. She was one hundred percent certain she wasn't on any rebound from Mark. What was happening was destiny. She was finding it incredibly exciting. She even felt truly young again as though she had been given a second chance to leave her unhappy past behind.

Mark had wounded her pride and self-esteem. With Rory she felt she wasn't so much taking a risk with their 'marriage of convenience'—she knew in her heart it wasn't—she was daring to dream. She wanted a husband she could love and respect; she wanted children before it was too late. If the timing appeared too soon after the breakdown of one marriage, to her it only offered proof there were miracles in life.

At some point on the way to her parked car, Allegra had the

unnerving feeling someone was following her. She stopped, looked back a few times, but everything appeared normal for 5:20 on a midweek working day. Crowds jostled. Shoppers, laden with carry bags, made their way, heads down, for the underground city car parks or the trains. Office workers were spilling out of the tall buildings and onto the streets; eager young single women raced home to change for dinner or the theatre, their faces alight with anticipation. She would return to Naroom at the weekend. It was now Wednesday. Saturday couldn't come soon enough!

She had arrived home, relaxing in her apartment, sipping a glass of chilled sauvignon blanc and watching a current affairs programme when there was a knock at her door. Probably Liz Delaney, an art dealer, from the adjoining apartment. Allegra had promised to have lunch with Liz before she went back. They had become good friends over the time since she had moved into the apartment post her break-up with Mark. An outside visitor would have had to get through security so it had to be someone in her section of the building that contained six apartments.

She looked through the peephole. No one there. That was odd. A number of times she'd come home to find a parcel outside her door kindly delivered by the management team, husband and wife. Maybe they'd come by. She opened the door slightly and as she did so there was Mark! As usual he looked wonderfully well tended, expensively dressed, flushed and cheerful, holding a very beautiful bouquet of dark red roses and a glittering ribboned box.

'Ally! You're a sight for sore eyes!' He smiled at her broadly, pleasure surging into his voice. 'May I come in for a minute.'

'I'm sorry. That's out of the question, Mark. We're divorced, remember?' Allegra's expression wasn't in the least hospitable, although she quickly adjusted to the shock of seeing him. Mark's turning up like this wasn't so extraordinary. He had always thought his manners and his monstrous brand of charm could gain him entrée anywhere.

Could it have been Mark who'd been following her? Possibly but he had never been violent or dangerous.

'Oh, don't be like that!' he begged, still looking enormously pleased with himself. Another woman? 'I've got some good news I'd like to share with you. You're not going out, are you?'

'As a matter of fact I am.' She found it easy to tell a white lie.

'I promise to be out of here in under twenty minutes,' he said. 'I have a date myself this evening. A wonderful violinist is in town A young woman, very good-looking, which will make her appearance on stage all the more exciting. You know I'm thrilled to see you, Ally. You don't mind if I say that? After all, we were very fond of one another. You can spare me a few minutes, surely?'

Even as she queried her own judgement, she found herself letting him in. Why was that, ingrained politeness?

He handed the roses and the ribboned box to her, still smiling as though he were riding the crest of a wave. Maybe he was remarrying? Anything was possible with Mark. She wondered if a phone call from her to his latest conquest might put a stop to it but reasoned with Mark's capacity for deception that wouldn't be a good idea.

'So what's the good news, Mark?' she asked, waving him into a chair while she set his offerings down on the kitchen counter. Her mobile was to hand if she needed it. He could take his little presents with him when he left. 'You'll have to be brief. I have yet to shower and dress.'

'You never answered any of my calls,' he said in a soft chiding voice. He had a very good speaking voice and he knew how to use it.

'No.' She didn't offer an explanation. None was needed. She had in fact given instructions to her secretary at work, not on any account to put him through. She had an unlisted number at the apartment, so that took care of that.

'You have to know I miss you terribly,' he said, looking at her with fervent eyes.

'That's not something I want to hear, Mark.' There was more than an edge of coldness in her manner.

'There's no one, absolutely no one like you,' he continued strongly.

'And here I was thinking you were about to tell me you're remarrying?' she scoffed, starting to feel very angry with herself. Her judgement about Mark had always been off.

'Listen, my girl!' Mark, a well built man, leaned forwards in the armchair, his attitude abruptly hardening. 'I don't think I'll ever get around to a second marriage, which is not to say I won't have women friends from time to time. I'd probably have stayed a happy bachelor, only you entered my life. So beautiful and so innocent, irresistible!'

Allegra's mouth went dry. 'Mark, this is all ancient history. And I'm *not* your girl.'

'Open your parcel,' he said as though that would surely soften her up. 'I bought it especially for you.'

She shook her head. 'Sorry. I'm not accepting gifts from you, Mark. My fiancé wouldn't like it.'

'Fiancé?' His expression changed dramatically. 'I don't believe you.'

She placed a hand over her eyes. 'Mark, it doesn't really matter if you believe me or not. I have a new life that doesn't include you.'

He looked shocked. 'I think you're just making this up. You want to punish me.' An odd look of weird excitement crept into his expression.

'From the stupid look on your face you're finding that incredibly erotic.' Allegra stared at him in disgust, ready to get rid of him. 'You haven't sought professional help, have you?'

'What a crosspatch you are!' he laughed heartily. '*You're* the one who really needs it. Come on, 'fess up. You miss me. God knows I want *you* back.'

Allegra moved swiftly behind the counter and picked up her mobile phone, holding it up for him to see. 'Mark, I'd like you to leave. I can summon help in precisely half a minute and my fiancé will be arriving in under an hour. He won't expect to see you and I assure you, you won't want to be around when he arrives. I've told him all about you, you see.'

Mark came to his feet, looking deeply offended. 'Damn it, what is there to tell? I wasn't a wife beater. I wasn't a bully. I didn't abuse you in any way. In fact I spoilt you rotten. What's this fiancé's name?'

His smile now looked more like a snarl. 'He's not anyone you know, Mark. His domain is the Outback.'

'And you're going to live in that godforsaken wilderness with him?' His expression was utterly scornful. 'How long do you think that would last? A beautiful creature like you willing to ditch a glamorous career and a lavish lifestyle for life in limbo with a *cowboy*? I mean where's the bloody culture?'

'I'm not chucking it as you seem to think. And I'm not decamping to Mars. The Outback is in my blood. I'm addicted to the vast open spaces. You never could believe that, but it's true. Besides, the man I'm going to marry is an achiever, Mark. A potential empire builder. He's also a cultured, sensitive man. We have many interests in common. Quite apart from that I've done what I never thought I'd get to do. I've fallen deeply in *love*.'

Mark just stood there. When he spoke his voice was quite calm, even sober. 'Ally, my darling, it's just another one of your little self-deceptions. You don't seem to have learned a thing married to me. You're so young and ignorant of the ways of the world. If you're speaking the truth and you are thinking of remarrying you'll only regret it. Despite everything you've done to me, I still love you. My God, didn't I prove it? You had everything you ever needed.'

'You should really have your head read, Mark,' she said wearily. 'You look so distinguished, so benign, but underneath I think you're mad. You can't love someone then betray them with extramarital affairs. We had some happy times, but they were quickly over. Our marriage was a big mistake for us both. *I'm* over it.'

'Well I'm *not!*' he said and looked at her like a wounded lion. 'I should never have let you go. But even I got sick of your parading your virtuous ways. For all you know, this Outback hero of yours could beat you up. Who would hear you in all that isolation? Who would know? You're taking a far greater risk with him than you ever did with me.'

'I doubt it!' she said with certainty. 'He doesn't have a personality disorder. Now, Mark, please go, or you might be the one who gets beaten up. My fiancé is six-three, years younger than you and superbly fit. I don't want him to hurt you.'

But Mark stood glued to the spot. 'Give me a kiss for old time's sake,' he begged.

'Don't attempt to touch me,' Allegra warned. 'This is all so undignified, Mark.'

Real tears stood in his eyes. 'You won't come back to me? I promise I'll never deceive you again.'

Allegra turned the mobile phone to her and started to punch in some numbers.

'All right, all right!' Mark held up a hand. 'I'm going.' He began to walk to the door.

Allegra followed, hugely relieved, but at the last moment Mark whirled about, clasping her in his arms and rocking her back and forth. 'I'll always be there for you, Ally. Will you remember that?'

'We're divorced, Mark. End of story.' Somehow Allegra managed to get a hand around him and turn the door knob. 'If I never lay eyes on you again, I *won't* miss you. Now *please*, go, or you might be late for your concert.'

Even as she pushed the door closed after him, he was still protesting. Oh God! The last thing she wanted was trouble.

Allegra gave it a minute, then she stared through the peephole. Either he was standing back from the door or he had walked off to the lift. She'd already turned the dead lock now she stood with her back to the door for a few minutes trying to calm herself.

Surely he had gone? And damn! In her agitation she had forgotten to give back his gifts. The scent of the roses reminded her. Their heady fragrance was like a mist in the air. After five minutes her pulses began to slow. Mark wasn't a complete fool. His public persona of sophisticated businessman about town was important to him.

It came as a double shock to hear another rap on her door a few minutes later. She stood silent, waiting for another one. It came and it wasn't gentle. Lord, was she going to have to ring the police? She loathed scenes. She was a very private person. Had Mark really taken leave of his senses? Allegra tossed her long hair over her shoulders and walked purposefully to the door, half afraid of what she might find.

It wasn't Mark standing there. It was Rory.

My God, *Rory*!

She started to shake with excitement. She 'd almost forgotten how tall he was.

She threw open the door on a wave of euphoria, her face radiant. 'Rory, how wonderful! What are you doing here? Why didn't you let me know you were coming?'

If she was expecting a long, lingering kiss or even a hug, preferably both, she didn't get either. He didn't smile. He had reverted to the dark, brooding look. 'Hello, Allegra. I'm here.'

'Of course you're here!' She grabbed his arm and tried to pull him in, dismayed by the resistance she felt in his powerful body. 'What's the matter?' she asked in perplexity, her euphoria dropping to dismay.

'Aren't you going to ask me how I got into the building?' He let his eyes slash over her, taking in her long flowing hair and the informality of her dress—a lovely yellow silk caftan banded in gold.

She stared at him in consternation. 'Isn't it enough you're here in the room? Okay, how *did* you get into the building?'

'One hell of a shock, too!' He walked past her into the living room, feeling so incredibly rattled he scarcely knew what he was doing. This was a far cry from when he had started out, feeling on top of the world. Here was the woman who could so easily make his life or break it. He had known that from the beginning but his decision to put his trust in her had been taken at the deepest level. Now *this*! All his old insecurities rushed to the fore like an unstoppable torrent. 'I ran into your ex-husband,' he said, as if that explained everything. 'You know, faithless old Mark. Imagine that! What timing! He'd just come from visiting you as I was about to make my way up.'

Her face paled. Surely he couldn't think he had caught her out? That made her angry. Here he was pushing her away when she had expected to be hauled close. 'How did you know it was Mark?' she countered. 'For that matter how did he know it was you? Heavens, you've never laid eyes on one another.'

'Ah, yes, but intuition is an amazing thing!' He rounded on her with a high, mettled look. 'Chloe had given me a fairly good description of him as well.'

'Ah, yes, Chloe, my little sister and my best friend. I don't think.' She wasn't about to confide in him about Chloe. Not at this stage, maybe never. 'So what did you say to each other?' She was becoming more agitated by the minute.

'Do you think I'd tell you?' His tone was near cutting *Stop, man, stop! Stay quiet until you calm down.* But he couldn't. He was jealous and incredibly distressed. To be so high, then plunged so low was hell. 'It was man stuff. Or at least it was man stuff my side. I think poor Mark is still mopping himself up.'

'You *hit* him?' Allegra felt a real pang of worry. Mark was enormously vain about his appearance. He wouldn't be any match for Rory.

'Just a tap on the nose. Relax,' he said sarcastically. 'Are those his roses?' He whipped his dark head in the direction of the counter where the roses lay in all their glory.

'Yes. I f-forgot to give them back to him.' Despite herself, Allegra stammered. Surely he would interpret that as a sign of guilt?

'What's in the box?' He coolly scrutinised her when his blood was on fire. She looked so beautiful she filled him with a furious desire. He had missed her so badly. Then the ex-husband appears. What was he supposed to think? The ex was giving notice of his intention to pay frequent visits? They could still be friends? What the hell was it all about? She let him in, didn't she?

'How should I know,' she answered him sharply, feeling goaded. 'I haven't opened it.'

'Let's open it now, shall we?' He strode off to the counter, the man of action.

Allegra spoke uneasily. 'I'd rather return it intact.'

'No, I want to see what sort of present he brought you,' he insisted. 'I seem to remember you're telling me once he was ancient history?'

'So he is. You're jealous?' She decided to do a little goading of her own.

'You bet I am, lady,' he clipped off.

At least that was good to hear. She began to settle. Jealousy she could handle. It was the lack of trust she couldn't. 'Surely you don't think I invited him here?' She gave him a cool, challenging look.

'He said you did!' He didn't rip at the glittering wrapping, neither did he lose any time getting it off.

'And you believed him?' She stared at him, horrified, fascinated, scarcely believing he was here with her. It should have been a wonderful reunion—she had been planning for it—instead they were into a ding dong fight.

'I didn't say that.' He realised calming down was going to

take a little time. He had invested so much of what was in him in her. He had allowed her to become his heart, damn it!

'Well, that's okay then.' Allegra said, only half mollified.

'But you did very foolishly open the door to him,' he pointed out with a deep, vertical frown between his brows.

The atmosphere was starting to get very heated. 'So? I made a mistake. Haven't *you* ever made a mistake?'

'Of course. But I'm not going to make one with you!' There was desire in his eyes. And suspicion. Both equally intense.

'What is that supposed to mean?' Her voice filled with disdain. 'When are you going to decide you can trust me?'

'I was sure I *did*, God, Allegra, I thought we were committed to one another, then your ex-husband shows up. Well, what do you know!' He withdrew an exquisite and what had to be on the body a very revealing nightgown from its tissue paper wrapping, draping it over his hand. 'And look, there's a note to go with it. Isn't that sweet!'

'Give me that.' She made a little run at him, clutching for the card.

He easily fended her off. 'You can have it in a minute. I'm *dying* to read it.'

'Rory, I *hate* this.' She gritted her teeth.

'You think I'm enjoying it?' He held her off with one arm. "Couldn't resist this one," he read out. 'It's so exactly you, my darling. All my love now and always, Marko.' Marko? You called him Marko?' He raised infuriatingly supercilious, black brows.

'I hate to admit my poor judgement, but I used to think I was in love with him,' she said tightly.

'I'm so glad you used the past tense. When *exactly* did the loving stop?' His voice was a velvet rasp.

'When it was replaced by disgust.' She gave a brittle, self-deprecating laugh. 'Put the damned thing away, Rory. You're upsetting me.'

'Do you have any idea how *I* feel?' he asked. 'I couldn't wait for the moment I would see you again. I'm just wondering why,' he added unforgivably, but hell he was desperate. He studied the lovely garment carefully.

'How dare you say that!' Allegra fired back.

'Okay, I'm sorry. But we're supposed to be getting married remember?' He stroked the silk-satin beneath his fingers as if to calm himself. 'You wear things like this?'

'I *said*, put it back.' She made a futile clutch for it.

Somehow they were pressed together, both trembling with anger, and a sexual excitement that was gaining strength by the minute.

His handsome face held a searing mockery. 'I confess I'm not surprised poor old Marko got a bit out of hand.'

She stared back at him, devastated by the taunting in his eyes. 'Stop that right now.'

'Sure. We don't need to talk about him. I have to say I wouldn't mind seeing you in this myself.' He pulled her ever closer, desperate for that closeness, knowing where it was going to take them.

'I've missed you.' She hadn't meant to say it, but something in his eyes drew it from her.

His eyes raced over her face. 'You're telling me I'm important to you?' His tone couldn't have been more intense.

'Of course you're important to me,' she said fierily. 'I thought *I* was important to you. Or have you decided you don't trust me after all?'

He heaved a breath, his arms tightening around her. 'He told me you left him because you tired of him. 'Sadly I wasn't enough for her!' he said. He admitted being unfaithful to you, but he said you drove him to it. 'Ally's everything a man could ever want!''

She broke his grip, shocked by the force of her outrage. 'Don't talk to me about Mark Hamilton. He's a man who places himself above the rules of common decency. He's my *past*. Can we get that straight? Or does something in you *want* to believe what he had to say. No, don't deny it. You've got problems, Rory Compton.'

'Hell yes!' He hauled her back into his arms, 'I'd been counting on you to wash them away. So I was angry and confused... incredibly jealous. Is that so unusual in a man in love? But I couldn't have believed him, could I? Or else why did I hit him?' The tension in his body wouldn't ease. His face remained taut, his arms like iron.

Allegra swallowed. *A man in love!* 'He actually needed a thrashing,' she said. 'He's such a liar. All he does is *act*. I refuse to talk about him anymore. He's not worth my breath. When he came to the door I thought he was going to tell me he'd found someone new. Honestly he can play any role. I intended to give him back his damned presents but it was more urgent to get him out the door.' Deep hurt rippled through her voice. 'You so fear betrayal, don't you?'

'Don't *you*?' he retorted, his eyes trained on her. 'After your experience—'

'Hush, that's enough!' She laid a finger against his lips. 'The all important thing is I trust *you*. But if you're going to make a habit of jumping to the wrong conclusions it could destroy everything we're trying to build. Tell me where are we now?' Her blue eyes were ablaze. *A man in love?*

'Here together,' he said more quietly. 'I'm just a fool of a man. You have to keep that in mind.' His voice broke under the pressure of his feelings. 'God, I don't want to argue any more, either. I've gone beyond arguing.'

'That's good, because I—'

He could take no more.

Her breath was cut off under the exquisite crush of his mouth.

Rory recognised he hadn't been in control of himself or the situation after what had seemed to him an eternity of denial. He had missed her so much. Now the only thing he could do was communicate his driving need of her through his fervent kisses. He had never imagined he could be so jealous. He was ashamed now. He knew from this day forth he could never claim he knew nothing about male jealousy getting out of hand.

For long moments they were locked together, like a warring couple, each frantically aroused and taking what they wanted from the other. Passion crackled like a bush fire, spurting out of control. Somehow he was free of his jacket. His shirt was open and she had thrust her hand into the opening, her slender fingers stroking over his chest and tugging at the curling coils of hair. She was muttering something to him but he was so far gone, the meaning of her words wasn't getting through to him. Only when she gave a little keening cry did he draw back.

'I've hurt you?' He was torn between the need for restraint and the pounding desire to go on doing what he was doing to her.

'You've no idea how you've hurt me.' Sexual excitement had her shaking. Suddenly she was pummelling his chest, training blazing eyes on him. 'I hate you for doing that to me, Rory.'

'No one will ever hate me better.' He felt exultant, almost not sorry for what had gone before because it was so incredibly exciting to make up.

'Either you trust me or you don't.' She issued the ultimatum.

'I do trust you. Kind of.' He drew back a little, staring down into her beautiful blue topaz eyes. There was wild colour under her skin. 'Is it possible you've grown *more* beautiful?'

'Don't soft soap me!' she warned, trying to break away again. This wasn't going to be any easy submission.

'Come here.' He wrestled her back into his arms, not extending even a tiny part of his strength. Both of them were at fever pitch instinctively aware it had only one outcome. 'Don't let's talk, Allegra. Not now anyway. Talk is important, but I desperately want to make love to you. My body can tell you what maybe my words can't. But first, you have to tell me quickly. Can I?'

She drew back in amazement. 'You're asking permission? How quaint after the way you've been arousing me.'

'You don't feel you were arousing me back?' he asked with a dry laugh. 'Oh God, Allegra, I'm not asking permission. I'm asking if it's okay? I told you I want children. But I want lots of *you* first.'

His meaning suddenly dawned on her. 'Oh!' she exclaimed, starting to melt.

'That's a beautiful gown.' His tone was so gentle, but incredibly seductive. 'A caftan isn't it?' His hands slid caressingly over the silk that covered her breasts.

'Yes.' She gave a stifled gasp, unbearably excited by his touch. 'And you're changing the subject.'

'What was the subject? Ah, yes. Can I take you to bed?' His eyes lingered on her mouth, so luscious and cushiony soft. 'Or are you going to find the strength to resist me?'

Such a question when he could see how much she was in thrall to him. 'How vain you are, how arrogant!'

'Not true!' His mood was elation. He resumed kissing her, making every part of her come throbbingly alive.

Allegra had to softly moan at the sheer wonder of it. His hands began to move down over the long line of her back. They cupped her taut buttocks, lifted them slightly as he pressed the sensitive delta of her body against him, showing her the strength of his arousal. He was all man, all muscle, all effortless mastery.

She felt her eyelids flutter. She had never been so conscious of her most intimate parts of her body and the changes that took place in them under sexual stimulation.

'I love you in yellow,' he murmured, working little nibbling kisses down the graceful line of her throat. ' It does marvellous things for your colouring.'

Her trembling was increasing so much so she could barely stand. In fact without his supporting arms she thought she would simply sag to the floor. 'I'll remember that.' She spoke jaggedly. 'You really should have told me you were coming.' She was getting weaker by the minute.

'I wanted to surprise you.' The kisses didn't halt, but became even more passionate. His strong arms took more of her weight.

'You succeeded.' What wonderful sensory powers he had! She felt as though a man had never touched her before. She had read about heroines of fiction swooning away under the weight of desire but she had never expected to experience the sensation herself.

'So it's all right to take you to bed?' Urgently he lifted his dark head waiting for her answer.

'To sleep?' She hooded her eyes, teasing, tempting and luring him on.

'You can. *Afterwards!*' His face was shadowed with strong emotion. 'That's if you *want* to.'

She was leaning the length of her body against him one minute, the next he held her high in his arms. 'Which way?'

'Down the hallway, last door on the right.' Her voice was as shaky as if she'd run the four-minute mile.

The night was endless magic. They didn't sleep. They made love—*loving* each other—right through the long, moonlit hours. By the time dawn broke over the city each knew every centimetre of the other's body and what pleasure exploration could bring.

Gradually light filled Allegra's bedroom, turning the broad expanses of glass on the sliding doors to molten gold.

Rory turned to her, pulled her in tight and kissed her. 'You're so beautiful,' he said. 'I want to spend the rest of my life with you. I want to wake every morning with you by my side. I want to go to bed with you every night of my life. Will you marry me, Allegra?'

'Haven't I said I would?' She pressed her own kiss onto his mouth.

'Not a marriage by arrangement,' he said firmly.

'Never! This is a true love match. Heart, body and soul. You're my future, the love of my life.'

'Thank the Lord for letting it happen!' He released a deep, heartfelt breath. 'We're part of each other.'

'We *are* each other,' she smiled tenderly. After last night they weren't two people, but one.

'That's exactly how I feel.' He leaned back to the bedside table. 'I meant to give you this last night, but we sort of got carried away.'

'It was wonderful!' She lifted her arms ecstatically above her head, stretching like a cat.

'And it's not over.' He gave her a beautiful smile over his shoulder.

She held it, treasuring it, treasuring him. 'What are you doing?' she asked.

'You'll see. I want to do this right.' He threw back the sheet and stood up, a bronze sculpture come to life.

'Rory, what *is* it?' Those silver sparkles in his eyes thrilled her.

He looked for some clothes; pulled them on. 'Stay there.' He held up his hand as she made to move out of bed. 'You couldn't look more beautiful if you tried.' He came around to her side, kneeling down on the carpet. 'My first proposal was utterly unworthy of you,' he said. 'I thought in my damned foolishness I had to put it like a business proposition. I didn't want to frighten you off. This proposal is more fitting. It carries with it all my love. Give me your hand, Allegra, love of my life. You're everything I've been looking for and never thought I'd find.'

Sometimes it was all a woman could do not to burst into tears. She couldn't take her eyes away from what he held in his palm. The slender hand she extended to him was visibly shaking.

'As blue as your eyes,' he said, his face transfigured by love. He showed her the sapphire and diamond ring he had commissioned for her.

Her voice went suddenly very small. 'This is the most beautiful thing that has ever happened to me,' she whispered, her eyes huge in her creamy face. Her hair tumbled around it and over her naked shoulders. Her breasts glowed in the golden wash of light.

'Our love is the one true thing,' he said, intensity in his gaze. He began to slide the beautiful ring down her finger to where it belonged.

'Oh, Rory!' Her eyes, glittering with tears, outshone the precious stone.

'Do you like it?' His voice was gentle, his upward glance full of desire.

She leaned forward to kiss his marvellous mouth. 'I *love* it. I'll never take if off.' Looking at him her voice turned husky. 'You on the other hand have to take off those clothes and get back into bed.'

He did.

CHAPTER EIGHT

THE CHANNEL COUNTRY was in flower.

It was a magnificent sight, Jay thought as he sat his beloved motor bike looking out over the phenomenal floral display he'd rejoiced in since early childhood. The miracle of the flowers! Why wasn't Rory here to enjoy it! His brother's absence had all but stripped him of any joy in life. But there were moments like now to lift the heart. The sad thing was very few people over the short one hundred and forty years of settlement of the vast Outback had been blessed by 'the vision splendid.' Ah well, such was the remoteness of their pocket of the world!

Good rains after long periods of drought always did bring forth the most spectacular displays he recalled. The longer the drought the more dormant seeds lay ready to germinate. Nature took with one hand and gave with another. The man on the land accepted that. This vast, remote, sixty thousand square mile area, a major flood plain system, had been endowed with marvellous rain and they were all rejoicing. Their three giant sprawling rivers, the Diamantina, the Georgina and the Cooper that in the Dry flowed sluggishly for many hundreds of miles, sometimes barely flowing at all, had all but met up. The Cooper alone ran fifty miles wide carrying the overflow from the monsoonal rains in the north, more than a thousand miles away.

It was the massive interlocking system of drainage channels that gave his riverine desert home its name. The twisting, multi-channelled water courses crisscrossed fiery-red sand plains, dune fields, alluvial clay plains and even found their way into areas of the hill country. This was about as good as it got. All the neighbouring stations were ecstatic. Stations that went by formidable names: Nocatunga, Nocundra, Monkira, Malagarga, Mooraberrie, Moondai, Currawilla, Coorabulka, Turrawin, Turrapirrie, Kinjarra, Keerongooloo... The list went on. Cattle stations on both sides of the mighty Simpson Desert had long been regarded as the premier cattle fattening stations in the land. Not only did zillions of wildflowers spring to life after flooding, like now, so, too, did the native grasses and clovers, the golden Spinifex, the pearl-grey saltbush, blue bush, cotton bush and the valuable succulent, the pink parakeelya to fatten the stock. Long after the rains had dried up, and the sweet fattening herbage had disappeared, dry herbage was still delivering rich feed, packed full of nutrients.

It was to take advantage of the peak conditions stock from two of Turrawin's outstations had been trucked in. Cattle that had roamed far into the Simpson in search of feed during the period of drought were being mustered and brought back within the boundaries of the run. It made for a lot of backbreaking toil. There never was an end to it. Never life without the spice of danger. Because of the flooding, Turrawin had been cut off from the mail run for a couple of weeks, so he had yet to receive longed for mail from Rory, last stop a place called Jimboorie. He seized upon it knowing Rory would always keep him informed of his whereabouts.

A new overseer had been hired by the name of Mike O'Connor. He came highly recommended. Better still, because it made for stability, Mike was a happily married man with a wife, Janine, who had made a very comfortable home for them in the old overseer's bungalow. They had a young son they were very proud of who was at boarding school in Brisbane. He would be coming home for vacations. From all accounts the boy was thrilled his father had landed the job on historic Turrawin. A seasoned stockman, Mike was proving invaluable support. In some respects he reminded Jay of Rory, calm in any situation, clear sighted, fair but authoritative with the men. As soon as the waters totally subsided and the scattered stock were brought in he was determined on going in search of his brother and after that, who knows? Jay thought himself capable of many things, but running a huge cattle enterprise wasn't one of them. Sooner or later, their father would come to his senses. He needed Rory far more than Rory needed him.

For the first time Jay was serious about wanting to start an entirely new life. Rory was the rightful heir to Turrawin by virtue of his special skills and leadership qualities. Rory was the son to take over. Jay was happy with that. An uneasy truce existed between him and his father these days. Jay knew his father hadn't taken his intention to make a new life for himself seriously. His father didn't give him credit for anything much yet he had pushed both his sons to the limit. Rory had thrived even in adversity. Jay thought he couldn't survive much more of the harsh treatment his father dished out. As soon as he could, he was moving out.

'So how's O'Connor coping?' Bernard Compton demanded to know the very instant Jay set foot on the homestead verandah. It was midafternoon and he had returned briefly to get another pair of boots. The ones he was wearing had all but packed it in.

'Why don't you come see for yourself?' Jay suggested, so weary he slumped into a wicker chair.

'I just might do that,' his father said.

'Better than sitting around the house,' Jay offered mildly, as though the outcome was self-evident. 'It's downright unhealthy, Dad. What's happened to you in this last year? You seem to have lost all interest in station work.'

'Why do I have to work when I've got you?' his father returned acidly. 'And this new bloke.'

'But you've always been so active,' Jay persisted, truly worried about his father. 'Are you ill, Dad? Is there something wrong with you? Something you're not saying?'

Bernard Compton took a deep breath. Held it in. 'There's nothing in my life I can change,' he said grimly.

'What do you *want* to change?' Jay stared across at his father, thinking no matter how much he tried he would never understand the man. 'Are you upset about Rory?'

'I suppose,' Bernard admitted grudgingly. Rory was vigour, vitality, hell, he was even *rage*! Too arrogant for his own good.

'It's not too late to say you're sorry, Dad. Get him home.' Jay's tone brightened with hope. He knew he just had to wait and his dad would weaken.

But his father laughed at him. A cruel laugh. 'No, thank you!' he said adamantly. 'Better he stays away. I'm sick of him challenging me. If only you had some of his guts!' he lamented. 'But you'll never make it as a cattleman, Jay. You're always going to need a good overseer.'

Jay sighed, well used to hearing his father's dismal opinion of him. 'Got it, Dad. You've told me a million times. But you weren't so crash hot at the job, were you? Sure Rory's strong. He walks tall and he walks fearlessly. But he's in the mould of Grandad, not you. I'd give anything to see Rory right now.' His voice gentled with love.

'Just listen to you!' Bernard Compton laughed so hard he began to wheeze. 'You sound like a damned girl.'

Sometimes Jay thought his inner wounds would run blood. 'You're not the father I wanted, either, Dad.' He rose to his feet, thinking he didn't give a damn about getting his boots now. 'Why don't you saddle up a horse and come down to the camp,' he suggested, forever tolerant. 'We're at the Five Mile. Your skin is blotched and your eyes bloodshot. You don't look well. You've got to put a stop to your drinking, Dad. You're coming at sixty. The life you're leading makes you a prime candidate for a heart attack or a stroke.'

Bernard Compton's heavy, handsome face turned a burning red. He glared up at his son. 'When I want advice from you I'll ask for it, *Doctor* Compton,' he sneered. 'Now bugger off and leave me in peace.'

Jay jumped the steps and strode off to his motor bike.

He hiked a leg over the high powered machine, turned the ignition, revved the engine, then tore off in a cloud of dust and fallen leaves. There were still more hours of driving cattle out of some very rough places. The chopper was in the air. He preferred riding the bike to mustering by chopper, which could be very dangerous, or mustering on horseback for that matter. He loved his motor bike—he maintained it extra well—but he didn't look as good on a bike as Rory. Hell, he could never hope to be as good as Rory at anything. The thought didn't make him feel bitter, rather sad.

You sound like a damned girl!

He wasn't ashamed of loving his brother. God no! He loved Rory far too much for bitterness. It was the way Rory loved him. Why couldn't Rory have been the firstborn? He'd asked that question for years on end. Futile question but he asked it all the same. Even then Rory would have needed to look like their father and not their beautiful mother.

Mum!

Flying along at speed, the motor roaring with power, Jay was filled with gut wrenching memories. Jay was a young man who had always felt with too much intensity. Most of the time he was able to block his worst memories out. For some reason when he was physically very stretched, like now, they flooded into his mind. He'd better get a check on them.

How the grasses had grown! In some places they were long enough to hide a man. Turrawin looked simply amazing after the rains. When they were kids he and Rory used to stay in the desert overnight, tucked up in their sleeping bags, telling one another stories, staring up at the trillions of glittering stars. In the dawn they awoke, floating on an ocean of white paper daisies with seeds that would endure forever. When they arrived back at the homestead their mother would be looking out for them, gathering them into her arms.

'Had fun, my darlings?'

Abruptly Jay changed direction, some overriding pressure bearing down on him and clouding his judgement. He followed not the course of the waterway that ran past the Five Mile camp, but headed out across the sea of Mitchell grasses relishing the scent of new-mown grass that rose from beneath the crush of the tyres. A great flight of budgerigar rode the thermal currents above him; a fluttering V shaped banner of green and gold. The wind was whistling in his ears and whipping his hair back. Only then did he realise he had left his helmet back on the verandah. Hell that was a mistake. But his father always managed to upset him. His feeling was his father was ailing in some way. No point in suggesting he see a doctor. Bernard Compton was a desperately stubborn man. He could be his undoing.

Once Jay heaved up then lunged as the front wheel hit something concealed in the grass. The impact almost unseated him. Not quite. Still he punched the gas, as if he were recharging his own batteries. It was only at the last minute he spotted through the screening a big ugly rock rearing up out of the grass dead set front of him.

It was too late to jump it. He hit the brakes knowing there was very little he could do now to avoid being badly injured or utterly extinguished. The motor bike crashed into the rock with bone-jarring impact, the front wheel bearing the brunt of it. Jay felt his body rise metres up into the air as if he had grown wings. Perhaps he had! His body hadn't fallen. It was soaring higher, into an infinite sky that was lightening and brightening, turning into the most shining...incandescent...white.

* * *

As Fate would have it, it was the new overseer, Mike O'Connor, who spotted the overturned machine from the chopper. No sign of Jay. This wasn't the only nightmare Mike had lived through in his life. He knew from experience Jay's body could be hidden by the long grasses. Whatever had persuaded the young man to cut a swathe through that particular area deeply shrouded in long concealing grasses? Mike hadn't found Jay in the least reckless. No rebel like his brother, Rory, who all the men spoke of with rough affection and respect. Rory, Mike had gathered, was the daring one. Neither Compton boys had been able to choose their ruthless old man.

'God Almighty! God Almighty!' A great lump stuck in O'Connor's neck and a rare rush of tears sprang into his eyes. Every instinct screamed this was bad. With anguish in his heart, Mike looked for a place to set the chopper down.

While this tragedy was unfolding, Allegra lay spooned against Rory's body, safe within the realm of his arm.

After that never-to-be-forgotten night, they had slept in. It was Saturday. No reason to get up. For that matter they could stay in bed all day. The very thought heated her skin. She held up her most precious ring to admire it. It suited her hand beautifully. It was the perfect symbol of their love. Very gently she turned her body towards him so that when he woke she would be looking into his eyes. Only she couldn't resist touching his face very softly, tracing a fingertip over the outline of his beautiful mouth. He had made her so happy she felt the tears swim into her eyes. Love with Rory was the sweetest, most meaningful experience, the distilled essence of her dreams. She knew she had been blessed with the greatest gift of all.

To love and be loved in return.

She must have drifted off again because she awoke to his warm lips against hers and his voice murmuring silkily. 'Time to wake up, Sleeping Princess.' The faint stubble of his beard deliciously grazed her skin.

'Lord, what time *is* it?' she asked, seeing heaven in those crystal clear eyes.

'Late.' He smiled back. 'But who cares. We can spend all day in bed.'

'Great! We don't need to get dressed at all.'

'Though we just might go out for a celebration dinner.' He kissed her again. 'So here we are.' He turned over on his back, taking a deep, voluptuous breath, then letting it out slowly.

'And it's wonderful,' she said, revelling in the flowing harmony.

'I've been watching you while you've been sleeping.' He drew her glowing head onto his shoulder. 'Even asleep you looked completely happy.'

'That's because I am.' It was so wonderful to be close. 'I've never been this happy in my life.'

'And it's highly contagious.' He kissed the top of her head, sharply aware of its clean fragrance. 'We're getting married.' He said it with enormous satisfaction, 'and it's got to be soon. Agreed?'

'Fine with me.' She snuggled even closer, laying the palm of her hand over his heart.

'We'll make it a wedding to dream about,' he promised her, his hands caressing her warm, silky flesh. 'Jay will be my best man.'

'Perfect!' she sighed.

He turned his attention to kissing her, engulfing her in pleasure. 'You taste of rose petals. I just *love* rose petals. I don't suppose you want to make love again?' he asked, with a quirk to his mouth.

She tilted her head to look at him. 'It looks like you can read my mind.'

'The wonder of you!' he said. One hand was in her billowing mane of hair, the other slipped down over her naked breasts.

His handsome face reflected the depth of his emotions. 'God, how I love you! You're everything I want.' He moved back into kissing her while Allegra gave herself up to the mounting heat.

The phone was ringing. For a moment neither of them were able to surface. Then Allegra turned her head, staring at it blankly. Let it go to message, she thought. Rory, too, rose up on one elbow. 'Are you going to answer it?' he asked, his eyes glinting with wry amusement.

'I guess.' She swung her legs to the carpet and he moved up behind her, locking his arms around her hips and resting his face against her satiny back, pressing kisses into her spine. 'Hello, Allegra speaking. I'm sorry, I can't hear you. Fine, it's okay now. Carrie!'

Her voice was infused with surprise. 'What is it? Is it the baby?'

Rory listened as surprise was replaced by warmth. Then abruptly her whole body language changed. She had been pliant to his touch, arching her back for him, now he felt tension. 'Yes, yes, he is,' she said. 'He's right here. Yes, Carrie, I'll put him on.'

She spoke in such a strange, hushed tone Rory moved back across the bed and sprang to his feet. 'What is it?' He swiftly pulled on some clothes, knowing in his bones this was serious. Allegra turned her head to him, her beautiful eyes that had been so filled with sensuality now glittering with tears.

'Clay Cunningham wants to speak to you,' she said, holding out the phone to him, 'It's not good news, Rory, I'm afraid.'

'My father, my brother?' Rory asked urgently, brushed by premonition. Something in her eyes gave him the answer. Denial laced with heartbreak poured into his voice. 'Not *Jay*?'

'I'm so sorry. So dreadfully sorry.' Allegra reached for her robe, unable to stop the tears pouring down her face.

Life would change for them now that his beloved brother was gone. She remembered, too, grief had a way of shattering dreams.

* * *

Mourners came from all over, wanting badly to pay their respects. It seemed incredible that young Jay Compton was being laid to rest. Rory was home. Folk were soothed by that. God knows what the reaction might have been had Bernard Compton not called his son home. Never a popular man—most people thought Bernard Compton was full of black holes—he had been virtually ostracised since the news got out Rory had been banished from Turrawin. Didn't everyone know Rory Compton was the brains and the brawn behind the whole outfit?

He'd brought his fiancée with him, a most beautiful young woman who stood close beside him while his brother's body was being interred. On Rory's other side stood another beautiful woman. No one had any difficulty recognising her. She looked scarcely different from the last time anyone had seen her. It was Laura Compton, the boys' mother.

People tried not to stare, but they were fascinated, wondering how this was possible she was back on Turrawin, standing at her estranged son's shoulder. Everyone had thought all family ties had been cut but death had a way of bringing the bereaved back together.

Afterwards at the homestead the huge crowd of mourners had an opportunity to meet Rory's fiancée and offer their condolences to him and to his mother who met everyone's eyes directly and even attempted a few smiles. This would not have been possible, everyone thought, only Bernard Compton was not able to attend his son's funeral. He was lying in a hospital bed far away hooked up to monitors that beeped and hummed.

Bernard Compton had suffered a serious heart attack not twenty minutes after Jay's body had been brought in, felled by a massive burden of guilt. He had been air lifted out by the Royal Flying Doctor. Now he was being monitored in case of a second attack. Bernard Compton's only wish was for release. He had nothing left to live for. Death would only free him from the pain and the guilt. No parent should have to lose a child.

That was the worst blow of all in life. He had never thought to lose Jay. He could only thank God he had never got around to disinheriting Rory. He'd lied about that. But look what it took to get Rory home!

To see them together, mother and son, was quite extraordinary, Allegra thought. Rory was the male version of his beautiful mother. No wonder the close resemblance had affected his father so powerfully. One could scarcely look at Rory—look into those remarkable silver-glinting eyes—without thinking of Laura. It was Allegra who had brought mother and son together.

Rory had reacted strongly when first she'd brought up his mother's name. She had tried to proceed with caution but he was so stricken he could scarcely handle his grief....

'How can these things happen?' he raged, prowling around the living room of her apartment like an agitated panther locked in a cage. 'Jay loved that bike. He was always tinkering with it. Now he's gone when Dad goes on living!' He threw up his arms embittered and stunned by the thought.

'Your father's end might be closer than you think, Rory.' Allegra was sitting very quietly, watching him prowl. It was amazing the energy he was giving off for all his grief. 'At least he wanted you home.'

'Really?' He sounded angry enough to choke. 'Well, there's no one else, is there?' he retorted, his handsome features locked into an impotent rage.

'What about your mother?' she asked, always courageous.

He walked to the back of the sofa where she was sitting, resting his hands on her shoulders. 'What about her?'

'Shouldn't she be told?' She didn't back down, seeing it as a duty to him and his mother.

'Sooner or later, my love. No rush!' he spoke with extreme sarcasm. 'She abandoned us years ago, remember?' He released her to resume his pacing. 'Maybe I'll wait the same time and tell her then.'

Allegra rose and went to where he was now standing by the window. Her lover. Her life. She wasn't at all confident, however, she could sway him no matter what argument she presented. She put her arms around him instead, kissing his cheek tenderly. 'Come and sit down with me,' she begged. 'I know the agony in your heart, but you have to be strong to face what's ahead. '

'Don't I know it!' He slicked his dark hair back from his face. 'I know your compassionate heart, Allegra, but I don't want to see my mother. I don't want to see my father, either. Does that make me a bad person?'

'No, only human.' Very gently she steered him to the sofa. 'Still, your mother haunts you?'

His eyes went glittery. 'Why wouldn't she? She *is* my mother She gave birth to me and Jay,' he said more quietly.

'Come on, sit down.'

'I don't know what I'd do if you weren't here with me.'

'Well, I am. All the way. You'll *have* to see your father, won't you?'

The knots in his stomach tightened. 'I guess I have to show up.'

'It takes a big man to make big moves,' she said. 'I'm sure your father is suffering because of this. Not just his heart attack, but overwhelming feelings of guilt...of taking the wrong path in life. He's lost Jay but he did reach out to *you.*'

'When it's all too late!' A dark shadow passed over Rory's face. 'I'm past caring. This tragedy mightn't have happened had I been home. Jay wasn't in the least reckless. He was as aware of the dangers as I am. He must have been deeply upset about something. My father has a vile tongue.'

'It was his moment, Rory,' Allegra said in a sad voice. 'Jay's time was up.'

'It seems like it.' He searched her face as though it held all the answers he needed to keep going 'I'm not religious, Allegra. How could I be after this? I can't imagine life without my brother.'

'I know.' She took his hands in hers. 'He was very special to you.'

'Well, he's gone now.' Grief filled his throat. 'And he won't be coming back. The worst part is being so unprepared. I never got a chance to say goodbye. It makes it all so much worse.'

Her smile was strained. 'You mightn't believe this now, but some time in the future you'll realise Jay is around. You'll have these little moments when he's more than just a memory. He'll be walking right beside you.'

He gave a harsh laugh. '*You're* my only moments of grace, Allegra,' he told her sombrely. 'Don't worry. I'm okay. I'll cope. It's just there was so much I wanted to say to him. Now I never will.'

'Say it all the same,' she urged, truly believing it would help. 'There will be ways to honour Jay, you'll see. I know you realise your mother might hear of his death from someone else?'

'Do you think she would care?' His handsome face was etched with misery.

'Of course she would!' Allegra found herself coming to Laura's defence. 'You told me when you were growing up she was a loving mother?'

That was met with silence.

'You told me she tried to see you after the divorce?' Her words continued at a rush. 'The visits went badly. All I'm saying is, some part of her is *still* the mother you knew. She's still *Jay's* mother.'

A turbulent edginess came into his face.. 'And it looks like she's got the woman I love for a powerful ally.'

She steadied herself. 'Being a woman I have to feel for her, Rory. More importantly, I'm trying to help you decide what's best. Please don't lock me out.' Her beautiful eyes were overbright in her pale face.

'As if I could!' His anger visibly cooled. 'Don't let's go on with this,' he begged. 'I can't contact my mother, not even for you, though you're mighty persuasive.'

'But it's you I'm thinking of, Rory. You spoke about missed chances. You won't get this chance again. I don't want you to suffer agonies later. Forgive me, but could I make a suggestion? Would you allow *me* to contact her? You said you knew where she lived?'

Rory's face was a study in conflicting emotions. 'I once stood outside her house, you know. I never went in.'

'When was this?' Hope quickened.

'A couple of years back when I was in Brisbane.'

'You wanted to talk to her?' She wanted him to go on.

'God knows why when there was nothing to say. We worshipped her. She left us. That's it in a nutshell. Jay was always the more sensitive one. I was the wild one, all mixed up. Jay had an even harder time than I did. My father's heart is made of stone.'

Allegra shook her head. 'That may very well be, but yours isn't!'

'We're talking about a man whose blood runs in my veins,' he reminded her with an ironic smile.

'There's a mingling of blood in all of us. It's possible your father has his own brand of love for you. He did, finally, give instructions for you be located and brought home.'

'So he did,' Rory acknowledged with a great sigh.

There was such an odd mix of expressions on his face. Grief, anger, indecision and something she clearly recognised as the hunger he felt for her, and the comfort her body could bring. And why not? The same swirl of emotions were in her as in him. It seemed odd to be sexually aroused at such a time, but Allegra saw it as a reaffirmation of life.'

'Do you want to go to bed, Rory?' she asked gently.

His answer was a long, deeply felt groan. He reached for her, enclosing her strongly in his arms. 'That's what I want more than anything in the world right now. I want to feel *alive*! You and me!'

* * *

She was at the airport with Rory to meet his mother when she arrived. It was an hour's flight from Brisbane to Sydney.

'Loving you has made me a better person already,' Rory told her with a wry smile. He had thrilled her by consenting to making that vital phone call.

She laughed in relief, knowing that if she started to cry, she mightn't be able to stop. 'You won't regret it, my darling. I promise you.'

The instant she laid eyes on Laura, Allegra lost any tiny lingering shred of doubt. She didn't know exactly how the family tragedy had happened, but she was absolutely certain Laura had suffered as much if not more than her sons.

She was there when mother and son fell into one another's arms. The long estrangement just vanished! Rory lost every vestige of the old bitterness as if it had been completely erased from his mind. It was as though somewhere up there Jay was already working miracles. Then Laura had turned to her and taken her hand, holding onto it as though it were a lifeline.

'Thank you, Allegra,' she said, her remarkable eyes filled with tears. 'Thank you from the bottom of my heart.'

Hadn't she just known what the exact colour of Rory's mother's eyes would be! In fact Laura was just as Allegra had pictured her. Time had been very kind to her. She looked surprisingly young. She had kept her figure, so her elegant pink linen suit hung perfectly on her body. Her thick sable hair curled softly around her beautiful oval face. Her smile was lovely. She looked a *gentle* woman. One it would be all too easy for a harsh man to hurt. Allegra took to her at once.

Rory, too, had found his answer. It's never too late for reconciliation. It's never too late to start a dialogue. It only takes a letter or a phone call. Rory's heart had melted at the first sound of his mother's voice.

Days slipped by after the funeral. They were alone on Turrawin. A charter flight had been arranged to fly Laura home but those few days together, though filled with pain, had healed many wounds. Laura had suffered just as badly as her sons when access to them had been closed off. The long silence she had so rigorously maintained now broke out of bounds. She told them stories of life with Bernard Compton, things Rory had never known or even imagined.

'It came to a time when I truly believed if I didn't leave Turrawin my very life would be threatened.'

It was impossible not to hear the stark truth in Laura's voice and to see the huge effort she was making not to break down.

'But you never said a word!' Shock glittered out of Rory's eyes.

'All I can do is beg you to forgive me.' Laura took her son's hand, immensely grateful she had been given this opportunity— however much grief surrounded it—to come back into his life. Had she not heard from him about Jay's death, she truly thought she wouldn't have been able to find the strength to go on.

'It was so incredibly hard for us all,' she said, her eyes full of sorrow. 'Bernard got incredible satisfaction out of making me suffer.'

'And he's going to have to answer for it,' Rory said.

But Bernard Compton's life was already running out.

That night Rory and Allegra lay in bed together, their limbs entwined. They had made the most extraordinary lyrical love in the moonlight, so close in body, mind and spirit Allegra thought of them as conjoined. Life was like navigating the open, unpredictable sea. There were the halcyon days to be treasured, the days the sea was rough; the times it turned pitiless, seemingly not to be overcome. They had encountered all three, braced themselves and somehow managed not only to survive but come out stronger and closer than ever.

The man they found in the hospital bed was a broken shell of the man he had once been. Weight had fallen off Bernard

Compton's heavy frame so he looked fragile beneath the white sheet that covered him. He was very deeply asleep when they arrived. Rory had been notified to come. 'There isn't much time!' a nurse told him, looking deeply sympathetic.

Rory pulled up a chair beside the bed and took his father's slack hand. Allegra stayed at a little distance near the window. The pain of losing her own father descended on her like a heavy cloak. She remembered how dreadful it had been; how much she missed him. She resolved there and then she couldn't let Chloe walk away from her, even though Chloe had betrayed her. Chloe was her own flesh and blood. In time she would find a way.

Rory sat with his father's hand in his for a long while. So long Allegra pulled her chair close up to the bed. She didn't really like looking at Bernard Compton as he lay there oblivious to their presence. She could see vestiges of his former handsomeness, but nothing of kindness. This had been a brutal man. Yet his own father, Rory's grandfather, had been much loved with a reputation for truth and integrity. It hurt her to know Bernard Compton's ruthless past had caught up with him. It had taken Jay's death to bring him to his knees.

To Allegra's eyes, it looked as though he had no hope of recovery. He looked like a man who had lost all will to survive.

It was deeply upsetting how much suffering he had brought into other people's lives, yet Rory was treating him gently. Just sitting there holding his father's hand as though he were much loved.

The same nurse's rubber soled shoes made funny squelching noises as she hurried down the corridor. There was a little irrepressible burst of laughter from a child and an admonishing, 'Be quiet, now, Hannah,' from a woman's voice. From the particular sound in it, it had to be the child's mother.

'He's gone,' Rory's voice startled her out of her sad reverie.

'Oh, Rory!' She placed her hand first on his shoulder, then

leaned forward to touch Bernard Compton's arm. He was unnervingly cold to the touch.

'He's gone, Allegra,' Rory said it again, as though she doubted it.

Two short words, she thought, though there could be few worse to be told.

He's gone!

This will change our world, Allegra thought, and closed her smarting eyes. Rory would be master of Turrawin. That was his destiny. And what of her childhood home, Naroom? What would happen there?

CHAPTER NINE

ALLEGRA STARED OUT over an ocean of bright yellow flowers. This was a world of a totally different kind to Naroom. Turrawin was *vast*! So new to it, it awed her. There were great flocks of kangaroos not in the hundreds she was used to, but thousands. They vastly outnumbered the people. Indeed the kangaroo population, some forty million, doubled the population of the nation. She had never thought it could be so exciting watching them bounding across the limitless plains in such numbers, no obstacle so high they couldn't take it in a flying leap. It was truly amazing to know a joey was only about the size of a bumble bee at birth.

The great flightless birds the emus, however, travelled not in huge flocks but in small groups. They made their nests on those plains, jealously stalking their territory and fixing anyone who came near with a baleful eye, although it was the male who had to stay home and sit on the eggs for an incredible couple of months. Emus could easily outrun the kangaroos and even keep pace with their vehicle. It was something to experience.

Great numbers of brumbies, too, roamed Turrawin in complete freedom. Allegra, the horse lover, found them beautiful to watch. The camels too fascinated her. In the one hundred fifty years since they had been introduced to the Outback by the

Afghans the flocks had thrived in the desert conditions, increasing to two or three hundred thousand. Seeing them standing on top of a fiery-red sand hill had become almost as synonymous with the Red Centre as the big red kangaroos. She had to admit the giant goannas, the perenties scared her, especially when standing up they were taller than Rory. Only Indonesia's Komodo Dragon was bigger.

'They've been known to leap at the horses,' Rory told her. 'But at least they're not crocs! There are plenty of dangerous critters around here. Taipans, tiger snakes, death adders, the king brown. Scorpions. You don't mess with them. Snakes, fortunately, like to keep out of our way. The tourists are greatly taken with our lizards and we have the most in the world. Australia's reptile emblem, the frilled lizard is a big favourite. When something disturbs them the frill, which usually lies along their back rises in a big circle—about the size of a dinner plate—around their neck.'

'It's all quite staggering!' Allegra mused. 'The *distances*! I thought I was used to distant horizons, but this is overwhelming. The land has a completely different feel to it too. It's primal yet thrilling.'

'It's dreamtime country,' Rory explained. 'Aboriginal country. The colours of the landscape are Namatjira colours, the wonderful dry ochres he used in his paintings.'

'Like the ones back at the homestead?'

'My mother bought those,' he said. 'I should give them to her.'

'You could,' Allegra agreed, 'but she'll be visiting often enough. I used to think those burnt umbers, the cinnabar, lapis lazuli, indigo, vermilion were too vivid to be true, but they're not. They're very closely observed.'

So, too, was the cloudless crystal-blue of the sky; the fiery-red of the sand hills at their door, the stark-white trunks of the ghost gums she thought so lovely. But what struck her most of all was the birdlife. Watching thousands upon thousands of them congregate at the bores, a favourite meeting place was an unforgettable sight. Orange and red chats, zebra finches, count-less species of parrots, galahs, sulphur crested cockatoos, the marvellous little emerald and gold gems, the lovebirds, the ab-original budgerigar. It was magic and Allegra abandoned her-self to Turrawin's spell.

Rory had sent their overseer, the man who had found Jay's body, Mike O'Connor to take charge at Naroom. He had al-ready settled in with his wife, living at the homestead as care-takers. Allegra had met both of them, husband and wife, and was happy with the arrangement. Naroom needed a good man in charge and they had decided O'Connor was it. It had been decided, too, Naroom would form a valuable link in the Comp-ton chain. It was part of Allegra's heritage so Rory had prom-ised her it would never be allowed to go out of the family. Who knows a future son might want to work it?

'You'd better enjoy all this while you can,' Rory advised, run-ning his hands lovingly across her shoulders and down her arms.

'It's a wonderland,' Allegra breathed. 'Could anyone believe on the driest continent on earth—right here on the edge of the desert—the entire landscape is mantled in wildflowers? I'm in awe of this place, Rory. It's so...'

'Haunting?' he suggested, a smile in his voice. 'The Great Spirits still roam this land. 'Be sure of it,' he said in such a voice it quickened all her pulses 'We're right in the path of the Great Rainbow Snake. The aborigines believe the spirits are beneath the earth, on it and above it. They believe someone, something, is always watching.'

'Well, it does have that feel.' She was ready to accept it. 'I believe in the Spirit of the Bush.'

'So do I!' Her deeply felt responses to his desert home gave him such comfort and joy they even managed to ease some of the misery Jay's passing had left in its wake. He mourned his father, too, but in an entirely different way. The what-might-have-been, the *if onlys*. A man was supposed to honour his fa-ther. He had certainly honoured his grandfather, but honouring his father had come too darn hard. Why was it some people were born full of a black fury? Was any of it their fault? All Rory knew was his father's death had come as a release. Not only to him, but to his mother, with whom he was reconciled, and in a way to the far flung Outback community.

Fate had made Rory master of Turrawin. To Turrawin's neighbours that seemed only proper and fitting. In Rory Compton they now had a neighbour and a helpmate they liked, respected and trusted. It was good to see him back at the helm; the place where he belonged.

Allegra sensed those feelings strongly when mourners came again to bury Bernard Compton in Turrawin's family cemetery, not far from his mother and father and his lost son. Bonds as strong as steel linked the people of the Inland. It was in part because of the *remoteness* in which they lived and part the national spirit.

'Just remember, you're seeing all this at its most magical,' Rory said. 'We might be carrying the fattest cattle in the nation at the moment but there are always the long years we have to get through the misery of drought. Far worse than anything you could ever have seen or suffered on Naroom. You need to know that. When the Dry returns all these wonderful everlastings will wilt and disintegrate, but the miraculous thing is they scatter their seeds far and wide. The birds help out, so do the desert winds. They pick the seeds up and blow them even further.'

'Hence mile after mile of desert flowers,' she said dreamily, resting contentedly against him.

He dropped a kiss on her smooth cheek then let his mouth linger over her cheekbone. 'The seeds can survive years and years of drought and scorching heat. They're clever little beggars, too. They germinate only when a successful display is assured. A brief shower wouldn't trigger this miracle. Only good rains and flooding have achieved this.'

'So we live here.'

'You're not going to tell me you don't really want to?' For an instant his heart turned over in his chest.

'Just teasing!' She gave a little laugh. 'Whither thou goest, I go. You've promised me my beautiful Taroom will stay in the family. I'm content with that.'

He nodded. 'Incidentally I have all sorts of plans for it I want to share with you.'

'Good,' she said cheerfully. 'Sharing is what it's all about.'

They stayed there for some time revelling in the urgent ecstasy of the desert flowering. For all the glamour of the city Allegra loved the wonderful wide-open spaces better. This was where she belonged. The desert country, too, was so rich in colour, laid on as vividly as a painting, she found it incredibly dramatic. These were the holy places, sacred to the aborigines. She could feel the powerful magic. Identify with it.

Rory pointed something out to her way to the North-East. She framed her eyes with her hands looking towards the silver-blue light that danced all over the vast landscape. 'It looks like an oasis,' she said. 'I can see a lagoon and palm trees. There are even people moving about.'

'Mirage,' he said. 'Fascinating isn't it? A quicksilver illusion. Do you want to go back to the house?'

'No way! I haven't come down to earth yet.' She gave him a smile of wondrous delight. 'There's something I want you to do for me first.'

'Just tell me.' He made a trail through the white paper daises as he walked back to her side. Something about her expression enthralled him.

'Make love to me amid the flowers,' she said softly, pulling him in close. The scene was set. The sky was so blue it was nearly violet. The rich red earth was covered by a glorious floral carpet one could walk on to the horizon. It was unbelievably perfect, a lovers' fantasy. Her fingers curled into the open neck of his denim shirt as she stood on tiptoes to kiss him gently, deeply on the mouth. She was such a happy woman and he had made it so.

Rory's eyes took on the sheen of silver coins in the sunlight. 'I'd be more than happy to, ma'am!' The vibrant tone of his voice held an embrace. 'I've never made love on a carpet of fragrant flowers before.'

'The first time with me.' She kissed him again, feeling as free as the air. Then a thought suddenly struck her. 'What if someone sees us?'

He laughed aloud. He was feeling like a prince in his own kingdom, his princess beside him. 'The only ones who are going to see us, my beautiful Allegra, have wings, like those little guys!' He lifted his head to mark another flyover of the ubiquitous budgerigar, a lovely light glinting off their emerald and gold feathers. They were heading towards the Pink Lady lagoon, one of the all time lovely places on the station. The two of them had visited it that morning to take in the exquisite sight of the cargo of pink waterlilies it was carrying. To cap off the entrancing experience they were witness to the ritual mating dance of a pair of brolgas who had performed for them on the lagoon's sandy banks.

'Don't keep me waiting, my love,' Allegra called to him as she sank oh so languorously onto the thick springy mat of wildflowers, then lay back. She held up her arms, her eyes brilliant with invitation.

'God you look beautiful like that.' Rory's face bore an expression of urgent excitement. 'I love you so much!' He fell to his knees, straddling her slender body. Gently he stroked her face, his expression breaking up a little as though to love was pain. Then quite unexpectedly he lifted his head and shouted in such a voice it seemed to echo around the hill country away to their west. *'I love you, Allegra!'*

'And I *hear* you!' She clutched him around the waist, laughing with delight while she pulled him down to her. 'For all our lives?' she asked very quietly, but with deep significance.

'For all our lives,' he answered with a fierce passion, as though reciting a vow that could never be broken except under pain of death. 'You're *my* woman!'

He heard her sigh, long and deep full of rapture. 'That's fine, because you're *my* man!'

'Then that's settled!' He gave a soft, playful growl then hunched over her; the all powerful male.

Passion licked along his veins like a flame shoots towards a powder keg.

'Isn't this glorious!' she cried, arching her body towards him with a sense of utter belonging.

'There's nobody like you,' he answered in a deep, velvety voice. He desired her so much he was in actual pain.

Swiftly, not losing a second, Rory began to peel off his clothes, feeling the desert air waft across his bare skin, cooling, caressing, fanning desire. To have her here among the flowers seemed to him so marvellous it was like an electric shock to his loins.

She was starting to undo her cotton shirt, fumbling a little with the buttons in her haste. Now he turned his attention to her and he shifted her hand away so he could have the infinite pleasure of undressing her himself. He could feel the delicious trembling that ran right through her body. Rejoiced in it. This was love. This was life.

Rory was overcome by a strong sense of destiny. It all seemed so beautiful to him it was almost a wedding ceremony. He was deeply, *deeply* committed to this woman. Everything in him craved what only she could offer.

'With my body I thee worship!' He intoned the line strongly as he bent to her. Then having stripped her he began to kiss her all over her beautiful woman's body so wondrously constructed for his loving. Kissed her until she was shaking and crying out his name.

'Rory!' The very air seemed to fracture into gold dust.

Both of them were overwhelmed by that extraordinary mix

of ecstasy and agony that was so much an element of passionate lovemaking. Yet nothing in the world could have seemed more romantic to them. They were cushioned in fragrance. Drowning in it. The scent of the crushed wildflowers was sinking into the very pores of their skin. To be young and alive and in love.

Allegra could feel moisture gathering in the cleft between her legs. She was ready for him. She had only to wait for him to enter her, to fill her, to touch off the wild tumult only he could arouse. One day they would have a baby...then, God willing, more children. They would be born on Turrawin.

A great wedge-tailed eagle circled them three times, as though astonished by what it saw. Such strange creatures humans! Then it flapped its great wings and flew off, soaring ever upwards as it made its way towards its eyrie in the ancient hills.

Neither Rory nor Allegra marked the eagle's flight or the thrilling stretch of its wings. But an eagle isn't the only creature that can soar. As the two lovers climaxed they, too, were borne up into the radiant blue sky...light...light...lighter than air.

Love when it's true has its own powerful magic. It's the closest a man and woman can get to Heaven.

EPILOGUE

Jimboorie Annual Picnic-Race Meeting.
Two years later.

THE WEATHER COULD hardly have been better.

After continuous years of drought, the good seasons had come. The best spell in ten years, and the whole Outback had come to life. The river flats and the flood plains of the Inland were covered in a riot of green herbage, one species with a sapphire-blue flower that grew so tall in places—up to seven feet—horsemen and cattle could disappear in it. The organisers of the annual event, one of the biggest and best on the social calendar—especially since Mrs. Caroline Cunningham of Jimboorie Station, had taken over as President of the Ladies' Committee—had chosen the first week of spring to take full advantage of the mild day temperatures and the balmy nights. As happened every year, a gala ball was held on the Saturday night, following the running of the very popular Jimboorie Cup in the afternoon with horses and jockeys coming from the cattle and sheep stations spread over a vast area.

The three pubs were full up with visitors. Outlying stations had accommodated more than their fair share of guests. The bulk of the crowd was station people, owners and their employees, but dedicated race-goers and those that liked 'one whale of a time' had come from all over the country, including the major cities. Many urbanite Australians, though they lived in the lush narrow corridors of the country's seaboards, really felt the need to identify with the vast Outback of their immense country. Attending the big picnic race meetings was a way of doing it.

A dozen and more private planes stood on the town airstrip and the town's streets were clogged with dusty four-wheel drive's and tourist buses. Outback people loved to party so with opportunities for them to come together limited, they ensured they made the most of every occasion.

This year entries in the race had been expanded to professional as well as amateur jockeys. Not as unfair as it might seem at first glance. The Outback riders, all station people, were splendid horsemen with a greater understanding of local conditions and the terrain, which was essentially a Wild West track. The field numbered twenty, the largest lineup since the Cup, sponsored by the pioneering sheep baron, William Cunningham, had begun in the late 1880s.

It was fast approaching three o'clock the traditional time for the running of the Cup, the main race. Caroline, who was to present the Cup and a fat cheque to the winner, made her way to the fenced off course—white post and rail—in time to see horses and riders showing themselves off to the crowd. Each jockey wore a numbered square on his back. Caroline's husband, Clay, the winning jockey for the past two years was riding his favourite Lightning Boy. Each year the competition got stiffer, this year in the form of Rory Compton master of Turrawin Station in the legendary Channel Country on Cezar. 'Kidman Country' as many people called the South-West corner because it was there when he was camped beneath a coolibah tree Sir Sydney Kidman, the original Cattle King planned his mighty cattle empire that at its zenith spread over more than one hundred thirty thousand square kilometres of the Outback.

Today rivalry was incredibly keen. This was the first time

the committee had received an entry from so far a field but she and Clay had pressed their friend Rory into entering. Over the past couple of years they had all become close. Clay actually took all the credit for introducing Rory to his beautiful Allegra. The rest was history. Caroline had been matron of honour at Allegra and Rory's wedding; Clay, best man. In turn the Comptons were godparents to their wonderful little son, Jeremy, who everyone at this stage called Jemmy.

Caroline caught sight of them now. Because she'd had her special duties to perform Allegra had offered to look after Jeremy for her. Allegra had quite a way with children. Caroline could see her son's blond curls shining like a cherub's in the sun. He really was the most beautiful little boy. Everyone adored him. There was no sign of the terrible twos about Jemmy. He was the sunniest natured child and he just loved Allegra's new baby. Caroline could see him standing protectively beside the pram, one hand tucked inside it, no doubt holding baby's little fingers. Caroline's heart melted with love. Children brought such incredible joy into one's life. She was so glad, too, she had Allegra for a friend. In fact she couldn't imagine life without her. Although separated by formidable distances, the fact Rory flew his own plane made it so much easier for two young married women to see one another fairly frequently when she and Clay visited. Both of them had been staying at Turrawin homestead the night Allegra gave birth to her daughter after a trouble-free pregnancy.

Could she ever forget the look of love and pride on the parents' faces! Caroline still had a lump in her throat at the memory.

Contentment written all over her, Allegra turned her head as Caroline hurried up to them. 'Hi, you're in good time!' Allegra's smile was radiant. Always beautiful, motherhood had endowed her expression with a tenderness that lent an extra bloom. 'I'm so glad we came, Carrie. The atmosphere is really exciting and so friendly! Don't the horses look marvellous? Groomed to perfection. Our riders, too, of course!' she laughed. 'Don't let's forget them. You look wonderful!' Allegra cast an expert eye over her friend's lovely outfit, thinking it absolutely right.

'I try.' Caroline smiled back and ran a loving hand over her son's platinum-blond curls. 'What a good boy you are, Jemmy,' she praised him. 'I see you're looking after baby.'

'She's boot-i-ful!' Jem pronounced softly. He took the baby's hand and kissed it. 'I jess love her.'

Both women laughed tenderly, their minds irresistibly jumping ahead to the time when their children would come of marriageable age. Wouldn't it be wonderful?

'Oh look, they're moving to the starting line,' Allegra exclaimed. 'Come on, my darling,' She swooped to lift her six-month-old daughter out of the pram and hold her up. 'Look at Daddy. There he is, sweetheart—Number 7. Uncle Clay is Number 4.'

Filled with excitement Jemmy began to jump up and down. 'Wave, Jaylene!' he cried, trying to help her do it. 'Wave!'

The beautiful baby must have known what her little friend meant, because Jaylene threw her rosy head back and twitched a tiny hand.

Jeremy looked on in amazement and pride. 'Good girl, Jaylene!'

What other name could we have given our first child, Allegra thought, herself amazed at what appeared to be her baby's response. It was a name to honour the memory of the young man who was Rory's brother. It felt so right!

'Oh, it's so exciting!' Caroline said. 'I just love these days!' An excellent horsewoman she wanted to join in the race herself.

'Who did you back?' Allegra laughingly asked. 'As if I don't know!' Caroline and Clay were very much in love.

'The winner, who else?' Caroline's eyes sparkled with mischief. 'I just know this is going to be the most exciting race ever!'

And so it turned out.

A great full-throated roar went up from the crowd. Racing was the nation's passion.

'They're off at the start of the Cunningham Cup!' The race caller's voice came blaring over the loud speaker.

It wasn't the winning that mattered. It was the great enjoyment of Outback people coming together; feeling the kinship and the pleasure right down to the heart.

* * * * *

Keep reading for an excerpt of
Second Chance With Her Guarded GP
by Kate Hardy.
Find it in the
Bestselling Authors Collection 2024 anthology,
out now!

CHAPTER ONE

OLIVER LANGLEY TOOK a deep breath.

This was it. His new start. Not the life he'd thought he'd have, six months ago: but that had been before the world had tilted on its axis and mixed everything up. Before his twin brother Rob had gone to work for a humanitarian aid organisation in the aftermath of an earthquake and his appendix had burst. Before Rob had ended up with severe blood poisoning that had wiped out his kidneys. Before Ollie had donated a kidney to his twin.

Before Ollie's fiancée had called off their wedding.

Which had been his own fault for asking her to move the wedding. 'Tab, with Rob being on dialysis, he's not well enough even to be at the wedding, let alone be my best man.' He'd been so sure his fiancée would see things the same way that he did. It made perfect sense to move the wedding until after the transplant, giving both him and Rob time to recover from the operation and meaning that Ollie's entire family would be there to share the day. 'Let's move the wedding back a few months. The transplant's hopefully going to be at the beginning of June, so we'll both be properly recovered by August. We can have a late summer wedding instead.'

'Move the wedding.' It had been a statement, not a question. She'd gone silent, as if considering it, then shaken her head. 'No.'

He'd stared at her. 'Tab, I know it'll be a bit of work, changing all the arrangements, but I'll do as much of it as I can.'

'That's not what I mean, Ollie.'

He'd stared at her, not understanding. 'Then what do you mean?'

'I—I've been thinking for a while. We should call it off.'

'Call it off?' He'd gone cold. 'Why? Have you met someone else?'

'No. It's not you. It's me.'

Which meant the problem *was* him and she was trying to be nice. 'Tab, whatever it is, we can work it out. Whatever I've done to upset you, I'm sorry.' He loved her. He wanted to marry her, to make a family with her. He'd thought she felt the same way and wanted the same things. But it was becoming horribly clear that he'd got it all wrong.

Her eyes had filled with tears. 'It's not you, it's me,' she said again. 'You're giving Rob a kidney—of course you are. He's your brother and you love him. Anyone would do the same, in your shoes.'

'But?' He'd forced himself to say the word she'd left out.

She'd looked him in the eye. 'What if something goes wrong? What if *you* get ill, and your one remaining kidney doesn't work any more, and you have to go on dialysis? What if they can't find a match for you, and you die?'

'That's not going to happen, Tab.' He'd tried to put his arms round her to comfort and reassure her but she'd pulled away.

'You're not listening, Ollie. I can't do this.'

'Why?'

'You know how it's been with my dad.'

'Yes.' Tabby's father had chronic fatigue syndrome. He'd been too ill to do much for years.

'Mum stuck by her wedding vows—in sickness and in health. I didn't realise when I was younger, but she worked herself to the bone, making sure my brother and I were OK, and keeping us financially afloat, and looking after Dad. Obviously when we got older and realised how ill Dad was, Tom and I did as much as we could do to help. But my mum's struggled every single day, Ollie. She's sacrificed her life to look after Dad. And I can't do that for you. I just *can't*.'

He'd frowned. 'But I'm not ill, Tab. OK, I'll need a bit of time to recover from the transplant, but I'll be fine. Rob will get better and everything will be back to normal soon enough.'

'But you can't promise me you'll always be well and I won't have to look after you, Ollie. You can't possibly promise something like that.' Tabby had shaken her head. 'I'm sorry, Ollie. I can't marry you.' She'd fought to hold back the tears. 'I know it's selfish and I know it's unfair, but I just don't love you enough to take that risk. I don't want a life like my mum's. I don't want to marry you.' She'd taken off the engagement ring and given it back to him. 'I'm so sorry, Ollie. But I can't do this.'

'Tab, you've just got an attack of cold feet. We'll get through this,' he said. 'We love each other. It'll be fine.'

'No, Ollie. That's the point. I do love you—but not *enough*. I'm sorry.'

He hadn't been able to change her mind.

She'd got in touch to wish him and Rob luck with the transplant, but she'd made it clear she didn't want him back. He wasn't enough for her. To the point where she hadn't even wanted him to help cancel all the arrangements; Tabby insisted on doing it all herself.

Ollie had spent a couple of weeks brooding after the operation, and he'd realised that he needed some time away from London. So he'd taken a six-month sabbatical from the practice in Camden where he was a salaried GP, lent his flat to a friend, and had gone back to Northumbria to stay with Rob and their parents. The open skies, hills and greenery had given him a breathing space from the bustle of London and time to think about what he wanted to do with his life.

Though the enforced time off after the transplant, once he'd untangled the wedding, had left Ollie with the fidgets. Much as he loved their parents and completely understood why their mum was fussing over her twin boys, Ollie liked having his own space and the smothering was driving him mad. He was pretty sure that doing the job he loved would help him get his equilibrium back and help him move on from the mess of his wedding-that-wasn't.

Then he'd seen the ad for a three-month maternity cover post at Ashermouth Bay Surgery, which would take him nearly up to the end of his sabbatical. He'd applied for the job; once the practice had given him a formal offer, he'd found a three-month let and moved into one of the old fishermen's cottages near the harbour, within walking distance of the practice.

And today was his first day at his new job. He might not have been enough for his fiancée, but he knew he was definitely good enough as a doctor.

The building was single-storey, built of red brick and with a tiled roof. There were window-boxes filled with welcoming bright red geraniums, and a raised brick flower bed in front of the door, filled with lavender. The whole place looked bright and welcoming; and next to the door was a sign listing the practice staff, from the doctors and nurses through to the reception and admin team.

Ollie was slightly surprised to see his own name on the sign, underneath that of Aadya Devi, the GP whose maternity leave he was covering, but it made him feel welcome. Part of the team. He really liked that.

He took a deep breath, pushed the door open and walked in to the reception area.

The receptionist was chatting to a woman in a nurse's uniform, who had her back to him. Clearly neither of them had heard him come in, because they were too busy talking about him.

'Dr Langley's starting this morning,' the receptionist said.

'Our newbie,' the nurse said, sounding pleased.

At thirty, Ollie didn't quite see himself as a 'newbie', but never mind. He was new to the practice, so he supposed it was an accurate description.

'Caroline's asked me to help him settle in, as she's away this week,' the nurse added.

Caroline was the senior partner at the practice: a GP in her late fifties, with a no-nonsense attitude and a ready laugh. Ollie had liked her very much at the interview.

He didn't really need someone to help him settle in, but OK. He got that this place was a welcoming one. That they believed in teamwork.

'And, of course, he's fresh meat,' the nurse said.

The receptionist laughed. 'Oh, Gem. Trust *you* to think of that.'

Ollie, who had just opened his mouth ready to say hello, stood there in silence, gobsmacked.

Fresh meat?

Right now, he was still smarting too much from the fallout from the wedding-that-wasn't to want any kind of relationship. And it rankled that someone was discussing him in that way. Fresh meat. A slab of beefcake. Clearly this 'Gem' woman made a habit of this, given the receptionist's comment.

Well, he'd just have to make sure she realised that she was barking up completely the wrong tree. And he didn't care if his metaphors were mixed.

He gave a loud cough. 'Good morning.'

'Oh! Good morning.' The receptionist smiled at him. 'We're not actually open yet, but can I help you?'

'I'm Oliver Langley,' he said.

The receptionist's cheeks went pink as she clearly realised that he'd overheard the end of their conversation.

Yeah. She might well be embarrassed. Fresh meat, indeed.

'I'm Maddie Jones, the receptionist—well, obviously,' she

said. 'Welcome to the practice. Can I get you a cup of coffee, Dr Langley?'

'Thank you, but I'm fine,' he said coolly. 'I don't expect to be waited on.'

The nurse next to her also turned round to greet him.

'Good morning, Dr Langley. Nice to meet you,' she said with a smile.

Surely she must realise that he'd overheard what she'd just said about him? And yet she was still being all smiley and sparkly-eyed. Brazening it out? That didn't sit well with him at all.

'I'm Gemma Baxter,' she said. 'I'm one of the practice nurse practitioners. Caroline asked me to look after you this week, as she's away on holiday.'

'That's kind of you, Nurse Baxter,' he said, keeping his voice expressionless, 'but quite unnecessary.'

'Call me Gemma. And, if nothing else,' she said, 'I can at least show you where everything is in the surgery.' She disappeared for a moment, then came through to join him in the waiting area. 'It's pretty obvious that this is the waiting area,' she said, gesturing to the chairs. 'The nurses' and HCA's rooms are this side of Reception—' she gestured to the corridor to their left '—the pharmacy's through the double doors to the right, the patient toilets are over there in the corner, and the doctors' rooms are this side.'

She gestured to the other corridor. 'If you'd like to follow me? The staff toilets, the kitchen and rest room are here, behind Reception and the admin team.' She led him into the kitchen. 'Coffee, tea, hot chocolate and fruit tea are in the cupboard above the kettle, along with the mugs. The dishwasher's next to the fridge, and there's a rota for emptying it; and the microwave's self-explanatory. We all put a couple of pounds into the kitty every week and Maddie keeps the supplies topped up. If there's anything you want that isn't here, just let Maddie know.'

She smiled at him. 'I need to start checking the out-of-hours notifications and hospital letters before my triage calls and vaccination clinic this morning, so I'm going to leave you here. Your room's the third on the right, but obviously you'll see your name on the door anyway.'

'Thank you for the tour,' he said. That 'fresh meat' comment had rubbed him up the wrong way, but he was going to have to work with her for the next three months so it'd be sensible to be polite and make the best of it.

'I'll come and find you at lunchtime,' she said. 'As it's your first day, lunch is on me.'

'That's—' But he didn't have time to tell her that it was totally unnecessary and he'd sort out his own lunch, thanks all the same, because she'd already gone through to the other corridor.

Ollie made himself a coffee, then headed for his consulting room. It was a bright, airy space; there was a watercolour on the wall of a castle overlooking the sea, which he vaguely recognised as a local attraction. A desk; a couple of chairs for his patient and a parent or support person; and a computer. Everything neatly ordered and in its place; nothing personal.

He checked his phone for the username and password the practice administrator had sent him last week, logged on to the system and changed the password. Then he put an alarm on his phone to remind him when telephone triage started, and once his emails came up he started to work through the discharge summaries, hospital letters and referrals from over the weekend.

Gemma knew she was making a bit of a snap judgement—the sort of thing she normally disapproved of—but Oliver Langley seemed so closed-off. He hadn't responded to the warmth of her smile or her greeting, and he'd been positively chilly when she'd said she'd show him round. She sincerely hoped he'd be a bit warmer with their patients. When you were worried about your health, the last thing you needed was a doctor being snooty with you. You needed someone who'd listen and who'd reassure you.

Yes, sure, he was gorgeous: tall, with dark floppy hair and

blue eyes, reminding her of a young Hugh Grant. But, when you were a medic, it didn't matter what you looked like; what mattered was how you behaved towards people. So far, from what Gemma had seen, Oliver Langley was very self-contained. If he was the best fit for the practice, as Caroline had claimed, Gemma hated to think what the other interviewees had been like. Robots, perhaps?

Hopefully she could work some kind of charm offensive on him over lunch. She intended to get a genuine smile out of him, even if she had to exhaust her entire stock of terrible jokes.

She took a gulp of the coffee she'd made earlier and checked the out-of-hours log, to see which of their patients had needed urgent treatment over the weekend and needed following up. Then she clicked onto the triage list Maddie had sent through, before starting her hour and a half of phone triage.

The system was one of the things the practice had kept from the Covid days. It was more efficient for dealing with minor illnesses and giving advice about coughs and colds and minor fevers; but in Gemma's view you could often tell a lot from a patient's body language—something that could prompt her to ask questions to unlock what her patient was *really* worrying about. That was something that telephone triage had taken away, since the Covid days. And trying to diagnose a rash or whether a wound had turned septic, from looking at a blurred photograph taken on a phone and sent in low resolution so it would actually reach the surgery email, had been next to impossible.

At least things were a bit easier now. They were all adjusting to the 'new normal'. She worked her way through the triage list until it was time to start her vaccination clinic. Even though the vaccination meant she had to make little ones cry, it also meant she got a chance for baby cuddles. Gemma would never admit to being broody, but if she was honest with herself her biological clock always sat up and took notice when she had this kind of clinic.

It had been twelve years since she'd lost her little sister—

since she'd lost her entire family, because her parents had closed off, too, unable to deal with their loss. Gemma had been so desperate to feel loved and to stop the pain of missing Sarah that she'd chosen completely the wrong way to do it; she'd gone off the rails and slept with way too many boys. Once her best friend's mum had sat her down and talked some sense into her, Gemma had ended up going the other way: so determined not to be needy that she wouldn't let her boyfriends close, and the relationships had fizzled out within weeks. She'd never managed to find anyone she'd really clicked with.

So the chances of her attending this particular clinic rather than running it were looking more and more remote. It was a good six months since she'd last had a casual date, let alone anything more meaningful. The nearest she'd get to having a real family of her own was being godmother to Scarlett, her best friend's daughter. She was grateful for that, but at the same time she wondered why she still hadn't been able to fix her own family. Why she still couldn't get through to her parents.

She shook herself. Ridiculous. Why was she thinking about this now?

Perhaps, she thought, because Oliver Langley was precisely the sort of man she'd gone for, back in her difficult days. Tall, dark-haired, blue-eyed and gorgeous. And his coolness towards her had unsettled her; she was used to people reacting to her warmth and friendliness in kind.

Well, tough. It was his problem, not hers, and she didn't have time to worry about it now. She had a job to do. She went into the corridor and called her first patient for her clinic.

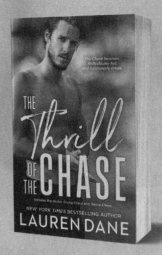 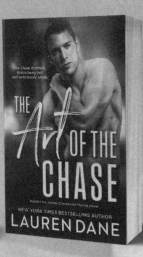

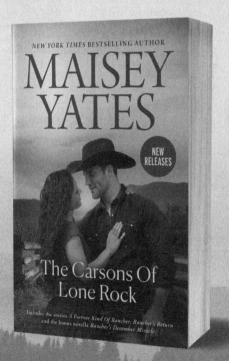

Subscribe and fall in love with a Mills & Boon series today!

You'll be among the first to read stories delivered to your door monthly and enjoy great savings.

WE SIMPLY LOVE ROMANCE

MILLS & BOON

JOIN US

Sign up to our newsletter to stay up to date with...

- Exclusive member discount codes
- Competitions
- New release book information
- All the latest news on your favourite authors

Plus...
get $10 off your first order.
What's not to love?

Sign up at **millsandboon.com.au/newsletter**